TALES OF MYSTERY & THE SUPERNATURAL

General Editor: David Stuart Davies

THE WITCH OF PRAGUE
and other tales

D1486651

The Witch of Prague

and other tales

by Francis Marion
Crawford

*with an introduction by
David Stuart Davies*

WORDSWORTH EDITIONS

In loving memory of
MICHAEL TRAYLER
the founder of Wordsworth Editions

I

Readers who are interested in other titles from
Wordsworth Editions are invited to visit our website at
www.wordsworth-editions.com

For our latest list and a full mail-order service contact
Bibliophile Books, Unit 5 Datapoint,
South Crescent, London E16 4TL
Tel: +44 020 74 74 24 74
Fax: +44 020 74 74 85 89
orders@bibliophilebooks.com
www.bibliophilebooks.com

This edition published 2008 by
Wordsworth Editions Limited
8B East Street, Ware, Hertfordshire SG12 9HJ

ISBN 978 1 84022 090 2

Typeset in Great Britain by Roperford Editorial
Printed by Clays Ltd, St Ives plc

CONTENTS

INTRODUCTION

I suppose it is quite fitting to commence a volume which is full of dark and unusual mystery stories designed to fuel the imagination by presenting the reader with a real life conundrum which concerns the author of 'The Screaming Skull' and the other tales in this collection. During his lifetime Francis Marion Crawford (1854–1909) wrote over forty books and was one of the most popular and commercially successful authors of his day. Such was Crawford's fame that when he fell ill in the year of his death, bulletins of his condition were reported on the front page of the *New York Times*. Yet strangely, quite soon after his death, his literary star faded in the heavens, his posthumous readership declined and gradually his books failed to be reprinted. Eventually one could only find the odd short story of his – usually 'For the Blood is the Life' or 'The Upper Berth' – in various anthologies of supernatural tales. Francis Marion Crawford became a forgotten writer and there seems to be no logical reason for the evaporation of interest in the work of this skilled author: it is a mystery.

Today, the man in the street has no real knowledge of Crawford or his stories. This collection aims to rectify that situation in a modest way. It contains all the tales from his best collection, *Wandering Ghosts*, and has the added bonus of his horror novel, *The Witch of Prague*. In reading these unnerving narratives, I hope you will not only enjoy them but be prompted to ponder the puzzle as to why they have been neglected by publishers in the years since Crawford's death.

F. Marion Crawford was born of American parents in Italy, a country which became his adopted home and where he lived for most of his life. As the youngest of four children – he had three sisters – he absorbed the strong artistic atmosphere in the family home. His father was the sculptor Thomas Crawford, whose most famous piece of statuary is the figure 'Armed Liberty' which stands on the top of the Capitol Building in Washington D.C. His mother, Louisa Ward, was the sister of Julia Ward Howe who wrote the 'Battle Hymn of the Republic'. Crawford's sister, Mary, was also a writer; she wrote novels and travel books under her married name Mrs Hugh Fraser. Crawford's education was eclectic and broad. He had a French governess before he attended school in Concord, New Hampshire. He went on to study Greek and mathematics in Rome and later studied German, Swedish and Spanish at Trinity College, Cambridge. He was fascinated by languages and mastered eighteen in all, but his passion was for Sanskrit, which he studied in Rome, India and at Harvard. To help fund this academic pursuit he turned his hand to writing newspaper articles and found that he had a talent for spinning words into an interesting and engrossing narrative. He eventually settled in Italy, where in 1884 he married Elizabeth Berdan, daughter of the American general Hiram Berdan, the inventor of the Berdan rifle.

By now he was passionately involved in his writing and produced at least one novel a year, sometimes two or three. Like so many Victorian authors he was interested in all aspects of the world, society and art, and so the subject-matter of his novels and stories varied. It is fair to say that only a few could be regarded as dealing with horror or the supernatural. Most authors of this period dabbled in stories of the ghostly and macabre as a matter of course. If we consider the output of such notables as Charles Dickens, Thomas Hardy, Henry James and Wilkie Collins we will find fine examples of the genre in their oeuvre. What is remarkable about these writers, Crawford included, is that while not specialising in the form they mastered the mechanics of the supernatural tale so effectively. It may be that they came to it with original ideas and fresh eyes, unlike some of those writers who dedicated their work to the uncanny and chilling.

Seven of the eight short stories collected in this edition were written at various times – one almost suspects idle moments – during the course of Crawford's life and were collected posthumously and published in 1911 under the title *Uncanny Tales* in Europe and *Wandering Ghosts* in the US. In this volume we have added the stray story 'The King's Messenger' as a bonus tale. For no obvious reason it was not included in the original collection.

'The Screaming Skull' appeared in two parts in *Collier's Magazine* in 1908. A cheap and unintentionally amusing film very loosely based on the story was made in 1958 and there was also a TV movie in 1973. As Crawford notes at the end of 'The Screaming Skull', the inspiration for his narrative was the legend associated with Bettiscombe Manor in Dorset. The fanciful nature of the legend connected with the old house appealed to the writer. It stated that the skull could not be removed from the house. To do so would cause great havoc. The legend suggests that the skull once belonged to an African slave whose dying wish was to be taken back to his native land to be buried there, instead of which he was interred locally. After the burial screams issued from the grave and the house was subject to poltergeist activity. Finally the body was disinterred and placed in the house. This seemed to placate the troubled spirit. Several attempts at reburial resulted in the same ghostly manifestation and over the years the skeleton became reduced to a skull. Crawford took elements from these supposedly true events and wove them into his own chilling tale.

'For the Blood is the Life' (1905), is generally regarded as one of the best vampire tales ever penned. It is poetic in mood with slow-burning terror and features a female vampire, Cristina. Her first appearance is beautifully conceived: 'The flickering light of the lantern played upon another face that looked up from the feast – upon two deep, dead eyes that saw in spite of death – upon parted lips redder than life itself – upon two gleaming teeth on which glistened a rosy drop.'

'The Upper Berth' (1886) is a ghost story of particular power which the respected American fantasy writer H. P. Lovecraft rated as Crawford's masterpiece. The plot concerns some supernatural being, never clearly seen but horribly felt, which haunts the upper berth of a fated steamship.

Crawford's love of the sea and sailing manifests itself again in 'Man Overboard' (1903), which was originally published as a small hardcover book. It is a tale of ghostly vengeance involving identical twins.

It may well be that Crawford's memory of him breaking a little girl's doll in a fit of temper when he was an infant prompted him to write 'The Doll's Ghost' (1911), a charming tale concerning a doll-maker and his lost child. It has all the elements of a Dickens Christmas story, including a benevolent spirit.

In 'The Dead Smile' (1899) Crawford excels at creating a wonderfully eerie atmosphere as a background to a tale of family secrets and death. On the brink of death, Sir Hugh Ockram's evil smile reflects the damnation he plans for his own son when Sir Hugh dies. The American writer of fantasy stories Seabury Quinn (1889–1969) was so enamoured with this tale that he rewrote it as 'The Jest of Warburg Tantaval' (1934), featuring his own occult detective, Jules de Grandin.

Atmosphere rather than supernatural happenings is the key attraction of 'By the Waters of Paradise' (1887), which is essentially a romance, but the character of the nurse who is gifted with second sight gives it a suitably unnerving twist.

The extra tale, 'The King's Messenger' is very clever, defying description without revealing the various twists in the plot and thus spoiling it for the reader. Suffice it to say that it involves a man who in a dream learns of the concurrent death of a friend.

You can see from these brief capsule descriptions of the short stories in the first section of this book that Crawford was able to provide varied canvases on which to paint his unnerving narratives. There is no sense of repetition or familiarity in his writing. Each tale covers fresh and interesting ground.

And so we come to the novel *The Witch of Prague*, a work that none other than the great writer of supernatural fiction Dennis Wheatley described as 'a classic of occult fiction'. The title suggests a dark fairy tale, which is perhaps an accurate description, for this is a story of witches and wizards and unrequited love. The period in which the story is set is not clearly stated, and while there is an air of timeless antiquity about the old city of Prague, electricity is mentioned several times and so it is clear that events take place in the late nineteenth century, around the time of the novel's publication in 1891. The narrative concerns a witch, although she is is not old and ugly as such creatures are usually presented, but an attractive and seductive young woman. Dennis Wheatley observes in his brief introduction to the 1974 edition of the novel: 'The mental picture conjured up in most people's minds by the word 'witch' is of an aged crook-backed hag with straggly grey hair beneath a steeple-crowned hat; but the records of history tell us that witches were often young and beautiful.'

Such is the case of the titular character in this novel. The alluring and wealthy Unorna is not herself evil, although she uses her powers selfishly, hypnotising the unwary with the power of her multi-coloured eyes to enslave them. It is her need for love which leads her into dealings with Keyork Arabian, a mysterious elderly dwarf, a powerful wizard who is the evil character in the novel.

The novel, which has a wonderful dreamlike quality at times, was written when Crawford endured an extended period of ill-health. That may be the reason that it is unusually full of dark moods and strong shifting emotions. Unorna is researching methods to prolong natural life with Keyork Arabian. In blending the elements of the occult powers of hypnotism and the new frontiers of scientific exploration,

Crawford's approach was highly individual and original for its time. He was in essence tapping into the disparate passions of the late Victorians, blending them into a powerfully dramatic potion. These elements of fantasy and science are not seen in his other narratives.

It was rare to have such a strongly drawn female character at the centre of a work of Victorian fiction. Unorna is a lady who knows what she wants and is determined to get it – but if she cannot get it, she will destroy it. She is unbending in her scornful rejection of Israel Kafka, the man who loves her but is too weak to resist her hypnotic powers. In turn, the witch desires the Wanderer but he loves another and is strong and resourceful enough to be able to resist Unorna and her hypnotic charms. Add to this potent mix the fierce passion of jealousy and the brew bubbles with high drama. And this is just the effect Crawford was striving for. He had no grandiose notions about the purpose of his fiction. It was there to entertain, engross and amuse.

In 1893 he produced *The Novel: What It Is*, which explained his thoughts on novel writing and fiction in general. In it he defended his literary approach, self-conceived as a combination of romanticism and realism, defining the art form in terms of its marketplace and audience. The novel, he wrote, is 'a marketable commodity' and 'intellectual artistic luxury' that 'must amuse, indeed, but should amuse reasonably, from an intellectual point of view. . . Its intention is to amuse and please, and certainly not to teach and preach; but in order to amuse well it must be a finely-balanced creation . . . ' He seems to have demonstrated this approach most effectively in *The Witch of Prague*, which is rich in detail and drama and makes no pretensions to preach or carry a message. It surprises me that some imaginative film maker has not tried to bring this fascinating novel to the screen.

This collection of F. Marion Crawford's work contains all his supernatural writings and therefore not only is it unique but it provides the modern reader with a wonderful insight into why this writer was so successful and popular in his day.

DAVID STUART DAVIES

THE WITCH OF PRAGUE

and other tales

The Screaming Skull

I have often heard it scream. No, I am not nervous, I am not imaginative, and I never believed in ghosts, unless that thing is one. Whatever it is, it hates me almost as much as it hated Luke Pratt, and it screams at me.

If I were you, I would never tell ugly stories about ingenious ways of killing people, for you never can tell but that someone at the table may be tired of his or her nearest and dearest. I have always blamed myself for Mrs Pratt's death, and I suppose I was responsible for it in a way, though heaven knows I never wished her anything but long life and happiness. If I had not told that story she might be alive yet. That is why the thing screams at me, I fancy.

She was a good little woman, with a sweet temper, all things considered, and a nice gentle voice; but I remember hearing her shriek once when she thought her little boy was killed by a pistol that went off though everyone was sure that it was not loaded. It was the same scream; exactly the same, with a sort of rising quaver at the end; do you know what I mean? Unmistakable.

The truth is, I had not realised that the doctor and his wife were not on good terms. They used to bicker a bit now and then when I was here, and I often noticed that little Mrs Pratt got very red and bit her lip hard to keep her temper, while Luke grew pale and said the most offensive things. He was that sort when he was in the nursery, I remember, and afterwards at school. He was my cousin, you know; that is how I came by this house; after he died, and his boy Charley was killed in South Africa, there were no relations left. Yes, it's a pretty little property, just the sort of thing for an old sailor like me who has taken to gardening.

One always remembers one's mistakes much more vividly than one's cleverest things, doesn't one? I've often noticed it. I was dining with the Pratts one night, when I told them the story that afterwards made so much difference. It was a wet night in November, and the sea was moaning. Hush! – if you don't speak you will hear it now . . .

Do you hear the tide? Gloomy sound, isn't it? Sometimes, about this time of year – hallo! – there it is! Don't be frightened, man – it won't eat you – it's only a noise, after all! But I'm glad you've heard it, because there are always people who think it's the wind, or my imagination, or something. You won't hear it again tonight, I fancy, for it doesn't often come more than once. Yes – that's right. Put another stick on the fire, and a little more stuff into that weak mixture you're so fond of. Do you remember old Blauklot the carpenter, on that German ship that picked us up when the *Clontarf* went to the bottom? We were hove to in a howling gale one night, as snug as you please, with no land within five hundred miles, and the ship coming up and falling off as regularly as clockwork – 'Biddy te boor beebles ashore tis night, poys!' old Blauklot sang out, as he went off to his quarters with the sail-maker. I often think of that, now that I'm ashore for good and all.

Yes, it was on a night like this, when I was at home for a spell, waiting to take the *Olympia* out on her first trip – it was on the next voyage that she broke the record, you remember – but that dates it. Ninety-two was the year, early in November.

The weather was dirty, Pratt was out of temper, and the dinner was bad, very bad indeed, which didn't improve matters, and cold, which made it worse. The poor little lady was very unhappy about it, and insisted on making a Welsh rarebit on the table to counteract the raw turnips and the half-boiled mutton. Pratt must have had a hard day. Perhaps he had lost a patient. At all events, he was in a nasty temper.

'My wife is trying to poison me, you see!' he said. 'She'll succeed some day.' I saw that she was hurt, and I made believe to laugh, and said that Mrs Pratt was much too clever to get rid of her husband in such a simple way; and then I began to tell them about Japanese tricks with spun glass and chopped horsehair and the like.

Pratt was a doctor, and knew a lot more than I did about such things, but that only put me on my mettle, and I told a story about a woman in Ireland who did for three husbands before anyone suspected foul play.

Did you never hear that tale? The fourth husband managed to keep awake and caught her, and she was hanged. How did she do it? She drugged them, and poured melted lead into their ears through a little horn funnel when they were asleep . . . No – that's the wind whistling. It's backing up to the southward again. I can tell by the sound. Besides, the other thing doesn't often come more than once in an evening even at this time of year – when it happened. Yes, it was in November. Poor Mrs Pratt died suddenly in her bed not long after I dined here. I can fix the date, because I got the news in New York by the steamer that followed the *Olympia* when I took her out on her first trip. You had the *Leofric* the same year? Yes, I remember. What a pair of old buffers we are coming to be, you and I. Nearly fifty years since we were apprentices together on the *Clontarf*. Shall you ever forget old Blauklot? 'Biddy te boor beebles ashore, poys!' Ha, ha! Take a little more, with all that water. It's the old Hulstkamp I found in the cellar when this house came to me, the same I brought Luke from Amsterdam five-and-twenty years ago. He had never touched a drop of it. Perhaps he's sorry now, poor fellow.

Where did I leave off? I told you that Mrs Pratt died suddenly – yes. Luke must have been lonely here after she was dead, I should think; I came to see him now and then, and he looked worn and nervous, and told me that his practice was growing too heavy for him, though he wouldn't take an assistant on any account. Years went on, and his son was killed in South Africa, and after that he began to be queer. There was something about him not like other people. I believe he kept his senses in his profession to the end; there was no complaint of his having made mad mistakes in cases, or anything of that sort, but he had a look about him –

Luke was a red-headed man with a pale face when he was young, and he was never stout; in middle age he turned a sandy grey, and after his son died he grew thinner and thinner, till his head looked like a skull with parchment stretched over it very tight, and his eyes had a sort of glare in them that was very disagreeable to look at.

He had an old dog that poor Mrs Pratt had been fond of, and that used to follow her everywhere. He was a bulldog, and the sweetest tempered beast you ever saw, though he had a way of hitching his upper lip behind one of his fangs that frightened strangers a good deal. Sometimes, of an evening, Pratt and Bumble – that was the dog's name – used to sit and look at each other a long time, thinking about old times, I suppose, when Luke's wife used to sit in that chair you've got. That was always her place, and this was the doctor's, where I'm sitting. Bumble used to climb up by the footstool – he was old and fat by that time, and could not jump much, and his teeth were getting shaky. He would look steadily at Luke, and Luke looked steadily at the dog, his face growing more and more like a skull with two little coals for eyes; and after about five minutes or so, though it may have been less, old Bumble would suddenly begin to shake all over, and all on a sudden he would set up an awful howl, as if he had been shot, and tumble out of the easy-chair and trot away, and hide himself under the sideboard, and lie there making odd noises.

Considering Pratt's looks in those last months, the thing is not surprising, you know. I'm not nervous or imaginative, but I can quite believe he might have sent a sensitive woman into hysterics – his head looked so much like a skull in parchment.

At last I came down one day before Christmas, when my ship was in dock and I had three weeks off. Bumble was not about, and I said casually that I supposed the old dog was dead.

'Yes,' Pratt answered, and I thought there was something odd in his tone even before he went on after a little pause. 'I killed him,' he said presently. 'I could stand it no longer.'

I asked what it was that Luke could not stand, though I guessed well enough.

'He had a way of sitting in her chair and glaring at me, and then howling,' Luke shivered a little. 'He didn't suffer at all, poor old Bumble,' he went on in a hurry, as if he thought I might imagine he had been cruel. 'I put dionine into his drink to make him sleep soundly, and then I chloroformed him gradually, so that he could not have felt suffocated even if he was dreaming. It's been quieter since then.'

I wondered what he meant, for the words slipped out as if he could not help saying them. I've understood since. He meant that he did not hear that noise so often after the dog was out of the way. Perhaps he thought at first that it was old Bumble in the yard howling at the moon, though it's not that kind of noise, is it? Besides, I know what it is, if Luke didn't. It's only a noise after all, and a noise never hurt anybody yet. But he was much more imaginative than I am. No doubt there really is something about this place that I don't understand; but when I don't understand a thing, I call it a phenomenon, and I don't take it for granted that it's going to kill me, as he did. I don't understand everything, by long odds, nor do you, nor does any man who has been to sea. We used to talk of tidal waves, for instance, and we could not account for them; now we account for them by calling them submarine earthquakes, and we branch off into fifty theories, any one of which might make earthquakes quite comprehensible if we only knew what they were. I fell in with one of them once, and the inkstand flew straight up from the table against the ceiling of my cabin. The same thing happened to Captain Lecky – I dare say you've read about it in his *Wrinkles*. Very good. If that sort of thing took place ashore, in this room for instance, a nervous person would talk about spirits and levitation and fifty things that mean nothing, instead of just quietly setting it down as a 'phenomenon' that has not been explained yet. My view of that voice, you see.

Besides, what is there to prove that Luke killed his wife? I would not even suggest such a thing to anyone but you. After all, there was nothing but the coincidence that poor little Mrs Pratt died suddenly in her bed a few days after I told that story at dinner. She was not the only woman who ever died like that. Luke got the doctor over from the next parish, and they agreed that she had died of something the matter with her heart Why not? It's common enough.

Of course, there was the ladle. I never told anybody about that, and it made me start when I found it in the cupboard in the bedroom. It was new, too – a little tinned iron ladle that had not been in the fire more than once or twice, and there was some lead in it that had been melted, and stuck to the bottom of the bowl, all grey, with hardened dross on it. But that proves nothing. A country doctor is generally a handy man, who does everything for himself, and Luke may have had a dozen reasons for melting a little lead in a ladle. He was fond of sea-fishing, for instance, and he may have cast a sinker for a night-line; perhaps it was a weight for the hall clock, or something like that. All the same, when I found it I had a rather queer sensation, because it looked so much like the thing I had described when I told them the story. Do you understand? It affected me unpleasantly, and I threw it away; it's at the bottom of the sea a mile from the Spit, and it will be jolly well rusted beyond recognising if it's ever washed up by the tide.

You see, Luke must have bought it in the village, years ago, for the man sells just such ladles still. I suppose they are used in cooking. In any case, there was no reason why an inquisitive housemaid should find such a thing lying about, with lead in it, and wonder what it was, and perhaps talk to the maid who heard me tell the story at dinner – for that girl married the plumber's son in the village, and may remember the whole thing.

You understand me, don't you? Now that Luke Pratt is dead and gone, and lies buried beside his wife, with an honest man's tombstone at his head, I should not care to stir up anything that could hurt his memory. They are both dead, and their son, too. There was trouble enough about Luke's death, as it was.

How? He was found dead on the beach one morning, and there was a coroner's inquest. There were marks on his throat, but he had not been robbed. The verdict was that he had come to his end 'by the hands or teeth of some person or animal unknown', for half the jury thought it might have been a big dog that had thrown him down and gripped his windpipe, though the skin of his throat was not broken. No one knew at what time he had gone out, nor where he had been. He was found lying on his back above high-water mark, and an old cardboard bandbox that had belonged to his wife lay under his hand, open. The lid had fallen off. He seemed to have been carrying home a skull in the box – doctors are fond of collecting such things. It had rolled out and lay near his head, and it was a remarkably fine skull, rather small, beautifully shaped and very white, with perfect teeth. That is to say, the upper jaw was perfect, but there was no lower one at all, when I first saw it.

Yes, I found it here when I came. You see, it was very white and polished, like a thing meant to be kept under a glass case, and the people did not know where it came from, nor what to do with it; so they put it back into the bandbox and set it on the shelf of the cupboard in the best bedroom, and of course they showed it to me when I took possession. I was taken down to the beach, too, to be shown the place where Luke was found, and the old fisherman explained just how he was lying, and the skull beside him. The only point he could not explain was why the skull had rolled up the sloping sand towards Luke's head instead of rolling downhill to his feet. It did not seem odd to me at the time, but I have often thought of it since, for the place is rather steep. I'll take you there tomorrow if you like – I made a sort of cairn of stones there afterwards.

When he fell down, or was thrown down – whichever happened – the bandbox struck the sand, and the lid came off, and the thing came out and ought to have rolled down. But it didn't. It was close to his head almost touching it, and turned with the face towards it. I say it didn't strike me as odd when the man told me; but I could not help thinking about it afterwards, again and again, till I saw a picture of it all when I closed my eyes; and then I began to ask myself why the plaguey thing had rolled up instead of down, and why it had stopped near Luke's head instead of anywhere else, a yard away, for instance.

You naturally want to know what conclusion I reached, don't you? None that at all explained the rolling, at all events. But I got something else into my head, after a time, that made me feel downright uncomfortable.

Oh, I don't mean as to anything supernatural! There may be ghosts, or there may not be. If there are, I'm not inclined to believe that they can hurt living people except by frightening them, and, for my part, I would rather face any shape of ghost than a fog in the

Channel when it's crowded. No. What bothered me was just a foolish idea, that's all, and I cannot tell how it began, nor what made it grow till it turned into a certainty.

I was thinking about Luke and his poor wife one evening over my pipe and a dull book, when it occurred to me that the skull might possibly be hers, and I have never got rid of the thought since. You'll tell me there's no sense in it, no doubt, that Mrs Pratt was buried like a Christian and is lying in the churchyard where they put her, and that it's perfectly monstrous to suppose her husband kept her skull in her old bandbox in his bedroom. All the same, in the face of reason and common sense and probability, I'm convinced that he did. Doctors do all sorts of queer things that would make men like you and me feel creepy, and those are just the things that don't seem probable, nor logical, nor sensible to us.

Then, don't you see? – if it really was her skull, poor woman, the only way of accounting for his having it is that he really killed her, and did it in that way, as the woman killed her husbands in the story, and that he was afraid there might be an examination some day which would betray him. You see, I told that too, and I believe it had really happened some fifty or sixty years ago. They dug up the three skulls, you know, and there was a small lump of lead rattling about in each one. That was what hanged the woman. Luke remembered that, I'm sure. I don't want to know what he did when he thought of it; my taste never ran in the direction of horrors, and I don't fancy you care for them either, do you? No. If you did, you might supply what is wanting to the story.

It must have been rather grim, eh? I wish I did not see the whole thing so distinctly, just as everything must have happened. He took it the night before she was buried, I'm sure, after the coffin had been shut, and when the servant girl was asleep. I would bet anything, that when he'd got it, he put something under the sheet in its place, to fill up and look like it. What do you suppose he put there, under the sheet?

I don't wonder you take me up on what I'm saying! First I tell you that I don't want to know what happened, and that I hate to think about horrors, and then I describe the whole thing to you as if I had seen it. I'm quite sure that it was her work-bag that he put there. I remember the bag very well, for she always used it of an evening; it was made of brown plush, and when it was stuffed full it was about the size of – you understand. Yes, there I am, at it again! You may laugh at me, but you don't live here alone, where it was done, and you didn't tell Luke the story about the melted lead. I'm not nervous, I tell you, but sometimes I begin to feel that I understand why some people are. I dwell on all this when I'm alone, and I dream of it, and when that thing screams – well, frankly, I don't like the noise any more than you do, though I should be used to it by this time.

I ought not to be nervous. I've sailed in a haunted ship. There was a Man in the Top, and two-thirds of the crew died of the West Coast fever inside of ten days after we anchored; but I was all right, then and afterwards. I have seen some ugly sights, too, just as you have, and all the rest of us. But nothing ever stuck in my head in the way this does.

You see, I've tried to get rid of the thing, but it doesn't like that. It wants to be there in its place, in Mrs Pratt's bandbox in the cupboard in the best bedroom. It's not happy anywhere else. How do I know that? Because I've tried it. You don't suppose that I've not tried, do you? As long as it's there it only screams now and then, generally at this time of year, but if I put it out of the house it goes on all night, and no servant will stay here twenty-four hours. As it is, I've often been left alone and have been obliged to shift for myself for a fortnight at a time. No one from the village would ever pass a night under the roof now, and as for selling the place, or even letting it, that's out of the question. The old women say that if I stay here I shall come to a bad end myself before long.

I'm not afraid of that. You smile at the mere idea that anyone could take such nonsense seriously. Quite right. It's utterly blatant nonsense, I agree with you. Didn't I tell you that it's only a noise after all when you started and looked round as if you expected to see a ghost standing behind your chair?

I may be all wrong about the skull, and I like to think that I am when I can. It may be just a fine specimen which Luke got somewhere long ago, and what rattles about inside when you shake it may be nothing but a pebble, or a bit of hard clay, or anything. Skulls that have lain long in the ground generally have something inside them that rattles don't they? No, I've never tried to get it out, whatever it is; I'm afraid it might be lead, don't you see? And if it is, I don't want to know the fact, for I'd much rather not be sure. If it really is lead, I killed her quite as much as if I had done the deed myself. Anybody must see that, I should think. As long as I don't know for certain, I have the consolation of saying that it's all utterly ridiculous nonsense, that Mrs Pratt died a natural death and that the beautiful skull belonged to Luke when he was a student in London. But if I were quite sure, I believe I should have to leave the house; indeed I do, most certainly. As it is, I had to give up trying to sleep in the best bedroom where the cupboard is.

You ask me why I don't throw it into the pond – yes, but please don't call it a 'confounded bugbear' – it doesn't like being called names.

There! Lord, what a shriek! I told you so! You're quite pale, man. Fill up your pipe and draw your chair nearer to the fire, and take some more drink. Old Hollands never hurt anybody yet. I've seen a Dutchman in Java drink half a jug of Hulstkamp in a morning without turning a hair. I don't take much rum myself, because it doesn't agree with my rheumatism, but you are not rheumatic and it won't damage you Besides, it's a very damp night outside. The wind is howling again, and it will soon be in the south-west; do you hear how the windows rattle? The tide must have turned too, by the moaning.

We should not have heard the thing again if you had not said that. I'm pretty sure we should not. Oh yes, if you choose to describe it as a coincidence, you are quite welcome, but I would rather that you should not call the thing names again, if you don't mind. It may be that the poor little woman hears, and perhaps it hurts her, don't you know? Ghosts? No! you don't call anything a ghost that you can take in your hands and look at in broad daylight, and that rattles when you shake it, do you, now? But it's something that hears and understands; there's no doubt about that.

I tried sleeping in the best bedroom when I first came to the house just because it was the best and most comfortable, but I had to give it up. It was their room, and there's the big bed she died in, and the cupboard is in the thickness of the wall, near the head, on the left. That's where it likes to be kept, in its bandbox. I only used the room for a fortnight after I came, and then I turned out and took the little room downstairs, next to the surgery, where Luke used to sleep when he expected to be called to a patient during the night.

I was always a good sleeper ashore; eight hours is my dose, eleven to seven when I'm alone, twelve to eight when I have a friend with me. But I could not sleep after three o'clock in the morning in that room – a quarter past, to be accurate – as a matter of fact, I timed it with my old pocket chronometer, which still keeps good time, and it was always at exactly seventeen minutes past three. I wonder whether that was the hour when she died?

It was not what you have heard. If it had been that, I could not have stood it two nights. It was just a start and a moan and hard breathing for a few seconds in the cupboard, and it could never have waked me under ordinary circumstances, I'm sure. I suppose you are like me in that, and we are just like other people who have been to sea. No natural sounds disturb us at all, not all the racket of a square-rigger hove to in a heavy gale, or rolling on her beam ends before the wind. But if a lead pencil gets adrift and rattles in the drawer of your cabin table you are awake in a moment. Just so – you always understand. Very well, the noise in the cupboard was no louder than that, but it waked me instantly.

I said it was like a 'start'. I know what I mean, but it's hard to explain without seeming to talk nonsense. Of course you cannot exactly 'hear' a person 'start'; at the most, you might hear the quick drawing of the breath between the parted lips and closed teeth, and the almost imperceptible sound of clothing that moved suddenly though very slightly. It was like that.

You know how one feels what a sailing vessel is going to do, two or three seconds before she does it, when one has the wheel. Riders say the same of a horse, but that's less strange, because the horse is a live animal with feelings of its own, and only poets and landsmen talk about a ship being alive, and all that. But I have always felt somehow that besides being a steaming machine or a sailing machine for carrying weights, a vessel at sea is a sensitive instrument, and a means of communication between nature and man, and most particularly the man at the wheel, if she is steered by hand. She takes her impressions directly from wind and sea, tide and stream, and transmits them to the man's hand, just as the wireless telegraphy picks up the interrupted currents aloft and turns them out below in the form of a message.

You see what I am driving at; I felt that something started in the cupboard, and I felt it so vividly that I heard it, though there may have been nothing to hear, and the sound inside my head waked me suddenly. But I really heard the other noise. It was as if it were muffled inside a box, as far away as if it came through a long-distance telephone; and yet I knew that it was inside the cupboard near the head of my bed. My hair did not bristle and my blood did not run cold that time. I simply resented being waked up by something that had no business to make a noise, any more than a pencil should rattle in the drawer of my cabin table on board ship. For I did not understand; I just supposed that the cupboard had some communication with the outside air, and that the wind had got in and was moaning through it with a sort of very faint screech. I struck a light and looked at my watch, and it was seventeen minutes past three. Then I turned over and went to sleep on my right ear. That's my good one; I'm pretty deaf with the other, for I struck the water with it when I was a lad in diving from the fore-topsail yard. Silly thing to do, it was, but the result is very convenient when I want to go to sleep when there's a noise.

That was the first night, and the same thing happened again and several times afterwards, but not regularly, though it was always at the same time, to a second; perhaps I was sometimes sleeping on my good ear, and sometimes not. I overhauled the cupboard and there was no way by which the wind could get in, or anything else, for the door makes a good fit, having been meant to keep out moths, I suppose; Mrs Pratt must have kept her winter things in it, for it still smells of camphor and turpentine.

After about a fortnight I had had enough of the noises. So far I had said to myself that it would be silly to yield to it and take the skull out of the room. Things always look differently by daylight, don't they? But the voice grew louder – I suppose one may call it a voice – and it got inside my deaf ear, too, one night. I realised that when I was wide awake, for my good ear was jammed down on the pillow, and I ought not to have heard a foghorn in that position. But I heard that, and it made me lose my temper, unless it scared me, for sometimes the two are not far apart. I struck a light and got up, and I opened the cupboard, grabbed the bandbox and threw it out of the window, as far as I could.

Then my hair stood on end. The thing screamed in the air, like a shell from a twelve-inch gun. It fell on the other side of the road. The night was very dark, and I could not see it fall, but I know it fell beyond the road The window is just over the front door, it's fifteen yards to the fence, more or less, and the road is ten yards wide. There's a thick-set hedge beyond, along the glebe that belongs to the vicarage.

I did not sleep much more than night. It was not more than half an hour after I had thrown the bandbox out when I heard a shriek outside – like what we've had tonight, but worse, more despairing, I should call it; and it may have been my imagination, but I could have sworn that the screams came nearer and nearer each time. I lit a pipe, and walked up and down for a bit, and then took a book and sat up reading, but I'll be hanged if I can remember what I read nor even what the book was, for every now and then a shriek came up that would have made a dead man turn in his coffin.

A little before dawn someone knocked at the front door. There was no mistaking that for anything else, and I opened my window and looked down, for I guessed that someone wanted the doctor, supposing that the new man had taken Luke's house. It was rather a relief to hear a human knock after that awful noise.

You cannot see the door from above, owing to the little porch. The knocking came again, and I called out, asking who was there, but nobody answered, though the knock was repeated. I sang out again, and said that the doctor did not live here any longer. There was no answer, but it occurred to me that it might be some old countryman who was stone deaf. So I took my candle and went down to open the door. Upon my word, I was not thinking of the thing yet, and I had almost forgotten the other noises. I went down convinced that I should find somebody outside, on the doorstep, with a message. I set the candle on the hall table, so that the wind should not blow it out when I opened. While I was drawing the old-fashioned bolt I heard the knocking again. It was not loud, and it had a queer, hollow sound, now that I was close to it, I remember, but I certainly thought it was made by some person who wanted to get in.

It wasn't. There was nobody there, but as I opened the door inward, standing a little on one side, so as to see out at once, something rolled across the threshold and stopped against my foot.

I drew back as I felt it, for I knew what it was before I looked down. I cannot tell you how I knew, and it seemed unreasonable, for I am still quite sure that I had thrown it across the road. It's a French window, that opens wide, and I got a good swing when I flung it out. Besides, when I went out early in the morning, I found the bandbox beyond the thick hedge.

You may think it opened when I threw it, and that the skull dropped out; but that's impossible, for nobody could throw an empty cardboard box so far. It's out of the question; you might as well try to fling a ball of paper twenty-five yards, or a blown bird's egg.

To go back, I shut and bolted the hall door, picked the thing up carefully, and put it on the table beside the candle. I did that mechanically, as one instinctively does the right thing in danger without thinking at all – unless one does the opposite. It may seem odd, but I believe my first thought had been that somebody might come and find me there on the threshold while it was resting against my foot, lying a little on its side, and turning one hollow eye up at my face, as if it meant to accuse me. And the light and shadow from the candle played in the hollows of the eyes as it stood on the table, so that they seemed to open and shut at me. Then the candle went out quite unexpectedly, though the door was fastened and there was not the least draught; and I used up at least half a dozen matches before it would burn again.

I sat down rather suddenly, without quite knowing why. Probably I had been badly frightened, and perhaps you will admit there was no great shame in being scared. The thing had come home, and it wanted to go upstairs, back to its cupboard. I sat still and stared at it for a bit till I began to feel very cold; then I took it and carried it up and set it in its place, and I remember that I spoke to it, and promised that it should have its bandbox again in the morning.

You want to know whether I stayed in the room till daybreak? Yes, but I kept a light burning, and sat up smoking and reading, most likely out of fright; plain, undeniable fear, and you need not call it cowardice either, for that's not the same thing. I could not have stayed alone with that thing in the cupboard; I should have been scared to death, though I'm not more timid than other people. Confound it all, man, it had crossed the road alone, and had got up the doorstep and had knocked to be let in.

When the dawn came, I put on my boots and went out to find the bandbox. I had to go a good way round, by the gate near the high road, and I found the box open and hanging on the other side of the hedge. It had caught on the twigs by the string, and the lid had fallen off and was lying on the ground below it. That shows that it did not open till it was well over; and if it had not opened as soon as it left my hand, what was inside it must have gone beyond the road too.

That's all. I took the box upstairs to the cupboard, and put the skull back and locked it up. When the girl brought me my breakfast she said she was sorry, but that she must go, and she did not care if she lost her month's wages. I looked at her, and her face was a sort of greenish yellowish white. I pretended to be surprised, and asked what was the matter; but that was of no use, for she just turned on me and wanted to know whether I meant to stay in a haunted house, and how long I expected to live if I did, for though she noticed I was sometimes a little hard of hearing, she did not believe that even I could sleep through those screams again – and if I could, why had I been moving about the house and opening and shutting the front door, between three and four in the morning? There was no answering that, since she had heard me, so off she went, and I was left to myself. I went down to the village during the morning and found a woman who was willing to come and do the little work there is and cook my dinner, on condition that she might go home every night. As for me, I moved downstairs that day, and I have never tried to sleep in the best bedroom since. After a little while I got a brace of middle-aged Scotch servants from London, and things were quiet enough for a long time. I began by telling them that the house was in a very exposed position, and that the wind whistled round it a good deal in the autumn and winter, which had given it a bad name in the village, the Cornish people being inclined to superstition and telling ghost stories. The two hard-faced, sandy-haired sisters almost smiled, and they answered with great contempt that they had no great opinion of any Southern bogey whatever, having been in service in two English haunted houses, where they had never seen so much as the Boy in Grey, whom they reckoned no very particular rarity in Forfarshire.

They stayed with me several months, and while they were in the house we had peace and quiet. One of them is here again now, but she went away with her sister within the year. This one – she was the cook – married the sexton, who works in my garden. That's the way of it. It's a small village and he has not much to do, and he knows enough about flowers to help me nicely, besides doing most of the hard work; for though I'm fond of exercise, I'm getting a little stiff in the hinges. He's a sober, silent sort of fellow, who minds his own business, and he was a widower when I came here – Trehearn is his name, James Trehearn. The Scottish sisters would not admit that there was anything wrong about the house, but when November came they gave me warning that they were going, on the ground that the chapel was such a long walk from here, being in the next parish, and that they could not possibly go to our church. But the younger one came back in the spring, and as soon as the banns could be published she was married to James Trehearn by the vicar, and she seems to have had no scruples about hearing him preach since then. I'm quite satisfied, if she is! The couple live in a small cottage that looks over the churchyard.

I suppose you are wondering what all this has to do with what I was talking about. I'm alone so much that when an old friend comes to see me, I sometimes go on talking just for the sake of hearing my own voice. But in this case there is really a connection of ideas. It was James Trehearn who buried poor Mrs Pratt, and her husband after her in the same grave, and it's not far from the back of his cottage. That's the connection in my mind, you see. It's plain enough. He knows something, I'm quite sure that he does, though he's such a reticent beggar.

Yes, I'm alone in the house at night now, for Mrs Trehearn does everything herself, and when I have a friend the sexton's niece comes in to wait on the table. He takes his wife home every evening in winter, but in summer, when there's light, she goes by herself. She's not a nervous woman, but she's less sure than she used to be that there are no bogies in England worth a Scotch-woman's notice. Isn't it amusing, the idea that Scotland has a monopoly of the super-natural? Odd sort of national pride, I call that, don't you?

That's a good fire, isn't it? When driftwood gets started at last there's nothing like it, I think. Yes, we get lots of it, for I'm sorry to say there are still a great many wrecks about here. It's a lonely coast, and you may have all the wood you want for the trouble of bringing it in. Trehearn and I borrow a cart now and then, and load it between here and the Spit. I hate a coal fire when I can get wood of any sort A log is company, even if it's only a piece of a deck beam or timber sawn off, and the salt in it makes pretty sparks. See how they fly, like Japanese hand-fireworks! Upon my word, with an old friend and a good fire and a pipe, one forgets all about that thing upstairs, especially now that the wind has moderated. It's only a lull, though, and it will blow a gale before morning.

You think you would like to see the skull? I've no objection. There's no reason why you shouldn't have a look at it, and you never saw a more perfect one in your life, except that there are two front teeth missing in the lower jaw.

Oh yes – I had not told you about the jaw yet. Trehearn found it in the garden last spring when he was digging a pit for a new asparagus bed. You know we make asparagus beds six or eight feet deep here. Yes, yes – I had forgotten to tell you that. He was digging straight down, just as he digs a grave; if you want a good asparagus bed made, I advise you to get a sexton to make it for you. Those fellows have a wonderful knack at that sort of digging.

Trehearn had got down about three feet when he cut into a mass of white lime in the side of the trench. He had noticed that the earth was a little looser there, though he says it had not been disturbed for a number of years. I suppose he thought that even old lime might not be good for asparagus, so he broke it out and threw it up. It was pretty hard, he says, in biggish lumps, and out of sheer force of habit he cracked the lumps with his spade as they lay outside the pit beside him; the jaw bone of the skull dropped out of one of the pieces. He thinks he must have knocked out the two front teeth in breaking up the lime, but he did not see them anywhere. He's a very experienced man in such things, as you may imagine, and he said at once that the jaw had probably belonged to a young woman, and that the teeth had been complete when she died. He brought it to me, and asked me if I wanted to keep it; if I did not, he said he would drop it into the next grave he made in the churchyard, as he supposed it was a Christian jaw, and ought to have decent burial, wherever the rest of the body might be. I told him that doctors often put bones into quicklime to whiten them nicely, and that I supposed Dr Pratt had once had a little lime pit in the garden for that purpose, and had forgotten the jaw. Trehearn looked at me quietly.

'Maybe it fitted that skull that used to be in the cupboard upstairs, sir,' he said. 'Maybe Dr Pratt had put the skull into the lime to clean it, or something, and when he took it out he left the lower jaw behind. There's some human hair sticking in the lime, sir.'

I saw there was, and that was what Trehearn said. If he did not suspect something, why in the world should he have suggested that the jaw might fit the skull? Besides, it did. That's proof that he knows more than he cares to tell. Do you suppose he looked before she was buried? Or perhaps – when he buried Luke in the same grave –

Well, well, it's of no use to go over that, is it? I said I would keep the jaw with the skull, and I took it upstairs and fitted it into its place. There's not the slightest doubt about the two belonging together, and together they are.

Trehearn knows several things. We were talking about plastering the kitchen a while ago, and he happened to remember that it had not been done since the very week when Mrs Pratt died. He did not say that the mason must have left some lime on the place, but he thought it, and that it was the very same lime he had found in the asparagus pit. He knows a lot. Trehearn is one of your silent beggars who can put two and two together. That grave is very near the back of his cottage, too, and he's one of the quickest men with a spade I ever saw. If he wanted to know the truth, he could, and no one else would ever be the wiser unless he chose to tell. In a quiet village like ours, people don't go and spend the night in the churchyard to see whether the sexton potters about by himself between ten o'clock and daylight.

What is awful to think of, is Luke's deliberation, if he did it; his cool certainty that no one would find him out; above all, his nerve, for that must have been extraordinary. I sometimes think it's bad enough to live in the place where it was done, if it really was done. I always put in the condition, you see, for the sake of his memory, and a little bit for my own sake, too.

I'll go upstairs and fetch the box in a minute. Let me light my pipe; there's no hurry! We had supper early, and it's only half-past nine o'clock. I never let a friend go to bed before twelve, or with less than three glasses – you may have as many more as you like, but you shan't have less, for the sake of old times.

It's breezing up again, do you hear? That was only a lull just now, and we are going to have a bad night.

A thing happened that made me start a little when I found that the jaw fitted exactly. I'm not very easily startled in that way myself, but I have seen people make a quick movement, drawing their breath sharply, when they had thought they were alone and suddenly turned and saw someone very near them. Nobody can call that fear. You wouldn't, would you? No. Well, just when I had set the jaw in its place under the skull, the teeth closed sharply on my finger. It felt exactly as if it were biting me hard, and I confess that I jumped before I realised that I had been pressing the jaw and the skull together with my other hand. I assure you I was not at all nervous. It was broad daylight, too, and a fine day, and the sun was streaming into the best bedroom. It would have been absurd to be nervous, and it was only a quick mistaken impression, but it really made me feel queer. Somehow it made me think of the funny verdict of the coroner's jury on Luke's death, 'by the hand or teeth of some person or animal unknown'. Ever since that I've wished I had seen those marks on his throat, though the lower jaw was missing then.

I have often seen a man do insane things with his hands that he does not realise at all. I once saw a man hanging on by an old awning stop with one hand, leaning backward, outboard, with all his weight on it, and he was just cutting the stop with the knife in his other hand when I got my arms round him. We were in mid-ocean, going twenty knots. He had not the smallest idea what he was doing; neither had I when I managed to pinch my finger between the teeth of that thing. I can feel it now. It was exactly as if it were alive and were trying to bite me. It would if it could, for I know it hates me, poor thing! Do you suppose that what rattles about inside is really a bit of lead? Well, I'll get the box down presently, and if whatever it is happens to drop out into your hands, that's your affair. If it's only a clod of earth or a pebble, the whole matter would be off my mind, and I don't believe I should ever think of the skull again; but somehow I cannot bring myself to shake out the bit of hard stuff myself. The mere idea that it may be lead makes me confoundedly uncomfortable, yet I've got the conviction that I shall know before long. I shall certainly know. I'm sure Trehearn knows, but he's such a silent beggar.

I'll go upstairs now and get it. What? You had better go with me? Ha, ha! do you think I'm afraid of a bandbox and a noise? Nonsense!

Bother the candle, it won't light! As if the ridiculous thing understood what it's wanted for! Look at that – the third match. They light fast enough for my pipe. There, do you see? It's a fresh box, just out of the tin safe where I keep the supply on account of the dampness. Oh, you think the wick of the candle may be damp, do you? All right, I'll light the beastly thing in the fire. That won't go out, at all events. Yes, it sputters a bit, but it will keep lighted now. It burns just like any other candle, doesn't it? The fact is, candles are not very good about here. I don't know where they come from, but they have a way of burning low occasionally, with a greenish flame that spits tiny sparks, and I'm often annoyed by their going out of themselves. It cannot be helped, for it will be long before we have electricity in our village. It really is rather a poor light, isn't it?

You think I had better leave you the candle and take the lamp, do you? I don't like to carry lamps about, that's the truth. I never dropped one in my life, but I have always thought I might, and it's so confoundedly dangerous if you do. Besides, I am pretty well used to these rotten candles by this time.

You may as well finish that glass while I'm getting it, for I don't mean to let you off with less than three before you go to bed. You won't have to go upstairs, either, for I've put you in the old study next to the surgery – that's where I live myself. The fact is, I never ask a friend to sleep upstairs now. The last man who did was Crackenthorpe, and he said he was kept awake all night. You remember old Crack, don't you? He stuck to the Service, and they've just made him an admiral. Yes, I'm off now – unless the candle goes out. I couldn't help asking if you remembered Crackenthorpe. If anyone had told us that the skinny little idiot he used to be was to turn out the most successful of the lot of us, we should have laughed at the idea, shouldn't we? You and I did not do badly, it's true – but I'm really going now. I don't mean to let you think that I've been putting it off by talking! As if there were anything to be afraid of! If I were scared, I should tell you so quite frankly, and get you to go upstairs with me.

*   *   *

Here's the box. I brought it down very carefully, so as not to disturb it, poor thing. You see, if it were shaken, the jaw might get separated from it again, and I'm sure it wouldn't like that. Yes, the candle went out as I was coming downstairs, but that was the draught from the leaky window on the landing. Did you hear anything? Yes, there was another scream. Am I pale, do you say? That's nothing. My heart is a little queer sometimes, and I went upstairs too fast. In fact, that's one reason why I really prefer to live altogether on the ground floor.

Wherever the shriek came from, it was not from the skull, for I had the box in my hand when I heard the noise, and here it is now; so we have proved definitely that the screams are produced by something else. I've no doubt I shall find out some day what makes them. Some crevice in the wall, of course, or a crack in a chimney, or a chink in the frame of a window. That's the way all ghost stories end in real life. Do you know, I'm jolly glad I thought of going up and bringing it down for you to see, for that last shriek settles the question. To think that I should have been so weak as to fancy that the poor skull could really cry out like a living thing!

Now I'll open the box, and we'll take it out and look at it under the bright light. It's rather awful to think that the poor lady used to sit there, in your chair, evening after evening, in just the same light, isn't it? But then – I've made up my mind that it's all rubbish from beginning to end, and that it's just an old skull that Luke had when he was a student and perhaps he put it into the lime merely to whiten it, and could not find the jaw.

I made a seal on the string, you see, after I had put the jaw in its place, and I wrote on the cover. There's the old white label on it still, from the milliner's, addressed to Mrs Pratt when the hat was sent to her, and as there was room I wrote on the edge: 'A skull, once the property of the late Luke Pratt, MD.' I don't quite know why I wrote that, unless it was with the idea of explaining how the thing happened to be in my possession. I cannot help wondering sometimes what sort of hat it was that came in the bandbox. What colour was it, do you think? Was it a gay spring hat with a bobbing feather and pretty ribands? Strange that the very same box should hold the head that wore the finery – perhaps. No – we made up our minds that it just came from the hospital in London where Luke did his time. It's far better to look at it in that light, isn't it? There's no more connection between that skull and poor Mrs Pratt than there was between my story about the lead and –

Good Lord! Take the lamp – don't let it go out, if you can help it – I'll have the window fastened again in a second – I say, what a gale! There, it's out! I told you so! Never mind, there's the firelight – I've got the window shut – the bolt was only half down. Was the box blown off the table? Where the deuce is it? There! That won't open again, for I've put up the bar. Good dodge, an old-fashioned bar – there's nothing like it. Now, you find the bandbox while I light the lamp. Confound those wretched matches! Yes, a pipe spill is better – it must light in the fire – hadn't thought of it – thank you – there we are again. Now, where's the box? Yes, put it back on the table, and we'll open it.

That's the first time I have ever known the wind to burst that window open; but it was partly carelessness on my part when I last shut it. Yes, of course I heard the scream. It seemed to go all round the house before it broke in at the window. That proves that it's always been the wind and nothing else, doesn't it? When it was not the wind, it was my imagination. I've always been a very imaginative man: I must have been, though I did not know it. As we grow older we understand ourselves better, don't you know?

I'll have a drop of the Hulstkamp neat, by way of an exception, since you are filling up your glass. That damp gust chilled me, and with my rheumatic tendency I'm very much afraid of a chill, for the cold sometimes seems to stick in my joints all winter when it once gets in.

By George, that's good stuff! I'll just light a fresh pipe, now that everything is snug again, and then we'll open the box. I'm so glad we heard that last scream together, with the skull here on the table between us, for a thing cannot possibly be in two places at the same time, and the noise most certainly came from outside, as any noise the wind makes must. You thought you heard it scream through the room after the window was burst open? Oh yes, so did I, but that was natural enough when everything was open. Of course we heard the wind. What could one expect?

Look here, please. I want you to see that the seal is intact before we open the box together. Will you take my glasses? No, you have your own. All right. The seal is sound, you see, and you can read the words of the motto easily. 'Sweet and low' – that's it – because the poem goes on 'Wind of the Western Sea', and says, 'blow him again to me', and all that. Here is the seal on my watch chain, where it's hung for more than forty years. My poor little wife gave it to me when I was courting, and I never had any other. It was just like her to think of those words – she was always fond of Tennyson.

It's no use to cut the string, for it's fastened to the box, so I'll just break the wax and untie the knot, and afterwards we'll seal it up again. You see, I like to feel that the thing is safe in its place, and that nobody can take it out. Not that I should suspect Trehearn of meddling with it, but I always feel that he knows a lot more than he tells.

You see, I've managed it without breaking the string, though when I fastened it I never expected to open the bandbox again. The lid comes off easily enough. There! Now look!

What! Nothing in it! Empty! It's gone, man, the skull is gone!

No, there's nothing the matter with me. I'm only trying to collect my thoughts. It's so strange. I'm positively certain that it was inside when I put on the seal last spring. I can't have imagined that: it's utterly impossible. If I ever took a stiff glass with a friend now and then, I would admit that I might have made some idiotic mistake when I had taken too much. But I don't, and I never did. A pint of ale at supper and half a go of rum at bedtime was the most I ever took in my good days. I believe it's always we sober fellows who get rheumatism and gout! Yet there was my seal, and there is the empty bandbox. That's plain enough.

I say, I don't half like this. It's not right. There's something wrong about it, in my opinion. You needn't talk to me about supernatural manifestations, for I don't believe in them, not a little bit! Somebody must have tampered with the seal and stolen the skull. Sometimes, when I go out to work in the garden in summer, I leave my watch and chain on the table. Trehearn must have taken the seal then, and used it, for he would be quite sure that I should not come in for at least an hour.

If it was not Trehearn – oh, don't talk to me about the possibility that the thing has got out by itself! If it has, it must be somewhere about the house, in some out-of-the-way corner, waiting. We may come upon it anywhere, waiting for us, don't you know? – just waiting in the dark. Then it will scream at me; it will shriek at me in the dark, for it hates me, I tell you!

The bandbox is quite empty. We are not dreaming, either of us. There, I turn it upside down.

What's that? Something fell out as I turned it over. It's on the floor, it s near your feet. I know it is, and we must find it. Help me to find it, man. Have you got it? For God's sake, give it to me, quickly!

Lead! I knew it when I heard it fall. I knew it couldn't be anything else by the little thud it made on the hearthrug. So it was lead after all and Luke did it.

I feel a little bit shaken up – not exactly nervous, you know, but badly shaken up, that's the fact. Anybody would, I should think. After all, you cannot say that it's fear of the thing, for I went up and brought it down – at least, I believed I was bringing it down, and that's the same thing, and by George, rather than give in to such silly nonsense, I'll take the box upstairs again and put it back in its place. It's not that. It's the certainty that the poor little woman came to her end in that way, by my fault, because I told the story. That's what is so dreadful. Somehow, I had always hoped that I should never be quite sure of it, but there is no doubting it now. Look at that!

Look at it! That little lump of lead with no particular shape. Think of what it did, man! Doesn't it make you shiver? He gave her something to make her sleep, of course, but there must have been one moment of awful agony. Think of having boiling lead poured into your brain. Think of it. She was dead before she could scream, but only think of – oh! there it is again – it's just outside – I know it's just outside – I can't keep it out of my head! – oh! – oh!

You thought I had fainted? No, I wish I had, for it would have stopped sooner. It's all very well to say that it's only a noise, and that a noise never hurt anybody – you're as white as a shroud yourself. There's only one thing to be done, if we hope to close an eye tonight. We must find it and put it back into its bandbox and shut it up in the cupboard, where it likes to be. I don't know how it got out, but it wants to get in again. That's why it screams so awfully tonight – it was never so bad as this – never since I first –

Bury it? Yes, if we can find it, we'll bury it, if it takes us all night. We'll bury it six feet deep and ram down the earth over it, so that it shall never get out again, and if it screams, we shall hardly hear it so deep down. Quick, we'll get the lantern and look for it. It cannot be far away; I'm sure it's just outside – it was coming in when I shut the window, I know it.

Yes, you're quite right. I'm losing my senses, and I must get hold of myself. Don't speak to me for a minute or two; I'll sit quite still and keep my eyes shut and repeat something I know. That's the best way.

'Add together the altitude, the latitude, and the polar distance, divide by two and subtract the altitude from the half-sum; then add the logarithm of the secant of the latitude, the cosecant of the polar distance, the cosine of the half-sum and the sine of the half-sum minus the altitude' – there! Don't say that I'm out of my senses, for my memory is all right, isn't it?

Of course, you may say that it's mechanical, and that we never forget the things we learned when we were boys and have used almost every day for a lifetime. But that's the very point. When a man is going crazy, it's the mechanical part of his mind that gets out of order and won't work right; he remembers things that never happened, or he sees things that aren't real, or he hears noises when there is perfect silence. That's not what is the matter with either of us, is it?

Come, we'll get the lantern and go round the house. It's not raining – only blowing like old boots, as we used to say. The lantern is in the cupboard under the stairs in the hall, and I always keep it trimmed in case of a wreck.

No use to look for the thing? I don't see how you can say that. It was nonsense to talk of burying it, of course, for it doesn't want to be buried; it wants to go back into its bandbox and be taken upstairs, poor thing! Trehearn took it out, I know, and made the seal over again. Perhaps he took it to the churchyard, and he may have meant well. I dare say he thought that it would not scream any more if it were quietly laid in consecrated ground, near where it belongs. But it has come home. Yes, that's it. He's not half a bad fellow, Trehearn, and rather religiously inclined, I think. Does not that sound natural, and reasonable, and well meant? He supposed it screamed because it was not decently buried – with the rest. But he was wrong. How should he know that it screams at me because it hates me, and because it's my fault that there was that little lump of lead in it?

No use to look for it, anyhow? Nonsense! I tell you it wants to be found – Hark! what's that knocking? Do you hear it? Knock – knock – knock – three times, then a pause, and then again. It has a hollow sound, hasn't it?

It has come home. I've heard that knock before. It wants to come in and be taken upstairs in its box. It's at the front door.

Will you come with me? We'll take it in. Yes, I own that I don't like to go alone and open the door. The thing will roll in and stop against my foot, just as it did before, and the light will go out. I'm a good deal shaken by finding that bit of lead, and, besides, my heart isn't quite right – too much strong tobacco, perhaps. Besides, I'm quite willing to own that I'm a bit nervous tonight, if I never was before in my life.

That's right, come along! I'll take the box with me, so as not to come back. Do you hear the knocking? It's not like any other knocking I ever heard. If you will hold this door open, I can find the lantern under the stairs by the light from this room without bringing the lamp into the hall – it would only go out.

The thing knows we are coming – hark! it's impatient to get in. Don't shut the door till the lantern is ready, whatever you do. There will be the usual trouble with the matches, I suppose – no, the first one, by Jove! I tell you it wants to get in, so there's no trouble. All right with that door now; shut it, please. Now come and hold the lantern, for it's blowing so hard outside that I shall have to use both hands. That's it, hold the light low. Do you hear the knocking still? Here goes – I'll open just enough with my foot against the bottom of the door – now!

Catch it! it's only the wind that blows it across the floor, that's all – there's half a hurricane outside, I tell you! Have you got it? The bandbox is on the table. One minute, and I'll have the bar up. There!

Why did you throw it into the box so roughly? It doesn't like that, you know.

What do you say? Bitten your hand? Nonsense, man! You did just what I did. You pressed the jaws together with your other hand and pinched yourself. Let me see. You don't mean to say you have drawn blood? You must have squeezed hard, by Jove, for the skin is certainly torn. I'll give you some carbolic solution for it before we go to bed, for they say a scratch from a skull's tooth may go bad and give trouble.

Come inside again and let me see it by the lamp. I'll bring the bandbox – never mind the lantern, it may just as well burn in the hall for I shall need it presently when I go up the stairs. Yes, shut the door if you will; it makes it more cheerful and bright. Is your finger still bleeding? I'll get you the carbolic in an instant; just let me see the thing.

Ugh! There's a drop of blood on the upper jaw. It's on the eye-tooth. Ghastly, isn't it? When I saw it running along the floor of the hall, the strength almost went out of my hands, and I felt my knees bending, then I understood that it was the gale, driving it over the smooth boards. You don t blame me? No, I should think not! We were boys together, and we've seen a thing or two, and we may just as well own to each other that we were both in a beastly funk when it slid across the floor at you. No wonder you pinched your finger picking it up, after that, if I did the same thing out of sheer nervousness, in broad daylight, with the sun streaming in on me.

Strange that the jaw should stick to it so closely, isn't it? I suppose it's the dampness, for it shuts like a vice – I have wiped off the drop of blood, for it was not nice to look at. I'm not going to try to open the jaws, don't be afraid! I shall not play any tricks with the poor thing, but I'll just seal the box again, and we'll take it upstairs and put it away where it wants to be. The wax is on the writing-table by the window. Thank you. It will be long before I leave my seal lying about again, for Trehearn to use, I can tell you. Explain? I don't explain natural phenomena, but if you choose to think that Trehearn had hidden it somewhere in the bushes, and that the gale blew it to the house against the door, and made it knock, as if it wanted to be let in, you're not thinking the impossible, and I'm quite ready to agree with you.

Do you see that? You can swear that you've actually seen me seal it this time, in case anything of the kind should occur again. The wax fastens the strings to the lid, which cannot possibly be lifted, even enough to get in one finger. You're quite satisfied, aren't you? Yes. Besides, I shall lock the cupboard and keep the key in my pocket hereafter.

Now we can take the lantern and go upstairs. Do you know, I'm very much inclined to agree with your theory that the wind blew it against the house. I'll go ahead, for I know the stairs; just hold the lantern near my feet as we go up. How the wind howls and whistles! Did you feel the sand on the floor under your shoes as we crossed the hall?

Yes – this is the door of the best bedroom. Hold up the lantern, please. This side, by the head of the bed. I left the cupboard open when I got the box. Isn't it queer how the faint odour of women's dresses will hang about an old closet for years? This is the shelf. You've seen me set the box there, and now you see me turn the key and put it into my pocket. So that's done!

Goodnight. Are you sure you're quite comfortable? It's not much of a room, but I dare say you would as soon sleep here as upstairs tonight. If you want anything, sing out; there's only a lath and plaster partition between us. There's not so much wind on this side by half. There's the Hollands on the table, if you'll have one more nightcap. No? Well, do as you please. Goodnight again, and don't dream about that thing, if you can.

The following paragraph appeared in the *Penraddon News*, 23 November 1906:

MYSTERIOUS DEATH OF A RETIRED SEA CAPTAIN

The village of Tredcombe is much disturbed by the strange death of Captain Charles Braddock, and all sorts of impossible stories are circulating with regard to the circumstances, which certainly seem difficult of explanation. The retired captain, who had successfully commanded in his time the largest and fastest liners belonging to one of the principal transatlantic steamship companies, was found dead in his bed on Tuesday morning in his own cottage, a quarter of a mile from the village. An examination was made at once by the local practitioner, which revealed the horrible fact that the deceased had been bitten in the throat by a human assailant, with such amazing force as to crush the windpipe and cause death. The marks of the teeth of both jaws were so plainly visible on the skin that they could be counted, but the perpetrator of the deed had evidently lost the two lower middle incisors. It is hoped that this peculiarity may help to identify the murderer, who can only be a dangerous escaped maniac. The deceased, though over sixty-five years of age, is said to have been a hale man of considerable physical strength, and it is remarkable that no signs of any struggle were visible in the room, nor could it be ascertained how the murderer had entered the house. Warning has been sent to all the insane asylums in the United Kingdom, but as yet no information has been received regarding the escape of any dangerous patient.

The coroner's Jury returned the somewhat singular verdict that Captain Braddock came to his death 'by the hands or teeth of some person unknown'. The local surgeon is said to have expressed privately the opinion that the maniac is a woman, a view he deduces from the small size of the jaws, as shown by the marks of the teeth. The whole affair is shrouded in mystery. Captain Braddock was a widower, and lived alone. He leaves no children.

(Author's Note. – Students of ghost lore and haunted houses will find the foundation of the foregoing story in the legends about a skull which is still preserved in the farmhouse called Bettiscombe Manor, situated, I believe, on the Dorsetshire coast.)

For the Blood is The Life

We had dined at sunset on the broad roof of the old tower, because it was cooler there during the great heat of summer. Besides, the little kitchen was built at one corner of the great square platform, which made it more convenient than if the dishes had to be carried down the steep stone steps, broken in places and everywhere worn with age. The tower was one of those built all down the west coast of Calabria by the Emperor Charles V early in the sixteenth century, to keep off the Barbary pirates, when the unbelievers were allied with Francis I against the Emperor and the Church. They have gone to ruin, a few still stand intact, and mine is one of the largest. How it came into my possession ten years ago, and why I spend a part of each year in it, are matters which do not concern this tale. The tower stands in one of the loneliest spots in southern Italy, at the extremity of a curving rocky promontory, which forms a small but safe natural harbour at the southern extremity of the Gulf of Policastro, and just north of Cape Scalea, the birthplace of Judas Iscariot, according to the old local legend. The tower stands alone on this hooked spur of the rock, and there is not a house to be seen within three miles of it. When I go there I take a couple of sailors, one of whom is a fair cook, and when I am away it is in charge of a gnomelike little being who was once a miner and who attached himself to me long ago.

My friend, who sometimes visits me in my summer solitude, is an artist by profession, a Scandinavian by birth, and a cosmopolitan by force of circumstances. We had dined at sunset; the sunset glow had reddened and faded again, and the evening purple steeped the vast chain of the mountains that embrace the deep gulf to eastward and rear themselves higher and higher toward the south. It was hot, and we sat at the landward corner of the platform, waiting for the night breeze to come down from the lower hills. The colour sank out of the air, there was a little interval of deep-grey twilight, and a lamp sent a yellow streak from the open door of the kitchen, where the men were getting their supper.

Then the moon rose suddenly above the crest of the promontory, flooding the platform and lighting up every little spur of rock and knoll of grass below us, down to the edge of the motionless water. My friend lighted his pipe and sat looking at a spot on the hillside. I knew that he was looking at it, and for a long time past I had wondered whether he would ever see anything there that would fix his attention. I knew that spot well. It was clear that he was interested at last, though it was a long time before he spoke. Like most painters, he trusts to his own eyesight, as a lion trusts his strength and a stag his speed, and he is always disturbed when he cannot reconcile what he sees with what he believes that he ought to see.

'It's strange,' he said. 'Do you see that little mound just on this side of the boulder?'

'Yes,' I said, and I guessed what was coming.

'It looks like a grave,' observed Holger.

'Very true. It does look like a grave.'

'Yes,' continued my friend, his eyes still fixed on the spot. 'But the strange thing is that I see the body lying on the top of it. Of course,' continued Holger, turning his head on one side as artists do, 'it must be an effect of light. In the first place, it is not a grave at all. Secondly, if it were, the body would be inside and not outside. Therefore, it's an effect of the moonlight. Don't you see it?'

'Perfectly; I always see it on moonlight nights.'

'It doesn't seem to interest you much,' said Holger.

'On the contrary, it does interest me, though I am used to it. You're not so far wrong, either. The mound is really a grave.'

'Nonsense!' cried Holger, incredulously. 'I suppose you'll tell me what I see lying on it is really a corpse!'

'No,' I answered, 'it's not. I know, because I have taken the trouble to go down and see.'

'Then what is it?' asked Holger.

'It's nothing.'

'You mean that it's an effect of light, I suppose?'

'Perhaps it is. But the inexplicable part of the matter is that it makes no difference whether the moon is rising or setting, or waxing or waning. If there's any moonlight at all, from east or west or overhead, so long as it shines on the grave you can see the outline of the body on top.'

Holger stirred up his pipe with the point of his knife, and then used his finger for a stopper. When the tobacco burned well he rose from his chair.

'If you don't mind,' he said, 'I'll go down and take a look at it.'

He left me, crossed the roof, and disappeared down the dark steps. I did not move, but sat looking down until he came out of the tower below. I heard him humming an old Danish song as he crossed the open space in the bright moonlight, going straight to the mysterious mound. When he was ten paces from it, Holger stopped short, made two steps forward, and then three or four backward, and then stopped again. I knew what that meant. He had reached the spot where the Thing ceased to be visible – where, as he would have said, the effect of light changed.

Then he went on till he reached the mound and stood upon it. I could see the Thing still, but it was no longer lying down; it was on its knees now, winding its white arms round Holger's body and looking up into his face. A cool breeze stirred my hair at that moment, as the night wind began to come down from the hills, but it felt like a breath from another world.

The Thing seemed to be trying to climb to its feet, helping itself up by Holger's body while he stood upright, quite unconscious of it and apparently looking toward the tower, which is very picturesque when the moonlight falls upon it on that side.

'Come along!' I shouted. 'Don't stay there all night!'

It seemed to me that he moved reluctantly as he stepped from the mound, or else with difficulty. That was it. The Thing's arms were still round his waist, but its feet could not leave the grave. As he came slowly forward it was drawn and lengthened like a wreath of mist, thin and white, till I saw distinctly that Holger shook himself, as a man does who feels a chill. At the same instant a little wail of pain came to me on the breeze – it might have been the cry of the small owl that lives among the rocks – and the misty presence floated swiftly back from Holger's advancing figure and lay once more at its length upon the mound.

Again I felt the cool breeze in my hair, and this time an icy thrill of dread ran down my spine. I remembered very well that I had once gone down there alone in the moonlight; that presently, being near, I had seen nothing; that, like Holger, I had gone and had stood upon the mound; and I remembered how, when I came back, sure that there was nothing there, I had felt the sudden conviction that there was something after all if I would only look behind me. I remembered the strong temptation to look back, a temptation I had resisted as unworthy of a man of sense, until, to get rid of it, I had shaken myself just as Holger did.

And now I knew that those white, misty arms had been round me too; I knew it in a flash, and I shuddered as I remembered that I had heard the night owl then too. But it had not been the night owl. It was the cry of the Thing.

I refilled my pipe and poured out a cup of strong southern wine; in less than a minute Holger was seated beside me again.

'Of course there's nothing there,' he said, 'but it's creepy, all the same. Do you know, when I was coming back I was so sure that there was something behind me that I wanted to turn round and look? It was an effort not to.'

He laughed a little, knocked the ashes out of his pipe, and poured himself out some wine. For a while neither of us spoke, and the moon rose higher, and we both looked at the Thing that lay on the mound.

'You might make a story about that,' said Holger after a long time.

'There is one,' I answered. 'If you're not sleepy, I'll tell it to you.'

'Go ahead,' said Holger, who likes stories.

Old Alario was dying up there in the village behind the hill. You remember him, I have no doubt. They say that he made his money by selling sham jewellery in South America, and escaped with his gains when he was found out. Like all those fellows, if they bring anything back with them, he at once set to work to enlarge his house; and, as there are no masons here, he sent all the way to Paola for two workmen. They were a rough-looking pair of scoundrels – a Neapolitan who had lost one eye and a Sicilian with an old scar half an inch deep across his left cheek. I often saw them, for on Sundays they used to come down here and fish off the rocks. When Alario caught the fever that killed him the masons were still at work. As he had agreed that part of their pay should be their board and lodging, he made them sleep in the house. His wife was dead, and he had an only son called Angelo, who was a much better sort than himself. Angelo was to marry the daughter of the richest man in the village, and, strange to say, though the marriage was arranged by their parents, the young people were said to be in love with each other.

For that matter, the whole village was in love with Angelo, and among the rest a wild, good-looking creature called Cristina, who was more like a gipsy than any girl I ever saw about here. She had very red lips and very black eyes, she was built like a greyhound, and had the tongue of the devil. But Angelo did not care a straw for her. He was rather a simple-minded fellow, quite different from his old scoundrel of a father, and under what I should call normal circumstances I really believe that he would never have looked at any girl except the nice plump little creature, with a fat dowry, whom his father meant him to marry. But things turned up which were neither normal nor natural.

On the other hand, a very handsome young shepherd from the hills above Maratea was in love with Cristina, who seems to have been quite indifferent to him. Cristina had no regular means of subsistence, but she was a good girl and willing to do any work or go on errands to any distance for the sake of a loaf of bread or a mess of beans, and permission to sleep under cover. She was especially glad when she could get something to do about the house of Angelo's father. There is no doctor in the village, and when the neighbours saw that old Alario was dying they sent Cristina to Scalea to fetch one. That was late in the afternoon, and if they had waited so long, it was because the dying miser refused to allow any such extravagance while he was able to speak. But while Cristina was gone, matters grew rapidly worse, the priest was brought to the bedside, and when he had done what he could he gave it as his opinion to the bystanders that the old man was dead, and left the house.

You know these people. They have a physical horror of death. Until the priest spoke, the room had been full of people. The words were hardly out of his mouth before it was empty. It was night now. They hurried down the dark steps and out into the street.

Angelo was away, Cristina had not come back – the simple woman servant who had nursed the sick man fled with the rest, and the body was left alone in the flickering light of the earthen oil lamp.

Five minutes later two men looked in cautiously and crept forward toward the bed. They were the one-eyed Neapolitan mason and his Sicilian companion. They knew what they wanted. In a moment they had dragged from under the bed a small but heavy iron-bound box, and long before any one thought of coming back to the dead man they had left the house and the village under cover of the darkness. It was easy enough, for Alario's house is the last toward the gorge which leads down here, and the thieves merely went out by the back door, got over the stone wall, and had nothing to risk after that except the possibility of meeting some belated countryman, which was very small indeed, since few of the people use that path. They had a mattock and shovel, and they made their way here without accident.

I am telling you this story as it must have happened, for, of course, there were no witnesses to this part of it. The men brought the box down by the gorge, intending to bury it until they should be able to come back and take it away in a boat. They must have been clever enough to guess that some of the money would be in paper notes, for they would otherwise have buried it on the beach in the wet sand, where it would have been much safer. But the paper would have rotted if they had been obliged to leave it there long, so they dug their hole down there, close to that boulder. Yes, just where the mound is now.

Cristina did not find the doctor in Scalea, for he had been sent for from a place up the valley, halfway to San Domenico. If she had found him, he would have come on his mule by the upper road, which is smoother but much longer. But Cristina took the short cut by the rocks, which passes about fifty feet above the mound, and goes round that corner. The men were digging when she passed, and she heard them at work. It would not have been like her to go by without finding out what the noise was, for she was never afraid of anything in her life, and, besides, the fishermen sometimes came ashore here at night to get a stone for an anchor or to gather sticks to make a little fire. The night was dark, and Cristina probably came close to the two men before she could see what they were doing. She knew them, of course, and they knew her, and understood instantly that they were in her power. There was only one thing to be done for their safety, and they did it. They knocked her on the head, they dug the hole deep, and they buried her quickly with the iron-bound chest. They must have understood that their only chance of escaping suspicion lay in getting back to the village before their absence was noticed, for they returned immediately, and were found half an hour later gossiping quietly with the man who was making Alario's coffin. He was a crony of theirs, and had been working at the repairs in the old man's house. So far as I have been able to make out, the only persons who were supposed to know where Alario kept his treasure were Angelo and the one woman servant I have mentioned. Angelo was away; it was the woman who discovered the theft.

It is easy enough to understand why no one else knew where the money was. The old man kept his door locked and the key in his pocket when he was out, and did not let the woman enter to clean the place unless he was there himself. The whole village knew that he had money somewhere, however, and the masons had probably discovered the whereabouts of the chest by climbing in at the window in his absence. If the old man had not been delirious until he lost consciousness, he would have been in frightful agony of mind for his riches. The faithful woman servant forgot their existence only for a few moments when she fled with the rest, overcome by the horror of death. Twenty minutes had not passed before she returned with the two hideous old hags who are always called in to prepare the dead for burial. Even then she had not at first the courage to go near the bed with them, but she made a pretence of dropping something, went down on her knees as if to find it, and looked under the bedstead. The walls of the room were newly whitewashed down to the floor, and she saw at a glance that the chest was gone. It had been there in the afternoon, it had therefore been stolen in the short interval since she had left the room.

There are no carabineers stationed in the village; there is not so much as a municipal watchman, for there is no municipality. There never was such a place, I believe. Scalea is supposed to look after it in some mysterious way, and it takes a couple of hours to get anybody from there. As the old woman had lived in the village all her life, it did not even occur to her to apply to any civil authority for help. She simply set up a howl and ran through the village in the dark, screaming out that her dead master's house had been robbed. Many of the people looked out, but at first no one seemed inclined to help her. Most of them, judging her by themselves, whispered to each other that she had probably stolen the money herself. The first man to move was the father of the girl whom Angelo was to marry; having collected his household, all of whom felt a personal interest in the wealth which was to have come into the family, he declared it to be his opinion that the chest had been stolen by the two journeyman masons who lodged in the house. He headed a search for them, which naturally began in Alario's house and ended in the carpenter's workshop, where the thieves were found discussing a measure of wine with the carpenter over the half-finished coffin, by the light of one earthen lamp filled with oil and tallow. The search party at once accused the delinquents of the crime, and threatened to lock them up in the cellar till the carabineers could be fetched from Scalea. The two men looked at each other for one moment, and then without the slightest hesitation they put out the single light, seized the unfinished coffin between them, and using it as a sort of battering ram, dashed upon their assailants in the dark. In a few moments they were beyond pursuit.

That is the end of the first part of the story. The treasure had disappeared, and as no trace of it could be found the people naturally supposed that the thieves had succeeded in carrying it off. The old man was buried, and when Angelo came back at last he had to borrow money to pay for the miserable funeral, and had some difficulty in doing so. He hardly needed to be told that in losing his inheritance he had lost his bride. In this part of the world marriages are made on strictly business principles, and if the promised cash is not forthcoming on the appointed day the bride or the bridegroom whose parents have failed to produce it may as well take themselves off, for there will be no wedding. Poor Angelo knew that well enough. His father had been possessed of hardly any land, and now that the hard cash which he had brought from South America was gone, there was nothing left but debts for the building materials that were to have been used for enlarging and improving the old house. Angelo was beggared, and the nice plump little creature who was to have been his turned up her nose at him in the most approved fashion. As for Cristina, it was several days before she was missed, for no one remembered that she had been sent to Scalea for the doctor, who had never come. She often disappeared in the same way for days together, when she could find a little work here and there at the distant farms among the hills. But when she did not come back at all, people began to wonder, and at last made up their minds that she had connived with the masons and had escaped with them.

I paused and emptied my glass.

'That sort of thing could not happen anywhere else,' observed Holger, filling his everlasting pipe again. 'It is wonderful what a natural charm there is about murder and sudden death in a romantic country like this. Deeds that would be simply brutal and disgusting anywhere else become dramatic and mysterious because this is Italy and we are living in a genuine tower of Charles V built against genuine Barbary pirates.'

'There's something in that,' I admitted. Holger is the most romantic man in the world inside of himself, but he always thinks it necessary to explain why he feels anything.

'I suppose they found the poor girl's body with the box,' he said presently.

'As it seems to interest you,' I answered, 'I'll tell you the rest of the story.'

The moon had risen high by this time; the outline of the Thing on the mound was clearer to our eyes than before.

The village very soon settled down to its small, dull life. No one missed old Alario, who had been away so much on his voyages to South America that he had never been a familiar figure in his native place. Angelo lived in the half-finished house, and because he had no money to pay the old woman servant she would not stay with him, but once in a long time she would come and wash a shirt for him for old acquaintance' sake. Besides the house, he had inherited a small patch of ground at some distance from the village; he tried to cultivate it, but he had no heart in the work, for he knew he could never pay the taxes on it and on the house, which would certainly be confiscated by the Government, or seized for the debt of the building material, which the man who had supplied it refused to take back.

Angelo was very unhappy. So long as his father had been alive and rich, every girl in the village had been in love with him; but that was all changed now. It had been pleasant to be admired and courted, and invited to drink wine by fathers who had girls to marry. It was hard to be stared at coldly, and sometimes laughed at because he had been robbed of his inheritance. He cooked his miserable meals for himself, and from being sad became melancholy and morose.

At twilight, when the day's work was done, instead of hanging about in the open space before the church with young fellows of his own age, he took to wandering in lonely places on the outskirts of the village till it was quite dark. Then he slunk home and went to bed to save the expense of a light. But in those lonely twilight hours he began to have strange waking dreams. He was not always alone, for often when he sat on the stump of a tree, where the narrow path turns down the gorge, he was sure that a woman came up noiselessly over the rough stones, as if her feet were bare; and she stood under a clump of chestnut trees only half a dozen yards down the path, and beckoned to him without speaking. Though she was in the shadow he knew that her lips were red, and that when they parted a little and smiled at him she showed two small sharp teeth. He knew this at first rather than saw it, and he knew that it was Cristina, and that she was dead. Yet he was not afraid; he only wondered whether it was a dream, for he thought that if he had been awake he should have been frightened.

Besides, the dead woman had red lips, and that could only happen in a dream. Whenever he went near the gorge after sunset she was already there waiting for him, or else she very soon appeared, and he began to be sure that she came a little nearer to him every day. At first he had only been sure of her blood-red mouth, but now each feature grew distinct, and the pale face looked at him with deep and hungry eyes.

It was the eyes that grew dim. Little by little he came to know that some day the dream would not end when he turned away to go home, but would lead him down the gorge out of which the vision rose. She was nearer now when she beckoned to him. Her cheeks were not livid like those of the dead, but pale with starvation, with the furious and unappeased physical hunger of her eyes that devoured him. They feasted on his soul and cast a spell over him, and at last they were close to his own and held them. He could not tell whether her breath was as hot as fire or as cold as ice; he could not tell whether her red lips burned his or froze them, or whether her five fingers on his wrists seared scorching scars or bit his flesh like frost; he could not tell whether he was awake or asleep, whether she was alive or dead, but he knew that she loved him, she alone of all creatures, earthly or unearthly, and her spell had power over him.

When the moon rose high that night the shadow of that Thing was not alone down there upon the mound.

Angelo awoke in the cool dawn, drenched with dew and chilled through flesh, and blood, and bone. He opened his eyes to the faint grey light, and saw the stars still shining overhead. He was very weak, and his heart was beating so slowly that he was almost like a man fainting. Slowly he turned his head on the mound, as on a pillow, but the other face was not there. Fear seized him suddenly, a fear unspeakable and unknown; he sprang to his feet and fled up the gorge, and he never looked behind him until he reached the door of the house on the outskirts of the village. Drearily he went to his work that day, and wearily the hours dragged themselves after the sun, till at last he touched the sea and sank, and the great sharp hills above Maratea turned purple against the dove-coloured eastern sky.

Angelo shouldered his heavy hoe and left the field. He felt less tired now than in the morning when he had begun to work, but he promised himself that he would go home without lingering by the gorge, and eat the best supper he could get himself, and sleep all night in his bed like a Christian man. Not again would he be tempted down the narrow way by a shadow with red lips and icy breath; not again would he dream that dream of terror and delight. He was near the village now; it was half an hour since the sun had set, and the cracked church bell sent little discordant echoes across the rocks and ravines to tell all good people that the day was done. Angelo stood still a moment where the path forked, where it led toward the village on the left, and down to the gorge on the right, where a clump of chestnut trees overhung the narrow way. He stood still a minute, lifting his battered hat from his head and gazing at the fast-fading sea westward, and his lips moved as he silently repeated the familiar evening prayer. His lips moved, but the words that followed them in his brain lost their meaning and turned into others, and ended in a name that he spoke aloud – 'Cristina!' With the name, the tension of his will relaxed suddenly, reality went out and the dream took him again and bore him on swiftly and surely like a man walking in his sleep, down, down, by the steep path in the gathering darkness. And as she glided beside him, Cristina whispered strange sweet things in his ear, which somehow, if he had been awake, he knew that he could not quite have understood; but now they were the most wonderful words he had ever heard in his life. And she kissed him also, but not upon his mouth. He felt her sharp kisses upon his white throat, and he knew that her lips were red. So the wild dream sped on through twilight and darkness and moonrise, and all the glory of the summer's night. But in the chilly dawn he lay as one half dead upon the mound down there, recalling and not recalling, drained of his blood, yet strangely longing to give those red lips more. Then came the fear, the awful nameless panic, the mortal horror that guards the confines of the world we see not, neither know of as we know of other things, but which we feel when its icy chill freezes our bones and stirs our hair with the touch of a ghostly hand. Once more Angelo sprang from the mound and fled up the gorge in the breaking day, but his step was less sure this time, and he panted for breath as he ran; and when he came to the bright spring of water that rises halfway up the hillside, he dropped upon his knees and hands and plunged his whole face in and drank as he had never drunk before – for it was the thirst of the wounded man who has lain bleeding all night long upon the battlefield.

She had him fast now, and he could not escape her, but would come to her every evening at dusk until she had drained him of his last drop of blood. It was in vain that when the day was done he tried to take another turning and to go home by a path that did not lead near the gorge. It was in vain that he made promises to himself each morning at dawn when he climbed the lonely way up from the shore to the village. It was all in vain, for when the sun sank burning into the sea, and the coolness of the evening stole out as from a hiding-place to delight the weary world, his feet turned toward the old way, and she was waiting for him in the shadow under the chestnut trees; and then all happened as before, and she fell to kissing his white throat even as she flitted lightly down the way, winding one arm about him. And as his blood failed, she grew more hungry and more thirsty every day, and every day when he awoke in the early dawn it was harder to rouse himself to the effort of climbing the steep path to the village; and when he went to his work his feet dragged painfully, and there was hardly strength in his arms to wield the heavy hoe. He scarcely spoke to any one now, but the people said he was 'consuming himself' for love of the girl he was to have married when he lost his inheritance; and they laughed heartily at the thought, for this is not a very romantic country. At this time, Antonio, the man who stays here to look after the tower, returned from a visit to his people, who live near Salerno. He had been away all the time since before Alario's death and knew nothing of what had happened. He has told me that he came back late in the afternoon and shut himself up in the tower to eat and sleep, for he was very tired. It was past midnight when he awoke, and when he looked out the waning moon was rising over the shoulder of the hill. He looked out toward the mound, and he saw something, and he did not sleep again that night. When he went out again in the morning it was broad daylight, and there was nothing to be seen on the mound but loose stones and driven sand. Yet he did not go very near it; he went straight up the path to the village and directly to the house of the old priest.

'I have seen an evil thing this night,' he said; 'I have seen how the dead drink the blood of the living. And the blood is the life.'

'Tell me what you have seen,' said the priest in reply.

Antonio told him everything he had seen.

'You must bring your book and your holy water tonight,' he added. 'I will be here before sunset to go down with you, and if it pleases your reverence to sup with me while we wait, I will make ready.'

'I will come,' the priest answered, 'for I have read in old books of these strange beings which are neither quick nor dead, and which lie ever fresh in their graves, stealing out in the dusk to taste life and blood.'

Antonio cannot read, but he was glad to see that the priest understood the business; for, of course, the books must have instructed him as to the best means of quieting the half-living Thing forever.

So Antonio went away to his work, which consists largely in sitting on the shady side of the tower, when he is not perched upon a rock with a fishing line catching nothing. But on that day he went twice to look at the mound in the bright sunlight, and he searched round and round it for some hole through which the being might get in and out; but he found none. When the sun began to sink and the air was cooler in the shadows, he went up to fetch the old priest, carrying a little wicker basket with him; and in this they placed a bottle of holy water, and the basin, and sprinkler, and the stole which the priest would need; and they came down and waited in the door of the tower till it should be dark. But while the light still lingered very grey and faint, they saw something moving, just there, two figures, a man's that walked, and a woman's that flitted beside him, and while her head lay on his shoulder she kissed his throat. The priest has told me that, too, and that his teeth chattered and he grasped Antonio's arm. The vision passed and disappeared into the shadow. Then Antonio got the leathern flask of strong liquor, which he kept for great occasions, and poured such a draught as made the old man feel almost young again; and he got the lantern, and his pick and shovel, and gave the priest his stole to put on and the holy water to carry, and they went out together toward the spot where the work was to be done. Antonio says that in spite of the rum his own knees shook together, and the priest stumbled over his Latin. For when they were yet a few yards from the mound the flickering light of the lantern fell upon Angelo's white face, unconscious as if in sleep, and on his upturned throat, over which a very thin red line of blood trickled down into his collar; and the flickering light of the lantern played upon another face that looked up from the feast – upon two deep, dead eyes that saw in spite of death – upon parted lips redder than life itself – upon two gleaming teeth on which glistened a rosy drop. Then the priest, good old man, shut his eyes tight and showered holy water before him, and his cracked voice rose almost to a scream; and then Antonio, who is no coward after all, raised his pick in one hand and the lantern in the other, as he sprang forward, not knowing what the end should be; and then he swears that he heard a woman's cry, and the Thing was gone, and Angelo lay alone on the mound un- conscious, with the red line on his throat and the beads of deathly sweat on his cold forehead. They lifted him, half-dead as he was, and laid him on the ground close by; then Antonio went to work, and the priest helped him, though he was old and could not do much; and they dug deep, and at last Antonio, standing in the grave, stooped down with his lantern to see what he might see.

His hair used to be dark brown, with grizzled streaks about the temples; in less than a month from that day he was as grey as a badger. He was a miner when he was young, and most of these fellows have seen ugly sights now and then, when accidents have happened, but he had never seen what he saw that night – that Thing which is neither alive nor dead, that Thing that will abide neither above ground nor in the grave. Antonio had brought something with him which the priest had not noticed. He had made it that afternoon – a sharp stake shaped from a piece of tough old driftwood. He had it with him now, and he had his heavy pick, and he had taken the lantern down into the grave. I don't think any power on earth could make him speak of what happened then, and the old priest was too frightened to look in. He says he heard Antonio breathing like a wild beast, and moving as if he were fighting with something almost as strong as himself; and he heard an evil sound also, with blows, as of something violently driven through flesh and bone: and then the most awful sound of all – a woman's shriek, the unearthly scream of a woman neither dead nor alive, but buried deep for many days. And he, the poor old priest, could only rock himself as he knelt there in the sand, crying aloud his prayers and exorcisms to drown these dreadful sounds. Then suddenly a small ironbound chest was thrown up and rolled over against the old man's knee, and in a moment more Antonio was beside him, his face as white as tallow in the flickering light of the lantern, shovelling the sand and pebbles into the grave with furious haste, and looking over the edge till the pit was half full; and the priest had said that there was much fresh blood on Antonio's hands and on his clothes.

I had come to the end of my story. Holger finished his wine and leaned back in his chair.

'So Angelo got his own again,' he said. 'Did he marry the prim and plump young person to whom he had been betrothed?'

'No; he had been badly frightened. He went to South America, and has not been heard of since.'

'And that poor thing's body is there still, I suppose,' said Holger. 'Is it quite dead yet, I wonder?'

I wonder, too. But whether it is dead or alive, I should hardly care to see it, even in broad daylight.

Antonio is as grey as a badger, and he has never been quite the same man since that night.

The Upper Berth

Somebody asked for the cigars. We had talked long, and the conversation was beginning to languish; the tobacco smoke had got into the heavy curtains, the wine had got into those brains which were liable to become heavy, and it was already perfectly evident that, unless somebody did something to rouse our oppressed spirits, the meeting would soon come to its natural conclusion, and we, the guests, would speedily go home to bed, and most certainly to sleep. No one had said anything very remarkable; it may be that no one had anything very remarkable to say. Jones had given us every particular of his last hunting adventure in Yorkshire. Mr Tompkins, of Boston, had explained at elaborate length those working principles, by the due and careful maintenance of which the Atchison, Topeka, and Santa Fe Railroad not only extended its territory, increased its departmental influence, and transported livestock without starving them to death before the day of actual delivery, but also, had for years succeeded in deceiving those passengers who bought its tickets into the fallacious belief that the corporation aforesaid was really able to transport human life without destroying it. Signor Tombola had endeavoured to persuade us, by arguments which we took no trouble to oppose, that the unity of his country in no way resembled the average modern torpedo, carefully planned, constructed with all the skill of the greatest European arsenals, but, when constructed, destined to be directed by feeble hands into a region where it must undoubtedly explode, unseen, unfeared, and unheard, into the illimitable wastes of political chaos.

It is unnecessary to go into further details. The conversation had assumed proportions which would have bored Prometheus on his rock, which would have driven Tantalus to distraction, and which would have impelled Ixion to seek relaxation in the simple but instructive dialogues of Herr Ollendorff, rather than submit to the greater evil of listening to our talk. We had sat at table for hours; we were bored, we were tired, and nobody showed signs of moving.

Somebody called for cigars. We all instinctively looked towards the speaker. Brisbane was a man of five-and-thirty years of age, and remarkable for those gifts which chiefly attract the attention of men. He was a strong man. The external proportions of his figure presented nothing extraordinary to the common eye, though his size was above the average. He was a little over six feet in height, and moderately broad in the shoulder; he did not appear to be stout but, on the other hand, he was certainly not thin; his small head was supported by a strong and sinewy neck; his broad muscular hands appeared to possess a peculiar skill in breaking walnuts without the assistance of the ordinary cracker, and, seeing him in profile, one could not help remarking the extraordinary breadth of his sleeves, and the unusual thickness of his chest. He was one of those men who are commonly spoken of among men as deceptive; that is to say, that though he looked exceedingly strong he was in reality very much stronger than he looked. Of his features I need say little. His head is small, his hair is thin, his eyes are blue, his nose is large, he has a small moustache, and a square jaw. Everybody knows Brisbane, and when he asked for a cigar everybody looked at him.

'It is a very singular thing,' said Brisbane.

Everybody stopped talking. Brisbane's voice was not loud, but possessed a peculiar quality of penetrating general conversation, and cutting it like a knife. Everybody listened. Brisbane, perceiving that he had attracted their general attention, lit his cigar with great equanimity.

'It is very singular,' he continued, 'that thing about ghosts. People are always asking whether anybody has seen a ghost. I have.'

'Bosh! What, you? You don't mean to say so, Brisbane? Well, for a man of his intelligence!'

A chorus of exclamations greeted Brisbane's remarkable statement. Everybody called for cigars, and Stubbs the butler suddenly appeared from the depths of nowhere with a fresh bottle of dry champagne. The situation was saved; Brisbane was going to tell a story.

I am an old sailor, said Brisbane, and as I have to cross the Atlantic pretty often, I have my favourites. Most men have their favourites. I have seen a man wait in a Broadway bar for three-quarters of an hour for a particular car which he liked. I believe the bar-keeper made at least one-third of his living by that man's preference. I have a habit of waiting for certain ships when I am obliged to cross that duck-pond. It may be a prejudice, but I was never cheated out of a good passage but once in my life. I remember it very well; it was a warm morning in June, and the Custom House officials, who were hanging about waiting for a steamer already on her way up from the Quarantine, presented a peculiarly hazy and thoughtful appearance. I had not much luggage – I never have. I mingled with the crowd of passengers, porters, and officious individuals in blue coats and brass buttons, who seemed to spring up like mushrooms from the deck of a moored steamer to obtrude their unnecessary services upon the independent passenger. I have often noticed with a certain interest the spontaneous evolution of these fellows. They are not there when you arrive; five minutes after the pilot has called 'Go ahead!' they, or at least their blue coats and brass buttons, have disappeared from deck and gang-way as completely as though they had been consigned to that locker which tradition unanimously ascribes to Davy Jones. But, at the moment of starting, they are there, clean-shaved, blue-coated, and ravenous for fees. I hastened on board. The *Kamtschatka* was one of my favourite ships. I say was, because she emphatically no longer is. I cannot conceive of any inducement which could entice me to make another voyage in her. Yes, I know what you are going to say. She is uncommonly clean in the run aft, she has enough bluffing off in the bows to keep her dry, and the lower berths are most of them double. She has a lot of advantages, but I won't cross in her again. Excuse the digression. I got on board. I hailed a steward, whose red nose and redder whiskers were equally familiar to me.

'One hundred and five, lower berth,' said I, in the businesslike tone peculiar to men who think no more of crossing the Atlantic than taking a whisky cocktail at downtown Delmonico's.

The steward took my portmanteau, greatcoat, and rug. I shall never forget the expression of his face. Not that he turned pale. It is maintained by the most eminent divines that even miracles cannot change the course of nature. I have no hesitation in saying that he did not turn pale; but, from his expression, I judged that he was either about to shed tears, to sneeze, or to drop my port-manteau. As the latter contained two bottles of particularly fine old sherry presented to me for my voyage by my old friend Snigginson van Pickyns, I felt extremely nervous. But the steward did none of these things.

'Well, I'm d—d!' said he in a low voice, and led the way.

I supposed my Hermes, as he led me to the lower regions, had had a little grog, but I said nothing, and followed him. One hundred and five was on the port side, well aft. There was nothing remarkable about the state-room. The lower berth, like most of those upon the *Kamtschatka*, was double. There was plenty of room; there was the usual washing apparatus, calculated to convey an idea of luxury to the mind of a North-American Indian; there were the usual inefficient racks of brown wood, in which it is more easy to hang a large-sized umbrella than the common tooth-brush of commerce. Upon the uninviting mattresses were carefully folded together those blankets which a great modern humourist has aptly compared to cold buck-wheat cakes. The question of towels was left entirely to the imagin-ation. The glass decanters were filled with a transparent liquid faintly tinged with brown, but from which an odour less faint, but not more pleasing, ascended to the nostrils, like a far-off sea-sick reminiscence of oily machinery. Sad-coloured curtains half-closed the upper berth. The hazy June daylight shed a faint illumination upon the desolate little scene. Ugh! how I hate that state-room!

The steward deposited my traps and looked at me, as though he wanted to get away – probably in search of more passengers and more fees. It is always a good plan to start in favour with those functionaries, and I accordingly gave him certain coins there and then.

'I'll try and make yer comfortable all I can,' he remarked, as he put the coins in his pocket. Nevertheless, there was a doubtful intonation in his voice which surprised me. Possibly his scale of fees had gone up, and he was not satisfied; but on the whole I was inclined to think that, as he himself would have expressed it, he was 'the better for a glass'. I was wrong, however, and did the man injustice.

2

Nothing especially worthy of mention occurred during that day. We left the pier punctually, and it was very pleasant to be fairly under way, for the weather was warm and sultry, and the motion of the steamer produced a refreshing breeze. Everybody knows what the first day at sea is like. People pace the decks and stare at each other, and occasionally meet acquaintances whom they did not know to be on board. There is the usual uncertainty as to whether the food will be good, bad, or indifferent, until the first two meals have put the matter beyond a doubt; there is the usual uncertainty about the weather, until the ship is fairly off Fire Island. The tables are crowded at first, and then suddenly thinned. Pale-faced people spring from their seats and precipitate themselves towards the door, and each old sailor breathes more freely as his sea-sick neighbour rushes from his side, leaving him plenty of elbow room and an unlimited command over the mustard.

One passage across the Atlantic is very much like another, and we who cross very often do not make the voyage for the sake of novelty. Whales and icebergs are indeed always objects of interest, but after all, one whale is very much like another whale, and one rarely sees an iceberg at close quarters. To the majority of us the most delightful moment of the day on board an ocean steamer is when we have taken our last turn on deck, have smoked our last cigar, and having succeeded in tiring ourselves, feel at liberty to turn in with a clear conscience. On that first night of the voyage I felt particularly lazy, and went to bed in one hundred and five rather earlier than I usually do. As I turned in, I was amazed to see that I was to have a companion. A portmanteau, very like my own, lay in the opposite corner, and in the upper berth had been deposited a neatly folded rug with a stick and umbrella. I had hoped to be alone, and I was disappointed; but I wondered who my room-mate was to be, and I determined to have a look at him.

Before I had been long in bed he entered. He was, as far as I could see, a very tall man, very thin, very pale, with sandy hair and whiskers and colourless grey eyes. He had about him, I thought, an air of rather dubious fashion; the sort of man you might see in Wall Street, without being able precisely to say what he was doing there – the sort of man who frequents the Café Anglais, who always seems to be alone and who drinks champagne; you might meet him on a race-course, but he would never appear to be doing anything there either. A little over-dressed – a little odd. There are three or four of his kind on every ocean steamer. I made up my mind that I did not care to make his acquaintance, and I went to sleep saying to myself that I would study his habits in order to avoid him. If he rose early, I would rise late; if he went to bed late, I would go to bed early. I did not care to know him. If you once know people of that kind they are always turning up. Poor fellow! I need not have taken the trouble to come to so many decisions about him, for I never saw him again after that first night in one hundred and five.

I was sleeping soundly when I was suddenly waked by a loud noise. To judge from the sound, my room-mate must have sprung with a single leap from the upper berth to the floor. I heard him fumbling with the latch and bolt of the door, which opened almost immediately, and then I heard his footsteps as he ran at full speed down the passage, leaving the door open behind him. The ship was rolling a little, and I expected to hear him stumble or fall, but he ran as though he were running for his life. The door swung on its hinges with the motion of the vessel, and the sound annoyed me. I got up and shut it, and groped my way back to my berth in the darkness. I went to sleep again; but I have no idea how long I slept.

When I awoke it was still quite dark, but I felt a disagreeable sensation of cold, and it seemed to me that the air was damp. You know the peculiar smell of a cabin which has been wet with sea water. I covered myself up as well as I could and dozed off again, framing complaints to be made the next day, and selecting the most powerful epithets in the language. I could hear my room-mate turn over in the upper berth. He had probably returned while I was asleep. Once I thought I heard him groan, and I argued that he was sea-sick. That is particularly unpleasant when one is below. Nevertheless I dozed off and slept till early daylight.

The ship was rolling heavily, much more than on the previous evening, and the grey light which came in through the porthole changed in tint with every movement according as the angle of the vessel's side turned the glass seawards or skywards. It was very cold – unaccountably so for the month of June. I turned my head and looked at the porthole, and saw to my surprise that it was wide open and hooked back. I believe I swore audibly. Then I got up and shut it. As I turned back I glanced at the upper berth. The curtains were drawn close together; my companion had probably felt cold as well as I. It struck me that I had slept enough. The state-room was uncomfortable, though, strange to say, I could not smell the damp-ness which had annoyed me in the night. My room-mate was still asleep – excellent opportunity for avoiding him – so I dressed at once and went on deck. The day was warm and cloudy, with an oily smell on the water. It was seven o'clock as I came out – much later than I had imagined. I came across the doctor, who was taking his first sniff of the morning air. He was a young man from the West of Ireland – a tremendous fellow, with black hair and blue eyes, already inclined to be stout; he had a happy-go-lucky, healthy look about him which was rather attractive.

'Fine morning,' I remarked, by way of introduction.

'Well,' said he, eyeing me with an air of ready interest, 'it's a fine morning and it's not a fine morning. I don't think it's much of a morning.'

'Well, no – it is not so very fine,' said I.

'It's just what I call fuggly weather,' replied the doctor.

'It was very cold last night, I thought,' I remarked. 'However, when I looked about, I found that the porthole was wide open. I had not noticed it when I went to bed. And the state-room was damp, too.'

'Damp!' said he. 'Whereabouts are you?'

'One hundred and five – '

To my surprise the doctor started visibly, and stared at me.

'What is the matter?' I asked.

'Oh – nothing,' he answered; 'only everybody has complained of that state-room for the last three trips.'

'I shall complain too,' I said. 'It has certainly not been properly aired. It is a shame!'

'I don't believe it can be helped,' answered the doctor. 'I believe there is something – well, it is not my business to frighten passengers.'

'You need not be afraid of frightening me,' I replied. 'I can stand any amount of damp. If I should get a bad cold I will come to you.'

I offered the doctor a cigar, which he took and examined very critically.

'It is not so much the damp,' he remarked. 'However, I dare say you will get on very well. Have you a room-mate?'

'Yes; a deuce of a fellow, who bolts out in the middle of the night and leaves the door open.'

Again the doctor glanced curiously at me. Then he lit the cigar and looked grave.

'Did he come back?' he asked presently.

'Yes. I was asleep, but I waked up and heard him moving. Then I felt cold and went to sleep again. This morning I found the porthole open.'

'Look here,' said the doctor, quietly, 'I don't care much for this ship. I don't care a rap for her reputation. I tell you what I will do. I have a good-sized place up here. I will share it with you, though I don't know you from Adam.'

I was very much surprised at the proposition. I could not imagine why he should take such a sudden interest in my welfare. However, his manner as he spoke of the ship was peculiar.

'You are very good, doctor,' I said. 'But really, I believe even now the cabin could be aired, or cleaned out, or something. Why do you not care for the ship?'

'We are not superstitious in our profession, sir,' replied the doctor. 'But the sea makes people so. I don't want to prejudice you, and I don't want to frighten you, but if you will take my advice you will move in here. I would as soon see you overboard,' he added, 'as know that you or any other man was to sleep in one hundred and five.'

'Good gracious! Why?' I asked.

'Just because on the last three trips the people who have slept there actually have gone overboard,' he answered, gravely.

The intelligence was startling and exceedingly unpleasant, I confess. I looked hard at the doctor to see whether he was making game of me, but he looked perfectly serious. I thanked him warmly for his offer, but told him I intended to be the exception to the rule by which everyone who slept in that particular state-room went overboard. He did not say much, but looked as grave as ever, and hinted that before we got across I should probably reconsider his proposal. In the course of time we went to breakfast, at which only an inconsiderable number of passengers assembled. I noticed that one or two of the officers who breakfasted with us looked grave. After breakfast I went into my state-room in order to get a book. The curtains of the upper berth were still closely drawn. Not a word was to be heard. My room-mate was probably still asleep.

As I came out I met the steward whose business it was to look after me. He whispered that the captain wanted to see me, and then scuttled away down the passage as if very anxious to avoid any questions. I went toward the captain's cabin, and found him waiting for me.

'Sir,' said he, 'I want to ask a favour of you.'

I answered that I would do anything to oblige him.

'Your room-mate has disappeared,' he said. 'He is known to have turned in early last night. Did you notice anything extraordinary in his manner?'

The question coming, as it did, in exact confirmation of the fears the doctor had expressed half an hour earlier, staggered me.

'You don't mean to say he has gone overboard?' I asked.

'I fear he has,' answered the captain.

'This is the most extraordinary thing – ' I began.

'Why?' he asked.

'He is the fourth, then?' I explained. In answer to another question from the captain, I explained, without mentioning the doctor, that I had heard the story concerning one hundred and five. He seemed very much annoyed at hearing that I knew of it. I told him what had occurred in the night.

'What you say,' he replied, 'coincides almost exactly with what was told me by the room-mates of two of the other three. They bolt out of bed and run down the passage. Two of them were seen to go overboard by the watch; we stopped and lowered boats, but they were not found. Nobody, however, saw or heard the man who was lost last night – if he is really lost. The steward, who is a superstitious fellow, perhaps, and expected something to go wrong, went to look for him this morning, and found his berth empty, but his clothes lying about, just as he had left them. The steward was the only man on board who knew him by sight, and he has been searching everywhere for him. He has disappeared! Now, sir, I want to beg you not to mention the circumstance to any of the passengers; I don't want the ship to get a bad name, and nothing hangs about an ocean-goer like stories of suicides. You shall have your choice of any one of the officers' cabins you like, including my own, for the rest of the passage. Is that a fair bargain?'

'Very,' said I; 'and I am much obliged to you. But since I am alone, and have the state-room to myself, I would rather not move. If the steward will take out that unfortunate man's things, I would as lief stay where I am. I will not say anything about the matter, and I think I can promise you that I will not follow my room-mate.'

The captain tried to dissuade me from my intention, but I preferred having a state-room alone to being the chum of any officer on board. I do not know whether I acted foolishly, but if I had taken his advice I should have had nothing more to tell. There would have remained the disagreeable coincidence of several suicides occurring among men who had slept in the same cabin, but that would have been all.

That was not the end of the matter, however, by any means. I obstinately made up my mind that I would not be disturbed by such tales, and I even went so far as to argue the question with the captain. There was something wrong about the state-room, I said. It was rather damp. The porthole had been left open last night. My room-mate might have been ill when he came on board, and he might have become delirious after he went to bed. He might even now be hiding somewhere on board, and might be found later. The place ought to be aired and the fastening of the port looked to. If the captain would give me leave, I would see that what I thought necessary were done immediately.

'Of course you have a right to stay where you are if you please,' he replied, rather petulantly; 'but I wish you would turn out and let me lock the place up, and be done with it.'

I did not see it in the same light, and left the captain, after promising to be silent concerning the disappearance of my companion. The latter had had no acquaintances on board, and was not missed in the course of the day. Towards evening I met the doctor again, and he asked me whether I had changed my mind. I told him I had not.

'Then you will before long,' he said, very gravely.

3

We played whist in the evening, and I went to bed late. I will confess now that I felt a disagreeable sensation when I entered my state-room. I could not help thinking of the tall man I had seen on the previous night, who was now dead, drowned, tossing about in the long swell, two or three hundred miles astern. His face rose very distinctly before me as I undressed, and I even went so far as to draw back the curtains of the upper berth, as though to persuade myself that he was actually gone. I also bolted the door of the state-room. Suddenly I became aware that the porthole was open, and fastened back. This was more than I could stand. I hastily threw on my dressing-gown and went in search of Robert, the steward of my passage. I was very angry, I remember, and when I found him I dragged him roughly to the door of one hundred and five, and pushed him towards the open porthole.

'What the deuce do you mean, you scoundrel, by leaving that port open every night? Don't you know it is against the regulations? Don't you know that if the ship heeled and the water began to come in, ten men could not shut it? I will report you to the captain, you blackguard, for endangering the ship!'

I was exceedingly wroth. The man trembled and turned pale, and then began to shut the round glass plate with the heavy brass fittings.

'Why don't you answer me?' I said, roughly.

'If you please, sir,' faltered Robert, 'there's nobody on board as can keep this 'ere port shut at night. You can try it yourself, sir. I ain't a-going to stop hany longer on board o' this vessel, sir; I ain't, indeed. But if I was you, sir, I'd just clear out and go and sleep with the surgeon, or something, I would. Look 'ere, sir, is that fastened what you may call securely, or not, sir? Try it, sir, see if it will move a hinch.'

I tried the port, and found it perfectly tight.

'Well, sir,' continued Robert, triumphantly, 'I wager my reputation as a AI steward, that in 'arf an hour it will be open again; fastened back, too, sir, that's the horful thing – fastened back!'

I examined the great screw and the looped nut that ran on it.

'If I find it open in the night, Robert, I will give you a sovereign. It is not possible. You may go.'

'Soverin' did you say, sir? Very good, sir. Thank ye, sir. Good night, sir. Pleasant reepose, sir, and all manner of hinchantin' dreams, sir.'

Robert scuttled away, delighted at being released. Of course, I thought he was trying to account for his negligence by a silly story, intended to frighten me, and I disbelieved him. The consequence was that he got his sovereign, and I spent a very peculiarly unpleasant night.

I went to bed, and five minutes after I had rolled myself up in my blankets the inexorable Robert extinguished the light that burned steadily behind the ground-glass pane near the door. I lay quite still in the dark trying to go to sleep, but I soon found that impossible. It had been some satisfaction to be angry with the steward, and the diversion had banished that unpleasant sensation I had at first experienced when I thought of the drowned man who had been my chum; but I was no longer sleepy, and I lay awake for some time, occasionally glancing at the porthole, which I could just see from where I lay, and which, in the darkness, looked like a faintly-luminous soup-plate suspended in blackness. I believe I must have lain there for an hour, and, as I remember, I was just dozing into sleep when I was roused by a draught of cold air and by distinctly feeling the spray of the sea blown upon my face. I started to my feet, and not having allowed in the dark for the motion of the ship, I was instantly thrown violently across the state-room upon the couch which was placed beneath the porthole. I recovered myself immediately, however, and climbed upon my knees. The porthole was again wide open and fastened back!

Now these things are facts. I was wide awake when I got up, and I should certainly have been waked by the fall had I still been dozing. Moreover, I bruised my elbows and knees badly, and the bruises were there on the following morning to testify to the fact, if I myself had doubted it. The porthole was wide open and fastened back – a thing so unaccountable that I remember very well feeling astonishment rather than fear when I discovered it. I at once closed the plate again and screwed down the loop nut with all my strength. It was very dark in the state-room. I reflected that the port had certainly been opened within an hour after Robert had at first shut it in my presence, and I determined to watch it and see whether it would open again. Those brass fittings are very heavy and by no means easy to move; I could not believe that the clump had been turned by the shaking of the screw. I stood peering out through the thick glass at the alternate white and grey streaks of the sea that foamed beneath the ship's side. I must have remained there a quarter of an hour.

Suddenly, as I stood, I distinctly heard something moving behind me in one of the berths, and a moment afterwards, just as I turned instinctively to look – though I could, of course, see nothing in the darkness – I heard a very faint groan. I sprang across the state-room, and tore the curtains of the upper berth aside, thrusting in my hands to discover if there were anyone there. There was someone.

I remember that the sensation as I put my hands forward was as though I were plunging them into the air of a damp cellar, and from behind the curtain came a gust of wind that smelled horribly of stagnant sea-water. I laid hold of something that had the shape of a man's arm, but was smooth, and wet, and icy cold. But suddenly, as I pulled, the creature sprang violently forward against me, a clammy, oozy mass, as it seemed to me, heavy and wet, yet endowed with a sort of supernatural strength. I reeled across the state-room, and in an instant the door opened and the thing rushed out. I had not had time to be frightened, and quickly recovering myself, I sprang through the door and gave chase at the top of my speed, but I was too late. Ten yards before me I could see – I am sure I saw it – a dark shadow moving in the dimly lighted passage, quickly as the shadow of a fast horse thrown before a dog-cart by the lamp on a dark night. But in a moment it had disappeared, and I found myself holding on to the polished rail that ran along the bulkhead where the passage turned towards the companion. My hair stood on end, and the cold perspiration rolled down my face. I am not ashamed of it in the least: I was very badly frightened.

Still I doubted my senses, and pulled myself together. It was absurd, I thought. The Welsh rarebit I had eaten had disagreed with me. I had been in a nightmare. I made my way back to my state-room, and entered it with an effort. The whole place smelled of stagnant sea-water, as it had when I had waked on the previous evening. It required my utmost strength to go in and grope among my things for a box of wax lights. As I lighted a railway reading lantern which I always carry in case I want to read after the lamps are out, I perceived that the porthole was again open, and a sort of creeping horror began to take possession of me which I never felt before, nor wish to feel again. But I got a light and proceeded to examine the upper berth, expecting to find it drenched with sea-water.

But I was disappointed. The bed had been slept in, and the smell of the sea was strong; but the bedding was as dry as a bone. I fancied that Robert had not had the courage to make the bed after the accident of the previous night – it had all been a hideous dream. I drew the curtains back as far as I could and examined the place very carefully. It was perfectly dry. But the porthole was open again. With a sort of dull bewilderment of horror, I closed it and screwed it down, and thrusting my heavy stick through the brass loop, wrenched it with all my might, till the thick metal began to bend under the pressure. Then I hooked my reading lantern into the red velvet at the head of the couch, and sat down to recover my senses if I could. I sat there all night, unable to think of rest – hardly able to think at all. But the porthole remained closed, and I did not believe it would now open again without the application of a considerable force.

The morning dawned at last, and I dressed myself slowly, thinking over all that had happened in the night. It was a beautiful day and I went on deck, glad to get out in the early, pure sunshine, and to smell the breeze from the blue water, so different from the noisome, stagnant odour from my state-room. Instinctively I turned aft, towards the surgeon's cabin. There he stood, with a pipe in his mouth, taking his morning airing precisely as on the preceding day.

'Good-morning,' said he, quietly, but looking at me with evident curiosity.

'Doctor, you were quite right,' said I. 'There is something wrong about that place.'

'I thought you would change your mind,' he answered, rather triumphantly. 'You have had a bad night, eh? Shall I make you a pick-me-up? I have a capital recipe.'

'No, thanks,' I cried. 'But I would like to tell you what happened.'

I then tried to explain as clearly as possible precisely what had occurred, not omitting to state that I had been scared as I had never been scared in my whole life before. I dwelt particularly on the phenomenon of the porthole, which was a fact to which I could testify, even if the rest had been an illusion. I had closed it twice in the night, and the second time I had actually bent the brass in wrenching it with my stick. I believe I insisted a good deal on this point.

'You seem to think I am likely to doubt the story,' said the doctor, smiling at the detailed account of the state of the porthole. 'I do not doubt it in the least. I renew my invitation to you. Bring your traps here, and take half my cabin.'

'Come and take half of mine for one night,' I said. 'Help me to get at the bottom of this thing.'

'You will get to the bottom of something else if you try,' answered the doctor.

'What?' I asked.

'The bottom of the sea. I am going to leave the ship. It is not canny.'

'Then you will not help me to find out – '

'Not I,' said the doctor, quickly. 'It is my business to keep my wits about me – not to go fiddling about with ghosts and things.'

'Do you really believe it is a ghost?' I inquired, rather contemptuously. But as I spoke I remembered very well the horrible sensation of the supernatural which had got possession of me during the night. The doctor turned sharply on me –

'Have you any reasonable explanation of these things to offer?' he asked. 'No; you have not. Well, you say you will find an explanation. I say that you won't, sir, simply because there is not any.'

'But, my dear sir,' I retorted, 'do you, a man of science, mean to tell me that such things cannot be explained?'

'I do,' he answered, stoutly. 'And, if they could, I would not be concerned in the explanation.'

I did not care to spend another night alone in the state-room, and yet I was obstinately determined to get at the root of the disturbances. I do not believe there are many men who would have slept there alone, after passing two such nights. But I made up my mind to try it, if I could not get anyone to share a watch with me. The doctor was evidently not inclined for such an experiment. He said he was a surgeon, and that in case any accident occurred on board he must always be in readiness. He could not afford to have his nerves unsettled. Perhaps he was quite right, but I am inclined to think that his precaution was prompted by his inclination. On enquiry, he informed me that there was no one on board who would be likely to join me in my investigations, and after a little more conversation I left him. A little later I met the captain, and told him my story. I said that if no one would spend the night with me I would ask leave to have the light burning all night, and would try it alone.

'Look here,' said he, 'I will tell you what I will do. I will share your watch myself, and we will see what happens. It is my belief that we can find out between us. There may be some fellow skulking on board, who steals a passage by frightening the passengers. It is just possible that there may be something queer in the carpentering of that berth.'

I suggested taking the ship's carpenter below and examining the place; but I was overjoyed at the captain's offer to spend the night with me. He accordingly sent for the workman and ordered him to do anything I required. We went below at once. I had all the bedding cleared out of the upper berth, and we examined the place thoroughly to see if there was a board loose anywhere, or a panel which could be opened or pushed aside. We tried the planks everywhere, tapped the flooring, unscrewed the fittings of the lower berth and took it to pieces – in short, there was not a square inch of the state-room which was not searched and tested. Everything was in perfect order, and we put everything back in its place. As we were finishing our work, Robert came to the door and looked in.

'Well, sir – find anything, sir?' he asked with a ghastly grin.

'You were right about the porthole, Robert,' I said, and I gave him the promised sovereign. The carpenter did his work silently and skilfully, following my directions. When he had done he spoke.

'I'm a plain man, sir,' he said. 'But it's my belief you had better just turn out your things and let me run half a dozen four inch screws through the door of this cabin. There's no good never came o' this cabin yet, sir, and that's all about it. There's been four lives lost out o' here to my own remembrance, and that in four trips. Better give it up, sir – better give it up!'

'I will try it for one night more,' I said.

'Better give it up, sir – better give it up! It's a precious bad job,' repeated the workman, putting his tools in his bag and leaving the cabin.

But my spirits had risen considerably at the prospect of having the captain's company, and I made up my mind not to be prevented from going to the end of the strange business. I abstained from Welsh rarebits and grog that evening, and did not even join in the customary game of whist. I wanted to be quite sure of my nerves, and my vanity made me anxious to make a good figure in the captain's eyes.

4

The captain was one of those splendidly tough and cheerful specimens of seafaring humanity whose combined courage, hardihood, and calmness in difficulty leads them naturally into high positions of trust. He was not the man to be led away by an idle tale, and the mere fact that he was willing to join me in the investigation was proof that he thought there was something seriously wrong, which could not be accounted for on ordinary theories, nor laughed down as a common superstition. To some extent, too, his reputation was at stake, as well as the reputation of the ship. It is no light thing to lose passengers overboard, and he knew it.

About ten o'clock that evening, as I was smoking a last cigar, he came up to me and drew me aside from the beat of the other passengers who were patrolling the deck in the warm darkness.

'This is a serious matter, Mr Brisbane,' he said. 'We must make up our minds either way – to be disappointed or to have a pretty rough time of it. You see, I cannot afford to laugh at the affair, and I will ask you to sign your name to a statement of whatever occurs. If nothing happens tonight we will try it again tomorrow and next day. Are you ready?'

So we went below, and entered the state-room. As we went in I could see Robert the steward, who stood a little further down the passage, watching us, with his usual grin, as though certain that something dreadful was about to happen. The captain closed the door behind us and bolted it.

'Supposing we put your portmanteau before the door,' he suggested. 'One of us can sit on it. Nothing can get out then. Is the port screwed down?'

I found it as I had left it in the morning. Indeed, without using a lever, as I had done, no one could have opened it. I drew back the curtains of the upper berth so that I could see well into it. By the captain's advice I lighted my reading-lantern, and placed it so that it shone upon the white sheets above. He insisted upon sitting on the portmanteau, declaring that he wished to be able to swear that he had sat before the door.

Then he requested me to search the state-room thoroughly, an operation very soon accomplished, as it consisted merely in looking beneath the lower berth and under the couch below the porthole. The spaces were quite empty.

'It is impossible for any human being to get in,' I said, 'or for any human being to open the port.'

'Very good,' said the captain, calmly. 'If we see anything now, it must be either imagination or something supernatural.'

I sat down on the edge of the lower berth.

'The first time it happened,' said the captain, crossing his legs and leaning back against the door, 'was in March. The passenger who slept here, in the upper berth, turned out to have been a lunatic – at all events, he was known to have been a little touched, and he had taken his passage without the knowledge of his friends. He rushed out in the middle of the night, and threw himself overboard, before the officer who had the watch could stop him. We stopped and lowered a boat; it was a quiet night, just before that heavy weather came on; but we could not find him. Of course his suicide was afterwards accounted for on the ground of his insanity.'

'I suppose that often happens?' I remarked, rather absently.

'Not often – no,' said the captain; 'never before in my experience, though I have heard of it happening on board of other ships. Well, as I was saying, that occurred in March. On the very next trip – what are you looking at?' he asked, stopping suddenly in his narration.

I believe I gave no answer. My eyes were riveted upon the port-hole. It seemed to me that the brass loop-nut was beginning to turn very slowly upon the screw – so slowly, however, that I was not sure it moved at all. I watched it intently, fixing its position in my mind, and trying to ascertain whether it changed. Seeing where I was looking, the captain looked too.

'It moves!' he exclaimed, in a tone of conviction. 'No, it does not,' he added, after a minute.

'If it were the jarring of the screw,' said I, 'it would have opened during the day; but I found it this evening jammed tight as I left it this morning.'

I rose and tried the nut. It was certainly loosened, for by an effort I could move it with my hands.

'The queer thing,' said the captain, 'is that the second man who was lost is supposed to have got through that very port. We had a terrible time over it. It was in the middle of the night, and the weather was very heavy; there was an alarm that one of the ports was open and the sea running in. I came below and found everything flooded, the water pouring in every time she rolled, and the whole port swinging from the top bolts – not the porthole in the middle. Well, we managed to shut it, but the water did some damage. Ever since that the place smells of sea-water from time to time. We supposed the passenger had thrown himself out, though the Lord only knows how he did it. The steward kept telling me that he could not keep anything shut here. Upon my word – I can smell it now, cannot you?' he inquired, sniffing the air suspiciously.

'Yes – distinctly,' I said, and I shuddered as that same odour of stagnant sea-water grew stronger in the cabin. 'Now, to smell like this, the place must be damp,' I continued, 'and yet when I examined it with the carpenter this morning everything was perfectly dry. It is most extraordinary – hallo!'

My reading-lantern, which had been placed in the upper berth, was suddenly extinguished. There was still a good deal of light from the pane of ground glass near the door, behind which loomed the regulation lamp. The ship rolled heavily, and the curtain of the upper berth swung far out into the state-room and back again. I rose quickly from my seat on the edge of the bed, and the captain at the same moment started to his feet with a loud cry of surprise. I had turned with the intention of taking down the lantern to examine it, when I heard his exclamation, and immediately afterwards his call for help. I sprang towards him. He was wrestling with all his might, with the brass loop of the port. It seemed to turn against his hands in spite of all his efforts. I caught up my cane, a heavy oak stick I always used to carry, and thrust it through the ring and bore on it with all my strength. But the strong wood snapped suddenly, and I fell upon the couch. When I rose again the port was wide open, and the captain was standing with his back against the door, pale to the lips.

'There is something in that berth!' he cried, in a strange voice, his eyes almost starting from his head. 'Hold the door, while I look – it shall not escape us, whatever it is!'

But instead of taking his place, I sprang upon the lower bed, and seized something which lay in the upper berth.

It was something ghostly, horrible beyond words, and it moved in my grip. It was like the body of a man long drowned, and yet it moved, and had the strength of ten men living; but I gripped it with all my might – the slippery, oozy, horrible thing. The dead white eyes seemed to stare at me out of the dusk; the putrid odour of rank sea-water was about it, and its shiny hair hung in foul wet curls over its dead face. I wrestled with the dead thing; it thrust itself upon me and forced me back and nearly broke my arms; it wound its corpse's arms about my neck, the living death, and overpowered me, so that I, at last, cried aloud and fell, and left my hold.

As I fell the thing sprang across me, and seemed to throw itself upon the captain. When I last saw him on his feet his face was white and his lips set. It seemed to me that he struck a violent blow at the dead being, and then he, too, fell forward upon his face, with an inarticulate cry of horror.

The thing paused an instant, seeming to hover over his prostrate body, and I could have screamed again for very fright, but I had no voice left. The thing vanished suddenly, and it seemed to my disturbed senses that it made its exit through the open port, though how that was possible, considering the smallness of the aperture, is more than anyone can tell. I lay a long time upon the floor, and the captain lay beside me. At last I partially recovered my senses and moved, and I instantly knew that my arm was broken – the small bone of the left forearm near the wrist.

I got upon my feet somehow, and with my remaining hand I tried to raise the captain. He groaned and moved, and at last came to himself. He was not hurt, but he seemed badly stunned.

*   *   *

Well, do you want to hear any more? There is nothing more. That is the end of my story. The carpenter carried out his scheme of running half a dozen four-inch screws through the door of one hundred and five; and if ever you take a passage in the *Kamtschatka*, you may ask for a berth in that state-room. You will be told that it is engaged – yes – it is engaged by that dead thing.

I finished the trip in the surgeon's cabin. He doctored my broken arm, and advised me not to 'fiddle about with ghosts and things' any more. The captain was very silent, and never sailed again in that ship, though it is still running. And I will not sail in her either. It was a very disagreeable experience, and I was very badly frightened, which is a thing I do not like. That is all. That is how I saw a ghost – if it was a ghost. It was dead, anyhow.

Man Overboard!

Yes – I have heard 'Man overboard!' a good many times since I was a boy, and once or twice I have seen the man go. There are more men lost in that way than passengers on ocean steamers ever learn of. I have stood looking over the rail on a dark night, when there was a step beside me, and something flew past my head like a big black bat – and then there was a splash! Stokers often go like that. They go mad with the heat, and they slip up on deck and are gone before anybody can stop them, often without being seen or heard. Now and then a passenger will do it, but he generally has what he thinks a pretty good reason. I have seen a man empty his revolver into a crowd of emigrants forward, and then go over like a rocket. Of course, any officer who respects himself will do what he can to pick a man up, if the weather is not so heavy that he would have to risk his ship; but I don't think I remember seeing a man come back when he was once fairly gone more than two or three times in all my life, though we have often picked up the life-buoy, and sometimes the fellow's cap. Stokers and passengers jump over; I never knew a sailor to do that, drunk or sober. Yes, they say it has happened on hard ships, but I never knew a case myself. Once in a long time a man is fished out when it is just too late, and dies in the boat before you can get him aboard, and – well, I don't know that I ever told that story since it happened – I knew a fellow who went over, and came back dead. I didn't see him after he came back; only one of us did, but we all knew he was there.

No, I am not giving you 'sharks'. There isn't a shark in this story, and I don't know that I would tell it at all if we weren't alone, just you and I. But you and I have seen things in various parts, and maybe you will understand. Anyhow, you know that I am telling what I know about, and nothing else; and it has been on my mind to tell you ever since it happened, only there hasn't been a chance.

It's a long story, and it took some time to happen; and it began a good many years ago, in October, as well as I can remember. I was mate then; I passed the local Marine Board for master about three years later. She was the *Helen B. Jackson*, of New York, with lumber for the West Indies, four-masted schooner, Captain Hackstaff. She was an old-fashioned one, even then – no steam donkey, and all to do by hand. There were still sailors in the coasting trade in those days, you remember. She wasn't a hard ship, for the old man was better than most of them, though he kept to himself and had a face like a monkey-wrench. We were thirteen, all told, in the ship's company; and some of them afterwards thought that might have had something to do with it, but I had all that nonsense knocked out of me when I was a boy. I don't mean to say that I like to go to sea on a Friday, but I *have* gone to sea on a Friday, and nothing has happened; and twice before that we have been thirteen, because one of the hands didn't turn up at the last minute, and nothing ever happened either – nothing worse than the loss of a light spar or two, or a little canvas. Whenever I have been wrecked, we had sailed as cheerily as you please – no thirteens, no Fridays, no dead men in the hold. I believe it generally happens that way.

I dare say you remember those two Benton boys that were so much alike? It is no wonder, for they were twin brothers. They shipped with us as boys on the old *Boston Belle*, when you were mate and I was before the mast. I never was quite sure which was which of those two, even then; and when they both had beards it was harder than ever to tell them apart. One was Jim, and the other was Jack; James Benton and John Benton. The only difference I ever could see was, that one seemed to be rather more cheerful and inclined to talk than the other; but one couldn't even be sure of that. Perhaps they had moods. Anyhow, there was one of them that used to whistle when he was alone. He only knew one tune, and that was 'Nancy Lee', and the other didn't know any tune at all; but I may be mistaken about that, too. Perhaps they both knew it.

Well, those two Benton boys turned up on board the *Helen B. Jackson*. They had been on half a dozen ships since the *Boston Belle*, and they had grown up and were good seamen. They had reddish beards and bright blue eyes and freckled faces; and they were quiet fellows, good workmen on rigging, pretty willing, and both good men at the wheel. They managed to be in the same watch – it was the port watch on the *Helen B.*, and that was mine, and I had great confidence in them both. If there was any job aloft that needed two hands, they were always the first to jump into the rigging; but that doesn't often happen on a fore-and-aft schooner. If it breezed up, and the jib-topsail was to be taken in, they never minded a wetting, and they would be out at the bowsprit end before there was a hand at the downhaul. The men liked them for that, and because they didn't blow about what the could do. I remember one day in a reefing job, the downhaul parted and came down on deck from the peak of the spanker. When the weather moderated, and we shook the reefs out, the downhaul was forgotten until we happened to think we might soon need it again. There was some sea on, and the boom was off and the gaff was slamming. One of those Benton boys was at the wheel, and before I knew what he was doing, the other was out on the gaff with the end of the new downhaul, trying to reeve it through its block. The one who was steering watched him, and got as white as cheese. The other one was swinging about on the gaff end, and every time she rolled to leeward he brought up with a jerk that would have sent anything but a monkey flying into space. But he didn't leave it until he had rove the new rope, and he got back all right. I think it was Jack at the wheel, the one that seemed more cheerful, the one that whistled 'Nancy Lee'. He had rather have been doing the job himself than watch his brother do it, and he had a scared look; but he kept her as steady as he could in the swell, and he drew a long breath when Jim had worked his way back to the peak-halliard block, and had something to hold on to. I think it was Jim.

They had good togs, too, and they were neat and clean men in the forecastle. I knew they had nobody belonging to them ashore – no mother, no sisters, and no wives; but somehow they both looked as if a woman overhauled them now and then. I remember that they had one ditty bag between them, and they had a woman's thimble in it. One of the men said something about it to them, and they looked at each other; and one smiled, but the other didn't. Most of their clothes were alike, but they had one red guernsey between them. For some time I used to think it was always the same one that wore it, and I thought that might be a way to tell them apart. But then I heard one asking the other for it, and saying that the other had worn it last. So that was no sign either. The cook was a West Indiaman, called James Lawley; his father had been hanged for putting lights in cocoanut trees where they didn't belong. But he was a good cook, and knew his business; and it wasn't soup-and-bully and dogsbody every Sunday. That's what I meant to say. On Sunday the cook called both those boys Jim, and on weekdays he called them Jack. He used to say he must be right sometimes if he did that, because even the hands on a painted clock point right twice a day.

What started me to trying for some way of telling the Bentons apart was this. I heard them talking about a girl. It was at night, in our watch, and the wind had headed us off a little rather suddenly, and when we had flattened in the jibs, we clewed down the topsails, while the two Benton boys got the spanker sheet aft. One of them was at the helm. I coiled down the mizzen-topsail downhaul myself, and was going aft to see how she headed up, when I stopped to look at a light, and leaned against the deck-house. While I was standing there I heard the two boys talking. It sounded as if they had talked of the same thing before, and as far as I could tell, the voice I heard first belonged to the one who wasn't quite so cheerful as the other – the one who was Jim when one knew which he was.

'Does Mamie know?' Jim asked.

'Not yet,' Jack answered quietly. He was at the wheel. 'I mean to tell her next time we get home.'

'All right.'

That was all I heard, because I didn't care to stand there listening while they were talking about their own affairs; so I went aft to look into the binnacle, and I told the one at the wheel to keep her so as long as she had way on her, for I thought the wind would back up again before long, and there was land to leeward. When he answered, his voice, somehow, didn't sound like the cheerful one. Perhaps his brother had relieved the wheel while they had been speaking, but what I had heard set me wondering which of them it was that had a girl at home. There's lots of time for wondering on a schooner in fair weather.

After that I thought I noticed that the two brothers were more silent when they were together. Perhaps they guessed that I had overheard something that night, and kept quiet when I was about. Some men would have amused themselves by trying to chaff them separately about the girl at home, and I suppose whichever one it was would have let the cat out of the bag if I had done that. But somehow, I didn't like to. Yes, I was thinking of getting married myself at that time, so I had a sort of fellow-feeling for whichever one it was, that made me not want to chaff him.

They didn't talk much, it seemed to me; but in fair weather, when there was nothing to do at night, and one was steering, the other was everlastingly hanging round as if he were waiting to relieve the wheel, though he might have been enjoying a quiet nap for all I cared in such weather. Or else, when one was taking his turn at the look-out, the other would be sitting on an anchor beside him. One kept near the other, at night more than in the daytime. I noticed that. They were fond of sitting on that anchor, and they generally tucked away their pipes under it, for the *Helen B.* was a dry boat in most weather, and like most fore-and-afters was better on a wind than going free. With a beam sea we sometimes shipped a little water aft. We were by the stern, anyhow, on that voyage, and that is one reason why we lost the man.

We fell in with a southerly gale, southeast at first; and then the barometer began to fall while you could watch it, and a long swell began to come up from the south'ard. A couple of months earlier we might have been in for a cyclone, but it's 'October all over' in those waters, as you know better than I. It was just going to blow, and then it was going to rain, that was all; and we had plenty of time to make everything snug before it breezed up much. It blew harder after sunset, and by the time it was quite dark it was a full gale. We had shortened sail for it, but as we were by the stern we were carrying the spanker close-reefed instead of the storm trysail. She steered better so, as long as we didn't have to heave to. I had the first watch with the Benton boys, and we had not been on deck an hour when a child might have seen that the weather meant business.

The old man came up on deck and looked round, and in less than a minute he told us to give her the trysail. That meant heaving to, and I was glad of it; for though the *Helen B.* was a good vessel enough, she wasn't a new ship by a long way, and it did her no good to drive her in that weather. I asked whether I should call all hands, but just then the cook came aft, and the old man said he thought we could manage the job without waking the sleepers, and the trysail was handy on deck already, for we hadn't been expecting anything better. We were all in oilskins, of course, and the night was as black as a coal mine, with only a ray of light from the slit in the binnacle shield, and you couldn't tell one man from another except by his voice. The old man took the wheel; we got the boom amidships, and he jammed her into the wind until she had hardly any way. It was blowing now, and it was all that I and two others could do to get in the slack of the downhaul, while the others lowered away at the peak and throat, and we had our hands full to get a couple of turns round the wet sail. It's all child's play on a fore-and-after compared with reefing topsails in anything like weather, but the gear of a schooner sometimes does unhandy things that you don't expect, and those everlasting long halliards get foul of everything if they get adrift. I remember thinking how unhandy that particular job was. Somebody unhooked the throat-halliard block, and thought he had hooked it into the head-cringle of the trysail, and sang out to hoist away, but he had missed it in the dark, and the heavy block went flying into the lee rigging, and nearly killed him when it swung back with the weather roll. Then the old man got her up into the wind until the jib was shaking like thunder; then he held her off, and she went off as soon as the headsails filled, and he couldn't get her back again without the spanker. Then the *Helen B.* did her favourite trick, and before we had time to say much we had a sea over the quarter and were up to our waists, with the parrels of the trysail only half becketed round the mast, and the deck so full of gear that you couldn't put your foot on a plank, and the spanker beginning to get adrift again, being badly stopped, and the general confusion and hell's delight that you can only have on a fore-and-after when there's nothing really serious the matter. Of course, I don't mean to say that the old man couldn't have steered his trick as well as you or I or any other seaman; but I don't believe he had ever been on board the *Helen B.* before, or had his hand on her wheel till then; and he didn't know her ways. I don't mean to say that what happened was his fault. I don't know whose fault it was. Perhaps nobody was to blame. But I knew something happened somewhere on board when we shipped that sea, and you'll never get it out of my head. I hadn't any spare time myself, for I was becketing the rest of the trysail to the mast. We were on the starboard tack, and the throat-halliard came down to port as usual, and I suppose there were at least three men at it, hoisting away, while I was at the beckets.

Now I am going to tell you something. You have known me, man and boy, several voyages; and you are older than I am; and you have always been a good friend to me. Now, do you think I am the sort of man to think I hear things where there isn't anything to hear, or to think I see things when there is nothing to see? No, you don't. Thank you. Well now, I had passed the last becket, and I sang out to the men to sway away, and I was standing on the jaws of the spanker-gaff, with my left hand on the bolt-rope of the trysail, so that I could feel when it was board-taut, and I wasn't thinking of anything except being glad the job was over, and that we were going to heave her to. It was as black as a coal-pocket, except that you could see the streaks on the seas as they went by, and abaft the deck-house I could see the ray of light from the binnacle on the captain's yellow oilskin as he stood at the wheel – or rather I might have seen it if I had looked round at that minute. But I didn't look round. I heard a man whistling. It was 'Nancy Lee', and I could have sworn that the man was right over my head in the crosstrees. Only somehow I knew very well that if anybody could have been up there, and could have whistled a tune, there were no living ears sharp enough to hear it on deck then. I heard it distinctly, and at the same time I heard the real whistling of the wind in the weather rigging, sharp and clear as the steam-whistle on a Dago's peanut-cart in New York. That was all right, that was as it should be; but the other wasn't right; and I felt queer and stiff, as if I couldn't move, and my hair was curling against the flannel lining of my sou'wester, and I thought somebody had dropped a lump of ice down my back.

I said that the noise of the wind in the rigging was real, as if the other wasn't, for I felt that it wasn't, though I heard it. But it was, all the same; for the captain heard it, too. When I came to relieve the wheel, while the men were clearing up decks, he was swearing. He was a quiet man, and I hadn't heard him swear before, and I don't think I did again, though several queer things happened after that. Perhaps he said all he had to say then; I don't see how he could have said anything more. I used to think nobody could swear like a Dane, except a Neapolitan or a South American; but when I had heard the old man I changed my mind. There's nothing afloat or ashore that can beat one of your quiet American skippers, if he gets off on that tack. I didn't need to ask him what was the matter, for I knew he had heard 'Nancy Lee', as I had, only it affected us differently.

He did not give me the wheel, but told me to go forward and get the second bonnet off the staysail, so as to keep her up better. As we tailed on to the sheet when it was done, the man next me knocked his sou'wester off against my shoulder, and his face came so close to me that I could see it in the dark. It must have been very white for me to see it, but I only thought of that afterwards. I don't see how any light could have fallen upon it, but I knew it was one of the Benton boys. I don't know what made me speak to him. 'Hullo, Jim! Is that you?' I asked. I don't know why I said Jim, rather than Jack.

'I am Jack,' he answered.

We made all fast, and things were much quieter.

'The old man heard you whistling "Nancy Lee", just now,' I said, 'and he didn't like it.'

It was as if there were a white light inside his face, and it was ghastly. I know his teeth chattered. But he didn't say anything, and the next minute he was somewhere in the dark trying to find his sou'wester at the foot of the mast.

When all was quiet, and she was hove to, coming to and falling off her four points as regularly as a pendulum, and the helm lashed a little to the lee, the old man turned in again, and I managed to light a pipe in the lee of the deckhouse, for there was nothing more to be done till the gale chose to moderate, and the ship was as easy as a baby in its cradle. Of course the cook had gone below, as he might have done an hour earlier; so there were supposed to be four of us in the watch. There was a man at the lookout, and there was a hand by the wheel, though there was no steering to be done, and I was having my pipe in the lee of the deck-house, and the fourth man was some-where about decks, probably having a smoke too. I thought some skippers I had sailed with would have called the watch aft, and given them a drink after that job, but it wasn't cold, and I guessed that our old man wouldn't be particularly generous in that way. My hands and feet were red-hot, and it would be time enough to get into dry clothes when it was my watch below; so I stayed where I was, and smoked. But by and by, things being so quiet, I began to wonder why nobody moved on deck; just that sort of restless wanting to know where every man is that one sometimes feels in a gale of wind on a dark night. So when I had finished my pipe I began to move about. I went aft, and there was a man leaning over the wheel, with his legs apart and both hands hanging down in the light from the binnacle, and his sou'wester over his eyes. Then I went forward, and there was a man at the lookout, with his back against the foremast, getting what shelter he could from the staysail. I knew by his small height that he was not one of the Benton boys. Then I went round by the weather side, and poked about in the dark, for I began to wonder where the other man was. But I couldn't find him, though I searched the decks until I got right aft again. It was certainly one of the Benton boys that was missing, but it wasn't like either of them to go below to change his clothes in such warm weather. The man at the wheel was the other, of course. I spoke to him.

'Jim, what's become of your brother?'

'I am Jack, sir.'

'Well, then, Jack, where's Jim? He's not on deck.'

'I don't know, sir.'

When I had come up to him he had stood up from force of instinct, and had laid his hands on the spokes as if he were steering, though the wheel was lashed; but he still bent his face down, and it was half hidden by the edge of his sou'wester, while he seemed to be staring at the compass. He spoke in a very low voice, but that was natural, for the captain had left his door open when he turned in, as it was a warm night in spite of the storm, and there was no fear of shipping any more water now.

'What put it into your head to whistle like that, Jack? You've been at sea long enough to know better.'

He said something, but I couldn't hear the words; it sounded as if he were denying the charge.

'Somebody whistled,' I said.

He didn't answer, and then, I don't know why, perhaps because the old man hadn't given us a drink, I cut half an inch off the plug of tobacco I had in my oilskin pocket, and gave it to him. He knew my tobacco was good, and he shoved it into his mouth with a word of thanks. I was on the weather side of the wheel.

'Go forward and see if you can find Jim,' I said.

He started a little, and then stepped back and passed behind me, and was going along the weather side. Maybe his silence about the whistling had irritated me, and his taking it for granted that because we were hove to and it was a dark night, he might go forward any way he pleased. Anyhow, I stopped him, though I spoke good-naturedly enough.

'Pass to leeward, Jack,' I said.

He didn't answer, but crossed the deck between the binnacle and the deckhouse to the lee side. She was only falling off and coming to, and riding the big seas as easily as possible, but the man was not steady on his feet and reeled against the corner of the deck-house and then against the lee rail. I was quite sure he couldn't have had anything to drink, for neither of the brothers were the kind to hide rum from their shipmates, if they had any, and the only spirits that were aboard were locked up in the captain's cabin. I wondered whether he had been hit by the throat-halliard block and was hurt.

I left the wheel and went after him, but when I got to the corner of the deck-house I saw that he was on a full run forward, so I went back. I watched the compass for a while, to see how far she went off, and she must have come to again half a dozen times before I heard voices, more than three or four, forward; and then I heard the little West Indies cook's voice, high and shrill above' the rest: 'Man overboard!'

There wasn't anything to be done, with the ship hove-to and the wheel lashed. If there was a man overboard, he must be in the water right alongside. I couldn't imagine how it could have happened, but

I ran forward instinctively. I came upon the cook first, half-dressed in his shirt and trousers, just as he had tumbled out of his bunk. He was jumping into the main rigging, evidently hoping to see the man, as if anyone could have seen anything on such a night, except the foam-streaks on the black water, and now and then the curl of a breaking sea as it went away to leeward. Several of the men were peering over the rail into the dark. I caught the cook by the foot, and asked who was gone.

'It's Jim Benton,' he shouted down to me. 'He's not aboard this ship!'

There was no doubt about that. Jim Benton was gone; and I knew in a flash that he had been taken off by that sea when we were setting the storm trysail. It was nearly half an hour since then; she had run like wild for a few minutes until we got her hove-to, and no swimmer that ever swam could have lived as long as that in such a sea. The men knew it as well as I, but still they stared into the foam as if they had any chance of seeing the lost man. I let the cook get into the rigging and joined the men, and asked if they had made a thorough search on board, though I knew they had and that it could not take long, for he wasn't on deck, and there was only the forecastle below.

'That sea took him over, sir, as sure as you're born,' said one of the men close beside me.

We had no boat that could have lived in that sea, of course, and we all knew it. I offered to put one over, and let her drift astern two or three cable's-lengths by a line, if the men thought they could haul me aboard again; but none of them would listen to that, and I should probably have been drowned if I had tried it, even with a life-belt; for it was a breaking sea. Besides, they all knew as well as I did that the man could not be right in our wake. I don't know why I spoke again.

'Jack Benton, are you there? Will you go if I will?'

'No, sir,' answered a voice; and that was all.

By that time the old man was on deck, and I felt his hand on my shoulder rather roughly, as if he meant to shake me.

'I'd reckoned you had more sense, Mr Torkeldsen,' he said. 'God knows I would risk my ship to look for him, if it were any use; but he must have gone half an hour ago.'

He was a quiet man, and the men knew he was right, and that they had seen the last of Jim Benton when they were bending the trysail – if anybody had seen him then. The captain went below again, and for some time the men stood around Jack, quite near him, without saying anything, as sailors do when they are sorry for a man and can't help him; and then the watch below turned in again, and we were three on deck.

Nobody can understand that there can be much consolation in a funeral, unless he has felt that blank feeling there is when a man's gone overboard whom everybody likes. I suppose landsmen think it would be easier if they didn't have to bury their fathers and mothers and friends; but it wouldn't be. Somehow the funeral keeps up the idea of something beyond. You may believe in that something just the same; but a man who has gone in the dark, between two seas, without a cry, seems much more beyond reach than if he were still lying on his bed, and had only just stopped breathing. Perhaps Jim Benton knew that, and wanted to come back to us. I don't know, and I am only telling you what happened, and you may think what you like.

Jack stuck by the wheel that night until the watch was over. I don't know whether he slept afterwards, but when I came on deck four hours later, there he was again, in his oilskins, with his sou'wester over his eyes, staring into the binnacle. We saw that he would rather stand there, and we left him alone. Perhaps it was some consolation to him to get that ray of light when everything was so dark. It began to rain, too, as it can when a southerly gale is going to break up, and we got every bucket and tub on board, and set them under the booms to catch the fresh water for washing our clothes. The rain made it very thick, and I went and stood under the lee of the staysail, looking out. I could tell that day was breaking, because the foam was whiter in the dark where the seas crested, and little by little the black rain grew grey and steamy, and I couldn't see the red glare of the port light on the water when she went off and rolled to leeward. The gale had moderated considerably, and in another hour we should be under way again. I was still standing there when Jack Benton came forward. He stood still a few minutes near me. The rain came down in a solid sheet, and I could see his wet beard and a corner of his cheek, too, grey in the dawn. Then he stooped down and began feeling under the anchor for his pipe. We had hardly shipped any water forward, and I suppose he had some way of tucking the pipe in, so that the rain hadn't floated it off. Presently he got on his legs again, and I saw that he had two pipes in his hand. One of them had belonged to his brother, and after looking at them a moment I suppose he recognised his own, for he put it in his mouth, dripping with water. Then he looked at the other fully a minute without moving. When he had made up his mind, I suppose, he quietly chucked it over the lee rail, without even looking round to see whether I was watching him. I thought it was a pity, for it was a good wooden pipe, with a nickel ferrule, and somebody would have been glad to have it. But I didn't like to make any remark, for he had a right to do what he pleased with what had belonged to his dead brother. He blew the water out of his own pipe, and dried it against his jacket, putting his hand inside his oilskin; he filled it, standing under the lee of the foremast, got a light after wasting two or three matches, and turned the pipe upside down in his teeth, to keep the rain out of the bowl. I don't know why I noticed everything he did, and remember it now; but somehow I felt sorry for him, and I kept wondering whether there was anything I could say that would make him feel better. But I didn't think of anything, and as it was broad daylight I went aft again, for I guessed that the old man would turn out before long and order the spanker set and the helm up. But he didn't turn out before seven bells, just as the clouds broke and showed blue sky to leeward – 'the Frenchman's barometer', you used to call it.

Some people don't seem to be so dead, when they are dead, as others are. Jim Benton was like that. He had been on my watch, and I couldn't get used to the idea that he wasn't about decks with me. I was always expecting to see him, and his brother was so exactly like him that I often felt as if I did see him and forgot he was dead, and made the mistake of calling Jack by his name; though I tried not to, because I knew it must hurt. If ever Jack had been the cheerful one of the two, as I had always supposed he had been, he had changed very much, for he grew to be more silent than Jim had ever been.

One fine afternoon I was sitting on the main-hatch, overhauling the clockwork of the taffrail-log, which hadn't been registering very well of late, and I had got the cook to bring me a coffee-cup to hold the small screws as I took them out, and a saucer for the sperm-oil I was going to use. I noticed that he didn't go away, but hung round without exactly watching what I was doing, as if he wanted to say something to me. I thought if it were worth much he would say it anyhow, so I didn't ask him questions; and sure enough he began of his own accord before long. There was nobody on deck but the man at the wheel, and the other man away forward.

'Mr Torkeldsen,' the cook began, and then stopped.

I supposed he was going to ask me to let the watch break out a barrel of flour, or some salt horse.

'Well, doctor?' I asked, as he didn't go on.

'Well, Mr Torkeldsen,' he answered, 'I somehow want to ask you whether you think I am giving satisfaction on this ship, or not?'

'So far as I know, you are, doctor. I haven't heard any complaints from the forecastle, and the captain has said nothing, and I think you know your business, and the cabin-boy is bursting out of his clothes. That looks as if you are giving satisfaction. What makes you think you are not?'

I am not good at giving you that West Indies talk, and shan't try; but the doctor beat about the bush a while, and then he told me he thought the men were beginning to play tricks on him, and he didn't like it, and thought he hadn't deserved it, and would like his discharge at our next port. I told him he was a d—d fool, of course, to begin with; and that men were more apt to try a joke with a chap they liked than with anybody they wanted to get rid of; unless it was a bad joke, like flooding his bunk, or filling his boots with tar. But it wasn't that kind of practical joke. The doctor said that the men were trying to frighten him, and he didn't like it, and that they put things in his way that frightened him. So I told him he was a d—d fool to be frightened, anyway, and I wanted to know what things they put in his way. He gave me a queer answer. He said they were spoons and forks, and odd plates, and a cup now and then, and such things.

I set down the taffrail-log on the bit of canvas I had put under it, and looked at the doctor. He was uneasy, and his eyes had a sort of hunted look, and his yellow face looked grey. He wasn't trying to make trouble. He was in trouble. So I asked him questions.

He said he could count as well as anybody, and do sums without using his fingers, but that when he couldn't count any other way he did use his fingers, and it always came out the same. He said that when he and the cabin-boy cleared up after the men's meals there were more things to wash than he had given out. There'd be a fork more, or there'd be a spoon more, and sometimes there'd be a spoon and a fork, and there was always a plate more. It wasn't that he complained of that. Before poor Jim Benton was lost they had a man more to feed, and his gear to wash up after meals, and that was in the contract, the doctor said. It would have been if there were twenty in the ship's company; but he didn't think it was right for the men to play tricks like that. He kept his things in good order, and he counted them, and he was responsible for them, and it wasn't right that the men should take more things than they needed when his back was turned, and just soil them and mix them up with their own, so as to make him think –

He stopped there, and looked at me, and I looked at him. I didn't know what he thought, but I began to guess. I wasn't going to humour any such nonsense as that, so I told him to speak to the men himself, and not come bothering me about such things.

'Count the plates and forks and spoons before them when they sit down to table, and tell them that's all they'll get; and when they have finished, count the things again, and if the count isn't right, find out who did it. You know it must be one of them. You're not a green hand; you've been going to sea ten or eleven years, and don't want any lesson about how to behave if the boys play a trick on you.'

'If I could catch him,' said the cook, 'I'd have a knife into him before he could say his prayers.'

Those West India men are always talking about knives, especially when they are badly frightened. I knew what he meant, and didn't ask him, but went on cleaning the brass cog-wheels of the patent log and oiling the bearings with a feather. 'Wouldn't it be better to wash it out with boiling water, sir?' asked the cook, in an insinuating tone. He knew that he had made a fool of himself, and was anxious to make it right again.

I heard no more about the odd platter and gear for two or three days, though I thought about his story a good deal. The doctor evidently believed that Jim Benton had come back, though he didn't quite like to say so. His story had sounded silly enough on a bright afternoon, in fair weather, when the sun was on the water, and every rag was drawing in the breeze, and the sea looked as pleasant and harmless as a cat that has just eaten a canary. But when it was toward the end of the first watch, and the waning moon had not risen yet, and the water was like still oil, and the jibs hung down flat and helpless like the wings of a dead bird – it wasn't the same then. More than once I have started then, and looked round when a fish jumped, expecting to see a face sticking up out of the water with its eyes shut. I think we all felt something like that at the time.

One afternoon we were putting a fresh service on the jib-sheet-pennant. It wasn't my watch, but I was standing by looking on. Just then Jack Benton came up from below, and went to look for his pipe under the anchor. His face was hard and drawn, and his eyes were cold like steel balls. He hardly ever spoke now, but he did his duty as usual and nobody had to complain of him, though we were all beginning to wonder how long his grief for his dead brother was going to last like that. I watched him as he crouched down, and ran his hand into the hiding-place for the pipe. When he stood up, he had two pipes in his hand.

Now, I remembered very well seeing him throw one of those pipes away, early in the morning after the gale; and it came to me now, and I didn't suppose he kept a stock of them under the anchor. I caught sight of his face, and it was greenish white, like the foam on shallow water, and he stood a long time looking at the two pipes. He wasn't looking to see which was his, for I wasn't five yards from him as he stood, and one of those pipes had been smoked that day, and was shiny where his hand had rubbed it, and the bone mouthpiece was chafed white where his teeth had bitten it. The other was water-logged. It was swelled and cracking with wet, and it looked to me as if there were a little green weed on it.

Jack Benton turned his head rather stealthily as I looked away, and then he hid the thing in his trousers pocket, and went aft on the lee side, out of sight. The men had got the sheet pennant on a stretch to serve it, but I ducked under it and stood where I could see what Jack did, just under the fore-staysail. He couldn't see me, and he was looking about for something. His hand shook as he picked up a bit of half-bent iron rod, about a foot long, that had been used for turning an eyebolt, and had been left on the mainhatch. His hand shook as he got a piece of marline out of his pocket, and made the water-logged pipe fast to the iron. He didn't mean it to get adrift, either, for he took his turns carefully, and hove them taut and then rode them, so that they couldn't slip, and made the end fast with two half-hitches round the iron, and hitched it back on itself. Then he tried it with his hands, and looked up and down the deck furtively, and then quietly dropped the pipe and iron over the rail, so that I didn't even hear the splash. If anybody was playing tricks on board, they weren't meant for the cook.

I asked some questions about Jack Benton, and one of the men told me that he was off his feed, and hardly ate anything, and swallowed all the coffee he could lay his hands on, and had used up all his own tobacco and had begun on what his brother had left.

'The doctor says it ain't so, sir,' said the man, looking at me shyly, as if he didn't expect to be believed; 'the doctor says there's as much eaten from breakfast to breakfast as there was before Jim fell over-board, though there's a mouth less and another that eats nothing. I says it's the cabin-boy that gets it. He's bu'sting.'

I told him that if the cabin-boy ate more than his share, he must work more than his share, so as to balance things. But the man laughed queerly, and looked at me again.

'I only said that, sir, just like that. We all know it ain't so.'

'Well, how is it?'

'How is it?' asked the man, half-angry all at once. 'I don't know how it is, but there's a hand on board that's getting his whack along with us as regular as the bells.'

'Does he use tobacco?' I asked, meaning to laugh it out of him, but as I spoke I remembered the waterlogged pipe.

'I guess he's using his own still,' the man answered, in a queer, low voice. 'Perhaps he'll take someone else's when his is all gone.'

It was about nine o'clock in the morning, I remember, for just then the captain called to me to stand by the chronometer while he took his fore observation. Captain Hackstaff wasn't one of those old skippers who do everything themselves with a pocket watch, and keep the key of the chronometer in their waistcoat pocket, and won't tell the mate how far the dead reckoning is out. He was rather the other way, and I was glad of it, for he generally let me work the sights he took, and just ran his eye over my figures afterwards. I am bound to say his eye was pretty good, for he would pick out a mistake in a logarithm, or tell me that I had worked the 'Equation of Time' with the wrong sign, before it seemed to me that he could have got as far as 'half the sum, minus the altitude'. He was always right, too, and besides he knew a lot about iron ships and local deviation, and adjusting the compass, and all that sort of thing. I don't know how he came to be in command of a fore-and-aft schooner. He never talked about himself, and maybe he had just been mate on one of those big steel square-riggers, and something had put him back. Perhaps he had been captain, and had got his ship aground, through no particular fault of his, and had to begin over again. Sometimes he talked just like you and me, and sometimes he would speak more like books do, or some of those Boston people I have heard. I don't know. We have all been shipmates now and then with men who have seen better days. Perhaps he had been in the Navy, but what makes me think he couldn't have been, was that he was a thorough good seaman, a regular old wind-jammer, and understood sail, which those Navy chaps rarely do. Why, you and I have sailed with men before the mast who had their master's certificates in their pockets – English Board of Trade certificates, too – who could work a double altitude if you would lend them a sextant and give them a look at the chronometer, as well as many a man who commands a big square-rigger. Navigation ain't everything, nor seamanship, either. You've got to have it in you, if you mean to get there.

I don't know how our captain heard that there was trouble forward. The cabin-boy may have told him, or the men may have talked outside his door when they relieved the wheel at night. Anyhow, he got wind of it, and when he had got his sight that morning he had all hands aft, and gave them a lecture. It was just the kind of talk you might have expected from him. He said he hadn't any complaint to make, and that so far as he knew everybody on board was doing his duty, and that he was given to understand that the men got their whack, and were satisfied. He said his ship was never a hard ship, and that he liked quiet, and that was the reason he didn't mean to have any nonsense, and the men might just as well understand that, too. We'd had a great misfortune, he said, and it was nobody's fault. We had lost a man we all liked and respected, and he felt that everybody in the ship ought to be sorry for the man's brother, who was left behind, and that it was rotten lubberly childishness, and unjust and unmanly and cowardly, to be playing schoolboy tricks with forks and spoons and pipes, and that sort of gear. He said it had got to stop right now, and that was all, and the men might go forward. And so they did.

It got worse after that, and the men watched the cook, and the cook watched the men, as if they were trying to catch each other; but I think everybody felt that there was something else. One evening, at supper-time, I was on deck, and Jack came aft to relieve the wheel while the man who was steering got his supper. He hadn't got past the main-hatch on the lee side, when I heard a man running in slippers that slapped on the deck, and there was a sort of a yell and I saw the coloured cook going for Jack, with a carving-knife in his hand. I jumped to get between them, and Jack turned round short, and put out his hand. I was too far to reach them, and the cook jabbed out with his knife. But the blade didn't get anywhere near Benton. The cook seemed to be jabbing it into the air again and again, at least four feet short of the mark. Then he dropped his right hand, and I saw the whites of his eyes in the dusk, and he reeled up against the pin-rail, and caught hold of a belaying-pin with his left. I had reached him by that time, and grabbed hold of his knife-hand and the other too, for I thought he was going to use the pin; but Jack Benton was standing staring stupidly at him, as if he didn't understand. But instead, the cook was holding on because he couldn't stand, and his teeth were chattering, and he let go of the knife, and the point stuck into the deck.

'He's crazy!' said Jack Benton, and that was all he said and he went aft.

When he was gone, the cook began to come to, and he spoke quite low, near my ear.

'There were two of them!' So help me God, there were two of them!'

I don't know why I didn't take him by the collar, and give him a good shaking; but I didn't. I just picked up the knife and gave it to him, and told him to go back to his galley, and not to make a fool of himself. You see, he hadn't struck at Jack, but at something he thought he saw, and I knew what it was, and I felt that same thing, like a lump of ice sliding down my back, that I felt that night when we were bending the trysail.

When the men had seen him running aft, they jumped up after him, but they held off when they saw that I had caught him. By and by, the man who had spoken to me before told me what had happened. He was a stocky little chap, with a red head.

'Well,' he said, 'there isn't much to tell. Jack Benton had been eating his supper with the rest of us. He always sits at the after corner of the table, on the port side. His brother used to sit at the end, next him. The doctor gave him a thundering big piece of pie to finish up with, and when he had finished he didn't stop for a smoke, but went off quick to relieve the wheel. Just as he had gone, the doctor came in from the galley, and when he saw Jack's empty plate he stood stock still staring at it; and we all wondered what was the matter, till we looked at the plate. There were two forks in it, sir, lying side by side. Then the doctor grabbed his knife, and flew up through the hatch like a rocket. The other fork was there all right, Mr Torkeldsen, for we all saw it and handled it; and we all had our own. That's all I know.'

I didn't feel that I wanted to laugh when he told me that story; but I hoped the old man wouldn't hear it, for I knew he wouldn't believe it, and no captain that ever sailed likes to have stories like that going round about his ship. It gives her a bad name. But that was all anybody ever saw except the cook, and he isn't the first man who has thought he saw things without having any drink in him. I think, if the doctor had been weak in the head as he was afterwards, he might have done something foolish again, and there might have been serious trouble. But he didn't. Only, two or three times I saw him looking at Jack Benton in a queer, scared way, and once, I heard him talking to himself.

'There's two of them! So help me God, there's two of them!'

He didn't say anything more about asking for his discharge, but I knew well enough that if he got ashore at the next port we should never see him again, if he had to leave his kit behind him, and his money, too. He was scared all through, for good and all; and he wouldn't be right again till he got another ship. It's no use to talk to a man when he gets like that, any more than it is to send a boy to the main truck when he has lost his nerve.

Jack Benton never spoke of what happened that evening. I don't know whether he knew about the two forks, or not; or whether he understood what the trouble was. Whatever he knew from the other men, he was evidently living under a hard strain. He was quiet enough, and too quiet; but his face was set, and sometimes it twitched oddly when he was at the wheel, and he would turn his head round sharp to look behind him. A man doesn't do that naturally, unless there's a vessel that he thinks is creeping up on the quarter. When that happens, if the man at the wheel takes a pride in his ship, he will almost always keep glancing over his shoulder to see whether the other fellow is gaining. But Jack Benton used to look round when there was nothing there; and what is curious, the other men seemed to catch the trick when they were steering. One day the old man turned out just as the man at the wheel looked behind him.

'What are you looking at?' asked the captain.

'Nothing, sir,' answered the man.

'Then keep your eye on the mizzen-royal,' said the old man, as if he were forgetting that we weren't a square-rigger.

'Ay, ay, sir,' said the man.

The captain told me to go below and work up the latitude from the dead-reckoning, and he went forward of the deckhouse and sat down to read, as he often did. When I came up, the man at the wheel was looking round again, and I stood beside him and just asked him quietly what everybody was looking at, for it was getting to be a general habit. He wouldn't say anything at first, but just answered that it was nothing. But when he saw that I didn't seem to care, and just stood there as if there were nothing more to be said, he naturally began to talk.

He said that it wasn't that he saw anything, because there wasn't anything to see except the spanker sheet just straining a little, and working in the sheaves of the blocks as the schooner rose to the short seas. There wasn't anything to be seen, but it seemed to him that the sheet made a queer noise in the blocks. It was a new manilla sheet; and in dry weather it did make a little noise, something between a creak and a wheeze. I looked at it and looked at the man, and said nothing; and presently he went on. He asked me if I didn't notice anything peculiar about the noise. I listened awhile, and said I didn't notice anything. Then he looked rather sheepish, but said he didn't think it could be his own ears, because every man who steered his trick heard the same thing now and then – sometimes once in a day, sometimes once in a night, sometimes it would go on a whole hour.

'It sounds like sawing wood,' I said, just like that.

'To us it sounds a good deal more like a man whistling "Nancy Lee".' He started nervously as he spoke the last words. 'There, sir, don't you hear it?' he asked suddenly.

I heard nothing but the creaking of the manilla sheet. It was getting near noon, and fine, clear weather in southern waters – just the sort of day and the time when you would least expect to feel creepy. But I remembered how I had heard that same tune overhead at night in a gale of wind a fortnight earlier, and I am not ashamed to say that the same sensation came over me now, and I wished myself well out of the *Helen B.*, and aboard of any old cargo-dragger, with a windmill on deck, and an eighty-nine-forty-eighter for captain, and a fresh leak whenever it breezed up.

Little by little during the next few days life on board that vessel came to be about as unbearable as you can imagine. It wasn't that there was much talk, for I think the men were shy even of speaking to each other freely about what they thought. The whole ship's company grew silent, until one hardly ever heard a voice, except giving an order and the answer. The men didn't sit over their meals when their watch was below, but either turned in at once or sat about on the forecastle smoking their pipes without saying a word. We were all thinking of the same thing. We all felt as if there were a hand on board, sometimes below, sometimes about decks, sometimes aloft, sometimes on the boom end; taking his full share of what the others got, but doing no work for it. We didn't only feel it, we knew it. He took up no room, he cast no shadow, and we never heard his footfall on deck; but he took his whack with the rest as regular as the bells, and he whistled 'Nancy Lee'. It was like the worst sort of dream you can imagine; and I dare say a good many of us tried to believe it was nothing else sometimes, when we stood looking over the weather rail in fine weather with the breeze in our faces; but if we happened to turn round and look into each other's eyes, we knew it was something worse than any dream could be; and we would turn away from each other with a queer, sick feeling, wishing that we could just for once see somebody who didn't know what we knew.

There's not much more to tell about the *Helen B. Jackson* so far as I am concerned. We were more like a shipload of lunatics than anything else when we ran in under Morro Castle, and anchored in Havana. The cook had brain fever and was raving mad in his delirium; and the rest of the men weren't far from the same state. The last three or four days had been awful, and we had been as near to having a mutiny on board as I ever want to be. The men didn't want to hurt anybody; but they wanted to get away out of that ship, if they had to swim for it; to get away from that whistling, from that dead shipmate who had come back, and who filled the ship with his unseen self. I know that if the old man and I hadn't kept a sharp lookout the men would have put a boat over quietly on one of those calm nights, and pulled away, leaving the captain and me and the mad cook to work the schooner into harbour. We should have done it somehow, of course, for we hadn't far to run if we could get a breeze; and once or twice I found myself wishing that the crew were really gone, for the awful state of fright in which they lived was beginning to work on me too. You see I partly believed and partly didn't; but anyhow I didn't mean to let the thing get the better of me, whatever it was. I turned crusty, too, and kept the men at work on all sorts of jobs, and drove them to it until they wished I was overboard, too. It wasn't that the old man and I were trying to drive them to desert without their pay, as I am sorry to say a good many skippers and mates do, even now. Captain Hackstaff was as straight as a string, and I didn't mean those poor fellows should be cheated out of a single cent; and I didn't blame them for wanting to leave the ship, but it seemed to me that the only chance to keep everybody sane through those last days was to work the men till they dropped. When they were dead tired they slept a little, and forgot the thing until they had to tumble up on deck and face it again. That was a good many years ago. Do you believe that I can't hear 'Nancy Lee' now without feeling cold down my back? For I heard it too, now and then, after the man had explained why he was always looking over his shoulder. Perhaps it was imagination. I don't know. When I look back it seems to me that I only remember a long fight against something I couldn't see, against an appalling presence, against something worse than cholera or Yellow Jack or the plague – and goodness knows the mildest of them is bad enough when it breaks out at sea. The men got as white as chalk, and wouldn't go about decks alone at night, no matter what I said to them. With the cook raving in his bunk the forecastle would have been a perfect hell, and there wasn't a spare cabin on board. There never is on a fore-and-after. So I put him into mine, and he was more quiet there, and at last fell into a sort of stupor as if he were going to die. I don't know what became of him, for we put him ashore alive and left him in the hospital.

The men came aft in a body, quiet enough, and asked the captain if he wouldn't pay them off, and let them go ashore. Some men wouldn't have done it, for they had shipped for the voyage, and had signed articles. But the captain knew that when sailors get an idea into their heads they're no better than children; and if he forced them to stay aboard he wouldn't get much work out of them, and couldn't rely on them in a difficulty. So he paid them off, and let them go. When they had gone forward to get their kits, he asked me whether I wanted to go too, and for a minute I had a sort of weak feeling that I might just as well. But I didn't, and he was a good friend to me afterwards. Perhaps he was grateful to me for sticking to him.

When the men went off he didn't come on deck; but it was my duty to stand by while they left the ship. They owed me a grudge for making them work during the last few days, and most of them dropped into the boat without so much as a word or a look, as sailors will. Jack Benton was the last to go over the side, and he stood still a minute and looked at me, and his white face twitched. I thought he wanted to say something.

'Take care of yourself, Jack,' said I. 'So long!'

It seemed as if he couldn't speak for two or three seconds; then his words came thick.

'It wasn't my fault, Mr Torkeldsen. I swear it wasn't my fault!'

That was all; and he dropped over the side, leaving me to wonder what he meant.

The captain and I stayed on board, and the ship-chandler got a West India boy to cook for us.

That evening, before turning in, we were standing by the rail having a quiet smoke, watching the lights of the city, a quarter of a mile off, reflected in the still water. There was music of some sort ashore, in a sailors' dance-house, I dare say; and I had no doubt that most of the men who had left the ship were there, and already full of jiggy-jiggy. The music played a lot of sailors' tunes that ran into each other, and we could hear the men's voices in the chorus now and then. One followed another, and then it was 'Nancy Lee' loud and clear, and the men singing 'Yo-ho, heave-ho!'

'I have no ear for music,' said Captain Hackstaff, 'but it appears to me that's the tune that man was whistling the night we lost the man overboard. I don't know why it has stuck in my head, and of course it's all nonsense; but it seems to me that I have heard it all the rest of the trip.'

I didn't say anything to that, but I wondered just how much the old man had understood. Then we turned in, and I slept ten hours without opening my eyes.

I stuck to the *Helen B. Jackson* after that as long as I could stand a fore-and-after; but that night when we lay in Havana was the last time I ever heard 'Nancy Lee' on board of her. The spare hand had gone ashore with the rest, and he never came back, and he took his tune with him; but all those things are just as clear in my memory as if they had happened yesterday. After that I was in deep water for a year or more, and after I came home I got my certificate, and what with having friends and having saved a little money, and having had a small legacy from an uncle in Norway, I got the command of a coastwise vessel, with a small share in her. I was at home three weeks before going to sea, and Jack Benton saw my name in the local papers, and wrote to me.

He said that he had left the sea, and was trying farming, and he was going to be married, and he asked if I wouldn't come over for that, for it wasn't more than forty minutes by train; and he and Mamie would be proud to have me at the wedding. I remembered how I had heard one brother ask the other whether Mamie knew. That meant, whether she knew, he wanted to marry her, I suppose. She had taken her time about it, for it was pretty nearly three years then since we had lost Jim Benton overboard.

I had nothing particular to do while we were getting ready for sea; nothing to prevent me from going over for a day, I mean; and I thought I'd like to see Jack Benton, and have a look at the girl he was going to marry. I wondered whether he had grown cheerful again, and had got rid of that drawn look he had when he told me it wasn't his fault. How could it have been his fault, anyhow? So I wrote to Jack that I would come down and see him married; and when the day came I took the train, and got there about ten o'clock in the morning. I wish I hadn't. Jack met me at the station, and he told me that the wedding was to be late in the afternoon, and that they weren't going off on any silly wedding trip, he and Mamie, but were just going to walk home from her mother's house to his cottage. That was good enough for him, he said. I looked at him hard for a minute after we met. When we had parted I had a sort of idea that he might take to drink, but he hadn't. He looked very respectable and well-to-do in his black coat and high city collar; but he was thinner and bonier than when I had known him, and there were lines in his face, and I thought his eyes had a queer look in them, half shifty, half scared. He needn't have been afraid of me, for I didn't mean to talk to his bride about the *Helen B. Jackson*.

He took me to his cottage first, and I could see that he was proud of it. It wasn't above a cable's-length from high-water mark, but the tide was running out, and there was already a broad stretch of hard wet sand on the other side of the beach road. Jack's bit of land ran back behind the cottage about a quarter of a mile, and he said that some of the trees we saw were his. The fences were neat and well kept, and there was a fair-sized barn a little way from the cottage, and I saw some nice-looking cattle in the meadows; but it didn't look to me to be much of a farm, and I thought that before long Jack would have to leave his wife to take care of it, and go to sea again. But I said it was a nice farm, so as to seem pleasant, and as I don't know much about these things I dare say it was, all the same. I never saw it but that once. Jack told me that he and his brother had been born in the cottage, and that when their father and mother died they leased the land to Mamie's father, but had kept the cottage to live in when they came home from sea for a spell. It was as neat a little place as you would care to see: the floors as clean as the decks of a yacht, and the paint as fresh as a man-o'-war. Jack always was a good painter. There was a nice parlour on the ground floor, and Jack had papered it and had hung the walls with photographs of ships and foreign ports, and with things he had brought home from his voyages: a boomerang, a South Sea club, Japanese straw hats and a Gibraltar fan with a bull-fight on it, and all that sort of gear. It looked to me as if Miss Mamie had taken a hand in arranging it. There was a brand-new polished iron Franklin stove set into the old fireplace, and a red table-cloth from Alexandria, embroidered with those outlandish Egyptian letters. It was all as bright and homelike as possible, and he showed me everything, and was proud of everything, and I liked him the better for it. But I wished that his voice would sound more cheerful, as it did when we first sailed in the *Helen B.*, and that the drawn look would go out of his face for a minute. Jack showed me everything, and took me upstairs, and it was all the same: bright and fresh and ready for the bride. But on the upper landing there was a door that Jack didn't open. When we came out of the bedroom I noticed that it was ajar, and Jack shut it quickly and turned the key.

'That lock's no good,' he said, half to himself. 'The door is always open.'

I didn't pay much attention to what he said, but as we went down the short stairs, freshly painted and varnished so that I was almost afraid to step on them, he spoke again.

'That was his room, sir. I have made a sort of store-room of it.'

'You may be wanting it in a year or so,' I said, wishing to be pleasant.

'I guess we won't use his room for that,' Jack answered in a low voice.

Then he offered me a cigar from a fresh box in the parlour, and he took one, and we lit them, and went out; and as we opened the front door there was Mamie Brewster standing in the path as if she were waiting for us. She was a fine-looking girl, and I didn't wonder that Jack had been willing to wait three years for her. I could see that she hadn't been brought up on steam-heat and cold storage, but had grown into a woman by the sea-shore. She had brown eyes, and fine brown hair, and a good figure.

'This is Captain Torkeldsen,' said Jack. 'This is Miss Brewster, captain; and she is glad to see you.'

'Well, I am,' said Miss Mamie, 'for Jack has often talked to us about you, captain.'

She put out her hand, and took mine and shook it heartily, and I suppose I said something, but I know I didn't say much.

The front door of the cottage looked toward the sea, and there was a straight path leading to the gate on the beach road. There was another path from the steps of the cottage that turned to the right, broad enough for two people to walk easily, and it led straight across the fields through gates to a larger house about a quarter of a mile away. That was where Mamie's mother lived, and the wedding was to be there. Jack asked me whether I would like to look round the farm before dinner, but I told him I didn't know much about farms. Then he said he just wanted to look round himself a bit, as he mightn't have much more chance that day; and he smiled, and Mamie laughed.

'Show the captain the way to the house, Mamie,' he said. 'I'll be along in a minute.'

So Mamie and I began to walk along the path, and Jack went up toward the barn.

'It was sweet of you to come, captain,' Miss Mamie began, 'for I have always wanted to see you.'

'Yes,' I said, expecting something more.

'You see, I always knew them both,' she went on. 'They used to take me out in a dory to catch codfish when I was a little girl, and I liked them both,' she added thoughtfully. 'Jack doesn't care to talk about his brother now. That's natural. But you won't mind telling me how it happened, will you? I should so much like to know.'

Well, I told her about the voyage and what happened that night when we fell in with a gale of wind, and that it hadn't been anybody's fault, for I wasn't going to admit that it was my old captain's, if it was. But I didn't tell her anything about what happened afterwards. As she didn't speak, I just went on talking about the two brothers, and how like they had been, and how when poor Jim was drowned and Jack was left, I took Jack for him. I told her that none of us had ever been sure which was which.

'I wasn't always sure myself,' she said, 'unless they were together. Leastways, not for a day or two after they came home from sea. And now it seems to me that Jack is more like poor Jim, as I remember him, than he ever was, for Jim was always more quiet, as if he were thinking.'

I told her I thought so, too. We passed the gate and went into the next field, walking side by side. Then she turned her head to look for Jack, but he wasn't in sight. I shan't forget what she said next.

'Are you sure now?' she asked.

I stood stock-still, and she went on a step, and then turned and looked at me. We must have looked at each other while you could count five or six.

'I know it's silly,' she went on, 'it's silly, and it's awful, too, and I have got no right to think it, but sometimes I can't help it. You see it was always Jack I meant to marry.'

'Yes,' I said stupidly, 'I suppose so.'

She waited a minute, and began walking on slowly before she went on again.

'I am talking to you as if you were an old friend, captain, and I have only known you five minutes. It was Jack I meant to marry, but now he is so like the other one.'

When a woman gets a wrong idea into her head, there is only one way to make her tired of it, and that is to agree with her. That's what I did, and she went on, talking the same way for a little while, and I kept on agreeing and agreeing until she turned round on me.

'You know you don't believe what you say,' she said, and laughed. 'You know that Jack is Jack, right enough;. and it's Jack I am going to marry.'

'Of course I said so, for I didn't care whether she thought me a weak creature or not. I wasn't going to say a word that could interfere with her happiness, and I didn't intend to go back on Jack Benton; but I remembered what he had said when he left the ship in Havana: that it wasn't his fault.

'All the same,' Miss Mamie went on, as a woman will, without realising what she was saying, 'all the same, I wish I had seen it happen. Then I should know.'

Next minute she knew that she didn't mean that, and was afraid that I would think her heartless, and began to explain that she would really rather have died herself than have seen poor Jim go overboard. Women haven't got much sense, anyhow. All the same, I wondered how she could marry Jack if she had a doubt that he might be Jim after all. I suppose she had really got used to him since he had given up the sea and had stayed ashore, and she cared for him.

Before long we heard Jack coming up behind us, for we had walked very slowly to wait for him.

'Promise not to tell anybody what I said, captain,' said Mamie, as girls do as soon as they have told their secrets.

Anyhow, I know I never did tell anyone but you. This is the first time I have talked of all that, the first time since I took the train from that place. I am not going to tell you all about the day. Miss Mamie introduced me to her mother, who was a quiet, hard-faced old New England farmer's widow, and to her cousins and relations; and there were plenty of them too at dinner, and there was the parson besides. He was what they call a Hard-shell Baptist in those parts, with a long, shaven upper lip and a whacking appetite, and a sort of superior look, as if he didn't expect to see many of us hereafter – the way a New York pilot looks round, and orders things about when he boards an Italian cargo-dragger, as if the ship weren't up to much anyway, though it was his business to see that she didn't get aground. That's the way a good many parsons look, I think. He said grace as if he were ordering the men to sheet home the topgallant-sail and get the helm up. After dinner we went out on the piazza, for it was warm autumn weather; and the young folks went off in pairs along the beach road, and the tide had turned and was beginning to come in. The morning had been clear and fine, but by four o'clock it began to look like a fog, and the damp came up out of the sea and settled on everything. Jack said he'd go down to his cottage and have a last look, for the wedding was to be at five o'clock, or soon after, and he wanted to light the lights, so as to have things look cheerful.

'I will just take a last look,' he said again, as we reached the house. We went in, and he offered me another cigar, and I lit it and sat down in the parlour. I could hear him moving about, first in the kitchen and then upstairs, and then I heard him in the kitchen again; and then before I knew anything I heard somebody moving upstairs again. I knew he couldn't have got up those stairs as quick as that. He came into the parlour, and he took a cigar himself, and while he was lighting it I heard those steps again overhead. His hand shook, and he dropped the match.

'Have you got in somebody to help?' I asked.

'No,' Jack answered sharply, and struck another match.

'There's somebody upstairs, Jack,' I said. 'Don't you hear footsteps?'

'It's the wind, captain,' Jack answered; but I could see he was trembling.

'That isn't any wind, Jack,' I said; it's still and foggy. I'm sure there's somebody upstairs.'

'If you are so sure of it, you'd better go and see for yourself, captain,' Jack answered, almost angrily.

He was angry because he was frightened. I left him before the fireplace, and went upstairs. There was no power on earth that could make me believe I hadn't heard a man's footsteps overhead. I knew there was somebody there. But there wasn't. I went into the bedroom, and it was all quiet, and the evening light was streaming in, reddish through the foggy air; and I went out on the landing and looked in the little back room that was meant for a servant girl or a child. And as I came back again I saw that the door of the other room was wide open, though I knew Jack had locked it. He had said the lock was no good. I looked in. It was a room as big as the bedroom, but almost dark, for it had shutters, and they were closed. There was a musty smell, as of old gear, and I could make out that the floor was littered with sea chests, and that there were oilskins and such stuff piled on the bed. But I still believed that there was somebody upstairs, and I went in and struck a match and looked round. I could see the four walls and the shabby old paper, an iron bed and a cracked looking-glass, and the stuff on the floor. But there was nobody there. So I put out the match, and came out and shut the door and turned the key. Now, what I am telling you is the truth. When I had turned the key, I heard footsteps walking away from the door inside the room. Then I felt queer for a minute, and when I went downstairs I looked behind me, as the men at the wheel used to look behind them on board the *Helen B.*

Jack was already outside on the steps, smoking. I have an idea that he didn't like to stay inside alone.

'Well?' he asked, trying to seem careless.

'I didn't find anybody,' I answered, 'but I heard somebody moving about.'

'I told you it was the wind,' said Jack contemptuously. 'I ought to know, for I live here, and I hear it often.'

There was nothing to be said to that, so we began to walk down toward the beach. Jack said there wasn't any hurry, as it would take Miss Mamie some time to dress for the wedding. So we strolled along, and the sun was setting through the fog, and the tide was coming in. I knew the moon was full, and that when she rose the fog would roll away from the land, as it does sometimes. I felt that Jack didn't like my having heard that noise, so I talked of other things, and asked him about his prospects, and before long we were chatting as pleasantly as possible. I haven't been at many weddings in my life, and I don't suppose you have, but that one seemed to me to be all right until it was pretty near over; and then, I don't know whether it was part of the ceremony or not, but Jack put out his hand and took Mamie's and held it a minute, and looked at her, while the parson was still speaking.

Mamie turned as white as a sheet and screamed. It wasn't a loud scream, but just a sort of stifled little shriek, as if she were half frightened to death; and the parson stopped, and asked her what was the matter, and the family gathered round.

'Your hand's like ice,' said Mamie to Jack, 'and it's all wet!'

She kept looking at it, as she got hold of herself again.

'It don't feel cold to me,' said Jack, and he held the back of his hand against his cheek. 'Try it again.'

Mamie held out hers, and touched the back of his hand, timidly at first, and then took hold of it.

'Why, that's funny,' she said.

'She's been as nervous as a witch all day,' said Mrs Brewster, severely.

'It is natural,' said the parson, 'that young Mrs Benton should experience a little agitation at such a moment.'

Most of the bride's relations lived at a distance, and were busy people, so it had been arranged that the dinner we'd had in the middle of the day was to take the place of a dinner afterwards, and that we should just have a bite after the wedding was over, and then that everybody should go home, and the young couple would walk down to the cottage by themselves. When I looked out I could see the light burning brightly in Jack's cottage, a quarter of a mile away.

I said I didn't think I could get any train to take me back before half-past nine, but Mrs Brewster begged me to stay until it was time, as she said her daughter would want to take off her wedding dress before she went home; for she had put on something white with a wreath, that was very pretty, and she couldn't walk home like that, could she?

So when we had all had a little supper the party began to break up, and when they were all gone Mrs Brewster and Mamie went upstairs, and Jack and I went out on the piazza to have a smoke, as the old lady didn't like tobacco in the house.

The full moon had risen now, and it was behind me as I looked down toward Jack's cottage, so that everything was clear and white, and there was only the light burning in the window. The fog had rolled down to the water's edge, and a little beyond, for the tide was high, or nearly, and was lapping up over the last reach of sand, within fifty feet of the beach road.

Jack didn't say much as we sat smoking, but he thanked me for coming to his wedding, and I told him I hoped he would be happy; and so I did. I dare say both of us were thinking of those footsteps upstairs, just then, and that the house wouldn't seem so lonely with a woman in it. By and by we heard Mamie's voice talking to her mother on the stairs, and in a minute she was ready to go. She had put on again the dress she had worn in the morning, and it looked black at night, almost as black as Jack's coat.

Well, they were ready to go now. It was all very quiet after the day's excitement, and I knew they would like to walk down that path alone now that they were man and wife at last. I bade them good-night, although Jack made a show of pressing me to go with them by the path as far as the cottage, instead of going to the station by the beach road. It was all very quiet, and it seemed to me a sensible way of getting married; and when Mamie kissed her mother good-night I just looked the other way, and knocked my ashes over the rail of the piazza. So they started down the straight path to Jack's cottage, and I waited a minute with Mrs Brewster, looking after them, before taking my hat to go. They walked side by side, a little shyly at first, and then I saw Jack put his arm round her waist. As I looked he was on her left, and I saw the outline of the two figures very distinctly against the moonlight on the path; and the shadow on Mamie's right was broad and black as ink, and it moved along, lengthening and shortening with the unevenness of the ground beside the path.

I thanked Mrs Brewster, and bade her good-night; and though she was a hard New England woman her voice trembled a little as she answered, but being a sensible person she went in and shut the door behind her as I stepped out on the path. I looked after the couple in the distance a last time, meaning to go down to the road, so as not to overtake them; but when I had made a few steps I stopped and looked again, for I knew I had seen something queer, though I had only real-ised it afterwards. I looked again, and it was plain enough now; and I stood stock-still, staring at what I saw. Mamie was walking between two men. The second man was just the same height as Jack, both being about a half ahead taller than she; Jack on her left in his black tail-coat and round hat, and the other man on her right – well, he was a sailor-man in wet oilskins. I could see the moonlight shining on the water that ran down him, and on the little puddle that had settled where the flap of his sou'wester was turned up behind: and one of his wet, shiny arms was round Mamie's waist, just above Jack's. I was fast to the spot where I stood, and for a minute I thought I was crazy. We'd had nothing but some cider for dinner, and tea in the evening, otherwise I'd have thought something had got into my head, though I was never drunk in my life. It was more like a bad dream after that.

I was glad Mrs Brewster had gone in. As for me, I couldn't help following the three, in a sort of wonder to see what would happen, to see whether the sailorman in his wet togs would just melt away into the moonshine. But he didn't.

I moved slowly, and I remembered afterwards that I walked on the grass, instead of on the path, as if I were afraid they might hear me coming. I suppose it all happened in less than five minutes after that, but it seemed as if it must have taken an hour. Neither Jack nor Mamie seemed to notice the sailor. She didn't seem to know that his wet arm was round her, and little by little they got near the cottage, and I wasn't a hundred yards from them when they reached the door. Something made me stand still then. Perhaps it was fright, for I saw everything that happened just as I see you now.

Mamie set her foot on the step to go up, and as she went forward I saw the sailor slowly lock his arm in Jack's, and Jack didn't move to go up. Then Mamie turned round on the step, and they all three stood that way for a second or two. She cried out then – I heard a man cry like that once, when his arm was taken off by a steam-crane, – and she fell back in a heap on the little piazza.

I tried to jump forward, but I couldn't move, and I felt my hair rising under my hat. The sailor turned slowly where he stood, and swung Jack round by the arm steadily and easily, and began to walk him down the pathway from the house. He walked him straight down that path, as steadily as Fate; and all the time I saw the moonlight shining on his wet oilskins. He walked him through the gate, and across the beach road, and out upon the wet sand, where the tide was high. Then I got my breath with a gulp, and ran for them across the grass, and vaulted over the fence, and stumbled across the road. But when I felt the sand under my feet, the two were at the water's edge; and when I reached the water they were far out, and up to their waists; and I saw that Jack Benton's head had fallen forward on his breast, and his free arm hung limp beside him, while his dead brother steadily marched him to his death. The moonlight was on the dark water, but the fog-bank was white beyond, and I saw them against it; and they went slowly and steadily down. The water was up to their armpits, and then up to their shoulders, and then I saw it rise up to the black rim of Jack's hat. But they never wavered; and the two heads went straight on, straight on, till they were under, and there was just a ripple in the moonlight where Jack had been.

It has been on my mind to tell you that story, whenever I got a chance. You have known me, man and boy, a good many years; and I thought I would like to hear your opinion. Yes, that's what I always thought. It wasn't Jim that went overboard; it was Jack, and Jim just let him go when he might have saved him; and then Jim passed himself off for Jack with us, and with the girl. If that's what happened, he got what he deserved. People said the next day that Mamie found it out as they reached the house, and that her husband just walked out into the sea, and drowned himself; and they would have blamed me for not stopping him if they'd known that I was there. But I never told what I had seen, for they wouldn't have believed me. I just let them think I had come too late.

When I reached the cottage and lifted Mamie up, she was raving mad. She got better afterwards, but she was never right in her head again.

Oh, you want to know if they found Jack's body? I don't know whether it was his, but I read in a paper at a Southern port where I was with my new ship that two dead bodies had come ashore in a gale down East, in pretty bad shape. They were locked together, and one was a skeleton in oilskins.

The Doll's Ghost

It was a terrible accident, and for one moment the splendid machinery of Cranston House got out of gear and stood still. The butler emerged from the retirement in which he spent his elegant leisure. Two grooms of the chambers appeared simultaneously from opposite directions. There were actually housemaids on the grand staircase, and those who remember the facts most exactly assert that Mrs Pringle herself positively stood upon the landing. Mrs Pringle was the housekeeper.

As for the head nurse, the under-nurse, and the nursery maid, their feelings cannot be described. The head nurse laid one hand upon the polished marble balustrade and stared stupidly before her. The under-nurse stood rigid and pale, leaning against the polished marble wall while the nursery maid collapsed and sat down upon the polished marble step – just beyond the limits of the velvet carpet – and burst into tears.

The Lady Gwendolen Lancaster-Douglas-Scroop, youngest daughter of the ninth Duke of Cranston – of the age of six years and three months – picked herself up quite alone, and sat down on the third step from the foot of the grand staircase in Cranston House.

'Oh!' exclaimed the butler before he disappeared again.

'Ah!' responded the grooms of the chambers, as they also went away.

'It's only that doll,' Mrs Pringle was distinctly heard to say, in a tone of contempt.

The under-nurse heard her say it. Then the three nurses gathered round Lady Gwendolen and patted her, gave her unhealthy things out of their pockets, and hurried her out of Cranston House as fast as they could, lest it should be found out upstairs that they had allowed the Lady Gwendolen Lancaster-Douglas-Scroop to tumble down the grand staircase with her doll in her arms. And as the doll was badly broken, the nursery-maid carried it, and the pieces, wrapped up in Lady Gwendolen's little cloak. It was not far to Hyde Park, and when they had reached a quiet place they took means to find out that Lady Gwendolen had no bruises – for the carpet was very thick and soft, and there was thick stuff under it to make it softer.

Lady Gwendolen Douglas-Scroop sometimes yelled, but she never cried. It was because she had yelled that the nurse had allowed her to go downstairs alone, with Nina the doll under one arm, steadying herself with her other hand on the balustrade as she trod upon the polished marble steps beyond the edge of the carpet. So she had fallen, and Nina had come to grief.

When the nurses were quite sure that she was not hurt, they unwrapped the doll and looked at her in her turn. She had been a very beautiful doll, very large, and fair, and healthy. She had real yellow hair and eyelids that would open and shut over very grown-up dark eyes. Moreover, when you moved her right arm up and down, she said 'Pa-pa', and when you moved the left, she said 'Ma-ma', very distinctly.

'I heard her say "Pa" when she fell,' said the under-nurse, who heard everything. 'But she ought to have said "Pa-pa".'

'That's because her arm went up when she hit the step,' said the head nurse. 'She'll say the other "Pa" when I put it down again.'

'Pa', said Nina, as her right arm was pushed down. She spoke through a face that was cracked, with a hideous gash, from the upper corner of the forehead, through the nose, and down to the little frilled collar of the pale green silk Mother Hubbard frock – where two little three-cornered pieces of porcelain had fallen out. 'I'm sure it's a wonder she can speak at all, being all smashed,' said the under-nurse.

'You'll have to take her to Mr Puckler,' said her superior. 'It's not far, and you'd better go at once.'

Lady Gwendolen was occupied with digging a hole in the ground with a little spade, and paid no attention to the nurses.

'What are you doing?' inquired the nursery maid, looking on.

'Nina's dead, and I'm diggin' her a grave,' replied her ladyship thoughtfully.

'Oh, she'll come to life again all right,' said the nursery maid.

The under-nurse wrapped Nina up again and departed. Fortunately a kind soldier, with very long legs and a very small cap, happened to be there; and as he had nothing to do, he offered to see the under-nurse safely to Mr Puckler's and back.

Mr Bernard Puckler and his little daughter lived in a little house in a little alley, which led out off a quiet little street not very far from Belgrave Square. He was the great doll doctor whose extensive practice lay in the most aristocratic quarter. He mended dolls of all sizes and ages, boy dolls and girl dolls, baby dolls in long clothes, grown-up dolls in fashionable gowns. He repaired talking dolls and dumb dolls, dolls that shut their eyes when they lay down, and those whose eyes had to be shut for them by means of a mysterious wire. His daughter Else was only twelve years old, but she was already very clever at mending dolls' clothes and at doing their hair – which is harder than you might think, though the dolls sit quite still while it is being done.

Mr Puckler had originally been a German, but he had dissolved his nationality in the ocean of London many years ago, like a great many foreigners. He still had one or two German friends, however, who came on Saturday evenings to smoke with him and play picquet or 'skat' for farthing points. They called him 'Herr Doctor', which seemed to please Mr Puckler very much.

He looked older than he was, for his beard was rather long and ragged, his hair was grizzled and thin, and he wore horn-rimmed spectacles. As for Else, she was a thin, pale child – very quiet and neat – with dark eyes and brown hair that was plaited down her back and tied with a bit of black ribbon. She mended the dolls' clothes and took the dolls back to their homes when they were strong again.

The house was a little one, but too big for the two people who lived in it. There was a small sitting room facing the street, three rooms upstairs, and the workshop was at the back. But the father and daughter lived most of their time in the workshop, because they were generally at work, even in the evenings.

Mr Puckler laid Nina on the table and looked at her a long time – until the tears began to fill his eyes behind the horn-rimmed spectacles. He was a very sensitive man who often fell in love with the dolls he mended, and who found it hard to part with them when they had smiled at him for a few days. They were real little people to him, with characters and thoughts and feelings of their own, and he was very tender with them all. But some attracted him especially from the first, and when they were brought to him maimed and injured, their state seemed so pitiful to him that the tears came easily. You must remember that he had lived among dolls during a great part of his life, and understood them.

'How do you know that they feel nothing?' he went on to say to Else. 'You must be gentle with them. It costs nothing to be kind to the little beings, and perhaps it makes a difference to them.'

And Else understood him, because she was a child, and she knew that she was more to him than all the dolls.

He fell in love with Nina at first sight, perhaps because her beautiful brown glass eyes were something like Else's, and he loved Else first and best, with all his heart. And, besides, it was a very sorrowful case.

Nina had not been long in the world. Her complexion was perfect, her hair was smooth where it should be smooth, curly where it should be curly, and her silk clothes were perfectly new. But across her face was that frightful gash, like a sabre cut, deep and shadowy within, but clean and sharp at the edges. When he tenderly pressed her head to close the gaping wound, the edges made a fine grating sound that was painful to hear, and the lids of the dark eyes quivered and trembled as though Nina were suffering dreadfully.

'Poor Nina!' he exclaimed sorrowfully. 'I shall not hurt you much, but you will take a long time to get strong.'

He always asked the names of the broken dolls when they were brought to him. Sometimes the people knew what the children called them, and told him. He liked 'Nina' for a name. Altogether and in every way she pleased him more than any doll he had seen for many years, and he felt drawn to her. He made up his mind to make her perfectly strong and sound, no matter how much labour it might cost him.

Mr Puckler worked patiently a little at a time while Else watched him. She could do nothing for poor Nina, whose clothes needed no mending. The longer the doll doctor worked, the more fond he became of the yellow hair and the beautiful brown glass eyes. He sometimes forgot all the other dolls that were waiting to be mended, lying side by side on a shelf, and sat for an hour gazing at Nina's face while he racked his ingenuity for some new invention by which to hide even the smallest trace of the terrible accident.

Eventually she was wonderfully mended. Even he was obliged to admit that. All the conditions had been most favourable for a cure, since the cement had set quite hard at the first attempt and the weather had been fine and dry, which makes a great difference in a dolls' hospital. But the scar – a very fine line right across the face, downwards from right to left – was still visible to his keen eyes.

At last he knew that he could do no more, and the under-nurse had already come twice to see whether the job was finished, as she coarsely expressed it.

'Nina is not quite strong yet,' Mr Puckler had answered each time, for he could not make up his mind to face the parting.

And now he sat before the square table at which he worked. Nina lay before him for the last time with a big brown-paper box beside her. It stood there like her coffin, waiting for her, he thought. At the thought of placing her into it, laying tissue paper over her dear face, putting on the lid, and tying the string, his sight was dim with tears again. He was never to look into the glassy depths of the beautiful brown eyes any more nor to hear the little wooden voice say 'Pa-pa' and 'Ma-ma'. It was a very painful moment.

In the vain hope of gaining time before the separation, he took up the little sticky bottles of cement, glue, gum and colour, looking at each one in turn, and then at Nina's face. And all his small tools lay there, neatly arranged in a row, but he knew that he could not use them again for Nina. She was quite strong at last, and in a country where there should be no cruel children to hurt her, she might live a hundred years with only that almost imperceptible line across her face to tell of the fearful thing that had befallen her on the marble steps of Cranston House.

Suddenly Mr Puckler's heart was quite full, and he rose abruptly from his seat and turned away.

'Else,' he said unsteadily, 'you must do it for me. I cannot bear to see her go into the box.' So he went and stood at the window with his back turned, while Else did what he had not the heart to do.

'Is it done?' he asked, not turning round. 'Then take her away, my dear. Put on your hat, and take her to Cranston House quickly. When you are gone I will turn round.'

Else was used to her father's queer ways with the dolls, and though she had never seen him so much moved by a parting, she was not much surprised.

'Come back quickly,' he said, when he heard her hand on the latch. 'It is growing late. I should not send you at this hour. But I cannot bear to look forward to it any more.'

When Else was gone, he left the window and sat down in his place before the table again, to wait for the child to come back. He touched the place where Nina had lain, very gently, and he recalled the softly tinted pink face, the glass eyes, and the ringlets of yellow hair, till he could almost see them.

The evenings were long, for it was late in the spring, but it began to grow dark soon and Else had not come back. She had been gone an hour and a half, much longer than he had expected, for it was barely half a mile from Belgrave Square to Cranston House. He reasoned that the child might have been kept waiting, but as the twilight deepened he grew anxious and walked up and down in the dim workshop, no longer thinking of Nina, but of Else, his own living child, whom he loved.

An undefinable, disquieting sensation came upon him by fine degrees, a chilliness and a faint stirring of his thin hair, joined with a wish to be in any company rather than be alone much longer. It was the beginning of fear.

He told himself in strong German-English that he was a foolish old man, and began to feel about for the matches in the dusk. He knew just where they should be, for he always kept them in the same place, close to the little tin box that held bits of sealing wax of various colours for some kinds of mending. But somehow he could not find the matches in the gloom.

Something had happened to Else, he was sure. As his fear increased, he felt as though it might be allayed if he could get a light and see what time it was. He called himself a foolish old man again and the sound of his own voice startled him in the dark. He could not find the matches.

The window was grey. Still, he thought he might see what time it was if he went close to it. He could go and get matches out of the cupboard afterwards. He stood back from the table, to get out of the way of the chair, and began to cross the board floor.

He stopped. Something was following him in the dark. There was a small pattering, as of tiny feet, upon the boards. He stopped and listened, as the roots of his hair tingled. It was nothing. He was a foolish old man, he thought. Then he made two steps more and he was sure that he heard the little pattering again. He turned his back to the window, leaning against the sash until the panes began to crack, and he faced the dark. Everything was quite still and it smelt of paste and cement and wood filings as usual.

'Is that you, Else?' he asked, and he was surprised by the fear in his voice.

There was no answer in the room, and he held up his watch and tried to make out what time it was by the grey dusk that was just not quite darkness. So far as he could see, it was within two or three minutes of ten o'clock. He had been a long time alone. He was shocked, and frightened for Else, out in London so late. He ran across the room to the door and as he fumbled for the latch, he distinctly heard the running of little feet after him.

'Mice!' he exclaimed feebly, just as he got the door open. He shut it quickly behind him, feeling as though some cold thing had settled on his back and was writhing upon him. The passage was quite dark, but he found his hat and was out in the alley in a moment – breathing more freely – and surprised to find how much light there still was in the open air. He could see the pavement clearly under his feet, and far off in the street to which the alley led, he could hear the laughter and calls of children playing some game out of doors. He wondered how he could have been so nervous and for an instant he thought of going back into the house to wait quietly for Else, but instantly he felt that nervous fright of something stealing over him again. In any case it was better to walk up to Cranston House and ask the servants about the child. One of the women had perhaps taken a fancy to her, and was even now giving her tea and cake.

He walked quickly to Belgrave Square, and then up the broad streets, listening as he went – whenever there was no other sound – for the tiny footsteps. But he heard nothing and was laughing at himself when he rang the servants' bell at the big house. Of course, the child must be there.

The person who opened the door was quite an inferior person, for it was a back door, but affected the manners of the front while staring superciliously at Mr Puckler under the strong light. 'No little girl had been seen,' he said and he knew 'nothing about no dolls'.

'She is my little girl,' said Mr Puckler tremulously, for all his anxiety was returning tenfold, 'and I am afraid something has happened.'

The inferior person said rudely that 'nothing could have happened to her in that house, because she had not been there'. Mr Puckler was obliged to admit that the man ought to know, as it was his business to keep the door and let people in, still he wished to be allowed to speak to the under-nurse, who knew him. But the man was ruder than ever, and finally shut the door in his face.

When the doll doctor was alone in the street, he steadied himself by the railing, for he felt as though he were breaking in two – just as some dolls break – in the middle of the backbone.

Presently he knew that he must be doing something to find Else, and that gave him strength. He began to walk as quickly as he could through the streets, following every highway and byway which his little girl might have taken on her errand. He also asked several policemen in vain if they had seen her. Most of them answered him kindly, for they saw that he was a sober man, in his right senses, and some of them had little girls of their own.

It was one o'clock in the morning when he returned to his own door, worn out, hopeless and broken-hearted. As he turned the key in the lock, his heart stood still, for he knew that he was awake and had not been dreaming. He had really heard those tiny footsteps pattering to meet him inside the house along the passage. But he was too unhappy to be much frightened any more, and his heart was a dull regular pain, that found its way all through him with every pulse. Sadly he went in, hung up his hat in the dark, and found the matches in the cupboard and the candlestick in its place in the corner.

Mr Puckler was so overcome and so completely worn out that he sat down in his chair before the work table and almost fainted; his face dropped forward upon his folded hands. Beside him the solitary candle burned steadily with a low flame in the still warm air.

'Else! Else!' he moaned against his yellow knuckles. It was all he could say, but it was of no relief to him. On the contrary, the very sound of her name was a new and sharp pain that pierced his ears and his head and his very soul. For every time he repeated her name it meant that little Else was dead, somewhere out in the streets of London in the dark.

He was so terribly hurt that he did not even feel something pulling gently at the skirt of his old coat, so gently that it was like the nibbling of a tiny mouse. He might have thought that it was really a mouse if he had noticed it.

'Else! Else!' he groaned against his hands. Then a cool breath stirred his thin hair and the low flame of the one candle dropped down almost to a mere spark, not flickering as though a draught were going to blow it out, but just dropping down as if it were tired out. Mr Puckler felt his hands stiffening with fright. Then he heard a faint rustling sound, like some small silk thing blown in a gentle breeze. He sat up straight, stark and scared, as a small wooden voice spoke in the stillness.

'Pa-pa,' it said, with a break between the syllables.

Mr Puckler stood up in a single jump. His chair fell over backwards with a smashing noise upon the wooden floor. The candle had almost gone out.

It was Nina's doll voice that had spoken. He would have known it among the voices of a hundred other dolls, yet there was something more in it, a little human ring with a pitiful cry, a call for help, and the wail of a hurt child. Mr Puckler stood up, stark and stiff, and tried to look round, but at first he could not, for he seemed to be frozen from head to foot.

He made a great effort and raised one hand to each of his temples to press his own head around as he would have turned a doll's. The candle was burning so low that it might as well have been out altogether. The room seemed quite dark at first, then he saw something. He would not have believed that he could be more frightened than he had been just before, but he was. His knees shook, for he saw Nina the doll, standing in the middle of the floor. She was shining with a faint and ghostly radiance. Her beautiful glassy brown eyes fixed on his. And across her face the very thin line of the break he had mended shone as though it were drawn in light with a fine point of white flame.

But there was something more in the eyes, something human, like Else's, but as if only the doll saw him through them, and not Else. Still there was enough of Else to bring back all his pain and to make him forget his fear.

'Else! My little Else!' he cried aloud.

The small ghost moved. Its doll arm slowly rose and fell with a stiff, mechanical motion. 'Pa-pa,' it said.

It seemed this time that there was even more of Else's tone echoing somewhere between the wooden notes that reached his ears so distinctly, and yet so far away. Else was calling him, he was sure.

His face was perfectly white in the gloom, but his knees did not shake any more. He felt that he was less frightened.

'Yes, child! But where? Where?' he asked. 'Where are you, Else?'

'Pa-pa!'

The syllables died away in the quiet room. There was a low rustling of silk, the glassy brown eyes turned slowly away, and Mr Puckler heard the pitter-patter of the small feet in the bronze kid slippers as the figure ran straight to the door. The candle burned high again. The room was full of light, and he was alone.

Mr Puckler passed his hand over his eyes and looked about him. He could see everything quite clearly and he felt that he must have been dreaming, though he was standing instead of sitting down, as he should have been if he had just awakened. The candle burned brightly now. There on the shelf were the dolls to be mended, lying in a row with their toes up. The third one had lost her right shoe, and Else had been making a new one.

He knew that. He certainly was not dreaming now. And he had not been dreaming when he had come in from his fruitless search and had heard the doll's footsteps running to the door. He had not fallen asleep in his chair. How could he possibly have fallen asleep when his heart was breaking? He had been awake all the time.

He steadied himself, set the fallen chair upon its legs, and said to himself again, very emphatically, that he was a foolish old man. He ought to be out in the streets looking for his child, asking questions, and inquiring at the police stations where all accidents were reported as soon as they were known, or at the hospitals.

'Pa-pa!'

The longing, wailing, pitiful little wooden cry rang from the passage outside the door. Mr Puckler stood for an instant, his white face transfixed and rooted to the spot. A moment later his hand was on the latch. Then he was in the passage, with the light streaming from the open door behind him.

Quite at the other end he saw the little phantom shining clearly in the shadow. The right hand seemed to beckon to him as it rose and fell once more. He knew all at once that it had not come to frighten him but to lead him. When it disappeared and he walked boldly towards the door, he knew that it was in the street outside waiting for him. He forgot that he was tired and had eaten no supper, and had walked many miles, for a sudden hope ran through him, like a golden stream of life.

And sure enough, at the corner of the alley, at the corner of the street, and out in Belgrave Square, he saw the small ghost flitting before him. Sometimes it was only a shadow, where there was other light, but then the glare of the lamps made a pale green sheen on its little Mother Hubbard frock of silk; and sometimes, where the streets were dark and silent, the whole figure shone out brightly with its yellow curls and rosy neck. It seemed to trot along like a tiny child. Mr Puckler could almost hear the pattering of the bronze kid slippers on the pavement as it ran. It went so very fast that he could only just keep up with it, tearing along with his hat on the back of his head and his thin hair blown by the night breeze, his horn-rimmed spectacles firmly set upon his broad nose.

On and on he went with no idea where he was. He did not even care, for he knew certainly that he was going the right way. Then at last, in a wide, quiet street, he was standing before a big, sober-looking door that had two lamps on each side of it, and a polished brass bell-handle, which he pulled.

Just inside, when the door was opened, in the bright light, there was the pale green sheen of the little silk dress, and once more the small cry came to his ears, less pitiful, more longing.

'Pa-pa!'

The shadow turned suddenly bright, and out of the brightness the beautiful brown glass eyes were turned up happily to his, while the rosy mouth smiled so divinely that the phantom doll looked almost like a little angel.

'A little girl was brought in soon after ten o'clock,' said the quiet voice of the hospital doorkeeper. 'I think they thought she was only stunned. She was holding a big brown paper box against her, they could not get it out of her arms, and she had a long plait of brown hair that hung down as they carried her.'

'She is my little girl,' said Mr Puckler, but he hardly heard his own voice.

He leaned over Else's face in the gentle light of the children's ward, and when he had stood there a minute the beautiful brown eyes opened and looked up to his.

'Pa-pa!' cried Else, softly, 'I knew you would come!'

Mr Puckler did not know what he did or said for a moment and what he felt was worth all the fear and terror and despair that had almost killed him that night. But by and by Else was telling her story, and the nurse let her speak, for there were only two other children in the room, who were getting well and were sound asleep.

'They were big boys with bad faces,' said Else, 'and they tried to get Nina away from me, but I held on and fought as well as I could till one of them hit me with something. I don't remember any more, for I tumbled down. I suppose the boys ran away and somebody found me there, but I'm afraid Nina is all smashed.'

'Here is the box,' said the nurse. 'We could not take it out of her arms till she came to herself. Would you like to see if the doll is broken?'

She undid the string quickly. There Nina lay, all smashed to pieces, but the gentle light of the children's ward made a pale green sheen in the folds of her little Mother Hubbard frock.

The Dead Smile

Chapter 1

Sir Hugh Ockram smiled as he sat by the open window of his study, in the late August afternoon. A curiously yellow cloud obscured the low sun, and the clear summer light turned lurid, as if it had been suddenly poisoned and polluted by the foul vapours of a plague. Sir Hugh's face seemed, at best, to be made of fine parchment drawn skin-tight over a wooden mask, in which two sunken eyes peered from far within. The eyes peered from under wrinkled lids, alive and watchful like toads in their holes, side by side and exactly alike. But as the light changed, a little yellow glare flashed in each. He smiled, stretching pale lips across discoloured teeth in an expression of profound self-satisfaction, blended with the most unforgiving hatred and contempt for the human doll.

Nurse Macdonald, who was a hundred years old, said that when Sir Hugh smiled he saw the faces of two women in hell – two dead women he had betrayed. The smile widened.

The hideous disease of which Sir Hugh was dying had touched his brain. His son stood beside him, tall, white, and delicate as an angel in a primitive picture. And though there was deep distress in his violet eyes as he looked at his father's face, he felt the shadow of that sickening smile stealing across his own lips, parting and drawing them against his will. It was like a bad dream, for he tried not to smile and smiled the more.

Beside him – strangely like him in her wan, angelic beauty, with the same shadowy golden hair, the same sad violet eyes, the same luminously pale face – Evelyn Warburton rested one hand upon his arm. As she looked into her uncle's eyes, she could not turn her own away, and she too knew that the deathly smile was hovering on her own red lips, drawing them tightly across her little teeth, while two bright tears ran down her cheeks to her mouth, and dropped from the upper to the lower lip. The smile was like the shadow of death and the seal of damnation upon her pure young face.

'Of course,' said Sir Hugh very slowly, still looking out at the trees, 'if you have made your mind up to be married, I cannot hinder you, and I don't suppose you attach the smallest importance to my consent – '

'Father!' exclaimed Gabriel reproachfully.

'No. I do not deceive myself,' continued the old man, smiling terribly. 'You will marry when I am dead, though there is a very good reason why you had better not – why you had better not,' he repeated very emphatically, and he slowly turned his toad eyes upon the lovers.

'What reason?' asked Evelyn in a frightened voice.

'Never mind the reason, my dear. You will marry just as if it did not exist.' There was a long pause. 'Two gone,' he said, his voice lowering strangely, 'and two more will be four all together forever and ever, burning, burning, burning bright.'

At the last words his head sank slowly back, and the little glare of his toad eyes disappeared under the swollen lids. Sir Hugh had fallen asleep, as he often did in his illness, even while speaking.

Gabriel Ockram drew Evelyn away, and from the study they went out into the dim hall. Softly closing the door behind them, each audibly drew a breath, as though some sudden danger had been passed. As they laid their hands each in the other's, their strangely-like eyes met in a long look in which love and perfect understanding were darkened by the secret terror of an unknown thing. Their pale faces reflected each other's fear.

'It is his secret,' said Evelyn at last. 'He will never tell us what it is.'

'If he dies with it,' answered Gabriel, 'let it be on his own head!'

'On his head!' echoed the dim hall. It was a strange echo. Some were frightened by it, for they said that if it were a real echo it should repeat everything and not give back a phrase here and there – now speaking, now silent. Nurse Macdonald said that the great hall would never echo a prayer when an Ockram was to die, though it would give back curses ten for one.

'On his head!' it repeated quite softly, and Evelyn started and looked round.

'It is only the echo,' said Gabriel, leading her away.

They went out into the late afternoon light, and sat upon a stone seat behind the chapel, which had been built across the end of the east wing. It was very still. Not a breath stirred, and there was no sound near them. Only far off in the park a song-bird was whistling the high prelude to the evening chorus.

'It is very lonely here,' said Evelyn, taking Gabriel's hand nervously and speaking as if she dreaded to disturb the silence. 'If it were dark, I should be afraid.'

'Of what? Of me?' Gabriel's sad eyes turned to her.

'Oh no! Never of you! But of the old Ockrams. They say they are just under our feet here in the north vault outside the chapel, all in their shrouds, with no coffins, as they used to bury them.'

'As they always will. As they will bury my father, and me. They say an Ockram will not lie in a coffin.'

'But it cannot be true. These are fairy tales, ghost stories!' Evelyn nestled nearer to her companion, grasping his hand more tightly as the sun began to go down.

'Of course. But there is the story of old Sir Vernon, who was beheaded for treason under James II. The family brought his body back from the scaffold in an iron coffin with heavy locks and put it in the north vault. But ever afterwards, whenever the vault was opened to bury another of the family, they found the coffin wide open, the body standing upright against the wall, and the head rolled away in a corner smiling at it.'

'As Uncle Hugh smiles?' Evelyn shivered.

'Yes, I suppose so,' answered Gabriel, thoughtfully. 'Of course I never saw it, and the vault has not been opened for thirty years. None of us have died since then.'

'And if . . . if Uncle Hugh dies, shall you . . . ?' Evelyn stopped. Her beautiful thin face was quite white.

'Yes. I shall see him laid there too, with his secret, whatever it is.' Gabriel sighed and pressed the girl's little hand.

'I do not like to think of it,' she said unsteadily. 'O Gabriel, what can the secret be? He said we had better not marry. Not that he forbade it, but he said it so strangely, and he smiled. Ugh!' Her small white teeth chattered with fear, and she looked over her shoulder while drawing still closer to Gabriel. 'And, somehow, I felt it in my own face.'

'So did I,' answered Gabriel in a low, nervous voice. 'Nurse Macdonald . . . ' He stopped abruptly.

'What? What did she say?'

'Oh, nothing. She has told me things . . . . They would frighten you, dear. Come, it is growing chilly.' He rose, but Evelyn held his hand in both of hers, still sitting and looking up into his face.

'But we shall be married just the same – Gabriel! Say that we shall!'

'Of course, darling, of course. But while my father is so very ill, it is impossible – '

'O Gabriel, Gabriel, dear! I wish we were married now!' Evelyn cried in sudden distress. 'I know that something will prevent it and keep us apart.'

'Nothing shall!'

'Nothing?'

'Nothing human,' said Gabriel Ockram, as she drew him down to her.

And their faces, that were so strangely alike, met and touched. Gabriel knew that the kiss had a marvellous savour of evil. Evelyn's lips were like the cool breath of a sweet and mortal fear that neither of them understood, for they were innocent and young. Yet she drew him to her by her lightest touch, as a sensitive plant shivers, waves its thin leaves, and bends and closes softly upon what it wants. He let himself be drawn to her willingly – as he would even if her touch had been deadly and poisonous – for he strangely loved that half voluptuous breath of fear, and he passionately desired the nameless evil something that lurked in her maiden lips.

'It is as if we loved in a strange dream,' she said.

'I fear the waking,' he murmured.

'We shall not wake, dear. When the dream is over it will have already turned into death, so softly that we shall not know it. But until then . . . '

She paused, her eyes seeking his, as their faces slowly came nearer. It was as if each had thoughts in their lips that foresaw and foreknew the other.

'Until then,' she said again, very low, her mouth near to his.

'Dream – till then,' he murmured.

Chapter 2

Nurse Macdonald slept sitting all bent together in a great old leather armchair with wings – many warm blankets wrapped about her, even in summer. She would rest her feet in a bag footstool lined with sheepskin while beside her, on a wooden table, there was a little lamp that burned at night, and an old silver cup, in which there was always something to drink.

Her face was very wrinkled, but the wrinkles were so small and fine and close together that they made shadows instead of lines.

Two thin locks of hair, that were turning from white to a smoky yellow, fell over her temples from under her starched white cap. Every now and then she would wake from her slumber, her eyelids drawn up in tiny folds like little pink silk curtains, and her queer blue eyes would look straight ahead through doors and walls and worlds to a far place beyond. Then she'd sleep again with her hands one upon the other on the edge of the blanket, her thumbs grown longer than the fingers with age.

It was nearly one o'clock in the night, and the summer breeze was blowing the ivy branch against the panes of the window with a hushing caress. In the small room beyond, with the door ajar, the young maid who took care of Nurse Macdonald was fast asleep. All was very quiet. The old woman breathed regularly, and her drawn lips trembled each time the breath went out.

But outside the closed window there was a face. Violet eyes were looking steadily at the ancient sleeper. Strange, as there were eighty feet from the sill of the window to the foot of the tower. It was like the face of Evelyn Warburton, yet the cheeks were thinner than Evelyn's and as white as a gleam. The eyes stared and the lips were red with life. They were dead lips painted with new blood.

Slowly Nurse Macdonald's wrinkled eyelids folded back, and she looked straight at the face at the window.

'Is it time?' she asked in her little old, faraway voice.

While she looked the face at the window changed, the eyes opened wider and wider till the white glared all round the bright violet and the bloody lips opened over gleaming teeth. The shadowy golden hair surrounding the face rose and streamed against the window in the night breeze and in answer to Nurse Macdonald's question came a sound that froze the living flesh.

It was a low-moaning voice, one that rose suddenly, like the scream of storm. Then it went from a moan to a wail, from a wail to a howl, and from a howl to the shriek of the tortured dead. He who has heard it before knows, and he can bear witness that the cry of the banshee is an evil cry to hear alone in the deep night.

When it was over and the face was gone, Nurse Macdonald shook a little in her great chair. She looked at the black square of the window, but there was nothing more there, nothing but the night and the whispering ivy branch. She turned her head to the door that was ajar, and there stood the young maid in her white gown, her teeth chattering with fright.

'It is time, child,' said Nurse Macdonald. 'I must go to him, for it is the end.'

She rose slowly, leaning her withered hands upon the arms of the chair as the girl brought her a woollen gown, a great mantle and her crutch-stick. But very often the girl looked at the window and was unjointed with fear, and often Nurse Macdonald shook her head and said words which the maid could not understand.

'It was like the face of Miss Evelyn,' said the girl, trembling.

But the ancient woman looked up sharply and angrily. Her queer blue eyes glared. She held herself up by the arm of the great chair with her left hand, and lifted up her crutch-stick to strike the maid with all her might. But she did not.

'You are a good girl,' she said, 'but you are a fool. Pray for wit, child. Pray for wit – or else find service in a house other than Ockram Hall. Now bring the lamp and help me up.'

Each step Nurse Macdonald took was a labour in itself, and as she moved, the maid's slippers clappered alongside. By the clacking noise the other servants knew that she was coming, very long before they saw her.

No one was sleeping now, and there were lights, and whisperings, and pale faces in the corridors near Sir Hugh's bedroom. Often someone would go in, and someone would come out, but everyone made way for Nurse Macdonald, who had nursed Sir Hugh's father more than eighty years ago.

The light was soft and clear in the room. Gabriel Ockram stood by his father's bedside, and there knelt Evelyn Warburton – her hair lying like a golden shadow down her shoulder, and her hands clasped nervously together. Opposite Gabriel, a nurse was trying to make Sir Hugh drink, but he would not. His lips parted, but his teeth were set. He was very, very thin now, and as his eyes caught the light sideways, they were as yellow coals.

'Do not torment him,' said Nurse Macdonald to the woman who held the cup. 'Let me speak to him, for his hour is come.'

'Let her speak to him,' said Gabriel in a dull voice.

The ancient nurse leaned to the pillow and laid the feather-weight of her withered hand – that was like a grown moth – upon Sir Hugh's yellow fingers. Then she spoke to him earnestly, while only Gabriel and Evelyn were left in the room to hear.

'Hugh Ockram,' she said, 'this is the end of your life; and as I saw you born, and saw your father born before you, I come to see you die. Hugh Ockram, will you tell me the truth?'

The dying man recognised the little faraway voice he had known all his life and he very slowly turned his yellow face to Nurse Macdonald, but he said nothing. Then she spoke again.

'Hugh Ockram, you will never see the daylight again. Will you tell the truth?'

His toad-like eyes were not yet dull. They fastened themselves on her face.

'What do you want of me?' he asked, each word sounding more hollow than the last. 'I have no secrets. I have lived a good life.'

Nurse Macdonald laughed – a tiny, cracked laugh that made her old head bob and tremble a little, as if her neck were on a steel spring. But Sir Hugh's eyes grew red, and his pale lips began to twist.

'Let me die in peace,' he said slowly.

But Nurse Macdonald shook her head, and her brown, mothlike hand left his and fluttered to his forehead.

'By the mother that bore you and died of grief for the sins you did, tell me the truth!'

Sir Hugh's lips tightened on his discoloured teeth.

'Not on earth,' he answered slowly.

'By the wife who bore your son and died heartbroken, tell me the truth!'

'Neither to you in life, nor to her in eternal death.'

His lips writhed, as if the words were coals between them, and a great drop of sweat rolled across the parchment of his forehead. Gabriel Ockram bit his hand as he watched his father die. But Nurse Macdonald spoke a third time.

'By the woman whom you betrayed, and who waits for you this night, Hugh Ockram, tell me the truth!'

'It is too late. Let me die in peace.'

His writhing lips began to smile across his yellow teeth, and his toadlike eyes glowed like evil jewels in his head.

'There is time,' said the ancient woman. 'Tell me the name of Evelyn Warburton's father. Then I will let you die in peace.'

Evelyn started. She stared at NurseMacdonald, and then at her uncle.

'The name of Evelyn's father?' he repeated slowly, while the awful smile spread upon his dying face.

The light was growing strangely dim in the great room. As Evelyn looked on, Nurse Macdonald's crooked shadow on the wall grew gigantic. Sir Hugh's breath was becoming thick, rattling in his throat, as death crept in like a snake and choked it back. Evelyn prayed aloud, high and clear.

Then something rapped at the window, and she felt her hair rise upon her head. She looked around in spite of herself. And when she saw her own white face looking in at the window, her own eyes staring at her through the glass – wide and fearful – her own hair streaming against the pane, and her own lips dashed with blood, she rose slowly from the floor and stood rigid for one moment before she screamed once and fell straight back into Gabriel's arms. But the shriek that answered hers was the fear-shriek of a tormented corpse out of which the soul cannot pass for shame of deadly sins.

Sir Hugh Ockram sat upright in his deathbed, and saw and cried aloud: 'Evelyn!'

His harsh voice broke and rattled in his chest as he sank down. But still Nurse Macdonald tortured him, for there was a little life left in him still.

'You have seen the mother as she waits for you, Hugh Ockram. Who was this girl Evelyn's father? What was his name?'

For the last time the dreadful smile came upon the twisted lips, very slowly, very surely now. The toad eyes glared red and the parchment face glowed a little in the flickering light; for the last time words came.

'They know it in hell.'

Then the glowing eyes went out quickly. The yellow face turned waxen pale, and a great shiver ran through the thin body as Hugh Ockram died.

But in death he still smiled, for he knew his secret and kept it still. He would take it with him to the other side, to lie with him forever in the north vault of the chapel where the Ockrams lie uncoffined in their shrouds – all but one. Though he was dead, he smiled, for he had kept his treasure of evil truth to the end. There was none left to tell the name he had spoken, but there was all the evil he had not undone left to bear fruit.

As they watched – Nurse Macdonald and Gabriel, who held the still unconscious Evelyn in his arms while he looked at the father – they felt the dead smile crawling along their own lips. Then they shivered a little as they both looked at Evelyn as she lay with her head on Gabriel's shoulder, for though she was very beautiful, the same sickening smile was twisting her young mouth too, and it was like the foreshadowing of a great evil that they could not understand.

By and by they carried Evelyn out, and when she opened her eyes the smile was gone. From far away in the great house the sound of weeping and crooning came up the stairs and echoed along the dismal corridors as the women had begun to mourn the dead master in the Irish fashion. The hall had echoes of its own all that night, like the far-off wail of the banshee among forest trees.

When the time was come they took Sir Hugh in his winding-sheet on a trestle bier and bore him to the chapel, through the iron door and down the long descent to the north vault lit with tapers, to lay him by his father. The two men went in first to prepare the place, and came back staggering like drunken men, their faces white.

But Gabriel Ockram was not afraid, for he knew. When he went in, alone, he saw the body of Sir Vernon Ockram leaning upright against the stone wall. Its head lay on the ground nearby with the face turned up. The dried leather lips smiled horribly at the dried-up corpse, while the iron coffin, lined with black velvet, stood open on the floor.

Gabriel took the body in his hands – for it was very light, being quite dried by the air of the vault – and those who peeped in the door saw him lay it in the coffin again. They heard it rustle a little, as it touched the sides and the bottom, like a bundle of reeds. He also placed the head upon the shoulders and shut down the lid, which fell to with the snap of its rusty spring.

After that they laid Sir Hugh beside his father, on the trestle bier on which they had brought him, and they went back to the chapel. But when they looked into one another's faces, master and men, they were all smiling with the dead smile of the corpse they had left in the vault. They could not bear to look at one another again until it had faded away.

Chapter 3

Gabriel Ockram became Sir Gabriel, inheriting the baronetcy with the half-ruined fortune left by his father, and Evelyn Warburton continued to lived at Ockram Hall, in the south room that had been hers ever since she could remember. She could not go away, for there were no relatives to whom she could have gone, and besides, there seemed to be no reason why she should not stay. The world would never trouble itself to care what the Ockrams did on their Irish estates. It was long since the Ockrams had asked anything of the world.

So Sir Gabriel took his father's place at the dark old table in the dining room, and Evelyn sat opposite to him – until such time as their mourning should be over – and they might be married at last.

Meanwhile, their lives went on as before – since Sir Hugh had been a hopeless invalid during the last year of his life, and they had seen him but once a day for a little while – spending most of their time together in a strangely perfect companionship.

Though the late summer saddened into autumn, and autumn darkened into winter, and storm followed storm, and rain poured on rain through the short days and the long nights, Ockram Hall seemed less gloomy since Sir Hugh had been laid in the north vault beside his father.

At Christmastide Evelyn decked the great hall with holly and green boughs. Huge fires blazed on every hearth. The tenants were all bid to come to a New Year's dinner at which they ate and drank well, while Sir Gabriel sat at the head of the table. Evelyn came in when the port wine was brought, and the most respected of the tenants made a speech to her health.

When the speechmaker said it had been a long time since there had been a Lady Ockram, Sir Gabriel shaded his eyes with his hand and looked down at the table; a faint colour came into Evelyn's transparent cheeks. And, said the grey-haired farmer, it was longer still since there had been a Lady Ockram so fair as the next was to be, and he drank to the health of Evelyn Warburton.

Then the tenants all stood up and shouted for her. Sir Gabriel stood up likewise, beside Evelyn. But when the men gave the last and loudest cheer of all, there was a voice not theirs, above them all, higher, fiercer, louder – an unearthly scream – shrieking for the bride of Ockram Hall. It was so loud that the holly and the green boughs over the great chimney shook and waved as if a cool breeze were blowing over them.

The men turned very pale. Many of them set down their glasses, but others let them fall upon the floor. Looking into one another's faces, they saw that they were all smiling strangely – a dead smile – like dead Sir Hugh's.

The fear of death was suddenly upon them all, so that they fled in a panic, falling over one another like wild beasts in the burning forest when the thick smoke runs along before the flame. Tables were overturned, drinking glasses and bottles were broken in heaps, and dark red wine crawled like blood upon the polished floor.

Sir Gabriel and Evelyn were left standing alone at the head of the table before the wreck of their feast, not daring to turn to look at one another, for each knew that the other smiled. But Gabriel's right arm held her and his left hand clasped her tight as they stared before them. But for the shadows of her hair, one might not have told their two faces apart.

They listened long, but the cry came not again, and eventually the dead smile faded from their lips as each remembered that Sir Hugh Ockram lay in the north vault smiling in his winding sheet, in the dark, because he had died with his secret.

So ended the tenants' New Year's dinner. But from that time on, Sir Gabriel grew more and more silent and his face grew even paler and thinner than before. Often, without warning and without words, he would rise from his seat as if something moved him against his will. He would go out into the rain or the sunshine to the north side of the chapel, sit on the stone bench and stare at the ground as if he could see through it, through the vault below, and through the white winding sheet in the dark, to the dead smile that would not die.

Always when he went out in that way Evelyn would come out presently and sit beside him. Once, as in the past, their beautiful faces came suddenly near; their lids drooped, and their red lips were almost joined together. But as their eyes met, they grew wide and wild, so that the white showed in a ring all round the deep violet. Their teeth chattered and their hands were like the hands of corpses, for fear of what was under their feet, and of what they knew but could not see.

Once, Evelyn found Sir Gabriel in the chapel alone, standing before the iron door that led down to the place of death with the key to the door in his hand, but he had not put it into the lock. Evelyn drew him away, shivering, for she had also been driven – in waking dreams – to see that terrible thing again, and to find out whether it had changed since it had been laid there.

'I'm going mad,' said Sir Gabriel, covering his eyes with his hand as he went with her. 'I see it in my sleep. I see it when I am awake. It draws me to it, day and night and unless I see it I shall die!'

'I know,' answered Evelyn, 'I know. It is as if threads were spun from it like a spider's, drawing us down to it.' She was silent for a moment and then she started violently and grasped his arm with a man's strength, and almost screamed the words she spoke. 'But we must not go there!' she cried. 'We must not go!'

Sir Gabriel's eyes were half shut, and he was not moved by the agony of her face.

'I shall die, unless I see it again,' he said, in a quiet voice not like his own. And all that day and that evening he scarcely spoke, thinking of it, always thinking, while Evelyn Warburton quivered from head to foot with a terror she had never known.

One grey winter morning, she went alone to Nurse Macdonald's room in the tower, and sat down beside the great leather easy chair, laying her thin white hand upon the withered fingers.

'Nurse,' she said, 'what was it that Uncle Hugh should have told you, that night before he died? It must have been an awful secret – and yet, though you asked him, I feel somehow that you know it, and that you know why he used to smile so dreadfully.'

The old woman's head moved slowly from side to side.

'I only guess . . . . I shall never know,' she answered slowly in her cracked little voice.

'But what do you guess? Who am I? Why did you ask who my father was? You know I am Colonel Warburton's daughter, and my mother was Lady Ockram's sister, so that Gabriel and I are cousins. My father was killed in Afghanistan. What secret can there be?'

'I do not know. I can only guess.'

'Guess what?' asked Evelyn imploringly, pressing the soft withered hands, as she leaned forward. But Nurse Macdonald's wrinkled lids dropped suddenly over her queer blue eyes, and her lips shook a little with her breath, as if she were asleep.

Evelyn waited. By the fire the Irish maid was knitting fast. Her needles clicked like three or four clocks ticking against each other. But the real clock on the wall solemnly ticked alone, checking off the seconds of the woman who was a hundred years old, and had not many days left. Outside the ivy branch beat the window in the wintry blast, as it had beaten against the glass a hundred years ago.

Then as Evelyn sat there she felt again the waking of a horrible desire – the sickening wish to go down, down to the thing in the north vault, and to open the winding-sheet, and see whether it had changed; and she held Nurse Macdonald's hands as if to keep herself in her place and fight against the appalling attraction of the evil dead.

But the old cat that kept Nurse Macdonald's feet warm, lying always on the footstool, got up and stretched itself, and looked up into Evelyn's eyes, while its back arched, and its tail thickened and bristled, and its ugly pink lips drew back in a devilish grin, showing its sharp teeth. Evelyn stared at it, half fascinated by its ugliness. Then the creature suddenly put out one paw with all its claws spread, and spat at the girl. All at once the grinning cat was like the smiling corpse far down below. Evelyn shivered down to her small feet, and covered her face with her free hand, lest Nurse Macdonald should wake and see the dead smile there, for she could feel it.

The old woman had already opened her eyes again, and she touched her cat with the end of her crutch-stick, whereupon its back went down and its tail shrank, and it sidled back to its place on the footstool. But its yellow eyes looked up sideways at Evelyn, between the slits of its lids.

'What is it that you guess, nurse?' asked the young girl again.

'A bad thing, a wicked thing. But I dare not tell you, lest it might not be true, and the very thought should blast your life. For if I guess right, he meant that you should not know, and that you two should marry and pay for his old sin with your souls.'

'He used to tell us that we ought not to marry.'

'Yes – he told you that, perhaps. But it was as if a man put poisoned meat before a starving beast, and said "do not eat", but never raised his hand to take the meat away. And if he told you that you should not marry, it was because he hoped you would; for of all men living or dead, Hugh Ockram was the falsest man that ever told a cowardly lie, and the crudest that ever hurt a weak woman, and the worst that ever loved a sin.'

'But Gabriel and I love each other,' said Evelyn very sadly.

Nurse Macdonald's old eyes looked far away, at sights seen long ago, and that rose in the grey winter air amid the mists of an ancient youth.

'If you love, you can die together,' she said, very slowly. 'Why should you live, if it is true? I am a hundred years old. What has life given me? The beginning is fire; the end is a heap of ashes; and between the end and the beginning lies all the pain of the world. Let me sleep, since I cannot die.'

Then the old woman's eyes closed again, and her head sank a little lower upon her breast.

So Evelyn went away and left her asleep, with the cat asleep on the footstool. The young girl tried to forget Nurse Macdonald's words, but she could not, for she heard them over and over again in the wind, and behind her on the stairs. And as she grew sick with fear of the frightful unknown evil to which her soul was bound, she felt a bodily something pressing her, pushing her, forcing her on from the other side. She felt threads that drew her mysteriously, and when she shut her eyes, she saw in the chapel behind the altar, the low iron door through which she must pass to go to the thing.

As she lay awake at night, she drew the sheet over her face, lest she should see shadows on the wall beckoning to her. The sound of her own warm breath made whisperings in her ears, while she held the mattress with her hands, to keep from getting up and going to the chapel. It would have been easier if there had not been a way thither through the library, by a door which was never locked. It would be fearfully easy to take her candle and go softly through the sleeping house. The key of the vault lay under the altar behind a stone that turned. She knew that little secret. She could go alone and see.

But when she thought of it, she felt her hair rise on her head. She shivered so that the bed shook, then the horror went through her in a cold thrill that was agony again, like a myriad of icy needles boring into her nerves.

Chapter 4

The old clock in Nurse Macdonald's tower struck midnight. From her room she could hear the creaking chains and weights in their box in the corner of the staircase, and the jarring of the rusty lever that lifted the hammer. She had heard it all her life. It struck eleven strokes clearly, and then came the twelfth with a dull half stroke, as though the hammer were too weary to go on and had fallen asleep against the bell.

The old cat got up from the footstool and stretched itself. Nurse Macdonald opened her ancient eyes and looked slowly round the room by the dim light of the night lamp. She touched the cat with her crutch-stick, and it lay down upon her feet. She drank a few drops from her cup and went to sleep again.

But downstairs Sir Gabriel sat straight up as the clock struck, for he had dreamed a fearful dream of horror, and his heart stood still. He awoke at its stopping and it beat again furiously with his breath, like a wild thing set free. No Ockram had ever known fear waking, but sometimes it came to Sir Gabriel in his sleep.

He pressed his hands to his temples as he sat up in bed. His hands were icy cold, but his head was hot. The dream faded far and in its place there came the master thought that racked his life. With the thought also came the sick twisting of his lips in the dark that would have been a smile. Far off, Evelyn Warburton dreamed that the dead smile was on her mouth, and awoke – starting with a little moan – her face in her hands, shivering.

But Sir Gabriel struck a light and got up and began to walk up and down his great room. It was midnight and he had barely slept an hour, and in the north of Ireland the winter nights are long.

'I shall go mad,' he said to himself, holding his forehead. He knew that it was true. For weeks and months the possession of the thing had grown upon him like a disease, till he could think of nothing without thinking first of that. And now all at once it outgrew his strength, and he knew that he must be its instrument or lose his mind. He knew that he must do the deed he hated and feared, if he could fear anything, or that something would snap in his brain and divide him from life while he was yet alive. He took the candlestick in his hand, the old-fashioned heavy candlestick that had always been used by the head of the house. He did not think of dressing, but went as he was – in his silk night clothes and his slippers – and opened the door.

Everything was very still in the great old house. He shut the door behind him and walked noiselessly on the carpet through the long corridor. A cool breeze blew over his shoulder and blew the flame of his candle straight out. Instinctively he stopped and looked round, but all was still, and the upright flame burned steadily. He walked on, and instantly a strong draught was behind him, almost extinguishing the light. It seemed to blow him on his way, ceasing whenever he turned, coming again when he went on – invisible, icy.

Down the great staircase to the echoing hall he went, seeing nothing but the flaring flame of the candle standing away from him over the guttering wax. The cold wind blew over his shoulder and through his hair. On he passed through the open door into the library dark with old books and carved bookcases. On he went through the door with shelves and the imitated backs of books painted on it, which shut itself after him with a soft click.

He entered the low arched passage, and though the door was shut behind him and fitted tightly in its frame, still the cold breeze blew the flame forward as he walked. He was not afraid; but his face was very pale and his eyes were wide and bright, seeing already in the dark air the picture of the thing beyond. But in the chapel he stood still, his hand on the little turning-stone tablet in the back of the stone altar. On the tablet were engraved the words:

CLAVIS SEPULCHRI CLARISSIMORUM DOMINORUM DE OCKRAM
[the key to the vault of the most illustrious lords of Ockram]

Sir Gabriel paused and listened. He fancied that he heard a sound far off in the great house where all had been so still, but it did not come again. Yet he waited at the last, and looked at the low iron door. Beyond it, down the long descent, lay his father uncoffined, six months dead, corrupt, terrible in his clinging shroud. The strangely preserving air of the vault could not yet have done its work completely. But on the thing's ghastly features, with their half-dried, open eyes, there would still be the frightful smile with which the man had died – the smile that haunted.

As the thought crossed Sir Gabriel's mind, he felt his lips writhing, and he struck his own mouth in wrath with the back of his hand so fiercely that a drop of blood ran down his chin, and another, and more, falling back in the gloom upon the chapel pavement. But still his bruised lips twisted themselves. He turned the tablet by the simple secret. It needed no safer fastening, for had each Ockram been coffined in pure gold, and had the door been open wide, there was not a man in Tyrone brave enough to go down to that place, save Gabriel Ockram himself, with his angel's face, his thin, white hands, and his sad unflinching eyes. He took the great old key and set it into the lock of the iron door. The heavy, rattling noise echoed down the descent beyond like footsteps, as if a watcher had stood behind the iron and were running away within, with heavy dead feet. And though he was standing still, the cool wind was from behind him, and blew the flame of the candle against the iron panel. He turned the key.

Sir Gabriel saw that his candle was short. There were new ones on the altar, with long candlesticks, so he lit one and left his own burning on the floor. As he set it down on the pavement his lip began to bleed again, and another drop fell upon the stones.

He drew the iron door open and pushed it back against the chapel wall, so that it should not shut of itself, while he was within; and the horrible draught of the sepulchre came up out of the depths in his face, foul and dark. He went in, but though the fetid air met him, yet the flame of the tall candle was blown straight from him against the wind while he walked down the easy incline with steady steps, his loose slippers slapping the pavement as he trod.

He shaded the candle with his hand, and his fingers seemed to be made of wax and blood as the light shone through them. And in spite of him the unearthly draught forced the flame forward, till it was blue over the black wick, and it seemed as if it must go out. But he went straight on, with shining eyes.

The downward passage was wide, and he could not always see the walls by the struggling light, but he knew when he was in the place of death by the larger, drearier echo of his steps in the greater space, and by the sensation of a distant blank wall. He stood still, almost enclosing the flame of the candle in the hollow of his hand. He could see a little, for his eyes were growing used to the gloom. Shadowy forms were outlined in the dimness, where the biers of the Ockrams stood crowded together, side by side, each with its straight, shrouded corpse, strangely preserved by the dry air, like the empty shell that the locust sheds in summer. And a few steps before him he saw clearly the dark shape of headless Sir Vernon's iron coffin, and he knew that nearest to it lay the thing he sought.

He was as brave as any of those dead men had been. They were his fathers, and he knew that sooner or later he should lie there himself, beside Sir Hugh, slowly drying to a parchment shell. But as yet, he was still alive. He closed his eyes a moment as three great drops stood on his forehead.

Then he looked again, and by the whiteness of the winding sheet he knew his father's corpse, for all the others were brown with age; and, moreover, the flame of the candle was blown toward it. He made four steps till he reached it, and suddenly the light burned straight and high, shedding a dazzling yellow glare upon the fine linen that was all white, save over the face, and where the joined hands were laid on the breast. And at those places ugly stains had spread, darkened with outlines of the features and of the tight clasped fingers. There was a frightful stench of drying death.

As Sir Gabriel looked down, something stirred behind him, softly at first, then more noisily, and something fell to the stone floor with a dull thud and rolled up to his feet. He started back and saw a withered head lying almost face upward on the pavement, grinning at him. He felt the cold sweat standing on his face, and his heart beat painfully.

For the first time in all his life that evil thing which men call fear was getting hold of him, checking his heart-strings as a cruel driver checks a quivering horse, clawing at his backbone with icy hands, lifting his hair with freezing breath, climbing up and gathering in his midriff with leaden weight.

Yet he bit his lip and bent down, holding the candle in one hand, to lift the shroud back from the head of the corpse with the other. Slowly he lifted it. It clove to the half-dried skin of the face, and his hand shook as if someone had struck him on the elbow, but half in fear and half in anger at himself, he pulled it, so that it came away with a little ripping sound. He caught his breath as he held it, not yet throwing it back, and not yet looking. The horror was working in him and he felt that old Vernon Ockram was standing up in his iron coffin, headless, yet watching him with the stump of his severed neck.

While he held his breath he felt the dead smile twisting his lips. In sudden wrath at his own misery, he tossed the death-stained linen backward, and looked at last. He ground his teeth lest he should shriek aloud. There it was, the thing that haunted him, that haunted Evelyn Warburton, that was like a blight on all that came near him.

The dead face was blotched with dark stains, and the thin, grey hair was matted about the discoloured forehead. The sunken lids were half open, and the candlelight gleamed on something foul where the toad eyes had lived.

But yet the dead thing smiled, as it had smiled in life. The ghastly lips were parted and drawn wide and tight upon the wolfish teeth, cursing still, and still defying hell to do its worst – defying, cursing, and always and forever smiling alone in the dark.

Sir Gabriel opened the sheet where the hands were. The blackened, withered fingers were closed upon something stained and mottled. Shivering from head to foot, but fighting like a man in agony for his life, he tried to take the package from the dead man's hold. But as he pulled at it the clawlike fingers seemed to close more tightly. When he pulled harder the shrunken hands and arms rose from the corpse with a horrible look of life following his motion – then as he wrenched the sealed packet loose at last, the hands fell back into their place still folded.

He set down the candle on the edge of the bier to break the seals from the stout paper. Kneeling on one knee, to get a better light, he read what was within, written long ago in Sir Hugh's queer hand. He was no longer afraid.

He read how Sir Hugh had written it all down that it might perchance be a witness of evil and of his hatred. He had written how he had loved Evelyn Warburton, his wife's sister; and how his wife had died of a broken heart with his curse upon her. He wrote how Warburton and he had fought side by side in Afghanistan, and Warburton had fallen; but Ockram had brought his comrade's wife back a full year later, and little Evelyn, her child, had been born in Ockram Hall. And he wrote how he had wearied of the mother, and she had died like her sister with his curse on her; and how Evelyn had been brought up as his niece, and how he had trusted that his son Gabriel and his daughter, innocent and unknowing, might love and marry, and the souls of the women he had betrayed might suffer yet another anguish before eternity was out. And, last of all, he hoped that some day, when nothing could be undone, the two might find his writing and live on, as man and wife, not daring to tell the truth for their children's sake and the world's word.

This he read, kneeling beside the corpse in the north vault, by the light of the altar candle. He had read it all and then he thanked God aloud that he had found the secret in time. When he finally rose to his feet and looked down at the dead face it had changed. The smile was gone from it. The jaw had fallen a little and the tired, dead lips were relaxed. And then there was a breath behind him and close to him, not cold like that which had blown the flame of the candle as he came, but warm and human. He turned suddenly.

There she stood, all in white, with her shadowy golden hair. She had risen from her bed and had followed him noiselessly. When she found him reading, she read over his shoulder.

He started violently when he saw her, for his nerves were unstrung. Then he cried out her name in that still place of death: 'Evelyn!'

'My brother!' she answered softly and tenderly, putting out both hands to meet his.

By the Waters of Paradise

I remember my childhood very distinctly. I do not think that the fact argues a good memory, for I have never been clever at learning words by heart, in prose or rhyme; so that I believe my remembrance of events depends much more upon the events themselves than upon my possessing any special facility for recalling them. Perhaps I am too imaginative, and the earliest impressions I received were of a kind to stimulate the imagination abnormally. A long series of little misfortunes, connected with each other as to suggest a sort of weird fatality, so worked upon my melancholy temperament when I was a boy that, before I was of age, I sincerely believed myself to be under a curse, and not only myself, but my whole family, and every individual who bore my name.

I was born in the old place where my father, and his father, and all his predecessors had been born, beyond the memory of man. It is a very old house, and the greater part of it was originally a castle, strongly fortified, and surrounded by a deep moat supplied with abundant water from the hills by a hidden aqueduct. Many of the fortifications have been destroyed, and the moat has been filled up. The water from the aqueduct supplies great fountains, and runs down into huge oblong basins in the terraced gardens, one below the other, each surrounded by a broad pavement of marble between the water and the flower-beds. The waste surplus finally escapes through an artificial grotto, some thirty yards long, into a stream, flowing down through the park to the meadows beyond, and thence to the distant river. The buildings were extended a little and greatly altered more than two hundred years ago, in the time of Charles II., but since then little has been done to improve them, though they have been kept in fairly good repair, according to our fortunes.

In the gardens there are terraces and huge hedges of box and evergreen, some of which used to be clipped into shapes of animals, in the Italian style. I can remember when I was a lad how I used to try to make out what the trees were cut to represent, and how I used to appeal for explanations to Judith, my Welsh nurse. She dealt in a strange mythology of her own, and peopled the gardens with griffins, dragons, good genii and bad, and filled my mind with them at the same time. My nursery window afforded a view of the great fountains at the head of the upper basin, and on moonlight nights the Welshwoman would hold me up to the glass and bid me look at the mist and spray rising into mysterious shapes, moving mystically in the white light like living things.

'It's the Woman of the Water,' she used to say; and sometimes she would threaten that if I did not go to sleep the Woman of the Water would steal up to the high window and carry me away in her wet arms.

The place was gloomy. The broad basins of water and the tall evergreen hedges gave it a funereal look, and the damp-stained marble causeways by the pools might have been made of tombstones. The grey and weather-beaten walls and towers without, the dark and massively-furnished rooms within, the deep, mysterious recesses and the heavy curtains, all affected my spirits. I was silent and sad from my childhood. There was a great clock tower above, from which the hours rang dismally during the day, and tolled like a knell in the dead of night. There was no light nor life in the house, for my mother was a helpless invalid, and my father had grown melancholy in his long task of caring for her. He was a thin, dark man, with sad eyes; kind, I think, but silent and unhappy. Next to my mother, I believe he loved me better than anything on earth, for he took immense pains and trouble in teaching me, and what he taught me I have never forgotten. Perhaps it was his only amusement, and that may be the reason why I had no nursery governess or teacher of any kind while he lived.

I used to be taken to see my mother every day, and sometimes twice a day, for an hour at a time. Then I sat upon a little stool near her feet, and she would ask me what I had been doing, and what I wanted to do. I daresay she saw already the seeds of a profound melancholy in my nature, for she looked at me always with a sad smile, and kissed me with a sigh when I was taken away.

One night, when I was just six years old, I lay awake in the nursery. The door was not quite shut, and the Welsh nurse was sitting sewing in the next room. Suddenly I heard her groan, and say in a strange voice, 'One – two – one – two!' I was frightened, and I jumped up and ran to the door, barefooted as I was.

'What is it, Judith?' I cried, clinging to her skirts. I can remember the look in her strange dark eyes as she answered.

'One – two leaden coffins, fallen from the ceiling!' she crooned, working herself in her chair. 'One – two – a light coffin and a heavy coffin, falling to the floor!'

Then she seemed to notice me, and she took me back to bed and sang me to sleep with a queer old Welsh song.

I do not know how it was, but the impression got hold of me that she had meant that my father and mother were going to die very soon. They died in the very room where she had been sitting that night. It was a great room, my day nursery, full of sun when there was any: and when the days were dark it was the most cheerful place in the house. My mother grew rapidly worse, and I was transferred to another part of the building to make place for her. They thought my nursery was gayer for her, I suppose; but she could not live. She was beautiful when she was dead, and I cried bitterly.

'The light one, the light one – the heavy one to come,' crooned the Welshwoman. And she was right. My father took the room after my mother was gone, and day by day he grew thinner and paler and sadder.

'The heavy one, the heavy one – all of lead,' moaned my nurse, one night in December, standing still, just as she was going to take away the light after putting me to bed. Then she took me up again and wrapped me in a little gown, and led me away to my father's room. She knocked, but no one answered. She opened the door, and we found him in his easy-chair before the fire, very white, quite dead.

So I was alone with the Welshwoman till strange people came, and relations whom I had never seen; and then I heard them saying that I must be taken away to some more cheerful place. They were kind people, and I will not believe that they were kind only because I was to be very rich when I grew to be a man. The world never seemed to be a very bad place to me, nor all the people to be miserable sinners, even when I was most melancholy. I do not remember that anyone ever did me any great injustice, nor that I was ever oppressed or ill-treated in any way, even by the boys at school. I was sad, I suppose, because my childhood was so gloomy, and, later, because I was unlucky in everything I undertook, till I finally believed I was pursued by fate, and I used to dream that the old Welsh nurse and the Woman of the Water between them had vowed to pursue me to my end. But my natural disposition should have been cheerful, as I have often thought.

Among lads of my age I was never last, or even among the last, in anything; but I was never first. If I trained for a race, I was sure to sprain my ankle on the day when I was to run. If I pulled an oar with others, my oar was sure to break. If I competed for a prize, some unforeseen accident prevented my winning it at the last moment. Nothing to which I put my hand succeeded, and I got the reputation of being unlucky, until my companions felt it was always safe to bet against me, no matter what the appearances might be. I became discouraged and listless in everything. I gave up the idea of competing for any distinction at the University, comforting myself with the thought that I could not fail in the examination for the ordinary degree. The day before the examination began I fell ill; and when at last I recovered, after a narrow escape from death, I turned my back upon Oxford, and went down alone to visit the old place where I had been born, feeble in health and profoundly disgusted and discouraged. I was twenty-one years of age, master of myself and of my fortune; but so deeply had the long chain of small unlucky circumstances affected me that I thought seriously of shutting myself up from the world to live the life of a hermit, and to die as soon as possible. Death seemed the only cheerful possibility in my existence, and my thoughts soon dwelt upon it altogether.

I had never shown any wish to return to my own home since I had been taken away as a little boy, and no one had ever pressed me to do so. The place had been kept in order after a fashion, and did not seem to have suffered during the fifteen years or more of my absence. Nothing earthly could affect those old grey walls that had fought the elements for so many centuries. The garden was more wild than I remembered it; the marble causeways about the pools looked more yellow and damp than of old, and the whole place at first looked smaller. It was not until I had wandered about the house and grounds for many hours that I realised the huge size of the home where I was to live in solitude. Then I began to delight in it, and my resolution to live alone grew stronger.

The people had turned out to welcome me, of course, and I tried to recognise the changed faces of the old gardener and the old housekeeper, and to call them by name. My old nurse I knew at once. She had grown very grey since she heard the coffins fall in the nursery fifteen years before, but her strange eyes were the same, and the look in them woke all my old memories. She went over the house with me.

'And how is the Woman of the Water?' I asked, trying to laugh a little. 'Does she still play in the moonlight?'

'She is hungry,' answered the Welshwoman, in a low voice.

'Hungry? Then we will feed her.' I laughed. But old Judith turned very pale, and looked at me strangely.

'Feed her? Ay – you will feed her well,' she muttered, glancing behind her at the ancient housekeeper, who tottered after us with feeble steps through the halls and passages.

I did not think much of her words. She had always talked oddly, as Welshwomen will, and though I was very melancholy I am sure I was not superstitious, and I was certainly not timid. Only, as in a far-off dream, I seemed to see her standing with the light in her hand and muttering, 'The heavy one – all of lead', and then leading a little boy through the long corridors to see his father lying dead in a great easy-chair before a smouldering fire. So we went over the house, and I chose the rooms where I would live; and the servants I had brought with me ordered and arranged everything, and I had no more trouble. I did not care what they did provided I was left in peace, and was not expected to give directions; for I was more listless than ever, owing to the effects of my illness at college.

I dined in solitary state, and the melancholy grandeur of the vast old dining-room pleased me. Then I went to the room I had selected for my study, and sat down in a deep chair, under a bright light, to think, or to let my thoughts meander through labyrinths of their own choosing, utterly indifferent to the course they might take.

The tall windows of the room opened to the level of the ground upon the terrace at the head of the garden. It was in the end of July, and everything was open, for the weather was warm. As I sat alone I heard the unceasing plash of the great fountains, and I fell to thinking of the Woman of the Water. I rose, and went out into the still night, and sat down upon a seat on the terrace, between two gigantic Italian flower-pots. The air was deliciously soft and sweet with the smell of the flowers, and the garden was more congenial to me than the house. Sad people always like running water and the sound of it at night, though I cannot tell why. I sat and listened in the gloom, for it was dark below, and the pale moon had not yet climbed over the hills in front of me, though all the air above was light with her rising beams. Slowly the white halo in the eastern sky ascended in an arch above the wooded crests, making the outlines of the mountains more intensely black by contrast, as though the head of some great white saint were rising from behind a screen in a vast cathedral, throwing misty glories from below. I longed to see the moon herself, and I tried to reckon the seconds before she must appear. Then she sprang up quickly, and in a moment more hung round and perfect in the sky. I gazed at her, and then at the floating spray of the tall fountains, and down at the pools, where the water-lilies were rocking softly in their sleep on the velvet surface of the moon-lit water. Just then a great swan floated out silently into the midst of the basin, and wreathed his long neck, catching the water in his broad bill, and scattering showers of diamonds around him.

Suddenly, as I gazed, something came between me and the light. I looked up instantly. Between me and the round disk of the moon rose a luminous face of a woman, with great strange eyes, and a woman's mouth, full and soft, but not smiling, hooded in black, staring at me as I sat still upon my bench. She was close to me – so close that I could have touched her with my hand. But I was transfixed and helpless. She stood still for a moment, but her expression did not change. Then she passed swiftly away, and my hair stood up on my head, while the cold breeze from her white dress was wafted to my temples as she moved. The moonlight, shining through the tossing spray of the fountain, made traceries of shadow on the gleaming folds of her garments. In an instant she was gone and I was alone.

I was strangely shaken by the vision, and some time passed before I could rise to my feet, for I was still weak from my illness, and the sight I had seen would have startled anyone. I did not reason with myself, for I was certain that I had looked on the unearthly, and no argument could have destroyed that belief. At last I got up and stood unsteadily, gazing in the direction in which I thought the face had gone; but there was nothing to be seen – nothing but the broad paths, the tall, dark evergreen hedges, the tossing water of the fountains and the smooth pool below. I fell back upon the seat and recalled the face I had seen. Strange to say, now that the first impression had passed, there was nothing startling in the recollection; on the contrary, I felt that I was fascinated by the face, and would give anything to see it again. I could retrace the beautiful straight features, the long dark eyes, and the wonderful mouth most exactly in my mind, and when I had reconstructed every detail from memory I knew that the whole was beautiful, and that I should love a woman with such a face.

'I wonder whether she is the Woman of the Water!' I said to myself. Then rising once more, I wandered down the garden, descending one short flight of steps after another, from terrace to terrace by the edge of the marble basins, through the shadow and through the moonlight; and I crossed the water by the rustic bridge above the artificial grotto, and climbed slowly up again to the highest terrace by the other side. The air seemed sweeter, and I was very calm, so that I think I smiled to myself as I walked, as though a new happiness had come to me. The woman's face seemed always before me, and the thought of it gave me an unwonted thrill of pleasure, unlike anything I had ever felt before.

I turned, as I reached the house, and looked back upon the scene. It had certainly changed in the short hour since I had come out, and my mood had changed with it. Just like my luck, I thought, to fall in love with a ghost! But in old times I would have sighed, and gone to bed more sad than ever, at such a melancholy conclusion. Tonight I felt happy, almost for the first time in my life. The gloomy old study seemed cheerful when I went in. The old pictures on the walls smiled at me, and I sat down in my deep chair with a new and delightful sensation that I was not alone. The idea of having seen a ghost, and of feeling much the better for it, was so absurd that I laughed softly, as I took up one of the books I had brought with me and began to read.

That impression did not wear off. I slept peacefully, and in the morning I threw open my windows to the summer air and looked down at the garden, at the stretches of green and at the coloured flower-beds, at the circling swallows and at the bright water.

'A man might make a paradise of this place,' I exclaimed. 'A man and a woman together!'

From that day the old castle no longer seemed gloomy, and I think I ceased to be sad; for some time, too, I began to take an interest in the place, and to try and make it more alive. I avoided my old Welsh nurse, lest she should damp my humour with some dismal prophecy, and recall my old self by bringing back memories of my dismal childhood. But what I thought of most was the ghostly figure I had seen in the garden that first night after my arrival. I went out every evening and wandered through the walks and paths; but, try as I might, I did not see my vision again. At last, after many days, the memory grew more faint, and my old moody nature gradually overcame the temporary sense of lightness I had experienced. The summer turned to autumn, and I grew restless. It began to rain. The dampness pervaded the gardens, and the outer halls smelled musty, like tombs; the grey sky oppressed me intolerably. I left the place as it was and went abroad, determined to try anything which might possibly make a second break in the monotonous melancholy from which I suffered.

2

Most people would be struck by the utter insignificance of the small events which, after the death of my parents, influenced my life and made me unhappy. The gruesome forebodings of a Welsh nurse, which chanced to be realised by an odd coincidence of events, should not seem enough to change the nature of a child, and to direct the bent of his character in after years. The little disappointments of schoolboy life, and the somewhat less childish ones of an uneventful and undistinguished academic career, should not have sufficed to turn me out at one-and-twenty years of age a melancholic, listless idler. Some weakness of my own character may have contributed to the result, but in a greater degree it was due to my having a reputation for bad luck. However, I will not try to analyse the causes of my state, for I should satisfy nobody, least of all myself. Still less will I attempt to explain why I felt a temporary revival of my spirits after my adventure in the garden. It is certain that I was in love with the face I had seen, and that I longed to see it again; that I gave up all hope of a second visitation, grew more sad than ever, packed up my traps, and finally went abroad. But in my dreams I went back to my home, and it always appeared to me sunny and bright, as it had looked on that summer's morning after I had seen the woman by the fountain.

I went to Paris. I went further, and wandered about Germany. I tried to amuse myself, and I failed miserably. With the aimless whims of an idle and useless man, come all sorts of suggestions for good resolutions. One day I made up my mind that I would go and bury myself in a German university for a time, and live simply like a poor student. I started with the intention of going to Leipsic, determined to stay there until some event should direct my life or change my humour, or make an end of me altogether. The express train stopped at some station of which I did not know the name. It was dusk on a winter's afternoon, and I peered through the thick glass from my seat. Suddenly another train came gliding in from the opposite direction, and stopped alongside of ours. I looked at the carriage which chanced to be abreast of mine, and idly read the black letters painted on a white board swinging from the brass handrail: BERLIN – COLOGNE – PARIS. Then I looked up at the window above. I started violently, and the cold perspiration broke out upon my forehead. In the dim light, not six feet from where I sat, I saw the face of a woman, the face I loved, the straight, fine features, the strange eyes, the wonderful mouth, the pale skin. Her head-dress was a dark veil, which seemed to be tied about her head and passed over the shoulders under her chin. As I threw down the window and knelt on the cushioned seat, leaning far out to get a better view, a long whistle screamed through the station, followed by a quick series of dull, clanking sounds; then there was a slight jerk, and my train moved on. Luckily the window was narrow, being the one over the seat, beside the door, or I believe I would have jumped out of it then and there. In an instant the speed increased, and I was being carried swiftly away in the opposite direction from the thing I loved.

For a quarter of an hour I lay back in my place, stunned by the suddenness of the apparition. At last one of the two other passengers, a large and gorgeous captain of the White Königsberg Cuirassiers, civilly but firmly suggested that I might shut my window, as the evening was cold. I did so, with an apology, and relapsed into silence. The train ran swiftly on, for a long time, and it was already beginning to slacken speed before entering another station, when I roused myself and made a sudden resolution. As the carriage stopped before the brilliantly lighted platform, I seized my belongings, saluted my fellow-passengers, and got out, determined to take the first express back to Paris.

This time the circumstances of the vision had been so natural that it did not strike me that there was anything unreal about the face, or about the woman to whom it belonged. I did not try to explain to myself how the face, and the woman, could be travelling by a fast train from Berlin to Paris on a winter's afternoon, when both were in my mind indelibly associated with the moonlight and the fountains in my own English home. I certainly would not have admitted that I had been mistaken in the dusk, attributing to what I had seen a resemblance to my former vision which did not really exist. There was not the slightest doubt in my mind, and I was positively sure that I had again seen the face I loved. I did not hesitate, and in a few hours I was on my way back to Paris. I could not help reflecting on my ill luck. Wandering as I had been for many months, it might as easily have chanced that I should be travelling in the same train with that woman, instead of going the other way. But my luck was destined to turn for a time.

I searched Paris for several days. I dined at the principal hotels; I went to the theatres; I rode in the Bois de Boulogne in the morning, and picked up an acquaintance, whom I forced to drive with me in the afternoon. I went to mass at the Madeleine, and I attended the services at the English Church. I hung about the Louvre and Nôtre Dame. I went to Versailles. I spent hours in parading the rue de Rivoli, in the neighbourhood of Meurice's corner, where foreigners pass and repass from morning till night. At last I received an invitation to a reception at the English Embassy. I went, and I found what I had sought so long.

There she was, sitting by an old lady in grey satin and diamonds, who had a wrinkled but kindly face and keen grey eyes that seemed to take in everything they saw, with very little inclination to give much in return. But I did not notice the chaperone. I saw only the face that had haunted me for months, and in the excitement of the moment I walked quickly towards the pair, forgetting such a trifle as the necessity for an introduction.

She was far more beautiful than I had thought, but I never doubted that it was she herself and no other. Vision or no vision before, this was the reality, and I knew it. Twice her hair had been covered, now at last I saw it, and the added beauty of its magnificence glorified the whole woman. It was rich hair, fine and abundant, golden, with deep ruddy tints in it like red bronze spun fine. There was no ornament in it, not a rose, not a thread of gold, and I felt that it needed nothing to enhance its splendour; nothing but her pale face, her dark strange eyes, and her heavy eyebrows. I could see that she was slender too, but strong withal, as she sat there quietly gazing at the moving scene in the midst of the brilliant lights and the hum of perpetual conversation.

I recollected the detail of introduction in time, and turned aside to look for my host. I found him at last. I begged him to present me to the two ladies, pointing them out to him at the same time.

'Yes – uh – by all means – uh – ' replied his Excellency with a pleasant smile. He evidently had no idea of my name, which was not to be wondered at.

'I am Lord Cairngorm,' I observed.

'Oh – by all means,' answered the Ambassador with the same hospitable smile. 'Yes – uh – the fact is, I must try and find out who they are; such lots of people, you know.'

'Oh, if you will present me, I will try and find out for you,' said I, laughing.

'Ah, yes – so kind of you – come along,' said my host. We threaded the crowd, and in a few minutes we stood before the two ladies.

' 'Lowmintrduce L'd Cairngorm,' he said; then, adding quickly to me, 'Come and dine tomorrow, won't you?' he glided away with his pleasant smile and disappeared in the crowd.

I sat down beside the beautiful girl, conscious that the eyes of the duenna were upon me.

'I think we have been very near meeting before,' I remarked, by way of opening the conversation.

My companion turned her eyes full upon me with an air of enquiry. She evidently did not recall my face, if she had ever seen me.

'Really – I cannot remember,' she observed, in a low and musical voice. 'When?'

'In the first place, you came down from Berlin by the express, ten days ago. I was going the other way, and our carriages stopped opposite each other. I saw you at the window.'

'Yes – we came that way, but I do not remember – ' She hesitated.

'Secondly,' I continued, 'I was sitting alone in my garden last summer – near the end of July – do you remember? You must have wandered in there through the park; you came up to the house and looked at me – '

'Was that you?' she asked, in evident surprise. Then she broke into a laugh. 'I told everybody I had seen a ghost; there had never been any Cairngorms in the place since the memory of man. We left the next day, and never heard that you had come there; indeed, I did not know the castle belonged to you.'

'Where were you staying?' I asked.

'Where? Why, with my aunt, where I always stay. She is your neighbour, since it *is* you.'

'I – beg your pardon – but then – is your aunt Lady Bluebell? I did not quite catch – '

'Don't be afraid. She is amazingly deaf. Yes. She is the relict of my beloved uncle, the sixteenth or seventeenth Baron Bluebell – I forget exactly how many of them there have been. And I – do you know who I am?' She laughed, well knowing that I did not.

'No,' I answered frankly. 'I have not the least idea. I asked to be introduced because I recognised you. Perhaps – perhaps you are a Miss Bluebell?'

'Considering that you are a neighbour, I will tell you who I am,' she answered. 'No; I am of the tribe of Bluebells, but my name is Lammas, and I have been given to understand that I was christened Margaret. Being a floral family, they call me Daisy. A dreadful American man once told me that my aunt was a Bluebell and that I was a Harebell – with two l's and an e – because my hair is so thick. I warn you, so that you may avoid making such a bad pun.'

'Do I look like a man who makes puns?' I asked, being very conscious of my melancholy face and sad looks.

Miss Lammas eyed me critically.

'No; you have a mournful temperament. I think I can trust you,' she answered. 'Do you think you could communicate to my aunt the fact that you are a Cairngorm and a neighbour? I am sure she would like to know.'

I leaned towards the old lady, inflating my lungs for a yell. But Miss Lammas stopped me.

'That is not of the slightest use,' she remarked. 'You can write it on a bit of paper. She is utterly deaf.'

'I have a pencil,' I answered; 'but I have no paper. Would my cuff do, do you think?'

'Oh, yes!' replied Miss Lammas, with alacrity; 'men often do that.'

I wrote on my cuff: 'Miss Lammas wishes me to explain that I am your neighbour, Cairngorm.' Then I held out my arm before the old lady's nose. She seemed perfectly accustomed to the proceeding, put up her glasses, read the words, smiled, nodded, and addressed me in the unearthly voice peculiar to people who hear nothing.

'I knew your grandfather very well,' she said. Then she smiled and nodded to me again, and to her niece, and relapsed into silence.

'It is all right,' remarked Miss Lammas. 'Aunt Bluebell knows she is deaf, and does not say much, like the parrot. You see, she knew your grandfather. How odd, that we should be neighbours! Why have we never met before?'

'If you had told me you knew my grandfather when you appeared in the garden, I should not have been in the least surprised,' I answered rather irrelevantly. 'I really thought you were the ghost of the old fountain. How in the world did you come there at that hour?'

'We were a large party and we went out for a walk. Then we thought we should like to see what your park was like in the moonlight, and so we trespassed. I got separated from the rest, and came upon you by accident, just as I was admiring the extremely ghostly look of your house, and wondering whether anybody would ever come and live there again. It looks like the castle of Macbeth, or a scene from the opera. Do you know anybody here?'

'Hardly a soul! Do you?'

'No. Aunt Bluebell said it was our duty to come. It is easy for her to go out; she does not bear the burden of the conversation.'

'I am sorry you find it a burden,' said I. 'Shall I go away?'

Miss Lammas looked at me with a sudden gravity in her beautiful eyes, and there was a sort of hesitation about the lines of her full, soft mouth.

'No,' she said at last, quite simply, 'don't go away. We may like each other, if you stay a little longer – and we ought to, because we are neighbours in the country.'

I suppose I ought to have thought Miss Lammas a very odd girl. There is, indeed, a sort of freemasonry between people who discover that they live near each other, and that they ought to have known each other before. But there was a sort of unexpected frankness and simplicity in the girl's amusing manner which would have struck anyone else as being singular, to say the least of it. To me, however, it all seemed natural enough. I had dreamed of her face too long not to be utterly happy when I met her at last, and could talk to her as much as I pleased. To me, the man of ill luck in everything, the whole meeting seemed too good to be true. I felt again that strange sensation of lightness which I had experienced after I had seen her face in the garden. The great rooms seemed brighter, life seemed worth living; my sluggish, melancholy blood ran faster, and filled me with a new sense of strength. I said to myself that without this woman I was but an imperfect being, but that with her I could accomplish everything to which I should set my hand. Like the great Doctor, when he thought he had cheated Mephistopheles at last, I could have cried aloud to the fleeting moment, *Verweile doch, du bist so schön*!

'Are you always gay?' I asked, suddenly. 'How happy you must be!'

'The days would sometimes seem very long if I were gloomy,' she answered, thoughtfully. 'Yes, I think I find life very pleasant, and I tell it so.'

'How can you "tell life" anything?' I inquired. 'If I could catch my life and talk to it, I would abuse it prodigiously, I assure you.'

'I dare say. You have a melancholy temper. You ought to live out of doors, dig potatoes, make hay, shoot, hunt, tumble into ditches, and come home muddy and hungry for dinner. It would be much better for you than moping in your rook tower, and hating everything.'

'It is rather lonely down there,' I murmured, apologetically, feeling that Miss Lammas was quite right.

'Then marry, and quarrel with your wife,' she laughed. 'Anything is better than being alone.'

'I am a very peaceable person. I never quarrel with anybody. You can try it. You will find it quite impossible.'

'Will you let me try?' she asked, still smiling.

'By all means – especially if it is to be only a preliminary canter,' I answered, rashly.

'What do you mean?' she inquired, turning quickly upon me.

'Oh – nothing. You might try my paces with a view to quarrelling in the future. I cannot imagine how you are going to do it. You will have to resort to immediate and direct abuse.'

'No. I will only say that if you do not like your life, it is your own fault. How can a man of your age talk of being melancholy, or of the hollowness of existence? Are you consumptive? Are you subject to hereditary insanity? Are you deaf, like Aunt Bluebell? Are you poor, like – lots of people? Have you been crossed in love? Have you lost the world for a woman, or any particular woman for the sake of the world? Are you feeble-minded, a cripple, an outcast? Are you – repulsively ugly?' She laughed again. 'Is there any reason in the world why you should not enjoy all you have got in life?'

'No. There is no reason whatever, except that I am dreadfully unlucky, especially in small things.'

'Then try big things, just for a change,' suggested Miss Lammas. 'Try and get married, for instance, and see how it turns out.'

'If it turned out badly it would be rather serious.'

'Not half so serious as it is to abuse everything unreasonably. If abuse is your particular talent, abuse something that ought to be abused. Abuse the Conservatives – or the Liberals – it does not matter which, since they are always abusing each other. Make yourself felt by other people. You will like it, if they don't. It will make a man of you. Fill your mouth with pebbles, and howl at the sea, if you cannot do anything else. It did Demosthenes no end of good, you know. You will have the satisfaction of imitating a great man.'

'Really, Miss Lammas, I think the list of innocent exercises you propose – '

'Very well – if you don't care for that sort of thing, care for some other sort of thing. Care for something, or hate something. Don't be idle. Life is short, and though art may be long, plenty of noise answers nearly as well.'

'I do care for something – I mean, somebody,' I said.

'A woman? Then marry her. Don't hesitate.'

'I do not know whether she would marry me,' I replied. 'I have never asked her.'

'Then ask her at once,' answered Miss Lammas. 'I shall die happy if I feel I have persuaded a melancholy fellow-creature to rouse himself to action. Ask her, by all means, and see what she says. If she does not accept you at once, she may take you the next time. Meanwhile, you will have entered for the race. If you lose, there are the "All-aged Trial Stakes", and the "Consolation Race".'

'And plenty of selling races into the bargain. Shall I take you at your word, Miss Lammas?'

'I hope you will,' she answered.

'Since you yourself advise me, I will. Miss Lammas, will you do me the honour to marry me?'

For the first time in my life the blood rushed to my head and my sight swam. I cannot tell why I said it. It would be useless to try to explain the extraordinary fascination the girl exercised over me, nor the still more extraordinary feeling of intimacy with her which had grown in me during that half-hour. Lonely, sad, unlucky as I had been all my life, I was certainly not timid, nor even shy. But to propose to marry a woman after half an hour's acquaintance was a piece of madness of which I never believed myself capable, and of which I should never be capable again, could I be placed in the same situation. It was as though my whole being had been changed in a moment by magic – by the white magic of her nature brought into contact with mine. The blood sank back to my heart, and a moment later I found myself staring at her with anxious eyes. To my amazement she was as calm as ever, but her beautiful mouth smiled, and there was a mischievous light in her dark-brown eyes.

'Fairly caught,' she answered. 'For an individual who pretends to be listless and sad you are not lacking in humour. I had really not the least idea what you were going to say. Wouldn't it be singularly awkward for you if I had said "Yes"? I never saw anybody begin to practise so sharply what was preached to him – with so very little loss of time!'

'You probably never met a man who had dreamed of you for seven months before being introduced.'

'No, I never did,' she answered, gaily. 'It smacks of the romantic. Perhaps you are a romantic character, after all. I should think you were if I believed you. Very well; you have taken my advice, entered for a Stranger's Race and lost it. Try the All-aged Trial Stakes. You have another cuff, and a pencil. Propose to Aunt Bluebell; she would dance with astonishment, and she might recover her hearing.'

3

That was how I first asked Margaret Lammas to be my wife, and I will agree with anyone who says I behaved very foolishly. But I have not repented of it, and I never shall. I have long ago understood that I was out of my mind that evening, but I think my temporary insanity on that occasion has had the effect of making me a saner man ever since. Her manner turned my head, for it was so different from what I had expected. To hear this lovely creature, who, in my imagination, was a heroine of romance, if not of tragedy, talking familiarly and laughing readily was more than my equanimity could bear, and I lost my head as well as my heart. But when I went back to England in the spring, I went to make certain arrangements at the Castle – certain changes and improvements which would be absolutely necessary. I had won the race for which I had entered myself so rashly, and we were to be married in June.

Whether the change was due to the orders I had left with the gardener and the rest of the servants, or to my own state of mind, I cannot tell. At all events, the old place did not look the same to me when I opened my window on the morning after my arrival. There were the grey walls below me, and the grey turrets flanking the huge building; there were the fountains, the marble causeways, the smooth basins, the tall box hedges, the water-lilies and the swans, just as of old. But there was something else there, too – something in the air, in the water, and in the greenness that I did not recognise – a light over everything by which everything was transfigured. The clock in the tower struck seven, and the strokes of the ancient bell sounded like a wedding chime. The air sang with the thrilling treble of the songbirds, with the silvery music of the plashing water and the softer harmony of the leaves stirred by the fresh morning wind. There was a smell of new-mown hay from the distant meadows, and of blooming roses from the beds below, wafted up together to my window. I stood in the pure sunshine and drank the air and all the sounds and the odours that were in it; and I looked down at my garden and said: 'It is Paradise, after all.' I think the men of old were right when they called heaven a garden, and Eden, a garden inhabited by one man and one woman, the Earthly Paradise.

I turned away, wondering what had become of the gloomy memories I had always associated with my home. I tried to recall the impression of my nurse's horrible prophecy before the death of my parents – an impression which hitherto had been vivid enough. I tried to remember my old self, my dejection, my listlessness, my bad luck, and my petty disappointments. I endeavoured to force myself to think as I used to think, if only to satisfy myself that I had not lost my individuality. But I succeeded in none of these efforts. I was a different man, a changed being, incapable of sorrow, of ill luck, or of sadness. My life had been a dream, not evil, but infinitely gloomy and hopeless. It was now a reality, full of hope, gladness, and all manner of good. My home had been like a tomb; today it was paradise. My heart had been as though it had not existed; today it beat with strength and youth, and the certainty of realised happiness. I revelled in the beauty of the world, and called loveliness out of the future to enjoy it before time should bring it to me, as a traveller in the plains looks up to the mountains, and already tastes the cool air through the dust of the road.

Here, I thought, we will live and live for years. There we will sit by the fountain towards evening and in the deep moonlight. Down those paths we will wander together. On those benches we will rest and talk. Among those eastern hills we will ride through the soft twilight, and in the old house we will tell tales on winter nights, when the logs burn high, and the holly berries are red, and the old clock tolls out the dying year. On these old steps, in these dark passages and stately rooms, there will one day be the sound of little pattering feet, and laughing child-voices will ring up to the vaults of the ancient hall. Those tiny footsteps shall not be slow and sad as mine were, nor shall the childish words be spoken in an awed whisper. No gloomy Welshwoman shall people the dusky corners with weird horrors, nor utter horrid prophecies of death and ghastly things. All shall be young, and fresh, and joyful, and happy, and we will turn the old luck again, and forget that there was ever any sadness.

So I thought, as I looked out of my window that morning and for many mornings after that, and every day it all seemed more real than ever before, and much nearer. But the old nurse looked at me askance, and muttered odd sayings about the Woman of the Water. I cared little what she said, for I was far too happy.

At last the time came near for the wedding. Lady Bluebell and all the tribe of Bluebells, as Margaret called them, were at Bluebell Grange, for we had determined to be married in the country, and to come straight to the Castle afterwards. We cared little for travelling, and not at all for a crowded ceremony at St George's in Hanover Square, with all the tiresome formalities afterwards. I used to ride over to the Grange every day, and very often Margaret would come

with her aunt and some of her cousins to the Castle. I was suspicious
of my own taste, and was only too glad to let her have her way about
the alterations and improvements in our home.

We were to be married on the thirtieth of July, and on the evening
of the twenty-eighth Margaret drove over with some of the Bluebell
party. In the long summer twilight we all went out into the garden.
Naturally enough, Margaret and I were left to ourselves, and we
wandered down by the marble basins.

'It is an odd coincidence,' I said; 'it was on this very night last year
that I first saw you.'

'Considering that it is the month of July,' answered Margaret with
a laugh, 'and that we have been here almost every day, I don't think
the coincidence is so extraordinary, after all.'

'No, dear,' said I, 'I suppose not. I don't know why it struck me.
We shall very likely be here a year from today, and a year from that.
The odd thing, when I think of it, is that you should be here at all.
But my luck has turned. I ought not to think anything odd that
happens now that I have you. It is all sure to be good.'

'A slight change in your ideas since that remarkable performance
of yours in Paris,' said Margaret. 'Do you know, I thought you were
the most extraordinary man I had ever met.'

'I thought you were the most charming woman I had ever seen. I
naturally did not want to lose any time in frivolities. I took you at
your word, I followed your advice, I asked you to marry me, and this
is the delightful result – what's the matter?'

Margaret had started suddenly, and her hand tightened on my
arm. An old woman was coming up the path, and was close to us
before we saw her, for the moon had risen, and was shining full in
our faces. The woman turned out to be my old nurse.

'It's only old Judith, dear – don't be frightened,' I said. Then I
spoke to the Welshwoman: 'What are you about, Judith? Have you
been feeding the Woman of the Water?'

'Ay – when the clock strikes, Willie – my lord, I mean,' muttered
the old creature, drawing aside to let us pass, and fixing her strange
eyes on Margaret's face.

'What does she mean?' asked Margaret, when we had gone by.

'Nothing, darling. The old thing is mildly crazy, but she is a good
soul.'

We went on in silence for a few moments, and came to the rustic
bridge just above the artificial grotto through which the water ran
out into the park, dark and swift in its narrow channel. We stopped,

and leaned on the wooden rail. The moon was now behind us, and shone full upon the long vista of basins and on the huge walls and towers of the Castle above.

'How proud you ought to be of such a grand old place!' said Margaret, softly.

'It is yours now, darling,' I answered. 'You have as good a right to love it as I – but I only love it because you are to live in it, dear.'

Her hand stole out and lay on mine, and we were both silent. Just then the clock began to strike far off in the tower. I counted – eight – nine – ten – eleven – I looked at my watch – twelve – thirteen – I laughed. The bell went on striking.

'The old clock has gone crazy, like Judith,' I exclaimed. Still it went on, note after note ringing out monotonously through the still air. We leaned over the rail, instinctively looking in the direction whence the sound came. On and on it went. I counted nearly a hundred, out of sheer curiosity, for I understood that something had broken, and that the thing was running itself down.

Suddenly there was a crack as of breaking wood, a cry and a heavy splash, and I was alone, clinging to the broken end of the rail of the rustic bridge.

I do not think I hesitated while my pulse beat twice. I sprang clear of the bridge into the black rushing water, dived to the bottom, came up again with empty hands, turned and swam downwards through the grotto in the thick darkness, plunging and diving at every stroke, striking my head and hands against jagged stones and sharp corners, clutching at last something in my fingers, and dragging it up with all my might. I spoke, I cried aloud, but there was no answer. I was alone in the pitchy blackness with my burden, and the house was five hundred yards away. Struggling still, I felt the ground beneath my feet, I saw a ray of moonlight – the grotto widened, and the deep water became a broad and shallow brook as I stumbled over the stones and at last laid Margaret's body on the bank in the park beyond.

'Ay, Willie, as the clock struck!' said the voice of Judith, the Welsh nurse, as she bent down and looked at the white face. The old woman must have turned back and followed us, seen the accident, and slipped out by the lower gate of the garden. 'Ay,' she groaned, 'you have fed the Woman of the Water this night, Willie, while the clock was striking.'

I scarcely heard her as I knelt beside the lifeless body of the woman I loved, chafing the wet white temples, and gazing wildly into the

wide-staring eyes. I remember only the first returning look of consciousness, the first heaving breath, the first movement of those dear
hands stretching out towards me.

* * *

That is not much of a story, you say. It is the story of my life. That
is all. It does not pretend to be anything else. Old Judith says my
luck turned on that summer's night, when I was struggling in the
water to save all that was worth living for. A month later there was
a stone bridge above the grotto, and Margaret and I stood on it and
looked up at the moonlit Castle, as we had done once before, and as
we have done many times since. For all those things happened ten
years ago last summer, and this is the tenth Christmas Eve we have
spent together by the roaring logs in the old hall, talking of old
times; and every year there are more old times to talk of. There are
curly-headed boys, too, with red-gold hair and dark-brown eyes
like their mother's, and a little Margaret, with solemn black eyes
like mine. Why could not she look like her mother, too, as well as
the rest of them?

The world is very bright at this glorious Christmas time, and
perhaps there is little use in calling up the sadness of long ago,
unless it be to make the jolly firelight seem more cheerful, the
good wife's face look gladder, and to give the children's laughter a
merrier ring, by contrast with all that is gone. Perhaps, too, some
sad-faced, listless, melancholy youth, who feels that the world is
very hollow, and that life is like a perpetual funeral service, just as I
used to feel myself, may take courage from my example, and having
found the woman of his heart, ask her to marry him after half an
hour's acquaintance. But, on the whole, I would not advise any man
to marry, for the simple reason that no man will ever find a wife like
mine, and being obliged to go further, he will necessarily fare
worse. My wife has done miracles, but I will not assert that any
other woman is able to follow her example.

Margaret always said that the old place was beautiful, and that I
ought to be proud of it. I daresay she is right. She has even more
imagination than I. But I have a good answer and a plain one, which
is this – that all the beauty of the Castle comes from her. She has
breathed upon it all, as the children blow upon the cold glass
window-panes in winter; and as their warm breath crystallises into
landscapes from fairyland, full of exquisite shapes and traceries
upon the blank surface, so her spirit has transformed every grey

stone of the old towers, every ancient tree and hedge in the gardens, every thought in my once melancholy self. All that was old is young, and all that was sad is glad, and I am the gladdest of all. Whatever heaven may be, there is no earthly paradise without woman, nor is there anywhere a place so desolate, so dreary, so unutterably miserable that a woman cannot make it seem heaven to the man she loves and who loves her.

I hear certain cynics laugh, and cry that all that has been said before. Do not laugh, my good cynic. You are too small a man to laugh at such a great thing as love. Prayers have been said before now by many, and perhaps you say yours, too. I do not think they lose anything by being repeated, nor you by repeating them. You say that the world is bitter, and full of the Waters of Bitterness. Love, and so live that you may be loved – the world will turn sweet for you, and you shall rest like me by the Waters of Paradise.

The King's Messenger

It was a rather dim daylight dinner. I remember that quite distinctly, for I could see the glow of the sunset over the trees in the park, through the high window at the west end of the dining-room. I had expected to find a larger party, I believe, for I recollect being a little surprised at seeing only a dozen people assembled at table. It seemed to me that in old times, ever so long ago, when I had last stayed in that house, there had been as many as thirty or forty guests. I recognised some of them among a number of beautiful portraits that hung on the walls. There was room for a great many because there was only one huge window, at one end, and one large door at the other. I was very much surprised, too, to see a portrait of myself, evidently painted about twenty years ago by Lenbach. It seemed very strange that I should have so completely forgotten the picture, and that I should not be able to remember having sat for it. We were good friends, it is true, and he might have painted it from memory, without my knowledge, but it was certainly strange that he should never have told me about it. The portraits that hung in the dining- room were all very good indeed and all, I should say, by the best painters of that time.

My left-hand neighbour was a lovely young girl whose name I had forgotten, though I had known her long, and I fancied that she looked a little disappointed when she saw that I was beside her. On my right there was a vacant seat, and beyond it sat an elderly woman with features as hard as the overwhelmingly splendid diamonds she wore. Her eyes made me think of grey glass marbles cemented into a stone mask. It was odd that her name should have escaped me, too, for I had often met her.

The table looked irregular, and I counted the guests mechanically while I ate my soup. We were only twelve, but the empty chair beside me was the thirteenth place.

I suppose it was not very tactful of me to mention this, but I wanted to say something to the beautiful girl on my left, and no other subject for a general remark suggested itself. Just as I was going to speak I remembered who she was.

'Miss Lorna,' I said, to attract her attention, for she was looking away from me toward the door. 'I hope you are not superstitious about there being thirteen at table, are you?'

'We are only twelve,' she said, in the sweetest voice in the world.

'Yes; but someone else is coming. There's an empty chair here beside me.'

'Oh, he doesn't count,' said Miss Lorna quietly. 'At least, not for everybody. When did you get here? Just in time for dinner, I suppose.'

'Yes,' I answered. 'I'm in luck to be beside you. It seems an age since we were last here together.'

'It does indeed,' Miss Lorna sighed and looked at the pictures on the opposite wall. 'I've lived a lifetime since I saw you last.'

I smiled at the exaggeration. 'When you are thirty, you won't talk of having your life behind you,' I said.

'I shall never be thirty,' Miss Lorna answered, with such an odd little air of conviction that I did not think of anything to say. 'Besides, life isn't made up of years or months or hours, or of anything that has to do with time,' she continued. 'You ought to know that. Our bodies are something better than mere clocks, wound up to show just how old we are at every moment, by our hair turning grey and our teeth falling out and our faces getting wrinkled and yellow, or puffy and red. Look at your own portrait over there. I don't mind saying that you must have been twenty years younger when that was painted, but I'm sure you are just the same man today, improved by age, perhaps.'

I heard a sweet little echoing laugh that seemed very far away; and indeed I could not have sworn that it rippled from Miss Lorna's beautiful lips, for though they were parted and smiling, my impression is that they did not move, even as little as most women's lips are moved by laughter.

'Thank you for thinking me improved,' I said. 'I find you a little changed, too. I was just going to say that you seem sadder, but you laughed just then.'

'Did I? I suppose that's the right thing to do when the play is over, isn't it?'

'If it has been an amusing play,' I answered, humoring her.

The wonderful violet eyes turned to me, full of light. 'It's not been a bad play. I don't complain.'

'Why do you speak of it as over?'

'I'll tell you, because I'm sure you will keep my secret. You will, won't you? We were always such good friends, you and I, even two years ago when I was young and silly. Will you promise not to tell anyone till I'm gone?'

'Gone?'

'Yes. Will you promise?'

'Of course I will. But . . . ' I did not finish the sentence, because Miss Lorna bent nearer to me, so as to speak in a much lower tone. While I listened, I felt her sweet young breath on my cheek. 'I'm going away tonight with the man who is to sit at your other side,' she said. 'He's a little late; he often is, for he is tremendously busy; but he'll come presently, and after dinner we shall just stroll out into the garden and never come back. That's my secret. You won't betray me, will you?' Again, as she looked at me, I heard that far-off silver laugh, sweet and low – I was almost too much surprised by what she had told me to notice how still her parted lips were, but that comes back to me now, with many other details.

'My dear Miss Lorna,' I said, 'do think of your parents before taking such a step.'

'I have thought of them,' she answered. 'Of course they would never consent, and I am very sorry to leave them, but it can't be helped.'

At this moment, as often happens when two people are talking in low tones at a large dinner-table, there was a momentary lull in the general conversation, and I was spared the trouble of making any further answer to what Miss Lorna had told me so unexpectedly, and with such profound confidence in my discretion.

To tell the truth, she would very probably not have listened, whether my words expressed sympathy or protest, for she had turned suddenly pale, and her eyes were wide and dark. The lull in the talk at table was due to the appearance of the man who was to occupy the vacant place beside me.

He had entered the room very quietly, and he made no elaborate apology for being late, as he sat down, bending his head courteously to our hostess and her husband, and smiling in a gentle sort of way as he nodded to the others.

'Please forgive me,' he said quietly. 'I was detained by a funeral and missed the train.'

It was not until he had taken his place that he looked across me at Miss Lorna and exchanged a glance of recognition with her. I noticed that the lady with the hard face and the splendid diamonds, who was at his other side, drew away from him a little, as if not wishing even to let his sleeve brush against her bare arm. It occurred to me at the same time that Miss Lorna must be wishing me anywhere else than between her and the man with whom she was just about to run away, and I wished for their sake and mine that I could change places with him. He was certainly not like other men, and though few people would have called him handsome there was something about him that instantly fixed the attention; rarely beautiful though Miss Lorna was, almost everyone would have noticed him first on entering the room, and most people, I think, would have been more interested by his face than by hers. I could well imagine that some women might love him, even to distraction, though it was just as easy to understand that others might be strongly repelled by him, and might even fear him.

For my part, I shall not try to describe him as one describes an ordinary man, with a dozen or so adjectives that leave nothing to the imagination but yet offer it no picture that it can grasp. My instinct was to fear him rather than think of him as a possible friend, but I could not help feeling instant admiration for him, as one does at first sight for anything that is very complete, harmonious, and strong. He was dark, and pale with a shadowy pallor I never saw in any other face; the features of thrice-great Hermes were not modelled in more perfect symmetry, his luminous eyes were not unkind, but there was something fateful in them, and they were set very deep under the grand white brow. His age I could not guess, but I should have called him young; standing, I had seen that he was tall and sinewy, and now that he was seated, he had the unmistakable look of a man accustomed to be in authority, to be heard and to be obeyed. His hands were white, his fingers straight, lean, and very strong.

Everyone at the table seemed to know him, but as often happens among civilised people no one called him by name in speaking to him.

'We were beginning to be afraid that you might not get here,' said our host.

'Really?' The Thirteenth Guest smiled quietly, but shook his head. 'Did you ever know me to break an engagement, under any circumstances?'

The master of the house laughed, though not very cordially, I thought. 'No,' he answered. 'Your reputation for keeping your appointments is proverbial. Even your enemies must admit that.'

The Guest nodded and smiled again. Miss Lorna bent toward me.

'What do you think of him?' she asked, almost in a whisper.

'Very striking sort of man,' I answered, in a low tone. 'But I'm inclined to be a little afraid of him.'

'So was I, at first,' she said, and I heard the silver laugh again. 'But that soon wears off,' she went on. 'You'll know him better some day.'

'Shall I?'

'Yes; I'm quite sure you will. Oh, I don't pretend that I fell in love with him at first sight. I went through a phase of feeling afraid of him, as almost everyone does. You see, when people first meet him they cannot possibly know how kind and gentle he can be, though he is so tremendously strong. I've heard him called cruel and ruthless and cold, but it's not true. Indeed it's not. He can be as gentle as a woman, and he's the truest friend in all the world.'

I was going to ask her to tell me his name, but just then I saw that she was looking at him, across me, and I sat as far back in my chair as I could, so that they might speak to each other if they wished to. Their eyes met, and there was a longing light in both. I could not help glancing from one to the other; and Miss Lorna's sweet lips moved almost imperceptibly, though no sound came from them. I have seen young lovers make that small sign to each other even across a room, the signal of a kiss given and returned in the heart's thoughts.

If she had been less beautiful and young, if the man she loved had not been so magnificently manly, it would have irritated me, but it seemed natural that they should love and not be ashamed of it, and I only hoped that no one else at the table had noticed the tenderly quivering little contraction of the young girl's exquisite mouth.

'You remembered,' said the man quietly. 'I got your message this morning. Thank you.'

'I hope it's not going to be very hard,' murmured Miss Lorna, smiling. 'Not that it would make any great difference if it were,' she added more thoughtfully.

'It's the easiest thing in life,' he said, 'And I promise that you shall never regret it.'

'I trust you,' the young girl answered simply.

Then she turned away, for she no doubt felt the awkwardness of talking to him across me of a secret which she had confided to me without letting him know that she had done so. Instinctively I turned to him, feeling that the moment had come for disregarding formality and making his acquaintance, since we were neighbours at table in a friend's house and I had known Miss Lorna so long.

Besides, it is always interesting to talk with a man who is just going to do something very dangerous or dramatic and who does not guess that you know what he is about.

'I suppose you motored here from town, as you said you missed the train,' I said. 'It's a good road, isn't it?'

'Yes, I literally flew,' replied the dark man, with his gentle smile. 'I hope you're not superstitious about thirteen at table?'

'Not in the least,' I answered. 'In the first place, I'm a fatalist about everything that doesn't depend on my own free will. As I have not the slightest intention of doing anything to shorten my life, it will certainly not come to an abrupt end by any autosuggestion arising from a silly superstition like that about thirteen.'

'Autosuggestion? That's rather a new light on the old beliefs.'

'And secondly,' I continued, 'I don't believe in death. There is no such thing.'

'Really?' My neighbour seemed greatly surprised. 'How do you mean?' he asked. 'I don't think I understand you.'

'I'm sure I don't,' put in Miss Lorna, and the silver laugh followed. She had overheard the conversation, and some of the others were listening, too.

'You don't kill a book by translating it,' I said, rather glad to expound my views. 'Death is only a translation of life into another language. That's what I mean.'

'That's a most interesting point of view,' observed the Thirteenth Guest thoughtfully. 'I never thought of the matter in that way before, though I've often seen the expression "translated" in epitaphs. Are you sure that you are not indulging in a little paronomasia?'

'What's that?' inquired the hard-faced lady, with all the contempt which a scholarly word deserves in polite society.

'It means punning,' I answered. 'No, I am not making a pun. Grave subjects do not lend themselves to low forms of humour. I assure you, I am quite in earnest. Death, in the ordinary sense, is not a real phenomenon at all, so long as there is any life in the universe. It's a name we apply to a change we only partly understand.'

'Learned discussions are an awful bore,' said the hard-faced lady very audibly.

'I don't advise you to argue the question too sharply with your neighbour there,' laughed the master of the house, leaning forward and speaking to me. 'He'll get the better of you. He's an expert at what you call "translating people into another language".'

If the man beside me was a famous surgeon, as our host perhaps meant, it seemed to me that the remark was not in very good taste. He looked more like a soldier.

'Does our friend mean that you are in the army, and that you are a dangerous person?' I asked of him.

'No,' he answered quietly. 'I'm only a King's Messenger, and in my own opinion I'm not at all dangerous.'

'It must be rather an active life,' I said, in order to say something; 'constantly coming and going, I suppose?'

'Yes, constantly.'

I felt that Miss Lorna was watching and listening, and I turned to her, only to find that she was again looking beyond me, at my neighbour, though he did not see her. I remember her face very distinctly as it was just then; the recollection is, in fact the last impression I retain of her matchless beauty, for I never saw her after that evening.

It is something to have seen one of the most beautiful women in the world gazing at the man who was more to her than life and all it held; it is something I cannot forget. But he did not return her look just then, for he had joined in the general conversation, and very soon afterward he practically absorbed it.

He talked well; more than well, marvellously; for before long even the lady with the hard face was listening spellbound, with the rest of us, to his stories of nations and tales of men, brilliant descriptions, anecdotes of heroism and tenderness that were each a perfect coin from the mint of humanity, with dashes of daring wit, glimpses of a profound insight into the great mystery of the beyond, and now and then a manly comment on life that came straight from the heart; never, in all my long experience, have I heard poet, or scholar, or soldier, or ruler of men talk as he did that evening. And as I listened I was more and more amazed that such a man should be but a simple King's Messenger, as he said he was, earning a poor gentleman's living by carrying his majesty's dispatches from London to the ends of the earth, and I made some sad and sober inward reflections on the vast difference between the gift of talking supremely well and the genius a man must have to accomplish even one little thing that may endure in history, in literature, or in art.

'Do you wonder that I love him?' whispered Miss Lorna.

Even in a whisper I heard the glorious pride of a woman who loves altogether and wholly believes there is no one like her chosen man.

'No,' I answered, 'for it is no wonder. I only hope – ' I stopped, feeling that it would be foolish and unkind to express the doubt I felt.

'You hope that I may not be disappointed,' said Miss Lorna, still almost in a whisper. 'That was what you were going to say, I'm sure.'

I nodded, in spite of myself, and met her eyes; they were full of a wonderful light.

'No one was ever disappointed in him,' she murmured – 'no living being, neither man, nor woman, nor child. With him I shall have peace and love without end.'

'Without end?'

'Yes. For ever and ever.'

After dinner we scattered through the great rooms in the soft evening light of mid-June, and by and by I was standing at an open window, looking out across the garden.

In the distance, Lorna was walking slowly away down the broad avenue with a tall man; and while they were still in sight, though far away, I am sure that I saw his arm steal round her as if he were drawing her on, and her head bent lovingly to his shoulder; and so they glided away into the twilight and disappeared.

Then at last I turned to my hostess. 'Do you mind telling me the name of that man who came in late and talked so well?' I asked. 'You all seemed to know him like an old friend.'

She looked at me in profound surprise. 'Do you mean to say that you do not know who he is?' she asked.

'No. I never met him before. He is a most extraordinary man to be only a King's Messenger.'

'He is indeed *the* King's Messenger, my dear friend. His name is Death.'

I dreamed this dream one afternoon last summer, dozing in my chair on deck, under the double awning, when the *Alda* was anchored off Goletta, in sight of Carthage, and the cool north breeze was blowing down the deep gulf of Tunis. I must have been wakened by some slight sound from a boat alongside, for when I opened my eyes my man was standing a little way off, evidently waiting till I should finish my nap. He brought me a telegram which had just come on board, and I opened it rather drowsily, not expecting any particular news.

It was from England, from a very dear friend.

LORNA DIED SUDDENLY LAST NIGHT AT CHURCH HADLEY.

That was all. The dream had been a message.

'With him I shall have peace and love without end.'

Thank God, I hear those words in her own voice whenever I think of her.

The Witch of Prague

Chapter 1

A great multitude of people filled the church, crowded together in the old black pews, standing closely thronged in the nave and aisles, pressing shoulder to shoulder even in the two chapels on the right and left of the apse, a vast gathering of pale men and women whose eyes were sad and in whose faces was written the history of their nation. The mighty shafts and pilasters of the Gothic edifice rose like the stems of giant trees in a primeval forest from a dusky undergrowth, spreading out and uniting their stony branches far above in the upper gloom. From the clerestory windows of the nave an uncertain light descended halfway to the depths and seemed to float upon the darkness below as oil upon the water of a well. Over the western entrance the huge fantastic organ bristled with blackened pipes and dusty gilded ornaments of colossal size, like some enormous kingly crown long forgotten in the lumber room of the universe, tarnished and overlaid with the dust of ages. Eastwards, before the rail which separated the high altar from the people, wax torches, so thick that a man might not span one of them with both his hands, were set up at irregular intervals, some taller, some shorter, burning with steady, golden flames, each one surrounded with heavy funeral wreaths, and each having a tablet below it, whereon were set forth in the Bohemian idiom, the names, titles, and qualities of him or her in whose memory it was lighted. Innumerable lamps and tapers before the side altars and under the strange canopied shrines at the bases of the pillars, struggled ineffectually with the gloom, shedding but a few sickly yellow rays upon the pallid faces of the persons nearest to their light.

Suddenly the heavy vibration of a single pedal note burst from the organ upon the breathing silence, long drawn out, rich, voluminous, and imposing. Presently, upon the massive bass, great chords grew up, succeeding each other in a simple modulation, rising then with the blare of trumpets and the simultaneous crash of mixtures, fifteenths and coupled pedals to a deafening peal, then subsiding quickly again and terminating in one long sustained common chord. And now, as the celebrant bowed at the lowest step before the high altar, the voices of the innumerable congregation joined the harmony of the organ, ringing up to the groined roof in an ancient Slavonic melody, melancholy and beautiful, and rendered yet more unlike all other music by the undefinable character of the Bohemian language, in which tones softer than those of the softest southern tongue alternate so oddly with rough gutturals and strident sibilants.

The Wanderer stood in the midst of the throng, erect, taller than the men near him, holding his head high, so that a little of the light from the memorial torches reached his thoughtful, manly face, making the noble and passionate features to stand out clearly, while losing its power of illumination in the dark beard and among the shadows of his hair. His was a face such as Rembrandt would have painted, seen under the light that Rembrandt loved best; for the expression seemed to overcome the surrounding gloom by its own luminous quality, while the deep grey eyes were made almost black by the wide expansion of the pupils; the dusky brows clearly defined the boundary in the face between passion and thought, and the pale forehead, by its slight recession into the shade from its middle prominence, proclaimed the man of heart, the man of faith, the man of devotion, as well as the intuitive nature of the delicately sensitive mind and the quick, elastic qualities of the man's finely organised, but nervous bodily constitution. The long white fingers of one hand stirred restlessly, twitching at the fur of his broad lapel which was turned back across his chest, and from time to time he drew a deep breath and sighed, not painfully, but wearily and hopelessly, as a man sighs who knows that his happiness is long past and that his liberation from the burden of life is yet far off in the future.

The celebrant reached the reading of the Gospel and the men and women in the pews rose to their feet. Still the singing of the long-drawn-out stanzas of the hymn continued with unflagging devotion, and still the deep accompaniment of the ancient organ sustained the mighty chorus of voices. The Gospel over, the people sank into their seats again, not standing, as is the custom in some countries, until the Creed had been said. Here and there, indeed, a woman, perhaps a stranger in the country, remained upon her feet, noticeable among the many figures seated in the pews. The Wanderer, familiar with many lands and many varying traditions of worship, unconsciously noted these exceptions, looking with a vague curiosity from one to the other. Then, all at once, his tall frame shivered from head to foot, and his fingers convulsively grasped the yielding sable on which they lay.

She was there, the woman he had sought so long, whose face he had not found in the cities and dwellings of the living, neither her grave in the silent communities of the dead. There, before the un-couth monument of dark red marble beneath which Tycho Brahe rests in peace, there she stood; not as he had seen her last on that day when his senses had left him in the delirium of his sickness, not in the freshness of her bloom and of her dark loveliness, but changed as he had dreamed in evil dreams that death would have power to change her. The warm olive of her cheek was turned to the hue of wax, the soft shadows beneath her velvet eyes were deepened and hardened, her expression, once yielding and changing under the breath of thought and feeling as a field of flowers when the west wind blows, was now set, as though for ever, in a death-like fixity. The delicate features were drawn and pinched, the nostrils contracted, the colour-less lips straightened out of the lines of beauty into the mould of a lifeless mask. It was the face of a dead woman, but it was her face still, and the Wanderer knew it well; in the kingdom of his soul the whole resistless commonwealth of the emotions revolted together to dethrone death's regent – sorrow, while the thrice-tempered springs of passion, bent but not broken, stirred suddenly in the palace of his body and shook the strong foundations of his being.

During the seconds that followed, his eyes were riveted upon the beloved head. Then, as the Creed ended, the vision sank down and was lost to his sight. She was seated now, and the broad sea of humanity hid her from him, though he raised himself the full height of his stature in the effort to distinguish even the least part of her head-dress. To move from his place was all but impossible, though the fierce longing to be near her bade him trample even upon the shoulders of the throng to reach her, as men have done more than once to save themselves from death by fire in crowded places. Still the singing of the hymn continued, and would continue, as he knew, until the moment of the Elevation. He strained his hearing to catch the sounds that came from the quarter where she sat. In a chorus of a thousand singers he fancied that he could have distinguished the tender, heart-stirring vibration of her tones. Never woman sang, never could woman sing again, as she had once sung, though her voice had been as soft as it had been sweet, and tuned to vibrate in the heart rather than in the ear. As the strains rose and fell, the

Wanderer bowed his head and closed his eyes, listening, through the maze of sounds, for the silvery ring of her magic note. Something he heard at last, something that sent a thrill from his ear to his heart, unless indeed his heart itself were making music for his ears to hear. The impression reached him fitfully, often interrupted and lost, but as often renewing itself and reawakening in the listener the certainty of recognition which he had felt at the sight of the singer's face.

He who loves with his whole soul has a knowledge and a learning which surpass the wisdom of those who spend their lives in the study of things living or long dead, or never animate. They, indeed, can construct the figure of a flower from the dried web of a single leaf, or by the examination of a dusty seed, and they can set up the scheme of life of a shadowy mammoth out of a fragment of its skeleton, or tell the story of hill and valley from the contemplation of a handful of earth or of a broken pebble. Often they are right, sometimes they are driven deeper and deeper into error by the complicated imperfections of their own science. But he who loves greatly possesses in his intuition the capacities of all instruments of observation which man has invented and applied to his use. The lenses of his eyes can magnify the infinitesimal detail to the dimensions of common things, and bring objects to his vision from immeasurable distances; the labyrinth of his ear can choose and distinguish amidst the harmonies and the discords of the world, muffling in its tortuous passages the reverberation of ordinary sounds while multiplying a hundredfold the faint tones of the one beloved voice. His whole body and his whole intelligence form together an instrument of exquisite sensibility whereby the perceptions of his inmost soul are hourly tortured, delighted, caught up into ecstasy, torn and crushed by jealousy and fear, or plunged into the frigid waters of despair.

The melancholy hymn resounded through the vast church, but though the Wanderer stretched the faculty of hearing to the utmost, he could no longer find the note he sought amongst the vibrations of the dank and heavy air. Then an irresistible longing came upon him to turn and force his way through the dense throng of men and women, to reach the aisle and press past the huge pillar till he could slip between the tombstone of the astronomer and the row of back wooden seats. Once there, he should see her face to face.

He turned, indeed, as he stood, and he tried to move a few steps. On all sides curious looks were directed upon him, but no one offered to make way, and still the monotonous singing continued until he felt himself deafened, as he faced the great congregation.

'I am ill,' he said in a low voice to those nearest to him. 'Pray let me pass!'

His face was white, indeed, and those who heard his words believed him. A mild old man raised his sad blue eyes, gazed at him, and while trying to draw back, gently shook his head. A pale woman, whose sickly features were half veiled in the folds of a torn black shawl, moved as far as she could, shrinking as the very poor and miserable shrink when they are expected to make way before the rich and the strong. A lad of fifteen stood upon tiptoe to make himself even slighter than he was and thus to widen the way, and the Wanderer found himself, after repeated efforts, as much as two steps distant from his former position. He was still trying to divide the crowd when the music suddenly ceased, and the tones of the organ died away far up under the western window. It was the moment of the Elevation, and at the first silvery tinkling of the bell, the people swayed a little, all those who were able kneeling, and those whose movements were impeded by the press of worshippers bending towards the altar as a field of grain before the gale. The Wanderer turned again and bowed himself with the rest, devoutly and humbly, with half-closed eyes, as he strove to collect and control his thoughts in the presence of the chief mystery of his Faith. Three times the tiny bell was rung, a pause followed, and thrice again the clear jingle of the metal broke the solemn stillness. Then once more the people stirred, and the soft sound of their simultaneous motion was like a mighty sigh breathed up from the secret vaults and the deep foundations of the ancient church; again the pedal note of the organ boomed through the nave and aisles, and again the thousands of human voices took up the strain of song.

The Wanderer glanced about him, measuring the distance he must traverse to reach the monument of the Danish astronomer and confronting it with the short time which now remained before the end of the Mass. He saw that in such a throng he would have no chance of gaining the position he wished to occupy in less than half an hour, and he had not but a scant ten minutes at his disposal. He gave up the attempt therefore, determining that when the celebration should be over he would move forward with the crowd, trusting to his superior stature and energy to keep him within sight of the woman he sought, until both he and she could meet, either just within or just without the narrow entrance of the church.

Very soon the moment of action came. The singing died away, the benediction was given, the second Gospel was read, the priest and the people repeated the Bohemian prayers, and all was over. The countless heads began to move onward, the shuffling of innumerable feet sent heavy, tuneless echoes through vaulted space, broken every moment by the sharp, painful cough of a suffering child whom no one could see in the multitude, or by the dull thud of some heavy foot striking against the wooden seats in the press. The Wanderer moved forward with the rest. Reaching the entrance of the pew where she had sat he was kept back during a few seconds by the half dozen men and women who were forcing their way out of it before him. But at the farthest end, a figure clothed in black was still kneeling. A moment more and he might enter the pew and be at her side. One of the other women dropped something before she was out of the narrow space, and stooped, fumbling and searching in the darkness. At the minute, the slight, girlish figure rose swiftly and passed like a shadow before the heavy marble monument. The Wanderer saw that the pew was open at the other end, and without heeding the woman who stood in his way, he sprang upon the low seat, passed her, stepped to the floor upon the other side and was out in the aisle in a moment. Many persons had already left the church and the space was comparatively free.

She was before him, gliding quickly toward the door. Ere he could reach her, he saw her touch the thick ice which filled the marble basin, cross herself hurriedly and pass out. But he had seen her face again, and he knew that he was not mistaken. The thin, waxen features were as those of the dead, but they were hers, nevertheless. In an instant he could be by her side. But again his progress was momentarily impeded by a number of persons who were entering the building hastily to attend the next Mass. Scarcely ten seconds later he was out in the narrow and dismal passage which winds between the north side of the Teyn Kirche and the buildings behind the Kinsky Palace. The vast buttresses and towers cast deep shadows below them, and the blackened houses opposite absorb what remains of the uncertain winter's daylight. To the left of the church a low arch spans the lane, affording a covered communication between the north aisle and the sacristy. To the right the open space is somewhat broader, and three dark archways give access to as many passages, leading in radiating directions and under the old houses to the streets beyond.

The Wanderer stood upon the steps, beneath the rich stone carvings which set forth the Crucifixion over the door of the church, and his quick eyes scanned everything within sight. To the left, no figure resembling the one he sought was to be seen, but on the right, he fancied that among a score of persons now rapidly dispersing he could distinguish just within one of the archways a moving shadow, black against the blackness. In an instant he had crossed the way and was hurrying through the gloom. Already far before him, but visible and, as he believed, unmistakable, the shade was speeding onward, light as mist, noiseless as thought, but yet clearly to be seen and followed. He cried aloud, as he ran,

'Beatrice! Beatrice!'

His strong voice echoed along the dank walls and out into the court beyond. It was intensely cold, and the still air carried the sound clearly to the distance. She must have heard him, she must have known his voice, but as she crossed the open place, and the grey light fell upon her, he could see that she did not raise her bent head nor slacken her speed.

He ran on, sure of overtaking her in the passage she had now entered, for she seemed to be only walking, while he was pursuing her at a headlong pace. But in the narrow tunnel, when he reached it, she was not, though at the farther end he imagined that the fold of a black garment was just disappearing. He emerged into the street, in which he could now see in both directions to a distance of fifty yards or more. He was alone. The rusty iron shutters of the little shops were all barred and fastened, and every door within the range of his vision was closed. He stood still in surprise and listened. There was no sound to be heard, not the grating of a lock, nor the tinkling of a bell, nor the fall of a footstep.

He did not pause long, for he made up his mind as to what he should do in the flash of a moment's intuition. It was physically impossible that she should have disappeared into any one of the houses which had their entrances within the dark tunnel he had just traversed. Apart from the presumptive impossibility of her being lodged in such a quarter, there was the self-evident fact that he must have heard the door opened and closed. Secondly, she could not have turned to the right, for in that direction the street was straight and without any lateral exit, so that he must have seen her. Therefore she must have gone to the left, since on that side there was a narrow alley leading out of the lane, at some distance from the point where he was now standing – too far, indeed, for her to have reached it unnoticed, unless, as was possible, he had been greatly deceived in the distance which had lately separated her from him.

Without further hesitation, he turned to the left. He found no one in the way, for it was not yet noon, and at that hour the people were either at their prayers or at their Sunday morning's potations, and the place was as deserted as a disused cemetery. Still he hastened onward, never pausing for breath, till he found himself all at once in the great Ring. He knew the city well, but in his race he had bestowed no attention upon the familiar windings and turnings, thinking only of overtaking the fleeting vision, no matter how, no matter where. Now, on a sudden, the great, irregular square opened before him, flanked on the one side by the fantastic spires of the Teyn Church, and the blackened front of the huge Kinsky Palace, on the other by the half-modern Town Hall with its ancient tower, its beautiful porch, and the graceful oriel which forms the apse of the chapel in the second storey.

One of the city watchmen, muffled in his military overcoat, and conspicuous by the great bunch of dark feathers that drooped from his black hat, was standing idly at the corner from which the Wanderer emerged. The latter thought of inquiring whether the man had seen a lady pass, but the fellow's vacant stare convinced him that no questioning would elicit a satisfactory answer. Moreover, as he looked across the square he caught sight of a retreating figure dressed in black, already at such a distance as to make positive recognition impossible. In his haste he found no time to convince himself that no living woman could have thus outrun him, and he instantly resumed his pursuit, gaining rapidly upon her he was following. But it is not an easy matter to overtake even a woman, when she has an advantage of a couple of hundred yards, and when the race is a short one. He passed the ancient astronomical clock, just as the little bell was striking the third quarter after eleven, but he did not raise his head to watch the sad-faced apostles as they presented their stiff figures in succession at the two square windows. When the blackened cock under the small Gothic arch above flapped his wooden wings and uttered his melancholy crow, the Wanderer was already at the corner of the little Ring, and he could see the object of his pursuit disappearing before him into the Karlsgasse. He noticed uneasily that the resemblance between the woman he was following and the object of his loving search seemed now to diminish, as in a bad dream, as the distance between himself and her decreased. But he held resolutely on, nearing her at every step, round a sharp corner to the right, then to the left, to the right again, and once more in the opposite direction, always, as he knew, approaching the old stone bridge. He was not a dozen paces behind her as she turned quickly a third time to the right, round the wall of the ancient house which faces the little square over against the enormous buildings comprising the Clementine Jesuit monastery and the astronomical observatory. As he sprang past the corner he saw the heavy door just closing and heard the sharp resounding clang of its iron fastening. The lady had disappeared, and he felt sure that she had gone through that entrance.

He knew the house well, for it is distinguished from all others in Prague, both by its shape and its oddly ornamented, unnaturally narrow front. It is built in the figure of an irregular triangle, the blunt apex of one angle facing the little square, the sides being erected on the one hand along the Karlsgasse and on the other upon a narrow alley which leads away towards the Jews' quarter. Overhanging passages are built out over this dim lane, as though to facilitate the interior communications of the dwelling, and in the shadow beneath them there is a small door studded with iron nails which is invariably shut. The main entrance takes in all the scant breadth of the truncated angle which looks towards the monastery. Immediately over it is a great window, above that another, and, highest of all, under the pointed gable, a round and unglazed aperture, within which there is inky darkness. The windows of the first and second storeys are flanked by huge figures of saints, standing forth in strangely contorted attitudes, black with the dust of ages, black as all old Prague is black, with the smoke of the brown Bohemian coal, with the dark and unctuous mists of many autumns, with the cruel, petrifying frosts of ten score winters.

He who knew the cities of men as few have known them, knew also this house. Many a time had he paused before it by day and by night, wondering who lived within its massive, irregular walls, behind those uncouth, barbarously sculptured saints who kept their interminable watch high up by the lozenged windows. He would know now. Since she whom he sought had entered, he would enter too; and in some corner of that dwelling which had long possessed a mysterious attraction for his eyes, he would find at last that being who held power over his heart, that Beatrice whom he had learned to think of as dead, while still believing that somewhere she must be yet alive, that dear lady whom, dead or living, he loved beyond all others, with a great love, passing words.

Chapter 2

The Wanderer stood still before the door. In the freezing air, his quick-drawn breath made fantastic wreaths of mist, white and full of odd shapes as he watched the tiny clouds curling quickly into each other before the blackened oak. Then he laid his hand boldly upon the chain of the bell. He expected to hear the harsh jingling of cracked metal, but he was surprised by the silvery clearness and musical quality of the ringing tones which reached his ear. He was pleased, and unconsciously took the pleasant infusion for a favourable omen. The heavy door swung back almost immediately, and he was confronted by a tall porter in dark green cloth and gold lacings, whose imposing appearance was made still more striking by the magnificent fair beard which flowed down almost to his waist. The man lifted his heavy cocked hat and held it low at his side as he drew back to let the visitor enter. The latter had not expected to be admitted thus without question, and paused under the bright light which illuminated the arched entrance, intending to make some inquiry of the porter. But the latter seemed to expect nothing of the sort. He carefully closed the door, and then, bearing his hat in one hand and his gold-headed staff in the other, he proceeded gravely to the other end of the vaulted porch, opened a great glazed door and held it back for the visitor to pass.

The Wanderer recognised that the farther he was allowed to penetrate unhindered into the interior of the house, the nearer he should be to the object of his search. He did not know where he was, nor what he might find. For all that he knew, he might be in a club, in a great banking-house, or in some semi-public institution of the nature of a library, an academy or a conservatory of music. There are many such establishments in Prague, though he was not acquainted with any in which the internal arrangements so closely resembled those of a luxurious private residence. But there was no time for hesitation, and he ascended the broad staircase with a firm step, glancing at the rich tapestries which covered the walls, at the polished surface of the marble steps on either side of the heavy carpet, and at the elaborate and beautiful iron-work of the hand-rail. As he mounted higher, he heard the quick rapping of an electric signal above him, and he understood that the porter had announced his coming. Reaching the landing, he was met by a servant in black, as correct at all points as the porter himself, and who bowed low as he held back the thick curtain which hung before the entrance. Without a word the man followed the visitor into a high room of irregular shape, which served as a vestibule, and stood waiting to receive the guest's furs, should it please him to lay them aside. To pause now, and to enter into an explanation with a servant, would have been to reject an opportunity which might never return. In such an establishment, he was sure of finding himself before long in the presence of some more or less intelligent person of his own class, of whom he could make such inquiries as might enlighten him, and to whom he could present such excuses for his intrusion as might seem most fitting in so difficult a case. He let his sables fall into the hands of the servant and followed the latter along a short passage.

The man introduced him into a spacious hall and closed the door, leaving him to his own reflections. The place was very wide and high and without windows, but the broad daylight descended abundantly from above through the glazed roof and illuminated every corner. He would have taken the room for a conservatory, for it contained a forest of tropical trees and plants, and whole gardens of rare southern flowers. Tall letonias, date palms, mimosas and rubber trees of many varieties stretched their fantastic spikes and heavy leaves half-way up to the crystal ceiling; giant ferns swept the polished marble floor with their soft embroideries and dark green laces; Indian creepers, full of bright blossoms, made screens and curtains of their intertwining foliage; orchids of every hue and of every exotic species bloomed in thick banks along the walls. Flowers less rare, violets and lilies of the valley, closely set and luxuriant, grew in beds edged with moss around the roots of the larger plants and in many open spaces. The air was very soft and warm, moist and full of heavy odours as the still atmosphere of an island in southern seas, and the silence was broken only by the light plash of softly-falling water.

Having advanced a few steps from the door, the Wanderer stood still and waited, supposing that the owner of the dwelling would be made aware of a visitor's presence and would soon appear. But no one came. Then a gentle voice spoke from amidst the verdure, apparently from no great distance.

'I am here,' it said.

He moved forward amidst the ferns and the tall plants, until he found himself on the farther side of a thick network of creepers. Then he paused, for he was in the presence of a woman, of her who dwelt among the flowers. She was sitting before him, motionless and upright in a high, carved chair, and so placed that the pointed leaves of the palm which rose above her cast sharp, star-shaped shadows over the broad folds of her white dress. One hand, as white, as cold, as heavily perfect as the sculpture of a Praxiteles or a Phidias, rested with drooping fingers on the arm of the chair. The other pressed the pages of a great book which lay open on the lady's knee. Her face was turned toward the visitor, and her eyes examined his face; calmly and with no surprise in them, but not without a look of interest. Their expression was at once so unusual, so disquieting, and yet so inexplicably attractive as to fascinate the Wanderer's gaze. He did not remember that he had ever seen a pair of eyes of distinctly different colours, the one of a clear, cold grey, the other of a deep, warm brown, so dark as to seem almost black, and he would not have believed that nature could so far transgress the canons of her own art and yet preserve the appearance of beauty. For the lady was beautiful, from the diadem of her red gold hair to the proud curve of her fresh young lips; from her broad, pale forehead, prominent and boldly modelled at the angles of the brows, to the strong mouldings of the well-balanced chin, which gave evidence of strength and resolution wherewith to carry out the promise of the high aquiline features and of the wide and sensitive nostrils.

'Madame,' said the Wanderer, bending his head courteously and advancing another step, 'I can neither frame excuses for having entered your house unbidden, nor hope to obtain indulgence for my intrusion, unless you are willing in the first place to hear my short story. May I expect so much kindness?'

He paused, and the lady looked at him fixedly and curiously. Without taking her eyes from his face, and without speaking, she closed the book she had held on her knee, and laid it beside her upon a low table. The Wanderer did not avoid her gaze, for he had nothing to conceal, nor any sense of timidity. He was an intruder upon the privacy of one whom he did not know, but he was ready to explain his presence and to make such amends as courtesy required, if he had given offence.

The heavy odours of the flowers filled his nostrils with an unknown, luxurious delight, as he stood there, gazing into the lady's eyes; he fancied that a gentle breath of perfumed air was blowing softly over his hair and face out of the motionless palms, and the faint plashing of the hidden fountain was like an exquisite melody in his ears. It was good to be in such a place, to look on such a woman, to breathe such odours, and to hear such tuneful music. A dreamlike, half-mysterious satisfaction of the senses dulled the keen self-knowledge of body and soul for one short moment. In the stormy play of his troubled life there was a brief interlude of peace. He tasted the fruit of the lotus, his lips were moistened in the sweet waters of forgetfulness.

The lady spoke at last, and the spell left him, not broken, as by a sudden shock, but losing its strong power by quick degrees until it was wholly gone.

'I will answer your question by another,' said the lady. 'Let your reply be the plain truth. It will be better so.'

'Ask what you will. I have nothing to conceal.'

'Do you know who and what I am? Do you come here out of curiosity, in the vain hope of knowing me, having heard of me from others?'

'Assuredly not.' A faint flush rose in the man's pale and noble face. 'You have my word,' he said, in the tone of one who is sure of being believed, 'that I have never, to my knowledge, heard of your existence, that I am ignorant even of your name – forgive my ignorance – and that I entered this house, not knowing whose it might be, seeking and following after one for whom I have searched the world, one dearly loved, long lost, long sought.'

'It is enough. Be seated. I am Unorna.'

'Unorna?' repeated the Wanderer, with an unconscious question in his voice, as though the name recalled some half-forgotten association.

'Unorna – yes. I have another name,' she added, with a shade of bitterness, 'but it is hardly mine. Tell me your story. You loved – you lost – you seek – so much I know. What else?'

The Wanderer sighed.

'You have told in those few words the story of my life – the unfinished story. A wanderer I was born, a wanderer I am, a wanderer I must ever be, until at last I find her whom I seek. I knew her in a strange land, far from my birthplace, in a city where I was known but to a few, and I loved her. She loved me, too, and that against her father's will. He would not have his daughter wed with one not of her race; for he himself had taken a wife among strangers, and while she was yet alive he had repented of what he had done. But I would have overcome his reasons and his arguments – she and I could have overcome them together, for he did not hate me, he bore me no ill-will. We were almost friends when I last took his hand. Then the hour of destiny came upon me. The air of that city was treacherous and deadly. I had left her with her father, and my heart was full of many things, and of words both spoken and unuttered. I lingered upon an ancient bridge that spanned the river, and the sun went down. Then the evil fever of the south laid hold upon me and poisoned the blood in my veins, and stole the consciousness from my understanding. Weeks passed away, and memory returned, with the strength to speak. I learned that she I loved and her father were gone, and none knew whither. I rose and left the accursed city, being at that time scarce able to stand upright upon my feet. Finding no trace of those I sought, I journeyed to their own country, for I knew where her father held his lands. I had been ill many weeks and much time had passed, from the day on which I had left her, until I was able to move from my bed. When I reached the gates of her home, I was told that all had been lately sold, and that others now dwelt within the walls. I inquired of those new owners of the land, but neither they or any of all those whom I questioned could tell me whither I should direct my search. The father was a strange man, loving travel and change and movement, restless and unsatisfied with the world, rich and free to make his own caprice his guide through life; reticent he was, moreover, and thoughtful, not given to speaking out his intentions. Those who administered his affairs in his absence were honourable men, bound by his especial injunction not to reveal his ever-varying plans. Many times, in my ceaseless search, I met persons who had lately seen him and his daughter and spoken with them. I was ever on their track, from hemisphere to hemisphere, from continent to continent, from country to country, from city to city, often believing myself close upon them, often learning suddenly that an ocean lay between them and me. Was he eluding me, purposely, resolutely, or was he unconscious of my desperate pursuit, being served by chance alone and by his own restless temper? I do not know. At last, someone told me that she was dead, speaking thoughtlessly, not knowing that I loved her. He who told me had heard the news from another, who had received it on hearsay from a third. None knew in what place her spirit had parted; none knew by what manner of sickness she had died. Since then, I have heard others say that she is not dead, that they have heard in their turn from others that she yet lives. An hour ago, I knew not what to think. Today, I saw her in a crowded church. I heard her voice, though I could not reach her in the throng, struggle how I would. I followed her in haste, I lost her at one turning, I saw her before me at the next. At last a figure, clothed as she had been clothed, entered your house. Whether it was she I know not certainly, but I do know that in the church I saw her. She cannot be within your dwelling without your knowledge; if she be here – then I have found her, my journey is ended, my wanderings have led me home at last. If she be not here, if I have been mistaken, I entreat you to let me set eyes on that other whom I mistook for her, to forgive then my mannerless intrusion and to let me go.'

Unorna had listened with half-closed eyes, but with unfaltering attention, watching the speaker's face from beneath her drooping lids, making no effort to read his thoughts, but weighing his words and impressing every detail of his story upon her mind. When he had done there was silence for a time, broken only by the plash and ripple of the falling water.

'She is not here,' said Unorna at last. 'You shall see for yourself. There is indeed in this house a young girl to whom I am deeply attached, who has grown up at my side and has always lived under my roof. She is very pale and dark, and is dressed always in black.'

'Like her I saw.'

'You shall see her again. I will send for her.' Unorna pressed an ivory key in the silver ball which lay beside her, attached to a thick cord of white silk. 'Ask Sletchna Axenia to come to me,' she said to the servant who opened the door in the distance, out of sight behind the forest of plants.

Amid less unusual surroundings the Wanderer would have rejected with contempt the last remnants of his belief in the identity of Unorna's companion, with Beatrice. But, being where he was, he felt unable to decide between the possible and the impossible, between what he might reasonably expect and what lay beyond the bounds of reason itself. The air he breathed was so loaded with rich exotic perfumes, the woman before him was so little like other women, her strangely mismatched eyes had for his own such a disquieting attraction, all that he saw and felt and heard was so far removed from the commonplaces of daily life as to make him feel that he himself was becoming a part of some other person's existence, that he was being gradually drawn away from his identity, and was losing the power of thinking his own thoughts. He reasoned as the shadows reason in dreamland, the boundaries of common probability receded to an immeasurable distance, and he almost ceased to know where reality ended and where imagination took up the sequence of events.

Who was this woman, who called herself Unorna? He tried to consider the question, and to bring his intelligence to bear upon it. Was she a great lady of Prague, rich, capricious, creating a mysterious existence for herself, merely for her own good pleasure? Her language, her voice, her evident refinement gave colour to the idea, which was in itself attractive to a man who had long ceased to expect novelty in this working-day world. He glanced at her face, musing and wondering, inhaling the sweet, intoxicating odours of the flowers and listening to the tinkling of the hidden fountain. Her eyes were gazing into his, and again, as if by magic, the curtain of life's stage was drawn together in misty folds, shutting out the past, the present, and the future, the fact, the doubt, and the hope, in an interval of perfect peace.

He was roused by the sound of a light footfall upon the marble pavement. Unorna's eyes were turned from his, and with something like a movement of surprise he himself looked towards the new-comer. A young girl was standing under the shadow of a great letonia at a short distance from him. She was very pale indeed, but not with that death-like, waxen pallor which had chilled him when he had looked upon that other face. There was a faint resemblance in the small, aquiline features, the dress was black, and the figure of the girl before him was assuredly neither much taller nor much shorter than that of the woman he loved and sought. But the likeness went no further, and he knew that he had been utterly mistaken.

Unorna exchanged a few indifferent words with Axenia and dismissed her.

'You have seen,' she said, when the young girl was gone. 'Was it she who entered the house just now?'

'Yes. I was misled by a mere resemblance. Forgive me for my importunity – let me thank you most sincerely for your great kindness.' He rose as he spoke.

'Do not go,' said Unorna, looking at him earnestly.

He stood still, silent, as though his attitude should explain itself, and yet expecting that she would say something further. He felt that her eyes were upon him, and he raised his own to meet the look frankly, as was his wont. For the first time since he had entered her presence he felt that there was more than a mere disquieting attraction in her steady gaze; there was a strong, resistless fascination, from which he had no power to withdraw himself. Almost unconsciously he resumed his seat, still looking at her, while telling himself with a severe effort that he would look but one instant longer and then turn away. Ten seconds passed, twenty, half a minute, in total silence. He was confused, disturbed, and yet wholly unable to shut out her penetrating glance. His fast ebbing consciousness barely allowed him to wonder whether he was weakened by the strong emotions he had felt in the church, or by the first beginning of some unknown and unexpected malady. He was utterly weak and unstrung. He could neither rise from his seat, nor lift his hand, nor close the lids of his eyes. It was as though an irresistible force were drawing him into the depths of a fathomless whirlpool, down, down, by its endless giddy spirals, robbing him of a portion of his consciousness at every gyration, so that he left behind him at every instant something of his individuality, something of the central faculty of self-recognition. He felt no pain, but he did not feel that inexpressible delight of peace which already twice had descended upon him. He experienced a rapid diminution of all perception, of all feeling, of all intelligence. Thought, and the memory of thought, ebbed from his brain and left it vacant, as the waters of a lock subside when the gates are opened, leaving emptiness in their place.

Unorna's eyes turned from him, and she raised her hand a moment, letting it fall again upon her knee. Instantly the strong man was restored to himself; his weakness vanished, his sight was clear, his intelligence was awake. Instantly the certainty flashed upon him that Unorna possessed the power of imposing the hypnotic sleep and had exercised that gift upon him, unexpectedly and against his will. He would have more willingly supposed that he had been the victim of a momentary physical faintness, for the idea of having been thus subjected to the influence of a woman, and of a woman whom he hardly knew, was repugnant to him, and had in it something humiliating to his pride, or at least to his vanity. But he could not escape the conviction forced upon him by the circumstances.

'Do not go far, for I may yet help you,' said Unorna, quietly. 'Let us talk of this matter and consult what is best to be done. Will you accept a woman's help?'

'Readily. But I cannot accept her will as mine, nor resign my consciousness into her keeping.'

'Not for the sake of seeing her whom you say you love?'

The Wanderer was silent, being yet undetermined how to act, and still unsteadied by what he had experienced. But he was able to reason, and he asked of his judgment what he should do, wondering what manner of woman Unorna might prove to be, and whether she was anything more than one of those who live and even enrich themselves by the exercise of the unusual faculties of powers nature has given them. He had seen many of that class, and he considered most of them to be but half fanatics, half charlatans, worshipping in themselves as something almost divine that which was but a physical power, or weakness, beyond their own limited comprehension. Though a whole school of wise and thoughtful men had already produced remarkable results and elicited astounding facts by sifting the truth through a fine web of closely logical experiment, it did not follow that either Unorna, or any other self-convinced, self-taught operator could do more than grope blindly towards the light, guided by intuition alone amongst the varied and misleading phenomena of hypnotism. The thought of accepting the help of one who was probably, like most of her kind, a deceiver of herself and therefore, and thereby, of others, was an affront to the dignity of his distress, a desecration of his love's sanctity, a frivolous invasion of love's holiest ground. But, on the other hand, he was stimulated to catch at the veriest shadows of possibility by the certainty that he was at last within the same city with her he loved, and he knew that hypnotic subjects are sometimes able to determine the abode of persons whom no one else can find. Tomorrow it might be too late. Even before today's sun had set Beatrice might be once more taken from him, snatched away to the ends of the earth by her father's ever-changing caprice. To lose a moment now might be to lose all.

He was tempted to yield, to resign his will into Unorna's hands, and his sight to her leading, to let her bid him sleep and see the truth. But then, with a sudden reaction of his individuality, he realised that he had another course, surer, simpler, more dignified. Beatrice was in Prague. It was little probable that she was permanently established in the city, and in all likelihood she and her father were lodged in one of the two or three great hotels. To be driven from the one to the other of these would be but an affair of minutes. Failing information from this source, there remained the registers of the Austrian police, whose vigilance takes note of every stranger's name and dwelling-place.

'I thank you,' he said. 'If all my inquiries fail, and if you will let me visit you once more today, I will then ask your help.'

'You are right,' Unorna answered.

Chapter 3

He had been deceived in supposing that he must inevitably find the names of those he sought upon the ordinary registers which chronicle the arrival and departure of travellers. He lost no time, he spared no effort, driving from place to place as fast as two sturdy Hungarian horses could take him, hurrying from one office to another, and again and again searching endless pages and columns which seemed full of all the names of earth, but in which he never found the one of all others which he longed to read. The gloom in the narrow streets was already deepening, though it was scarcely two hours after midday, and the heavy air had begun to thicken with a cold grey haze, even in the broad, straight Przikopy, the wide thoroughfare which has taken the place and name of the moat before the ancient fortifications, so that distant objects and figures lost the distinctness of their outlines. Winter in Prague is but one long, melancholy dream, broken sometimes at noon by an hour of sunshine, by an intermittent visitation of reality, by the shock and glare of a little broad daylight. The morning is not morning, the evening is not evening; as in the land of the Lotus, it is ever afternoon, grey, soft, misty, sad, save when the sun, being at his meridian height, pierces the dim streets and sweeps the open places with low, slanting waves of pale brightness. And yet these same dusky streets are thronged with a moving multitude, are traversed ever by ceaseless streams of men and women, flowing onward, silently, swiftly, eagerly. The very beggars do not speak above a whisper, the very dogs are dumb. The stillness of all voices leaves nothing for the perception of the hearing save the dull thread of many thousand feet and the rough rattle of an occasional carriage. Rarely, the harsh tones of a peasant, or the clear voices of a knot of strangers, unused to such oppressive silence, startle the ear, causing hundreds of eager, half-suspicious, half-wondering eyes to turn in the direction of the sound.

And yet Prague is a great city, the capital of the Bohemian Crown-land, the centre of a not unimportant nation, the focus in which are concentrated the hottest, if not the brightest, rays from the fire of regeneration kindled within the last half century by the Slavonic race. There is an ardent furnace of life hidden beneath the crust of ashes: there is a wonderful language behind that national silence.

The Wanderer stood in deep thought under the shadow of the ancient Powder Tower. Haste had no further object now, since he had made every inquiry within his power, and it was a relief to feel the pavement beneath his feet and to breathe the misty frozen air after having been so long in the closeness of his carriage. He hesitated as to what he should do, unwilling to return to Unorna and acknowledge himself vanquished, yet finding it hard to resist his desire to try every means, no matter how little reasonable, how evidently useless, how puerile and revolting to his sounder sense. The street behind him led directly towards Unorna's house. Had he found himself in a more remote quarter, he might have come to another and a wiser conclusion. Being so near to the house of which he was thinking, he yielded to the temptation. Having reached this stage of resolution, his mind began to recapitulate the events of the day, and he suddenly felt a strong wish to revisit the church, to stand in the place where Beatrice had stood, to touch in the marble basin beside the door the thick ice which her fingers had touched so lately, to traverse again the dark passages through which he had pursued her. To accomplish his purpose he need only turn aside a few steps from the path he was now following. He left the street almost immediately, passing under a low arched way that opened on the right-hand side, and a moment later he was within the walls of the Teyn Kirche.

The vast building was less gloomy than it had been in the morning. It was not yet the hour of vespers, the funeral torches had been extinguished, as well as most of the lights upon the high altar, there were not a dozen persons in the church, and high up beneath the roof broad shafts of softened sunshine, floating above the mists of the city without, streamed through the narrow lancet windows and were diffused in the great gloom below. The Wanderer went to the monument of Brahe and sat down in the corner of the blackened pew. His hands trembled a little as he clasped them upon his knee, and his head sank slowly towards his breast.

He thought of all that might have been if he had risked everything that morning. He could have used his strength to force a way for himself through the press, he could have thrust the multitude to the right and left, and he could have reached her side. Perhaps he had been weak, indolent, timid, and he accused himself of his own failure. But then, again, he seemed to see about him the closely packed crowd, the sea of faces, the thick, black mass of humanity, and he knew the tremendous power that lay in the inert, passive resistance of a vast gathering such as had been present. Had it been anywhere else, in a street, in a theatre, anywhere except in a church, all would have been well. It had not been his fault, for he knew, when he thought of it calmly, that the strength of his body would have been but as a breath of air against the silent, motionless, and immovable barrier presented by a thousand men, standing shoulder to shoulder against him. He could have done nothing. Once again his fate had defeated him at the moment of success.

He was aware that someone was standing very near to him. He looked up and saw a very short, grey-bearded man engaged in a minute examination of the dark red marble face on the astronomer's tomb. The man's head, covered with closely-cropped grey hair, was half buried between his high, broad shoulders, in an immense collar of fur, but the shape of the skull was so singular as to distinguish its possessor, when hatless, from all other men. The cranium was abnormally shaped, reaching a great elevation at the summit, then sinking suddenly, then spreading forward to an enormous development at the temple just visible as he was then standing, and at the same time forming unusual protuberances behind the large and pointed ears. No one who knew the man could mistake his head, when even the least portion of it could be seen. The Wanderer recognised him at once.

As though he were conscious of being watched, the little man turned sharply, exhibiting his wrinkled forehead, broad at the brows, narrow and high in the middle, showing, too, a Socratic nose half buried in the midst of the grey hair which grew as high as the prominent cheek bones, and suggesting the idea of a polished ivory ball lying in a nest of greyish wool. Indeed all that was visible of the face above the beard might have been carved out of old ivory, so far as the hue and quality of the surface were concerned; and if it had been necessary to sculpture a portrait of the man, no material could have been chosen more fitted to reproduce faithfully the deep cutting of the features, to render the close network of the wrinkles which covered them like the shadings of a line engraving, and at the same time to give the whole that appearance of hardness and smoothness which was peculiar to the clear, tough skin. The only positive colour which relieved the half tints of the face lay in the sharp bright eyes which gleamed beneath the busy eyebrows like tiny patches of vivid blue sky seen through little rifts in a curtain of cloud. All expression, all mobility, all life were concentrated in those two points.

The Wanderer rose to his feet.

'Keyork Arabian!' he exclaimed, extending his hand. The little man immediately gripped it in his small fingers, which, soft and delicately made as they were, possessed a strength hardly to have been expected either from their shape, or from the small proportions of him to whom they belonged.

'Still wandering?' asked the little man, with a slightly sarcastic intonation. He spoke in a deep, caressing bass, not loud, but rich in quality and free from that jarring harshness which often belongs to very manly voices. A musician would have discovered that the pitch was that of those Russian choristers whose deep throats yield organ tones, a full octave below the compass of ordinary singers in other lands.

'You must have wandered, too, since we last met,' replied the taller man.

'I never wander,' said Keyork. 'When a man knows what he wants, knows where it is to be found, and goes thither to take it, he is not wandering. Moreover, I have no thought of removing myself or my goods from Prague. I live here. It is a city for old men. It is saturnine. The foundations of its houses rest on the silurian formation, which is more than can be said for any other capital, as far as I know.'

'Is that an advantage?' inquired the Wanderer.

'To my mind. I would say to my son, if I had one – my thanks to a blind but intelligent destiny for preserving me from such a calamity! – I would say to him, "Spend thy youth among flowers in the land where they are brightest and sweetest; pass thy manhood in all lands where man strives with man, thought for thought, blow for blow; choose for thine old age that spot in which, all things being old, thou mayest for the longest time consider thyself young in comparison with thy surroundings." A man can never feel old if he contemplates and meditates upon those things only which are immeasurably older than himself. Moreover the imperishable can preserve the perishable.'

'It was not your habit to talk of death when we were together.'

'I have found it interesting of late years. The subject is connected with one of my inventions. Did you ever embalm a body? No? I could tell you something singular about the newest process.'

'What is the connection?'

'I am embalming myself, body and mind. It is but an experiment, and unless it succeeds it must be the last. Embalming, as it is now understood, means substituting one thing for another. Very good. I am trying to purge from my mind its old circulating medium; the new thoughts must all be selected from a class which admits of no decay. Nothing could be simpler.'

'It seems to me that nothing could be more vague.'

'You were not formerly so slow to understand me,' said the strange little man with some impatience.

'Do you know a lady of Prague who calls herself Unorna?' the Wanderer asked, paying no attention to his friend's last remark.

'I do. What of her?' Keyork Arabian glanced keenly at his companion.

'What is she? She has an odd name.'

'As for her name, it is easily accounted for. She was born on the twenty-ninth day of February, the year of her birth being bisextile. Unor means February, Unorna, derivative adjective, "belonging to February". Someone gave her the name to commemorate the circumstance.'

'Her parents, I suppose.'

'Most probably – whoever they may have been.'

'And what is she?' the Wanderer asked.

'She calls herself a witch,' answered Keyork with considerable scorn. 'I do not know what she is, or what to call her – a sensitive, an hysterical subject, a medium, a witch – a fool, if you like, or a charlatan if you prefer the term. Beautiful she is, at least, whatever else she may not be.'

'Yes, she is beautiful.'

'So you have seen her, have you?' The little man again looked sharply up at his tall companion. 'You have had a consultation – '

'Does she give consultations? Is she a professional seer?' The Wanderer asked the question in a tone of surprise. 'Do you mean that she maintains an establishment upon such a scale out of the proceeds of fortune-telling?'

'I do not mean anything of the sort. Fortune-telling is excellent! Very good!' Keyork's bright eyes flashed with amusement. 'What are you doing here – I mean in this church?' He put the question suddenly.

'Pursuing – an idea, if you please to call it so.'

'Not knowing what you mean I must please to call your meaning by your own name for it. It is your nature to be enigmatic. Shall we go out? If I stay here much longer I shall be petrified instead of embalmed. I shall turn into dirty old red marble like Tycho's effigy there, an awful warning to future philosophers, and an example for the edification of the faithful who worship here.'

They walked towards the door, and the contrast between the appearance of the two brought the ghost of a smile to the thin lips of the pale sacristan, who was occupied in renewing the tapers upon one of the side altars. Keyork Arabian might have stood for the portrait of the gnome-king. His high and pointed head, his immense beard, his stunted but powerful and thickset limbs, his short, sturdy strides, the fiery, half-humorous, half-threatening twinkle of his bright eyes gave him all the appearance of a fantastic figure from a fairy tale, and the diminutive height of his compact frame set off the noble stature and graceful motion of his companion.

'So you were pursuing an idea,' said the little man as they emerged into the narrow street. 'Now ideas may be divided variously into classes, as, for instance, ideas which are good, bad, or indifferent. Or you may contrast the idea of Plato with ideas anything but platonic – take it as you please. Then there is my idea, which is in itself, good, interesting, and worthy of the embalming process; and there is your idea, which I am human enough to consider altogether bad, worthless, and frivolous, for the plain and substantial reason that it is not mine. Perhaps that is the best division of all. Thine eye is necessarily, fatally, irrevocably evil, because mine is essentially, predestinately, and unchangeably good. If I secretly adopt your idea, I openly assert that it was never yours at all, but mine from the beginning, by the prerogatives of greater age, wider experience, and immeasurably superior wisdom. If you have an idea upon any subject, I will utterly annihilate it to my own most profound satisfaction; if you have none concerning any special point, I will force you to accept mine, as mine, or to die the intellectual death. That is the general theory of the idea.'

'And what does it prove?' inquired the Wanderer.

'If you knew anything,' answered Keyork, with twinkling eyes, 'you would know that a theory is not a demonstration, but an explanation. But, by the hypothesis, since you are not I, you can know nothing certainly. Now my theory explains many things, and, among others, the adamantine, imperishable, impenetrable nature of the substance vanity upon which the showman, Nature, projects in fast fading colours the unsubstantial images of men. Why do you drag me through this dismal passage?'

'I passed through it this morning and missed my way.'

'In pursuit of the idea, of course. That was to be expected. Prague is constructed on the same principle as the human brain, full of winding ways, dark lanes, and gloomy arches, all of which may lead somewhere, or may not. Its topography continually misleads its inhabitants as the convolutions of the brain mislead the thoughts that dwell there, sometimes bringing them out at last, after a patient search for daylight, upon a fine broad street where the newest fashions in thought are exposed for sale in brightly illuminated shop windows and showcases; conducting them sometimes to the dark, unsavoury court where the miserable self drags out its unhealthy existence in the single room of its hired earthly lodging.'

'The self which you propose to preserve from corruption,' observed the tall man, who was carefully examining every foot of the walls between which he was passing with his companion, 'since you think so poorly of the lodger and the lodging, I wonder that you should be anxious to prolong the sufferings of the one and his lease of the other.'

'It is all I have,' answered Keyork Arabian. 'Did you think of that?'

'That circumstance may serve as an excuse, but it does not constitute a reason.'

'Not a reason! Is the most abject poverty a reason for throwing away the daily crust? My self is all I have. Shall I let it perish when an effort may preserve it from destruction? On the one side of the line stands Keyork Arabian, on the other floats the shadow of an annihilation, which threatens to swallow up Keyork's self, while leaving all that he has borrowed of life to be enjoyed or wasted by others. Could Keyork be expected to hesitate, so long as he may hope to remain in possession of that inestimable treasure, his own individuality, which is his only means for enjoying all that is not his, but borrowed?'

'So soon as you speak of enjoyment, argument ceases,' answered the Wanderer.

'You are wrong, as usual,' returned the other. 'It is the other way. Enjoyment is the universal solvent of all arguments. No reason can resist its mordant action. It will dissolve any philosophy not founded upon it and modelled out of its substance, as Aqua Regia will dissolve all metals, even to gold itself. Enjoyment? Enjoyment is the protest of reality against the tyranny of fiction.'

The little man stopped short in his walk, striking his heavy stick sharply upon the pavement and looking up at his companion, very much as a man of ordinary size looks up at the face of a colossal statue.

'Have wisdom and study led you no farther than that conclusion?'

Keyork's eyes brightened suddenly, and a peal of laughter, deep and rich, broke from his sturdy breast and rolled long echoes through the dismal lane, musical as a hunting-song heard among great trees in winter. But his ivory features were not discomposed, though his white beard trembled and waved softly like a snowy veil blown about by the wind.

'If wisdom can teach how to prolong the lease, what study can be compared with that of which the results may beautify the dwelling? What more can any man do for himself than make himself happy? The very question is absurd. What are you trying to do for yourself at the present moment? Is it for the sake of improving the physical condition or of promoting the moral case of mankind at large that you are dragging me through the slums and byways and alleys of the gloomiest city on this side of eternal perdition? It is certainly not for my welfare that you are sacrificing yourself. You admit that you are pursuing an idea. Perhaps you are in search of some new and curious form of mildew, and when you have found it – or something else – you will name your discovery *Fungus Pragensis*, or *Cryptogamus minor Errantis* – 'the Wanderer's toadstool'. But I know you of old, my good friend. The idea you pursue is not an idea at all, but that specimen of the *genus homo* known as "woman", species "lady", variety "true love", vulgar designation "sweetheart".'

The Wanderer stared coldly at his companion.

'The vulgarity of the designation is indeed only equalled by that of your taste in selecting it,' he said slowly. Then he turned away, intending to leave Keyork standing where he was.

But the little man had already repented of his speech. He ran quickly to his friend's side and laid one hand upon his arm. The Wanderer paused and again looked down.

'Is it of any use to be offended with my speeches? Am I an acquaintance of yesterday? Do you imagine that it could ever be my intention to annoy you?' the questions were asked rapidly in tones of genuine anxiety.

'Indeed, I hardly know how I could suppose that. You have always been friendly – but I confess – your names for things are not – always – '

The Wanderer did not complete the sentence, but looked gravely at Keyork as though wishing to convey very clearly again what he had before expressed in words.

'If we were fellow-countrymen and had our native language in common, we should not so easily misunderstand one another,' replied the other. 'Come, forgive my lack of skill, and do not let us quarrel. Perhaps I can help you. You may know Prague well, but I know it better. Will you allow me to say that I know also whom it is you are seeking here?'

'Yes. You know. I have not changed since we last met, nor have circumstances favoured me.'

'Tell me – have you really seen this Unorna, and talked with her?'

'This morning.'

'And she could not help you?'

'I refused to accept her help, until I had done all that was in my own power to do.'

'You were rash. And have you now done all, and failed?'

'I have.'

'Then, if you will accept a humble suggestion from me, you will go back to her at once.'

'I know very little of her. I do not altogether trust her – '

'Trust! Powers of Eblis – or any other powers! Who talks of trust? Does the wise man trust himself? Never. Then how can he dare trust anyone else?'

'Your cynical philosophy again!' exclaimed the Wanderer.

'Philosophy? I am a mysosophist! All wisdom is vanity, and I hate it! Autology is my study, autosophy my ambition, autonomy my pride. I am the great Panegoist, the would-be Conservator of Self, the inspired prophet of the Universal I. I – I – I! My creed has but one word, and that word but one letter, that letter represents Unity, and Unity is Strength. I am I, one, indivisible, central! O I! Hail and live for ever!'

Again the little man's rich bass voice rang out in mellow laughter. A very faint smile appeared upon his companion's sad face.

'You are happy, Keyork,' he said. 'You must be, since you can laugh at yourself so honestly.'

'At myself? Vain man! I am laughing at you, and at everyone else, at everything except myself. Will you go to Unorna? You need not trust her any more than the natural infirmity of your judgment suggests.'

'Can you tell me nothing more of her? Do you know her well?'

'She does not offer her help to everyone. You would have done well to accept it in the first instance. You may not find her in the same humour again.'

'I had supposed from what you said of her that she made a profession of clairvoyance, or hypnotism, or mesmerism – whatever may be the right term nowadays.'

'It matters very little,' answered Keyork, gravely. 'I used to wonder at Adam's ingenuity in naming all living things, but I think he would have made but a poor figure in a tournament of modern terminologists. No. Unorna does not accept remuneration for her help when she vouchsafes to give it.'

'And yet I was introduced to her presence without even giving my name.'

'That is her fancy. She will see anyone who wishes to see her, beggar, gentleman, or prince. But she only answers such questions as she pleases to answer.'

'That is to say, inquiries for which she is already prepared with a reply,' suggested the Wanderer.

'See for yourself. At all events, she is a very interesting specimen. I have never known anyone like her.'

Keyork Arabian was silent, as though he were reflecting upon Unorna's character and peculiar gifts, before describing them to his friend. His ivory features softened almost imperceptibly, and his sharp blue eyes suddenly lost their light, as though they no longer saw the outer world. But the Wanderer cared for none of these things, and bestowed no attention upon his companion's face. He preferred the little man's silence to his wild talk, but he was determined, if possible, to extract some further information concerning Unorna, and before many seconds had elapsed he interrupted Keyork's meditations with a question.

'You tell me to see for myself,' he said. 'I would like to know what I am to expect. Will you not enlighten me?'

'What?' asked the other vaguely, as though roused from sleep.

'If I go to Unorna and ask a consultation of her, as though she were a common somnambulist, and if she deigns to place her powers at my disposal what sort of assistance shall I most probably get?'

They had been walking slowly forward, and Keyork again stopped, rapping the pavement with his iron-shod stick, and looking up from under his bushy, overhanging eyebrows.

'Of two things, one will happen,' he answered. 'Either she will herself fall into the abnormal state and will answer correctly any questions you put to her, or she will hypnotise you, and you will yourself see – what you wish to see.'

'I myself?'

'You yourself. The peculiarity of the woman is her duality, her double power. She can, by an act of volition, become hypnotic, clairvoyant – whatever you choose to call it. Or, if her visitor is at all sensitive, she can reverse the situation and play the part of the hypnotiser. I never heard of a like case.'

'After all, I do not see why it should not be so,' said the Wanderer thoughtfully. 'At all events, whatever she can do, is evidently done by hypnotism, and such extraordinary experiments have succeeded of late – '

'I did not say that there was nothing but hypnotism in her processes.'

'What then? Magic?' The Wanderer's lip curled scornfully.

'I do not know,' replied the little man, speaking slowly. 'Whatever her secret may be, she keeps it, even when speaking in sleep. This I can tell you. I suspect that there is some other being, or person, in that queer old house of hers whom she consults on grave occasions. At a loss for an answer to a difficult scientific question, I have known her to leave the room and to come back in the course of a few minutes with a reply which I am positive she could never have framed herself.'

'She may have consulted books,' suggested the Wanderer.

'I am an old man,' said Keyork Arabian suddenly. 'I am a very old man; there are not many books which I have not seen and partially read at one time or at another, and my memory is surprisingly good. I have excellent reasons for believing that her information is not got from anything that was ever written or printed.'

'May I ask of what general nature your questions were?' inquired the other, more interested than he had hitherto been in the conversation.

'They referred to the principles of embalmment.'

'Much has been written about that since the days of the Egyptians.'

'The Egyptians!' exclaimed Keyork with great scorn. 'They embalmed their dead after a fashion. Did you ever hear that they embalmed the living?' The little man's eyes shot fire.

'No, nor will I believe in any such outrageous impossibilities! If that is all, I have little faith in Unorna's mysterious counsellor.'

'The faith which removes mountains is generally gained by experience when it is gained at all, and the craving for explanation takes the place, in some minds, of a willingness to learn. It is not my business to find explanations, nor to raise my little self to your higher level, by standing upon this curbstone, in order to deliver a lecture in the popular form, upon matters that interest me. It is enough that I have found what I wanted. Go and do likewise. See for yourself. You have nothing to lose and everything to gain. You are unhappy, and unhappiness is dangerous, in rare cases fatal. If you tell me tomorrow that Unorna is a charlatan, you will be in no worse plight than today, nor will your opinion of her influence mine. If she helps you to find what you want – so much the better for you – how much the better, and how great the risk you run, are questions for your judgment.'

'I will go,' answered the Wanderer, after a moment's hesitation.

'Very good,' said Keyork Arabian. 'If you want to find me again, come to my lodging. Do you know the house of the Black Mother of God?'

'Yes – there is a legend about a Spanish picture of our Lady once preserved there – '

'Exactly, it takes its name from that black picture. It is on the corner of the Fruit Market, over against the window at which the Princess Windischgratz was shot. I live in the upper storey. Goodbye.'

'Goodbye.'

Chapter 4

After the Wanderer had left her, Unorna continued to hold in her hand the book she had again taken up, following the printed lines mechanically from left to right, from the top of the page to the foot. Having reached that point, however, she did not turn over the leaf. She was vaguely aware that she had not understood the sense of the words, and she returned to the place at which she had begun, trying to concentrate her attention upon the matter, moving her fresh lips to form the syllables, and bending her brows in the effort of understanding, so that a short, straight furrow appeared, like a sharp vertical cut extending from between the eyes to the midst of the broad forehead. One, two and three sentences she grasped and comprehended; then her thoughts wandered again, and the groups of letters passed meaningless before her sight. She was accustomed to directing her intelligence without any perceptible effort, and she was annoyed at being thus led away from her occupation, against her will and in spite of her determination. A third attempt showed her that it was useless to force herself any longer, and with a gesture and look of irritation she once more laid the volume upon the table at her side.

During a few minutes she sat motionless in her chair, her elbow leaning on the carved arm-piece, her chin supported upon the back of her half-closed hand, of which the heavy, perfect fingers were turned inwards, drooping in classic curves towards the lace about her throat. Her strangely mismatched eyes stared vacantly towards an imaginary horizon, not bounded by banks of flowers, nor obscured by the fantastic foliage of exotic trees.

Presently she held up her head, her white hand dropped upon her knee, she hesitated an instant, and then rose to her feet, swiftly, as though she had made a resolution and was about to act upon it. She made a step forward, and then paused again, while a half-scornful smile passed like a shadow over her face. Very slowly she began to pace the marble floor, up and down in the open space before her chair, turning and turning again, the soft folds of her white gown following her across the smooth pavement with a gentle, sweeping sound, such as the breeze makes among flowers in spring.

'Is it he?' she asked aloud in a voice ringing with the joy and the fear of a passion that has waited long and is at last approaching the fulfilment of satisfaction.

No answer came to her from among the thick foliage, nor in the scented breath of the violets and the lilies. The murmuring song of the little fountain alone disturbed the stillness, and the rustle of her own garments as she moved.

'Is it he? Is it he? Is it he?' she repeated again and again, in varying tones, chiming the changes of hope and fear, of certainty and vacillation, of sadness and of gladness, of eager passion and of chilling doubt.

She stood still, staring at the pavement, her fingers clasped together, the palms of her hands turned downward, her arms relaxed. She did not see the dark red squares of marble, alternating with the white and the grey, but as she looked a face and a form rose before her, in the contemplation of which all her senses and faculties concentrated themselves. The pale and noble head grew very distinct in her inner sight, the dark grey eyes gazed sadly upon her, the passionate features were fixed in the expression of a great sorrow.

'Are you indeed he?' she asked, speaking softly and doubtfully, and yet unconsciously projecting her strong will upon the vision, as though to force it to give the answer for which she longed.

And the answer came, imposed by the effort of her imagination upon the thing imagined. The face suddenly became luminous, as with a radiance within itself; the shadows of grief melted away, and in their place trembled the rising light of a dawning love. The lips moved and the voice spoke, not as it had spoken to her lately, but in tones long familiar to her in dreams by day and night.

'I am he, I am that love for whom you have waited; you are that dear one whom I have long sought throughout the world. The hour of our joy has struck, the new life begins today, and there shall be no end.'

Unorna's arms went out to grasp the shadow, and she drew it to her in her fancy and kissed its radiant face.

'To ages of ages!' she cried.

Then she covered her eyes as though to impress the sight they had seen upon the mind within, and groping blindly for her chair sank back into her seat. But the mechanical effort of will and memory could not preserve the image. In spite of all inward concentration of thought, its colours faded, its outlines trembled, grew faint and vanished, and darkness was in its place. Unorna's hand dropped to her side, and a quick throb of pain stabbed her through and through, agonising as the wound of a blunt and jagged knife, though it was gone almost before she knew where she had felt it. Then her eyes flashed with unlike fires, the one dark and passionate as the light of a black diamond, the other keen and daring as the gleam of blue steel in the sun.

'Ah, but I will!' she exclaimed. 'And what I will – shall be.'

As though she were satisfied with the promise thus made to herself, she smiled, her eyelids drooped, the tension of her frame was relaxed, and she sank again into the indolent attitude in which the Wanderer had found her. A moment later the distant door turned softly upon its hinges and a light footfall broke the stillness. There was no need for Unorna to speak in order that the sound of her voice might guide the newcomer to her retreat. The footsteps approached swiftly and surely. A young man of singular beauty came out of the green shadows and stood beside the chair in the open space.

Unorna betrayed no surprise as she looked up into her visitor's face. She knew it well. In form and feature the youth represented the noblest type of the Jewish race. It was impossible to see him without thinking of a young eagle of the mountains, eager, swift, sure, instinct with elasticity, far-sighted and untiring, strong to grasp and to hold, beautiful with the glossy and unruffled beauty of a plumage continually smoothed in the sweep and the rush of high, bright air.

Israel Kafka stood still, gazing down upon the woman he loved, and drawing his breath hard between his parted lips. His piercing eyes devoured every detail of the sight before him, while the dark blood rose in his lean olive cheek, and the veins of his temples swelled with the beating of his quickened pulse.

'Well?'

The single indifferent word received the value of a longer speech from the tone in which it was uttered, and from the look and gesture which accompanied it. Unorna's voice was gentle, soft, half-indolent, half-caressing, half-expectant, and half-careless. There was something almost insolent in its assumption of superiority, which was borne out by the little defiant tapping of two long white fingers upon the arm of the carved chair. And yet, with the rising inflection of the monosyllable there went a raising of the brows, a sidelong glance of the eyes, a slowly wreathing smile that curved the fresh lips just enough to unmask two perfect teeth, all of which lent to the voice a meaning, a familiarity, a pliant possibility of favourable interpretation, fit rather to flatter a hope than to chill a passion.

The blood beat more fiercely in the young man's veins, his black eyes gleamed yet more brightly, his pale, high-curved nostrils quivered at every breath he drew. The throbbings of his heart unseated his thoughts and strongly took possession of the government of his body. Under an irresistible impulse he fell upon his knees beside Unorna, covering her marble hand with all his lean, dark fingers and pressing his forehead upon them, as though he had found and grasped all that could be dear to him in life.

'Unorna! My golden Unorna!' he cried, as he knelt.

Unorna looked down upon his bent head. The smile faded from her face, and for a moment a look of hardness lingered there, which gave way to an expression of pain and regret. As though collecting her thoughts she closed her eyes, as she tried to draw back her hand; then as he held it still, she leaned back and spoke to him.

'You have not understood me,' she said, as quietly as she could.

The strong fingers were not lifted from hers, but the white face, now bloodless and transparent, was raised to hers, and a look of such fear as she had never dreamed of was in the wide black eyes.

'Not – understood?' he repeated in startled, broken tones.

Unorna sighed, and turned away, for the sight hurt her and accused her.

'No, you have not understood. Is it my fault? Israel Kafka, that hand is not yours to hold.'

'Not mine? Unorna!' Yet he could not quite believe what she said.

'I am in earnest,' she answered, not without a lingering tenderness in the intonation. 'Do you think I am jesting with you, or with myself?'

Neither of the two stirred during the silence which followed. Unorna sat quite still, staring fixedly into the green shadows of the foliage, as though not daring to meet the gaze she felt upon her. Israel Kafka still knelt beside her, motionless and hardly breathing, like a dangerous wild animal startled by an unexpected enemy, and momentarily paralysed in the very act of springing, whether backward in flight, or forward in the teeth of the foe, it is not possible to guess.

'I have been mistaken,' Unorna continued at last. 'Forgive – forget –'

Israel Kafka rose to his feet and drew back a step from her side. All his movements were smooth and graceful. The perfect man is most beautiful in motion, the perfect woman in repose.

'How easy it is for you!' exclaimed the Moravian. 'How easy! How simple! You call me, and I come. You let your eyes rest on me, and I kneel before you. You sigh, and I speak words of love. You lift your hand and I crouch at your feet. You frown – and I humbly leave you. How easy!'

'You are wrong, and you speak foolishly. You are angry, and you do not weigh your words.'

'Angry! What have I to do with so common a madness as anger? I am more than angry. Do you think that because I have submitted to the veering gusts of your good and evil humours these many months, I have lost all consciousness of myself? Do you think that you can blow upon me as upon a feather, from east and west, from north and south, hotly or coldly, as your unstable nature moves you? Have you promised me nothing? Have you given me no hope? Have you said and done nothing whereby you are bound? Or can no pledge bind you, no promise find a foothold in your slippery memory, no word of yours have meaning for those who hear it?'

'I never gave you either pledge or promise,' answered Unorna in a harder tone. 'The only hope I have ever extended to you was this, that I would one day answer you plainly. I have done so. You are not satisfied. Is there anything more to be said? I do not bid you leave my house for ever, any more than I mean to drive you from my friendship.'

'From your friendship! Ah, I thank you, Unorna; I most humbly thank you! For the mercy you extend in allowing me to linger near you, I am grateful! Your friend, you say? Ay, truly, your friend and servant, your servant and your slave, your slave and your dog. Is the friend impatient and dissatisfied with his lot? A soft word shall turn away his anger. Is the servant over-presumptuous? Your scorn will soon teach him his duty. Is the slave disobedient? Blows will cure him of his faults. Does your dog fawn upon you too familiarly? Thrust him from you with your foot and he will cringe and cower till you smile again. Your friendship – I have no words for thanks!'

'Take it, or take it not – as you will.' Unorna glanced at his angry face and quickly looked away.

'Take it? Yes, and more too, whether you will give it or not,' answered Israel Kafka, moving nearer to her. 'Yes. Whether you will, or whether you will not, I have all, your friendship, your love, your life, your breath, your soul – all, or nothing!'

'You are wise to suggest the latter alternative as a possibility,' said Unorna coldly and not heeding his approach.

The young man stood still, and folded his arms. The colour had returned to his face and a deep flush was rising under his olive skin.

'Do you mean what you say?' he asked slowly. 'Do you mean that I shall not have all, but nothing? Do you still dare to mean that, after all that has passed between you and me?'

Unorna raised her eyes and looked steadily into his.

'Israel Kafka, do not speak to me of daring.'

But the young man's glance did not waver. The angry expression of his features did not relax; he neither drew back nor bent his head. Unorna seemed to be exerting all the strength of her will in the attempt to dominate him, but without result. In the effort she made to concentrate her determination her face grew pale and her lips trembled. Kafka faced her resolutely, his eyes on fire, the rich colour mantling in his cheeks.

'Where is your power now?' he asked suddenly. 'Where is your witchery? You are only a woman, after all. You are only a weak woman!'

Very slowly he drew nearer to her side, his lithe figure bending a little as he looked down upon her. Unorna leaned far back, withdrawing her face from his as far as she could, but still trying to impose her will upon him.

'You cannot,' he said between his teeth, answering her thought.

Men who have tamed wild beasts alone know what such a moment is like. A hundred times the brave man has held the tiger spell-bound and crouching under his cold, fearless gaze. The beast, ever docile and submissive, has cringed at his feet, fawned to his touch, and licked the hand that snatched away the half-devoured morsel. Obedient to voice and eye, the giant strength and sinewy grace have been debased to make the sport of multitudes; the noble, pliant frame has contorted itself to execute the mean antics of the low-comedy ape – to counterfeit death like a poodle dog; to leap through gaudily-painted rings at the word of command; to fetch and carry like a spaniel. A hundred times the changing crowd has paid its paltry fee to watch the little play that is daily acted behind the stout iron bars by the man and the beast. The man, the nobler, braver creature, is arrayed in a wretched flimsy finery of tights and spangles, parading his physical weakness and inferiority in the toggery of a mountebank. The tiger, vast, sleepy-eyed, mysterious, lies motionless in the front of his cage, the gorgeous stripes of his velvet coat following each curve of his body, from the cushions of his great fore paws to the arch of his gathered haunches. The watchfulness and flexible activity of the serpent and the strength that knows no master are clothed in the magnificent robes of the native-born sovereign. Time and time again the beautiful giant has gone through the slavish round of his mechanical tricks, obedient to the fragile creature of intelligence, to the little dwarf, man, whose power is in his eyes and heart only. He is accustomed to the lights, to the spectators, to the laughter, to the applause, to the frightened scream of the hysterical women in the audience, to the close air and to the narrow stage behind the bars. The tamer in his tights and tinsel has grown used to his tiger, to his emotions, to his hourly danger. He even finds at last that his mind wanders during the performance, and that at the very instant when he is holding the ring for the leap, or thrusting his head into the beast's fearful jaws, he is thinking of his wife, of his little child, of his domestic happiness or household troubles, rather than of what he is doing. Many times, perhaps many hundreds of times, all passes off quietly and successfully. Then, inevitably, comes the struggle. Who can tell the causes? The tiger is growing old, or is ill fed, or is not well, or is merely in one of those evil humours to which animals are subject as well as their masters. One day he refuses to go through with the performance. First one trick fails, and then another. The public grows impatient, the man in spangles grows nervous, raises his voice, stamps loudly with his foot, and strikes his terrible slave with his light switch. A low, deep sound breaks from the enormous throat, the spectators hold their breath, the huge, flexible limbs are gathered for the leap, and in the gaslight and the dead silence man and beast are face to face. Life hangs in the balance, and death is at the door.

Then the tamer's heart beats loud, his chest heaves, his brows are furrowed. Even then, in the instant that still separates him from triumph or destruction, the thought of his sleeping child or of his watching wife darts through his brain. But the struggle has begun and there is no escape. One of two things must happen: he must overcome or he must die. To draw back, to let his glance waver, to show so much as the least sign of fear, is death. The moment is supreme, and he knows it.

Unorna grasped the arms of her chair as though seeking for physical support in her extremity. She could not yield. Before her eyes arose a vision unlike the reality in all its respects. She saw an older face, a taller figure, a look of deeper thought between her and the angry man who was trying to conquer her resistance with a glance. Between her and her mistake the image of what should be stood out, bright, vivid, and strong. A new conviction had taken the place of the old, a real passion was flaming upon the altar whereon she had fed with dreams the semblance of a sacred fire.

'You do not really love me,' she said softly.

Israel Kafka started, as a man who is struck unawares. The monstrous untruth which filled the words broke down his guard, sudden tears veiled the penetrating sharpness of his gaze, and his hand trembled.

'I do not love you? I! Unorna – Unorna!'

The first words broke from him in a cry of horror and stupefaction. But her name, when he spoke it, sounded as the death moan of a young wild animal wounded beyond all power to turn at bay.

He moved unsteadily and laid hold of the tall chair in which she sat. He was behind her now, standing, but bending down so that his forehead pressed his fingers. He could not bear to look upon her hair, still less upon her face. Even his hands were white and bloodless. Unorna could hear his quick breathing just above her shoulder. She sat quite still, and her lips were smiling, though her brow was thoughtful and almost sad. She knew that the struggle was over and that she had gained the mastery, though the price of victory might be a broken heart.

'You thought I was jesting,' she said in a low voice, looking before her into the deep foliage, but knowing that her softest whisper would reach him. 'But there was no jest in what I said – nor any unkindness in what I meant, though it is all my fault. But that is true – you never loved me as I would be loved.'

'Unorna – '

'No, I am not unkind. Your love is young, fierce, inconstant; half terrible, half boyish, aflame today, asleep tomorrow, ready to turn into hatred at one moment, to melt into tears at the next, intermittent, unstable as water, fleeting as a cloud's shadow on the mountain side – '

'It pleased you once,' said Israel Kafka in broken tones. 'It is not less love because you are weary of it, and of me.'

'Weary, you say? No, not weary – and very truly not of you. You will believe that today, tomorrow, you will still try to force life into your belief – and then it will be dead and gone like all thoughts which have never entered into the shapes of reality. We have not loved each other. We have but fancied that it would be sweet to love, and the knife of truth has parted the web of our dreams, keenly, in the midst, so that we see before us what is, though the ghost of what might have been is yet lingering near.'

'Who wove that web, Unorna? You, or I?' He lifted his heavy eyes and gazed at her coiled hair.

'What matters it whether it was your doing or mine? But we wove it together – and together we must see the truth.'

'If this is true, there is no more "together" for you and me.'

'We may yet glean friendship in the fields where love has grown.'

'Friendship! The very word is a wound! Friendship! The very dregs and lees of the wine of life! Friendship! The sour drainings of the heart's cup, left to moisten the lips of the damned when the blessed have drunk their fill! I hate the word, as I hate the thought!'

Unorna sighed, partly, perhaps, that he might hear the sigh, and put upon it an interpretation soothing to his vanity, but partly, too, from a sincere regret that he should need to suffer as he was evidently suffering. She had half believed that she loved him, and she owed him pity. Women's hearts pay such debts unwillingly, but they do pay them, nevertheless. She wished that she had never set eyes upon Israel Kafka; she wished that she might never see him again; even his death would hardly have cost her a pang, and yet she was sorry for him. Diana, the huntress, shot her arrows with unfailing aim; Diana, the goddess, may have sighed and shed one bright immortal tear, as she looked into the fast-glazing eyes of the dying stag – may not Diana, the maiden, have felt a touch of human sympathy and pain as she listened to the deep note of her hounds baying on poor Actaeon's track! No one is all bad, or all good. No woman is all earthly, nor any goddess all divine.

'I am sorry,' said Unorna. 'You will not understand – '

'I have understood enough. I have understood that a woman can have two faces and two hearts, two minds, two souls; it is enough, my understanding need go no farther. You sighed before you spoke. It was not for me; it was for yourself. You never felt pain or sorrow for another.'

He was trying hard to grow cold and to find cold words to say, which might lead her to believe him stronger than he was and able to master his grief. But he was too young, too hot, too changeable for such a part. Moreover, in his first violent outbreak Unorna had dominated him, and he could not now regain the advantage.

'You are wrong, Israel Kafka. You would make me less than human. If I sighed, it was indeed for you. See – I confess that I have done you wrong, not in deeds, but in letting you hope. Truly, I myself have hoped also. I have thought that the star of love was trembling just below the east, and that you and I might be one to another – what we cannot be now. My wisdom has failed me, my sight has been deceived. Am I the only woman in this world who has been mistaken? Can you not forgive? If I had promised, if I had said one word – and yet, you are right, too, for I have let you think in earnest what has been but a passing dream of my own thoughts. It was all wrong; it was all my fault. There, lay your hand in mine and say that you forgive, as I ask forgiveness.'

He was still standing behind her, leaning against the back of her chair. Without looking round she raised her hand above her shoulder as though seeking for his. But he would not take it.

'Is it so hard?' she asked softly. 'Is it even harder for you to give than for me to ask? Shall we part like this – not to meet again – each bearing a wound, when both might be whole? Can you not say the word?'

'What is it to you whether I forgive you or not?'

'Since I ask it, believe that it is much to me,' she answered, slowly turning her head until, without catching sight of his face, she could just see where his fingers were resting on her chair. Then, over her shoulder, she touched them, and drew them to her cheek. He made no resistance.

'Shall we part without one kind thought?' Her voice was softer still and so low and sweet that it seemed as though the words were spoken in the ripple of the tiny fountain. There was magic in the place, in the air, in the sounds, above all in the fair woman's touch.

'Is this friendship?' asked Kafka. Then he sank upon his knees beside her, and looked up into her face.

'It is friendship; yes – why not? Am I like other women?'

'Then why need there be any parting?'

'If you will be my friend there need be none. You have forgiven me now – I see it in your eyes. Is it not true?'

He was at her feet, passive at last under the superior power which he had never been able to resist. Unorna's fascination was upon him, and he could only echo her words, as he would have executed her slightest command, without consciousness of free will or individual thought. It was enough that for one moment his anger should cease to give life to his resistance; it was sufficient that Unorna should touch him thus, and speak softly, his eyelids quivered and his look became fixed, his strength was absorbed in hers and incapable of acting except under her direction. So long as she might please the spell would endure.

'Sit beside me now, and let us talk,' she said.

Like a man in a dream, he rose and sat down near her.

Unorna laughed, and there was something in the tone that was not good to hear. A moment earlier it would have wounded Israel Kafka to the quick and brought the hot, angry blood to his face. Now he laughed with her, vacantly, as though not knowing the cause of his mirth.

'You are only my slave, after all,' said Unorna scornfully.

'I am only your slave, after all,' he repeated.

'I could touch you with my hand and you would hate me, and forget that you ever loved me.'

This time the man was silent. There was a contraction of pain in his face, as though a violent mental struggle were going on within him. Unorna tapped the pavement impatiently with her foot and bent her brows.

'You would hate me and forget that you ever loved me,' she repeated, dwelling on each word as though to impress it on his consciousness. 'Say it. I order you.'

The contraction of his features disappeared.

'I should hate you and forget that I ever loved you,' he said slowly.

'You never loved me.'

'I never loved you.'

Again Unorna laughed, and he joined in her laughter, unintelligently, as he had done before. She leaned back in her seat, and her face grew grave. Israel Kafka sat motionless in his chair, staring at her with unwinking eyes. But his gaze did not disturb her. There was no more meaning in it than in the expression of a marble statue, far less than in that of a painted portrait. Yet the man was alive and in the full strength of his magnificent youth, supple, active, fierce by nature, able to have killed her with his hands in the struggle of a moment. Yet she knew that without a word from her he could neither turn his head nor move in his seat.

For a long time Unorna was absorbed in her meditations. Again and again the vision of a newer happiness took shape and colour before her, so clearly and vividly that she could have clasped it and held it and believed in its reality, as she had done before Israel Kafka had entered. But there was a doubt now, which constantly arose between her and it, the dark and shapeless shadow of a reasoning she hated and yet knew to be strong.

'I must ask him,' she said unconsciously.

'You must ask him,' repeated Israel Kafka from his seat.

For the third time Unorna laughed aloud as she heard the echo of her own words.

'Whom shall I ask?' she inquired contemptuously, as she rose to her feet.

The dull, glassy eyes sought hers in painful perplexity, following her face as she moved.

'I do not know,' answered the powerless man.

Unorna came close to him and laid her hand upon his head.

'Sleep, until I wake you,' she said.

The eyelids drooped and closed at her command, and instantly the man's breathing became heavy and regular. Unorna's full lips curled as she looked down at him.

'And you would be my master!' she exclaimed.

Then she turned and disappeared among the plants, leaving him alone.

Chapter 5

Unorna passed through a corridor which was, indeed, only a long balcony covered in with arches and closed with windows against the outer air. At the farther end three steps descended to a dark door, through the thickness of a massive wall, showing that at this point Unorna's house had at some former time been joined with another building beyond, with which it thus formed one habitation. Unorna paused, holding the key as though hesitating whether she should put it into the lock. It was evident that much depended upon her decision, for her face expressed the anxiety she felt. Once she turned away, as though to abandon her intention, hesitated, and then, with an impatient frown, opened the door and went in. She passed through a small, well-lighted vestibule and entered the room beyond.

The apartment was furnished with luxury, but a stranger would have received an oddly disquieting impression of the whole at a first glance. There was everything in the place which is considered necessary for a bedroom, and everything was perfect of its kind, spotless and dustless, and carefully arranged in order. But almost everything was of an unusual and unfamiliar shape, as though designed for some especial reason to remain in equilibrium in any possible position, and to be moved from place to place with the smallest imaginable physical effort. The carved bedstead was fitted with wheels which did not touch the ground, and levers so placed as to be within the reach of a person lying in it. The tables were each supported at one end only by one strong column, fixed to a heavy base set on broad rollers, so that the board could be run across a bed or a lounge with the greatest ease. There was but one chair made like ordinary chairs; the rest were so constructed that the least motion of the occupant must be accompanied by a corresponding change of position of the back and arms, and some of them bore a curious resemblance to a surgeon's operating table, having attachments of silver-plated metal at many points, of which the object was not immediately evident. Before a closed door a sort of wheeled conveyance, partaking of the nature of a chair and of a perambulator, stood upon polished rails, which disappeared under the door itself, showing that the thing was intended to be moved from one room to another in a certain way and in a fixed line. The rails, had the door been opened, would have been seen to descend upon the other side by a gentle inclined plane into the centre of a huge marble basin, and the contrivance thus made it possible to wheel a person into a bath and out again without necessitating the slightest effort or change of position in the body. In the bedroom the windows were arranged so that the light and air could be regulated to a nicety. The walls were covered with fine basket work, apparently adapted in panels; but these panels were in reality movable trays, as it were, forming shallow boxes fitted with closely-woven wicker covers, and filled with charcoal and other porous substances intended to absorb the impurities of the air, and thus easily changed and renewed from time to time. Immediately beneath the ceiling were placed delicate glass globes of various soft colours, with silken shades, movable from below by means of brass rods and handles. In the ceiling itself there were large ventilators, easily regulated as might be required, and there was a curious arrangement of rails and wheels from which depended a sort of swing, apparently adapted for moving a person or a weight to different parts of the room without touching the floor. In one of the lounges, not far from the window, lay a colossal old man, wrapped in a loose robe of warm white stuff, and fast asleep.

He was a very old man, so old, indeed, as to make it hard to guess his age from his face and his hands, the only parts visible as he lay at rest, the vast body and limbs lying motionless under his garment, as beneath a heavy white pall. He could not be less than a hundred years old, but how much older than that he might really be, it was impossible to say. What might be called the waxen period had set in, and the high colourless features seemed to be modelled in that soft, semi-transparent material. The time had come when the stern furrows of age had broken up into countless minutely-traced lines, so close and fine as to seem a part of the texture of the skin, mere shadings, evenly distributed throughout, and no longer affecting the expression of the face as the deep wrinkles had done in former days; at threescore and ten, at fourscore, and even at ninety years. The century that had passed had taken with it its marks and scars, leaving the great features in their original purity of design, lean, smooth, and clearly defined. That last change in living man is rare enough, but when once seen is not to be forgotten. There is something in the faces of the very, very old which hardly suggests age at all, but rather the vague possibility of a returning prime. Only the hands tell the tale, with their huge, shining, fleshless joints, their shadowy hollows, and their unnatural yellow nails.

The old man lay quite still, breathing softly through his snowy beard. Unorna came to his side. There was something of wonder and admiration in her own eyes as she stood there gazing upon the face which other generations of men and women, all long dead, had looked upon and known. The secret of life and death was before her each day when she entered that room, and on the very verge of solution. The wisdom hardly gained in many lands was striving with all its concentrated power to preserve that life; the rare and subtle gifts which she herself possessed were daily exercised to their full in the suggestion of vitality; the most elaborate inventions of skilled mechanicians were employed in reducing the labour of living to the lowest conceivable degree of effort. The great experiment was being tried. What Keyork Arabian described as the embalming of a man still alive was being attempted. And he lived. For years they had watched him and tended him, and looked critically for the least signs of a diminution or an augmentation in his strength. They knew that he was now in his one hundred and seventh year, and yet he lived and was no weaker. Was there a limit; or was there not, since the destruction of the tissues was arrested beyond doubt, so far as the most minute tests could show? Might there not be, in the slow oscillations of nature, a degree of decay, on this side of death, from which a return should be possible, provided that the critical moment were passed in a state of sleep and under perfect conditions? How do we know that all men must die? We suppose the statement to be true by induction, from the undoubted fact that men have hitherto died within a certain limit of age. By induction, too, our fathers, our grandfathers, knew that it was impossible for man to traverse the earth faster than at the full speed of a galloping horse. After several thousand years of experience that piece of knowledge, which seemed to be singularly certain, was suddenly proved to be the grossest ignorance by a man who had been in the habit of playing with a tea-kettle when a boy. We ourselves, not very long ago, knew positively, as all men had known since the beginning of the world, that it was quite impossible to converse with a friend at a distance beyond the carrying power of a speaking trumpet. Today, a boy who does not know that one may talk very agreeably with a friend a thousand miles away is an ignoramus; and experimenters whisper among themselves that, if the undulatory theory of light have any foundation, there is no real reason why we may not see that same friend at that same distance, as well as talk with him. Ten years ago we were quite sure that it was beyond the bounds of natural possibility to produce a bad burn upon the human body by touching the flesh with a bit of card-board or a common lead pencil. Now we know with equal certainty that if upon one arm of a hypnotised patient we impress a letter of the alphabet cut out of wood, telling him that it is red-hot iron, the shape of the letter will on the following day be found on a raw and painful wound not only in the place we selected but on the other arm, in the exactly corresponding spot, and reversed as though seen in a looking-glass; and we very justly consider that a physician who does not know this and similar facts is dangerously behind the times, since the knowledge is open to all. The inductive reasoning of many thousands of years has been knocked to pieces in the last century by a few dozen men who have reasoned little but attempted much. It would be rash to assert that bodily death may not some day, and under certain conditions, be altogether escaped. It is nonsense to pretend that human life may not possibly, and before long, be enormously prolonged, and that by some shorter cut to longevity than temperance and sanitation. No man can say that it will, but no man of average intelligence can now deny that it may.

Unorna had hesitated at the door, and she hesitated now. It was in her power, and in hers only, to wake the hoary giant, or at least to modify his perpetual sleep so far as to obtain from him answers to her questions. It would be an easy matter to lay one hand upon his brow, bidding him see and speak – how easy, she alone knew. But on the other hand, to disturb his slumber was to interfere with the continuity of the great experiment, to break through a rule lately made, to incur the risk of an accident, if not of death itself.

She drew back at the thought, as though fearing to startle him, and then she smiled at her own nervousness. To wake him she must exercise her will. There was no danger of his ever being roused by any sound or touch not proceeding from herself. The crash of thunder had no reverberation for his ears, the explosion of a cannon would not have penetrated into his lethargy. She might touch him, move him, even speak to him, but unless she laid her hand upon his waxen forehead and bid him feel and hear, he would be as unconscious as the dead. She returned to his side and gazed into his placid face. Strange faculties were asleep in that ancient brain, and strange wisdom was stored there, gathered from many sources long ago, and treasured unconsciously by the memory to be recalled at her command.

The man had been a failure in his day, a scholar, a student, a searcher after great secrets, a wanderer in the labyrinths of higher thought. He had been a failure and had starved, as failures must, in order that vulgar success may fatten and grow healthy. He had outlived the few that had been dear to him, he had outlived the power to feed on thought, he had outlived generations of men, and cycles of changes, and yet there had been life left in the huge gaunt limbs and sight in the sunken eyes. Then he had outlived pride itself, and the ancient scholar had begged his bread. In his hundredth year he had leaned for rest against Unorna's door, and she had taken him in and cared for him, and since that time she had preserved his life. For his history was known in the ancient city, and it was said that he had possessed great wisdom in his day. Unorna knew that this wisdom could be hers if she could keep alive the spark of life, and that she could employ his own learning to that end. Already she had much experience of her powers, and knew that if she once had the mastery of the old man's free will he must obey her fatally and unresistingly. Then she conceived the idea of embalming, as it were, the living being, in a perpetual hypnotic lethargy, from whence she recalled him from time to time to an intermediate state, in which she caused him to do mechanically all those things which she judged necessary to prolong life.

Seeing her success from the first, she had begun to fancy that the present condition of things might be made to continue indefinitely. Since death was today no nearer than it had been seven years ago, there was no reason why it might not be guarded against during seven years more, and if during seven, why not during ten, twenty, fifty? She had for a helper a physician of consummate practical skill – a man whose interest in the result of the trial was, if anything, more keen than her own; a friend, above all, whom she believed she might trust, and who appeared to trust her.

But in the course of their great experiment they had together made rules by which they had mutually agreed to be bound. They had of late determined that the old man must not be disturbed in his profound rest by any question tending to cause a state of mental activity. The test of a very fine instrument had proved that the shortest interval of positive lucidity was followed by a slight but distinctly perceptible rise of temperature in the body, and this could mean only a waste of the precious tissues they were so carefully preserving. They hoped and believed that the grand crisis was at hand, and that, if the body did not now lose strength and vitality for a considerable time, both would slowly though surely increase, in consequence of the means they were using to instil new blood into the system. But the period was supreme, and to interfere in any way with the progress of the experiment was to run a risk of which the whole extent could only be realised by Unorna and her companion.

She hesitated therefore, well knowing that her ally would oppose her intention with all his might, and dreading his anger, bold as she was, almost as much as she feared the danger to the old man's life. On the other hand, she had a motive which the physician could not have, and which, as she was aware, he would have despised and condemned. She had a question to ask, which she considered of vital importance to herself, to which she firmly believed that the true answer would be given, and which, in her womanly impetuosity and impatience, she could not bear to leave unasked until the morrow, much less until months should have passed away. Two very powerful incentives were at work, two of the very strongest which have influence with mankind, love and a superstitious belief in an especial destiny of happiness, at the present moment on the very verge of realisation.

She believed profoundly in herself and in the suggestions of her own imagination. So fixed and unalterable was that belief that it amounted to positive knowledge, so far as it constituted a motive of action. In her strange youth wild dreams had possessed her, and some of them, often dreamed again, had become realities to her now. Her powers were natural, those gifts which from time to time are seen in men and women, which are alternately scoffed at as impostures, or accepted as facts, but which are never understood either by their possessor or by those who witness the results. She had from childhood the power to charm with eye and hand all living things, the fascination which takes hold of the consciousness through sight and touch and word, and lulls it to sleep. It was witchery, and she was called a witch. In earlier centuries her hideous fate would have been sealed from the first day when, under her childish gaze, a wolf that had been taken alive in the Bohemian forest crawled fawning to her feet, at the full length of its chain, and laid its savage head under her hand, and closed its bloodshot eyes and slept before her. Those who had seen had taken her and taught her how to use what she possessed according to their own shadowy beliefs and dim traditions of the half-forgotten magic in a distant land. They had filled her heart with longings and her brain with dreams, and she had grown up to believe that one day love would come suddenly upon her and bear her away through the enchanted gates of the earthly paradise; once only that love would come, and the supreme danger of her life would be that she should not know it when it was at hand.

And now she knew that she loved, for the place of her fondness for the one man had been taken by her passion for the other, and she felt without reasoning, where, before, she had tried to reason herself into feeling. The moment had come. She had seen the man in whom her happiness was to be, the time was short, the danger great if she should not grasp what her destiny would offer her but once. Had the Wanderer been by her side, she would have needed to ask no question, she would have known and been satisfied. But hours must pass before she could see him again, and every minute spent without him grew more full of anxiety and disturbing passion than the last. The wild love-blossom that springs into existence in a single moment has elements which do not enter into the gentler being of that other love which is sown in indifference, and which grows up in slowly increasing interest, tended and refreshed in the pleasant intercourse of close acquaintance, to bud and bloom at last as a mild-scented garden flower. Love at first sight is impatient, passionate, ruthless, cruel, as the year would be, if from the calendar of the season the months of slow transition were struck out; if the raging heat of August followed in one day upon the wild tempests of the winter; if the fruit of the vine but yesterday in leaf grew rich and black today, to be churned to foam tomorrow under the feet of the laughing wine-treaders.

Unorna felt that the day would be intolerable if she could not hear from other lips the promise of a predestined happiness. She was not really in doubt, but she was under the imperious impulse of a passion which must needs find some response, even in the useless confirmation of its reality uttered by an indifferent person – the spirit of a mighty cry seeking its own echo in the echoless, flat waste of the Great Desert.

Then, too, she placed a sincere faith in the old man's answers to her questions, regardless of the matter inquired into. She believed that in the mysterious condition between sleep and waking which she could command, the knowledge of things to be was with him as certainly as the memory of what had been and of what was even now passing in the outer world. To her, the one direction of the faculty seemed no less possible than the others, though she had not yet attained alone to the vision of the future. Hitherto the old man's utterances had been fulfilled to the letter. More than once, as Keyork Arabian had hinted, she had consulted his second sight in preference to her own, and she had not been deceived. His greater learning and his vast experience lent to his sayings something divine in her eyes; she looked upon him as the Pythoness of Delphi looked upon the divinity of her inspiration.

The irresistible longing to hear the passionate pleadings of her own heart solemnly confirmed by the voice in which she trusted overcame at last every obstacle. Unorna bent over the sleeper, looking earnestly into his face, and she laid one hand upon his brow.

'You hear me,' she said, slowly and distinctly. 'You are conscious of thought, and you see into the future.'

The massive head stirred, the long limbs moved uneasily under the white robe, the enormous, bony hands contracted, and in the cavernous eyes the great lids were slowly lifted. A dull stare met her look.

'Is it he?' she asked, speaking more quickly in spite of herself. 'Is it he at last?'

There was no answer. The lips did not part, there was not even the attempt to speak. She had been sure that the one word would be spoken unhesitatingly, and the silence startled her and brought back the doubt which she had half forgotten.

'You must answer my question. I command you to answer me. Is it he?'

'You must tell me more before I can answer.'

The words came in a feeble piping voice, strangely out of keeping with the colossal frame and imposing features.

Unorna's face was clouded, and the ready gleam of anger flashed in her eyes as it ever did at the smallest opposition to her will.

'Can you not see him?' she asked impatiently.

'I cannot see him unless you lead me to him and tell me where he is.'

'Where are you?'

'In your mind.'

'And what are you?'

'I am the image in your eyes.'

'There is another man in my mind,' said Unorna. 'I command you to see him.'

'I see him. He is tall, pale, noble, suffering. You love him.'

'Is it he who shall be my life and my death? Is it he who shall love me as other women are not loved?'

The weak voice was still for a moment, and the face seemed covered with a veil of perplexity.

'I see with your eyes,' said the old man at last.

'And I command you to see into the future with your own!' cried Unorna, concentrating her terrible will as she grew more impatient.

There was an evident struggle in the giant's mind, an effort to obey which failed to break down an obstacle. She bent over him eagerly and her whole consciousness was centered in the words she desired him to speak.

Suddenly the features relaxed into an expression of rest and satisfaction. There was something unearthly in the sudden smile that flickered over the old waxen face – it was as strange and unnatural as though the cold marble effigy upon a sepulchre had laughed aloud in the gloom of an empty church.

'I see. He will love you,' said the tremulous tones.

'Then it is he?'

'It is he.'

With a suppressed cry of triumph Unorna lifted her head and stood upright. Then she started violently and grew very pale.

'You have probably killed him and spoiled everything,' said a rich bass voice at her elbow – the very sub-bass of all possible voices.

Keyork Arabian was beside her. In her intense excitement she had not heard him enter the room, and he had surprised her at once in the breaking of their joint convention and in the revelation of her secret. If Unorna could be said to know the meaning of the word fear in any degree whatsoever, it was in relation to Keyork Arabian, the man who during the last few years had been her helper and associate in the great experiment. Of all men she had known in her life, he was the only one whom she felt to be beyond the influence of her powers, the only one whom she felt that she could not charm by word, or touch, or look. The odd shape of his head, she fancied, figured the outline and proportions of his intelligence, which was, as it were, pyramidal, standing upon a base so broad and firm as to place the centre of its ponderous gravity far beyond her reach to disturb. There was certainly no other being of material reality that could have made Unorna start and turn pale by its inopportune appearance.

'The best thing you can do is to put him to sleep at once,' said the little man. 'You can be angry afterwards, and, I thank heaven, so can I – and shall.'

'Forget,' said Unorna, once more laying her hand upon the waxen brow. 'Let it be as though I had not spoken with you. Drink, in your sleep, of the fountain of life, take new strength into your body and new blood into your heart. Live, and when I next wake you be younger by as many months as there shall pass hours till then. Sleep.'

A low sigh trembled in the hoary beard. The eyelids drooped over the sunken eyes, there was a slight motion of the limbs, and all was still, save for the soft and regular breathing.

'The united patience of the seven archangels, coupled with that of Job and Simon Stylites, would not survive your acquaintance for a day,' observed Keyork Arabian.

'Is he mine or yours?' Unorna asked, turning to him and pointing to the sleeper.

She was quite ready to face her companion after the first shock of his unexpected appearance. His small blue eyes sparkled angrily.

'I am not versed in the law concerning real estate in human kind in the Kingdom of Bohemia,' he answered. 'You may have property in a couple of hundredweight, more or less, of old bones rather the worse for the wear and tear of a century, but I certainly have some ownership in the life. Without me, you would have been the possessor of a remarkably fine skeleton by this time – and of nothing more.'

As he spoke, his extraordinary voice ran over half a dozen notes of portentous depth, like the opening of a fugue on the pedals of an organ. Unorna laughed scornfully.

'He is mine, Keyork Arabian, alive or dead. If the experiment fails, and he dies, the loss is mine, not yours. Moreover, what I have done is done, and I will neither submit to your reproaches nor listen to your upbraidings. Is that enough?'

'Of its kind, quite. I will build an altar to Ingratitude, we will bury our friend beneath the shrine, and you shall serve in the temple. You could deify all the cardinal sins if you would only give your attention to the subject, merely by the monstrously imposing proportions you would know how to give them.'

'Does it ease you to make such an amazing noise?' inquired Unorna, raising her eyebrows.

'Immensely. Our friend cannot hear it, and you can. You dare to tell me that if he dies you are the only loser. Do fifty years of study count for nothing? Look at me. I am an old man, and unless I find the secret of life here, in this very room, before many years are over, I must die – die, do you understand? Do you know what it means to die? How can you comprehend that word – you girl, you child, you thing of five and twenty summers!'

'It was to be supposed that your own fears were at the root of your anger,' observed Unorna, sitting down upon her chair and calmly folding her hands as though to wait until the storm should pass over.

'Is there anything at the root of anything except Self? You moth, you butterfly, you thread of floating gossamer! How can you understand the incalculable value of Self – of that which is all to me and nothing to you, or which, being yours, is everything to you and to me nothing? You are so young – you still believe in things, and interests, and good and evil, and love and hate, truth and falsehood, and a hundred notions which are not facts, but only contrasts between one self and another! What were you doing here when I found you playing with life and death, perhaps with my life, for a gipsy trick, in the crazy delusion that this old parcel of humanity can see the shadows of things which are not yet? I saw, I heard. How could he answer anything save that which was in your own mind, when you were forcing him with your words and your eyes to make a reply of some sort, or perish? Ah! You see now. You understand now. I have opened your eyes a little. Why did he hesitate, and suffer? Because you asked that to which he knew there was no answer. And you tortured him with your will until his individuality fell into yours, and spoke your words.'

Unorna's head sank a little and she covered her eyes. The truth of what he said flashed upon her suddenly and unexpectedly, bringing with it the doubt which had left her at the moment when the sleeper had spoken. She could not hide her discomfiture and Keyork Arabian saw his advantage.

'And for what?' he asked, beginning to pace the broad room. 'To know whether a man will love you or not! You seem to have forgotten what you are. Is not such a poor and foolish thing as love at the command of those who can say to the soul, be this, or be that, and who are obeyed? Have you found a second Keyork Arabian, over whom your eyes have no power – neither the one nor the other?'

He laughed rather brutally at the thought of her greatest physical peculiarity, but then suddenly stopped short. She had lifted her face and those same eyes were fastened upon him, the black and the grey, in a look so savage and fierce that even he was checked, if not startled.

'They are certainly very remarkable eyes,' he said, more calmly, and with a certain uneasiness which Unorna did not notice. 'I wonder whom you have found who is able to look you in the face without losing himself. I suppose it can hardly be my fascinating self whom you wish to enthrall,' he added, conscious after a moment's trial that he was proof against her influence.

'Hardly,' answered Unorna, with a bitter laugh.

'If I were the happy man you would not need that means of bringing me to your feet. It is a pity that you do not want me. We should make a very happy couple. But there is much against me. I am an old man, Unorna. My figure was never of divine proportions, and as for my face, Nature made it against her will. I know all that – and yet, I was young once, and eloquent. I could make love then – I believe that I could still if it would amuse you.'

'Try it,' said Unorna, who, like most people, could not long be angry with the gnome-like little sage.

Chapter 6

'I could make love – yes, and since you tell me to try, I will.'

He came and stood before her, straightening his diminutive figure in a comical fashion as though he were imitating a soldier on parade.

'In the first place,' he said, 'in order to appreciate my skill, you should realise the immense disadvantages under which I labour. I am a dwarf, my dear Unorna. In the presence of that kingly wreck of a Homeric man' – he pointed to the sleeper beside them – 'I am a Thersites, if not a pigmy. To have much chance of success I should ask you to close your eyes, and to imagine that my stature matches my voice. That gift at least, I flatter myself, would have been appreciated on the plains of Troy. But in other respects I resemble neither the long-haired Greeks nor the trousered Trojans. I am old and hideous, and in outward appearance I am as like Socrates as in inward disposition I am totally different from him. Admit, since I admit it, that I am the ugliest and smallest man of your acquaintance.'

'It is not to be denied,' said Unorna with a smile.

'The admission will make the performance so much the more interesting. And now, as the conjurer says when he begins, observe that there is no deception. That is the figure of speech called lying, because there is to be nothing but deception from beginning to end. Did you ever consider the nature of a lie, Unorna? It is a very interesting subject.'

'I thought you were going to make love to me.'

'True; how easily one forgets those little things! And yet no woman ever forgave a man who forgot to make love when she expected him to do so. For a woman who is a woman, never forgets to be exigent. And now there is no reprieve, for I have committed myself, am sentenced, and condemned to be made ridiculous in your eyes. Can there be anything more contemptible, more laughable, more utterly and hopelessly absurd, than an old and ugly man declaring his un-requited passion for a woman who might be his granddaughter? Is he not like a hoary old owl, who leaves his mousing to perch upon one leg and hoot love ditties at the evening star, or screech out amorous sonnets to the maiden moon?'

'Very like,' said Unorna with a laugh.

'And yet – my evening star – dear star of my fast-sinking evening – golden Unorna – shall I be cut off from love because my years are many? Or rather, shall I not love you the more, because the years that are left are few and scantily blessed? May not your dawn blend with my sunset and make together one short day?'

'That is very pretty,' said Unorna, thoughtfully. He had the power of making his speech sound like a deep, soft music.

'For what is love?' he asked. 'Is it a garment, a jewel, a fanciful ornament which only boys and girls may wear upon a summer's holiday? May we take it or leave it, as we please? Wear it, if it shows well upon our beauty, or cast it off for others to put on when we limp aside out of the race of fashion to halt and breathe before we die? Is love beauty? Is love youth? Is love yellow hair or black? Is love the rose upon the lip or the peach blossom in the cheek, that only the young may call it theirs? Is it an outward grace, which can live but so long as the other outward graces are its companions, to perish when the first grey hair streaks the dark locks? Is it a glass, shivered by the first shock of care as a mirror by a sword-stroke? Is it a painted mask, washed colourless by the first rain of autumn tears? Is it a flower, so tender that it must perish miserably in the frosty rime of earliest winter? Is love the accident of youth, the complement of a fresh complexion, the corollary of a light step, the physical concomitant of swelling pulses and unstrained sinews?'

Keyork Arabian laughed softly. Unorna was grave and looked up into his face, resting her chin upon her hand.

'If that is love, if that is the idol of your shrine, the vision of your dreams, the familiar genius of your earthly paradise, why then, indeed, he who worships by your side, and who would share the habitation of your happiness, must wear Absalom's anointed curls and walk with Agag's delicate step. What matter if he be but a half-witted puppet? He is fair. What matter if he be foolish, faithless, forgetful, inconstant, changeable as the tide of the sea? He is young. His youth shall cover all his deficiencies and wipe out all his sins! Imperial love, monarch and despot of the human soul, is become the servant of boys for the wage of a girl's first thoughtless kiss. If that is love, let it perish out of the world, with the bloom of the wood violet in spring, with the flutter of the bright moth in June, with the song of the nightingale and the call of the mocking-bird, with all things that are fair and lovely and sweet but for a few short days. If that is love, why then love never made a wound, nor left a scar, nor broke a heart in this easy-going rose-garden of a world. The rose blooms, blows, fades and withers and feels nothing. If that is love, we may yet all develop into passionless promoters of a flat and unprofitable commonwealth; the earth may yet be changed to a sweetmeat for us to feed on, and the sea to sugary lemonade for us to drink, as the mad philosopher foretold, and we may yet all be happy after love has left us.'

Unorna smiled, while he laughed again.

'Good,' she said. 'You tell me what love is not, but you have not told me what it is.'

'Love is the immortal essence of mortal passion, together they are as soul and body, one being; separate them, and the body without the soul is a monster, the soul without the body is no longer human, nor earthly, nor real to us at all, though still divine. Love is the world's maker, master and destroyer, the magician whose word can change water to blood, and blood to fire, the dove to a serpent, and the serpent to a dove – ay, and can make of that same dove an eagle, with an eagle's beak and talons, and air-cleaving wing-stroke. Love is the spirit of life and the angel of death. He speaks, and the thorny wilderness of the lonely heart is become a paradise of flowers. He is silent, and the garden is but a blackened desert over which a destroying flame has passed in the arms of the east wind. Love stands at the gateway of each human soul, holding in his hands a rose and a drawn sword – the sword is for the many, the rose for the one.'

He sighed and was silent. Unorna looked at him curiously.

'Have you ever loved, that you should talk like that?' she asked. He turned upon her almost fiercely.

'Loved? Yes, as you can never love; as you, in your woman's heart, can never dream of loving – with every thought, with every fibre, with every pulse, with every breath; with a love that is burning the old oak through and through, root and branch, core and knot, to feathery ashes that you may scatter with a sigh – the only sigh you will ever breathe for me, Unorna. Have I loved? Can I love? Do I love today as I loved yesterday and shall love tomorrow? Ah, child! That you should ask that, with your angel's face, when I am in hell for you! When I would give my body to death and my soul to darkness for a touch of your hand, for as much kindness and gentleness in a word from your dear lips as you give the beggars in the street! When I would tear out my heart with my hands to feed the very dog that fawns on you – and who is more to you than I, because he is yours, and all that is yours I love, and worship, and adore!'

Unorna had looked up and smiled at first, believing that it was all but a comedy, as he had told her that it should be. But as he spoke, and the strong words chased each other in the torrent of his passionate speech, she was startled and surprised. There was a force in his language, a fiery energy in his look, a ring of half-desperate hope in his deep voice, which moved her to strange thoughts. His face, too, was changed and ennobled, his gestures larger, even his small stature ceased, for once, to seem dwarfish and gnome-like.

'Keyork Arabian, is it possible that you love me?' she cried, in her wonder.

'Possible? True? There is neither truth nor possibility in anything else for me, in anything, in anyone, but you, Unorna. The service of my love fills the days and the nights and the years with you – fills the world with you only; makes heaven to be on earth, since heaven is but the air that is made bright with your breath, as the temple of all temples is but the spot whereon your dear feet stand. The light of life is where you are, the darkness of death is everywhere where you are not. But I am condemned to die, cut off, predestined to be lost – for you have no pity, Unorna, you cannot find it in you to be sorry for the poor old man whose last pulse will beat for you; whose last word will be your name; whose last look upon your beauty will end the dream in which he lived his life. What can it be to you, that I love you so? Why should it be anything to you? When I am gone – with the love of you in my heart, Unorna – when they have buried the ugly old body out of your sight, you will not even remember that I was once your companion, still less that I knelt before you, that I kissed the ground on which you stood; that I loved you as men love whose hearts are breaking, that I touched the hem of your garment and was for one moment young – that I besought you to press my hand but once, with one thought of kindness, with one last and only word of human pity –'

He broke off suddenly, and there was a tremor in his voice which lent intense expression to the words. He was kneeling upon one knee beside Unorna, but between her and the light, so that she saw his face indistinctly. She could not but pity him. She took his outstretched hand in hers.

'Poor Keyork!' she said, very kindly and gently. 'How could I have ever guessed all this?'

'It would have been exceedingly strange if you had,' answered Keyork, in a tone that made her start.

Then a magnificent peal of bass laughter rolled through the room, as the gnome sprang suddenly to his feet.

'Did I not warn you?' asked Keyork, standing back and contemplating Unorna's surprised face with delight. 'Did I not tell you that I was going to make love to you? That I was old and hideous and had everything against me? That it was all a comedy for your amusement? That there was to be nothing but deception from beginning to end? That I was like a decrepit owl screeching at the moon, and many other things to a similar effect?'

Unorna smiled somewhat thoughtfully.

'You are the greatest of great actors, Keyork Arabian. There is something diabolical about you. I sometimes almost think that you are the devil himself!'

'Perhaps I am,' suggested the little man cheerfully.

'Do you know that there is a horror about all this?' Unorna rose to her feet. Her smile had vanished and she seemed to feel cold.

As though nothing had happened, Keyork began to make his daily examination of his sleeping patient, applying his thermometer to the body, feeling the pulse, listening to the beatings of the heart with his stethoscope, gently drawing down the lower lid of one of the eyes to observe the colour of the membrane, and, in a word, doing all those things which he was accustomed to do under the circumstances with a promptness and briskness which showed how little he feared that the old man would wake under his touch. He noted some of the results of his observations in a pocket-book. Unorna stood still and watched him.

'Do you remember ever to have been in the least degree like other people?' she asked, speaking after a long silence, as he was returning his notes to his pocket.

'I believe not,' he answered. 'Nature spared me that indignity – or denied me that happiness – as you may look at it. I am not like other people, as you justly remark. I need not say that it is the other people who are the losers.'

'The strange thing is, that you should be able to believe so much of yourself when you find it so hard to believe good of your fellow-men.'

'I object to the expression, "fellow-men",' returned Keyork promptly. 'I dislike phrases, and, generally, maxims as a whole, and all their component parts. A woman must have invented that particular phrase of yours in order to annoy a man she disliked.'

'And why, if you please?'

'Because no one ever speaks of "fellow-women". The question of woman's duty to man has been amply discussed since the days of Menes the Thinite – but no one ever heard of a woman's duty to her fellow-women; unless, indeed, her duty is to try and outdo them by fair means or foul. Then why talk of man and his fellow-men? I can put the wisest rule of life into two short phrases.'

'Give me the advantage of your wisdom.'

'The first rule is, beware of women.'

'And the second?'

'Beware of men,' laughed the little sage. 'Observe the simplicity and symmetry. Each rule has three words, two of which are the same in each, so that you have the result of the whole world's experience at your disposal at the comparatively small expenditure of one verb, one preposition, and two nouns.'

'There is little room for love in your system,' remarked Unorna, 'for such love, for instance, as you described to me a few minutes ago.'

'There is too much room for it in yours,' retorted Keyork. 'Your system is constantly traversed in all directions by bodies, sometimes nebulous and sometimes fiery, which move in unknown orbits at enormous rates of speed. In astronomy they call them comets, and astronomers would be much happier without them.'

'I am not an astronomer.'

'Fortunately for the peace of the solar system. You have been sending your comets dangerously near to our sick planet,' he added, pointing to the sleeper. 'If you do it again he will break up into asteroids. To use that particularly disagreeable and suggestive word invented by men, he will die.'

'He seems no worse,' said Unorna, contemplating the massive, peaceful face.

'I do not like the word "seems",' answered Keyork. 'It is the refuge of inaccurate persons, unable to distinguish between facts and appearances.'

'You object to everything today. Are there any words which I may use without offending your sense of fitness in language?'

'None which do not express a willing affirmation of all I say. I will receive any original speech on your part at the point of the sword. You have done enough damage today, without being allowed the luxury of dismembering common sense. Seems, you say! By all that is unholy! By Eblis, Ahriman, and the Three Black Angels! He is worse, and there is no seeming. The heat is greater, the pulse is weaker, the heart flutters like a sick bird.'

Unorna's face showed her anxiety.

'I am sorry,' she said, in a low voice.

'Sorry! No doubt you are. It remains to be seen whether your sorrow can be utilised as a simple, or macerated in tears to make a tonic, or sublimated to produce a corrosive which will destroy the canker, death. But be sorry by all means. It occupies your mind without disturbing me, or injuring the patient. Be sure that if I can find an active application for your sentiment, I will give you the rare satisfaction of being useful.'

'You have the art of being the most intolerably disagreeable of living men when it pleases you.'

'When you displease me, you should say. I warn you that if he dies – our friend here – I will make further studies in the art of being unbearable to you. You will certainly be surprised by the result.'

'Nothing that you could say or do would surprise me.'

'Indeed? We shall see.'

'I will leave you to your studies, then. I have been here too long as it is.'

She moved and arranged the pillow under the head of the sleeping giant and adjusted the folds of his robe. Her touch was tender and skilful in spite of her ill-suppressed anger. Then she turned away and went towards the door. Keyork Arabian watched her until her hand was upon the latch. His sharp eyes twinkled, as though he expected something amusing to occur.

'Unorna!' he said, suddenly, in an altered voice. She stopped and looked back.

'Well?'

'Do not be angry, Unorna. Do not go away like this.'

Unorna turned, almost fiercely, and came back a step.

'Keyork Arabian, do you think you can play upon me as on an instrument? Do you suppose that I will come and go at your word like a child – or like a dog? Do you think you can taunt me at one moment, and flatter me the next, and find my humour always at your command?'

The gnome-like little man looked down, made a sort of inclination of his short body, and laid his hand upon his heart.

'I was never presumptuous, my dear lady. I never had the least intention of taunting you, as you express it, and as for your humour – can you suppose that I could expect to command, where it is only mine to obey?'

'It is of no use to talk in that way,' said Unorna, haughtily. 'I am not prepared to be deceived by your comedy this time.'

'Nor I to play one. Since I have offended you, I ask your pardon. Forgive the expression, for the sake of the meaning; the thoughtless word for the sake of the unworded thought.'

'How cleverly you turn and twist both thoughts and words!'

'Do not be so unkind, dear friend.'

'Unkind to you? I wish I had the secret of some unkindness that you should feel!'

'The knowledge of what I can feel is mine alone,' answered Keyork, with a touch of sadness. 'I am not a happy man. The world, for me, holds but one interest and one friendship. Destroy the one, or embitter the other, and Keyork's remnant of life becomes but a foretaste of death.'

'And that interest – that friendship – where are they?' asked Unorna in a tone still bitter, but less scornful than before.

'Together, in this room, and both in danger, the one through your young haste and impetuosity, the other through my wretched weakness in being made angry; forgive me, Unorna, as I ask forgiveness –'

'Your repentance is too sudden; it savours of the death-bed.'

'Small wonder, when my life is in the balance.'

'Your life?' She uttered the question incredulously, but not without curiosity.

'My life – and for your word,' he answered, earnestly. He spoke so impressively, and in so solemn a tone, that Unorna's face became grave. She advanced another step towards him, and laid her hand upon the back of the chair in which she previously had sat.

'We must understand each other – today or never,' she said. 'Either we must part and abandon the great experiment – for, if we part, it must be abandoned –'

'We cannot part, Unorna.'

'Then, if we are to be associates and companions – '

'Friends,' said Keyork in a low voice.

'Friends? Have you laid the foundation for a friendship between us? You say that your life is in the balance. That is a figure of speech, I suppose. Or has your comedy another act? I can believe well enough that your greatest interest in life lies there, upon that couch, asleep. I know that you can do nothing without me, as you know it yourself. But in your friendship I can never trust – never! – still less can I believe that any words of mine can affect your happiness, unless they be those you need for the experiment itself. Those, at least, I have not refused to pronounce.'

While she was speaking, Keyork began to walk up and down the room, in evident agitation, twisting his fingers and bending down his head.

'My accursed folly!' he exclaimed, as though speaking to himself. 'My damnable ingenuity in being odious! It is not to be believed! That a man of my age should think one thing and say another – like a tetchy girl or a spoilt child! The stupidity of the thing! And then, to have the idiotic utterances of the tongue registered and judged as a confession of faith – or rather, of faithlessness! But it is only just – it is only right – Keyork Arabian's self is ruined again by Keyork Arabian's vile speeches, which have no more to do with his self than the clouds on earth have with the sun above them! Ruined, ruined – lost, this time. Cut off from the only living being he respects – the only being whose respect he covets; sent back to die in his loneliness, to perish like a friendless beast, as he is, to the funereal music of his own irrepressible snarling! To growl himself out of the world, like a broken-down old tiger in the jungle, after scaring away all possible peace and happiness and help with his senseless growls! Ugh! It is perfectly just, it is absolutely right and supremely horrible to think of! A fool to the last, Keyork, as you always were – and who would make a friend of such a fool?'

Unorna leaned upon the back of the chair watching him, and wondering whether, after all, he were not in earnest this time. He jerked out his sentences excitedly, striking his hands together and then swinging his arms in strange gestures. His tone, as he gave utterance to his incoherent self-condemnation, was full of sincere conviction and of anger against himself. He seemed not to see Unorna, nor to notice her presence in the room. Suddenly, he stopped, looked at her and came towards her. His manner became very humble.

'You are right, my dear lady,' he said. 'I have no claim to your forbearance for my outrageous humours. I have offended you, insulted
you, spoken to you as no man should speak to any woman. I cannot
even ask you to forgive me, and, if I tell you that I am sorry, you will
not believe me. Why should you? But you are right. This cannot go
on. Rather than run the risk of again showing you my abominable
temper, I will go away.'

His voice trembled and his bright eyes seemed to grow dull and
misty.

'Let this be our parting,' he continued, as though mastering his
emotion. 'I have no right to ask anything, and yet I ask this of you.
When I have left you, when you are safe for ever from my humours
and my tempers and myself – then, do not think unkindly of Keyork
Arabian. He would have seemed the friend he is, but for his unruly
tongue.'

Unorna hesitated a moment. Then she put out her hand, convinced of his sincerity in spite of herself.

'Let bygones be bygones, Keyork,' she said. 'You must not go, for
I believe you.'

At the words, the light returned to his eyes, and a look of ineffable
beatitude overspread the face which could be so immovably expressionless.

'You are as kind as you are good, Unorna, and as good as you are
beautiful,' he said, and with a gesture which would have been courtly
in a man of nobler stature, but which was almost grotesque in such a
dwarf, he raised her fingers to his lips.

This time, no peal of laugher followed to destroy the impression
he had produced upon Unorna. She let her hand rest in his a few
seconds, and then gently withdrew it.

'I must be going,' she said.

'So soon?' exclaimed Keyork regretfully. 'There were many things
I had wished to say to you today, but if you have no time – '

'I can spare a few minutes,' answered Unorna, pausing. 'What is
it?'

'One thing is this.' His face had again become impenetrable as a
mask of old ivory, and he spoke in his ordinary way. 'This is the
question. I was in the Teyn Kirche before I came here.'

'In church!' exclaimed Unorna in some surprise, and with a slight
smile.

'I frequently go to church,' answered Keyork gravely. 'While there,
I met an old acquaintance of mine, a strange fellow whom I have not

seen for years. The world is very small. He is a great traveller – a wanderer through the world.'

Unorna looked up quickly, and a very slight colour appeared in her cheeks.

'Who is he?' she asked, trying to seem indifferent. 'What is his name?'

'His name? It is strange, but I cannot recall it. He is very tall, wears a dark beard, has a pale, thoughtful face. But I need not describe him, for he told me that he had been with you this morning. That is not the point.'

He spoke carelessly and scarcely glanced at Unorna while speaking.

'What of him?' she inquired, trying to seem as indifferent as her companion.

'He is a little mad, poor man, that is all. It struck me that, if you would, you might save him. I know something of his story, though not much. He once loved a young girl, now doubtless dead, but whom he still believes to be alive, and he spends – or wastes – his life in a useless search for her. You might cure him of the delusion.'

'How do you know that the girl is dead?'

'She died in Egypt, four years ago,' answered Keyork. 'They had taken her there in the hope of saving her, for she was at death's door already, poor child.'

'But if you convince him of that.'

'There is no convincing him, and if he were really convinced he would die himself. I used to take an interest in the man, and I know that you could cure him in a simpler and safer way. But of course it lies with you.'

'If you wish it, I will try,' Unorna answered, turning her face from the light. 'But he will probably not come back to me.'

'He will. I advised him very strongly to come back, very strongly indeed. I hope I did right. Are you displeased?'

'Not at all!' Unorna laughed a little. 'And if he comes, how am I to convince him that he is mistaken, and that the girl is dead?'

'That is very simple. You will hypnotise him, he will yield very easily, and you will suggest to him very forcibly to forget the girl's existence. You can suggest to him to come back tomorrow and the next day, or as often as you please, and you can renew the suggestion each time. In a week he will have forgotten – as you know people can forget – entirely, totally, without hope of recalling what is lost.'

'That is true,' said Unorna, in a low voice. 'Are you sure that the effect will be permanent?' she asked with sudden anxiety.

'A case of the kind occurred in Hungary last year. The cure was effected in Pesth. I was reading it only a few months ago. The oblivion was still complete, as long as six months after the treatment, and there seems no reason to suppose that the patient's condition will change. I thought it might interest you to try it.'

'It will interest me extremely. I am very grateful to you for telling me about him.'

Unorna had watched her companion narrowly during the conversation, expecting him to betray his knowledge of a connection between the Wanderer's visit and the strange question she had been asking of the sleeper when Keyork had surprised her. She was agreeably disappointed in this however. He spoke with a calmness and ease of manner which disarmed suspicion.

'I am glad I did right,' said he.

He stood at the foot of the couch upon which the sleeper was lying, and looked thoughtfully and intently at the calm features.

'We shall never succeed in this way,' he said at last. 'This condition may continue indefinitely, till you are old, and I – until I am older than I am by many years. He may not grow weaker, but he cannot grow stronger. Theories will not renew tissues.'

Unorna looked up.

'That has always been the question,' she answered. 'At least, you have told me so. Will lengthened rest and perfect nourishment alone give a new impulse to growth or will they not?'

'They will not. I am sure of it now. We have arrested decay, or made it so slow as to be imperceptible. But we have made many attempts to renew the old frame, and we are no farther advanced than we were nearly four years ago. Theories will not make tissues.'

'What will?'

'Blood,' answered Keyork Arabian very softly.

'I have heard of that being done for young people in illness,' said Unorna.

'It has never been done as I would do it,' replied the gnome, shaking his head and gathering his great beard in his hand, as he gazed at the sleeper.

'What would you do?'

'I would make it constant for a day, or for a week if I could – a constant circulation; the young heart and the old should beat together; it could be done in the lethargic sleep – an artery and a vein – a vein and an artery – I have often thought of it; it could not fail. The new young blood would create new tissue, because it would itself constantly be renewed in the young body which is able to renew it, only expending itself in the old. The old blood would itself become young again as it passed to the younger man.'

'A man!' exclaimed Unorna.

'Of course. An animal would not do, because you could not produce the lethargy nor make use of suggestion for healing purposes – '

'But it would kill him!'

'Not at all, as I would do it, especially if the young man were very strong and full of life. When the result is obtained, an antiseptic ligature, suggestion of complete healing during sleep, proper nourishment, such as we are giving at present, by recalling the patient to the hypnotic state, sleep again, and so on; in eight and forty hours your young man would be waked and would never know what had happened to him – unless he felt a little older, by nervous sympathy,' added the sage with a low laugh.

'Are you perfectly sure of what you say?' asked Unorna eagerly.

'Absolutely. I have examined the question for years. There can be no doubt of it. Food can maintain life, blood alone can renew it.'

'Have you everything you need here?' inquired Unorna.

'Everything. There is no hospital in Europe that has the appliances we have prepared for every emergency.'

He looked at her face curiously. It was ghastly pale with excitement. The pupil of her brown eye was so widely expanded that the iris looked black, while the aperture of the grey one was contracted to the size of a pin's head, so that the effect was almost that of a white and sightless ball.

'You seem interested,' said the gnome.

'Would such a man – such a man as Israel Kafka answer the purpose?' she asked.

'Admirably,' replied the other, beginning to understand.

'Keyork Arabian,' whispered Unorna, coming close to him and bending down to his ear, 'Israel Kafka is alone under the palm tree where I always sit. He is asleep, and he will not wake.'

The gnome looked up and nodded gravely. But she was gone almost before she had finished speaking the words.

'As upon an instrument,' said the little man, quoting Unorna's angry speech. 'Truly I can play upon you, but it is a strange music.'

Half an hour later Unorna returned to her place among the flowers, but Israel Kafka was gone.

Chapter 7

The Wanderer, when Keyork Arabian had left him, had intended to revisit Unorna without delay, but he had not proceeded far in the direction of her house when he turned out of his way and entered a deserted street which led towards the river. He walked slowly, drawing his furs closely about him, for it was very cold.

He found himself in one of those moments of life in which the presentiment of evil almost paralyses the mind's power of making any decision. In general, a presentiment is but the result upon the consciousness of conscious or unconscious fear. This fear is very often the natural consequence of the reaction which, in melancholy natures, comes almost inevitably after a sudden and unexpected satisfaction or after a period in which the hopes of the individual have been momentarily raised by some unforeseen circumstance. It is by no means certain that hope is of itself a good thing. The wise and mournful soul prefers the blessedness of that non-expectancy which shall not be disappointed, to the exhilarating pleasures of an anticipation which may prove empty. In this matter lies one of the great differences between the normal moral state of the heathen and that of the Christian. The Greek hoped for all things in this world and for nothing in the next; the Christian, on the contrary, looks for a happiness to come hereafter, while fundamentally denying the reality of any earthly joy whatsoever in the present. Man, however, is so constituted as to find it almost impossible to put faith in either bliss alone, without helping his belief by borrowing some little refreshment from the hope of the other. The wisest of the Greeks believed the soul to be immortal; the sternest of Christians cannot forget that once or twice in his life he had been contemptibly happy, and condemns himself for secretly wishing that he might be as happy again before all is over. Faith is the evidence of things unseen, but hope is the unreasoning belief that unseen things may soon become evident. The definition of faith puts earthly disappointment out of the question; that of hope introduces it into human affairs as a constant and imminent probability.

The development of psychologic research in our day has proved beyond a doubt that individuals of a certain disposition may be conscious of events actually occurring, or which have recently occurred, at a great distance; but it has not shown satisfactorily that things yet to happen are foreshadowed by that restless condition of the sensibilities which we call presentiment. We may, and perhaps must, admit that all that is or has been produces a real and perceptible impression upon all else that is. But there is as yet no good reason for believing that an impression of what shall be can be conveyed by anticipation – without reasoning – to the mind of man.

But though the realisation of a presentiment may be as doubtful as any event depending upon chance alone, yet the immense influence which a mere presentiment may exercise is too well known to be denied. The human intelligence has a strong tendency to believe in its own reasonings, of which, indeed, the results are often more accurate and reliable than those reached by the physical perceptions alone. The problems which can be correctly solved by inspection are few indeed compared with those which fall within the province of logic. Man trusts to his reason, and then often confounds the impressions produced by his passions with the results gained by semi-conscious deduction. His love, his hate, his anger create fears, and these supply him with presentiments which he is inclined to accept as so many well-reasoned grounds of action. If he is often deceived, he becomes aware of his mistake, and, going to the other extreme, considers a presentiment as a sort of warning that the contrary of what he expects will take place; if he chances to be often right he grows superstitious.

The lonely man who was pacing the icy pavement of the deserted street on that bitter winter's day felt the difficulty very keenly. He would not yield and he could not advance. His heart was filled with forebodings which his wisdom bade him treat with indifference, while his passion gave them new weight and new horror with every minute that passed.

He had seen with his eyes and heard with his ears. Beatrice had been before him, and her voice had reached him among the voices of thousands, but now, since the hours has passed and he had not found her, it was as though he had been near her in a dream, and the strong certainty took hold of him that she was dead and that he had looked upon her wraith in the shadowy church.

He was a strong man, not accustomed to distrust his senses, and his reason opposed itself instantly to the suggestion of the supernatural. He had many times, on entering a new city, felt himself suddenly elated by the irresistible belief that his search was at an end, and that within a few hours he must inevitably find her whom he had sought so long. Often as he passed through the gates of some vast burying-place, he had almost hesitated to walk through the silent ways, feeling all at once convinced that upon the very first headstone he was about to see the name that was ever in his heart. But the expectation of final defeat, like the anticipation of final success, had been always deceived. Neither living nor dead had he found her.

Two common, reasonable possibilities lay before him, and two only. He had either seen Beatrice, or he had not. If she had really been in the Teyn Kirche, she was in the city and not far from him. If she had not been there, he had been deceived by an accidental but extraordinary likeness. Within the logical concatenation of cause and effect there was no room for any other supposition, and it followed that his course was perfectly clear. He must continue his search until he should find the person he had seen, and the result would be conclusive, for he would again see the same face and hear the same voice. Reason told him that he had in all likelihood been mistaken after all. Reason reminded him that the church had been dark, the multitude of worshippers closely crowded together, the voices that sang almost innumerable and wholly undistinguishable from each other. Reason showed him a throng of possibilities, all pointing to an error of his perceptions and all in direct contradiction with the one fact which his loving instinct held for true.

The fear of evil, the presentiment of death, defied logic and put its own construction and interpretation upon the strange event. He neither believed, nor desired to believe, in a supernatural visitation, yet the inexplicable certainty of having seen a ghostly vision overwhelmed reason and all her arguments. Beatrice was dead. Her spirit had passed in that solemn hour when the Wanderer had stood in the dusky church; he had looked upon her shadowy wraith, and had heard the echo of a voice from beyond the stars, whose crystal tones already swelled the diviner harmony of an angelic strain.

The impression was so strong at first as to be but one step removed from conviction. The shadow of a great mourning fell upon him, of a grief too terrible for words, too solemn for tears, too strong to find any expression save in death itself. He walked heavily, bending his head, his eyes half closed as though in bodily pain, the icy pavement rang like iron under his tread, the frozen air pierced through him, as his sorrow pierced his heart, the gloom of the fast-sinking winter's day deepened as the darkness in his own soul. He, who was always alone, knew at last what loneliness could mean. While she had lived she had been with him always, a living, breathing woman, visible to his inner eyes, speaking to his inward hearing, waking in his sleepless love. He had sought her with restless haste and untiring strength through the length and breadth of the whole world, but yet she had never left him, he had never been separated from her for one moment, never, in the years of his wandering, had he entered the temple of his heart without finding her in its most holy place. Men had told him that she was dead, but he had looked within himself and had seen that she was still alive; the dread of reading her sacred name carved upon the stone that covered her resting-place, had chilled him and made his sight tremble, but he had entered the shrine of his soul and had found her again, untouched by death, unchanged by years, living, loved, and loving. But now, when he shut out the dismal street from view, and went to the sanctuary and kneeled upon the threshold, he saw but a dim vision, as of something lying upon an altar in the dark, something shrouded in white, something shapely and yet shapeless, something that had been and was not any more.

He reached the end of the street, but he felt a reluctance to leave it, and turned back again, walking still more slowly and heavily than before. So far as any outward object or circumstance could be said to be in harmony with his mood, the dismal lane, the failing light, the bitter air, were at that moment sympathetic to him. The tomb itself is not more sepulchral than certain streets and places in Prague on a dark winter's afternoon. In the certainty that the last and the greatest of misfortunes had befallen him, the Wanderer turned back into the gloomy by-way as the pale, wreathing ghosts, fearful of the sharp daylight and the distant voices of men, sink back at dawn into the graves out of which they have slowly risen to the outer air in the silence of the night.

Death, the arch-steward of eternity, walks the bounds of man's entailed estate, and the headstones of men's graves are landmarks in the great possession committed to his stewardship, enclosing within their narrow ring the wretched plot of land which makes up all of life's inheritance. From ever to always the generations of men do bondsmen's service in that single field, to plough it and sow it, and harrow it and water it, to lay the sickle to the ripe corn if so be that their serfdom falls in the years of plenty and the ear is full, to eat the bread of tears, if their season of servitude be required of them in a time of scarcity and famine. Bondsmen of death, from birth, they are sent forth out of the sublime silence of the pathless forest which hems in the open glebeland of the present and which is eternity, past and to come; bondsmen of death, from youth to age, they join in the labour of the field, they plough, they sow, they reap perhaps, tears they shed many, and of laughter there is also a little amongst them; bondsmen of death to the last, they are taken in the end, when they have served their tale of years, many or few, and they are led from furrow and grassland, willing or unwilling, mercifully or cruelly, to the uttermost boundary, and they are thrust out quickly into the darkness whence they came. For their place is already filled, and the new husbandmen, their children, have in their turn come into the field, to eat of the fruit they sowed, to sow in turn a seed of which they themselves shall not see the harvest, whose sheaves others shall bind, whose ears others shall thresh, and of whose corn others shall make bread after them. With our eyes we may yet see the graves of two hundred generations of men, whose tombs serve but to mark that boundary more clearly, whose fierce warfare, when they fought against the master, could not drive back that limit by a handbreadth, whose uncomplaining labour, when they accepted their lot patiently, earned them not one scant foot of soil wherewith to broaden their inheritance as reward for their submission; and of them all, neither man nor woman was ever forgotten in the day of reckoning, nor was one suffered to linger in the light. Death will bury a thousand generations more, in graves as deep, strengthening year by year the strong chain of his grim landmarks. He will remember us every one when the time comes; to some of us he will vouchsafe a peaceful end, but some shall pass away in mortal agony, and some shall be dragged unconscious to the other side; but all must go. Some shall not see him till he is at hand, and some shall dream of him in year-long dreams of horror, to be taken unawares at the last. He will remember us every one and will come to us, and the place of our rest shall be marked for centuries, for years, or for seconds, for each a stone, or a few green sods laid upon a mound beneath the sky, or the ripple on a changing wave when the loaded sack has slipped from the smooth plank, and the sound of a dull splash has died away in the wind. There be strong men, as well as weak, who shudder and grow cold when they think of that yet undated day which must close with its black letter their calendar of joy and sorrow; there are weaklings, as well as giants, who fear death for those they love, but who fear not anything else at all. The master treats courage and cowardice alike; Achilles and Thersites must alike perish, and none will be so bold as to say that he can tell the dust of the misshapen varlet from the ashes of the swift-footed destroyer, whose hair was once so bright, whose eyes were so fierce, whose mighty heart was so slothless, so wrathful, so inexorable and so brave.

The Wanderer was of those who dread nothing save for the one dearly-beloved object, but who, when that fear is once roused by a real or an imaginary danger, can suffer in one short moment the agony which should be distributed through a whole lifetime. The magnitude of his passion could lend to the least thought or presentiment connected with it the force of a fact and the overwhelming weight of a real calamity.

In order to feel any great or noble passion a man must have an imagination both great and sensitive in at least one direction. The execution of a rare melody demands as a prime condition an instrument of wide compass and delicate construction, and one of even more rich and varied capabilities is needed to render those grand harmonies which are woven in the modulation of sonorous chords. A skilful hand may draw a scale from wooden blocks set upon ropes of straw, but the great musician must hold the violin, or must feel the keys of the organ under his fingers and the responsive pedals at his feet, before he can expect to interpret fittingly the immortal thought of the composer. The strings must vibrate in perfect tune, the priceless wood must be seasoned and penetrated with the melodies of years, and scores of years, the latent music must be already trembling to be free, before the hand that draws the bow can command the ears and hearts of those who hear. So too love, the chief musician of this world, must find an instrument worthy of his touch before he can show all his power, and make heart and soul ring with the lofty strains of a sublime passion. Not everyone knows what love means; few indeed know all that love can mean. There is no more equality among men than there is likeness between them, and no two are alike. The many have little, the few have much. To the many is given the faint perception of higher things, which is either the vestige, or the promise, of a nobler development, past or yet to come. As through a veil they see the line of beauty which it is not theirs to trace; as in a dream they hear the succession of sweet tones which they can themselves never bring together, though their half-grown instinct feels a vague satisfaction in the sequence; as from another world, they listen to the poet's song, wondering, admiring, but powerless over the great instrument of human speech, from whose 15,000 keys their touch can draw but the dull, tuneless prose of daily question and answer; as in a mirage of things unreal, they see the great deeds that are done in their time for love or hate, for race or country, for ambition and for vengeance, but though they see the result, and know the motive, the inward meaning and spirit of it all escapes them. It is theirs to be, and existence is in itself their all. To think, to create, to act, to feel can be only for the few. To one is given the transcendent genius that turns the very stones along life's road to precious gems of thought; whose gift it is to find speech in dumb things and eloquence in the ideal half of the living world; to whom sorrow is a melody and joy sweet music; to whom the humblest effort of a humble life can furnish an immortal lyric, and in whom one thought of the Divine can inspire a sublime hymn. Another stoops and takes a handful of clay from the earth, and with the pressure of his fingers moulds it to the reality of an unreal image seen in dreams; or, standing before the vast, rough block of marble, he sees within the mass the perfection of a faultless form – he lays the chisel to the stone, the mallet strikes the steel, one by one the shapeless fragments fly from the shapely limbs, the matchless curves are uncovered, the breathing mouth smiles through the petrifaction of a thousand ages, the shroud of stone falls from the godlike brow, and the Hermes of Olympia stands forth in all his deathless beauty. Another is born to the heritage of this world's power, fore-destined to rule and fated to destroy; the naked sword of destiny lies in his cradle; the axe of a king-maker awaits the awakening of his strength; the sceptre of supreme empire hangs within his reach. Unknown, he dreams and broods over the future; unheeded, he begins to move among his fellows; a smile, half of encouragement, half of indifference, greets his first effort; he advances a little farther, and thoughtful men look grave; another step, and suddenly all mankind cries out and faces him and would beat him back, but it is too late; one struggle more, and the hush of a great and unknown fear falls on the wrangling nations; they are silent, and the world is his. He is the man who is already thinking when others have scarcely begun to feel; who is creating before the thoughts of his rivals have reached any conclusion; who acts suddenly, terribly and irresistibly, before their creations have received life. And yet, the greatest and the richest inheritance of all is not his, for it has fallen to another, to the man of heart, and it is the inheritance of the kingdom of love.

In all ages the reason of the world has been at the mercy of brute force. The reign of law has never had more than a passing reality, and never can have more than that so long as man is human. The individual intellect and the aggregate intelligence of nations and races have alike perished in the struggles of mankind, to revive again, indeed, but as surely to be again put to the edge of the sword. Here and there great thoughts and great masterpieces have survived the martyrdom of a thinker, the extinction of a school, the death of a poet, the wreck of a high civilisation. Socrates is murdered with the creed of immortality on his very lips; hardly had he spoken the wonderful words recorded in the *Phaedo* when the fatal poison sent its deathly chill through his limbs; the Greeks are gone, yet the Hermes of Olympia remains, mutilated and maimed, indeed, but faultless still, and still supreme. The very name of Homer is grown well-nigh as mythic as his blindness. There are those today who, standing by the grave of William Shakespeare, say boldly that he was not the creator of the works that bear his name. And still, through the centuries, Achilles wanders lonely by the shore of the sounding sea; Paris loves, and Helen is false; Ajax raves, and Odysseus steers his sinking ship through the raging storm. Still, Hamlet the Avenger swears, hesitates, kills at last, and then himself is slain; Romeo sighs in the ivory moon-light, and love-bound Juliet hears the triumphant lark carolling his ringing hymn high in the cool morning air, and says it is the night-ingale – Immortals all, the marble god, the Greek, the Dane, the love-sick boy, the maiden foredoomed to death. But how short is the roll-call of these deathless ones! Through what raging floods of destruc-tion have they lived, through what tempests have they been tossed, upon what inhospitable shores have they been cast up by the changing tides of time! Since they were called to life by the great, half-nameless departed, how often has their very existence been forgotten by all but a score in tens of millions? Has it been given to those embodied thoughts of transcendent genius to ride in the whirlwind of men's passions or to direct the stormy warfare of half-frantic nations? Since they were born in all their bright perfection, to live on in unchanging beauty, violence has ruled the world; many a time since then the sword has mown down its harvest of thinkers, many a time has the iron harrow of war torn up and scarred the face of the earth. Athens still stands in broken loveliness, and the Tiber still rolls its tawny waters heavily through Rome; but Rome and Athens are today but places of departed spirits; they are no longer the seats of life, their broken hearts are petrified. All men may see the ports through which the blood flowed to the throbbing centre, the traces of the mighty arteries through which it was driven to the ends of the earth. But the blood is dried up, the hearts are broken, and though in their stony ruins those dead world-hearts be grander and more endur-ing than any which in our time are whole and beating, yet neither their endurance nor their grandeur have saved them from man, the destroyer, nor was the beauty of their thoughts or the thoughtfully-devised machinery of their civilisation a shield against a few score thousand rough-hammered blades, wielded by rough-hewn mortals who recked neither of intellect nor of civilisation, nor yet of beauty, being but very human men, full of terribly strong and human passions. Look where you will, throughout the length and breadth of all that was the world five thousand, or five hundred years ago; everywhere passion has swept thought before it, and belief, reason. And we, too, with our reason and our thoughts, shall be swept from existence and the memory of it. Is this the age of reason, and is this the reign of law? In the midst of this civilisation of ours three millions of men lie down nightly by their arms, men trained to handle rifle and sword, taught to destroy and to do nothing else; and nearly as many more wait but a summons to leave their homes and join the ranks. And often it is said that we are on the eve of a universal war. At the command of a few individuals, at the touch of a few wires, more than five millions of men in the very prime and glory of strength, armed as men never were armed since time began, will arise and will kill civilisation and thought, as both the one and the other have been slain before by fewer hands and less deadly weapons. Is this reason, or is this law? Passion rules the world, and rules alone. And passion is neither of the head, nor of the hand, but of the heart. Passion cares nothing for the mind. Love, hate, ambition, anger, avarice, either make a slave of intelligence to serve their impulses, or break down its impotent opposition with the unanswerable argument of brute force, and tear it to pieces with iron hands.

Love is the first, the greatest, the gentlest, the most cruel, the most irresistible of passions. In his least form he is mighty. A little love has destroyed many a great friendship. The merest outward semblance of love has made such havoc as no intellect could repair. The reality has made heroes and martyrs, traitors and murderers, whose names will not be forgotten, for glory or for shame. Helen is not the only woman whose smile has kindled the beacon of a ten years' war, nor Antony the only man who has lost the world for a caress. It may be that the Helen who shall work our destruction is even now twisting and braiding her golden hair; it may be that the new Antony, who is to lose this same old world again, already stands upon the steps of Cleopatra's throne. Love's day is not over yet, nor has man outgrown the love of woman.

But the power to love greatly is a gift, differing much in kind, though little in degree, from the inspiration of the poet, the genius of the artist, or the unerring instinct and eagle's glance of the conqueror; for conqueror, artist and poet are moved by passion and not by reason, which is but their servant in so far as it can be commanded to move others, and their deadliest enemy when it would move themselves. Let the passion and the instrument but meet, being suited to each other, and all else must go down before them. Few, indeed, are they to whom is given that rich inheritance, and they themselves alone know all their wealth, and all their misery, all the boundless possibilities of happiness that are theirs, and all the dangers and the terrors that beset their path. He who has won woman in the face of daring rivals, of enormous odds, of gigantic obstacles, knows what love means; he who has lost her, having loved her, alone has measured with his own soul the bitterness of earthly sorrow, the depth of total loneliness, the breadth of the wilderness of despair. And he who has sorrowed long, who has long been alone, but who has watched the small, twinkling ray still burning upon the distant border of his desert – the faint glimmer of a single star that was still above the horizon of despair – he only can tell what utter darkness can be upon the face of the earth when that last star has set for ever. With it are gone suddenly the very quarters and cardinal points of life's chart, there is no longer any right hand or any left, any north or south, any rising of the sun or any going down, any forward or backward direction in his path, any heaven above, or any hell below. The world has stood still and there is no life in the thick, black stillness. Death himself is dead, and one living man is forgotten behind, to mourn him as a lost friend, to pray that some new destroyer, more sure of hand than death himself, may come striding through the awful silence to make an end at last of the tormented spirit, to bear it swiftly to the place where that last star ceased to shine, and to let it down into the restful depths of an unremembering eternity. But into that place, which is the soul of man, no destroyer can penetrate; that solitary life neither the sword, nor pestilence, nor age, nor eternity can extinguish; that immortal memory no night can obscure. There was a beginning indeed, but end there can be none.

Such a man was the Wanderer, as he paced the deserted street in the cruel, gloomy cold of the late day. Between his sight and the star of his own hope an impenetrable shadow had arisen, so that he saw it no more. The memory of Beatrice was more than ever distinct to his inner sense, but the sudden presentiment of her death, real in its working as any certainty, had taken the reality of her from the ground on which he stood. For that one link had still been between them. Somewhere, near or far, during all these years, she too had trodden the earth with her light footsteps, the same universal mother earth on which they both moved and lived. The very world was hers, since she was touching it, and to touch it in his turn was to feel her presence. For who could tell what hidden currents ran in the secret depths, or what mysterious interchange of sympathy might not be maintained through them? The air itself was hers, since she was somewhere breathing it; the stars, for she looked on them; the sun, for it warmed her; the cold of winter, for it chilled her too; the breezes of spring, for they fanned her pale cheek and cooled her dark brow. All had been hers, and at the thought that she had passed away, a cry of universal mourning broke from the world she had left behind, and darkness descended upon all things, as a funeral pall.

Cold and dim and sad the ancient city had seemed before, but it was a thousandfold more melancholy now, more black, more saturated with the gloom of ages. From time to time the Wanderer raised his heavy lids, scarcely seeing what was before him, conscious of nothing but the horror which had so suddenly embraced his whole existence. Then, all at once, he was face to face with someone. A woman stood still in the way, a woman wrapped in rich furs, her features covered by a dark veil which could not hide the unequal fire of the unlike eyes so keenly fixed on his.

'Have you found her?' asked the soft voice.

'She is dead,' answered the Wanderer, growing very white.

Chapter 8

During the short silence which followed, and while the two were still standing opposite to each other, the unhappy man's look did not change. Unorna saw that he was sure of what he said, and a thrill of triumph, as jubilant as his despair was profound, ran through her. If she had cared to reason with herself and to examine into her own sincerity, she would have seen that nothing but genuine passion, good or bad, could have lent the assurance of her rival's death such power to flood the dark street with sunshine. But she was already long past doubt upon that question. The enchanter had bound her heart with his spells at the first glance, and the wild nature was already on fire. For one instant the light shot from her eyes, and then sank again as quickly as it had come. She had other impulses than those of love, and subtle gifts of perception that condemned her to know the truth, even when the delusion was most glorious. He was himself deceived, and she knew it. Beatrice might, indeed, have died long ago. She could not tell. But as she sought in the recesses of his mind, she saw that he had no certainty of it, she saw the black presentiment between him and the image, for she could see the image too. She saw the rival she already hated, not receiving a vision of the reality, but perceiving it through his mind, as it had always appeared to him. For one moment she hesitated still, and she knew that her whole life was being weighed in the trembling balance of that hesitation. For one moment her face became an impenetrable mask, her eyes grew dull as uncut jewels, her breathing ceased, her lips were set like cold marble. Then the stony mask took life again, the sight grew keen, and a gentle sigh stirred the chilly air.

'She is not dead.'

'Not dead!' The Wanderer started, but fully two seconds after she had spoken, as a man struck by a bullet in battle, in whom the suddenness of the shock has destroyed the power of instantaneous sensation.

'She is not dead. You have dreamed it,' said Unorna, looking at him steadily.

He pressed his hand to his forehead and then moved it, as though brushing away something that troubled him.

'Not dead? Not dead!' he repeated, in changing tones.

'Come with me. I will show her to you.'

He gazed at her and his senses reeled. Her words sounded like rarest music in his ear; in the darkness of his brain a soft light began to diffuse itself.

'Is it possible? Have I been mistaken?' he asked in a low voice, as though speaking to himself.

'Come!' said Unorna again very gently.

'Whither? With you? How can you bring me to her? What power have you to lead the living to the dead?'

'To the living. Come.'

'To the living – yes. I have dreamed an evil dream – a dream of death. She is not – no, I see it now. She is not dead. She is only very far from me, very, very far. And yet it was this morning – but I was mistaken, deceived by some faint likeness. Ah, God! I thought I knew her face! What is it that you want with me?'

He asked the question as though again suddenly aware of Unorna's presence. She had lifted her veil and her eyes drew his soul into their mysterious depths.

'She calls you. Come.'

'She? She is not here. What can you know of her? Why do you look at me so?'

He felt an unaccountable uneasiness under her gaze, like a warning of danger not far off. The memory of his meeting with her on that same morning was not clear at that moment, but he had not forgotten the odd disturbance of his faculties which had distressed him at the time. He was inclined to resist any return of the doubtful state and to oppose Unorna's influence. He felt the fascination of her glance, and he straightened himself rather proudly and coldly as though to withdraw himself from it. It was certain that Unorna, at the surprise of meeting her, had momentarily dispelled the gloomy presentiment which had given him such terrible pain. And yet, even his disturbed and anxious consciousness found it more than strange that she should thus press him to go with her, and so boldly promise to bring him to the object of his search. He resisted her, and found that resistance was not easy.

'And yet,' said she, dropping her eyes and seeming to abandon the attempt, 'you said that if you failed today you would come back to me. Have you succeeded, that you need no help?'

'I have not succeeded.'

'And if I had not come to you – if I had not met you here, you would have failed for the last time. You would have carried with you the conviction of her death to the moment of your own.'

'It was a horrible delusion, but since it was a delusion it would have passed away in time.'

'With your life, perhaps. Who would have waked you, if I had not?'

'I was not sleeping. Why do you reason? What would you prove?'

'Much, if I knew how. Will you walk with me? It is very cold.'

They had been standing where they had met. As she spoke, Unorna looked up with an expression wholly unlike the one he had seen a few moments earlier. Her strong will was suddenly veiled by the most gentle and womanly manner, and a little shiver, real or feigned, passed over her as she drew the folds of her fur more closely round her. The man before her could resist the aggressive manifestation of her power, but he was far too courteous to refuse her request.

'Which way?' he asked quietly.

'To the river,' she answered.

He turned and took his place by her side. For some moments they walked on in silence. It was already almost twilight.

'How short the days are!' exclaimed Unorna, rather suddenly.

'How long, even at their shortest!' replied her companion.

'They might be short – if you would.'

He did not answer her, though he glanced quickly at her face. She was looking down at the pavement before her, as though picking her way, for there were patches of ice upon the stones. She seemed very quiet. He could not guess that her heart was beating violently, and that she found it hard to say six words in a natural tone.

So far as he himself was concerned he was in no humour for talking. He had seen almost everything in the world, and had read or heard almost everything that mankind had to say. The streets of Prague had no novelty for him, and there was no charm in the chance acquaintance of a beautiful woman, to bring words to his lips. Words had long since grown useless in the solitude of a life that was spent in searching for one face among the millions that passed before his sight. Courtesy had bidden him to walk with her, because she had asked it, but courtesy did not oblige him to amuse her, he thought, and she had not the power that Keyork Arabian had to force him into conversation, least of all into conversing upon his own inner life. He regretted the few words he had spoken, and would have taken them back, had it been possible. He felt no awkwardness in the long silence.

Unorna for the first time in her life felt that she had not full control of her faculties. She who was always so calm, so thoroughly mistress of her own powers, whose judgment Keyork Arabian could deceive, but whose self-possession he could not move, except to anger, was at the present moment both weak and unbalanced. Ten minutes earlier she had fancied that it would be an easy thing to fix her eyes on his and to cast the veil of a half-sleep over his already half-dreaming senses. She had fancied that it would be enough to say 'Come', and that he would follow. She had formed the bold scheme of attaching him to herself, by visions of the woman whom he loved as she wished to be loved by him. She believed that if he were once in that state she could destroy the old love for ever, or even turn it to hate, at her will. And it had seemed easy. That morning, when he had first come to her, she had fastened her glance upon him more than once, and she had seen him turn a shade paler, had noticed the drooping of his lids and the relaxation of his hands. She had sought him in the street, guided by something surer than instinct, she had found him, had read his thoughts, and had felt him yielding to her fixed determination. Then, suddenly, her power had left her, and as she walked beside him, she knew that if she looked into his face she would blush and be confused like a shy girl. She almost wished that he would leave her without a word and without an apology.

It was not possible, however, to prolong the silence much longer. A vague fear seized her. Had she really lost all her dominating strength in the first moments of the first sincere passion she had ever felt? Was she reduced to weakness by his presence, and unable so much as to sustain a fragmentary conversation, let alone suggesting to his mind the turn it should take? She was ashamed of her poverty of spirit in the emergency. She felt herself tongue-tied, and the hot blood rose to her face. He was not looking at her, but she could not help fancying that he knew her secret embarrassment. She hung her head and drew her veil down so that it should hide even her mouth.

But her trouble increased with every moment, for each second made it harder to break the silence. She sought madly for something to say, and she knew that her cheeks were on fire. Anything would do, no matter what. The sound of her own voice, uttering the commonest of commonplaces, would restore her equanimity. But that simple, almost meaningless phrase would not be found. She would stammer, if she tried to speak, like a child that has forgotten its lesson and fears the schoolmaster as well as the laughter of its schoolmates. It would be so easy if he would say something instead of walking quietly by her side, suiting his pace to hers, shifting his position so that she might step upon the smoothest parts of the ill-paved street, and shielding her, as it were, from the passers-by. There was a courteous forethought for her convenience and safety in every movement of his, a something which a woman always feels when traversing a crowded thoroughfare by the side of a man who is a true gentleman in every detail of life, whether husband, or friend, or chance acquaintance. For the spirit of the man who is really thoughtful for woman, as well as sincerely and genuinely respectful in his intercourse with them, is manifest in his smallest outward action.

While every step she took increased the violence of the passion which had suddenly swept away her strength, every instant added to her confusion. She was taken out of the world in which she was accustomed to rule, and was suddenly placed in one where men are men, and women are women, and in which social conventionalities hold sway. She began to be frightened. The walk must end, and at the end of it they must part. Since she had lost her power over him he might go away, for there would be nothing to bring him to her. She wondered why he would not speak, and her terror increased. She dared not look up, lest she should find him looking at her.

Then they emerged from the street and stood by the river, in a lonely place. The heavy ice was grey with old snow in some places and black in others, where the great blocks had been cut out in long strips. It was lighter here. A lingering ray of sunshine, forgotten by the departing day, gilded the vast walls and turrets of venerable Hradschin, far above them on the opposite bank, and tinted the sharp dark spires of the half-built cathedral which crowns the fortress. The distant ring of fast-moving skates broke the stillness.

'Are you angry with me?' asked Unorna, almost humbly, and hardly knowing what she said. The question had risen to her lips without warning, and was asked almost unconsciously.

'I do not understand. Angry? At what? Why should you think I am angry?'

'You are so silent,' she answered, regaining courage from the mere sound of her own words. 'We have been walking a long time, and you have said nothing. I thought you were displeased.'

'You must forgive me. I am often silent.'

'I thought you were displeased,' she repeated. 'I think that you were, though you hardly knew it. I should be very sorry if you were angry.'

'Why would you be sorry?' asked the Wanderer with a civil indifference that hurt Unorna more than any acknowledgment of his displeasure could have done.

'Because I would help you, if you would let me.'

He looked at her with sudden keenness. In spite of herself she blushed and turned her head away. He hardly noticed the fact, and, if he had, would assuredly not have put upon it any interpretation approaching to the truth. He supposed that she was flushed with walking.

'No one has ever helped me, least of all in the way you mean,' he said. 'The counsels of wise men – of the wisest – have been useless, as well as the dreams of women who fancy they have the gift of mental sight beyond the limit of bodily vision.'

'Who fancy they see!' exclaimed Unorna, almost glad to find that she was still strong enough to feel annoyance at the slight.

'I beg your pardon. I do not mean to doubt your powers, of which I have had no experience.'

'I did not offer to see for you. I did not offer you a dream.'

'Would you show me that which I already see, waking and sleeping? Would you bring to my hearing the sound of a voice which I can hear even now? I need no help for that.'

'I can do more than that – for you.'

'And why for me?' he asked with some curiosity.

'Because – because you are Keyork Arabian's friend.' She glanced at his face, but he showed no surprise.

'You have seen him this afternoon, of course,' he remarked.

An odd smile passed over Unorna's face.

'Yes. I have seen him this afternoon. He is a friend of mine, and of yours – do you understand?'

'He is the wisest of men,' said the Wanderer. 'And also the maddest,' he added thoughtfully.

'And you think it was in his madness, rather than in his wisdom, that he advised you to come to me?'

'Possibly. In his belief in you, at least.'

'And that may be madness?' She was gaining courage.

'Or wisdom – if I am mad. He believes in you. That is certain.'

'He has no beliefs. Have you known him long, and do not know that? With him there is nothing between knowledge and ignorance.'

'And he knows, of course, by experience what you can do and what you cannot do?'

'By very long experience, as I know him.'

'Neither your gifts nor his knowledge of them can change dreams to facts.'

Unorna smiled again.

'You can produce a dream – nothing more,' continued the Wanderer, drawn at last into argument. 'I, too, know something of these things. The wisdom of the Egyptians is not wholly lost yet. You may possess some of it, as well as the undeveloped power which could put all their magic within your reach if you knew how to use it. Yet a dream is a dream.'

'Philosophers have disputed that,' answered Unorna. 'I am no philosopher, but I can overthrow the results of all their disputations.'

'You can do this. If I resign my will into your keeping you can cause me to dream. You can call up vividly before me the remembered and unremembered sights of my life. You can make me see clearly the sights impressed upon your own memory. You might do that, and yet you could be showing me nothing which I do not see now before me – of those things which I care to see.'

'But suppose that you were wrong, and that I had no dream to show you, but a reality?'

She spoke the words very earnestly, gazing into his eyes at last without fear. Something in her tone struck him and fixed his attention.

'There is no sleep needed to see realities,' he said.

'I did not say that there was. I only asked you to come with me to the place where she is.'

The Wanderer started slightly and forgot all the instinct of opposition to her which he had felt so strongly before.

'Do you mean that you know – that you can take me to her – ' he could not find words. A strange, overmastering astonishment took possession of him, and with it came wild hope and the wilder longing to reach its realisation instantly.

'What else could I have meant? What else did I say?' Her eyes were beginning to glitter in the gathering dusk.

The Wanderer no longer avoided their look, but he passed his hand over his brow, as though dazed.

'I only asked you to come with me,' she repeated softly. 'There is nothing supernatural about that. When I saw that you did not believe me I did not try to lead you then, though she is waiting for you. She bade me bring you to her.'

'You have seen her? You have talked with her? She sent you? Oh, for God's sake, come quickly! – come, come!'

He put out his hand as though to take hers and lead her away. She grasped it eagerly. He had not seen that she had drawn off her glove. He was lost. Her eyes held him and her fingers touched his bare wrist. His lids drooped and his will was hers. In the intolerable anxiety of the moment he had forgotten to resist, he had not even thought of resisting.

There were great blocks of stone in the desolate place, landed there before the river had frozen for a great building, whose gloomy, unfinished mass stood waiting for the warmth of spring to be completed. She led him by the hand, passive and obedient as a child, to a sheltered spot and made him sit down upon one of the stones. It was growing dark.

'Look at me,' she said, standing before him, and touching his brow. He obeyed.

'You are the image in my eyes,' she said, after a moment's pause.

'Yes. I am the image in your eyes,' he answered in a dull voice.

'You will never resist me again, I command it. Hereafter it will be enough for me to touch your hand, or to look at you, and if I say, "Sleep", you will instantly become the image again. Do you understand that?'

'I understand it.'

'Promise!'

'I promise,' he replied, without perceptible effort.

'You have been dreaming for years. From this moment you must forget all your dreams.'

His face expressed no understanding of what she said. She hesitated a moment and then began to walk slowly up and down before him. His half-glazed look followed her as she moved. She came back and laid her hand upon his head.

'My will is yours. You have no will of your own. You cannot think without me,' She spoke in a tone of concentrated determination, and a slight shiver passed over him.

'It is of no use to resist, for you have promised never to resist me again,' she continued. 'All that I command must take place in your mind instantly, without opposition. Do you understand?'

'Yes,' he answered, moving uneasily.

For some seconds she again held her open palm upon his head. She seemed to be evoking all her strength for a great effort.

'Listen to me, and let everything I say take possession of your mind for ever. My will is yours, you are the image in my eyes, my word is your law. You know what I please that you should know. You forget what I command you to forget. You have been mad these many years, and I am curing you. You must forget your madness. You have now forgotten it. I have erased the memory of it with my hand. There is nothing to remember any more.'

The dull eyes, deep-set beneath the shadows of the overhanging brow, seemed to seek her face in the dark, and for the third time there was a nervous twitching of the shoulders and limbs. Unorna knew the symptom well, but had never seen it return so often, like a protest of the body against the enslaving of the intelligence. She was nervous in spite of her success. The immediate results of hypnotic suggestion are not exactly the same in all cases, even in the first moments; its consequences may be widely different with different individuals. Unorna, indeed, possessed an extraordinary power, but on the other hand she had to deal with an extraordinary organisation. She knew this instinctively, and endeavoured to lead the sleeping mind by degrees to the condition in which she wished it to remain.

The repeated tremor in the body was the outward sign of a mental resistance which it would not be easy to overcome. The wisest course was to go over the ground already gained. This she was determined to do by means of a sort of catechism.

'Who am I?' she asked.

'Unorna,' answered the powerless man promptly, but with a strange air of relief.

'Are you asleep?'

'No.'

'Awake?'

'No.'

'In what state are you?'

'I am an image.'

'And where is your body?'

'Seated upon that stone.'

'Can you see your face?'

'I see it distinctly. The eyes in the body are glassy.'

'The body is gone now. You do not see it any more. Is that true?'

'It is true. I do not see it. I see the stone on which it was sitting.'

'You are still in my eyes. Now' – she touched his head again – 'now, you are no longer an image. You are my mind.'

'Yes. I am your mind.'

'You, my Mind, know that I met today a man called the Wanderer, whose body you saw when you were in my eyes. Do you know that or not?'

'I know it. I am your mind.'

'You know, Mind, that the man was mad. He had suffered for many years from a delusion. In pursuit of the fixed idea he had wandered far through the world. Do you know whither his travels had led him?'

'I do not know. That is not in your mind. You did not know it when I became your mind.'

'Good. Tell me, Mind, what was this man's delusion?'

'He fancied that he loved a woman whom he could not find.'

'The man must be cured. You must know that he was mad and is now sane. You, my Mind, must see that it was really a delusion. You see it now.'

'Yes. I see it.'

Unorna watched the waking sleeper narrowly. It was now night, but the sky had cleared and the starlight falling upon the snow in the lonely, open place, made it possible to see very well. Unorna seemed as unconscious of the bitter cold as her subject, whose body was in a state past all outward impressions. So far she had gone through all the familiar process of question and answer with success, but this was not all. She knew that if, when he awoke, the name he loved still remained in his memory, the result would not be accomplished.

She must produce entire forgetfulness, and to do this, she must wipe out every association, one by one. She gathered her strength during a short pause. She was greatly encouraged by the fact that the acknowledgment of the delusion had been followed by no convulsive reaction in the body. She was on the very verge of a complete triumph, and the concentration of her will during a few moments longer might win the battle.

She could not have chosen a spot better suited for her purpose. Within five minutes' walk of streets in which throngs of people were moving about, the scene which surrounded her was desolate and almost wild. The unfinished building loomed like a ruin behind her; the rough-hewn blocks lay like boulders in a stony desert; the broad grey ice lay like a floor of lustreless iron before her under the uncertain starlight. Only afar off, high up in the mighty Hradschin, lamps gleamed here and there from the windows, the distant evidences of human life. All was still. Even the steely ring of the skates had ceased.

'And so,' she continued, presently, 'this man's whole life has been a delusion, ever since he began to fancy in the fever of an illness that he loved a certain woman. Is this clear to you, my Mind?'

'It is quite clear,' answered the muffled voice.

'He was so utterly mad that he even gave that woman a name – a name, when she had never existed except in his imagination.'

'Except in his imagination,' repeated the sleeper, without resistance.

'He called her Beatrice. The name was suggested to him because he had fallen ill in a city of the South where a woman called Beatrice once lived and was loved by a great poet. That was the train of self-suggestion in his delirium. Mind, do you understand?'

'He suggested to himself the name in his illness.'

'In the same way that he suggested to himself the existence of the woman whom he afterwards believed he loved?'

'In exactly the same way.'

'It was all a curious and very interesting case of auto-hypnotic suggestion. It made him very mad. He is now cured of it. Do you see that he is cured?'

The sleeper gave no answer. The stiffened limbs did not move, indeed, nor did the glazed eyes reflect the starlight. But he gave no answer. The lips did not even attempt to form words. Had Unorna been less carried away by the excitement in her own thoughts, or less absorbed in the fierce concentration of her will upon its passive subject, she would have noticed the silence and would have gone back again over the old ground. As it was, she did not pause.

'You understand therefore, my Mind, that this Beatrice was entirely the creature of the man's imagination. Beatrice does not exist, because she never existed. Beatrice never had any real being. Do you understand?'

This time she waited for an answer, but none came.

'There never was any Beatrice,' she repeated firmly, laying her hand upon the unconscious head and bending down to gaze into the sightless eyes.

The answer did not come, but a shiver like that of an ague shook the long, graceful limbs.

'You are my Mind,' she said fiercely. 'Obey me! There never was any Beatrice, there is no Beatrice now, and there never can be.'

The noble brow contracted in a look of agonising pain, and the whole frame shook like an aspen leaf in the wind. The mouth moved spasmodically.

'Obey me! Say it!' cried Unorna with passionate energy.

The lips twisted themselves, and the face was as grey as the grey snow.

'There is – no – Beatrice.' The words came out slowly, and yet not distinctly, as though wrung from the heart by torture.

Unorna smiled at last, but the smile had not faded from her lips when the air was rent by a terrible cry.

'By the Eternal God of Heaven!' cried the ringing voice. 'It is a lie! – a lie! – a lie!'

She who had never feared anything earthly or unearthly, shrank back. She felt her heavy hair rising bodily upon her head.

The Wanderer had sprung to his feet. The magnitude and horror of the falsehood spoken had stabbed the slumbering soul to sudden and terrible wakefulness. The outline of his tall figure was distinct against the grey background of ice and snow. He was standing at his full height, his arms stretched up to heaven, his face luminously pale, his deep eyes on fire and fixed upon her face, forcing back her dominating will upon itself. But he was not alone!

'Beatrice!' he cried in long-drawn agony.

Between him and Unorna something passed by, something dark and soft and noiseless, that took shape slowly – a woman in black, a veil thrown back from her forehead, her white face turned towards the Wanderer, her white hands hanging by her side. She stood still, and the face turned, and the eyes met Unorna's, and Unorna knew that it was Beatrice.

There she stood, between them, motionless as a statue, impalpable as air, but real as life itself. The vision, if it was a vision, lasted fully a minute. Never, to the day of her death, was Unorna to forget that face, with its deathlike purity of outline, with its unspeakable nobility of feature.

It vanished as suddenly as it had appeared. A low broken sound of pain escaped from the Wanderer's lips, and with his arms extended he fell forwards. The strong woman caught him and he sank to the ground gently, in her arms, his head supported upon her shoulder, as she kneeled under the heavy weight.

There was a sound of quick footsteps on the frozen snow. A Bohemian watchman, alarmed by the loud cry, was running to the spot.

'What has happened?' he asked, bending down to examine the couple.

'My friend has fainted,' said Unorna calmly. 'He is subject to it. You must help me to get him home.'

'Is it far?' asked the man.

'To the House of the Black Mother of God.'

Chapter 9

The principal room of Keyork Arabian's dwelling was in every way characteristic of the man. In the extraordinary confusion which at first disturbed a visitor's judgment, some time was needed to discover the architectural bounds of the place. The vaulted roof was indeed apparent, as well as small portions of the wooden flooring. Several windows, which might have been large had they filled the arched embrasures in which they were set, admitted the daylight when there was enough of it in Prague to serve the purpose of illumination. So far as could be seen from the street, they were commonplace windows without shutters and with double casements against the cold, but from within it was apparent that the tall arches in the thick walls had been filled in with a thinner masonry in which the modern frames were set. So far as it was possible to see, the room had but two doors; the one, masked by a heavy curtain made of a Persian carpet, opened directly upon the staircase of the house; the other, exactly opposite, gave access to the inner apartments. On account of its convenient size, however, the sage had selected for his principal abiding place this first chamber, which was almost large enough to be called a hall, and here he had deposited the extraordinary and heterogeneous collection of objects, or more properly speaking, of remains, upon the study of which he spent a great part of his time.

Two large tables, three chairs and a divan completed the list of all that could be called furniture. The tables were massive, dark, and old-fashioned; the feet at each end consisted of thick flat boards sawn into a design of simple curves, and connected by strong crosspieces keyed to them with large wooden bolts. The chairs were ancient folding stools, with movable backs and well-worn cushions of faded velvet. The divan differed in no respect from ordinary oriental divans in appearance, and was covered with a stout dark Bokhara carpet of no great value; but so far as its use was concerned, the disorderly heaps of books and papers that lay upon it showed that Keyork was more inclined to make a book-case of it than a couch.

The room received its distinctive character, however, neither from its vaulted roof, nor from the deep embrasures of its windows, nor from its scanty furniture, but from the peculiar nature of the many curious objects, large and small, which hid the walls and filled almost all the available space on the floor. It was clear that every one of the specimens illustrated some point in the great question of life and death which formed the chief study of Keyork Arabian's latter years; for by far the greater number of the preparations were dead bodies, of men, of women, of children, of animals, to all of which the old man had endeavoured to impart the appearance of life, and in treating some of which he had attained results of a startling nature. The osteology of man and beast was indeed represented, for a huge case, covering one whole wall, was filled to the top with a collection of many hundred skulls of all races of mankind, and where real specimens were missing, their place was supplied by admirable casts of craniums; but this reredos, so to call it, of bony heads formed but a vast, grinning background for the bodies which stood and sat and lay in half-raised coffins and sarcophagi before them, in every condition produced by various known and lost methods of embalming. There were, it is true, a number of skeletons, disposed here and there in fantastic attitudes, gleaming white and ghostly in their mechanical nakedness, the bones of human beings, the bones of giant orang-outangs, of creatures large and small down to the flimsy little framework of a common bullfrog, strung on wires as fine as hairs, which squatted comfortably upon an old book near the edge of a table, as though it had just skipped to that point in pursuit of a ghostly fly and was pausing to meditate a farther spring. But the eye did not discover these things at the first glance. Solemn, silent, strangely expressive, lay three slim Egyptians, raised at an angle as though to give them a chance of surveying their fellow-dead, the linen bandages unwrapped from their heads and arms and shoulders, their jet-black hair combed and arranged and dressed by Keyork's hand, their faces softened almost to the expression of life by one of his secret processes, their stiffened joints so limbered by his art that their arms had taken natural positions again, lying over the edges of the sarcophagi in which they had rested motionless and immovable through thirty centuries. For the man had pursued his idea in every shape and with every experiment, testing, as it were, the potential imperishability of the animal frame by the degree of lifelike plumpness and softness and flexibility which it could be made to take after a mummification of three thousand years. And he had reached the conclusion that, in the nature of things, the human body might vie, in resisting the mere action of time, with the granite of the pyramids. Those had been his earliest trials. The results of many others filled the room. Here a group of South Americans, found dried in the hollow of an ancient tree, had been restored almost to the likeness of life, and were apparently engaged in a lively dispute over the remains of a meal – as cold as themselves and as human. There, towered the standing body of an African, leaning upon a knotted club, fierce, grinning, lacking only sight in the sunken eyes to be terrible. There again, surmounting a lay figure wrapped in rich stuffs, smiled the calm and gentle face of a Malayan lady – decapitated for her sins, so marvellously preserved that the soft dark eyes still looked out from beneath the heavy, half-drooping lids, and the full lips, still richly coloured, parted a little to show the ivory teeth. Other sights there were, more ghastly still, triumphs of preservation, if not of semi-resuscitation, over decay, won on its own most special ground. Triumphs all, yet almost failures in the eyes of the old student, they represented the mad efforts of an almost supernatural skill and superhuman science to revive, if but for one second, the very smallest function of the living body. Strange and wild were the trials he had made; many and great the sacrifices and blood offerings lavished on his dead in the hope of seeing that one spasm which would show that death might yet be conquered; many the engines, the machines, the artificial hearts, the applications of electricity that he had invented; many the powerful reactives he had distilled wherewith to excite the long dead nerves, or those which but two days had ceased to feel. The hidden essence was still undiscovered, the meaning of vitality eluded his profoundest study, his keenest pursuit. The body died, and yet the nerves could still be made to act as though alive for the space of a few hours – in rare cases for a day. With his eyes he had seen a dead man spring half across a room from the effects of a few drops of musk – on the first day; with his eyes he had seen the dead twist themselves, and move and grin under the electric current – provided it had not been too late. But that 'too late' had baffled him, and from his first belief that life might be restored when once gone, he had descended to what seemed the simpler proposition of the two, to the problem of maintaining life indefinitely so long as its magic essence lingered in the flesh and blood. And now he believed that he was very near the truth; how terribly near he had yet to learn.

On that evening when the Wanderer fell to the earth before the shadow of Beatrice, Keyork Arabian sat alone in his charnel-house. The brilliant light of two powerful lamps illuminated everything in the place, for Keyork loved light, like all those who are intensely attached to life for its own sake. The yellow rays flooded the lifelike faces of his dead companions, and streamed upwards to the heterogeneous objects that filled the shelves almost to the spring of the vault – objects which all reminded him of the conditions of lives long ago extinct, endless heaps of barbarous weapons, of garments of leather and of fish skin, Amurian, Siberian, Gothic, Mexican, and Peruvian; African and Red Indian masks, models of boats and canoes, sacred drums, Liberian idols, Runic calendars, fiddles made of human skulls, strange and barbaric ornaments, all producing together an amazing richness of colour – all things in which the man himself had taken but a passing interest, the result of his central study – life in all its shapes.

He sat alone. The African giant looked down at his dwarf-like form as though in contempt of such half-grown humanity; the Malayan lady's bodiless head turned its smiling face towards him; scores of dead beings seemed to contemplate half in pity, half in scorn, their would-be reviver. Keyork Arabian was used to their company and to their silence. Far beyond the common human horror of dead humanity, if one of them had all at once nodded to him and spoken to him he would have started with delight and listened with rapture. But they were all still dead, and they neither spoke or moved a finger. A thought that had more hope in it than any which had passed through his brain for many years now occupied and absorbed him. A heavy book lay open on the table by his side, and from time to time he glanced at a phrase which seemed to attract him. It was always the same phrase, and two words alone sufficed to bring him back to contemplation of it. Those two words were 'Immortality' and 'Soul'. He began to speak aloud to himself, being by nature fond of speech.

'Yes. The soul is immortal. I am quite willing to grant that. But it does not in any way follow that it is the source of life, or the seat of intelligence. The Buddhists distinguished it even from the individuality. And yet life holds it, and when life ends it takes its departure. How soon? I do not know. It is not a condition of life, but life is one of its conditions. Does it leave the body when life is artificially prolonged in a state of unconsciousness – by hypnotism, for instance? Is it more closely bound up with animal life, or with intelligence? If with either, has it a definite abiding place in the heart, or in the brain? Since its presence depends directly on life, so far as I know, it belongs to the body rather than to the brain. I once made a rabbit live an hour without its head. With a man that experiment would need careful manipulation – I would like to try it. Or is it all a question of that phantom, Vitality? Then the presence of the soul depends upon the potential excitability of the nerves, and, as far as we know, it must leave the body not more than twenty-four hours after death, and it certainly does not leave the body at the moment of dying. But if of the nerves, then what is the condition of the soul in the hypnotic state? Unorna hypnotises our old friend there – and our young one, too. For her, they have nerves. At her touch they wake, they sleep, they move, they feel, they speak. But they have no nerves for me. I can cut them with knives, burn them, turn the life-blood of the one into the arteries of the other – they feel nothing. If the soul is of the nerves – or of the vitality, then they have souls for Unorna, and none for me. That is absurd. Where is that old man's soul? He has slept for years. Has not his soul been somewhere else in the meanwhile? If we could keep him asleep for centuries, or for scores of centuries, like that frog found alive in a rock, would his soul – able by the hypothesis to pass through rocks or universes – stay by him? Could an ingenious sinner escape damnation for a few thousand years by being hypnotised? Verily the soul is a very unaccountable thing, and what is still more unaccountable is that I believe in it. Suppose the case of the ingenious sinner. Suppose that he could not escape by his clever trick. Then his soul must inevitably taste the condition of the damned while he is asleep. But when he is waked at last, and found to be alive, his soul must come back to him, glowing from the eternal flames. Unpleasant thought! Keyork Arabian, you had far better not go to sleep at present. Since all that is fantastic nonsense, on the face of it, I am inclined to believe that the presence of the soul is in some way a condition requisite for life, rather than depending upon it. I wish I could buy a soul. It is quite certain that life is not a mere mechanical or chemical process. I have gone too far to believe that. Take man at the very moment of death – have everything ready, do what you will – my artificial heart is a very perfect instrument, mechanically speaking – and how long does it take to start the artificial circulation through the carotid artery? Not a hundredth part so long a time as drowned people often lie before being brought back, without a pulsation, without a breath. Yet I never succeeded, though I have made the artificial heart work on a narcotised rabbit, and the rabbit died instantly when I stopped the machine, which proves that it was the machine that kept it alive. Perhaps if one applied it to a man just before death he might live on indefinitely, grow fat and flourish so long as the glass heart worked. Where would his soul be then? In the glass heart, which would have become the seat of life? Everything, sensible or absurd, which I can put into words makes the soul seem an impossibility – and yet there is something which I cannot put into words, but which proves the soul's existence beyond all doubt. I wish I could buy somebody's soul and experiment with it.'

He ceased and sat staring at his specimens, going over in his memory the fruitless experiments of a lifetime. A loud knocking roused him from his reverie. He hastened to open the door and was confronted by Unorna. She was paler than usual, and he saw from her expression that there was something wrong.

'What is the matter?' he asked, almost roughly.

'He is in a carriage downstairs,' she answered quickly. 'Something has happened to him. I cannot wake him, you must take him in – '

'To die on my hands? Not I!' laughed Keyork in his deepest voice. 'My collection is complete enough.'

She seized him suddenly by both arms, and brought her face near to his.

'If you dare to speak of death – '

She grew intensely white, with a fear she had not before known in her life. Keyork laughed again, and tried to shake himself free of her grip.

'You seem a little nervous,' he observed calmly. 'What do you want of me?'

'Your help, man, and quickly! Call your people! Have him carried upstairs! Revive him! Do something to bring him back!'

Keyork's voice changed.

'Is he in real danger?' he asked. 'What have you done to him?'

'Oh, I do not know what I have done!' cried Unorna desperately. 'I do not know what I fear – '

She let him go and leaned against the doorway, covering her face with her hands. Keyork stared at her. He had never seen her show so much emotion before. Then he made up his mind. He drew her into his room and left her standing and staring at him while he thrust a few objects into his pockets and threw his fur coat over him.

'Stay here till I come back,' he said, authoritatively, as he went out.

'But you will bring him here?' she cried, suddenly conscious of his going.

The door had already closed. She tried to open it, in order to follow him, but she could not. The lock was of an unusual kind, and either intentionally or accidentally Keyork had shut her in. For a few moments she tried to force the springs, shaking the heavy woodwork a very little in the great effort she made. Then, seeing that it was useless, she walked slowly to the table and sat down in Keyork's chair.

She had been in the place before, and she was as free from any unpleasant fear of the dead company as Keyork himself. To her, as to him, they were but specimens, each having a peculiar interest as a thing, but all destitute of that individuality, of that grim, latent malice, of that weird, soulless, physical power to harm, with which timid imaginations endow dead bodies.

She scarcely gave them a glance, and she certainly gave them no thought. She sat before the table, supporting her head in her hands and trying to think connectedly of what had just happened. She knew well enough how the Wanderer had lain upon the frozen ground, his head supported on her knee, while the watchman had gone to call a carriage. She remembered how she had summoned all her strength and had helped to lift him in, as few women could have done. She remembered every detail of the place, and everything she had done, even to the fact that she had picked up his hat and a stick he had carried and had taken them into the vehicle with her. The short drive through the ill-lighted streets was clear to her. She could still feel the pressure of his shoulder as he had leaned heavily against her; she could see the pale face by the fitful light of the lanterns as they passed, and of the lamps that flashed in front of the carriage with each jolting of the wheels over the rough paving-stones. She remembered exactly what she had done, her efforts to wake him, at first regular and made with the certainty of success, then more and more mad as she realised that something had put him beyond the sphere of her powers for the moment, if not for ever; his deathly pallor, his chilled hands, his unnatural stillness – she remembered it all, as one remembers circumstances in real life a moment after they have taken place. But there remained also the recollection of a single moment during which her whole being had been at the mercy of an impression so vivid that it seemed to stand alone divested of any outward sensations by which to measure its duration. She, who could call up visions in the minds of others, who possessed the faculty of closing her bodily eyes in order to see distant places and persons in the state of trance, she who expected no surprises in her own act, had seen something very vividly, which she could not believe had been a reality, and which she yet could not account for as a revelation of second sight. That dark, mysterious presence that had come bodily, yet without a body, between her and the man she loved was neither a real woman, nor the creation of her own brain, nor a dream seen in hypnotic state. She had not the least idea how long it had stood there; it seemed an hour, and it seemed but a second. But that incorporeal thing had a life and a power of its own. Never before had she felt that unearthly chill run through her, nor that strange sensation in her hair. It was a thing of evil omen, and the presage was already about to be fulfilled. The spirit of the dark woman had arisen at the sound of the words in which he denied her; she had risen and had come to claim her own, to rob Unorna of what seemed most worth coveting on earth – and she could take him, surely, to the place whence she came. How could Unorna tell that he was not already gone, that his spirit had not passed already, even when she was lifting his weight from the ground?

At the despairing thought she started and looked up. She had almost expected to see that shadow beside her again. But there was nothing. The lifeless bodies stood motionless in their mimicry of life under the bright light. The swarthy negro frowned, the face of the Malayan woman wore still its calm and gentle expression. Far in the background the rows of gleaming skulls grinned, as though at the memory of their four hundred lives; the skeleton of the orang-outang stretched out its long bony arms before it; the dead savages still squatted round the remains of their meal. The stillness was oppressive.

Unorna rose to her feet in sudden anxiety. She did not know how long she had been alone. She listened anxiously at the door for the sound of footsteps on the stairs, but all was silent. Surely, Keyork had not taken him elsewhere, to his lodgings, where he would not be cared for. That was impossible. She must have heard the sound of the wheels as the carriage drove away. She glanced at the windows and saw that the casements were covered with small, thick curtains which would muzzle the sound. She went to the nearest, thrust the curtain aside, opened the inner and the second glass and looked out. Though the street below was dim, she could see well enough that the carriage was no longer there. It was the bitterest night of the year and the air cut her like a knife, but she would not draw back. She strained her sight in both directions, searching in the gloom for the moving lights of a carriage, but she saw nothing. At last she shut the window and went back to the door. They must be on the stairs, or still below, perhaps, waiting for help to carry him up. The cold might kill him in his present state, a cold that would kill most things exposed to it. Furiously she shook the door. It was useless. She looked about for an instrument to help her strength. She could see nothing – no – yes – there was the iron-wood club of the black giant. She went and took it from his hand. The dead thing trembled all over, and rocked as though it would fall, and wagged its great head at her, but she was not afraid. She raised the heavy club and struck upon the door, upon the lock, upon the panels with all her might. The terrible blows sent echoes down the staircase, but the door did not yield, nor the lock either. Was the door of iron and the lock of granite? she asked herself. Then she heard a strange, sudden noise behind her. She turned and looked. The dead negro had fallen bodily from his pedestal to the floor, with a dull, heavy thud. She did not desist, but struck the oaken planks again and again with all her strength. Then her arms grew numb and she dropped the club. It was all in vain. Keyork had locked her in and had taken the Wanderer away.

She went back to her seat and fell into an attitude of despair. The reaction from the great physical efforts she had made overcame her. It seemed to her that Keyork's only reason for taking him away must be that he was dead. Her head throbbed and her eyes began to burn. The great passion had its will of her and stabbed her through and through with such pain as she had never dreamed of. The horror of it all was too deep for tears, and tears were by nature very far from her eyes at all times. She pressed her hands to her breast and rocked herself gently backwards and forwards. There was no reason left in her. To her there was no reason left in anything if he were gone. And if Keyork Arabian could not cure him, who could? She knew now what that old prophecy had meant, when they had told her that love would come but once, and that the chief danger of her life lay in a mistake on that decisive day. Love had indeed come upon her like a whirlwind, he had flashed upon her like the lightning, she had tried to grasp him and keep him, and he was gone again – for ever. Gone through her own fault, through her senseless folly in trying to do by art what love would have done for himself. Blind, insensate, mad! She cursed herself with unholy curses, and her beautiful face was strained and distorted. With unconscious fingers she tore at her heavy hair until it fell about her like a curtain. In the raging thirst of a great grief for tears that would not flow she beat her bosom, she beat her face, she struck with her white forehead the heavy table before her, she grasped her own throat, as though she would tear the life out of herself. Then again her head fell forward and her body swayed regularly to and fro, and low words broke fiercely from her trembling lips now and then, bitter words of a wild, strong language in which it is easier to curse than to bless. As the sudden love that had in a few hours taken such complete possession of her was boundless, so its consequences were illimitable. In a nature strange to fear, the fear for another wrought a fearful revolution. Her anger against herself was as terrible as her fear for him she loved was paralysing. The instinct to act, the terror lest it should be too late, the impossibility of acting at all so long as she was imprisoned in the room, all three came over her at once.

The mechanical effort of rocking her body from side to side brought no rest; the blow she struck upon her breast in her frenzy she felt no more than the oaken door had felt those she had dealt it with the club. She could not find even the soothing antidote of bodily pain for her intense moral suffering. Again the time passed without her knowing or guessing of its passage.

Driven to desperation she sprang at last from her seat and cried aloud. 'I would give my soul to know that he is safe!'

The words had not died away when a low groan passed, as it were, round the room. The sound was distinctly that of a human voice, but it seemed to come from all sides at once. Unorna stood still and listened.

'Who is in this room?' she asked in loud clear tones.

Not a breath stirred. She glanced from one specimen to another, as though suspecting that among the dead some living being had taken a disguise. But she knew them all. There was nothing new to her there. She was not afraid. Her passion returned.

'My soul! – yes!' she cried again, leaning heavily on the table, 'I would give it if I could know, and it would be little enough!'

Again that awful sound filled the room, and rose now almost to a wail and died away.

Unorna's brow flushed angrily. In the direct line of her vision stood the head of the Malayan woman, its soft, embalmed eyes fixed on hers.

'If there are people hidden here,' cried Unorna fiercely, 'let them show themselves! Let them face me! I say it again – I would give my immortal soul!'

This time Unorna saw as well as heard. The groan came, and the wail followed it and rose to a shriek that deafened her. And she saw how the face of the Malayan woman changed; she saw it move in the bright lamp-light, she saw the mouth open. Horrified, she looked away. Her eyes fell upon the squatting savages – their heads were all turned towards her, she was sure that she could see their shrunken chests heave as they took breath to utter that terrible cry again and again; even the fallen body of the African stirred on the floor, not five paces from her. Would their shrieking never stop? All of them – every one – even to the white skulls high up in the case; not one skeleton, not one dead body that did not mouth at her and scream and moan and scream again.

Unorna covered her ears with her hands to shut out the hideous, unearthly noise. She closed her eyes lest she should see those dead things move. Then came another noise. Were they descending from their pedestals and cases and marching upon her, a heavy-footed company of corpses?

Fearless to the last, she dropped her hands and opened her eyes.

'In spite of you all,' she cried defiantly, 'I will give my soul to have him safe!'

Something was close to her. She turned and saw Keyork Arabian at her elbow. There was an odd smile on his usually unexpressive face.

'Then give me that soul of yours, if you please,' he said. 'He is quite safe and peacefully asleep. You must have grown a little nervous while I was away.'

Chapter 10

Unorna let herself sink into a chair. She stared almost vacantly at Keyork, then glanced uneasily at the motionless specimens, then stared at him again.

'Yes,' she said at last. 'Perhaps I was a little nervous. Why did you lock me in? I would have gone with you. I would have helped you.'

'An accident – quite an accident,' answered Keyork, divesting himself of his fur coat. 'The lock is a peculiar one, and in my hurry I forgot to show you the trick of it.'

'I tried to get out,' said Unorna with a forced laugh. 'I tried to break the door down with a club. I am afraid I have hurt one of your specimens.'

She looked about the room. Everything was in its usual position, except the body of the African. She was quite sure that when she had heard that unearthly cry, the dead faces had all been turned towards her.

'It is no matter,' replied Keyork in a tone of indifference which was genuine. 'I wish somebody would take my collection off my hands. I should have room to walk about without elbowing a failure at every step.'

'I wish you would bury them all,' suggested Unorna, with a slight shudder.

Keyork looked at her keenly. 'Do you mean to say that those dead things frightened you?' he asked incredulously.

'No; I do not. I am not easily frightened. But something odd happened – the second strange thing that has happened this evening. Is there anyone concealed in this room?'

'Not a rat – much less a human being. Rats dislike creosote and corrosive sublimate, and as for human beings – '

He shrugged his shoulders and smiled.

'Then I have been dreaming,' said Unorna, attempting to look relieved. 'Tell me about him. Where is he?'

'In bed – at his hotel. He will be perfectly well tomorrow.'

'Did he wake?' she asked anxiously.

'Yes. We talked together.'

'And he was in his right mind?'

'Apparently. But he seems to have forgotten something.'

'Forgotten? What? That I had made him sleep?'

'Yes. He had forgotten that too.'

'In Heaven's name, Keyork, tell me what you mean! Do not keep me – '

'How impatient women are!' exclaimed Keyork with exasperating calm. 'What is it that you most want him to forget?'

'You cannot mean – '

'I can, and I do. He has forgotten Beatrice. For a witch – well, you are a very remarkable one, Unorna. As a woman of business – ' He shook his head.

'What do you mean this time? What did you say?' Her questions came in a strained tone and she seemed to have difficulty in concentrating her attention, or in controlling her emotions, or both.

'You paid a large price for the information,' observed Keyork.

'What price? What are you speaking of? I do not understand.'

'Your soul,' he answered, with a laugh. 'That was what you offered to anyone who would tell you that the Wanderer was safe. I immediately closed with your offer. It was an excellent one for me.'

Unorna tapped the table impatiently.

'It is odd that a man of your learning should never be serious,' she said.

'I supposed that you were serious,' he answered. 'Besides, a bargain is a bargain, and there were numerous witnesses to the transaction,' he added, looking round the room at his dead specimens.

Unorna tried to laugh with him.

'Do you know, I was so nervous that I fancied all those creatures were groaning and shrieking and gibbering at me, when you came in.'

'Very likely they were,' said Keyork Arabian, his small eyes twinkling.

'And I imagined that the Malayan woman opened her mouth to scream, and that the Peruvian savages turned their heads; it was very strange – at first they groaned, and then they wailed, and then they howled and shrieked at me.'

'Under the circumstances, that is not extraordinary.'

Unorna stared at him rather angrily. He was jesting, of course, and she had been dreaming, or had been so overwrought by excitement as to have been made the victim of a vivid hallucination. Nevertheless there was something disagreeable in the matter-of-fact gravity of his jest.

'I am tired of your kind of wit,' she said.

'The kind of wit which is called wisdom is said to be fatiguing,' he retorted.

'I wish you would give me an opportunity of being wearied in that way.'

'Begin by opening your eyes to facts, then. It is you who are trying to jest. It is I who am in earnest. Did you, or did you not, offer your soul for a certain piece of information? Did you, or did you not, hear those dead things moan and cry? Did you, or did you not, see them move?'

'How absurd!' cried Unorna. 'You might as well ask whether, when one is giddy, the room is really going round? Is there any practical difference, so far as sensation goes, between a mummy and a block of wood?'

'That, my dear lady, is precisely what we do not know, and what we most wish to know. Death is not the change which takes place at a moment which is generally clearly defined, when the heart stops beating, and the eye turns white, and the face changes colour. Death comes some time after that, and we do not know exactly when. It varies very much in different individuals. You can only define it as the total and final cessation of perception and apperception, both functions depending on the nerves. In ordinary cases Nature begins of herself to destroy the nerves by a sure process. But how do you know what happens when decay is not only arrested but prevented before it has begun? How can you foretell what may happen when a skilful hand has restored the tissues of the body to their original flexibility, or preserved them in the state in which they were last sensitive?'

'Nothing can ever make me believe that a mummy can suddenly hear and understand,' said Unorna. 'Much less that it can move and produce a sound. I know that the idea has possessed you for many years, but nothing will make me believe it possible.'

'Nothing?'

'Nothing short of seeing and hearing.'

'But you have seen and heard.'

'I was dreaming.'

'When you offered your soul?'

'Not then, perhaps. I was only mad then.'

'And on the ground of temporary insanity you would repudiate the bargain?'

Unorna shrugged her shoulders impatiently and did not answer. Keyork relinquished the fencing.

'It is of no importance,' he said, changing his tone. 'Your dream – or whatever it was – seems to have been the second of your two experiences. You said there were two, did you not? What was the first?'

Unorna sat silent for some minutes, as though collecting her thoughts. Keyork, who never could have enough light, busied himself with another lamp. The room was now brighter than it generally was in the daytime.

Unorna watched him. She did not want to make confidences to him, and yet she felt irresistibly impelled to do so. He was a strange compound of wisdom and levity, in her opinion, and his light-hearted moods were those which she most resented. She was never sure whether he was in reality tactless, or frankly brutal. She inclined to the latter view of his character, because he always showed such masterly skill in excusing himself when he had gone too far. Neither his wisdom nor his love of jesting explained to her the powerful attraction which he exercised over her whole nature, and of which she was, in a manner, ashamed. She could quarrel with him as often as they met, and yet she could not help being always glad to meet him again. She could not admit that she liked him because she dominated him; on the contrary, he was the only person she had ever met over whom she had no influence whatever, who did as he pleased without consulting her, and who laughed at her mysterious power so far as he himself was concerned. Nor was her liking founded upon any consciousness of obligation. If he had helped her to the best of his ability in the great experiment, it was also clear enough that he had the strongest personal interest in doing so. He loved life with a mad passion for its own sake, and the only object of his study was to find a means of living longer than other men. All the aims and desires and complex reasonings of his being tended to this simple expression – the wish to live. To what idolatrous self-worship Keyork Arabian might be capable of descending, if he ever succeeded in eliminating death from the equation of his immediate future, it was impossible to say. The wisdom of ages bids us beware of the man of one idea. He is to be feared for his ruthlessness, for his concentration, for the singular strength he has acquired in the centralisation of his intellectual power, and because he has welded, as it were, the rough metal of many passions and of many talents into a single deadly weapon which he wields for a single purpose. Herein lay, perhaps, the secret of Unorna's undefined fear of Keyork and of her still less definable liking for him.

She leaned one elbow on the table and shaded her eyes from the brilliant light.

'I do not know why I should tell you,' she said at last. 'You will only laugh at me, and then I shall be angry, and we shall quarrel as usual.'

'I may be of use,' suggested the little man gravely. 'Besides, I have made up my mind never to quarrel with you again, Unorna.'

'You are wise, my dear friend. It does no good. As for your being of use in this case, the most I can hope is that you may find me an explanation of something I cannot understand.'

'I am good at that. I am particularly good at explanations – and, generally, at all *post facto* wisdom.'

'Keyork, do you believe that the souls of the dead can come back and be visible to us?'

Keyork Arabian was silent for a few seconds.

'I know nothing about it,' he answered.

'But what do you think?'

'Nothing. Either it is possible, or it is not, and until the one proposition or the other is proved I suspend my judgment. Have you seen a ghost?'

'I do not know. I have seen something – ' She stopped, as though the recollections were unpleasant.

'Then' said Keyork, 'the probability is that you saw a living person. Shall I sum up the question of ghosts for you?'

'I wish you would, in some way that I can understand.'

'We are, then, in precisely the same position with regard to the belief in ghosts which we occupy towards such questions as the abolition of death. The argument in both cases is inductive and all but conclusive. We do not know of any case, in the two hundred generations of men, more or less, with whose history we are in some degree acquainted, of any individual who has escaped death. We conclude that all men must die. Similarly, we do not know certainly – not from real, irrefutable evidence at least – that the soul of any man or woman dead has ever returned visibly to earth. We conclude, therefore, that none ever will. There is a difference in the two cases, which throws a slight balance of probability on the side of the ghost. Many persons have asserted that they have seen ghosts, though none have ever asserted that men do not die. For my own part, I have had a very wide, practical, and intimate acquaintance with dead people – sometimes in very queer places – but I have never seen anything even faintly suggestive of a ghost. Therefore, my dear lady, I advise you to take it for granted that you have seen a living person.'

'I never shivered with cold and felt my hair rise upon my head at the sight of any living thing,' said Unorna dreamily, and still shading her eyes with her hand.

'But might you not feel that if you chanced to see someone whom you particularly disliked?' asked Keyork, with a gentle laugh.

'Disliked?' repeated Unorna in a harsh voice. She changed her position and looked at him. 'Yes, perhaps that is possible. I had not thought of that. And yet – I would rather it had been a ghost.'

'More interesting, certainly, and more novel,' observed Keyork, slowly polishing his smooth cranium with the palm of his hand. His head, and the perfect hemisphere of his nose, reflected the light like ivory balls of different sizes.

'I was standing before him,' said Unorna. 'The place was lonely and it was already night. The stars shone on the snow, and I could see distinctly. Then she – that woman – passed softly between us. He cried out, calling her by name, and then fell forward. After that, the woman was gone. What was it that I saw?'

'You are quite sure that it was not really a woman?'

'Would a woman, and of all women that one, have come and gone without a word?'

'Not unless she is a very singularly reticent person,' answered Keyork, with a laugh. 'But you need not go so far as the ghost theory for an explanation. You were hypnotised, my dear friend, and he made you see her. That is as simple as anything need be.'

'But that is impossible, because – ' Unorna stopped and changed colour.

'Because you had hypnotised him already,' suggested Keyork gravely.

'The thing is not possible,' Unorna repeated, looking away from him.

'I believe it to be the only natural explanation. You had made him sleep. You tried to force his mind to something contrary to its firmest beliefs. I have seen you do it. He is a strong subject. His mind rebelled, yielded, then made a final and desperate effort, and then collapsed. That effort was so terrible that it momentarily forced your will back upon itself, and impressed his vision on your sight. There are no ghosts, my dear colleague. There are only souls and bodies. If the soul can be defined as anything it can be defined as Pure Being in the Mode of Individuality but quite removed from the Mode of Matter. As for the body – well, there it is before you, in a variety of shapes, and in various states of preservation, as incapable of producing a ghost as a picture or a statue. You are altogether in a very nervous condition today. It is really quite indifferent whether that good lady be alive or dead.'

'Indifferent!' exclaimed Unorna fiercely. Then she was silent.

'Indifferent to the validity of the theory. If she is dead, you did not see her ghost, and if she is alive you did not see her body, because, if she had been there in the flesh, she would have entered into an explanation – to say the least. Hypnosis will explain anything and everything, without causing you a moment's anxiety for the future.'

'Then I did not hear shrieks and moans, nor see your specimens moving when I was here alone just now?'

'Certainly not! Hypnosis again. Auto-hypnosis this time. You should really be less nervous. You probably stared at the lamp without realising the fact. You know that any shining object affects you in that way, if you are not careful. It is a very bright lamp, too. Instantaneous effect – bodies appear to move and you hear unearthly yells – you offer your soul for sale and I buy it, appearing in the nick of time. If your condition had lasted ten seconds longer you would have taken me for his majesty and lived, in imagination, through a dozen years or so of sulphurous purgatorial treatment under my personal supervision, to wake up and find yourself unscorched – and unredeemed, as ever.'

'You are a most comforting person, Keyork,' said Unorna, with a faint smile. 'I only wish I could believe everything you tell me.'

'You must either believe me or renounce all claim to intelligence,' answered the little man, climbing from his chair and sitting upon the table at her elbow. His short, sturdy legs swung at a considerable height above the floor, and he planted his hands firmly upon the board on either side of him. The attitude was that of an idle boy, and was so oddly out of keeping with his age and expression that Unorna almost laughed as she looked at him.

'At all events,' he continued, 'you cannot doubt my absolute sincerity. You come to me for an explanation. I give you the only sensible one that exists, and the only one which can have a really sedative effect upon your excitement. Of course, if you have any especial object in believing in ghosts – if it affords you any great and lasting pleasure to associate, in imagination, with spectres, wraiths, and airily-malicious shadows, I will not cross your fancy. To a person of solid nerves a banshee may be an entertaining companion, and an apparition in a well-worn winding-sheet may be a pretty toy. For all I know, it may be a delight to you to find your hair standing on end at the unexpected appearance of a dead woman in a black cloak between you and the person with whom you are engaged in animated conversation. All very well, as a mere pastime, I say. But if you find that you are reaching a point on which your judgment is clouded, you had better shut up the magic lantern and take the rational view of the case.'

'Perhaps you are right.'

'Will you allow me to say something very frank, Unorna?' asked Keyork with unusual diffidence.

'If you can manage to be frank without being brutal.'

'I will be short, at all events. It is this. I think you are becoming superstitious.' He watched her closely to see what effect the speech would produce. She looked up quickly.

'Am I? What is superstition?'

'Gratuitous belief in things not proved.'

'I expected a different definition from you.'

'What did you expect me to say?'

'That superstition is belief.'

'I am not a heathen,' observed Keyork sanctimoniously.

'Far from it,' laughed Unorna. 'I have heard that devils believe and tremble.'

'And you class me with those interesting things, my dear friend?'

'Sometimes: when I am angry with you.'

'Two or three times a day, then? Not more than that?' inquired the sage, swinging his heels, and staring at the rows of skulls in the background.

'Whenever we quarrel. It is easy for you to count the occasions.'

'Easy, but endless. Seriously, Unorna, I am not the devil. I can prove it to you conclusively on theological grounds.'

'Can you? They say that his majesty is a lawyer, and a successful one, in good practice.'

'What caused Satan's fall? Pride. Then pride is his chief characteristic. Am I proud, Unorna? The question is absurd, I have nothing to be proud of – a little old man with a grey beard, of whom nobody ever heard anything remarkable. No one ever accused me of pride. How could I be proud of anything? Except of your acquaintance, my dear lady,' he added gallantly, laying his hand on his heart, and leaning towards her as he sat.

Unorna laughed at the speech, and threw back her dishevelled hair with a graceful gesture. Keyork paused.

'You are very beautiful,' he said thoughtfully, gazing at her face and at the red-gold lights that played in the tangled tresses.

'Worse and worse!' she exclaimed, still laughing. 'Are you going to repeat the comedy you played so well this afternoon, and make love to me again?'

'If you like. But I do not need to win your affections now.'

'Why not?'

'Have I not bought your soul, with everything in it, like a furnished house?' he asked merrily.

'Then you are the devil after all?'

'Or an angel. Why should the evil one have a monopoly in the soul-market? But you remind me of my argument. You would have distracted Demosthenes in the heat of a peroration, or Socrates in the midst of his defence, if you had flashed that hair of yours before their old eyes. You have almost taken the life out of my argument. I was going to say that my peculiarity is not less exclusive than Lucifer's, though it takes a different turn. I was going to confess with the utmost frankness and the most sincere truth that my only crime against Heaven is a most perfect, unswerving, devotional love for my own particular Self. In that attachment I have never wavered yet – but I really cannot say what may become of Keyork Arabian if he looks at you much longer.'

'He might become a human being,' suggested Unorna.

'How can you be so cruel as to suggest such a horrible possibility?' cried the gnome with a shudder, either real or extremely well feigned.

'You are betraying yourself, Keyork. You must control your feelings better, or I shall find out the truth about you.'

He glanced keenly at her, and was silent for a while. Unorna rose slowly to her feet, and standing beside him, began to twist her hair into a great coil upon her head.

'What made you let it down?' asked Keyork with some curiosity, as he watched her.

'I hardly know,' she answered, still busy with the braids. 'I was nervous, I suppose, as you say, and so it got loose and came down.'

'Nervous about our friend?'

She did not reply, but turned from him with a shake of the head and took up her fur mantle.

'You are not going?' said Keyork quietly, in a tone of conviction.

She started slightly, dropped the sable, and sat down again.

'No,' she said, 'I am not going yet. I do not know what made me take my cloak.'

'You have really no cause for nervousness now that it is all over,' remarked the sage, who had not descended from his perch on the table. 'He is very well. It is one of those cases which are interesting as being new, or at least only partially investigated. We may as well speak in confidence, Unorna, for we really understand each other. Do you not think so?'

'That depends on what you have to say.'

'Not much – nothing that ought to offend you. You must consider, my dear,' he said, assuming an admirably paternal tone, 'that I might be your father, and that I have your welfare very much at heart, as well as your happiness. You love this man – no, do not be angry, do not interrupt me. You could not do better for yourself, nor for him. I knew him years ago. He is a grand man – the sort of man I would like to be. Good. You find him suffering from a delusion, or a memory, whichever it be. Not only is this delusion – let us call it so – ruining his happiness and undermining his strength, but so long as it endures, it also completely excludes the possibility of his feeling for you what you feel for him. Your own interest coincides exactly with the promptings of real, human charity. And yours is in reality a charitable nature, dear Unorna, though you are sometimes a little hasty with poor old Keyork. Good again. You, being moved by a desire for this man's welfare, most kindly and wisely take steps to cure him of his madness. The delusion is strong, but your will is stronger. The delusion yields after a violent struggle during which it has even impressed itself upon your own senses. The patient is brought home, properly cared for, and disposed to rest. Then he wakes, apparently of his own accord, and behold! he is completely cured. Everything has been successful, everything is perfect, everything has followed the usual course of such mental cures by means of hypnosis. The only thing I do not understand is the waking. That is the only thing which makes me uneasy for the future, until I can see it properly explained. He had no right to wake without your suggestion, if he was still in the hypnotic state; and if he had already come out of the hypnotic state by a natural reaction, it is to be feared that the cure may not be permanent.'

Unorna had listened attentively, as she always did when Keyork delivered himself of a serious opinion upon a psychiatric case. Her eyes gleamed with satisfaction as he finished.

'If that is all that troubles you,' she said, 'you may set your mind at rest. After he had fallen, and while the watchman was getting the carriage, I repeated my suggestion and ordered him to wake without pain in an hour.'

'Perfect! Splendid!' cried Keyork, clapping his hands loudly together. 'I did you an injustice, my dear Unorna. You are not so nervous as I thought, since you forgot nothing. What a woman! Ghost-proof, and able to think connectedly even at such a moment! But tell me, did you not take the opportunity of suggesting something else?' His eyes twinkled merrily, as he asked the question.

'What do you mean?' inquired Unorna, with sudden coldness.

'Oh, nothing so serious as you seem to think. I was only wondering whether a suggestion of reciprocation might not have been wise.'

She faced him fiercely.

'Hold your peace, Keyork Arabian!' she cried.

'Why?' he asked with a bland smile, swinging his little legs and stroking his long beard.

'There is a limit! Must you for ever be trying to suggest, and trying to guide me in everything I do? It is intolerable! I can hardly call my soul my own!'

'Hardly, considering my recent acquisition of it,' returned Keyork calmly.

'That wretched jest is threadbare.'

'A jest! Wretched? And threadbare, too? Poor Keyork! His wit is failing at last.'

He shook his head in mock melancholy over his supposed intellectual dotage. Unorna turned away, this time with the determination to leave him.

'I am sorry if I have offended you,' he said, very meekly. 'Was what I said so very unpardonable?'

'If ignorance is unpardonable, as you always say, then your speech is past forgiveness,' said Unorna, relenting by force of habit, but gathering her fur around her. 'If you know anything of women – '

'Which I do not,' observed the gnome in a low-toned interruption.

'Which you do not – you would know how much such love as you advise me to manufacture by force of suggestion could be worth in a woman's eyes. You would know that a woman will be loved for herself, for her beauty, for her wit, for her virtues, for her faults, for her own love, if you will, and by a man conscious of all his actions and free of his heart; not by a mere patient reduced to the proper state of sentiment by a trick of hypnotism, or psychiatry, or of whatever you choose to call the effect of this power of mine which neither you, nor I, nor anyone can explain. I will be loved freely, for myself, or not at all.'

'I see, I see,' said Keyork thoughtfully, 'something in the way Israel Kafka loves you.'

'Yes, as Israel Kafka loves me, I am not afraid to say it. As he loves me, of his own free will, and to his own destruction – as I should have loved him, had it been so fated.'

'So you are a fatalist, Unorna,' observed her companion, still stroking and twisting his beard. 'It is strange that we should differ upon so many fundamental questions, you and I, and yet be such good friends. Is it not?'

'The strangest thing of all is that I should submit to your exasperating ways as I do.'

'It does not strike me that it is I who am quarrelling this time,' said Keyork.

'I confess, I would almost prefer that to your imperturbable coolness. What is this new phase? You used not to be like this. You are planning some wickedness. I am sure of it.'

'And that is all the credit I get for keeping my temper! Did I not say a while ago that I would never quarrel with you again?'

'You said so, but – '

'But you did not expect me to keep my word,' said Keyork, slipping from his seat on the table with considerable agility and suddenly standing close before her. 'And do you not yet know that when I say a thing I do it, and that when I have got a thing I keep it?'

'So far as the latter point is concerned, I have nothing to say. But you need not be so terribly impressive; and unless you are going to break your word, by which you seem to set such store, and quarrel with me, you need not look at me so fiercely.'

Keyork suddenly let his voice drop to its deepest and most vibrating key.

'I only want you to remember this,' he said. 'You are not an ordinary woman, as I am not an ordinary man, and the experiment we are making together is an altogether extraordinary one. I have told you the truth. I care for nothing but my individual self, and I seek nothing but the prolongation of life. If you endanger the success of the great trial again, as you did today, and if it fails, I will never forgive you. You will make an enemy of me, and you will regret it while you live, and longer than that, perhaps. So long as you keep the compact there is nothing I will not do to help you – nothing within the bounds of your imagination. And I can do much. Do you understand?'

'I understand that you are afraid of losing my help.'

'That is it – of losing your help. I am not afraid of losing you – in the end.'

Unorna smiled rather scornfully at first, as she looked down upon the little man's strange face and gazed fearlessly into his eyes. But as she looked, the smile faded, and the colour slowly sank from her face, until she was very pale. And as she felt herself losing courage before something which she could not understand, Keyork's eyes grew brighter and brighter till they glowed like drops of molten metal. A sound as of many voices wailing in agony rose and trembled and quavered in the air. With a wild cry, Unorna pressed her hands to her ears and fled towards the entrance.

'You are very nervous tonight,' observed Keyork, as he opened the door.

Then he went silently down the stairs by her side and helped her into the carriage, which had been waiting since his return.

Chapter 11

A month had passed since the day on which Unorna had first seen the Wanderer, and since the evening when she had sat so long in conversation with Keyork Arabian. The snow lay heavily on all the rolling moorland about Prague, covering everything up to the very gates of the black city; and within, all things were as hard and dark and frozen as ever. The sun was still the sun, no doubt, high above the mist and the gloom which he had no power to pierce, but no man could say that he had seen him in that month. At long intervals indeed, a faint rose-coloured glow touched the high walls of the Hradschin and transfigured for an instant the short spires of the unfinished cathedral, hundreds of feet above the icebound river and the sepulchral capital; sometimes, in the dim afternoons, a little gold filtered through the heavy air and tinged the snow-steeples of the Teyn Kirche, and yellowed the stately tower of the town hall; but that was all, so far as the moving throngs of silent beings that filled the streets could see. The very air men breathed seemed to be stiffening with damp cold. For that is not the glorious winter of our own dear north, where the whole earth is a jewel of gleaming crystals hung between two heavens, between the heaven of the day and the heaven of the night, beautiful alike in sunshine and in starlight, under the rays of the moon, at evening and again at dawn; where the pines and hemlocks are as forests of plumes powdered thick with dust of silver; where the black ice rings like a deep-toned bell beneath the heel of the sweeping skate – the ice that you may follow a hundred miles if you have breath and strength; where the harshest voice rings musically among the icicles and the snow-laden boughs; where the quick jingle of sleigh bells far off on the smooth, deep track brings to the listener the vision of our own merry Father Christmas, with snowy beard, and apple cheeks, and peaked fur cap, and mighty gauntlets, and hampers and sacks full of toys and good things and true northern jollity; where all is young and fresh and free; where eyes are bright and cheeks are red, and hands are strong and hearts are brave; where children laugh and tumble in the diamond dust of the dry, driven snow; where men and women know what happiness can mean; where the old are as the giant pines, green, silver-crowned landmarks in the human forest, rather than as dried, twisted, sapless trees fit only to be cut down and burned, in that dear north to which our hearts and memories still turn for refreshment, under the Indian suns, and out of the hot splendour of calm southern seas. The winter of the black city that spans the frozen Moldau is the winter of the grave, dim as a perpetual afternoon in a land where no lotus ever grew, cold with the unspeakable frigidness of a reeking air that thickens as oil but will not be frozen, melancholy as a stony island of death in a lifeless sea.

A month had gone by, and in that time the love that had so suddenly taken root in Unorna's heart had grown to great proportions, as love will when, being strong and real, it is thwarted and repulsed at every turn. For she was not loved. She had destroyed the idol and rooted out the memory of it, but she could not take its place. She had spoken the truth when she had told Keyork that she would be loved for herself, or not at all, and that she would use neither her secret arts nor her rare gifts to manufacture a semblance when she longed for a reality.

Almost daily she saw him. As in a dream he came to her and sat by her side, hour after hour, talking of many things, calm apparently, and satisfied in her society, but strangely apathetic and indifferent. Never once in those many days had she seen his pale face light up with pleasure, nor his deep eyes show a gleam of interest; never had the tone of his voice been disturbed in its even monotony; never had the touch of his hand, when they met and parted, felt the communication of the thrill that ran through hers.

It was very bitter, for Unorna was proud with the scarcely reasoning pride of a lawless, highly gifted nature, accustomed to be obeyed and little used to bending under any influence. She brought all the skill she could command to her assistance; she talked to him, she told him of herself, she sought his confidence, she consulted him on every matter, she attempted to fascinate his imagination with tales of a life which even he could never have seen; she even sang to him old songs and snatches of wonderful melodies which, in her childhood, had still survived the advancing wave of silence that has overwhelmed the Bohemian people within the memory of living man, bringing a change into the daily life and temperament of a whole nation which is perhaps unparalleled in any history. He listened, he smiled, he showed a faint pleasure and a great understanding in all these things, and he came back day after day to talk and listen again. But that was all. She felt that she could amuse him without charming him.

And Unorna suffered terribly. Her cheek grew thinner and her eyes gleamed with sudden fires. She was restless, and her beautiful hands, from seeming to be carved in white marble, began to look as though they were chiselled out of delicate transparent alabaster. She slept little and thought much, and if she did not shed tears, it was because she was too strong to weep for pain and too proud to weep from anger and disappointment. And yet her resolution remained firm, for it was part and parcel of her inmost self, and was guarded by pride on the one hand and an unalterable belief in fate on the other.

Today they sat together, as they had so often sat, among the flowers and the trees in the vast conservatory, she in her tall, carved chair and he upon a lower seat before her. They had been silent for some minutes. It was not yet noon, but it might have been early morning in a southern island, so soft was the light, so freshly scented the air, so peaceful the tinkle of the tiny fountain. Unorna's expression was sad, as she gazed in silence at the man she loved. There was something gone from his face, she thought, since she had first seen him, and it was to bring that something back that she would give her life and her soul if she could.

Suddenly her lips moved and a sad melody trembled in the air. Unorna sang, almost as though singing to herself. The Wanderer's deep eyes met hers and he listened.

> When in life's heaviest hour
>   Grief crowds upon the heart,
> One wondrous prayer
>   My memory repeats.
>
> The harmony of the living words
>   Is full of strength to heal,
> There breathes in them a holy charm
>   Past understanding.
>
> Then, as a burden from my soul,
>   Doubt rolls away,
> And I believe – believe in tears,
>   And all is light – so light!

She ceased, and his eyes were still upon her, calm, thoughtful, dispassionate. The colour began to rise in her cheek. She looked down and tapped upon the carved arm of the chair with an impatient gesture familiar to her.

'And what is that one prayer?' asked the Wanderer. 'I knew the song long ago, but I have never guessed what that magic prayer can be like.'

'It must be a woman's prayer; I cannot tell you what it is.'

'And are you so sad today, Unorna? What makes you sing that song?'

'Sad? No, I am not sad,' she answered with an effort. 'But the words rose to my lips and so I sang.'

'They are pretty words,' said her companion, almost indifferently. 'And you have a very beautiful voice,' he added thoughtfully.

'Have I? I have been told so, sometimes.'

'Yes. I like to hear you sing, and talk, too. My life is a blank. I do not know what it would be without you.'

'I am little enough to – those who know me,' said Unorna, growing pale, and drawing a quick breath.

'You cannot say that. You are not little to me.'

There was a long silence. He gazed at the plants, and his glance wandered from one to the other, as though he did not see them, being lost in meditation. The voice had been calm and clear as ever, but it was the first time he had ever said so much, and Unorna's heart stood still, half fire and half ice. She could not speak.

'You are very much to me,' he said again, at last. 'Since I have been in this place a change has come over me. I seem to myself to be a man without an object, without so much as a real thought. Keyork tells me that there is something wanting, that the something is woman, and that I ought to love. I cannot tell. I do not know what love is, and I never knew. Perhaps it is the absence of it that makes me what I am – a body and an intelligence without a soul. Even the intelligence I begin to doubt. What sense has there ever been in all my wanderings? Why have I been in every place, in every city? What went I forth to see? Not even a reed shaken by the wind! I have spoken all languages, read thousands of books, known men in every land – and for what? It is as though I had once had an object in it all, though I know that there was none. But I have realised the worthlessness of my life since I have been here. Perhaps you have shown it to me, or helped me to see it. I cannot tell. I ask myself again and again what it was all for, and I ask in vain. I am lonely, indeed, in the world, but it has been my own choice. I remember that I had friends once, when I was younger, but I cannot tell what has become of one of them. They wearied me, perhaps, in those days, and the weariness drove me from my own home. For I have a home, Unorna, and I fancy that when old age gets me at last I shall go there to die, in one of those old towers by the northern sea. I was born there, and there my mother died and my father, before I knew them; it is a sad place! Meanwhile, I may have thirty years, or forty, or even more to live. Shall I go on living this wandering, aimless life? And if not, what shall I do? Love, says Keyork Arabian – who never loved anything but himself, but to whom that suffices, for it passes the love of woman!'

'That is true, indeed,' said Unorna in a low voice.

'And what he says might be true also, if I were capable of loving. But I feel that I am not. I am as incapable of that as of anything else. I ought to despise myself, and yet I do not. I am perfectly contented, and if I am not happy I at least do not realise what unhappiness means. Am I not always of the same even temper?'

'Indeed you are.' She tried not to speak bitterly, but something in her tone struck him.

'Ah, I see! You despise me a little for my apathy. Yes, you are quite right. Man is not made to turn idleness into a fine art, nor to manufacture contentment out of his own culpable indifference! It is despicable – and yet, here I am.'

'I never meant that,' cried Unorna with sudden heat. 'Even if I had, what right have I to make myself the judge of your life?'

'The right of friendship,' answered the Wanderer very quietly. 'You are my best friend, Unorna.'

Unorna's anger rose within her. She remembered how in that very place, and but a month earlier, she had offered Israel Kafka her friendship, and it was as though a heavy retribution were now meted out to her for her cruelty on that day. She remembered his wrath and his passionate denunciations of friendship, his scornful refusal, his savage attempt to conquer her will, his failure and his defeat. She remembered how she had taken her revenge, delivering him over in his sleep to Keyork Arabian's will. She wished that, like him, she could escape from the wound of the word in a senseless lethargy of body and mind. She knew now what he had suffered, for she suffered it all herself. He, at least, had been free to speak his mind, to rage and storm and struggle. She must sit still and hide her agony, at the risk of losing all. She bit her white lips and turned her head away, and was silent.

'You are my best friend,' the Wanderer repeated in his calm voice, and every syllable pierced her like a glowing needle. 'And does not friendship give rights which ought to be used? If, as I think, Unorna, you look upon me as an idler, as a worthless being, as a man without so much as the shadow of a purpose in the world, it is but natural that you should despise me a little, even though you may be very fond of me. Do you not see that?'

Unorna stared at him with an odd expression for a moment.

'Yes – I am fond of you!' she exclaimed, almost harshly. Then she laughed. He seemed not to notice her tone.

'I never knew what friendship was before,' he went on. 'Of course, as I said, I had friends when I was little more than a boy, boys and young men like myself, and our friendship came to this, that we laughed, and feasted and hunted together, and sometimes even quarrelled, and caring little, thought even less. But in those days there seemed to be nothing between that and love, and love I never understood, that I can remember. But friendship like ours, Unorna, was never dreamed of among us. Such friendship as this, when I often think that I receive all and give nothing in return.'

Again Unorna laughed, so strangely that the sound of her own voice startled her.

'Why do you laugh like that?' he asked.

'Because what you say is so unjust to yourself,' she answered, nervously and scarcely seeing him where he sat. 'You seem to think it is all on your side. And yet, I just told you that I was fond of you.'

'I think it is a fondness greater than friendship that we feel for each other,' he said, presently, thrusting the probe of a new hope into the tortured wound.

'Yes?' she spoke faintly, with averted face.

'Something more – a stronger tie, a closer bond. Unorna, do you believe in the migration of the soul throughout ages, from one body to another?'

'Sometimes,' she succeeded in saying.

'I do not believe in it,' he continued. 'But I see well enough how men may, since I have known you. We have grown so intimate in these few weeks, we seem to understand each other so wholly, with so little effort, we spend such happy, peaceful hours together every day, that I can almost fancy our two selves having been together through a whole lifetime in some former state, living together, thinking together, inseparable from birth, and full of an instinctive, mutual understanding. I do not know whether that seems an exaggeration to you or not. Has the same idea ever crossed your mind?'

She said something, or tried to say something, but the words were inaudible; he interpreted them as expressive of assent, and went on, in a musing tone, as though talking quite as much to himself as to her.

'And that is the reason why it seems as though we must be more than friends, though we have known each other so short a time. Perhaps it is too much to say.'

He hesitated, and paused. Unorna breathed hard, not daring to think of what might be coming next. He talked so calmly, in such an easy tone, it was impossible that he could be making love. She remembered the vibrations in his voice when, a month ago, he had told her his story. She remembered the inflection of the passionate cry he had uttered when he had seen the shadow of Beatrice stealing between them, she knew the ring of his speech when he loved, for she had heard it. It was not there now. And yet, the effort not to believe would have been too great for her strength.

'Nothing that you could say would be – ' she stopped herself – 'would pain me,' she added, desperately, in the attempt to complete the sentence.

He looked somewhat surprised, and then smiled.

'No. I shall never say anything, nor do anything, which could give you pain. What I meant was this. I feel towards you, and with you, as I can fancy a man might feel to a dear sister. Can you understand that?'

In spite of herself she started. He had but just said that he would never give her pain. He did not guess what cruel wounds he was inflicting now.

'You are surprised,' he said, with intolerable self-possession. 'I cannot wonder. I remember to have very often thought that there are few forms of sentimentality more absurd than that which deceives a man into the idea that he can with impunity play at being a brother to a young and beautiful woman. I have always thought so, and I suppose that in whatever remains of my indolent intelligence I think so still. But intelligence is not always so reliable as instinct. I am not young enough nor foolish enough either, to propose that we should swear eternal brother-and-sisterhood – or perhaps I am not old enough, who can tell? Yet I feel how perfectly safe it would be for either of us.'

The steel had been thrust home, and could go no farther. Unorna's unquiet temper rose at his quiet declaration of his absolute security. The colour came again to her cheek, a little hotly, and though there was a slight tremor in her voice when she spoke, yet her eyes flashed beneath the drooping lids.

'Are you sure it would be safe?' she asked.

'For you, of course there can be no danger possible,' he said, in perfect simplicity of good faith. 'For me – well, I have said it. I cannot imagine love coming near me in any shape, by degrees or unawares. It is a strange defect in my nature, but I am glad of it since it makes this pleasant life possible.'

'And why should you suppose that there is no danger for me?' asked Unorna, with a quick glance and a silvery laugh. She was recovering her self-possession.

'For you? Why should there be? How could there be? No woman ever loved me, then why should you? Besides – there are a thousand reasons, one better than the other.'

'I confess I would be glad to hear a few of them, my friend. You were good enough just now to call me young and beautiful. You are young too, and certainly not repulsive in appearance. You are gifted, you have led an interesting life – indeed, I cannot help laughing when I think how many reasons there are for my falling in love with you. But you are very reassuring, you tell me there is no danger. I am willing to believe.'

'It is safe to do that,' answered the Wanderer with a smile, 'unless you can find at least one reason far stronger than those you give. Young and passably good-looking men are not rare, and as for men of genius who have led interesting lives, many thousands have been pointed out to me. Then why, by any conceivable chance, should your choice fall on me?'

'Perhaps because I am so fond of you already,' said Unorna, looking away lest her eyes should betray what was so far beyond fondness. 'They say that the most enduring passions are either born in a single instant, or are the result of a treacherously increasing liking. Take the latter case. Why is it impossible, for you or for me? We are slipping from mere liking into friendship, and for all I know we may some day fall headlong from friendship into love. It would be very foolish no doubt, but it seems to me quite possible. Do you not see it?'

The Wanderer laughed lightly. It was years since he had laughed, until this friendship had begun.

'What can I say?' he asked. 'If you, the woman, acknowledge yourself vulnerable, how can I, the man, be so discourteous as to assure you that I am proof? And yet, I feel that there is no danger for either of us.'

'You are still sure?'

'And if there were, what harm would be done?' he laughed again. 'We have no plighted word to break, and I, at least, am singularly heart-free. The world would not come to an untimely end if we loved each other. Indeed, the world would have nothing to say about it.'

'To me, it would not,' said Unorna, looking down at her clasped hands. 'But to you – what would the world say, if it learned that you were in love with Unorna, that you were married to the Witch?'

'The world? What is the world to me, or what am I to it? What is my world? If it is anything, it consists of a score of men and women who chance to be spending their allotted time on earth in that corner of the globe in which I was born, who saw me grow to manhood, and who most inconsequently arrogate to themselves the privilege of criticising my actions, as they criticise each other's; who say loudly that this is right and that is wrong, and who will be gathered in due time to their insignificant fathers with their own insignificance thick upon them, as is meet and just. If that is the world I am not afraid of its judgments in the very improbable case of my falling in love with you.'

Unorna shook her head. There was a momentary relief in discussing the consequences of a love not yet born in him.

'That would not be all,' she said. 'You have a country, you have a home, you have obligations – you have all those things which I have not.'

'And not one of those which you have.'

She glanced at him again, for there was a truth in the words which hurt her. Love, at least, was hers in abundance, and he had it not.

'How foolish it is to talk like this!' she exclaimed. 'After all, when people love, they care very little what the world says. If I loved anyone' – she tried to laugh carelessly – 'I am sure I should be indifferent to everything or everyone else.'

'I am sure you would be,' assented the Wanderer.

'Why?' She turned rather suddenly upon him. 'Why are you sure?'

'In the first place because you say so, and secondly because you have the kind of nature which is above common opinion.'

'And what kind of nature may that be?'

'Enthusiastic, passionate, brave.'

'Have I so many good qualities?'

'I am always telling you so.'

'Does it give you pleasure to tell me what you think of me?'

'Does it pain you to hear it?' asked the Wanderer, somewhat surprised at the uncertainty of her temper, and involuntarily curious as to the cause of the disturbance.

'Sometimes it does,' Unorna answered.

'I suppose I have grown awkward and tactless in my lonely life. You must forgive me if I do not understand my mistake. But since I have annoyed you, I am sorry for it. Perhaps you do not like such speeches because you think I am flattering you and turning compliments. You are wrong if you think that. I am sincerely attached to you, and I admire you very much. May I not say as much as that?'

'Does it do any good to say it?'

'If I may speak of you at all I may express myself with pleasant truths.'

'Truths are not always pleasant. Better not to speak of me at any time.'

'As you will,' answered the Wanderer bending his head as though in submission to her commands. But he did not continue the conversation, and a long silence ensued.

He wondered what was passing in her mind, and his reflections led to no very definite result. Even if the idea of her loving him had presented itself to his intelligence he would have scouted it, partly on the ground of its apparent improbability, and partly, perhaps, because he had of late grown really indolent, and would have resented any occurrence which threatened to disturb the peaceful, objectless course of his days. He put down her quick changes of mood to sudden caprice, which he excused readily enough.

'Why are you so silent?' Unorna asked, after a time.

'I was thinking of you,' he answered, with a smile. 'And since you forbade me to speak of you, I said nothing.'

'How literal you are!' she exclaimed impatiently.

'I could see no figurative application of your words,' he retorted, beginning to be annoyed at her prolonged ill humour.

'Perhaps there was none.'

'In that case – '

'Oh, do not argue! I detest argument in all shapes, and most of all when I am expected to answer it. You cannot understand me – you never will – ' She broke off suddenly and looked at him.

She was angry with him, with herself, with everything, and in her anger she loved him tenfold better than before. Had he not been blinded by his own absolute coldness he must have read her heart in the look she gave him, for his eyes met hers. But he saw nothing. The glance had been involuntary, but Unorna was too thoroughly a woman not to know all that it had expressed and would have conveyed to the mind of anyone not utterly incapable of love, all that it might have betrayed even to this man who was her friend and talked of being her brother. She realised with terrible vividness the extent of her own passion and the appalling indifference of its objet. A wave of despair rose and swept over her heart. Her sight grew dim and she was conscious of sharp physical pain. She did not even attempt to speak, for she had no thoughts which could take the shape of words. She leaned back in her chair, and tried to draw her breath, closing her eyes, and wishing she were alone.

'What is the matter?' asked the Wanderer, watching her in surprise.

She did not answer. He rose and stood beside her, and lightly touched her hand.

'Are you ill?' he asked again.

She pushed him away, almost roughly.

'No,' she answered shortly.

Then, all at once, as though repenting of her gesture, her hand sought his again, pressed it hard for a moment, and let it fall.

'It is nothing,' she said. 'It will pass. Forgive me.'

'Did anything I said – ' he began.

'No, no; how absurd!'

'Shall I go. Yes, you would rather be alone – ' he hesitated.

'No – yes – yes, go away and come back later. It is the heat perhaps; is it not hot here?'

'I dare say,' he answered absently.

He took her hand and then left her, wondering exceedingly over a matter which was of the simplest.

It was some time before Unorna realised that he was gone. She had suffered a severe shock, not to be explained by any word or words which he had spoken, so much as by the revelation of her own utter powerlessness, of her total failure to touch his heart, but most directly of all the consequence of a sincere passion which was assuming dangerous proportions and which threatened to sweep away even her pride in its irresistible course.

She grew calmer when she found herself alone, but in a manner she grew also more desperate. A resolution began to form itself in her mind which she would have despised and driven out of her thoughts a few hours earlier; a resolution destined to lead to strange results. She began to think of resorting once more to a means other than natural in order to influence the man she loved.

In the first moments she had felt sure of herself, and the certainty that the Wanderer had forgotten Beatrice as completely as though she had never existed had seemed to Unorna a complete triumph. With little or no common vanity she had nevertheless felt sure that the man must love her for her own sake. She knew, when she thought of it, that she was beautiful, unlike other women, and born to charm all living things. She compared in her mind the powers she controlled at will, and the influence she exercised without effort over everyone who came near her. It had always seemed to her enough to wish in order to see the realisation of her wishes. But she had herself never understood how closely the wish was allied with the despotic power of suggestion which she possessed. But in her love she had put a watch over her mysterious strength and had controlled it, saying that she would be loved for herself or not at all. She had been jealous of every glance, lest it should produce a result not natural. She had waited to be won, instead of trying to win. She had failed, and passion could be restrained no longer.

'What does it matter how, if only he is mine!' she exclaimed fiercely, as she rose from her carved chair an hour after he had left her.

Chapter 12

Israel Kafka found himself seated in the corner of a comfortable carriage with Keyork Arabian at his side. He opened his eyes quite naturally, and after looking out of the window stretched himself as far as the limits of the space would allow. He felt very weak and very tired. The bright colour had left his olive cheeks, his lips were pale and his eyes heavy.

'Travelling is very tiring,' he said, glancing at Keyork's face.

The old man rubbed his hands briskly and laughed.

'I am as fresh as ever,' he answered. 'It is true that I have the happy faculty of sleeping when I get a chance and that no preoccupation disturbs my appetite.'

Keyork Arabian was in a very cheerful frame of mind. He was conscious of having made a great stride towards the successful realisation of his dream. Israel Kafka's ignorance, too, amused him, and gave him a fresh and encouraging proof of Unorna's amazing powers.

By a mere exercise of superior will this man, in the very prime of youth and strength, had been deprived of a month of his life. Thirty days were gone, as in the flash of a second, and with them was gone also something less easily replaced, or at least more certainly missed. In Kafka's mind the passage of time was accounted for in a way which would have seemed supernatural twenty years ago, but which at the present day is understood in practice if not in theory. For thirty days he had been stationary in one place, almost motionless, an instrument in Keyork's skilful hands, a mere reservoir of vitality upon which the sage had ruthlessly drawn to the fullest extent of its capacities. He had been fed and tended in his unconsciousness, he had, unknown to himself, opened his eyes at regular intervals, and had absorbed through his ears a series of vivid impressions destined to disarm his suspicions, when he was at last allowed to wake and move about the world again. With unfailing forethought Keyork had planned the details of a whole series of artificial reminiscences, and at the moment when Kafka came to himself in the carriage the machinery of memory began to work as Keyork had intended that it should.

Israel Kafka leaned back against the cushions and reviewed his life during the past month. He remembered very well the afternoon when, after a stormy interview with Unorna, he had been persuaded by Keyork to accompany the latter upon a rapid southward journey. He remembered how he had hastily packed together a few necessaries for the expedition, while Keyork stood at his elbow advising him what to take and what to leave, with the sound good sense of an experienced traveller, and he could almost repeat the words of the message he had scrawled on a sheet of paper at the last minute to explain his sudden absence from his lodging – for the people of the house had all been away when he was packing his belongings. Then the hurry of the departure recalled itself to him, the crowds of people at the Franz Josef station, the sense of rest in finding himself alone with Keyork in a compartment of the express train; after that he had slept during most of the journey, waking to find himself in a city of the snow-driven Tyrol. With tolerable distinctness he remembered the sights he had seen, and fragments of conversation – then another departure, still southward, the crossing of the Alps, Italy, Venice – a dream of water and sun and beautiful buildings, in which the varied conversational powers of his companion found constant material. As a matter of fact the conversation was what was most clearly impressed upon Kafka's mind, as he recalled the rapid passage from one city to another, and realised how many places he had visited in one short month. From Venice southwards again, Florence, Rome, Naples, Sicily, by sea to Athens and on to Constantinople, familiar to him already from former visits – up the Bosporus, by the Black Sea to Varna, and then, again, a long period of restful sleep during the endless railway journey – Pesth, Vienna rapidly revisited, and back at last to Prague, to the cold and the grey snow and the black sky. It was not strange, he thought, that his recollections of so many cities should be a little confused. A man would need a fine memory to catalogue the myriad sights which such a trip offers to the eye, the innumerable sounds, familiar and unfamiliar, which strike the ear, the countless sensations of comfort, discomfort, pleasure, annoyance and admiration, which occupy the nerves without intermission. There was something not wholly disagreeable in the hazy character of the retrospect, especially to a nature such as Kafka's, full of undeveloped artistic instincts and of a passionate love of all sensuous beauty, animate and inanimate. The gorgeous pictures rose one after the other in his imagination, and satisfied a longing of which he felt that he had been vaguely aware before beginning the journey. None of these lacked reality, any more than Keyork himself, though it seemed strange to the young man that he should actually have seen so much in so short a time.

But Keyork and Unorna understood their art and knew how much more easy it is to produce a fiction of continuity where an element of confusion is introduced by a multitude and variety of quickly succeeding impressions, almost destitute of incident. One occurrence, indeed, he remembered with extraordinary distinctness, and could have affirmed under oath in all its details. It had taken place in Palermo. The heat had seemed intense by contrast with the bitter north he had left behind. Keyork had gone out and he had been alone in a strange hotel. His head swam in the stifling scirocco. He had sent for a local physician, and the old-fashioned doctor had then and there taken blood from his arm. He had lost so much that he had fainted. The doctor had been gone when Keyork returned, and the sage had been very angry, abusing in most violent terms the ignorance which could still apply such methods. Israel Kafka knew that the lancet had left a wound on his arm and that the scar was still visible. He remembered, too, that he had often felt tired since, and that Keyork had invariably reminded him of the circumstances, attributing to it the weariness from which he suffered, and indulging each time in fresh abuse of the benighted doctor.

Very skilfully had the whole story been put together in all its minutest details, carefully thought out and written down in the form of a journal before it had been impressed upon his sleeping mind with all the tyrannic force of Unorna's strong will. And there was but little probability that Israel Kafka would ever learn what had actually been happening to him while he fancied that he had been travelling swiftly from place to place. He could still wonder, indeed, that he should have yielded so easily to Keyork's pressing invitation to accompany the latter upon such an extraordinary flight, but he remembered then his last interview with Unorna and it seemed almost natural that in his despair he should have chosen to go away. Not that his passion for the woman was dead. Intentionally, or by an oversight, Unorna had not touched upon the question of his love for her, in the course of her otherwise well-considered suggestions. Possibly she had believed that the statement she had forced from his lips was enough and that he would forget her without any further action on her part. Possibly, too, Unorna was indifferent and was content to let him suffer, believing that his devotion might still be turned to some practical use. However that may be, when Israel Kafka opened his eyes in the carriage he still loved her, though he was conscious that in his manner of loving a change had taken place, of which he was destined to realise the consequences before another day had passed.

When Keyork answered his first remark, he turned and looked at the old man.

'I suppose you are tougher than I,' he said, languidly. 'You will hardly believe it, but I have been dozing already, here, in the carriage, since we left the station.'

'No harm in that. Sleep is a great restorative,' laughed Keyork.

'Are you so glad to be in Prague again?' asked Kafka. 'It is a melancholy place. But you laugh as though you actually liked the sight of the black houses and the grey snow and the silent people.'

'How can a place be melancholy? The seat of melancholy is the liver. Imagine a city with a liver – of brick and mortar, or stone and cement, a huge mass of masonry buried in its centre, like an enormous fetish, exercising a mysterious influence over the city's health – then you may imagine a city as suffering from melancholy.'

'How absurd!'

'My dear boy, I rarely say absurd things,' answered Keyork imperturbably. 'Besides, as a matter of fact, there is nothing absurd. But you suggested rather a fantastic idea to my imagination. The brick liver is not a bad conception. Far down in the bowels of the earth, in a black cavern hollowed beneath the lowest foundations of the oldest church, the brick liver was built by the cunning magicians of old, to last for ever, to purify the city's blood, to regulate the city's life, and in a measure to control its destinies by means of its passions. A few wise men have handed down the knowledge of the brick liver to each other from generation to generation, but the rest of the inhabitants are ignorant of its existence. They alone know that every vicissitude of the city's condition is traceable to that source – its sadness, its merriment, its carnivals and its lents, its health and its disease, its prosperity and the hideous plagues which at distant intervals kill one in ten of the population. Is it not a pretty thought?'

'I do not understand you,' said Kafka, wearily.

'It is a very practical idea,' continued Keyork, amused with his own fancies, 'and it will yet be carried out. The great cities of the next century will each have a liver of brick and mortar and iron and machinery, a huge mechanical purifier. You smile! Ah, my dear boy, truth and phantasm are very much the same to you! You are too young. How can you be expected to care for the great problem of problems, for the mighty question of prolonging life?'

Keyork laughed again, with a meaning in his laughter which escaped his companion altogether.

'How can you be expected to care?' he repeated. 'And yet men used to say that it was the duty of strong youth to support the trembling weakness of feeble old age.'

His eyes twinkled with a diabolical mirth.

'No,' said Kafka. 'I do not care. Life is meant to be short. Life is meant to be storm, broken with gleams of love's sunshine. Why prolong it? If it is unhappy you would only draw out the unhappiness to greater lengths, and such joy as it has is joy only because it is quick, sudden, violent. I would concentrate a lifetime into an instant, if I could, and then die content in having suffered everything, enjoyed everything, dared everything in the flash of a great lightning between two total darknesses. But to drag on through slow sorrows, or to crawl through a century of contentment – never! Better be mad, or asleep, and unconscious of the time.'

'You are a very desperate person!' exclaimed Keyork. 'If you had the management of this unstable world you would make it a very convulsive and nervous place. We should all turn into flaming ephemerides, fluttering about the crater of a perpetually active volcano. I prefer the system of the brick liver. There is more durability in it.'

The carriage stopped before the door of Kafka's dwelling. Keyork got out with him and stood upon the pavement while the porter took the slender luggage into the house. He smiled as he glanced at the leathern portmanteau which was supposed to have made such a long journey while it had in reality lain a whole month in a corner of Keyork's great room behind a group of specimens. He had opened it once or twice in that time, had disturbed the contents and had thrown in a few objects from his heterogeneous collection, as reminiscences of the places visited in imagination by Kafka, and of the acquisition of which the latter was only assured in his sleeping state. They would constitute a tangible proof of the journey's reality in case the suggestion proved less thoroughly successful than was hoped, and Keyork prided himself upon this supreme touch.

'And now,' he said, taking Kafka's hand, 'I would advise you to rest as long as you can. I suppose that it must have been a fatiguing trip for you, though I myself am as fresh as a May morning. There is nothing wrong with you, but you are tired. Repose, my dear boy, repose, and plenty of it. That infernal Sicilian doctor! I shall never forgive him for bleeding you as he did. There is nothing so weakening. Goodbye – I shall hardly see you again today, I fancy.'

'I cannot tell,' answered the young man absently. 'But let me thank you,' he added, with a sudden consciousness of obligation, 'for your pleasant company, and for making me go with you. I dare say it has done me good, though I feel unaccountably tired – I feel almost old.'

His tired eyes and haggard face showed that this at least was no illusion. The fancied journey had added ten years to his age in thirty days, and those who knew him best would have found it hard to recognise the brilliantly vital personality of Israel Kafka in the pale and exhausted youth who painfully climbed the stairs with unsteady steps, panting for breath and clutching at the hand-rail for support.

'He will not die this time,' remarked Keyork Arabian to himself, as he sent the carriage away and began to walk towards his own home. 'Not this time. But it was a sharp strain, and it would not be safe to try it again.'

He thrust his gloved hands into the pockets of his fur coat, so that the stick he held stood upright against his shoulder in a rather military fashion. The fur cap sat a little to one side on his strange head, his eyes twinkled, his long white beard waved in the cold wind, and his whole appearance was that of a jaunty gnome-king, well satisfied with the inspection of his treasure chamber.

And he had cause for satisfaction, as he knew well enough when he thought of the decided progress made in the great experiment. The cost at which that progress had been obtained was nothing. Had Israel Kafka perished altogether under the treatment he had received, Keyork Arabian would have bestowed no more attention upon the catastrophe than would have been barely necessary in order to conceal it and to protect himself and Unorna from the consequences of the crime. In the duel with death, the life of one man was of small consequence, and Keyork would have sacrificed thousands to his purposes with equal indifference to their intrinsic value and with a proportionately greater interest in the result to be attained. There was a terrible logic in his mental process. Life was a treasure literally inestimable in value. Death was the destroyer of this treasure, devised by the Supreme Power as a sure means of limiting man's activity and intelligence. To conquer Death on his own ground was to win the great victory over that Power, and to drive back to an indefinite distance the boundaries of human supremacy.

It was assuredly not for the sake of benefiting mankind at large that he pursued his researches at all sacrifices and at all costs. The prime object of all his consideration was himself, as he unhesitatingly admitted on all occasions, conceiving perhaps that it was easier to defend such a position than to disclaim it. There could be no doubt that in the man's enormous self-estimation, the Supreme Power occupied a place secondary to Keyork Arabian's personality, and hostile to it. And he had taken up arms, as Lucifer, assuming his individual right to live in spite of God, Man and Nature, convinced that the secret could be discovered and determined to find it and to use it, no matter at what price. In him there was neither ambition, nor pride, nor vanity in the ordinary meaning of these words. For passion ceases with the cessation of comparison between man and his fellows, and Keyork Arabian acknowledged no ground for such a comparison in his own case. He had matched himself in a struggle with the Supreme Power, and, directly, with that Power's only active representative on earth, with death. It was well said of him that he had no beliefs, for he knew of no intermediate position between total suspension of judgment, and the certainty of direct knowledge. And it was equally true that he was no atheist, as he had sanctimoniously declared of himself. He admitted the existence of the Power; he claimed the right to assail it, and he grappled with the greatest, the most terrible, the most universal and the most stupendous of Facts, which is the Fact that all men die. Unless he conquered, he must die also. He was past theories, as he was beyond most other human weaknesses, and facts had for him the enormous value they acquire in the minds of men cut off from all that is ideal.

In Unorna he had found the instrument he had sought throughout half a lifetime. With her he had tried the great experiment and pushed it to the very end; and when he conducted Israel Kafka to his home, he already knew that the experiment had succeeded. His plan was a simple one. He would wait a few months longer for the final result, he would select his victim, and with Unorna's help he would himself grow young again.

'And who can tell,' he asked himself, 'whether the life restored by such means may not be more resisting and stronger against deathly influences than before? Is it not true that the older we grow the more slowly we grow old? Is not the gulf which divides the infant from the man of twenty years far wider than that which lies between the twentieth and the fortieth years, and that again more full of rapid change than the third score? Take, too, the wisdom of my old age as against the folly of a scarce grown boy, shall not my knowledge and care and forethought avail to make the same material last longer on the second trial than on the first?'

No doubt of that, he thought, as he walked briskly along the pavement and entered his own house. In his great room he sat down by the table and fell into a long meditation upon the most immediate consequences of his success in the difficult undertaking he had so skilfully brought to a conclusion. His eyes wandered about the room from one specimen to another, and from time to time a short, scornful laugh made his white beard quiver. As he had said once to Unorna, the dead things reminded him of many failures; but he had never before been able to laugh at them and at the unsuccessful efforts they represented. It was different today. Without lifting his head he turned up his bright eyes, under the thick, finely-wrinkled lids, as though looking upward toward that Power against which he strove. The glance was malignant and defiant, human and yet half-devilish. Then he looked down again, and again fell into deep thought.

'And if it is to be so,' he said at last, rising suddenly and letting his open hand fall upon the table, 'even then, I am provided. She cannot free herself from that bargain, at all events.'

Then he wrapped his furs around him and went out again. Scarce a hundred paces from Unorna's door he met the Wanderer. He looked up into the cold, calm face, and put out his hand, with a greeting.

'You look as though you were in a very peaceful frame of mind,' observed Keyork.

'Why should I be anything but peaceful?' asked the other, 'I have nothing to disturb me.'

'True, true. You possess a very fine organisation. I envy you your magnificent constitution, my dear friend. I would like to have some of it, and grow young again.'

'On your principle of embalming the living, I suppose.'

'Exactly,' answered the sage with a deep, rolling laugh. 'By the bye, have you been with our friend Unorna? I suppose that is a legitimate question, though you always tell me I am tactless.'

'Perfectly legitimate, my dear Keyork. Yes, I have just left her. It is like a breath of spring morning to go there in these days.'

'You find it refreshing?'

'Yes. There is something about her that I could describe as sooth-ing, if I were aware of ever being irritable, which I am not.'

Keyork smiled and looked down, trying to dislodge a bit of ice from the pavement with the point of his stick.

'Soothing – yes. That is just the expression. Not exactly the quality most young and beautiful women covet, eh? But a good quality in its way, and at the right time. How is she today?'

'She seemed to have a headache – or she was oppressed by the heat. Nothing serious, I fancy, but I came away, as I fancied I was tiring her.'

'Not likely,' observed Keyork. 'Do you know Israel Kafka?' he asked suddenly.

'Israel Kafka,' repeated the Wanderer thoughtfully, as though searching in his memory.

'Then you do not,' said Keyork. 'You could only have seen him since you have been here. He is one of Unorna's most interesting patients, and mine as well. He is a little odd.'

Keyork tapped his ivory forehead significantly with one finger.

'Mad,' suggested the Wanderer.

'Mad, if you prefer the term. He has fixed ideas. In the first place, he imagines that he has just been travelling with me in Italy, and is always talking of our experiences. Humour him, if you meet him. He is in danger of being worse if contradicted.'

'Am I likely to meet him?'

'Yes. He is often here. His other fixed idea is that he loves Unorna to distraction. He has been dangerously ill during the last few weeks but is better now, and he may appear at any moment. Humour him a little if he wearies you with his stories. That is all I ask. Both Unorna and I are interested in the case.'

'And does not Unorna care for him at all?' inquired the other indifferently.

'No, indeed. On the contrary, she is annoyed at his insistance, but sees that it is a phase of insanity and hopes to cure it before long.'

'I see. What is he like? I suppose he is an Israelite.'

'From Moravia – yes. The wreck of a handsome boy,' said Keyork carelessly. 'This insanity is an enemy of good looks. The nerves give way – then the vitality – the complexion goes – men of five and twenty years look old under it. But you will see for yourself before long. Goodbye. I will go in and see what is the matter with Unorna.'

They parted, the Wanderer continuing on his way along the street with the same calm, cold, peaceful expression which had elicited Keyork's admiration, and Keyork himself going forward to Unorna's door. His face was very grave. He entered the house by a small side door and ascended by a winding staircase directly to the room from which, an hour or two earlier, he had carried the still unconscious Israel Kafka. Everything was as he had left it, and he was glad to be certified that Unorna had not disturbed the aged sleeper in his absence. Instead of going to her at once he busied himself in making a few observations and in putting in order certain of his instruments and appliances. Then at last he went and found Unorna. She was walking up and down among the plants and he saw at a glance that something had happened. Indeed the few words spoken by the Wanderer had suggested to him the possibility of a crisis, and he had purposely lingered in the inner apartment, in order to give her time to recover her self-possession. She started slightly when he entered, and her brows contracted, but she immediately guessed from his expression that he was not in one of his aggressive moods.

'I have just rectified a mistake which might have had rather serious consequences,' he said, stopping before her and speaking earnestly and quietly.

'A mistake?'

'We remembered everything, except that our wandering friend and Kafka were very likely to meet, and that Kafka would in all probability refer to his delightful journey to the south in my company.'

'That is true!' exclaimed Unorna with an anxious glance. 'Well? What have you done?'

'I met the Wanderer in the street. What could I do? I told him that Israel Kafka was a little mad, and that his harmless delusions referred to a journey he was supposed to have made with me, and to an equally imaginary passion which he fancies he feels for you.'

'That was wise,' said Unorna, still pale. 'How came we to be so imprudent! One word, and he might have suspected – '

'He could not have suspected all,' answered Keyork. 'No man could suspect that.'

'Nevertheless, I suppose what we have done is not exactly – justifiable.'

'Hardly. It is true that criminal law has not yet adjusted itself to meet questions of suggestion and psychic influence, but it draws the line, most certainly, somewhere between these questions and the extremity to which we have gone. Happily the law is at an immeasurable distance from science, and here, as usual in such experiments, no one could prove anything, owing to the complete unconsciousness of the principal witnesses.'

'I do not like to think that we have been near to such trouble,' said Unorna.

'Nor I. It was fortunate that I met the Wanderer when I did.'

'And the other? Did he wake as I ordered him to do? Is all right? Is there no danger of his suspecting anything?'

It seemed as though Unorna had momentarily forgotten that such a contingency might be possible, and her anxiety returned with the recollection. Keyork's rolling laughter reverberated among the plants and filled the whole wide hall with echoes.

'No danger there,' he answered. 'Your witchcraft is above criticism. Nothing of that kind that you have ever undertaken has failed.'

'Except against you,' said Unorna, thoughtfully.

'Except against me, of course. How could you ever expect anything of the kind to succeed against me, my dear lady?'

'And why not? After all, in spite of our jesting, you are not a supernatural being.'

'That depends entirely on the interpretation you give to the word supernatural. But, my dear friend and colleague, let us not deceive each other, though we are able between us to deceive other people into believing almost anything. There is nothing in all this witchcraft of yours but a very powerful moral influence at work – I mean apart from the mere faculty of clairvoyance which is possessed by hundreds of common somnambulists, and which, in you, is a mere accident. The rest, this hypnotism, this suggestion, this direction of others' wills, is a moral affair, a matter of direct impression produced by words. Mental suggestion may in rare cases succeed, when the person to be influenced is himself a natural clairvoyant. But these cases are not worth taking into consideration. Your influence is a direct one, chiefly exercised by means of your words and through the impression of power which you know how to convey in them. It is marvellous, I admit. But the very definition puts me beyond your power.'

'Why?'

'Because there is not a human being alive, and I do not believe that a human being ever lived, who had the sense of independent individuality which I have. Let a man have the very smallest doubt concerning his own independence – let that doubt be ever so transitory and produced by any accident whatsoever – and he is at your mercy.'

'And you are sure that no accident could shake your faith in yourself?'

'My consciousness of myself, you mean. No. I am not sure. But, my dear Unorna, I am very careful in guarding against accidents of all sorts, for I have attempted to resuscitate a great many dead people and I have never succeeded, and I know that a false step on a slippery staircase may be quite as fatal as a teaspoonful of prussic acid – or an unrequited passion. I avoid all these things and many others. If I did not, and if you had any object in getting me under your influence, you would succeed sooner or later. Perhaps the day is not far distant when I will voluntarily sleep under your hand.'

Unorna glanced quickly at him.

'And in that case,' he added, 'I am sure you could make me believe anything you pleased.'

'What are you trying to make me understand?' she asked, suspiciously, for he had never before spoken of such a possibility.

'You look anxious and weary,' he said in a tone of sympathy in which Unorna could not detect the least false modulation, though she fancied from his fixed gaze that he meant her to understand something which he could not say. 'You look tired,' he continued, 'though it is becoming to your beauty to be pale – I always said so. I will not weary you. I was only going to say that if I were under your influence – you might easily make me believe that you were not yourself, but another woman – for the rest of my life.'

They stood looking at each other in silence during several seconds. Then Unorna seemed to understand what he meant.

'Do you really believe that is possible?' she asked earnestly.

'I know it. I know of a case in which it succeeded very well.'

'Perhaps,' she said, thoughtfully. 'Let us go and look at him.'

She moved in the direction of the aged sleeper's room and they both left the hall together.

Chapter 13

Unorna was superstitious, as Keyork Arabian had once told her. She did not thoroughly understand herself and she had very little real comprehension of the method by which she produced such remarkable results. She was gifted with a sensitive and active imagination, which supplied her with semi-mystic formulae of thought and speech in place of reasoned explanations, and she undoubtedly attributed much of her own power to supernatural influences. In this respect, at least, she was no farther advanced than the witches of older days, and if her inmost convictions took a shape which would have seemed incomprehensible to those predecessors of hers, this was to be attributed in part to the innate superiority of her nature, and partly, also, to the high degree of cultivation in which her mental faculties had reached development.

Keyork Arabian might spend hours in giving her learned explanations of what she did, but he never convinced her. Possibly he was not convinced himself, and he still hesitated, perhaps, between the two great theories advanced to explain the phenomena of hypnotism. He had told her that he considered her influence to be purely a moral one, exerted by means of language and supported by her extraordinary concentrated will. But it did not follow that he believed what he told her, and it was not improbable that he might have his own doubts on the subject – doubts which Unorna was not slow to suspect, and which destroyed for her the whole force of his reasoning. She fell back upon a sort of grossly unreasonable mysticism, combined with a blind belief in those hidden natural forces and secret virtues of privileged objects, which formed the nucleus of mediaeval scientific research. The field is a fertile one for the imagination and possesses a strange attraction for certain minds. There are men alive in our own time to whom the transmutation of metals does not seem an impossibility, nor the brewing of the elixir of life a matter to be scoffed at as a matter of course. The world is full of people who, in their inmost selves, put faith in the latent qualities of precious stones and amulets, who believe their fortunes, their happiness, and their lives to be directly influenced by some trifling object which they have always upon them. We do not know enough to state with assurance that the constant handling of any particular metal, or gem, may not produce a real and invariable corresponding effect upon the nerves. But we do know most positively that, when the belief in such talismans is once firmly established, the moral influence they exert upon men through the imagination is enormous. From this condition of mind to that in which auguries are drawn from outward and apparently accidental circumstances, is but a step. If Keyork Arabian inclined to the psychic rather than to the physical school in his view of Unorna's witchcraft and in his study of hypnotism in general, his opinion resulted naturally from his great knowledge of mankind, and of the unacknowledged, often unsuspected, convictions which in reality direct mankind's activity. It was this experience, too, and the certainty to which it had led him, that put him beyond the reach of

Unorna's power so long as he chose not to yield himself to her will. Her position was in reality diametrically opposed to his, and although he repeated his reasonings to her from time to time, he was quite indifferent to the nature of her views, and never gave himself any real trouble to make her change them. The important point was that she should not lose anything of the gifts she possessed, and Keyork was wise enough to see that the exercise of them depended in a great measure upon her own conviction regarding their exceptional nature.

Unorna herself believed in everything which strengthened and developed that conviction, and especially in the influences of time and place. It appeared to her a fortunate circumstance, when she at last determined to overcome her pride, that the resolution should have formed itself exactly a month after she had so successfully banished the memory of Beatrice from the mind of the man she loved. She felt sure of producing a result as effectual if, this time, she could work the second change in the same place and under the same circumstances as the first. And to this end everything was in her favour. She needed not to close her eyes to fancy that thirty days had not really passed between then and now, as she left her house in the afternoon with the Wanderer by her side.

He had come back and had found her once more herself, calm, collected, conscious of her own powers. No suspicion of the real cause of the disturbance he had witnessed crossed his mind, still less could he guess what thing she meditated as she directed their walk towards that lonely place by the river which had been the scene of her first great effort. She talked lightly as they went, and he, in that strange humour of peaceful, well-satisfied indifference which possessed him, answered her in the same strain. It was yet barely afternoon, but there was already a foretaste of coming evening in the chilly air.

'I have been thinking of what you said this morning,' she said, suddenly changing the current of the conversation. 'Did I thank you for your kindness?' She smiled as she laid her hand gently upon his arm, to cross a crowded street, and she looked up into his quiet face.

'Thank me? For what? On the contrary – I fancied that I had annoyed you.'

'Perhaps I did not quite understand it all at first,' she answered thoughtfully. 'It is hard for a woman like me to realise what it would be to have a brother – or a sister, or anyone belonging to me. I needed to think of the idea. Do you know that I am quite alone in the world?'

The Wanderer had accepted her as he found her, strangely alone, indeed, and strangely independent of the world, a beautiful, singularly interesting woman, doing good, so far as he knew, in her own way, separated from ordinary existence by some unusual circumstances, and elevated above ordinary dangers by the strength and the pride of her own character. And yet, indolent and indifferent as he had grown of late, he was conscious of a vague curiosity in regard to her story. Keyork either really knew nothing, or pretended to know nothing, of her origin.

'I see that you are alone,' said the Wanderer. 'Have you always been so?'

'Always. I have had an odd life. You could not understand it, if I told you of it.'

'And yet I have been lonely too – and I believe I was once unhappy, though I cannot think of any reason for it.'

'You have been lonely – yes. But yours was another loneliness more limited, less fatal, more voluntary. It must seem strange to you – I do not even positively know of what nation I was born.'

Her companion looked at her in surprise, and his curiosity increased.

'I know nothing of myself,' she continued. 'I remember neither father nor mother. I grew up in the forest, among people who did not love me, but who taught me, and respected me as though I were their superior, and who sometimes feared me. When I look back, I am amazed at their learning and their wisdom – and ashamed of having learned so little.'

'You are unjust to yourself.'

Unorna laughed.

'No one ever accused me of that,' she said. 'Will you believe it? I do not even know where that place was. I cannot tell you even the name of the kingdom in which it lay. I learned a name for it and for the forest, but those names are in no map that has ever fallen into my hands. I sometimes feel that I would go to the place if I could find it.'

'It is very strange. And how came you here?'

'I was told the time had come. We started at night. It was a long journey, and I remember feeling tired as I was never tired before or since. They brought me here, they left me in a religious house among nuns. Then I was told that I was rich and free. My fortune was brought with me. That, at least, I know. But those who received it and who take care of it for me, know no more of its origin than I myself. Gold tells no tales, and the secret has been well kept. I would give much to know the truth – when I am in the humour.'

She sighed, and then laughed again.

'You see why it is that I find the idea of a brother so hard to understand,' she added, and then was silent.

'You have all the more need of understanding it, my dear friend,' the Wanderer answered, looking at her thoughtfully.

'Yes – perhaps so. I can see what friendship is. I can almost guess what it would be to have a brother.'

'And have you never thought of more than that?' He asked the question in his calmest and most friendly tone, somewhat deferentially as though fearing lest it should seem tactless and be unwelcome.

'Yes, I have thought of love also,' she answered, in a low voice. But she said nothing more, and they walked on for some time in silence.

They came out upon the open place by the river which she remembered so well. Unorna glanced about her and her face fell. The place was the same, but the solitude was disturbed. It was not Sunday as it had been on that day a month ago. All about the huge blocks of stone, groups of workmen were busy with great chisels and heavy hammers, hewing and chipping and fashioning the material that it might be ready for use in the early spring. Even the river was changed. Men were standing upon the ice, cutting it into long symmetrical strips, to be hauled ashore. Some of the great pieces were already separated from the main ice, and sturdy fellows, clad in dark woollen, were poling them over the dark water to the foot of the gently sloping road where heavy carts stood ready to receive the load when cut up into blocks. The dark city was taking in a great provision of its own coldness against the summer months.

Unorna looked about her. Everywhere there were people at work, and she was more disappointed than she would own to herself at the invasion of the solitude. The Wanderer looked from the stone-cutters to the ice-men with a show of curiosity.

'I have not seen so much life in Prague for many a day,' he observed.

'Let us go,' answered Unorna, nervously. 'I do not like it. I cannot bear the sight of people today.'

They turned in a new direction, Unorna guiding her companion by a gesture. They were near to the Jewish quarter, and presently were threading their way through narrow and filthy streets thronged with eager Hebrew faces, and filled with the hum of low-pitched voices chattering together, not in the language of the country, but in a base dialect of German. They were in the heart of Prague, in that dim quarter which is one of the strongholds of the Israelite, whence he directs great enterprises and sets in motion huge financial schemes, in which Israel sits, as a great spider in the midst of a dark web, dominating the whole capital with his eagle's glance and weaving the destiny of the Bohemian people to suit his intricate speculations. For throughout the length and breadth of Slavonic and German Austria the Jew rules, and rules alone.

Unorna gathered her furs more closely about her, in evident disgust at her surroundings, but still she kept on her way. Her companion, scarcely less familiar with the sights of Prague than she herself, walked by her side, glancing carelessly at the passing people, at the Hebrew signs, at the dark entrances that led to courts within courts and into labyrinths of dismal lanes and passages, looking at everything with the same serene indifference, and idly wondering what made Unorna choose to walk that way. Then he saw that she was going towards the cemetery. They reached the door, were admitted and found themselves alone in the vast wilderness.

In the midst of the city lies the ancient burial ground, now long disused but still undisturbed, many acres of uneven land, covered so thickly with graves, and planted so closely with granite and sandstone slabs, that the paths will scarce allow two persons to walk side by side. The stones stand and lie in all conceivable positions, erect, slanting at every angle, prostrate upon the earth or upon others already fallen before them – two, three, and even four upon a grave, where generations of men have been buried one upon the other – stones large and small, covered with deep-cut inscriptions in the Hebrew character, bearing the sculpture of two uplifted hands, wherever the Kohns, the children of the tribe of Aaron, are laid to rest, or the gracefully chiselled ewer of the Levites. Here they lie, thousands upon thousands of dead Jews, great and small, rich and poor, wise and ignorant, neglected individually, but guarded as a whole with all the tenacious determination of the race to hold its own, and to preserve the sacredness of its dead. In the dim light of the winter's afternoon it is as though a great army of men had fallen fighting there, and had been turned to stone as they fell. Rank upon rank they lie, with that irregularity which comes of symmetry destroyed, like columns and files of soldiers shot down in the act of advancing. And in winter, the grey light falling upon the untrodden snow throws a pale reflection upwards against each stone, as though from the myriad sepulchres a faintly luminous vapour were rising to the outer air. Over all, the rugged brushwood and the stunted trees intertwine their leafless branches and twigs in a thin, ghostly network of grey, that clouds the view of the farther distance without interrupting it, a forest of shadowy skeletons clasping fleshless, bony hands one with another, from grave to grave, as far as the eye can see.

The stillness in the place is intense. Not a murmur of distant life from the surrounding city disturbs the silence. At rare intervals a strong breath of icy wind stirs the dead branches and makes them crack and rattle against the gravestones and against each other as in a dance of death. It is a wild and dreary place. In the summer, indeed, the thick leafage lends it a transitory colour and softness, but in the depth of winter, when there is nothing to hide the nakedness of truth, when the snow lies thick upon the ground and the twined twigs and twisted trunks scarce cast a tracery of shadow under the sunless sky, the utter desolation and loneliness of the spot have a horror of their own, not to be described, but never to be forgotten.

Unorna walked forward in silence, choosing a path so narrow that her companion found himself obliged to drop behind and follow in her footsteps. In the wildest part of this wilderness of death there is a little rising of the ground. Here both the gravestones and the stunted trees are thickest, and the solitude is, if possible, even more complete than elsewhere. As she reached the highest point Unorna stood still, turned quickly towards the Wanderer and held out both her hands towards him.

'I have chosen this place, because it is quiet,' she said, with a soft smile.

Hardly knowing why he did so, he laid his hands in hers and looked kindly down to her upturned face.

'What is it?' he asked, meeting her eyes.

She was silent, and her fingers did not unclasp themselves. He looked at her, and saw for the hundredth time that she was very beautiful. There was a faint colour in her cheeks, and her full lips were just parted as though a loving word had escaped them which she would not willingly recall. Against the background of broken neutral tints, her figure stood out, an incarnation of youth and vitality. If she had often looked weary and pale of late, her strength and freshness had returned to her now in all their abundance. The Wanderer knew that he was watching her, and knew that he was thinking of her beauty and realising the whole extent of it more fully than ever before, but beyond this point his thoughts could not go. He was aware that he was becoming fascinated by her eyes, and he felt that with every moment it was growing harder for him to close his own, or to look away from her, and then, an instant later, he knew that it would be impossible. Yet he made no effort. He was passive, indifferent, will-less, and her gaze charmed him more and more. He was already in a dream, and he fancied that the beautiful figure shone with a soft, rosy light of its own in the midst of the gloomy waste. Looking into her sunlike eyes, he saw there twin images of himself, that drew him softly and surely into themselves until he was absorbed by them and felt that he was no longer a reality but a reflection. Then a deep unconsciousness stole over all his senses and he slept, or passed into that state which seems to lie between sleep and trance.

Unorna needed not to question him this time, for she saw that he was completely under her influence. Yet she hesitated at the supreme moment, and then, though to all real intents she was quite alone, a burning flush of shame rose to her face, and her heart sank within her. She felt that she could not do it.

She dropped his hands. They fell to his sides as though they had been of lead. Then she turned from him and pressed her aching forehead against a tall weather-worn stone that rose higher than her own height from the midst of the hillock.

Her woman's nature rebelled against the trick. It was the truest thing in her and perhaps the best, which protested so violently against the thing she meant to do; it was the simple longing to be loved for her own sake, and of the man's own free will, to be loved by him with the love she had despised in Israel Kafka. But would this be love at all, this artificial creation of her suggestion reacting upon his mind? Would it last? Would it be true, faithful, tender? Above all, would it be real, even for a moment? She asked herself a thousand questions in a second of time.

Then the ready excuse flashed upon her – the pretext which the heart will always find when it must have its way. Was it not possible, after all, that he was beginning to love her even now? Might not that outburst of friendship which had surprised her and wounded her so deeply, be the herald of a stronger passion? She looked up quickly and met his vacant stare.

'Do you love me?' she asked, almost before she knew what she was going to say.

'No.' The answer came in the far-off voice that told of his unconsciousness, a mere toneless monosyllable breathed upon the murky air. But it stabbed her like the thrust of a jagged knife. A long silence followed, and Unorna leaned against the great slab of carved sandstone.

Even to her there was something awful in his powerless, motion-less presence. The noble face, pale and set as under a mask, the thoughtful brow, the dominating features, were not those of a man born to be a plaything to the will of a woman. The commanding figure towered in the grim surroundings like a dark statue, erect, unmoving, and in no way weak. And yet she knew that she had but to speak and the figure would move, the lips would form words, the voice would reach her ear. He would raise this hand or that, step forwards or backwards, at her command, affirm what she bid him affirm, and deny whatever she chose to hear denied. For a moment she wished that he had been as Keyork Arabian, stronger than she; then, with the half-conscious comparison the passion for the man himself surged up and drowned every other thought. She almost forgot that for the time he was not to be counted among the living. She went to him, and clasped her hands upon his shoulder, and looked up into his scarce-seeing eyes.

'You must love me,' she said, 'you must love me because I love you so. Will you not love me, dear? I have waited so long for you!'

The soft words vibrated in his sleeping ear but drew forth neither acknowledgment nor response. Like a marble statue he stood still, and she leaned upon his shoulder.

'Do you not hear me?' she cried in a more passionate tone. 'Do you not understand me? Why is it that your love is so hard to win? Look at me! Might not any man be proud to love me? Am I not beautiful enough for you? And yet I know that I am fair. Or are you ashamed because people call me a witch? Why then I will never be one again, for your sake! What do I care for it all? Can it be anything to me – can anything have worth that stands between me and you? Ah, love – be not so very hard!'

The Wanderer did not move. His face was as calm as a sculptured stone.

'Do you despise me for loving you?' she asked again, with a sudden flush.

'No. I do not despise you.' Something in her tone had pierced through his stupor and had found an answer. She started at the sound of his voice. It was as though he had been awake and had known the weight of what she had been saying, and her anger rose at the cold reply.

'No – you do not despise me, and you never shall!' she exclaimed passionately. 'You shall love me, as I love you – I will it, with all my will! We are created to be all, one to the other, and you shall not break through the destiny of love. Love me, as I love you – love me with all your heart, love me with all your mind, love me with all your soul, love me as man never loved woman since the world began! I will it, I command it – it shall be as I say – you dare not disobey me – you cannot if you would.'

She paused, but this time no answer came. There was not even a contraction of the stony features.

'Do you hear all I say?' she asked.

'I hear.'

'Then understand and answer me,' she said.

'I do not understand. I cannot answer.'

'You must. You shall. I will have it so. You cannot resist my will, and I will it with all my might. You have no will – you are mine, your body, your soul, and your thoughts, and you must love me with them all from now until you die – until you die,' she repeated fiercely.

Again he was silent. She felt that she had no hold upon his heart or mind, seeing that he was not even disturbed by her repeated efforts.

'Are you a stone, that you do not know what love is?' she cried, grasping his hand in hers and looking with desperate eyes into his face.

'I do not know what love is,' he answered, slowly.

'Then I will tell you what love is,' she said, and she took his hand and pressed it upon her own brow.

The Wanderer started at the touch, as though he would have drawn back. But she held him fast, and so far, at least, he was utterly subject to her. His brow contracted darkly, and his face grew paler.

'Read it there,' she cried. 'Enter into my soul and read what love is, in his own great writing. Read how he steals suddenly into the sacred place, and makes it his, and tears down the old gods and sets up his dear image in their stead – read how he sighs, and speaks, and weeps, and loves – and forgives not, but will be revenged at the last. Are you indeed of stone, and have you a stone for a heart? Love can melt even stones, being set in man as the great central fire in the earth to burn the hardest things to streams of liquid flame! And see, again, how very soft and gentle he can be! See how I love you – see how sweet it is – how very lovely a thing it is to love as woman can. There – have you felt it now? Have you seen into the depths of my soul and into the hiding-places of my heart? Let it be so in your own, then, and let it be so for ever. You understand now. You know what it all is – how wild, how passionate, how gentle and how great! Take to yourself this love of mine – is it not all yours? Take it, and plant it with strong roots and seeds of undying life in your own sleeping breast, and let it grow, and grow, till it is even greater than it was in me, till it takes us both into itself, together, fast bound in its immortal bonds, to be two in one, in life and beyond life, for ever and ever and ever to the end of ends!'

She ceased and she saw that his face was no longer expressionless and cold. A strange light was upon his features, the passing radiance of a supreme happiness seen in the vision of a dream. Again she laid her hands upon his shoulder clasped together, as she had done at first. She knew that her words had touched him and she was confident of the result, confident as one who loves beyond reason. Already in imagination she fancied him returning to consciousness, not knowing that he had slept, but waking with a gentle word just trembling upon his lips, the words she longed to hear.

One moment more, she thought. It was good to see that light upon his face, to fancy how that first word would sound, to feel that the struggle was past and that there was nothing but happiness in the future, full, overflowing, overwhelming, reaching from earth to heaven and through time to eternity. One moment, only, before she let him wake – it was such glory to be loved at last! Still the light was there, still that exquisite smile was on his lips. And they would be always there now, she thought.

At last she spoke.

'Then love, since you are mine, and I am yours, wake from the dream to life itself – wake, not knowing that you have slept, knowing only that you love me now and always – wake, love, wake!'

She waved her delicate hand before his eyes and still resting the other upon his shoulder, watched the returning brightness in the dark pupils that had been glazed and fixed a moment before. And as she looked, her own beauty grew radiant in the splendour of a joy even greater than she had dreamed of. As it had seemed to him when he had lost himself in her gaze, so now she also fancied that the grim, grey wilderness was full of a soft rosy light. The place of the dead was become the place of life; the great solitude was peopled as the whole world could never be for her; the crumbling gravestones were turned to polished pillars in the temple of an immortal love, and the ghostly, leafless trees blossomed with the undying flowers of the earthly paradise.

One moment only, and then all was gone. The change came, sure, swift and cruel. As she looked, it came, gradual, in that it passed through every degree, but sudden also, as the fall of a fair and mighty building, which being undermined in its foundations passes in one short minute through the change from perfect completeness to hopeless and utter ruin.

All the radiance, all the light, all the glory were gone in an instant. Her own supremely loving look had not vanished, her lips still parted sweetly, as forming the word that was to answer his, and the calm indifferent face of the waking man was already before her.

'What is it?' he asked, in his kind and passionless voice. 'What were you going to ask me, Unorna?'

It was gone. The terribly earnest appeal had been in vain. Not a trace of that short vision of love remained impressed upon his brain.

With a smothered cry of agony Unorna leaned against the great slab of stone behind her and covered her eyes. The darkness of night descended upon her, and with it the fire of a burning shame.

Then a loud and cruel laugh rang through the chilly air, such a laugh as the devils in hell bestow upon the shame of a proud soul that knows its own infinite bitterness. Unorna started and uncovered her eyes, her suffering changed in a single instant to ungovernable and destroying anger. She made a step forwards and then stopped short, breathing hard. The Wanderer, too, had turned, more quickly than she. Between two tall gravestones, not a dozen paces away, stood a man with haggard face and eyes on fire, his keen, worn features contorted by a smile in which unspeakable satisfaction struggled for expression with a profound despair.

The man was Israel Kafka.

Chapter 14

The Wanderer looked from Unorna to Kafka with profound surprise. He had never seen the man and had no means of knowing who he was, still less of guessing what had brought him to the lonely place, or why he had broken into a laugh, of which the harsh, wild tones still echoed through the wide cemetery. Totally unconscious of all that had happened to himself during the preceding quarter of an hour, the Wanderer was deprived of the key to the situation. He only understood that the stranger was for some reason or other deeply incensed against Unorna, and he realised that the intruder had, on the moment of appearance, no control over himself.

Israel Kafka remained where he stood, between the two tall stones, one hand resting on each, his body inclined a little forward, his dark, sunken eyes, bloodshot and full of a turbid, angry brightness, bent intently upon Unorna's face. He looked as though he were about to move suddenly forwards, but it was impossible to foresee that he might not as suddenly retreat, as a lean and hungry tiger crouches for a moment in uncertainty whether to fight or fly, when after tracking down his man he finds him not alone and defenceless as he had anticipated, but well-armed and in company.

The Wanderer's indolence was only mental, and was moreover transitory and artificial. When he saw Unorna advance, he quickly placed himself between her and Israel Kafka, and looked from one to the other.

'Who is this man?' he asked. 'And what does he want of you?'

Unorna made as though she would pass him. But he laid his hand upon her arm with a gesture that betrayed his anxiety for her safety. At his touch, her face changed for a moment and a faint blush dyed her cheek.

'You may well ask who I am,' said the Moravian, speaking in a voice half-choked with passion and anger. 'She will tell you she does not know me – she will deny my existence to my face. But she knows me very well. I am Israel Kafka.'

The Wanderer looked at him more curiously. He remembered what he had heard but a few hours earlier from Keyork concerning the young fellow's madness. The situation now partially explained itself.

'I understand,' he said, looking at Unorna. 'He seems to be dangerous. What shall I do with him?'

He asked the question as calmly as though it had referred to the disposal of an inanimate object, instead of to the taking into custody of a madman.

'Do with me?' cried Kafka, advancing suddenly a step forwards from between the slabs. 'Do with me? Do you speak of me as though I were a dog – a dumb animal – but I will – '

He choked and coughed, and could not finish the sentence. There was a hectic flush in his cheek and his thin, graceful frame shook violently from head to foot. Unable to speak for the moment, he waved his hand in a menacing gesture. The Wanderer shook his head rather sadly.

'He seems very ill,' he said, in a tone of compassion.

But Unorna was pitiless. She knew what her companion could not know, namely, that Kafka must have followed them through the streets to the cemetery and must have overheard Unorna's passionate appeal and must have seen and understood the means she was using to win the Wanderer's love. Her anger was terrible. She had suffered enough secret shame already in stooping to the use of her arts in such a course. It had cost her one of the greatest struggles of her life, and her disappointment at the result had been proportionately bitter. In that alone she had endured almost as much pain as she could bear. But to find suddenly that her humiliation, her hot speech, her failure, the look which she knew had been on her face until the moment when the Wanderer awoke, that all this had been seen and heard by Israel Kafka was intolerable. Even Keyork's unexpected appearance could not have so fired her wrath. Keyork might have laughed at her afterwards, but her failure would have been no triumph to him. Was not Keyork enlisted on her side, ready to help her at all times, by word or deed, in accordance with the terms of their agreement? But of all men Kafka, whom she had so wronged, was the one man who should have been ignorant of her defeat and miserable shame.

'Go!' she cried, with a gesture of command. Her eyes flashed and her extended hand trembled.

There was such concentrated fury in a single word that the Wanderer started in surprise, ignorant as he was of the true state of things.

'You are uselessly unkind,' he said gravely. 'The poor man is mad. Let me take him away.'

'Leave him to me,' she answered imperiously. 'He will obey me.'

But Israel Kafka did not turn. He rested one hand upon the slab and faced her. As when many different forces act together at one point, producing after the first shock a resultant little expected, so the many passions that were at work in his face finally twisted his lips into a smile.

'Yes,' he said, in a low tone, which did not express submission. 'Leave me to her! Leave me to the Witch and to her mercy. It will be the end this time. She is drunk with her love of you and mad with her hatred of me.'

Unorna grew suddenly pale, and would have again sprung forward. But the Wanderer stopped her and held her arm. At the same time he looked into Kafka's eyes and raised one hand as though in warning.

'Be silent!' he exclaimed.

'And if I speak, what then?' asked the Moravian with his evil smile.

'I will silence you,' answered the Wanderer coldly. 'Your madness excuses you, perhaps, but it does not justify me in allowing you to insult a woman.'

Kafka's anger took a new direction. Even madmen are often calmed by the quiet opposition of a strong and self-possessed man.

And Kafka was not mad. He was no coward either, but the subtlety of his race was in him. As oil dropped by the board in a wild tempest does not calm the waves, but momentarily prevents their angry crests from breaking, so the Israelite's quick tact veiled the rough face of his dangerous humour.

'I insult no one,' he said, almost deferentially. 'Least of all her whom I have worshipped long and lost at last. You accuse me unjustly of that, and though my speech may have been somewhat rude, yet may I be forgiven for the sake of what I have suffered. For I have suffered much.'

Seeing that he was taking a more courteous tone, the Wanderer folded his arms and left Unorna free to move, awaiting her commands, or the further development of events. He saw in her face that her anger was not subsiding, and he wondered less at it after hearing Kafka's insulting speech. It was a pity, he thought, that anyone should take so seriously a maniac's words, but he was nevertheless resolved that they should not be repeated. After all, it would be an easy matter, if the man again overstepped the bounds of gentle speech, to take him bodily away from Unorna's presence.

'And are you going to charm our ears with a story of your sufferings?' Unorna asked, in a tone so cruel, that the Wanderer expected a quick outburst of anger from Kafka, in reply. But he was disappointed in this. The smile still lingered on the Moravian's face, when he answered, and his expressive voice, no longer choking with passion, grew very soft and musical.

'It is not mine to charm,' he said. 'It is not given to me to make slaves of all living things with hand and eye and word. Such power Nature does not give to all, she has given none to me. I have no spell to win Unorna's love – and if I had, I cannot say that I would take a love thus earned.'

He paused a moment and Unorna grew paler. She started, but then did not move again. His words had power to wound her, but she trembled lest the Wanderer should understand their hidden meaning, and she was silent, biding her time and curbing her passion.

'No,' continued Kafka, 'I was not thus favoured in my nativity. The star of love was not in the ascendant, the lord of magic charms was not trembling upon my horizon, the sun of earthly happiness was not enthroned in my mid-heaven. How could it be? She had it all, this Unorna here, and Nature, generous in one mad moment, lavished upon her all there was to give. For she has all, and we have nothing, as I have learned and you will learn before you die.'

He looked at the Wanderer as he spoke. His hollow eyes seemed calm enough, and in his dejected attitude and subdued tone there was nothing that gave warning of a coming storm. The Wanderer listened, half-interested and yet half-annoyed by his persistence. Unorna herself was silent still.

'The nightingale was singing on that night,' continued Kafka. 'It was a dewy night in early spring, and the air was very soft, when Unorna first breathed it. The world was not asleep but dreaming, when her eyes first opened to look upon it. Heaven had put on all its glories – across its silent breast was bound the milk-white riband, its crest was crowned with God's crown-jewels, the great northern stars, its mighty form was robed in the mantle of majesty set with the diamonds of suns and worlds, great and small, far and near – not one tiny spark of all the myriad million gems was darkened by a breath of wind-blown mist. The earth was very still, all wrapped in peace and lulled in love. The great trees pointed their dark spires upwards from the temple of the forest to the firmament of the greater temple on high. In the starlight the year's first roses breathed out the perfume gathered from the departed sun, and every dewdrop in the short, sweet grass caught in its little self the reflection of heaven's vast glory. Only, in the universal stillness, the nightingale sang the song of songs, and bound the angel of love with the chains of her linked melody and made him captive in bonds stronger than his own.'

Israel Kafka spoke dreamily, resting against the stone beside him, seemingly little conscious of the words that fell in oriental imagery from his lips. In other days Unorna had heard him speak like this to her, and she had loved the speech, though not the man, and sometimes for its sake she had wished her heart could find its fellow in his. And even now, the tone and the words had a momentary effect upon her. What would have sounded as folly, over-wrought, sentimental, almost laughable, perhaps, to other women, found an echo in her own childish memories and a sympathy in her belief in her own mysterious nature. The Wanderer had heard men talk as Israel Kafka talked, in other lands, where speech is prized by men and women not for its tough strength but for its wealth of flowers.

'And love was her first captive,' said the Moravian, 'and her first slave. Yes, I will tell you the story of Unorna's life. She is angry with me now. Well, let it be. It is my fault – or hers. What matter? She cannot quite forget me out of mind – and I? Has Lucifer forgotten God?'

He sighed, and a momentary light flashed in his eyes. Something in the blasphemous strength of the words attracted the Wanderer's attention. Utterly indifferent himself, he saw that there was something more than madness in the man before him. He found himself wondering what encouragement Unorna had given the seed of passion that it should have grown to such strength, and he traced the madness back to the love, instead of referring the love to the madness. But he said nothing.

'So she was born,' continued Kafka, dreaming on. 'She was born amid the perfume of the roses, under the starlight, when the nightingale was singing. And all things that lived, loved her, and submitted to her voice and hand, and to her eyes and to her unspoken will, as running water follows the course men give it, winding and gliding, falling and rushing, full often of a roar of resistance that covers the deep, quick-moving stream, flowing in spite of itself through the channel that is dug for it to the determined end. And nothing resisted her. Neither man nor woman nor child had any strength to oppose against her magic. The wolf-hounds licked her feet, the wolves themselves crouched fawning in her path. For she is without fear – as she is without mercy. Is that strange? What fear can there be for her who has the magic charm, who holds sleep in the one hand and death in the other, and between whose brows is set the knowledge of what shall be hereafter? Can anyone harm her? Has anyone the strength to harm her? Is there anything on earth which she covets and which shall not be hers?'

Though his voice was almost as soft as before, the evil smile flickered again about his drawn lips as he looked into Unorna's face. He wondered why she did not face him and crush him and force him to sleep with her eyes as he knew she could do. But he himself was past fear. He had suffered too much and cared not what chanced to him now. But she should know that he knew all, if he told her so with his latest breath. Despair had given him a strange control of his anger and of his words, and jealousy had taught him the art of wounding swiftly, surely and with a light touch. Sooner or later she would turn upon him and annihilate him in a dream of unconsciousness; he knew that, and he knew that such faint power of resisting her as he had ever possessed was gone. But so long as she was willing to listen to him, so long would he torture her with the sting of her own shame, and when her patience ended, or her caprice changed, he would find some bitter word to cast at her in the moment before losing his consciousness of thought and his power to speak. This one chance of wounding was given to him and he would use it to the utmost, with all subtlety, with all cruelty, with all determination to torture.

'Whatsoever she covets is hers to take. No one escapes the spell in the end, no one resists the charm. And yet it is written in the book of her fate that she shall one day taste the fruit of ashes, and drink of the bitter water. It is written that whosoever slays with the sword shall die by the sword also. She has killed with love, and by love she shall perish. I loved her once. I know what I am saying.'

Again he paused, lingering thoughtfully upon the words. The Wanderer glanced at Unorna as though asking her whether he should not put a sudden end to the strange monologue. She was pale and her eyes were bright; but she shook her head.

'Let him say what he will say,' she answered, taking the question as though it had been spoken. 'Let him say all he will. Perhaps it is the last time.'

'And so you give me your gracious leave to speak,' said Israel Kafka. 'And you will let me say all that is in my heart to say to you – before this other man. And then you will make an end of me. I see. I accept the offer. I can even thank you for your patience. You are kind today – I have known you harder. Well, then, I will speak out. I will tell my story, not that anyone may judge between you and me. There is neither judge nor justice for those who love in vain. So I loved you. That is the whole story. Do you understand me, sir? I loved this woman, but she would not love me. That is all. And what of it, and what then? Look at her, and look at me – the beginning and the end.'

In a manner familiar to Orientals the unhappy man laid one finger upon his own breast, and with the other hand pointed at Unorna's fair young face. The Wanderer's eyes obeyed the guiding gesture, and he looked from one to the other, and again the belief crossed his thoughts that there was less of madness about Israel Kafka than Keyork would have had him think. Trying to read the truth from Unorna's eyes, he saw that they avoided his, and he fancied he detected symptoms of distress in her pallor and contracted lips. And yet he argued that if it were all true she would silence the speaker, and that the only reason for her patience must be sought in her willingness to humour the diseased brain in its wanderings. In either case he pitied Israel Kafka profoundly, and his compassion increased from one moment to another.

'I loved her. There is a history in those three words which neither the eloquent tongue nor the skilled pen can tell. See how coldly I speak. I command my speech, I may pick and choose among ten thousand words and phrases, and describe love at my leisure. She grants me time; she is very merciful today. What would you have me say? You know what love is. Think of such love as yours can have been, and take twice that, and three times over, and a hundred thousand times, and cram it, burning, flaming, melting into your bursting heart – then you would know a tenth of what I have known. Love, indeed! Who can have known love but me? I stand alone. Since the dull, unlovely world first jarred and trembled and began to move, there has not been another of my kind, nor has man suffered as I have suffered, and been crushed and torn and thrown aside to die, without even the mercy of a death-wound. Describe it? Tell it? Look at me! I am both love's description and the epitaph on his gravestone. In me he lived, me he tortured, with me he dies never to live again as he has lived this once. There is no justice and no mercy! Think not that it is enough to love and that you will be loved in return. Do not think that – do not dream that. Do you not know that the fiercest drought is as a spring rain to the rocks, which thirst not and need no refreshment?'

Again he fixed his eyes on Unorna's face and faintly smiled. Apparently she was displeased.

'What is it that you would say?' she asked coldly. 'What is this that you tell us of rocks and rain, and death-wounds, and the rest? You say you loved me once – that was a madness. You say that I never loved you – that, at least, is truth. Is that your story? It is indeed short enough, and I marvel at the many words in which you have put so little!'

She laughed in a hard tone. But Israel Kafka's eyes grew dark and the sombre fire beamed in them as he spoke again. The weary, tortured smile left his wan lips, and his pale face grew stern.

'Laugh, laugh, Unorna!' he cried. 'You do not laugh alone. And yet – I love you still, I love you so well in spite of all that I cannot laugh at you as I would, even though I were to see you again clinging to the rock and imploring it to take pity on your thirst. And he who dies for you, Unorna – of him you ask nothing, save that he will crawl away and die alone, and not disturb your delicate life with such an unseemly sight.'

'You talk of death!' exclaimed Unorna scornfully. 'You talk of dying for me because you are ill today. Tomorrow, Keyork Arabian will have cured you, and then, for aught I know, you will talk of killing me instead. This is child's talk, boy's talk. If we are to listen to you, you must be more eloquent. You must give us such a tale of woe as shall draw tears from our eyes and sobs from our breasts – then we will applaud you and let you go. That shall be your reward.'

The Wanderer glanced at her in surprise. There was a bitterness in her tone of which he had not believed her soft voice capable.

'Why do you hate him so if he is mad?' he asked.

'The reason is not far to seek,' said Kafka. 'This woman here – God made her crooked-hearted! Love her, and she will hate you as only she has learned how to hate. Show her that cold face of yours, and she will love you so that she will make a carpet of her pride for you to walk on – ay, or spit on either, if you deign to be so kind. She has a wonderful kind of heart, for it freezes when you burn it, and melts when you freeze it.'

'Are you mad, indeed?' asked the Wanderer, suddenly planting himself in front of Kafka. 'They told me so – I can almost believe it.'

'No – I am not mad yet,' answered the younger man, facing him fearlessly. 'You need not come between me and her. She can protect herself. You would know that if you knew what I saw her do with you, first when I came here.'

'What did she do?' The Wanderer turned quickly as he stood, and looked at Unorna.

'Do not listen to his ravings,' she said. The words seemed weak and poorly chosen, and there was a strange look in her face as though she were either afraid or desperate, or both.

'She loves you,' said Israel Kafka calmly. 'And you do not know it. She has power over you, as she has over me, but the power to make you love her she has not. She will destroy you, and your state will be no better than mine today. We shall have moved on a step, for I shall be dead and you will be the madman, and she will have found another to love and to torture. The world is full of them. Her altar will never lack sacrifices.'

The Wanderer's face was grave.

'You may be mad or not,' he said. 'I cannot tell. But you say monstrous things, and you shall not repeat them.'

'Did she not say that I might speak?' asked Kafka with a bitter laugh.

'I will keep my word,' said Unorna. 'You seek your own destruction. Find it in your own way. It will not be the less sure. Speak – say what you will. You shall not be interrupted.'

The Wanderer drew back, not understanding what was passing, nor why Unorna was so long-suffering.

'Say all you have to say,' she repeated, coming forward so that she stood directly in front of Israel Kafka. 'And you,' she added, speaking to the Wanderer, 'leave him to me. He is quite right – I can protect myself if I need any protection.'

'You remember how we parted, Unorna?' said Kafka. 'It is a month today. I did not expect a greeting of you when I came back, or, if I did expect it, I was foolish and unthinking. I should have known you better. I should have known that there is one half of your word which you never break – the cruel half, and one thing which you cannot forgive, and which is my love for you. And yet that is the very thing which I cannot forget. I have come back to tell you so. You may as well know it.'

Unorna's expression grew cold, as she saw that he abandoned the strain of reproach and spoke once more of his love for her.

'Yes, I see what you mean,' he said, very quietly. 'You mean to show me by your face that you give me no hope. I should have known that by other things I have seen here. God knows, I have seen enough! But I meant to find you alone. I went to your home, I saw you go out, I followed you, I entered here – I heard all – and I understood, for I know your power, as this man cannot know it. Do you wonder that I followed you? Do you despise me? Do you think I still care, because you do? Love is stronger than the woman loved and for her we do deeds of baseness, unblushingly, which she would forbid our doing, and for which she despises us when she hates us, and loves us the more dearly when she loves us at all. You hate me – then despise me, too, if you will. It is too late to care. I followed you like a spy, I saw what I expected to see, I have suffered what I knew I should suffer. You know that I have been away during this whole month, and that I have travelled thousands of leagues in the hope of forgetting you.'

'And yet I fancied I had seen you within the month,' Unorna said, with a cruel smile.

'They say that ghosts haunt the places they have loved,' answered Kafka unmoved. 'If that be true I may have troubled your dreams and you may have seen me. I have come back broken in body and in heart. I think I have come back to die here. The life is going out of me, but before it is quite gone I can say two things. I can tell you that I know you at last, and that, in spite of the horror of knowing what you are, I love you still.'

'Am I so very horrible?' she asked scornfully.

'You know what you are, better than I can tell you, but not better than I know. I know even the secret meaning of your moods and caprices. I know why you are willing to listen to me, this last time, so patiently, with only now and then a sneer and a cutting laugh.'

'Why?'

'In order to make me suffer the more. You will never forgive me now, for you know that I know, and that alone is a sin past all forgiveness, and over and above that I am guilty of the crime of loving when you have no love for me.'

'And as a last resource you come to me and recapitulate your misdeeds. The plan is certainly original, though it lacks wit.'

'There is least wit where there is most love, Unorna. I take no account of the height of my folly when I see the depth of my love, which has swallowed up myself and all my life. In the last hour I have known its depth and breadth and strength, for I have seen what it can bear. And why should I complain of it? Have I not many times said that I would die for you willingly – and is it not dying for you to die of love for you? To prove my faith it were too easy a death. When I look into your face I know that there is in me the heart that made true Christian martyrs – '

Unorna laughed.

'Would you be a martyr?' she asked.

'Not for your Faith – but for the faith I once had in you, and for the love that no martyrdom could kill. Ay – to prove that love I would die a hundred deaths – and to gain yours I would die the death eternal.'

'And you would have deserved it. Have you not deserved enough already, enough of martyrdom, for tracking me today, following me stealthily, like a thief and a spy, to find out my ends and my doings?'

'I love you, Unorna.'

'And therefore you suspect me of unimaginable evil – and therefore you come out of your hiding-place and accuse me of things I have neither done nor thought of doing, building up falsehood upon lie, and lie upon falsehood in the attempt to ruin me in the eyes of one who has my friendship and who is my friend. You are foolish to throw yourself upon my mercy, Israel Kafka.'

'Foolish? Yes, and mad, too! And my madness is all you have left me – take it – it is yours! You cannot kill my love. Deny my words, deny your deeds! Let all be false in you – it is but one pain more, and my heart is not broken yet. It will bear another. Tell me that what I saw had no reality – that you did not make him sleep – here, on this spot, before my eyes – that you did not pour your love into his sleeping ears, that you did not command, implore, entreat – and fail!

What is it all to me, whether you speak truth or not? Tell me it is not true that I would die a thousand martyrdoms for your sake, as you are, and if you were a thousand times worse than you are! Your wrong, your right, your truth, your falsehood, you yourself are swallowed up in the love I bear you! I love you always, and I will say it, and say it again – ah, your eyes! I love them, too! Take me into them, Unorna – whether in hate or love – but in love – yes, love – Unorna, golden Unorna!'

With the cry on his lips – the name he had given her in other days – he made one mad step forwards, throwing out his arms as though to clasp her to him. But it was too late. Even while he had been speaking her mysterious influence had overpowered him, as he had known that it would, when she so pleased.

She caught his two hands in the air, and pressed him back and held him against the tall slab. The whole pitilessness of her nature gleamed like a cold light in her white face.

'There was a martyr of your race once,' she said in cruel tones. 'His name was Simon Abeles. You talk of martyrdom! You shall know what it means – though it be too good for you, who spy upon the woman whom you say you love.'

The hectic flush of passion sank from Israel Kafka's cheek. Rigid, with outstretched arms and bent head, he stood against the ancient gravestone. Above him, as though raised to heaven in silent supplication, were the sculptured hands that marked the last resting-place of a Kohn.

'You shall know now,' said Unorna. 'You shall suffer indeed.'

Chapter 15 *

Unorna's voice sank from the tone of anger to a lower pitch. She spoke quietly and very distinctly as though to impress every word upon the ear of the man who was in her power. The Wanderer listened, too, scarcely comprehending at first, but slowly yielding to

* The deeds here described were done in Prague on the twenty-first day of February in the year 1694. Lazarus and his accomplice Levi Kurtzhandel, or Brevimanus, or 'the short-handed', were betrayed by their own people. Lazarus hanged himself in prison, and Levi suffered death by the wheel – repentant, it is said, and himself baptized. A full account of the trial, written in Latin, was printed, and a copy of it may be seen in the State Museum in Prague. The body of Simon Abeles was exhumed and rests in the Teyn Kirche, in the chapel on the left of the high altar. The slight extension of certain scenes not fully described in the Latin volume will be pardoned in a work of fiction.

the influence she exerted until the vision rose before him also with all its moving scenes, in all its truth and in all its horror. As in a dream the deeds that had been passed before him, the desolate burial-ground was peopled with forms and faces of other days, the grave-stones rose from the earth and piled themselves into gloomy houses and remote courts and dim streets and venerable churches, the dry and twisted trees shrank down, and broadened and swung their branches as arms, and drew up their roots out of the ground as feet under them and moved hither and thither. And the knots and bosses and gnarls upon them became faces, dark, eagle-like and keen, and the creaking and crackling of the boughs and twigs under the pierc-ing blast that swept by, became articulate and like the voices of old men talking angrily together. There were sudden changes from day to night and from night to day. In dark chambers crouching men took counsel of blood together under the feeble rays of a flickering lamp. In the uncertain twilight of winter, muffled figures lurked at the corner of streets, waiting for someone to pass, who must not escape them. As the Wanderer gazed and listened, Israel Kafka was transformed. He no longer stood with outstretched arms, his back against a crumbling slab, his filmy eyes fixed on Unorna's face. He grew younger; his features were those of a boy of scarcely thirteen years, pale, earnest and brightened by a soft light which followed him hither and thither, and he was not alone. He moved with others through the old familiar streets of the city, clothed in a fashion of other times, speaking in accents comprehensible but unlike the speech of today, acting in a dim and far-off life that had once been.

The Wanderer looked, and, as in dreams, he knew that what he saw was unreal, he knew that the changing walls and streets and houses and public places were built up of gravestones which in truth were deeply planted in the ground, immovable and incapable of spontaneous motion; he knew that the crowds of men and women were not human beings but gnarled and twisted trees rooted in the earth, and that the hum of voices which reached his ears was but the sound of dried branches bending in the wind; he knew that Israel Kafka was not the pale-faced boy who glided from place to place followed everywhere by a soft radiance; he knew that Unorna was the source and origin of the vision, and that the mingling speeches of the actors, now shrill in angry altercation, now hissing in low, fierce whisper, were really formed upon Unorna's lips and made audible through her tones, as the chorus of indistinct speech proceeded from the swaying trees. It was to him an illusion of which he understood the key and penetrated the secret, but it was marvellous in its way, and he was held enthralled from the first moment when it began to unfold itself. He understood further that Israel Kafka was in a state different from this, that he was suffering all the reality of another life, which to the Wanderer was but a dream. For the moment all his faculties had a double perception of things and sounds, distinguishing clearly between the fact and the mirage that distorted and obscured it. For the moment he was aware that his reason was awake though his eyes and his ears might be sleeping. Then the unequal contest between the senses and the intellect ceased, and while still retaining the dim consciousness that the source of all he saw and heard lay in Unorna's brain, he allowed himself to be led quickly from one scene to another, absorbed and taken out of himself by the horror of the deeds done before him.

At first, indeed, the vision, though vivid, seemed objectless and of uncertain meaning. The dark depths of the Jews' quarter of the city were opened, and it was towards evening. Throngs of gowned men, crooked, bearded, filthy, vulture-eyed, crowded upon each other in a narrow public place, talking in quick, shrill accents, gesticulating, with hands and arms and heads and bodies, laughing, chuckling, chattering, hook-nosed and loose-lipped, grasping fat purses in lean fingers, shaking greasy curls that straggled out under caps of greasy fur, glancing to right and left with quick, gleaming looks that pierced the gloom like fitful flashes of lightning, plucking at each other by the sleeve and pointing long fingers and crooked nails, two, three and four at a time, as markers, in their ready reckoning, a writhing mass of humanity, intoxicated by the smell of gold, mad for its possession, half hysteric with the fear of losing it, timid yet dangerous, poisoned to the core by the sweet sting of money, terrible in intelligence, vile in heart, contemptible in body, irresistible in the unity of their greed – the Jews of Prague, two hundred years ago.

In one corner of the dusky place there was a little light. A boy stood there, beside a veiled woman, and the light that seemed to cling about him was not the reflection of gold. He was very young. His pale face had in it all the lost beauty of the Jewish race, the lips were clearly cut, even, pure in outline and firm, the forehead broad with thought, the features noble, aquiline – not vulture-like. Such a face might holy Stephen, deacon and protomartyr, have turned upon the young men who laid their garments at the feet of the unconverted Saul.

He stood there, looking on at the scene in the market-place, not wondering, for nothing of it was new to him, not scorning, for he felt no hate, not wrathful, for he dreamed of peace. He would have had it otherwise – that was all. He would have had the stream flow back upon its source and take a new channel for itself, he would have seen the strength of his people wielded in cleaner deeds for nobler aims. The gold he hated, the race for it he despised, the poison of it he loathed, but he had neither loathing nor contempt nor hatred for the men themselves. He looked upon them and he loved to think that the carrion vulture might once again be purified and lifted on strong wings and become, as in old days, the eagle of the mountains.

For many minutes he gazed in silence. Then he sighed and turned away. He held certain books in his hand, for he had come from the school of the synagogue where, throughout the short winter days, the rabbis taught him and his companions the mysteries of the sacred tongue. The woman by his side was a servant in his father's house, and it was her duty to attend him through the streets, until the day when, being judged a man, he should be suddenly freed from the bondage of childish things.

'Let us go,' he said in a low voice. 'The air is full of gold and heavy. I cannot breathe it.'

'Whither?' asked the woman.

'Thou knowest,' he answered. And suddenly the faint radiance that was always about him grew brighter, and spread out arms behind him, to the right and left, in the figure of a cross.

They walked together, side by side, quickly and often glancing behind them as though to see whether they were followed. And yet it seemed as though it was not they who moved, but the city about them which changed. The throng of busy Jews grew shadowy and disappeared, their shrill voices were lost in the distance. There were other people in the street, of other features and in different garbs, of prouder bearing and hot, restless manner, broad-shouldered, erect, manly, with spur on heel and sword at side. The outline of the old synagogue melted into the murky air and changed its shape, and stood out again in other and ever-changing forms. Now they were passing before the walls of a noble palace, now beneath long, low galleries of arches, now again across the open space of the Great Ring in the midst of the city – then all at once they were standing before the richly carved doorway of the Teyn Kirche, the very doorway out of which the Wanderer had followed the fleeting shadow of Beatrice's figure but a month ago. And then they paused, and looked again to the right and left, and searched the dark corners with piercing glances.

'Thy life is in thine hand,' said the woman, speaking close to the boy's ear. 'It is yet time. Turn with me and let us go back.'

The mysterious radiance lit up the youth's beautiful face in the dark street and showed the fearless yet gentle smile that was on his lips.

'What is there to fear?' he asked.

'Death,' answered the woman in a trembling tone. 'They will kill thee, and it shall be upon my head.'

'And what is Death?' he asked again, and the smile was still upon his face as he led the way up the steps.

The woman bowed her head and drew her veil more closely about her and followed him. Then they were within the church, darker, more ghostly, less rich in those days than now. The boy stood beside the hewn stone basin wherein was the blessed water, and he touched the frozen surface with his fingers, and held them out to his companion.

'Is it thus?' he asked. And the heavenly smile grew more radiant as he made the sign of the Cross.

Again the woman inclined her head.

'Be it not upon me!' she exclaimed earnestly. 'Though I would it might be for ever so with thee.'

'It is for ever,' the boy answered.

He went forward and prostrated himself before the high altar, and the soft light hovered above him. The woman knelt at a little distance from him, with clasped hands and upturned eyes. The church was very dark and silent.

An old man in a monk's robe came forward out of the shadow of the choir and stood behind the marble rails and looked down at the boy's prostrate figure, wonderingly. Then the low gateway was opened and he descended the three steps and bent down to the young head.

'What wouldest thou?' he asked.

Simon Abeles rose until he knelt, and looked up into the old man's face.

'I am a Jew. I would be a Christian. I would be baptized.'

'Fearest thou not thy people?' the monk asked.

'I fear not death,' answered the boy simply.

'Come with me.'

Trembling, the woman followed them both, and all were lost in the gloom of the church. They were not to be seen, and all was still for a space. Suddenly a clear voice broke the silence.

'*Ego baptizo te in nomine Patris, et Filii, et Spiritus Sancti.*'

Then the woman and the boy were standing again without the entrance in the chilly air, and the ancient monk was upon the threshold under the carved arch; his thin hands, white in the darkness, were lifted high, and he blessed them, and they went their way.

In the moving vision the radiance was brighter still and illuminated the streets as they moved on. Then a cloud descended over all, and certain days and weeks passed, and again the boy was walking swiftly toward the church. But the woman was not with him, and he believed that he was alone, though the messengers of evil were upon him. Two dark figures moved in the shadow, silent, noiseless in their walk, muffled in long garments. He went on, no longer deigning to look back, beyond fear as he had ever been, and beyond even the expectation of a danger. He went into the church, and the two men made gestures, and spoke in low tones, and hid themselves in the shade of the buttresses outside.

The vision grew darker and a terrible stillness was over everything, for the church was not opened to the sight this time. There was a horror of long waiting with the certainty of what was to come. The narrow street was empty to the eye, and yet there was the knowledge of evil presence, of two strong men waiting in the dark to take their victim to the place of expiation. And the horror grew in the silence and the emptiness, until it was unbearable.

The door opened and the boy was with the monk under the black arch. The old man embraced him and blessed him and stood still for a moment watching him as he went down. Then he also turned and went back, and the door was closed.

Swiftly the two men glided from their hiding-place and sped along the uneven pavement. The boy paused and faced them, for he felt that he was taken. They grasped him by the arms on each side, Lazarus his father, and Levi, surnamed the Short-handed, the strongest and the cruellest and the most relentless of the younger rabbis. Their grip was rough, and the older man held a coarse woollen cloth in his hand with which to smother the boy's cries if he should call out for help. But he was very calm and did not resist them.

'What would you?' he asked.

'And what doest thou in a Christian church?' asked Lazarus in low fierce tones.

'What Christians do, since I am one of them,' answered the youth, unmoved.

Lazarus said nothing, but he struck the boy on the mouth with his hard hand so that the blood ran down.

'Not here!' exclaimed Levi, anxiously looking about.

And they hurried him away through dark and narrow lanes. He opposed no resistance to Levi's rough strength, not only suffering himself to be dragged along but doing his best to keep pace with the man's long strides, nor did he murmur at the blows and thrusts dealt him from time to time by his father from the other side. During some minutes they were still traversing the Christian part of the city. A single loud cry for help would have brought a rescue, a few words to the rescuers would have roused a mob of fierce men and the two Jews would have paid with their lives for the deeds they had not yet committed. But Simon Abeles uttered no cry and offered no resistance. He had said that he feared not death, and he had spoken the truth, not knowing what manner of death was to be his. Onward they sped, and in the vision the way they traversed seemed to sweep past them, so that they remained always in sight though always hurrying on. The Christian quarter was passed; before them hung the chain of one of those gates which gave access to the city of the Jews. With a jeer and an oath the bearded sentry watched them pass – the martyr and his torturers. One word to him, even then, and the butt of his heavy halberd would have broken Levi's arm and laid the boy's father in the dust. The word was not spoken. On through the filthy ways, on and on, through narrow courts and tortuous passages to a dark low doorway. Then, again, the vision showed but an empty street and there was silence for a space, and a horror of long waiting in the falling night.

Lights moved within the house, and then one window after another was bolted and barred from within. Still the silence endured until the ear was grown used to it and could hear sounds very far off, from deep down below the house itself, but the walls did not open and the scene did not change. A dull noise, bad to hear, resounded as from beneath a vault, and then another and another – the sound of cruel blows upon a human body. Then a pause.

'Wilt thou renounce it?' asked the voice of Lazarus.

'*Kyrie eleison, Christe eleison!*' came the answer, brave and clear.

'Lay on, Levi, and let thy arm be strong!'

And again the sound of blows, regular, merciless, came up from the bowels of the earth.

'Dost thou repent? Dost thou renounce? Dost thou deny?'

'I repent of my sins – I renounce your ways – I believe in the Lord –'

The sacred name was not heard. A smothered groan as of one losing consciousness in extreme torture was all that came up from below.

'Lay on, Levi, lay on!'

'Nay,' answered the strong rabbi, 'the boy will die. Let us leave him here for this night. Perchance cold and hunger will be more potent than stripes, when he shall come to himself.'

'As thou sayest,' answered the father in angry reluctance.

Again all was silent. Soon the rays of light ceased to shine through the crevices of the outer shutters, and sleep descended upon the quarter of the Jews. Still the scene in the vision changed not. After a long stillness a clear young voice was heard speaking.

'Lord, if it be Thy will that I die, grant that I may bear all in Thy name, grant that I, unworthy, may endure in this body the punishments due to me in spirit for my sins. And if it be Thy will that I live, let my life be used also for Thy glory.'

The voice ceased and the cloud of passing time descended upon the vision and was lifted again and again. And each time the same voice was heard and the sound of torturing blows, but the voice of the boy was weaker every night, though it was not less brave.

'I believe,' it said, always. 'Do what you will, you have power over the body, but I have the Faith over which you have no power.'

So the days and the nights passed, and though the prayer came up in feeble tones, it was born of a mighty spirit and it rang in the ears of the tormentors as the voice of an angel which they had no power to silence, appealing from them to the tribunal of the Throne of God Most High.

Day by day, also, the rabbis and the elders began to congregate together at evening before the house of Lazarus and to talk with him and with each other, debating how they might break the endurance of his son and bring him again into the synagogue as one of themselves. Chief among them in their councils was Levi, the Short-handed, devising new tortures for the frail body to bear and boasting how he would conquer the stubborn boy by the might of his hands to hurt. Some of the rabbis shook their heads.

'He is possessed of a devil,' they said. 'He will die and repent not.'

But others nodded approvingly and wagged their filthy heads and said that when the fool had been chastised the evil spirit would depart from him.

Once more the cloud of passing time descended and was lifted. Then the walls of the house were opened and in a low arched chamber the rabbis sat about a black table. It was night and a single smoking lamp was lighted, a mere wick projecting out of a three-cornered vessel of copper which was full of oil and was hung from the vault with blackened wires. Seven rabbis sat at the board, and at the head sat Lazarus. Their crooked hands and claw-like nails moved uneasily and there was a lurid fire in their vultures' eyes. They bent forward, speaking to each other in low tones, and from beneath their greasy caps their anointed side-curls dangled and swung as they moved their heads. But Levi the Short-handed was not among them. Their muffled talk was interrupted from time to time by the sound of sharp, loud blows, as of a hammer striking upon nails, and as though a carpenter were at work not far from the room in which they sat.

'He has not repented,' said Lazarus, from his place. 'Neither many stripes, nor cold, nor hunger, nor thirst, have moved him to righteousness. It is written that he shall be cut off from his people.'

'He shall be cut off,' answered the rabbis with one voice.

'It is right and just that he should die,' continued the father. 'Shall we give him over to the Christians that he may dwell among them and become one of them, and be shown before the world to our shame?'

'We will not let him go,' said the dark man, and an evil smile flickered from one face to another as a firefly flutters from tree to tree in the night – as though the spirit of evil had touched each one in turn.

'We will not let him go,' said each again.

Lazarus also smiled as though in assent, and bowed his head a little before he spoke.

'I am obedient to your judgment. It is yours to command and mine to obey. If you say that he must die, let him die. He is my son. Take him. Did not our father Abraham lay Isaac upon the altar and offer him as a burnt sacrifice before the Lord?'

'Let him die,' said the rabbis.

'Then let him die,' answered Lazarus. 'I am your servant. It is mine to obey.'

'His blood be on our heads,' they said. And again, the evil smile went round.

'It is then expedient that we determine of what manner his death shall be,' continued the father, inclining his body to signify his submission.

'It is not lawful to shed his blood,' said the rabbis. 'And we cannot stone him, lest we be brought to judgment of the Christians. Determine thou the manner of his death.'

'My masters, if you will it, let him be brought once more before us. Let us all hear with our ears his denial, and if he repent at the last, it is well, let him live. But if he harden his heart against our entreaties, let him die. Levi hath brought certain pieces of wood hither to my house, and is even now at work. If the youth is still stubborn in his unbelief, let him die even as the Unbeliever died – by the righteous judgment of the Romans.'

'Let it be so. Let him be crucified!' said the rabbis with one voice.

Then Lazarus rose and went out, and, in the vision, the rabbis remained seated, motionless in their places awaiting his return. The noise of Levi's hammer echoed through the low vaulted chamber, and at each blow the smoking lamp quivered a little, casting strange shadows upon the evil faces beneath its light. At last footsteps, slow and uncertain, were heard without, the low door opened, and Lazarus entered, holding up the body of his son before him.

'I have brought him before you for the last time,' he said. 'Question him and hear his condemnation out of his own mouth. He repents not, though I have done my utmost to bring him back to the paths of righteousness. Question him, my masters, and let us see what he will say.'

White and exhausted with long hunger and thirst, his body broken by torture, scarcely any longer sensible to bodily pain, Simon Abeles would have fallen to the ground had his father not held him under the arms. His head hung forward and the pale and noble face was inclined towards the breast, but the deep, dark eyes were open and gazed calmly upon those who sat in judgment at the table. A rough piece of linen cloth was wrapped about the boy's shoulders and body, but his thin arms were bare.

'Hearest thou, Simon, son of Lazarus?' asked the rabbis. 'Knowest thou in whose presence thou standest?'

'I hear you and I know you all.' There was no fear in the voice though it trembled from weakness.

'Renounce then thy errors, and having suffered the chastisement of thy folly, return to the ways of thy father and of thy father's house and of all thy people.'

'I renounce my sins, and whatsoever is yet left for me to suffer, I will, by God's help, so bear it as to be not unworthy of Christ's mercy.'

The rabbis gazed at the brave young face, and smiled and wagged their beards, talking one with another in low tones.

'It is as we feared,' they said. 'He is unrepentant and he is worthy of death. It is not expedient that the young adder should live. There is poison under his tongue, and he speaks things not lawful for an

Israelite to hear. Let him die, that we may see him no more, and that our children be not corrupted by his false teachings.'

'Hearest thou? Thou shalt die.' It was Lazarus who spoke, while holding up the boy before the table and hissing the words into his ear.

'I hear. I am ready. Lead me forth.'

'There is yet time to repent. If thou wilt but deny what thou hast said these many days, and return to us, thou shalt be forgiven and thy days shall be long among us, and thy children's days after thee, and the Lord shall perchance have mercy and increase thy goods among thy fellows.'

'Let him alone,' said the rabbis. 'He is unrepentant.'

'Lead me forth,' said Simon Abeles.

'Lead him forth,' repeated the rabbis. 'Perchance, when he sees the manner of his death before his eyes, he will repent at the last.'

The boy's fearless eyes looked from one to the other.

'Whatsoever it be,' he said, 'I have but one life. Take it as you will. I die in the faith of the Lord Jesus Christ, and into His hands I commend my spirit – which you cannot take.'

'Lead him forth! Let him be crucified!' cried the rabbis together. 'We will hear him no longer.'

Then Lazarus led his son away from them, and left them talking together and shaking their heads and wagging their filthy beards. And in the vision the scene changed. The chamber with its flickering lamp and its black table and all the men who were in it grew dim and faded away, and in its place there was a dim inner court between high houses, upon which only the windows of the house of Lazarus opened. There, upon the ground, stood a lantern of horn, and the soft yellow light of it fell upon two pieces of wood, nailed one upon the other to form a small cross – small, indeed, but yet tall enough and broad enough and strong enough to bear the slight burden of the boy's frail body. And beside it stood Lazarus and Levi, the Short-handed, the strong rabbi, holding Simon Abeles between them. On the ground lay pieces of cord, ready, wherewith to bind him to the cross, for they held it unlawful to shed his blood.

It was soon done. The two men took up the cross and set it, with the body hanging thereon, against the wall of the narrow court, over against the house of Lazarus.

'Thou mayest still repent – during this night,' said the father, holding up the horn lantern and looking into his son's tortured face.

'Ay – there is yet time,' said Levi, brutally. 'He will not die so soon.'

'Lord, into Thy hands I commend my spirit,' said the weak voice once more.

Then Lazarus raised his hand and struck him once more on the mouth, as he had done on that first night when he had seized him near the church. But Levi, the Short-handed, as though in wrath at seeing all his torments fail, dealt him one heavy blow just where the ear joins the neck, and it was over at last. A radiant smile of peace flickered over the pale face, the eyelids quivered and closed, the head fell forward upon the breast and the martyrdom of Simon Abeles was consummated.

Into the dark court came the rabbis one by one from the inner chamber, and each as he came took up the horn lantern and held it to the dead face and smiled and spoke a few low words in the Hebrew tongue and then went out into the street, until only Lazarus and Levi were left alone with the dead body. Then they debated what they should do, and for a time they went into the house and refreshed themselves with food and wine, and comforted each other, well knowing that they had done an evil deed. And they came back when it was late and wrapped the body in the coarse cloth and carried it out stealthily and buried it in the Jewish cemetery, and departed again to their own houses.

'And there he lay,' said Unorna, 'the boy of your race who was faithful to death. Have you suffered? Have you for one short hour known the meaning of such great words as you dared to speak to me? Do you know now what it means to be a martyr, to suffer for standing on the very spot where he lay, to have felt in some small degree a part of what he must have felt. You live. Be warned. If again you anger me, your life shall not be spared you.'

The visions had all vanished. Again the wilderness of gravestones and lean, crooked trees appeared, wild and desolate as before. The Wanderer roused himself and saw Unorna standing before Israel Kafka's prostrate body. As though suddenly released from a spell he sprang forward and knelt down, trying to revive the unconscious man by rubbing his hands and chafing his temples.

Chapter 16

The Wanderer glanced at Unorna's face and saw the expression of relentless hatred which had settled upon her features. He neither understood it nor attempted to account for it. So far as he knew, Israel Kafka was mad, a man to be pitied, to be cared for, to be controlled perhaps, but assuredly not to be maltreated. Though the memories of the last half hour were confused and distorted, the Wanderer began to be aware that the young Hebrew had been made to suffer almost beyond the bounds of human endurance. So far as it was possible to judge, Israel Kafka's fault consisted in loving a woman who did not return his love, and his worst misdeed had been his sudden intrusion upon an interview in which the Wanderer could recall nothing which might not have been repeated to the whole world with impunity.

During the last month he had lived a life of bodily and mental indolence, in which all his keenest perceptions and strongest instincts had been lulled into a semi-dormant state. Unknown to himself, the mainspring of all thought and action had been taken out of his existence together with the very memory of it. For years he had lived and moved and wandered over the earth in obedience to one dominant idea. By a magic of which he knew nothing that idea had been annihilated, temporarily, if not for ever, and the immediate consequence had been the cessation of all interest and of all desire for individual action. The suspension of all anxiety, restlessness and mental suffering had benefited the physical man though it had reduced the intelligence to a state bordering upon total apathy.

But organisations, mental or physical, of great natural strength, are never reduced to weakness by a period of inactivity. It is those minds and bodies which have been artificially developed by a long course of training to a degree of power they were never intended to possess, which lose that force almost immediately in idleness. The really very strong man has no need of constant gymnastic exercise; he will be stronger than other men whatever he does. The strong character needs not be constantly struggling against terrible odds in the most difficult situations in order to be sure of its own solidity, nor must the deep intellect be ever plodding through the mazes of intricate theories and problems that it may feel itself superior to minds of less compass. There is much natural inborn strength of body and mind in the world, and on the whole those who possess either accomplish more than those in whom either is the result of long and well-regulated training.

The belief in a great cruelty and a greater injustice roused the man who throughout so many days had lived in calm indifference to every aspect of the humanity around him. Seeing that Israel Kafka could not be immediately restored to consciousness, he rose to his feet again and stood between the prostrate victim and Unorna.

'You are killing this man instead of saving him,' he said. 'His crime, you say, is that he loves you. Is that a reason for using all your powers to destroy him in body and mind?'

'Perhaps,' answered Unorna calmly, though there was still a dangerous light in her eyes.

'No. It is no reason,' answered the Wanderer with a decision to which Unorna was not accustomed. 'Keyork tells me that the man is mad. He may be. But he loves you and deserves mercy of you.'

'Mercy!' exclaimed Unorna with a cruel laugh. 'You heard what he said – you were for silencing him yourself. You could not have done it. I have – and most effectually.'

'Whatever your art really may be, you use it badly and cruelly. A moment ago I was blinded myself. If I had understood clearly while you were speaking that you were making this poor fellow suffer in himself the hideous agony you described I would have stopped you. You blinded me, as you dominated him. But I am not blind now. You shall not torment him any longer.

'And how would you have stopped me? How can you hinder me now?' asked Unorna.

The Wanderer gazed at her in silence for some moments. There was an expression in his face which she had never seen there. Towering above her he looked down. The massive brows were drawn together, the eyes were cold and impenetrable, every feature expressed strength.

'By force, if need be,' he answered very quietly.

The woman before him was not of those who fear or yield. She met his glance boldly. Scarcely half an hour earlier she had been able to steal away his senses and make him subject to her. She was ready to renew the contest, though she realised that a change had taken place in him.

'You talk of force to a woman!' she exclaimed, contemptuously. 'You are indeed brave!'

'You are not a woman. You are the incarnation of cruelty. I have seen it.'

His eyes were cold and his voice was stern. Unorna felt a very sharp pain and shivered as though she were cold. Whatever else was bad and cruel and untrue in her wild nature, her love for him was true and passionate and enduring. And she loved him the more for the strength he was beginning to show, and for his determined opposition. The words he had spoken had hurt her as he little guessed they could, not knowing that he alone of men had power to wound her.

'You do not know,' she answered. 'How should you?' Her glance fell and her voice trembled.

'I know enough,' he said. He turned coldly from her and knelt again beside Israel Kafka.

He raised the pale head and supported it upon his knee, and gazed anxiously into the face, raising the lids with his finger as though to convince himself that the man was not dead. Indeed there seemed to be but little life left in him as he lay there with outstretched arms and twisted fingers, scarcely breathing. In such a place, without so much as the commonest restorative to aid him, the Wanderer saw that he had but little chance of success.

Unorna stood aside, not looking at the two men. It was nothing to her whether Kafka lived or died. She was suffering herself, more than she had ever suffered in her life. He had said that she was not a woman – she whose whole woman's nature worshipped him. He had said that she was the incarnation of cruelty – and it was true, though it was her love for him that made her cruel to the other. Could he know what she had felt, when she had understood that Israel Kafka had heard her passionate words and seen her eager face, and had laughed her to scorn? Could any woman at such a time be less than cruel? Was not her hate for the man who loved her as great as her love for the man who loved her not? Even if she possessed instruments of torture for the soul more terrible than those invented in darker ages to rack the human body, was she not justified in using them all? Was not Israel Kafka guilty of the greatest of all crimes, of loving when he was not loved, and of witnessing her shame and discomfiture? She could not bear to look at him, lest she should lose herself and try to thrust the Wanderer aside and kill the man with her hands.

Then she heard footsteps on the frozen path, and turning quickly she saw that the Wanderer had lifted Kafka's body from the ground and was moving rapidly away, towards the entrance of the cemetery. He was leaving her in anger, without a word. She turned very pale and hesitated. Then she ran forward to overtake him, but he, hearing her approach, quickened his stride, seeming but little hampered in his pace by the burden he bore. But Unorna, too, was fleet of foot and strong.

'Stop!' she cried, laying her hand upon his arm. 'Stop! Hear me! Do not leave me so!'

But he would not pause, and hurried onward towards the gate, while she hung upon his arm, trying to hinder him and speaking in desperate agitation. She felt that if she let him go now, he would leave her for ever. In that moment even her hatred of Kafka sank into insignificance. She would do anything, bear anything, promise anything rather than lose what she loved so wildly.

'Stop!' she cried again. 'I will save him – I will obey you – I will be kind to him – he will die in your arms if you do not let me help you – oh! for the love of Heaven, wait one moment! Only one moment!'

She so thrust herself in the Wanderer's path, hanging upon him and trying to tear Kafka from his arms, that he was forced to stand still and face her.

'Let me pass!' he exclaimed, making another effort to advance. But she clung to him and he could not move.

'No – I will not let you go,' she murmured. 'You can do nothing without me, you will only kill him, as I would have done a moment ago – '

'And as you will do now,' he said sternly, 'if I let you have your way.'

'By all that is holy in Heaven, I will save him – he shall not even remember – '

'Do not swear. I shall not believe you.'

'You will believe when you see – you will forgive me – you will understand.'

Without answering he exerted his strength and clasping the insensible man more firmly in his arms he made one or two steps forward. Unorna's foot slipped on the frozen ground and she would have fallen to the earth, but she clung to him with desperate energy. Seeing that she was in danger of some bodily hurt if he used greater force, the Wanderer stopped again, uncertain how to act; Unorna stood before him, panting a little from the struggle, her face as white as death.

'Unless you kill me,' she said, 'you shall not take him away so. Hold him in your arms, if you will, but let me speak to him.'

'And how shall I know that you will not hurt him, you who hate him as you do?'

'Am I not at your mercy?' asked Unorna. 'If I deceive you, can you not do what you will with me, even if I try to resist you, which I will not? Hold me, if you choose, lest I should escape you, and if Israel Kafka does not recover his strength and his consciousness, then take me with you and deliver me up to justice as a witch – as a murderess, if you will.'

The Wanderer was silent for a moment. Then he realised that what she said was true. She was in his power.

'Restore him if you can,' he said.

Unorna laid her hands upon Kafka's forehead and bending down whispered into his ear words which were inaudible even to the man who held him. The mysterious change from sleep to consciousness was almost instantaneous. He opened his eyes and looked first at Unorna and then at the Wanderer. There was neither pain nor passion in his face, but only wonder. A moment more and his limbs regained their strength, he stood upright and passed his hand over his eyes as though trying to remember what had happened.

'How came I here?' he asked in surprise. 'What has happened to me?'

'You fainted,' said Unorna quietly. 'You remember that you were very tired after your journey. The walk was too much for you. We will take you home.'

'Yes – yes – I must have fainted. Forgive me – it comes over me sometimes.'

He evidently had complete control of his faculties at the present moment, when he glanced curiously from the one to the other of his two companions, as they all three began to walk towards the gate. Unorna avoided his eyes, and seemed to be looking at the irregular slabs they passed on their way.

The Wanderer had intended to free himself from her as soon as Kafka regained his senses, but he had not been prepared for such a sudden change. He saw, now, that he could not exchange a word with her without exciting the man's suspicion, and he was by no means sure that the first emotion might not produce a sudden and danger-ous effect. He did not even know how great the change might be, which Unorna's words had brought about. That Kafka had forgotten at once his own conduct and the fearful vision which Unorna had imposed upon him was clear, but it did not follow that he had ceased to love her. Indeed, to one only partially acquainted with the laws which govern hypnotics, such a transition seemed very far removed from possibility. He who in one moment had himself been made to forget utterly the dominant passion and love of his life, was so completely ignorant of the fact that he could not believe such a thing possible in any case whatsoever.

In the dilemma in which he found himself there was nothing to be done but to be guided by circumstances. He was not willing to leave Kafka alone with the woman who hated him, and he saw no means of escaping her society so long as she chose to impose it upon them both. He supposed, too, that Unorna realised this as well as he did, and he tried to be prepared for all events by revolving all the possibilities in his mind.

But Unorna was absorbed by very different thoughts. From time to time she stole a glance at his face, and she saw that it was stern and cold as ever. She had kept her word, but he did not relent. A terrible anxiety overwhelmed her. It was possible, even probable, that he would henceforth avoid her. She had gone too far. She had not reckoned upon such a nature as his, capable of being roused to implacable anger by mere sympathy for the suffering of another. Then, understanding it at last, she had thought it would be enough that those sufferings should be forgotten by him upon whom they had been inflicted. She could not comprehend the horror he felt for herself and for her hideous cruelty. She had entered the cemetery in the consciousness of her strong will and of her mysterious powers, certain of victory, sure that having once sacrificed her pride and stooped so low as to command what should have come of itself, she should see his face change and hear the ring of passion in that passionless voice. She had failed in that, and utterly. She had been surprised by her worst enemy. She had been laughed to scorn in the moment of her deepest humiliation, and she had lost the foundations of friendship in the attempt to build upon them the hanging gardens of an artificial love. In that moment, as they reached the gate, Unorna was not far from despair.

A Jewish boy, with puffed red lips and curving nostrils, was loitering at the entrance. The Wanderer told him to find a carriage.

'Two carriages,' said Unorna, quickly. The boy ran out. 'I will go home alone,' she added. 'You two can drive together.'

The Wanderer inclined his head in assent, but said nothing. Israel Kafka's dark eyes rested upon hers for a moment.

'Why not go together?' he asked.

Unorna started slightly and turned as though about to make a sharp answer. But she checked herself, for the Wanderer was looking at her. She spoke to him instead of answering Kafka.

'It is the best arrangement – do you not think so?' she asked.

'Quite the best.'

'I shall be gratified if you will bring me word of him,' she said, glancing at Kafka.

The Wanderer was silent as though he had not heard.

'Have you been in pain? Do you feel as though you had been suffering?' she asked of the younger man, in a tone of sympathy and solicitude.

'No. Why do you ask?'

Unorna smiled and looked at the Wanderer, with intention. He did not heed her. At that moment two carriages appeared and drew up at the end of the narrow alley which leads from the street to the entrance of the cemetery. All three walked forward together. Kafka went forward and opened the door of one of the conveyances for Unorna to get in. The Wanderer, still anxious for the man's safety, would have taken his place, but Kafka turned upon him almost defiantly.

'Permit me,' he said. 'I was before you here.'

The Wanderer stood civilly aside and lifted his hat. Unorna held out her hand, and he took it coldly, not being able to do otherwise.

'You will let me know, will you not?' she said. 'I am anxious about him.'

He raised his eyebrows a little and dropped her hand.

'You shall be informed,' he said.

Kafka helped her to get into the carriage. She drew him by the hand so that his head was inside the door and the other man could not hear her words.

'I am anxious about you,' she said very kindly. 'Make him come himself to me and tell me how you are.'

'Surely – if you have asked him – '

'He hates me,' whispered Unorna quickly. 'Unless you make him come he will send no message.'

'Then let me come myself – I am perfectly well – '

'Hush – no!' she answered hurriedly. 'Do as I say – it will be best for you – and for me. Goodbye.'

'Your word is my law,' said Kafka, drawing back. His eyes were bright and his thin cheek was flushed. It was long since she had spoken so kindly to him. A ray of hope entered his life.

The Wanderer saw the look and interpreted it rightly. He understood that in that brief moment Unorna had found time to do some mischief. Her carriage drove on, and left the two men free to enter the one intended for them. Kafka gave the driver the address of his lodgings. Then he sank back into the corner, exhausted and conscious of his extreme weakness. A short silence followed.

'You are in need of rest,' said the Wanderer, watching him curiously.

'Indeed, I am very tired, if not actually ill.'

'You have suffered enough to tire the strongest.'

'In what way?' asked Kafka. 'I have forgotten what happened. I know that I followed Unorna to the cemetery. I had been to her house, and I saw you afterwards together. I had not spoken to her since I came back from my long journey this morning. Tell me what occurred. Did she make me sleep? I feel as I have felt before when I have fancied that she has hypnotised me.'

The Wanderer looked at him in surprise. The question was asked as naturally as though it referred to an everyday occurrence of little or no weight.

'Yes,' he answered. 'She made you sleep.'

'Why? Do you know? If she has made me dream something, I have forgotten it.'

The Wanderer hesitated a moment.

'I cannot answer your question,' he said, at length.

'Ah – she told me that you hated her,' said Kafka, turning his dark eyes to his companion. 'But, yet,' he added, 'that is hardly a reason why you should not tell me what happened.'

'I could not tell you the truth without saying something which I have no right to say to a stranger – which I could not easily say to a friend.'

'You need not spare me – '

'It might save you.'

'Then say it – though I do not know from what danger I am to be saved. But I can guess, perhaps. You would advise me to give up the attempt to win her.'

'Precisely. I need say no more.'

'On the contrary,' said Kafka with sudden energy, 'when a man gives such advice as that to a stranger he is bound to give also his reasons.'

The Wanderer looked at him calmly as he answered.

'One man need hardly give a reason for saving another man's life. Yours is in danger.'

'I see that you hate her, as she said you did.'

'You and she are both mistaken in that. I am not in love with her and I have ceased to be her friend. As for my interest in you, it does not even pretend to be friendly – it is that which any man may feel for a fellow-being, and what any man would feel who had seen what I have seen this afternoon.'

The calm bearing and speech of the experienced man of the world carried weight with it in the eyes of the young Moravian, whose hot blood knew little of restraint and less of caution; with the keen instinct of his race in the reading of character he suddenly understood that his companion was at once generous and disinterested. A burst of confidence followed close upon the conviction.

'If I am to lose her love, I would rather lose my life also, and by her hand,' he said hotly. 'You are warning me against her. I feel that you are honest and I see that you are in earnest. I thank you. If I am in danger, do not try to save me. I saw her face a few moments ago, and she spoke to me. I cannot believe that she is plotting my destruction.'

The Wanderer was silent. He wondered whether it was his duty to do or say more. Unorna was a changeable woman. She might love the man tomorrow. But Israel Kafka was too young to let the conversation drop. Boy-like he expected confidence for confidence, and was surprised at his companion's taciturnity.

'What did she say to me when I was asleep?' he asked, after a short pause.

'Did you ever hear the story of Simon Abeles?' the Wanderer inquired by way of answer.

Kafka frowned and looked round sharply.

'Simon Abeles? He was a renegade Hebrew boy. His father killed him. He is buried in the Teyn Kirche. What of him? What has he to do with Unorna, or with me? I am myself a Jew. The time has gone by when we Jews hid our heads. I am proud of what I am, and I will never be a Christian. What can Simon Abeles have to do with me?'

'Little enough, now that you are awake.'

'And when I was asleep, what then? She made me see him, perhaps?'

'She made you live his life. She made you suffer all that he suffered –'

'What?' cried Israel Kafka in a loud and angry tone.

'What I say,' returned the other quietly.

'And you did not interfere? You did not stop her? No, of course, I forgot that you are a Christian.'

The Wanderer looked at him in surprise. It had not struck him that Israel Kafka might be a man of the deepest religious convictions, a Hebrew of the Hebrews, and that what he would resent most would be the fact that in his sleep Unorna had made him play the part and suffer the martyrdom of a convert to Christianity. This was exactly what took place. He would have suffered anything at Unorna's hands, and without complaint, even to bodily death, but his wrath rose furiously at the thought that she had been playing with what he held most sacred, that she had forced from his lips the denial of the faith of his people and the confession of the Christian belief, perhaps the very words of the hated Creed. The modern Hebrew of Western Europe might be indifferent in such a case, as though he had spoken in the delirium of a fever, but the Jew of the less civilised East is a different being, and in some ways a stronger. Israel Kafka represented the best type of his race, and his blood boiled at the insult that had been put upon him. The Wanderer saw, and understood, and at once began to respect him, as men who believe firmly in opposite creeds have been known to respect each other even in a life and death struggle.

'I would have stopped her if I could,' he said.

'Were you sleeping, too?' asked Kafka hotly.

'I cannot tell. I was powerless though I was conscious. I saw only Simon Abeles in it all, though I seemed to be aware that you and he were one person. I did interfere – so soon as I was free to move. I think I saved your life. I was carrying you away in my arms when she waked you.'

'I thank you – I suppose it is as you tell me. You could not move – but you saw it all, you say. You saw me play the part of the apostate, you heard me confess the Christian's faith?'

'Yes – I saw you die in agony, confessing it still.'

Israel Kafka ground his teeth and turned his face away. The Wanderer was silent. A few moments later the carriage stopped at the door of Kafka's lodging. The latter turned to his companion, who was startled by the change in the young face. The mouth was now closely set, the features seemed bolder, the eyes harder and more manly, a look of greater dignity and strength was in the whole.

'You do not love her?' he asked. 'Do you give me your word that you do not love her?'

'If you need so much to assure you of it, I give you my word. I do not love her.'

'Will you come with me for a few moments? I live here.'

The Wanderer made a gesture of assent. In a few moments they found themselves in a large room furnished almost in Eastern fashion, with few objects, but those of great value. Israel Kafka was alone in the world and was rich. There were two or three divans, a few low, octagonal, inlaid tables, a dozen or more splendid weapons hung upon the wall, and the polished wooden floor was partly covered with extremely rich carpets.

'Do you know what she said to me, when I helped her into the carriage?' asked Kafka.

'No, I did not attempt to hear.'

'She did not mean that you should hear her. She made me promise to send you to her with news of myself. She said that you hated her and would not go to her unless I begged you to do so. Is that true?'

'I have told you that I do not hate her. I hate her cruelty. I will certainly not go to her of my own choice.'

'She said that I had fainted. That was a lie. She invented it as an excuse to attract you, on the ground of her interest in my condition.'

'Evidently.'

'She hates me with an extreme hatred. Her real interest lay in showing you how terrible that hatred could be. It is not possible to conceive of anything more diabolically bad than what she did to me. She made me her sport – yours, too, perhaps, or she would at least have wished it. On that holy ground where my people lie in peace she made me deny my faith, she made me, in your eyes and her own, personate a renegade of my race, she made me confess in the Christian creed, she made me seem to die for a belief I abhor. Can you conceive of anything more devilish? A moment later she smiles upon me and presses my hand, and is anxious to know of my good health. And but for you, I should never have known what she had done to me. I owe you gratitude, though it be for the worst pain I have ever suffered. But do you think I will forgive her?'

'You would be very forgiving if you could,' said the Wanderer, his own anger rising again at the remembrance of what he had seen.

'And do you think that I can love still?'

'No.'

Israel Kafka walked the length of the room and then came back and stood before the Wanderer and looked into his eyes. His face was very calm and resolute, the flush had vanished from his thin cheeks, and the features were set in an expression of irrevocable determination. Then he spoke, slowly and distinctly.

'You are mistaken. I love her with all my heart. I will therefore kill her.'

The Wanderer had seen many men in many lands and had witnessed the effects of many passions. He gazed earnestly into Israel Kafka's face, searching in vain for some manifestation of madness. But he was disappointed. The Moravian had formed his resolution in cold blood and intended to carry it out. His only folly appeared to lie in the announcement of his intention. But his next words explained even that.

'She made me promise to send you to her if you would go,' he said. 'Will you go to her now?'

'What shall I tell her? I warn you that since – '

'You need not warn me. I know what you would say. But I will be no common murderer. I will not kill her as she would have killed me. Warn her, not me. Go to her and say, "Israel Kafka has promised before God that he will take your blood in expiation, and there is no escape from the man who is himself ready to die." Tell her to fly for her life, and that quickly.'

'And what will you gain by doing this murder?' asked the Wanderer, calmly. He was revolving schemes for Unorna's safety, and was half amazed to find himself forced in common humanity to take her part.

'I shall free myself of my shame in loving her, at the price of her blood and mine. Will you go?'

'And what is to prevent me from delivering you over to safe keeping before you do this deed?'

'You have no witness,' answered Kafka with a smile. 'You are a stranger in the city and in this country, and I am rich. I shall easily prove that you love Unorna, and that you wish to get rid of me out of jealousy.'

'That is true,' said the Wanderer, thoughtfully. 'I will go.'

'Go quickly, then,' said Israel Kafka, 'for I shall follow soon.'

As the Wanderer left the room he saw the Moravian turn toward the place where the keen, splendid Eastern weapons hung upon the wall.

Chapter 17

The Wanderer knew that the case was urgent and the danger great. There was no mistaking the tone of Israel Kafka's voice nor the look in his face. Nor did the savage resolution seem altogether unnatural in a man of the Moravian's breeding. The Wanderer had no time and but little inclination to blame himself for the part he had played in disclosing to the principal actor the nature of the scene which had taken place in the cemetery, and the immediate consequences of that disclosure, though wholly unexpected, did not seem utterly illogical. Israel Kafka's nature was eastern, violently passionate and, at the same time, long-suffering in certain directions as only the fatalist can be. He could have loved for a lifetime faithfully, without requital; he would have suffered in patience Unorna's anger, scorn, pity or caprice; he had long before now resigned his free will into the keeping of a passion which was degrading as it enslaved all his thoughts and actions, but which had something noble in it, inasmuch as it fitted him for the most heroic self-sacrifice.

Unorna's act had brought the several seemingly contradictory elements of his character to bear upon one point. He had realised in the same moment that it was impossible for her to love him; that her changing treatment of him was not the result of caprice but of a fixed plan of her own, in the execution of which she would spare him neither falsehood nor insult; that to love such a woman was the lowest degradation; that he could nevertheless not destroy that love; and, finally, that the only escape from his shame lay in her destruction, and that this must in all probability involve his own death also. At the same time he felt that there was something solemn in the expiation he was about to exact, something that accorded well with the fierce traditions of ancient Israel, and that the deed should not be done stealthily or in the dark. Unorna must know that she was to die by his hand, and why. He had no object in concealment, for his own life was already ended by the certainty that his love was hopeless, and on the other hand, fatalist as he was, he believed that Unorna could not escape him and that no warning could save her.

The Wanderer understood most of these things as he hastened towards her house through the darkening streets. Not a carriage was to be seen, and he was obliged to traverse the distance on foot, as often happens at supreme moments, when everything might be gained by the saving of a few minutes in conveying a warning.

He saw himself in a very strange position. Half an hour had not elapsed since he had watched Unorna driving away from the cemetery and had inwardly determined that he would never, if possible, set eyes on her again. Scarcely two hours earlier, he had been speaking to her of the sincere friendship which he felt was growing up for her in his heart. Since then he had learned, almost beyond the possibility of a doubt, that she loved him, and he had learned, too, to despise her; he had left her meaning that the parting should be final, and now he was hurrying to her house to give her the warning which alone could save her from destruction. And yet, he found it impossible to detect any inconsistency in his own conduct. As he had been conscious of doing his utmost to save Israel Kafka from her, so now he knew that he was doing all he could to save Unorna from the Moravian, and he recognised the fact that no man with the commonest feelings of humanity could have done less in either case. But he was conscious, also, of a change in himself which he did not attempt to analyse. His indolent, self-satisfied apathy was gone, the strong interests of human life and death stirred him, mind and body together acquired their activity, and he was at all points once more a man. He was ignorant, indeed, of what had been taken from him. The memory of Beatrice was gone, and he fancied himself one who had never loved woman. He looked back with horror and amazement upon the emptiness of his past life, wondering how such an existence as he had led, or fancied he had led, could have been possible.

But there was scant time for reflection upon the problem of his own mission in the world as he hastened towards Unorna's house. His present mission was clear enough and simple enough, though by no means easy of accomplishment. What Israel Kafka had told him was very true. Should he attempt a denunciation, he would have little chance of being believed. It would be easy enough for Kafka to bring witnesses to prove his own love for Unorna and the Wanderer's intimacy with her during the past month, and the latter's consequent interest in disposing summarily of his Moravian rival. A stranger in the land would have small hope of success against a man whose antecedents were known, whose fortune was reputed great, and who had at his back the whole gigantic strength of the Jewish interest in Prague, if he chose to invoke the assistance of his people. The matter would end in a few days in the Wanderer being driven from the country, while Israel Kafka would be left behind to work his will as might seem best in his own eyes.

There was Keyork Arabian. So far as it was possible to believe in the sincerity of any of the strange persons among whom the Wanderer found himself, it seemed certain that the sage was attached to Unorna by some bond of mutual interests which he would be loth to break. Keyork had many acquaintances and seemed to posses everywhere a certain amount of respect, whether because he was perhaps a member of some widespread, mysterious society of which the Wanderer knew nothing, or whether this importance of his was due to his personal superiority of mind and wide experience of travel, no one could say. But it seemed certain that if Unorna could be placed for the time being in a safe refuge, it would be best to apply to Keyork to ensure her further protection. Meanwhile that refuge must be found and Unorna must be conveyed to it without delay.

The Wanderer was admitted without question. He found Unorna in her accustomed place. She had thrown aside her furs and was sitting in an attitude of deep thought. Her dress was black, and in the soft light of the shaded lamps she was like a dark, marble statue set in the midst of thick shrubbery in a garden. Her elbow rested on her knee, her chin upon her beautiful, heavy hand; only in her hair was there bright colour.

She knew the Wanderer's footstep, but she neither moved her body nor turned her head. She felt that she grew paler than before, and she could hear her heart beating strongly.

'I come from Israel Kafka,' said the Wanderer, standing still before her.

She knew from his tone how hard his face must be, and she would not look up.

'What of him?' she asked in a voice without expression. 'Is he well?'

'He bids me say to you that he has promised before Heaven to take your life, and that there is no escape from a man who is ready to lay down his own.'

Unorna turned her head slowly towards him, and a very soft look stole over her strange face.

'And you have brought me his message – this warning – to save me?' she said.

'As I tried to save him from you an hour ago. But there is little time. The man is desperate, whether mad or sane, I cannot tell. Make haste. Determine where to go for safety, and I will take you there.'

But Unorna did not move. She only looked at him, with an expression he could no longer misunderstand. He was cold and impassive.

'I fancy it will not be safe to hesitate long,' he said. 'He is in earnest.'

'I do not fear Israel Kafka, and I fear death less,' answered Unorna deliberately. 'Why does he mean to kill me?'

'I think that in his place almost all human men would feel as he does, though religion, or prudence, or fear, or all three together, might prevent them from doing what they would wish to do.'

'You too? And which of the three would prevent you from murdering me?'

'None, perhaps – though pity might.'

'I want no pity, least of all from you. What I have done, I have done for you, and for you only.'

The Wanderer's face showed only a cold disgust. He said nothing.

'You do not seem surprised,' said Unorna. 'You know that I love you?'

'I know it.'

A silence followed, during which Unorna returned to her former attitude, turning her eyes away and resting her chin upon her hand. The Wanderer began to grow impatient.

'I must repeat that, in my opinion, you have not much time to spare,' he said. 'If you are not in a place of safety in half an hour, I cannot answer for the consequences.'

'No time? There is all eternity. What is eternity, or time, or life to me? I will wait for him here. Why did you tell him what I did, if you wished me to live?'

'Why – since there are to be questions – why did you exercise your cruelty upon an innocent man who loves you?'

'Why? There are reasons enough!' Unorna's voice trembled slightly. 'You do not know what happened. How should you? You were asleep. You may as well know, since I may be beyond telling you an hour from now. You may as well know how I love you, and to what depths I have gone down to win your love.'

'I would rather not receive your confidence,' the Wanderer answered haughtily. 'I came here to save your life, not to hear your confessions.'

'And when you have heard, you will no longer wish to save me. If you choose to leave me here, I will wait for Israel Kafka alone. He may kill me if he pleases. I do not care. But if you stay you shall hear what I have to say.'

She glanced at his face. He folded his arms and stood still. Whatever she had done, he would not leave her alone at the mercy of the desperate man whom he expected every moment to enter the room. If she would not save herself, he might nevertheless disarm Kafka and prevent the deed. As his long-sleeping energy revived in him the thought of a struggle was not disagreeable.

'I loved you from the moment when I first saw you,' said Unorna, trying to speak calmly. 'But you loved another woman. Do you remember her? Her name was Beatrice, and she was very dark, as I am fair. You had lost her and you had sought her for years. You entered my house, thinking that she had gone in before you. Do you remember that morning? It was a month ago today. You told me the story.'

'You have dreamed it,' said the Wanderer in cold surprise. 'I never loved any woman yet.'

Unorna laughed bitterly.

'How perfect it all was at first!' she exclaimed. 'How smooth it seemed! How easy! You slept before me, out there by the river that very afternoon. And in your sleep I bade you forget. And you forgot wholly, your love, the woman, her very name, even as Israel Kafka forgot today what he had suffered in the person of the martyr. You told him the story, and he believes you, because he knows me, and knows what I can do. You can believe me or not as you will. I did it.'

'You are dreaming,' the Wanderer repeated, wondering whether she were not out of her mind.

'I did it. I said to myself that if I could destroy your old love, root it out from your heart and from your memory and make you as one who had never loved at all, then you would love me as you had once loved her, with your whole free soul. I said that I was beautiful – it is true, is it not? And young I am, and I loved as no woman ever loved. And I said that it was enough, and that soon you would love me, too. A month has passed away since then. You are of ice – of stone – I do not know of what you are. This morning you hurt me. I thought it was the last hurt and that I should die then – instead of tonight. Do you remember? You thought I was ill, and you went away. When you were gone I fought with myself. My dreams – yes, I had dreamed of all that can make earth Heaven, and you had waked me. You said that you would be a brother to me – you talked of friendship. The sting of it! It is no wonder that I grew faint with pain. Had you struck me in the face, I would have kissed your hand. But your friendship! Rather be dead than, loving, be held a friend! And I had dreamed of being dear to you for my own sake, of being dearest, and first, and alone beloved, since that other was gone and I had burned her memory. That pride I had still, until that moment. I fancied that it was in my power, if I would stoop so low, to make you sleep again as you had slept before, and to make you at my bidding feel all I felt. I fought with myself. I would not go down to that depth. And then I said that even that were better than your friendship, even a false semblance of love inspired by my will, preserved by my suggestion. And so I fell. You came back to me and I led you to that lonely place, and made you sleep, and then I told you what was in my heart and poured out the fire of my soul into your ears. A look came into your face – I shall not forget it. My folly was upon me, and I thought it was for me. I know the truth now. Sleeping, the old memory revived in you of her whom waking you will never remember again. But the look was there, and I bade you awake. My soul rose in my eyes. I hung upon your lips. The loving word I longed for seemed already to tremble in the air. Then came the truth. You awoke, and your face was stone, calm, smiling, indifferent, unloving. And all this Israel Kafka had seen, hiding like a thief almost beside us. He saw it all, he heard it all, my words of love, my agony of waiting, my utter humiliation, my burning shame. Was I cruel to him? He had made me suffer, and he suffered in his turn. All this you did not know. You know it now. There is nothing more to tell. Will you wait here until he comes? Will you look on, and be glad to see me die? Will you remember in the years to come with satisfaction that you saw the witch killed for her many misdeeds, and for the chief of them all – for loving you?'

The Wanderer had listened to her words, but the tale they told was beyond the power of his belief. He stood still in his place, with folded arms, debating what he should do to save her. One thing alone was clear. She loved him to distraction. Possibly, he thought, her story was but an invention to excuse her cruelty and to win his commiseration. It failed to do either at first, but yet he would not leave her to her fate.

'You shall not die if I can help it,' he said simply.

'And if you save me, do you think that I will leave you?' she asked with sudden agitation, turning and half rising from her seat. 'Think what you will be doing, if you save me. Think well. You say that Israel Kafka is desperate. I am worse than desperate, worse than mad with my love.'

She sank back again and hid her face for a moment. He, on his part, began to see the terrible reality and strength of her passion, and silently wondered what the end would be. He too was human, and pity for her began at last to touch his heart.

'You shall not die, if I can save you,' he said again.

She sprang to her feet very suddenly and stood before him.

'You pity me!' she cried. 'What lie is that which says that there is a kinship between pity and love? Think well – beware – be warned. I have told you much, but you do not know me yet. If you save me, you save me but to love you more than I do already. Look at me. For me there is neither God, nor hell, nor pride, nor shame. There is nothing that I will not do, nothing I shall be ashamed or afraid of doing. If you save me, you save me that I may follow you as long as I live. I will never leave you. You shall never escape my presence, your whole life shall be full of me – you do not love me, and I can threaten you with nothing more intolerable than myself. Your eyes will weary of the sight of me and your ears at the sound of my voice. Do you think I have no hope? A moment ago I had none. But I see it now. Whether you will, or not, I shall be yours. You may make a prisoner of me – I shall be in your keeping then, and shall know it, and feel it, and love my prison for your sake, even if you will not let me see you. If you would escape from me, you must kill me, as Israel Kafka means to kill me now – and then, I shall die by your hand and my life will have been yours and given to you. How can you think that I have no hope! I have hope – and certainty, for I shall be near you always to the end – always, always, always! I will cling to you – as I do now –

and say, I love you, I love you – yes, and you will cast me off, but I will not go – I will clasp your feet, and say again, I love you, and you may spurn me – man, god, wanderer, devil – whatever you are – beloved always! Tread upon me, trample on me, crush me – you cannot save yourself, you cannot kill my love!'

She had tried to take his hand and he had withdrawn his, she had fallen upon her knees, and as he tried to free himself had fallen almost to her length upon the marble floor, clinging to his very feet, so that he could make no step without doing her some hurt. He looked down, amazed and silent, and as he looked she cast one glance upward to his stern face, the bright tears streaming like falling gems from her unlike eyes, her face pale and quivering, her rich hair all loosened and falling about her.

And then, neither body nor heart nor soul could bear the enormous strain that was laid upon them. A low cry broke from her lips, a stormy sob, another and another, like quick short waves breaking over the bar when the tide is low and the wind is rising suddenly.

The Wanderer was in sore straits, for the minutes were passing quickly and he remembered the last look on Kafka's face, and how he had left the Moravian standing before the weapons on the wall. And nothing had been done yet, not so much as an order given not to admit him if he came to the house. At any moment he might be upon them. And the storm showed no signs of being spent. Her wild, convulsive sobbing was painful to hear. If he tried to move, she dragged herself frantically at his feet so that he feared lest he should tread upon her hands. He pitied her now most truly, though he guessed rightly that to show his pity would be but to add fuel to the blazing flame.

Then, in the interval of a second, as she drew breath to weep afresh, he fancied that he heard sounds below as of the great door being opened and closed again. With a quick, strong movement, stooping low he put his arms about her and raised her from the floor. At his touch, her sobbing ceased for a moment, as though she had wanted only that to soothe her. In spite of him she let her head rest upon his shoulder, letting him still feel that if he did not support her weight with his arm she would fall again. In the midst of the most passionate and real outburst of despairing love there was no artifice which she would not use to be nearer to him, to extort even the semblance of a caress.

'I heard someone come in below,' he said, hurriedly. 'It must be he. Decide quickly what to do. Either stay or fly – you have not ten seconds for your choice.'

She turned her imploring eyes to his.

'Let me stay here and end it all – '

'That you shall not!' he exclaimed, dragging her towards the end of the hall opposite to the usual entrance, and where he knew that there must be a door behind the screen of plants. His hold tightened upon her yielding waist. Her head fell back and her full lips parted in an ecstasy of delight as she felt herself hurried along in his arms, scarcely touching the floor with her feet.

'Ah – now – now! Let it come now!' she sighed.

'It must be now – or never,' he said almost roughly. 'If you will leave this house with me now, very well. But leave this room you shall. If I am to meet that man and stop him, I will meet him alone.'

'Leave you alone? Ah no – not that – '

They had reached the exit now. At the same instant both heard someone enter at the other end and rapid footsteps on the marble pavement.

'Which is it to be?' asked the Wanderer, pale and calm. He had pushed her through before him and seemed ready to go back alone.

With violent strength she drew him to her, closed the door and slipped the strong steel bolt across below the lock. There was a dim light in the passage.

'Together, then,' she said. 'I shall at least be with you – a little longer.'

'Is there another way out of the house?' asked the Wanderer anxiously.

'More than one. Come with me.'

As they disappeared in the corridor, they heard behind them the noise of the door-lock as someone tried to force it open. Then a heavy sound as though a man's shoulder struck against the solid panel. Unorna led the way through a narrow, winding passage, illuminated here and there by small lamps with shades of soft colours, blown in Bohemian glass.

Pushing aside a curtain they came out into a small room. The Wanderer uttered an involuntary exclamation of surprise as he recognised the vestibule and saw before him the door of the great conservatory, open as Israel Kafka had left it. That the latter was still trying to pursue them through the opposite exit was clear enough, for the blows he was striking on the panel echoed loudly out into the hall. Swiftly and silently Unorna closed the entrance and locked it securely.

'He is safe for a little while,' she said. 'Keyork will find him there when he comes, an hour hence, and Keyork will perhaps bring him to his senses.'

She had regained control of herself, to all appearances, and she spoke with perfect calm and self-possession. The Wanderer looked at her in surprise and with some suspicion. Her hair was all falling about her shoulders, but saving this sign, there was no trace of the recent storm, nor the least indication of passion. If she had been acting a part throughout before an audience, she would have seemed less indifferent when the curtain fell. The Wanderer, having little cause to trust her, found it hard to believe that she had not been counterfeiting. It seemed impossible that she should be the same woman who but a moment earlier had been dragging herself at his feet, in wild tears and wilder protestations of her love.

'If you are sufficiently rested,' he said with a touch of sarcasm which he could not restrain, 'I would suggest that we do not wait any longer here.'

She turned and faced him, and he saw now how very white she was.

'So you think that even now I have been deceiving you? That is what you think. I see it in your face.'

Before he could prevent her she had opened the door wide again and was advancing calmly into the conservatory.

'Israel Kafka!' she cried in loud clear tones. 'I am here – I am waiting – come!'

The Wanderer ran forward. He caught sight in the distance of a pair of fiery eyes and of something long and thin and sharp-gleaming under the soft lamps. He knew then that all was deadly earnest. Swift as thought he caught Unorna and bore her from the hall, locking the door again and setting his broad shoulders against it, as he put her down. The daring act she had done appealed to him, in spite of himself.

'I beg your pardon,' he said almost deferentially. 'I misjudged you.'

'It is that,' she answered. 'Either I will be with you or I will die, by his hand, by yours, by my own – it will matter little when it is done. You need not lean against the door. It is very strong. Your furs are hanging there, and here are mine. Let us be going.'

Quietly, as though nothing unusual had happened, they descended the stairs together. The porter came forward with all due ceremony, to open the shut door. Unorna told him that if Keyork Arabian came while she was out, he was to be shown directly into the conservatory.

A moment later she and her companion were standing together in the small irregular square before the Clementinum.

'Where will you go?' asked the Wanderer.

'With you,' she answered, laying her hand upon his arm and looking into his face as though waiting to see what direction he would choose. 'Unless you send me back to him,' she added, glancing quickly at the house and making as though she would withdraw her hand once more. 'If it is to be that, I will go alone.'

There seemed to be no way out of the terrible dilemma, and the Wanderer stood still in deep thought. He knew that if he could but free himself from her for half an hour, he could get help from the right quarter and take Israel Kafka red-handed and armed as he was. For the man was caught as in a trap and must stay there until he was released, and there would be little doubt from his manner, when taken, that he was either mad or consciously attempting some crime. There was no longer any necessity, he thought, for Unorna to take refuge anywhere for more than an hour. In that time Israel Kafka would be in safe custody, and she could re-enter her house with nothing to fear. But he counted without Unorna's unyielding obstinacy. She threatened if he left her for a moment to go back to Israel Kafka. A few minutes earlier she had carried out her threat and the consequence had been almost fatal.

'If you are in your right mind,' he said at last, beginning to walk towards the corner, 'you will see that what you wish to do is utterly against reason. I will not allow you to run the risk of meeting Israel Kafka tonight, but I cannot take you with me. No – I will hold you, if you try to escape me, and I will bring you to a place of safety by force, if need be.'

'And you will leave me there, and I shall never see you again. I will not go, and you will find it hard to take me anywhere in the crowded city by force. You are not Israel Kafka, with the whole Jews' quarter at your command in which to hide me.'

The Wanderer was perplexed. He saw, however, that if he would yield the point and give his word to return to her, she might be induced to follow his advice.

'If I promise to come back to you, will you do what I ask?' he inquired.

'Will you promise truly?'

'I have never broken a promise yet.'

'Did you promise that other woman that you would never love again, I wonder? If so, you are faithful indeed. But you have forgotten that. Will you come back to me if I let you take me where I shall be safe tonight?'

'I will come back whenever you send for me.'

'If you fail, my blood is on your head.'

'Yes – on my head be it.'

'Very well. I will go to that house where I first stayed when I came here. Take me there quickly – no – not quickly either – let it be very long! I shall not see you until tomorrow.'

A carriage was passing at a foot pace. The Wanderer stopped it, and helped Unorna to get in. The place was very near, and neither spoke, though he could feel her hand upon his arm. He made no attempt to shake her off. At the gate they both got out, and he rang a bell that echoed through vaulted passages far away in the interior.

'Tomorrow,' said Unorna, touching his hand.

He could see even in the dark the look of love she turned upon him.

'Good-night,' he said, and in the next moment she had disappeared within.

Chapter 18

Having made the necessary explanations to account for her sudden appearance, Unorna found herself installed in two rooms of modest dimensions, and very simply though comfortably furnished. It was quite a common thing for ladies to seek retreat and quiet in the convent during two or three weeks of the year, and there was plenty of available space at the disposal of those who wished to do so. Such visits were indeed most commonly made during the lenten season, and on the day when Unorna sought refuge among the nuns it chanced that there was but one other stranger within the walls. She was glad to find that this was the case. Her peculiar position would have made it hard for her to bear with equanimity the quiet observation of a number of women, most of whom would probably have been to some extent acquainted with the story of her life, and some of whom would certainly have wished out of curiosity to enter into nearer acquaintance with her while within the convent, while not intending to prolong their intercourse with her any further. It could not be expected, indeed, that in a city like Prague such a woman as Unorna could escape notice, and the fact that little or nothing was known of her true history had left a very wide field for the imaginations of those who chose to invent one for her. The common story, and the one which on the whole was nearest to the truth, told that she was the daughter of a noble of eastern Bohemia who had died soon after her birth, the last of his family, having converted his ancestral possessions into money for Unorna's benefit, in order to destroy all trace of her relationship to him. The secret must, of course, have been confided to someone, but it had been kept faithfully, and Unorna herself was no wiser than those who amused themselves with fruitless speculations regarding her origin. If from the first, from the moment when, as a young girl, she left the convent to enter into possession of her fortune, she had chosen to assert some right to a footing in the most exclusive aristocracy in the world, it is not impossible that the protection of the Abbess might have helped her to obtain it. The secret of her birth would, however, have rendered a marriage with a man of that class all but impossible, and would have entirely excluded her from the only other position considered dignified for a well-born woman of fortune, unmarried and wholly without living relations or connections – that of a lady-canoness on the Crown foundation. Moreover, her wild bringing-up, and the singular natural gifts she possessed, and which she could not resist the impulse to exercise, had in a few months placed her in a position from which no escape was possible so long as she continued to live in Prague; and against those few – chiefly men – who for her beauty's sake, or out of curiosity, would gladly have made her acquaintance, she raised an impassable barrier of pride and reserve. Nor was her reputation altogether an evil one. She lived in a strange fashion, it is true, but the very fact of her extreme seclusion had kept her name free from stain. If people spoke of her as the Witch, it was more from habit and half in jest than in earnest. In strong contradiction to the cruelty which she could exercise ruthlessly when roused to anger, was her well-known kindness to the poor, and her charities to institutions founded for their benefit were in reality considerable, and were said to be boundless. These explanations seem necessary in order to account for the readiness with which she turned to the convent when she was in danger, and for the facilities which were then at once offered her for a stay long or short, as she should please to make it. Some of the more suspicious nuns looked grave when they heard that she was under their roof; others, again, had been attached to her during the time she had formerly spent among them; and there were not lacking those who, disapproving of her presence, held their peace, in the anticipation that the rich and eccentric lady would on departing present a gift of value to their order.

The rooms which were kept at the disposal of ladies desiring to make a religious retreat for a short time were situated on the first floor of one wing of the convent overlooking a garden which was not within the cloistered precincts, but which was cultivated for the convenience of the nuns, who themselves never entered it. The windows on this side were not latticed, and the ladies who occupied the apartments were at liberty to look out upon the small square of land, their view of the street beyond being cut off however by a wall in which there was one iron gate for the convenience of the gardeners, who were thus not obliged to pass through the main entrance of the convent in order to reach their work. Within the rooms all opened out upon a broad vaulted corridor, lighted in the day-time by a huge arched window looking upon an inner court, and at night by a single lamp suspended in the middle of the passage by a strong iron chain. The pavement of this passage was of broad stones, once smooth and even but now worn and made irregular by long use. The rooms for the guests were carpeted with sober colours and warmed by high stoves built up of glazed white tiles. The furniture, as has been said, was simple, but afforded all that was strictly necessary for ordinary comfort, each apartment consisting of a bedroom and sitting-room, small in lateral dimensions but relatively very high. The walls were thick and not easily penetrated by any sounds from without, and, as in many religious houses, the entrances from the corridor were all closed by double doors, the outer one of strong oak with a lock and a solid bolt, the inner one of lighter material, but thickly padded to exclude sound as well as currents of cold air. Each sitting-room contained a table, a sofa, three or four chairs, a small book-shelf, and a praying-stool provided with a hard and well-worn cushion for the knees. Over this a brown wooden crucifix was hung upon the grey wall.

In the majority of convents it is not usual, nor even permissible, for ladies in retreat to descend to the nuns' refectory. When there are many guests they are usually served by lay sisters in a hall set apart for the purpose; when there are few, their simple meals are brought to them in their rooms. Moreover they of course put on no religious robe, though they dress themselves in black. In the church, or chapel, as the case may be, they do not take places within the latticed choir with the sisters, but either sit in the body of the building, or occupy a side chapel reserved for their use, or else perform their devotions kneeling at high windows above the choir, which communicate within with rooms accessible from the convent.

It is usual for them to attend Mass, Vespers, the Benediction and Compline, but when there are midnight services they are not expected to be present.

Unorna was familiar with convent life and was aware that the Benediction was over, and that the hour for the evening meal was approaching. A fire had been lit in her sitting-room, but the air was still very cold and she sat wrapped in her furs as when she had arrived, leaning back in a corner of the sofa, her head inclined forward, and one white hand resting on the green baize cloth which covered the table.

She was very tired, and the absolute stillness was refreshing and restoring after the long-drawn-out emotions of the stormy day. Never, in her short and passionate life, had so many events been crowded into the space of a few hours. Since the morning she had felt almost everything that her wild, high-strung nature was capable of feeling – love, triumph, failure, humiliation – anger, hate, despair, and danger of sudden death. She was amazed when, looking back, she remembered that at noon on that day her life and all its interests had been stationary at the point familiar to her during a whole month, the point that still lay within the boundaries of hope's kingdom, the point at which the man she loved had wounded her by speaking of brotherly affection and sisterly regard. She could almost believe, when she thought of it all, that someone had done to her as she had done to others, that she had been cast into a state of sleep, and had been forced against her will to live through the storms of years in the lethargy of an hour. And yet, despite all, her memory was distinct, her faculties were awake, her intellect had lost none of its clearness, even in the last and worst hour of all. She could recall each look on the Wanderer's face, each tone of his cold speech, each intonation of her own passionate outpourings. Her strong memory had retained all, and there was not the slightest break in the continuity of her recollections. But there was little comfort to be derived from the certainty that she had not been dreaming, and that everything had really taken place precisely as she remembered it. She would have given all she possessed, which was much, to return to the hour of noon on that same day.

In so far as a very unruly nature can understand itself, Unorna understood the springs of the actions, she regretted and confessed that in all likelihood she would do again as she had done at each successive stage. Indeed, since the last great outbreak of her heart, she realised more than ever the great proportions which her love had of late assumed; and she saw that she was indeed ready, as she had said, to dare everything and risk everything for the sake of obtaining the very least show of passion in return. It was quite clear to her, since she had failed so totally, that she should have had patience, that she ought to have accepted gratefully the man's offer of brotherly devotion, and trusted in time to bring about a further and less platonic development. But she was equally sure that she could never have found the patience, and that if she had restrained herself today she would have given way tomorrow. She possessed all the blind indifference to consequences which is a chief characteristic of the Slav nature when dominated by passion. She had shown it in her rash readiness to face Israel Kafka at the moment of leaving her own home. If she could not have what she longed for, she cared as little what became of her as she cared for Kafka's own fate. She had but one object, one passion, one desire, and to all else her indifference was supreme. Life and death, in this world or the next, were less weighty than feathers in a scale that measures hundreds of tons. The very idea of balance was for the moment beyond her imagination. For a while indeed the pride of a woman at once young, beautiful, and accustomed to authority, had kept her firm in the determination to be loved for herself, as she believed that she deserved to be loved; and just so long as that remained, she had held her head high, confidently expecting that the mask of indifference would soon be shivered, that the eyes she adored would soften with warm light, that the hand she worshipped would tremble suddenly, as though waking to life within her own. But that pride was gone, and from its disappearance there had been but one step to the most utter degradation of soul to which a woman can descend, and from that again but one step more to a resolution almost stupid in its hardened obstinacy. But as though to show how completely she was dominated by the man whom she could not win even her last determination had yielded under the slightest pressure from his will. She had left her house beside him with the mad resolve never again to be parted from him, cost what it might, reputation, fortune, life itself. And yet ten minutes had not elapsed before she found herself alone, trusting to a mere word of his for the hope of ever seeing him again. She seemed to have no individuality left. He had spoken and she had obeyed. He had commanded and she had done his bidding. She was even more ashamed of this than of having wept, and sobbed, and dragged herself at his feet. In the first moment she had submitted, deluding herself with the idea she had expressed, that he was consigning her to a prison and that her freedom was dependent on his will. The foolish delusion vanished. She saw that she was free, when she chose, to descend the steps she had just mounted, to go out through the gate she had lately entered, and to go whithersoever she would, at the mere risk of meeting Israel Kafka. And that risk she heartily despised, being thoroughly brave by nature, and utterly indifferent to death by force of circumstance.

She comforted herself with the thought that the Wanderer would come to her, once at least, when she was pleased to send for him. She had that loyal belief inseparable from true love until violently overthrown by irrefutable evidence, and which sometimes has such power as to return even then, overthrowing the evidence of the senses themselves. Are there not men who trust women, and women who trust men, in spite of the vilest betrayals? Love is indeed often the inspirer of subjective visions, creating in the beloved object the qualities it admires and the virtues it adores, powerless to accept what it is not willing to see, dwelling in a fortress guarded by intangible, and therefore indestructible, fiction and proof against the artillery of facts. Unorna's confidence was, however, not misplaced. The man whose promise she had received had told the truth when he had said that he had never broken any promise whatsoever.

In this, at least, there was therefore comfort. On the morrow she would see him again. The moment of complete despair had passed when she had received that assurance from his lips, and as she thought of it, sitting in the absolute stillness of her room, the proportions of the storm grew less, and possible dimensions of a future hope greater – just as the seafarer when his ship lies in a flat calm of the oily harbour thinks half incredulously of the danger past, despises himself for the anxiety he felt, and vows that on the morrow he will face the waves again, though the winds blow ever so fiercely. In Unorna the master passion was as strong as ever. In a dim vision the wreck of her pride floated still in the stormy distance, but she turned her eyes away, for it was no longer a part of her. The spectre of her humiliation rose up and tried to taunt her with her shame – she almost smiled at the thought that she could still remember it. He lived, she lived, and he should yet be hers. As her physical weariness began to disappear in the absolute quiet and rest, her determination revived. Her power was not all gone yet. On the morrow she would see him again. She might still fix her eyes on his, and in an unguarded moment cast him into a deep sleep. She remembered that look on his face in the old cemetery. She had guessed rightly; it had been for the faint memory of Beatrice. But she would bring it back again, and it should be for her, for he should never wake again. Had she not done as much with the ancient scholar who for long years had lain in her home in that mysterious state, who obeyed when she commanded him to rise, and walk, to eat, to speak? Why not the Wanderer, then? To outward eyes he would be alive and awake, calm, natural, happy. And yet he would be sleeping. In that condition, at least, she could command his actions, his thoughts, and his words. How long could it be made to last? She did not know. Nature might rebel in the end and throw off the yoke of the heavily-imposed will. An interval might follow, full again of storm and passion and despair; but it would pass, and he would again fall under her influence. She had read, and Keyork Arabian had told her, of the marvels done every day by physicians of common power in the great hospitals and universities of the Empire, and elsewhere throughout Europe. None of them appeared to be men of extraordinary natural gifts. Their powers were but weakness compared with hers. Even with miserable, hysteric women they often had to try again and again before they could produce the hypnotic sleep for the first time. When they had got as far as that, indeed, they could bring their learning, their science, and their experience to bear – and they could make foolish experiments, familiar to Unorna from her childhood as the sights and sounds of her daily life. Few, if any of them, had even the power necessary to hypnotise an ordinarily strong man in health. She, on the contrary, had never failed in that, and at the first trial, except with Keyork Arabian, a man of whom she said in her heart, half in jest and half superstitiously, that he was not a man at all, but a devil or a monster over whom earthly influences had no control.

All her energy returned. The colour came back to her face, her eyes sparkled, her strong white hands contracted and opened, and closed again, as though she would grasp something. The room, too, had become warmer and she had forgotten to lay aside her furs. She longed for more air and, rising, walked across the room. It occurred to her that the great corridor would be deserted and as quiet as her own apartment, and she went out and began to pace the stone flags, her head high, looking straight before her.

She wished that she had him there now, and she was angry at the thought that she had not seen earlier how easily it could all be done. However strong he might be, having twice been under her influence before he could not escape it again. In those moments when they had stood together before the great dark buildings of the Clementinum, it might all have been accomplished; and now, she must wait until the morning. But her mind was determined. It mattered not how, it mattered not in what state, he should be hers. No one would know what she had done. It was nothing to her that he would be wholly unconscious of his past life – had she not already made him forget the most important part of it? He would still be himself, and yet he would love her, and speak lovingly to her, and act as she would have him act. Everything could be done, and she would risk nothing, for she would marry him and make him her lawful husband, and they would spend their lives together, in peace, in the house wherein she had so abased herself before him, foolishly believing that, as a mere woman, she could win him.

She paced the corridor, passing and repassing beneath the light of the single lamp that hung in the middle, walking quickly, with a sensation of pleasure in the movement and in the cold draught that fanned her cheek.

Then she heard footsteps distinct from the echo of her own and she stood still. Two women were coming towards her through the gloom. She waited near her own door, supposing that they would pass her. As they came near, she saw that the one was a nun, habited in the plain grey robe and black and white head-dress of the order. The other was a lady dressed, like herself, in black. The light burned so badly that as the two stopped and stood for a moment conversing together, Unorna could not clearly distinguish their faces. Then the lady entered one of the rooms, the third or the fourth from Unorna's, and the nun remained standing outside, apparently hesitating whether to turn to the right or to the left, or asking herself in which direction her occupations called her. Unorna made a movement, and at the sound of her foot the nun came towards her.

'Sister Paul!' Unorna exclaimed, recognising her as her face came under the glare of the lamp, and holding out her hands.

'Unorna!' cried the nun, with an intonation of surprise and pleasure. 'I did not know that you were here. What brings you back to us?'

'A caprice, Sister Paul – nothing but a caprice. I shall perhaps be gone tomorrow.'

'I am sorry,' answered the sister. 'One night is but a short retreat from the world.' She shook her head rather sadly.

'Much may happen in a night,' replied Unorna with a smile. 'You used to tell me that the soul knew nothing of time. Have you changed your mind? Come into my room and let us talk. I have not forgotten your hours. You can have nothing to do for the moment, unless it is supper-time.'

'We have just finished,' said Sister Paul, entering readily enough. 'The other lady who is staying here insisted upon supping in the guests' refectory – out of curiosity perhaps, poor thing – and I met her on the stairs as she was coming up.'

'Are she and I the only ones here?' Unorna asked carelessly.

'Yes. There is no one else, and she only came this morning. You see it is still the carnival season in the world. It is in Lent that the great ladies come to us, and then we have often not a room free.'

The nun smiled sadly, shaking her head again, in a way that seemed habitual with her.

'After all,' she added, as Unorna said nothing, 'it is better that they should come then, rather than not at all, though I often think it would be better still if they spent carnival in the convent and Lent in the world.'

'The world you speak of would be a gloomy place if you had the ordering of it, Sister Paul!' observed Unorna with a little laugh.

'Ah, well! I dare say it would seem so to you. I know little enough of the world as you understand it, save for what our guests tell me – and, indeed, I am glad that I do not know more.'

'You know almost as much as I do.'

The sister looked long and earnestly into Unorna's face as though searching for something. She was a thin, pale woman over forty years of age. Not a wrinkle marked her waxen skin, and her hair was entirely concealed under the smooth head-dress, but her age was in her eyes.

'What is your life, Unorna?' she asked suddenly. 'We hear strange tales of it sometimes, though we know also that you do great works of charity. But we hear strange tales and strange words.'

'Do you?' Unorna suppressed a smile of scorn. 'What do people say of me? I never asked.'

'Strange things, strange things,' repeated the nun with a shake of the head.

'What are they? Tell me one of them, as an instance.'

'I should fear to offend you – indeed I am sure I should, though we were good friends once.'

'And are still. The more reason why you should tell me what is said. Of course I am alone in the world, and people will always tell vile tales of women who have no one to protect them.'

'No, no,' Sister Paul hastened to assure her. 'As a woman, no word has reached us that touches your fair name. On the contrary, I have heard worldly women say much more that is good of you in that respect than they will say of each other. But there are other things,

Unorna – other things which fill me with fear for you. They call you by a name that makes me shudder when I hear it.'

'A name?' repeated Unorna in surprise and with considerable curiosity.

'A name – a word – what you will – no, I cannot tell you, and besides, it must be untrue.'

Unorna was silent for a moment and then understood. She laughed aloud with perfect unconcern.

'I know!' she cried. 'How foolish of me! They call me the Witch – of course.'

Sister Paul's face grew very grave, and she immediately crossed herself devoutly, looking askance at Unorna as she did so. But Unorna only laughed again.

'Perhaps it is very foolish,' said the nun, 'but I cannot bear to hear such a thing said of you.'

'It is not said in earnest. Do you know why they call me the Witch? It is very simple. It is because I can make people sleep – people who are suffering or mad or in great sorrow, and then they rest. That is all my magic.'

'You can put people to sleep? Anybody?' Sister Paul opened her faded eyes very wide. 'But that is not natural,' she added in a perplexed tone. 'And what is not natural cannot be right.'

'And is all right that is natural?' asked Unorna thoughtfully.

'It is not natural,' repeated the other. 'How do you do it? Do you use strange words and herbs and incantations?'

Unorna laughed again, but the nun seemed shocked by her levity and she forced herself to be grave.

'No, indeed!' she answered. 'I look into their eyes and tell them to sleep – and they do. Poor Sister Paul! You are behind the age in the dear old convent here. The thing is done in half of the great hospitals of Europe every day, and men and women are cured in that way of diseases that paralyse them in body as well as in mind. Men study to learn how it is done; it is as common today, as a means of healing, as the medicines you know by name and taste. It is called hypnotism.'

Again the sister crossed herself.

'I have heard the word, I think,' she said, as though she thought there might be something diabolical in it. 'And do you heal the sick in this way by means of this – thing?'

'Sometimes,' Unorna answered. 'There is an old man, for instance, whom I have kept alive for many years by making him sleep – a great deal.' Unorna smiled a little.

'But you have no words with it? Nothing?'

'Nothing. It is my will. That is all.'

'But if it is of good, and not of the Evil One, there should be a prayer with it. Could you not say a prayer with it, Unorna?'

'I dare say I could,' replied the other, trying not to laugh. 'But that would be doing two things at once; my will would be weakened.'

'It cannot be of good,' said the nun. 'It is not natural, and it is not true that the prayer can distract the will from the performance of a good deed.' She shook her head more energetically than usual. 'And it is not good either that you should be called a witch, you who have lived here amongst us.'

'It is not my fault!' exclaimed Unorna, somewhat annoyed by her persistence. 'And besides, Sister Paul, even if the devil is in it, it would be right all the same.'

The nun held up her hands in holy horror, and her jaw dropped.

'My child! My child! How can you say such things to me!'

'It is very true,' Unorna answered, quietly smiling at her amazement. 'If people who are ill are made well, is it not a real good, even if the Evil One does it? Is it not good to make him do good, if one can, even against his will?'

'No, no!' cried Sister Paul, in great distress. 'Do not talk like that – let us not talk of it at all! Whatever it is, it is bad, and I do not understand it, and I am sure that none of us here could, no matter how well you explained it. But if you will do it, Unorna, my dear child, then say a prayer each time, against temptation and the devil's works.'

With that the good nun crossed herself a third time, and unconsciously, from force of habit, began to tell her beads with one hand, mechanically smoothing her broad, starched collar with the other. Unorna was silent for a few minutes, plucking at the sable lining of the cloak which lay beside her upon the sofa where she had dropped it.

'Let us talk of other things,' she said at last. 'Talk of the other lady who is here. Who is she? What brings her into retreat at this time of year?'

'Poor thing – yes, she is very unhappy,' answered Sister Paul. 'It is a sad story, so far as I have heard it. Her father is just dead, and she is alone in the world. The Abbess received a letter yesterday from the Cardinal Archbishop, requesting that we would receive her, and this morning she came. His eminence knew her father, it appears. She is only to be here for a short time, I believe, until her relations come to take her home to her own country. Her father was taken ill in a country place near the city, which he had hired for the shooting season, and the poor girl was left all alone out there. The Cardinal thought she would be safer and perhaps less unhappy with us while she is waiting.'

'Of course,' said Unorna, with a faint interest. 'How old is she, poor child?'

'She is not a child, she must be five and twenty years old, though perhaps her sorrow makes her look older than she is.'

'And what is her name?'

'Beatrice. I cannot remember the name of the family.'

Unorna started.

Chapter 19

'What is it?' asked the nun, noticing Unorna's sudden movement.

'Nothing; the name of Beatrice is familiar to me, that is all. It suggested something.'

Though Sister Paul was as unworldly as five and twenty years of cloistered life can make a woman who is naturally simple in mind and devout in thought, she possessed that faculty of quick observation which is learned as readily, and exercised perhaps as constantly, in the midst of a small community, where each member is in some measure dependent upon all the rest for the daily pittance of ideas, as in wider spheres of life.

'You may have seen this lady, or you may have heard of her,' she said.

'I would like to see her,' Unorna answered thoughtfully.

She was thinking of all the possibilities in the case. She remembered the clearness and precision of the Wanderer's first impression, when he first told her how he had seen Beatrice in the Teyn Kirche, and she reflected that the name was a very uncommon one. The Beatrice of his story too had a father and no other relation, and was supposed to be travelling with him. By the uncertain light in the corridor Unorna had not been able to distinguish the lady's features, but the impression she had received had been that she was dark, as Beatrice was. There was no reason in the nature of things why this should not be the woman whom the Wanderer loved. It was natural enough that, being left alone in a strange city at such a moment, she should have sought refuge in a convent, and this being admitted it followed that she would naturally have been advised to retire to the one in which Unorna found herself, it being the one in which ladies were most frequently received as guests. Unorna could hardly trust herself to speak. She was conscious that Sister Paul was watching her, and she turned her face from the lamp.

'There can be no difficulty about your seeing her, or talking with her, if you wish it,' said the nun. 'She told me that she would be at Compline at nine o'clock. If you will be there yourself you can see her come in, and watch her when she goes out. Do you think you have ever seen her?'

'No,' answered Unorna in an odd tone. 'I am sure that I have not.'

Sister Paul concluded from Unorna's manner that she must have reason to believe that the guest was identical with someone of whom she had heard very often. Her manner was abstracted and she seemed ill at ease. But that might be the result of fatigue.

'Are you not hungry?' asked the nun. 'You have had nothing since you came, I am sure.'

'No – yes – it is true,' answered Unorna. 'I had forgotten. It would be very kind of you to send me something.'

Sister Paul rose with alacrity, to Unorna's great relief.

'I will see to it,' she said, holding out her hand. 'We shall meet in the morning. Good-night.'

'Good-night, dear Sister Paul. Will you say a prayer for me?' She added the question suddenly, by an impulse of which she was hardly conscious.

'Indeed I will – with all my heart, my dear child,' answered the nun looking earnestly into her face. 'You are not happy in your life,' she added, with a slow, sad movement of her head.

'No – I am not happy. But I will be.'

'I fear not,' said Sister Paul, almost under her breath, as she went out softly.

Unorna was left alone. She could not sit still in her extreme anxiety. It was agonising to think that the woman she longed to see was so near her, but that she could not, upon any reasonable pretext, go and knock at her door and see her and speak to her. She felt also a terrible doubt as to whether she would recognise her, at first sight, as the same woman whose shadow had passed between herself and the Wanderer on that eventful day a month ago. The shadow had been veiled, but she had a prescient consciousness of the features beneath the veil. Nevertheless, she might be mistaken. It would be necessary to seek her acquaintance by some excuse and endeavour to draw from her some portion of her story, enough to confirm Unorna's suspicions, or to prove conclusively that they were unfounded. To do this, Unorna herself needed all her strength and coolness, and she was glad when a lay sister entered the room bringing her evening meal.

There were moments when Unorna, in favourable circumstances, was able to sink into the so-called state of second sight, by an act of volition, and she wished now that she could close her eyes and see the face of the woman who was only separated from her by two or three walls. But that was not possible in this case. To be successful she would have needed some sort of guiding thread, or she must have already known the person she wished to see. She could not command that inexplicable condition as she could dispose of her other powers, at all times and in almost all moods. She felt that if she were at present capable of falling into the trance state at all, her mind would wander uncontrolled in some other direction. There was nothing to be done but to have patience.

The lay sister went out. Unorna ate mechanically what had been set before her and waited. She felt that a crisis perhaps more terrible than that through which she had lately passed was at hand, if the stranger should prove to be indeed the Beatrice whom the Wanderer loved. Her brain was in a whirl when she thought of being brought face to face with the woman who had been before her, and every cruel and ruthless instinct of her nature rose and took shape in plans for her rival's destruction.

She opened her door, careless of the draught of frozen air that rushed in from the corridor. She wished to hear the lady's footstep when she left her room to go to the church, and she sat down and remained motionless, fearing lest her own footfall should prevent the sound from reaching her. The heavy-toned bells began to ring, far off in the night.

At last it came, the opening of a door, the slight noise made by a light tread upon the pavement. She rose quietly and went out, following in the same direction. She could see nothing but a dark shadow moving before her towards the opposite end of the passage, farther and farther from the hanging lamp. Unorna could hear her own heart beating as she followed, first to the right, then to the left. There was another light at this point. The lady had noticed that someone was coming behind her and turned her head to look back. The delicate, dark profile stood out clearly. Unorna held her breath, walking swiftly forward. But in a moment the lady went on, and entered the chapel-like room from which a great balconied window looked down into the church above the choir. As Unorna went in, she saw her kneeling upon one of the stools, her hands folded, her head inclined, her eyes closed, a black veil loosely thrown over her still blacker hair and falling down upon her shoulder without hiding her face.

Unorna sank upon her knees, compressing her lips to restrain the incoherent exclamation that almost broke from them in spite of her, clasping her hands desperately, so that the faint blue veins stood out upon the marble surface.

Below, hundreds of candles blazed upon the altar in the choir and sent their full yellow radiance up to the faces of the two women, as they knelt there almost side by side, both young, both beautiful, but utterly unlike. In a single glance Unorna had understood that it was true. An arm's length separated her from the rival whose very existence made her own happiness an utter impossibility. With unchanging, unwilling gaze she examined every detail of that beauty which the Wanderer had so loved that even when forgotten there was no sight in his eyes for other women.

It was indeed such a face as a man would find it hard to forget. Unorna, seeing the reflection of it in the Wanderer's mind, had fancied it otherwise, though she could not but recognise the reality from the impression she had received. She had imagined it more ethereal, more faint, more sexless, more angelic, as she had seen it in her thoughts. Divine it was, but womanly beyond Unorna's own. Dark, delicately aquiline, tall and noble, the purity it expressed was of earth and not of heaven. It was not transparent, for there was life in every feature; it was sad indeed almost beyond human sadness, but it was sad with the mortal sorrows of this world, not with the unfathomable melancholy of the suffering saint. The lips were human, womanly, pure and tender, but not formed for speech of prayer alone. The drooping lids, not drawn, but darkened with faint, uneven shadows by the flow of many tears, were slowly lifted now and again, disclosing a vision of black eyes not meant for endless weeping, nor made so deep and warm only to strain their sight towards heaven above, forgetting earth below. Unorna knew that those same eyes could gleam, and flash, and blaze, with love and hate and anger, that under the rich, pale skin, the blood could rise and ebb with the changing tide of the heart, that the warm lips could part with passion and, moving, form words of love. She saw pride in the wide sensitive nostrils, strength in the even brow, and queenly dignity in the perfect poise of the head upon the slender throat. And the clasped hands were womanly, too, neither full and white and heavy like those of a marble statue, as Unorna's were, nor thin and over-sensitive like those of holy women in old pictures, but real and living, delicate in outline, but not without nervous strength, hands that might linger in another's, not wholly passive, but all responsive to the thrill of a loving touch.

It was very hard to bear. A better woman than Unorna might have felt something evil and cruel and hating in her heart, at the sight of so much beauty in one who held her place, in the queen of the kingdom where she longed to reign. Unorna's cheek grew very pale, and her unlike eyes were fierce and dangerous. It was well for her that she could not speak to Beatrice then, for she wore no mask, and the dark beauty would have seen the danger of death in the face of the fair, and would have turned and defended herself in time.

But the sweet singing of the nuns came softly up from below, echoing to the groined roof, rising and falling, high and low; and the full radiance of the many waxen tapers shone steadily from the great altar, gilding and warming statue and cornice and ancient moulding, and casting deep shadows into all the places that it could not reach. And still the two women knelt in their high balcony, the one rapt in fervent prayer, the other wondering that the presence of such hatred as hers should have no power to kill, and all the time making a supreme effort to compose her own features into the expression of friendly sympathy and interest which she knew she would need so soon as the singing ceased and it was time to leave the church again.

The psalms were finished. There was a pause, and then the words of the ancient hymn floated up to Unorna's ears, familiar in years gone by. Almost unconsciously she herself, by force of old habit, joined in the first verse. Then, suddenly, she stopped, not realising, indeed, the horrible gulf that lay between the words that passed her lips and the thoughts that were at work in her heart, but silenced by the near sound of a voice less rich and full, but far more exquisite and tender than her own. Beatrice was singing, too, with joined hands, and parted lips, and upturned face.

'Let dreams be far, and phantasms of the night – bind Thou our Foe,' sang Beatrice in long, sweet notes.

Unorna heard no more. The light dazzled her, and the blood beat in her heart. It seemed as though no prayer that was ever prayed could be offered up more directly against herself, and the voice that sang it, though not loud, had the rare power of carrying every syllable distinctly in its magic tones, even to a great distance. As she knelt, it was as if Beatrice had been even nearer, and had breathed the words into her very ear. Afraid to look round, lest her face should betray her emotion, Unorna glanced down at the kneeling nuns. She started. Sister Paul, alone of them all, was looking up, her faded eyes fixed on Unorna's with a look that implored and yet despaired, her clasped hands a little raised from the low desk before her, most evidently offering up the words with the whole fervent intention of her pure soul, as an intercession for Unorna's sins.

For one moment the strong, cruel heart almost wavered, not through fear, but under the nameless impression that sometimes takes hold of men and women. The divine voice beside her seemed to dominate the hundred voices below; the nun's despairing look chilled for one instant all her love and all her hatred, so that she longed to be alone, away from it all, and for ever. But the hymn ended, the voice was silent, and Sister Paul's glance turned again towards the altar. The moment was passed and Unorna was again what she had been before.

Then followed the canticle, the voice of the prioress in the versicles after that, and the voices of the nuns, no longer singing, as they made the responses; the Creed, a few more versicles and responses, the short, final prayers, and all was over. From the church below came up the soft sound that many women make when they move silently together. The nuns were passing out in their appointed order.

Beatrice remained kneeling a few moments longer, crossed herself and then rose. At the same moment Unorna was on her feet. The necessity for immediate action at all costs restored the calm to her face and the tactful skill to her actions. She reached the door first, and then, half turning her head, stood aside, as though to give Beatrice precedence in passing. Beatrice glanced at her face for the first time, and then by a courteous movement of the head signified that Unorna should go out first. Unorna appeared to hesitate, Beatrice to protest. Both women smiled a little, and Unorna, with a gesture of submission, passed through the doorway. She had managed it so well that it was almost impossible to avoid speaking as they threaded the long corridors together. Unorna allowed a moment to pass, as though to let her companion understand the slight awkwardness of the situation, and then addressed her in a tone of quiet and natural civility.

'We seem to be the only ladies in retreat,' she said.

'Yes,' Beatrice answered. Even in that one syllable something of the quality of her thrilling voice vibrated for an instant. They walked a few steps farther in silence.

'I am not exactly in retreat,' she said presently, either because she felt that it would be almost rude to say nothing, or because she wished her position to be clearly understood. 'I am waiting here for someone who is to come for me.'

'It is a very quiet place to rest in,' said Unorna. 'I am fond of it.'

'You often come here, perhaps.'

'Not now,' answered Unorna. 'But I was here for a long time when I was very young.'

By a common instinct, as they fell into conversation, they began to walk more slowly, side by side.

'Indeed,' said Beatrice, with a slight increase of interest. 'Then you were brought up here by the nuns?'

'Not exactly. It was a sort of refuge for me when I was almost a child. I was left here alone, until I was thought old enough to take care of myself.'

There was a little bitterness in her tone, intentional, but masterly in its truth to nature.

'Left by your parents?' Beatrice asked. The question seemed almost inevitable.

'I had none. I never knew a father or a mother.' Unorna's voice grew sad with each syllable.

They had entered the great corridor in which their apartments were situated, and were approaching Beatrice's door. They walked more and more slowly, in silence during the last few moments, after Unorna had spoken. Unorna sighed. The passing breath travelling on the air of the lonely place seemed both to invite and to offer sympathy.

'My father died last week,' Beatrice said in a very low tone, that was not quite steady. 'I am quite alone – here and in the world.'

She laid her hand upon the latch and her deep black eyes rested upon Unorna's, as though almost, but not quite, conveying an invitation, hungry for human comfort, yet too proud to ask it.

'I am very lonely, too,' said Unorna. 'May I sit with you for a while?'

She had but just time to make the bold stroke that was necessary. In another moment she knew that Beatrice would have disappeared within. Her heart beat violently until the answer came. She had been successful.

'Will you, indeed?' Beatrice exclaimed. 'I am poor company, but I shall be very glad if you will come in.'

She opened her door, and Unorna entered. The apartment was almost exactly like her own in size and shape and furniture, but it already had the air of being inhabited. There were books upon the table, and a square jewel-case, and an old silver frame containing a large photograph of a stern, dark man in middle age – Beatrice's father, as Unorna at once understood. Cloaks and furs lay in some confusion upon the chairs, a large box stood with the lid raised, against the wall, displaying a quantity of lace, among which lay silks and ribbons of soft colours.

'I only came this morning,' Beatrice said, as though to apologise for the disorder.

Unorna sank down in a corner of the sofa, shading her eyes from the bright lamp with her hand. She could not help looking at Beatrice, but she felt that she must not let her scrutiny be too apparent, nor her conversation too eager. Beatrice was proud and strong, and could doubtless be very cold and forbidding when she chose.

'And do you expect to be here long?' Unorna asked, as Beatrice established herself at the other end of the sofa.

'I cannot tell,' was the answer. 'I may be here but a few days, or I may have to stay a month.

'I lived here for years,' said Unorna thoughtfully. 'I suppose it would be impossible now – I should die of apathy and inanition.' She laughed in a subdued way, as though respecting Beatrice's mourning. 'But I was young then,' she added, suddenly withdrawing her hand from her eyes, so that the full light of the lamp fell upon her.

She chose to show that she, too, was beautiful, and she knew that Beatrice had as yet hardly seen her face as they passed through the gloomy corridors. It was an instinct of vanity, and yet, for her purpose, it was the right one. The effect was sudden and unexpected, and Beatrice looked at her almost fixedly, in undisguised admiration.

'Young then!' she exclaimed. 'You are young now!'

'Less young than I was then,' Unorna answered with a little sigh, followed instantly by a smile.

'I am five and twenty,' said Beatrice, woman enough to try and force a confession from her new acquaintance.

'Are you? I would not have thought it – we are nearly of an age – quite, perhaps, for I am not yet twenty-six. But then, it is not the years – ' She stopped suddenly.

Beatrice wondered whether Unorna were married or not. Considering the age she admitted and her extreme beauty it seemed probable that she must be. It occurred to her that the acquaintance had been made without any presentation, and that neither knew the other's name.

'Since I am a little the younger,' she said, 'I should tell you who I am.'

Unorna made a slight movement. She was on the point of saying that she knew already – and too well.

'I am Beatrice Varanger.'

'I am Unorna.' She could not help a sort of cold defiance that sounded in her tone as she pronounced the only name she could call hers.

'Unorna?' Beatrice repeated, courteously enough, but with an air of surprise.

'Yes – that is all. It seems strange to you? They called me so because I was born in February, in the month we call Unor. Indeed it is strange, and so is my story – though it would have little interest for you.'

'Forgive me, you are wrong, It would interest me immensely – if you would tell me a little of it; but I am such a stranger to you – '

'I do not feel as though you are that,' Unorna answered with a very gentle smile.

'You are very kind to say so,' said Beatrice quietly.

Unorna was perfectly well aware that it must seem strange, to say the least of it, that she should tell Beatrice the wild story of her life, when they had as yet exchanged barely a hundred words. But she cared little what Beatrice thought, provided that she could interest her. She had a distinct intention of making the time slip by unnoticed, until it should be late.

She related her history, so far as it was known to herself, simply and graphically, substantially as it has been already set forth, but with an abundance of anecdote and comment which enhanced the interest and at the same time extended its limits, interspersing her monologues with remarks which called for an answer and which served as tests of her companion's attention. She hinted but lightly at her possession of unusual power over animals, and spoke not at all of the influence she could exert upon people. Beatrice listened eagerly. She could have told, on her part, that for years her own life had been dull and empty, and that it was long since she had talked with anyone who had so roused her interest.

At last Unorna was silent. She had reached the period of her life which had begun a month before that time, and at that point her story ended.

'Then you are not married?' Beatrice's tone expressed an interrogation and a certain surprise.

'No,' said Unorna, 'I am not married. And you, if I may ask?'

Beatrice started visibly. It had not occurred to her that the question might seem a natural one for Unorna to ask, although she had said that she was alone in the world. Unorna might have supposed her to have lost her husband. But Unorna could see that it was not surprise alone that had startled her. The question, as she knew it must, had roused a deep and painful train of thought.

'No,' said Beatrice, in an altered voice. 'I am not married. I shall never marry.'

A short silence followed, during which she turned her face away.

'I have pained you,' said Unorna with profound sympathy and regret. 'Forgive me! How could I be so tactless!'

'How could you know?' Beatrice asked simply, not attempting to deny the suggestion.

But Unorna was suffering too. She had allowed herself to imagine that in the long years which had passed Beatrice might perhaps have forgotten. It had even crossed her mind that she might indeed be married. But in the few words, and in the tremor that accompanied them, as well as in the increased pallor of Beatrice's face, she detected a love not less deep and constant and unforgotten than the Wanderer's own.

'Forgive me,' Unorna repeated. 'I might have guessed. I have loved too.'

She knew that here, at least, she could not feign and she could not control her voice, but with supreme judgment of the effect she allowed herself to be carried beyond all reserve. In the one short sentence her whole passion expressed itself, genuine, deep, strong, ruthless. She let the words come as they would, and Beatrice was startled by the passionate cry that burst from the heart, so wholly unrestrained.

For a long time neither spoke again, and neither looked at the other. To all appearances Beatrice was the first to regain her self-possession. And then, all at once the words came to her lips which could be restrained no longer. For years she had kept silence, for there had been no one to whom she could speak. For years she had sought him, as best she could, as he had sought her, fruitlessly and at last hopelessly. And she had known that her father was seeking him also, everywhere, that he might drag her to the ends of the earth at the mere suspicion of the Wanderer's presence in the same country. It had amounted to a madness with him of the kind not seldom seen. Beatrice might marry whom she pleased, but not the one man she loved. Day by day and year by year their two strong wills had been silently opposed, and neither the one nor the other had ever been unconscious of the struggle, nor had either yielded a hair's-breadth. But Beatrice had been at her father's mercy, for he could take her whither he would, and in that she could not resist him. Never in that time had she lost faith in the devotion of the man she sought, and at last it was only in the belief that he was dead that she could discover an explanation of his failure to find her. Still she would not change, and still, through the years, she loved more and more truly, and passionately, and unchangingly.

The feeling that she was in the presence of a passion as great, as unhappy, and as masterful as her own, unloosed her tongue. Such things happen in this strange world. Men and women of deep and strong feelings, outwardly cold, reserved, taciturn and proud, have been known, once in their lives, to pour out the secrets of their hearts to a stranger or a mere acquaintance, as they could never have done to a friend.

Beatrice seemed scarcely conscious of what she was saying, or of Unorna's presence. The words, long kept back and sternly restrained, fell with a strange strength from her lips, and there was not one of them from first to last that did not sheathe itself like a sharp knife in Unorna's heart. The enormous jealousy of Beatrice which had been growing within her beside her love during the last month was reaching the climax of its overwhelming magnitude. She hardly knew when Beatrice ceased speaking, for the words were still all ringing in her ears, and clashing madly in her own breast, and prompting her fierce nature to do some violent deed. But Beatrice looked for no sympathy and did not see Unorna's face. She had forgotten Unorna herself at the last, as she sat staring at the opposite wall.

Then she rose quickly, and taking something from the jewel-box, thrust it into Unorna's hands.

'I cannot tell why I have told you – but I have. You shall see him too. What does it matter? We have both loved, we are both un-happy – we shall never meet again.'

'What is it?' Unorna tried to ask, holding the closed case in her hands. She knew what was within it well enough, and her self-command was forsaking her. It was almost more than she could bear. It was as though Beatrice were wreaking vengeance on her, instead of her destroying her rival as she had meant to do, sooner or later.

Beatrice took the thing from her, opened it, gazed at it a moment, and put it again into Unorna's hands. 'It was like him,' she said, watching her companion as though to see what effect the portrait would produce. Then she shrank back.

Unorna was looking at her. Her face was livid and unnaturally drawn, and the extraordinary contrast in the colour of her two eyes was horribly apparent. The one seemed to freeze, the other to be on fire. The strongest and worst passions that can play upon the human soul were all expressed with awful force in the distorted mask, and not a trace of the magnificent beauty so lately there was visible. Beatrice shrank back in horror.

'You know him!' she cried, half guessing at the truth.

'I know him – and I love him,' said Unorna slowly and fiercely, her eyes fixed on her enemy, and gradually leaning towards her so as to bring her face nearer and nearer to Beatrice.

The dark woman tried to rise, and could not. There was worse than anger, or hatred, or the intent to kill, in those dreadful eyes. There was a fascination from which no living thing could escape. She tried to scream, to shut out the vision, to raise her hand as a screen before it. Nearer and nearer it came, and she could feel the warm breath of it upon her cheek. Then her brain reeled, her limbs relaxed, and her head fell back against the wall.

'I know him, and I love him,' were the last words Beatrice heard.

Chapter 20 *

Unorna was hardly conscious of what she had done. She had not had the intention of making Beatrice sleep, for she had no distinct intention whatever at that moment. Her words and her look had been but the natural results of overstrained passion, and she repeated what she had said again and again, and gazed long and fiercely into Beatrice's face before she realised that she had unintentionally thrown her rival

* The deeds here recounted are not imaginary. Not very long ago the sacrilege which Unorna attempted was actually committed at night in a Catholic church in London, under circumstances that clearly proved the intention of some person or persons to defile the consecrated wafers. A case of hypnotic suggestion to the committal of a crime in a convent occurred in Hungary not many years since, with a different object, namely, a daring robbery, but precisely as here described. A complete account of the case will be found, with authority and evidence, in a pamphlet entitled *Eine experimentale Studie auf dem Gebiete des Hypnotismus*, by Dr. R. von Krafft-Ebing, Professor of Psychiatry and for nervous diseases, in the University of Gratz, second edition, Stuttgart, Ferdinand Enke, 1889. It is not possible, in a work of fiction, to quote learned authorities at every chapter, but it may be said here, and once for all, that all the most important situations have been taken from cases which have come under medical observation within the last few years.

and enemy into the intermediate state. It is rarely that the first stage of hypnotism produces the same consequences in two different individuals. In Beatrice it took the form of total unconsciousness, as though she had merely fainted away.

Unorna gradually regained her self-possession. After all, Beatrice had told her nothing which she did not either wholly know or partly guess, and her anger was not the result of the revelation but of the way in which the story had been told. Word after word, phrase after phrase had cut her and stabbed her to the quick, and when Beatrice had thrust the miniature into her hands her wrath had risen in spite of herself. But now that she had returned to a state in which she could think connectedly, and now that she saw Beatrice asleep before her, she did not regret what she had unwittingly done. From the first moment when, in the balcony over the church, she had realised that she was in the presence of the woman she hated, she had determined to destroy her. To accomplish this she would in any case have used her especial weapons, and though she had intended to steal by degrees upon her enemy, lulling her to sleep by a more gentle fascination, at an hour when the whole convent should be quiet, yet since the first step had been made unexpectedly and without her will, she did not regret it.

She leaned back and looked at Beatrice during several minutes, smiling to herself from time to time, scornfully and cruelly. Then she rose and locked the outer door and closed the inner one carefully. She knew from long ago that no sound could then find its way to the corridor without. She came back and sat down again, and again looked at the sleeping face, and she admitted for the hundredth time that evening, that Beatrice was very beautiful.

'If he could see us now!' she exclaimed aloud.

The thought suggested something to her. She would like to see herself beside this other woman and compare the beauty he loved with the beauty that could not touch him. It was very easy. She found a small mirror, and set it up upon the back of the sofa, on a level with Beatrice's head. Then she changed the position of the lamp and looked at herself, and touched her hair, and smoothed her brow, and loosened the black lace about her white throat. And she looked from herself to Beatrice, and back to herself again, many times.

'It is strange that black should suit us both so well – she so dark and I so fair!' she said. 'She will look well when she is dead.'

She gazed again for many seconds at the sleeping woman.

'But he will not see her, then,' she added, rising to her feet and laying the mirror on the table.

She began to walk up and down the room as was her habit when in deep thought, turning over in her mind the deed to be done and the surest and best way of doing it. It never occurred to her that Beatrice could be allowed to live beyond that night. If the woman had been but an unconscious obstacle in her path Unorna would have spared her life, but as matters stood, she had no inclination to be merciful.

There was nothing to prevent the possibility of a meeting between Beatrice and the Wanderer, if Beatrice remained alive. They were in the same city together, and their paths might cross at any moment. The Wanderer had forgotten, but it was not sure that the artificial forgetfulness would be proof against an actual sight of the woman once so dearly loved. The same consideration was true of Beatrice. She, too, might be made to forget, though it was always an experiment of uncertain issue and of more than uncertain result, even when successful, so far as duration was concerned. Unorna reasoned coldly with herself, recalling all that Keyork Arabian had told her and all that she had read. She tried to admit that Beatrice might be disposed of in some other way, but the difficulties seemed to be insurmountable. To effect such a disappearance Unorna must find some safe place in which the wretched woman might drag out her existence undiscovered. But Beatrice was not like the old beggar who in his hundredth year had leaned against Unorna's door, unnoticed and uncared for, and had been taken in and had never been seen again. The case was different. The aged scholar, too, had been cared for as he could not have been cared for elsewhere, and, in the event of an inquiry being made, he could be produced at any moment, and would even afford a brilliant example of Unorna's charitable doings. But Beatrice was a stranger and a person of some importance in the world. The Cardinal Archbishop himself had directed the nuns to receive her, and they were responsible for her safety. To spirit her away in the night would be a dangerous thing. Wherever she was to be taken, Unorna would have to lead her there alone. Unorna would herself be missed. Sister Paul already suspected that the name of Witch was more than a mere appellation. There would be a search made, and suspicion might easily fall upon Unorna, who would have been obliged, of course, to conceal her enemy in her own house for lack of any other convenient place.

There was no escape from the deed. Beatrice must die. Unorna could produce death in a form which could leave no trace, and it would be attributed to a weakness of the heart. Does anyone account otherwise for those sudden deaths which are no longer unfrequent in the world? A man, a woman, is to all appearances in perfect health. He or she was last seen by a friend, who describes the conversation accurately, and expresses astonishment at the catastrophe which followed so closely upon the visit. He or she is found alone by a servant, or a third person, in a profound lethargy from which neither restoratives nor violent shocks upon the nerves can produce any awakening. In one hour, or a few hours, it is over. There is an examination, and the authorities pronounce an ambiguous verdict – death from a syncope of the heart. Such things happen, they say, with a shake of the head. And, indeed, they know that such things really do happen, and they suspect that they do not happen naturally; but there is no evidence, not even so much as may be detected in a clever case of vegetable poisoning. The heart has stopped beating, and death has followed. There are wise men by the score today who do not ask 'What made it stop?' but 'Who made it stop?' But they have no evidence to bring, and the new jurisprudence, which in some countries covers the cases of thefts and frauds committed under hypnotic suggestion, cannot as yet lay down the law for cases where a man has been told to die, and dies – from 'weakness of the heart'. And yet it is known, and well known, that by hypnotic suggestion the pulse can be made to fall to the lowest number of beatings consistent with life, and that the temperature of the body can be commanded beforehand to stand at a certain degree and fraction of a degree at a certain hour, high or low, as may be desired. Let those who do not believe read the accounts of what is done from day to day in the great European seats of learning, accounts of which every one bears the name of some man speaking with authority and responsible to the world of science for every word he speaks, and doubly so for every word he writes. A few believe in the antiquated doctrine of electric animal currents, the vast majority are firm in the belief that the influence is a moral one – all admit that whatever force, or influence, lies at the root of hypnotism, the effects it can produce are practically unlimited, terrible in their comprehensiveness, and almost entirely unprovided for in the scheme of modern criminal law.

Unorna was sure of herself, and of her strength to perform what she contemplated. There lay the dark beauty in the corner of the sofa, where she had sat and talked so long, and told her last story, the story of her life which was now to end. A few determined words spoken in her ear, a pressure of the hand upon the brow and the heart, and she would never wake again. She would lie there still, until they found her, hour after hour, the pulse growing weaker and weaker, the delicate hands colder, the face more set. At the last, there would be a convulsive shiver of the queenly form, and that would be the end. The physicians and the authorities would come and would speak of a weakness of the heart, and there would be masses sung for her soul, and she would rest in peace.

Her soul? In peace? Unorna stood still. Was that to be all her vengeance upon the woman who stood between her and happiness? Was there to be nothing but that, nothing but the painless passing of the pure young spirit from earth to heaven? Was no one to suffer for all Unorna's pain? It was not enough. There must be more than that. And yet, what more? That was the question. What imaginable wealth of agony would be a just retribution for her existence? Unorna could lead her, as she had led Israel Kafka, through the life and death of a martyr, through a life of wretchedness and a death of shame, but then, the moment must come at last, since this was to be death indeed, and her spotless soul would be beyond Unorna's reach forever. No, that was not enough. Since she could not be allowed to live to be tormented, vengeance must follow her beyond the end of life.

Unorna stood still and an awful light of evil came into her face. A thought of which the enormity would have terrified a common being had entered her mind and taken possession of it. Beatrice was in her power. Beatrice should die in mortal sin, and her soul would be lost for ever.

For a long time she did not move, but stood looking down at the calm and lovely face of her sleeping enemy, devising a crime to be imposed upon her for her eternal destruction. Unorna was very superstitious, or the hideous scheme could never have presented itself to her. To her mind the deed was everything, whatever it was to be, and the intention or the unconsciousness in doing it could have nothing to do with the consequences to the soul of the doer. She made no theological distinctions. Beatrice should commit some terrible crime and should die in committing it. Then she would be lost, and devils would do in hell the worst torment which Unorna could not do on earth. A crime – a robbery, a murder – it must be done in the convent. Unorna hesitated, bending her brows and poring in imagination over the dark catalogue of all imaginable evil.

A momentary and vague terror cast its shadow on her thoughts. By some accident of connection between two ideas, her mind went back a month, and reviewed as in a flash of light all that she had thought and done since that day. She had greatly changed since then. She could think calmly now of deeds which even she would not have dared then. She thought of the evening when she had cried aloud that she would give her soul to know the Wanderer safe, of the quick answer that had followed, and of Keyork Arabian's face. Was he a devil, indeed, as she sometimes fancied, and had there been a reality and a binding meaning in that contract?

Keyork Arabian! He, indeed, possessed the key to all evil. What would he have done with Beatrice? Would he make her rob the church – murder the Abbess in her sleep? Bad, but not bad enough.

Unorna started. A deed suggested itself so hellish, so horrible in its enormity, so far beyond all conceivable human sin, that for one moment her brain reeled. She shuddered again and again, and groped for support and leaned against the wall in a bodily weakness of terror. For one moment she, who feared nothing, was shaken by fear from head to foot, her face turned white, her knees shook, her sight failed her, her teeth chattered, her lips moved hysterically.

But she was strong still. The thing she had sought had come to her suddenly. She set her teeth, and thought of it again and again, till she could face the horror of it without quaking. Is there any limit to the hardening of the human heart?

The distant bells rang out the call to midnight prayer. Unorna stopped and listened. She had not known how quickly time was passing. But it was better so. She was glad it was so late, and she said so to herself, but the evil smile that was sometimes in her face was not there now. She had thought a thought that left a mark on her forehead. Was there any reality in that jesting contract with Keyork Arabian?

She must wait before she did the deed. The nuns would go down into the lighted church, and kneel and pray before the altar. It would last some time, the midnight lessons, the psalms, the prayers – and she must be sure that all was quiet, for the deed could not be done in the room where Beatrice was sleeping.

She was conscious of the time now, and every minute seemed an hour, and every second was full of that one deed, done over and over again before her eyes, until every awful detail of the awful whole was stamped indelibly upon her brain. She had sat down now, and leaning forwards, was watching the innocent woman and wondering how she would look when she was doing it. But she was calm now, as she felt that she had never been in her life. Her breath came evenly, her heart beat naturally, she thought connectedly of what she was about to do. But the time seemed endless.

The distant clocks chimed the half hour, three-quarters, past midnight. Still she waited. At the stroke of one she rose from her seat, and standing beside Beatrice laid her hand upon the dark brow.

A few questions, a few answers followed. She must assure herself that her victim was in the right state to execute minutely all her commands. Then she opened the door upon the corridor and listened. Not a sound broke the intense stillness, and all was dark. The hanging lamp had been extinguished and the nuns had all returned from the midnight service to their cells. No one would be stirring now until four o'clock, and half an hour was all that Unorna needed.

She took Beatrice's hand. The dark woman rose with half-closed eyes and set features. Unorna led her out into the dark passage.

'It is light here,' Unorna said. 'You can see your way. But I am blind. Take my hand – so – and now lead me to the church by the nun's staircase. Make no noise.'

'I do not know the staircase,' said the sleeper in drowsy tones.

Unorna knew the way well enough, but not wishing to take a light with her, she was obliged to trust herself to her victim, for whose vision there was no such thing as darkness unless Unorna willed it.

'Go as you went today, to the room where the balcony is, but do not enter it. The staircase is on the right of the door, and leads into the choir. Go!'

Without hesitation Beatrice led her out into the impenetrable gloom, with swift, noiseless footsteps in the direction commanded, never wavering nor hesitating whether to turn to the right or the left, but walking as confidently as though in broad daylight. Unorna counted the turnings and knew that there was no mistake. Beatrice was leading her unerringly towards the staircase. They reached it, and began to descend the winding steps. Unorna, holding her leader by one hand, steadied herself with the other against the smooth, curved wall, fearing at every moment lest she should stumble and fall in the total darkness. But Beatrice never faltered. To her the way was as bright as though the noonday sun had shone before her.

The stairs ended abruptly against a door. Beatrice stood still. She had received no further commands and the impulse ceased.

'Draw back the bolt and take me into the church,' said Unorna, who could see nothing, but who knew that the nuns fastened the door behind them when they returned into the convent. Beatrice obeyed without hesitation and led her forward.

They came out between the high carved seats of the choir, behind the high altar. The church was not quite as dark as the staircase and passages had been, and Unorna stood still for a moment. In some of the chapels hanging lamps of silver were lighted, and their tiny flames spread a faint radiance upwards and sideways, though not downwards, sufficient to break the total obscurity to eyes accustomed for some minutes to no light at all. The church stood, too, on a little eminence in the city, where the air without was less murky and impenetrable with the night mists, and though there was no moon the high upper windows of the nave were distinctly visible in the gloomy height like great lancet-shaped patches of grey upon a black ground.

In the dimness, all objects took vast and mysterious proportions. A huge giant reared his height against one of the pillars, crowned with a high, pointed crown, stretching out one great shadowy hand into the gloom – the tall pulpit was there, as Unorna knew, and the hand was the wooden crucifix standing out in its extended socket. The black confessionals, too, took shape, like monster nuns, kneeling in their heavy hoods and veils, with heads inclined, behind the fluted pilasters, just within the circle of the feeble chapel lights. Within the choir, the deep shadows seemed to fill the carved stalls with the black ghosts of long dead sisters, returned to their familiar seats out of the damp crypt below. The great lectern in the midst of the half circle behind the high altar became a hideous skeleton, headless, its straight arms folded on its bony breast. The back of the high altar itself was a great throne whereon sat in judgment a misty being of awful form, judging the dead women all through the lonely night. The stillness was appalling. Not a rat stirred.

Unorna shuddered, not at what she saw, but at what she felt. She had reached the place, and the doing of the deed was at hand. Beatrice stood beside her erect, asleep, motionless, her dark face just outlined in the surrounding dusk.

Unorna took her hand and led her forwards. She could see now, and the moment had come. She brought Beatrice before the high altar and made her stand in front of it. Then she herself went back and groped for something in the dark. It was the pair of small wooden steps upon which the priest mounts in order to open the golden door of the high tabernacle above the altar, when it is necessary to take therefrom the Sacred Host for the Benediction, or other consecrated wafers for the administration of the Communion. To all Christians, of all denominations whatsoever, the bread-wafer when once consecrated is a holy thing. To Catholics and Lutherans there is there, substantially, the Presence of God.

No imaginable act of sacrilege can be more unpardonable than the desecration of the tabernacle and the wilful defilement and destruction of the Sacred Host.

This was Unorna's determination. Beatrice should commit this crime against Heaven, and then die with the whole weight of it upon her soul, and thus should her soul itself be tormented for ever and ever to ages of ages.

Considering what she believed, it is no wonder that she should have shuddered at the tremendous thought. And yet, in the distortion of her reasoning, the sin would be upon Beatrice who did the act, and not upon herself who commanded it. There was no diminution of her own faith in the sacredness of the place and the holiness of the consecrated object – had she been one whit less sure of that, her vengeance would have been vain and her whole scheme meaningless.

She came back out of the darkness and set the wooden steps in their place before the altar at Beatrice's feet. Then, as though to save herself from all participation in the guilt of the sacrilege which was to follow, she withdrew outside the Communion rail, and closed the gate behind her.

Beatrice, obedient to her smallest command, and powerless to move or act without her suggestion, stood still as she had been placed, with her back to the church and her face to the altar. Above her head the richly wrought door of the tabernacle caught what little light there was and reflected it from its own uneven surface.

Unorna paused a moment, looked at the shadowy figure, and then glanced behind her into the body of the church, not out of any ghostly fear, but to assure herself that she was alone with her victim. She saw that all was quite ready, and then she calmly knelt down just upon one side of the gate and rested her folded hands upon the marble railing. A moment of intense stillness followed. Again the thought of Keyork Arabian flashed across her mind. Had there been any reality, she vaguely wondered, in that compact made with him? What was she doing now? But the crime was to be Beatrice's, not hers. Her heart beat fast for a moment, and then she grew very calm again.

The clock in the church tower chimed the first quarter past one. She was able to count the strokes and was glad to find that she had lost no time. As soon as the long, singing echo of the bells had died away, she spoke, not loudly, but clearly and distinctly.

'Beatrice Varanger, go forward and mount the steps I have placed for you.'

The dark figure moved obediently, and Unorna heard the slight sound of Beatrice's foot upon the wood. The shadowy form rose higher and higher in the gloom, and stood upon the altar itself.

'Now do as I command you. Open wide the door of the tabernacle.'

Unorna watched the black form intently. It seemed to stretch out its hand as though searching for something, and then the arm fell again to the side.

'Do as I command you,' Unorna repeated with the angry and dominant intonation that always came into her voice when she was not obeyed.

Again the hand was raised for a moment, groped in the darkness and sank down into the shadow.

'Beatrice Varanger, you must do my will. I order you to open the door of the tabernacle, to take out what is within and to throw it to the ground!' Her voice rang clearly through the church. 'And may the crime be on your soul for ever and ever,' she added in a low voice.

A third time the figure moved. A strange flash of light played for a moment upon the tabernacle, the effect, Unorna thought, of the golden door being suddenly opened.

But she was wrong. The figure moved, indeed, and stretched out a hand and moved again. A sudden crash of something very heavy, falling upon stone, broke the great stillness – the dark form tottered, reeled and fell to its length upon the great altar. Unorna saw that the golden door was still closed, and that Beatrice had fallen. Unable to move or act by her own free judgment, and compelled by Unorna's determined command, she had made a desperate effort to obey. Unorna had forgotten that there was a raised step upon the altar itself, and that there were other obstacles in the way, including heavy candlesticks and the framed Canon of the Mass, all of which are usually set aside before the tabernacle is opened by the priest. In attempting to do as she was told, the sleeping woman had stumbled, had overbalanced herself, had clutched one of the great silver candlesticks so that it fell heavily beside her, and then, having no further support, she had fallen herself.

Unorna sprang to her feet and hastily opened the gate of the railing. In a moment she was standing by the altar at Beatrice's head. She could see that the dark eyes were open now. The great shock had recalled her to consciousness.

'Where am I?' she asked in great distress, seeing nothing in the darkness now, and groping with her hands.

'Sleep – be silent and sleep!' said Unorna in low, firm tones, pressing her palm upon the forehead.

'No – no!' cried the startled woman in a voice of horror. 'No – I will not sleep – no, do not touch me! Oh, where am I – help! Help!'

She was not hurt. With one strong, lithe movement, she sprang to the ground and stood with her back to the altar, her hands stretched out to defend herself from Unorna. But Unorna knew what extreme danger she was in if Beatrice left the church awake and conscious of what had happened. She seized the moving arms and tried to hold them down, pressing her face forward so as to look into the dark eyes she could but faintly distinguish. It was no easy matter, however, for Beatrice was young and strong and active. Then all at once she began to see Unorna's eyes, as Unorna could see hers, and she felt the terrible influence stealing over her again.

'No – no – no!' she cried, struggling desperately. 'You shall not make me sleep. I will not – I will not!'

There was a flash of light again in the church, this time from behind the high altar, and the noise of quick footsteps. But neither Unorna nor Beatrice noticed the light or the sound. Then the full glow of a strong lamp fell upon the faces of both and dazzled them, and Unorna felt a cool thin hand upon her own. Sister Paul was beside them, her face very white and her faded eyes turning from the one to the other.

It was very simple. Soon after Compline was over the nun had gone to Unorna's room, had knocked and had entered. To her surprise Unorna was not there, but Sister Paul imagined that she had lingered over her prayers and would soon return. The good nun had sat down to wait for her, and telling her beads had fallen asleep. The unaccustomed warmth and comfort of the guest's room had been too much for the weariness that constantly oppressed a constitution broken with ascetic practices. Accustomed by long habit to awake at midnight to attend the service, her eyes opened of themselves, indeed, but a full hour later than usual. She heard the clock strike one, and for a moment could not believe her senses. Then she understood that she had been asleep, and was amazed to find that Unorna had not come back. She went out hastily into the corridor. The lay sister had long ago extinguished the hanging lamp, but Sister Paul saw the light streaming from Beatrice's open door. She went in and called aloud. The bed had not been touched. Beatrice was not there. Sister Paul began to think that both the ladies must have gone to the midnight service. The corridors were dark and they might have lost their way. She took the lamp from the table and went to the balcony at which the guests performed their devotion. It had been her light that had flashed across the door of the tabernacle. She had looked down into the choir, and far below her had seen a figure, unrecognisable from that height in the dusk of the church, but clearly the figure of a woman standing upon the altar. Visions of horror rose before her eyes, of the sacrilegious practices of witch-craft, for she had thought of nothing else during the whole evening. Lamp in hand she descended the stairs to the choir and reached the altar, providentially, just in time to save Beatrice from falling a victim again to the evil fascination of the enemy who had planned the destruction of her soul as well as of her body.

'What is this? What are you doing in this holy place and at this hour?' asked Sister Paul, solemnly and sternly.

Unorna folded her arms and was silent. No possible explanation of the struggle presented itself even to her quick intellect. She fixed her eyes on the nun's face, concentrating all her will, for she knew that unless she could control her also, she herself was lost. Beatrice answered the question, drawing herself up proudly against the great altar and pointing at Unorna with her outstretched hand, her dark eyes flashing indignantly.

'We were talking together, this woman and I. She looked at me – she was angry – and then I fainted, or fell asleep, I cannot tell which. I awoke in the dark to find myself lying upon the altar here. Then she took hold of me and tried to make me sleep again. But I would not. Let her explain, herself, what she has done, and why she brought me here!'

Sister Paul turned to Unorna and met the full glare of the unlike eyes, with her own calm, half-heavenly look of innocence.

'What have you done, Unorna? What have you done?' she asked very sadly.

But Unorna did not answer. She only looked at the nun more fixedly and savagely. She felt that she might as well have looked upon some ancient picture of a saint in heaven, and bid it close its eyes. But she would not give up the attempt, for her only safety lay in its success. For a long time Sister Paul returned her gaze steadily.

'Sleep!' said Unorna, putting up her hand. 'Sleep, I command you!'

But Sister Paul's eyes did not waver. A sad smile played for a moment upon her waxen features.

'You have no power over me – for your power is not of good,' she said, slowly and softly.

Then she quietly turned to Beatrice, and took her hand.

'Come with me, my daughter,' she said. 'I have a light and will take you to a place where you will be safe. She will not trouble you any more tonight. Say a prayer, my child, and do not be afraid.'

'I am not afraid,' said Beatrice. 'But where is she?' she asked suddenly.

Unorna had glided away while they were speaking. Sister Paul held the lamp high and looked in all directions. Then she heard the heavy door of the sacristy swing upon its hinges and strike with a soft thud against the small leathern cushion. Both women followed her, but as they opened the door again a blast of cold air almost extinguished the lamp. The night wind was blowing in from the street.

'She is gone out,' said Sister Paul. 'Alone and at this hour – Heaven help her!' It was as she said, Unorna had escaped.

Chapter 21

After leaving Unorna at the convent, the Wanderer had not hesitated as to the course he should pursue. It was quite clear that the only person to whom he could apply at the present juncture was Keyork Arabian. Had he been at liberty to act in the most natural and simple way, he would have applied to the authorities for a sufficient force with which to take Israel Kafka into custody as a dangerous lunatic. He was well aware, however, that such a proceeding must lead to an inquiry of a more or less public nature, of which the consequences might be serious, or at least extremely annoying, to Unorna. Of the inconvenience to which he might himself be exposed, he would have taken little account, though his position would have been as difficult to explain as any situation could be. The important point was to prevent the possibility of Unorna's name being connected with an open scandal. Every present circumstance in the case was directly or indirectly the result of Unorna's unreasoning passion for himself, and it was clearly his duty, as a man of honour, to shield her from the consequences of her own acts, as far as lay in his power.

He did not indeed believe literally all that she had told him in her mad confession. Much of that, he was convinced, was but a delusion. It might be possible, indeed, for Unorna to produce forgetfulness of such a dream as she impressed upon Kafka's mind in the cemetery that same afternoon, or even, perhaps, of some real circumstance of merely relative importance in a man's life; but the Wanderer could not believe that it was in her power to destroy the memory of the great passion through which she pretended that he himself had passed. He smiled at the idea, for he had always trusted his own senses and his own memory. Unorna's own mind was clearly wandering, or else she had invented the story, supposing him credulous enough to believe it. In either case it did not deserve a moment's consideration except as showing to what lengths her foolish and ill-bestowed love could lead her.

Meanwhile she was in danger. She had aroused the violent and deadly resentment of Israel Kafka, a man who, if not positively insane, as Keyork Arabian had hinted, was by no means in a normal state of mind or body, a man beside himself with love and anger, and absolutely reckless of life for the time being, a man who, for the security of all concerned, must be at least temporarily confined in a place of safety, until a proper treatment and the lapse of a certain length of time should bring him to his senses. For the present, he was wholly intractable, being at the mercy of the most uncontrolled passions and of one of those intermittent phases of blind fatalism to which the Semitic races are peculiarly subject.

There were two reasons which determined the Wanderer to turn to Keyork Arabian for assistance, besides his wish to see the bad business end quickly and without publicity. Keyork, so far as the Wanderer was aware, was himself treating Israel Kafka's case, and would therefore know what to do, if anyone knew at all. Secondly, it was clear from the message which Unorna had left with the porter of her own house that she expected Keyork to come at any moment. He was then in immediate danger of being brought face to face with Israel Kafka without having received the least warning of his present condition, and it was impossible to say what the infuriated youth might do at such a moment. He had been shut up, caught in his own trap, as it were, for some time, and his anger and madness might reasonably be supposed to have been aggravated rather than cooled by his unexpected confinement. It was as likely as not that he would use the weapon he carried upon the first person with whom he found himself face to face, especially if that person made any attempt to overpower and disarm him.

The Wanderer drove to Keyork Arabian's house, and leaving his carriage to wait in case of need, ascended the stairs and knocked at the door. For some reason or other Keyork would not have a bell in his dwelling, whether because, like Mahomet, he regarded the bell as the devil's instrument, or because he was really nervously sensitive to the sound of one, nobody had ever discovered. The Wanderer knocked therefore, and Keyork answered the knock in person.

'My dear friend!' he exclaimed in his richest and deepest voice, as he recognised the Wanderer. 'Come in. I am delighted to see you. You will join me at supper. This is good indeed!'

He took his visitor by the arm and led him in. Upon one of the tables stood a round brass platter covered, so far as it was visible, with Arabic inscriptions, and highly polished – one of those commonly used all over the East at the present day for the same purpose. Upon this were placed at random several silver bowls, mere hemispheres without feet, remaining in a convenient position by their own weight. One of these contained snowy rice, in that perfectly dry but tender state dear to the taste of Orientals, in another there was a savoury, steaming mess of tender capon, chopped in pieces with spices and aromatic herbs, a third contained a pure white curd of milk, and a fourth was heaped up with rare fruits. A flagon of Bohemian glass, clear and bright as rock-crystal, and covered with very beautiful traceries of black and gold, with a drinking-vessel of the same design, stood upon the table beside the platter.

'My simple meal,' said Keyork, spreading out his hands, and smiling pleasantly. 'You will share it with me. There will be enough for two.'

'So far as I am concerned, I should say so,' the Wanderer answered with a smile. 'But my business is rather urgent.'

Suddenly he saw that there was a third person in the room, and glanced at Keyork in surprise.

'I want to speak a few words with you alone,' he said. 'I would not trouble you but – '

'Not in the least, not in the least, my dear friend!' asseverated Keyork, motioning him to a chair beside the board.

'But we are not alone,' observed the Wanderer, still standing and looking at the stranger. Keyork saw the glance and understood. He broke into peals of laughter.

'That!' he exclaimed, presently. 'That is only the Individual. He will not disturb us. Pray be seated.'

'I assure you that my business is very private – ' the Wanderer objected.

'Quite so – of course. But there is nothing to fear. The Individual is my servant – a most excellent creature who has been with me for many years. He cooks for me, cleans the specimens, and takes care of me in all ways. A most reliable man, I assure you.'

'Of course, if you can answer for his discretion – '

The Individual was standing at a little distance from the table observing the two men intently but respectfully with his keen little black eyes. The rest of his square, dark face expressed nothing. He had perfectly straight, jet-black hair which hung evenly all around his head and flat against his cheeks. He was dressed entirely in a black robe of the nature of a kaftan, gathered closely round his waist by a black girdle, and fitting tightly over his stalwart shoulders.

'His discretion is beyond all doubt,' Keyork answered, 'and for the best of all reasons. He is totally deaf and dumb and absolutely illiterate. I bought him years ago in Astrakhan, of a Russian friend. He is very clever with his fingers. It is he who stole for me the Malayan lady's head over there, after she was executed. And now, my dear friend, let us have supper.'

There were neither plates nor knives nor forks upon the table, and at a sign from Keyork the Individual retired to procure those Western encumbrances to eating. The Wanderer, acquainted as he had long been with his host's eccentricities, showed little surprise, but understood that whatever he said would not be overheard, any more than if they had been alone. He hesitated a moment, however, for he had not determined exactly how far it was necessary to acquaint Keyork with the circumstances, and he was anxious to avoid all reference to Unorna's folly in regard to himself. The Individual returned, bringing, with other things, a drinking-glass for the Wanderer. Keyork filled it and then filled his own. It was clear that ascetic practices formed no part of his scheme for the prolongation of life. As he raised his glass to his lips, his bright eyes twinkled.

'To Keyork's long life and happiness,' he said calmly, and then sipped the wine. 'And now for your story,' he added, brushing the brown drops from his white moustache with a small damask napkin which the Individual presented to him and immediately received again, to throw it aside as unfit for a second use.

'I hardly think that we can afford to linger over supper,' the Wanderer said, noticing Keyork's coolness with some anxiety. 'The case is urgent. Israel Kafka has lost his head completely. He has sworn to kill Unorna, and is at the present moment confined in the conservatory in her house.'

The effect of the announcement upon Keyork was so extraordinary that the Wanderer started, not being prepared for any manifestation of what seemed to be the deepest emotion. The gnome sprang from the table with a cry that would have been like the roar of a wounded wild beast if it had not articulated a terrific blasphemy.

'Unorna is quite safe,' the Wanderer hastened to say.

'Safe – where?' shouted the little man, his hands already on his furs. The Individual, too, had sprung across the room like a cat and was helping him. In five seconds Keyork would have been out of the house.

'In a convent. I took her there, and saw the gate close behind her.'

Keyork dropped his furs and stood still a moment. The Individual, always unmoved, rearranged the coat and cap neatly in their place, following all his master's movements, however, with his small eyes. Then the sage broke out in a different strain. He flung his arms round the Wanderer's body and attempted to embrace him.

'You have saved my life! – the curse of the three black angels on you for not saying so first!' he cried in an agony of ecstasy. 'Preserver! What can I do for you? – Saviour of my existence, how can I repay you! You shall live forever, as I will; you shall have all my secrets; the gold spider shall spin her web in your dwelling; the Part of Fortune shall shine on your path, it shall rain jewels on your roof; and your winter shall have snows of pearls – you shall – '

'Good Heavens! Keyork,' interrupted the Wanderer. 'Are you mad? What is the matter with you?'

'Mad? The matter? I love you! I worship you! I adore you! You have saved her life, and you have saved mine; you have almost killed me with fright and joy in two moments, you have – '

'Be sensible, Keyork. Unorna is quite safe, but we must do something about Kafka and – '

The rest of his speech was drowned in another shout from the gnome, ending in a portentous peal of laughter. He had taken his glass again and was toasting himself.

'To Keyork, to his long life, to his happiness!' he cried. Then he wet his lips again in the golden juice, and the Individual, unmoved, presented him with a second napkin.

The wine seemed to steady him, and he sat down again in his place.

'Come!' he said. 'Let us eat first. I have an amazing appetite, and Israel Kafka can wait.'

'Do you think so? Is it safe?' the Wanderer asked.

'Perfectly,' returned Keyork, growing quite calm again. 'The locks are very good on those doors. I saw to them myself.'

'But someone else – '

'There is no someone else,' interrupted the sage sharply. 'Only three persons can enter the house without question – you, I, and Kafka. You and I are here, and Kafka is there already. When we have eaten we will go to him, and I flatter myself that the last state of the young man will be so immeasurably worse than the first, that he will not recognise himself when I have done with him.'

He had helped his friend and began eating. Somewhat reassured the Wanderer followed his example. Under the circumstances it was as well to take advantage of the opportunity for refreshment. No one could tell what might happen before morning.

'It just occurs to me,' said Keyork, fixing his keen eyes on his companion's face, 'that you have told me absolutely nothing, except that Kafka is mad and that Unorna is safe.'

'Those are the most important points,' observed the Wanderer.

'Precisely. But I am sure that you will not think me indiscreet if I wish to know a little more. For instance, what was the immediate cause of Kafka's extremely theatrical and unreasonable rage? That would interest me very much. Of course he is mad, poor boy! But I take delight in following out the workings of an insane intellect. Now there are no phases of insanity more curious than those in which the patient is possessed with a desire to destroy what he loves best. These cases are especially worthy of study because they happen so often in our day.'

The Wanderer saw that some explanation was necessary and he determined to give one in as few words as possible.

'Unorna and I had strolled into the Jewish Cemetery,' he said. 'While we were talking there, Israel Kafka suddenly came upon us and spoke and acted very wildly. He is madly in love with her. She became very angry and would not let me interfere. Then, by way of punishment for his intrusion I suppose, she hypnotised him and made him believe that he was Simon Abeles, and brought the whole of the poor boy's life so vividly before me, as I listened, that I actually seemed to see the scenes. I was quite unable to stop her or to move from where I stood, though I was quite awake. But I realised what was going on and I was disgusted at her cruelty to the unfortunate man. He fainted at the end, but when he came to himself he seemed to remember nothing. I took him home and Unorna went away by herself. Then he questioned me so closely as to what had happened that I was weak enough to tell him the truth. Of course, as a fervent Hebrew, which he seems to be, he did not relish the idea of having played the Christian martyr for Unorna's amusement, and amidst the graves of his own people. He there and then impressed me that he intended to take Unorna's life without delay, but insisted that I should warn her of her danger, saying that he would not be a common murderer. Seeing that he was mad and in earnest I went to her. There was some delay, which proved fortunate, as it turned out, for we left the conservatory by the small door just as he was entering from the other end. We locked it behind us, and going round by the passages locked the other door upon him also, so that he was caught in a trap. And there he is, unless someone has let him out.'

'And then you took Unorna to the convent?' Keyork had listened attentively.

'I took her to the convent, promising to come to her when she should send for me. Then I saw that I must consult you before doing anything more. It will not do to make a scandal of the matter.'

'No,' answered Keyork thoughtfully. 'It will not do.'

The Wanderer had told his story with perfect truth and yet in a way which entirely concealed the very important part Unorna's passion for him had played in the sequence of events. Seeing that Keyork asked no further questions he felt satisfied that he had accomplished his purpose as he had intended, and that the sage suspected nothing. He would have been very much disconcerted had he known that the latter had long been aware of Unorna's love, and was quite able to guess at the cause of Kafka's sudden appearance and extreme excitement. Indeed, so soon as he had finished the short narrative, his mind reverted with curiosity to Keyork himself, and he wondered what the little man had meant by his amazing outburst of gratitude on hearing of Unorna's safety. Perhaps he loved her. More impossible things than that had occurred in the Wanderer's experience. Or, possibly, he had an object to gain in exaggerating his thankfulness to Unorna's preserver. He knew that Keyork rarely did anything without an object, and that, although he was occasionally very odd and excitable, he was always in reality perfectly well aware of what he was doing. He was roused from his speculations by Keyork's voice.

'There will be no difficulty in securing Kafka,' he said. 'The real question is, what shall we do with him? He is very much in the way at present, and he must be disposed of at once, or we shall have more trouble. How infinitely more to the purpose it would have been if he had wisely determined to cut his own throat instead of Unorna's! But young men are so thoughtless!'

'I will only say one thing,' said the Wanderer, 'and then I will leave the direction to you. The poor fellow has been driven mad by

Unorna's caprice and cruelty. I am determined that he shall not be made to suffer gratuitously anything more.'

'Do you think that Unorna was intentionally cruel to him?' inquired Keyork. 'I can hardly believe that. She has not a cruel nature.'

'You would have changed your mind, if you had seen her this afternoon. But that is not the question. I will not allow him to be ill-treated.'

'No, no! of course not!' Keyork answered with eager assent. 'But of course you will understand that we have to deal with a dangerous lunatic, and that it may be necessary to use whatever means are most sure and certain.'

'I shall not quarrel with your means,' the Wanderer said quietly, 'provided that there is no unnecessary brutality. If I see anything of the kind I will take the matter into my own hands.'

'Certainly, certainly!' said the other, eyeing with curiosity the man who spoke so confidently of taking out of Keyork Arabian's grasp whatever had once found its way into it.

'He shall be treated with every consideration,' the Wanderer continued. 'Of course, if he is very violent, we shall have to use force.'

'We will take the Individual with us,' said Keyork. 'He is very strong. He has a trick of breaking silver florins with his thumbs and fingers which is very pretty.'

'I fancy that you and I could manage him. It is a pity that neither of us has the faculty of hypnotising. This would be the proper time to use it.'

'A great pity. But there are other things that will do almost as well.'

'What, for instance?'

'A little ether in a sponge. He would only struggle a moment, and then he would be much more really unconscious than if he had been hypnotised.'

'Is it quite painless?'

'Quite, if you give it gradually. If you hurry the thing, the man feels as though he were being smothered. But the real difficulty is what to do with him, as I said before.'

'Take him home and get a keeper from the lunatic asylum,' the Wanderer suggested.

'Then comes the whole question of an inquiry into his sanity,' objected Keyork. 'We come back to the starting-point. We must settle all this before we go to him. A lunatic asylum is not a club in this country. There is a great deal of formality connected with getting into it, and a great deal more connected with getting out. Now, I could not get a keeper for Kafka without going to the physician in charge and making a statement, and demanding an examination, and all the rest of it. And Israel Kafka is a person of importance among his own people. He comes of great Jews in Moravia, and we should have the whole Jews' quarter – which means nearly the whole of Prague, in a broad sense – about our ears in twenty-four hours. No, no, my friend. To avoid an enormous scandal things must be done very quietly indeed.'

'I cannot see anything to be done, then, unless we bring him here,' said the Wanderer, falling into the trap from sheer perplexity. Everything that Keyork had said was undeniably true.

'He would be a nuisance in the house,' answered the sage, not wishing, for reasons of his own, to appear to accept the proposition too eagerly. 'Not but that the Individual would make a capital keeper. He is as gentle as he is strong, and as quick as a tiger-cat.'

'So far as that is concerned,' said the Wanderer coolly, 'I could take charge of him myself, if you did not object to my presence.'

'You do not trust me,' said the other, with a sharp glance.

'My dear Keyork, we are old acquaintances, and I trust you implicitly to do whatever you have predetermined to do for the advantage of your studies, unless someone interferes with you. You have no more respect for human life or sympathy for human suffering than you have belief in the importance of anything not conducive to your researches. I am perfectly well aware that if you thought you could learn something by making experiments upon the body of Israel Kafka, you would not scruple to make a living mummy of him, you would do it without the least hesitation. I should expect to find him with his head cut off, living by means of a glass heart and thinking through a rabbit's brain. That is the reason why I do not trust you. Before I could deliver him into your hands, I would require of you a contract to give him back unhurt – and a contract of the kind you would consider binding.'

Keyork Arabian wondered whether Unorna, in the recklessness of her passion, had betrayed the nature of the experiment they had been making together, but a moment's reflection told him that he need have no anxiety on this score. He understood the Wanderer's nature too well to suspect him of wishing to convey a covert hint instead of saying openly what was in his mind.

'Taste one of these oranges,' he said, by way of avoiding an answer. 'they have just come from Smyrna.' The Wanderer smiled as he took the proffered fruit.

'So that unless you have a serious objection to my presence,' he said, continuing his former speech, 'you will have me as a guest so long as Israel Kafka is here.'

Keyork Arabian saw no immediate escape.

'My dear friend!' he exclaimed with alacrity. 'If you are really in earnest, I am as really delighted. So far from taking your distrust ill, I regard it as a providentially fortunate bias of your mind, since it will keep us together for a time. You will be the only loser. You see how simply I live.'

'There is a simplicity which is the extremest development of refined sybarism,' the Wanderer said, smiling again. 'I know your simplicity of old. It consists of getting precisely what you want, and in producing local earthquakes and revolutions when you cannot get it. Moreover you want what is good – to the taste, at least.'

'There is something in that,' answered Keyork with a merry twinkle in his eye. 'Happiness is a matter of speculation. Comfort is a matter of fact. Most men are uncomfortable, because they do not know what they want. If you have tastes, study them. If you have intelligence, apply it to the question of gratifying your tastes. Consult yourself first – and nobody second. Consider this orange – I am fond of oranges and they suit my constitution admirably. Consider the difficulty I have had in procuring it at this time of year – not in the wretched condition in which they are sold in the market, plucked half green in Spain or Italy and ripened on the voyage in the fermenting heat of the decay of those which are already rotten – but ripe from the tree and brought to me directly by the shortest and quickest means possible. Consider this orange, I say. Do you vainly imagine that if I had but two or three like it I would offer you one?'

'I would not be so rash as to imagine anything of the kind, my dear Keyork. I know you very well. If you offer me one it is because you have a week's supply at least.'

'Exactly,' said Keyork. 'And a few to spare, because they will only keep a week as I like them, and because I would no more run the risk of missing my orange a week hence for your sake, than I would deprive myself of it today.'

'And that is your simplicity.'

'That is my simplicity. It is indeed a perfectly simple matter, for there is only one idea in it, and in all things I carry that one idea out to its ultimate expression. That one idea, as you very well put it, is to have exactly what I want in this world.'

'And will you be getting what you want in having me quartered upon you as poor Israel Kafka's keeper?' asked the Wanderer, with an expression of amusement. But Keyork did not wince.

'Precisely,' he answered without hesitation. 'In the first place you will relieve me of much trouble and responsibility, and the Individual will not be so often called away from his manifold and important household duties. In the second place I shall have a most agreeable and intelligent companion with whom I can talk as long as I like. In the third place I shall undoubtedly satisfy my curiosity.'

'In what respect, if you please?'

'I shall discover the secret of your wonderful interest in Israel Kafka's welfare. I always like to follow the workings of a brain essentially different from my own, philanthropic, of course. How could it be anything else? Philanthropy deals with a class of ideas wholly unfamiliar to me. I shall learn much in your society.'

'And possibly I shall learn something from you,' the Wanderer answered. 'There is certainly much to be learnt. I wonder whether your ideas upon all subjects are as simple as those you hold about oranges.'

'Absolutely. I make no secret of my principles. Everything I do is for my own advantage.'

'Then,' observed the Wanderer, 'the advantage of Unorna's life must be an enormous one to you, to judge by your satisfaction at her safety.'

Keyork stared at him a moment and then laughed – but less heartily and loudly than usual, his companion fancied.

'Very good!' he exclaimed. 'Excellent! I fell into the trap like a rat into a basin of water. You are indeed an interesting companion, my dear friend – so interesting that I hope we shall never part again.' There was a rather savage intonation in the last words.

They looked at each other intently, neither wincing nor lowering his gaze. The Wanderer saw that he had touched upon Keyork's greatest and most important secret, and Keyork fancied that his companion knew more than he actually did. But nothing further was said, for Keyork was far too wise to enter into explanation, and the Wanderer knew well enough that if he was to learn anything it must be by observation and not by questioning. Keyork filled both glasses in silence and both men drank before speaking again.

'And now that we have refreshed ourselves,' he said, returning naturally to his former manner, 'we will go and find Israel Kafka. It is as well that we should have given him a little time to himself. He may have returned to his senses without any trouble on our part. Shall we take the Individual?'

'As you please,' the Wanderer answered indifferently as he rose from his place.

'It is very well for you not to care,' observed Keyork. 'You are big and strong and young, whereas I am a little man and very old at that. I shall take him for my own protection. I confess that I value my life very highly. It is a part of that simplicity which you despise. That devil of a Jew is armed, you say?'

'I saw something like a knife in his hand, as we shut him in,' said the Wanderer with the same indifference as before.

'Then I will take the Individual,' Keyork answered promptly. 'A man's bare hands must be strong and clever to take a man's life in a scuffle, and few men can use a pistol to any purpose. But a knife is a weapon of precision. I will take the Individual, decidedly.'

He made a few rapid signs, and the Individual disappeared, coming back a moment later attired in a long coat not unlike his master's except that the fur of the great collar was of common fox instead of being of sable. Keyork drew his peaked cape comfortably down over the tips of his ears.

'The ether!' he exclaimed. 'How forgetful I am growing! Your charming conversation had almost made me forget the object of our visit!'

He went back and took the various things he needed. Then the three men went out together.

Chapter 22

More than an hour had elapsed since the Wanderer and Unorna had finally turned the key upon Israel Kafka, leaving him to his own reflections. During the first moments he made desperate efforts to get out of the conservatory, throwing himself with all his weight and strength against the doors and thrusting the point of his long knife into the small apertures of the locks. Then, seeing that every attempt was fruitless, he desisted and sat down, in a state of complete exhaustion. A reaction began to set in after the furious excitement of the afternoon, and he felt all at once that it would be impossible for him to make another step or raise his arm to strike. A man less sound originally in bodily constitution would have broken down sooner, and it was a proof of Israel Kafka's extraordinary vigour and energy that he did not lose his senses in a delirious fever at the moment when he felt that his strength could bear no further strain.

But his thoughts, such as they were, did not lack clearness. He saw that his opportunity was gone, and he began to think of the future, wondering what would take place next. Assuredly when he had come to Unorna's house with the fixed determination to take her life, the last thing that he had expected had been to be taken prisoner and left to his own meditations. It was clear that the Wanderer's warning had been conveyed without loss of time and had saved Unorna from her immediate fate. Nevertheless, he did not regret having given her the opportunity of defending herself. He had not meant that there should be any secret about the deed, for he was ready to sacrifice his own life in executing it.

Yet he was not altogether brave. He had neither Unorna's innate indifference to physical danger, nor the Wanderer's calm superiority to fear. He would not have made a good soldier, and he could not have faced another man's pistol at fifteen paces without experiencing a mental and bodily commotion not unlike terror, which he might or might not have concealed from others, but which would in any case have been painfully apparent to himself.

It is a noticeable fact in human nature that a man of even ordinary courage will at any time, when under excitement, risk his life rather than his happiness. Moreover, an immense number of individuals, naturally far from brave, destroy their own lives yearly in the moment when all chances of happiness are temporarily eclipsed. The inference seems to be that mankind, on the whole, values happiness more highly than life. The proportion of suicides from so-called 'honourable motives' is small as compared with the many committed out of despair.

Israel Kafka's case was by no means a rare one. The fact of having been made to play a part which to him seemed at once blasphemous and ignoble had indeed turned the scale, but was not the motive. In all things, the final touch which destroys the balance is commonly mistaken for the force which has originally produced a state of unstable equilibrium, whereas there is very often no connection between the one and the other. The Moravian himself believed that the sacrifice of Unorna, and of himself afterwards, was to be an expiation of the outrage Unorna had put upon his faith in his own person. He had merely seized upon the first excuse which presented itself for ending all, because he was in reality past hope.

We have, as yet, no absolute test of sanity, as we have of fever in the body and of many other unnatural conditions of the human organism.

The only approximately accurate judgments in the patient's favour are obtained from examinations into the relative consecutiveness and consistency of thought in the individual examined, when the whole tendency of that thought is towards an end conceivably approvable by a majority of men. A great many philosophers and thinkers have accordingly been pronounced insane at one period of history and have been held up as models of sanity at another. The most immediately destructive consequences of individual reasoning on a limited scale, murder and suicide, have been successively regarded as heroic acts, as criminal deeds, and as the deplorable but explicable actions of irresponsible beings in consecutive ages of violence, strict law and humanitarianism. It seems to be believed that the combination of murder and suicide is more commonly observed under the last of the three reigns than it was under the first; it was undoubtedly least common under the second. In other words it appears probable that the practice of considering certain crimes as the result of insanity has a tendency to make those crimes increase in number, as they undoubtedly increase in barbarity, from year to year. Meanwhile, however, no definite conclusion has been reached as to the state of mind of a man who murders the woman he loves and then ends his own life.

Israel Kafka may therefore be regarded as mad or sane. In favour of the theory of his madness the total uselessness of the deed he contemplated may be adduced; on the other hand the extremely consecutive and consistent nature of his thoughts and actions gives evidence of his sanity.

When he found himself a prisoner in Unorna's conservatory, his intention underwent no change though his body was broken with fatigue and his nerves with the long-continued strain of a terrible excitement. His determination was as cool and as fixed as ever.

These somewhat dry reflections seem necessary to the understanding of what followed.

The key turned in the lock and the bolt was slipped back. Instantly Israel Kafka's energy returned. He rose quickly and hid himself in the shrubbery, in a position from which he could observe the door. He had seen Unorna enter before and had of course heard her cry before the Wanderer had carried her away, and he had believed that she had wished to face him, either with the intention of throwing herself upon his mercy or in the hope of dominating him with her eyes as she had so often done before. Of course, he had no means of knowing that she had already left the house. He imagined that the Wanderer had gone and that Unorna, being freed from his restraint, was about to enter the place again. The door opened and the three men came in. Kafka's first idea, on seeing himself disappointed, was that they had come to take him into custody, and his first impulse was to elude them.

The Wanderer entered first, tall, stately, indifferent, the quick glance of his deep eyes alone betraying that he was looking for someone. Next came Keyork Arabian, muffled still in his furs, turning his head sharply from side to side in the midst of the sable collar that half buried it, and evidently nervous. Last of all the Individual, who had divested himself of his outer coat and whose powerful proportions did not escape Israel Kafka's observation. It was clear that if there were a struggle it could have but one issue. Kafka would be over-powered. His knowledge of the disposition of the plants and trees offered him a hope of escape. The three men had entered the con-servatory, and if he could reach the door before they noticed him, he could lock it upon them, as it had been locked upon himself. He could hear their footsteps on the marble pavement very near him, and he caught glimpses of their moving figures through the thick leaves.

With cat-like tread he glided along in the shadows of the foliage until he could see the door. From the entrance an open way was left in a straight line towards the middle of the hall, down which his pursuers were still slowly walking. He must cross an open space in the line of their vision in order to get out, and he calculated the distance to be traversed, while listening to their movements, until he felt sure that they were so far from the door as not to be able to reach him. Then he made his attempt, darting across the smooth pavement with his knife in his hand. There was no one in the way.

Then came a violent shock and he was held as in a vice, so tightly that he could not believe himself in the arms of a human being. His captors had anticipated that he would try to escape and has posted the Individual in the shadow of a tree near the doorway. The deaf and dumb man had received his instructions by means of a couple of quick signs, and not a whisper had betrayed the measures taken. Kafka struggled desperately, for he was within three feet of the door and still believed an escape possible. He tried to strike behind him with his sharp blade of which a single touch would have severed muscle and sinew like silk threads, but the bear-like embrace seemed to confine his whole body, his arms and even his wrists. Then he felt himself turned round and the Individual pushed him towards the middle of the hall. The Wanderer was advancing quickly, and Keyork Arabian, who had again fallen behind, peered at Kafka from behind his tall companion with a grotesque expression in which bodily fear and a desire to laugh at the captive were strongly intermingled.

'It is of no use to resist,' said the Wanderer quietly. 'We are too strong for you.'

Kafka said nothing, but his bloodshot eyes glared up angrily at the tall man's face.

'He looks dangerous, and he still has that thing in his hand,' said Keyork Arabian. 'I think I will give him ether at once while the Individual holds him. Perhaps you could do it.'

'You will do nothing of the kind,' the Wanderer answered. 'What a coward you are, Keyork!' he added contemptuously.

Going to Kafka's side he took him by the wrist of the hand which held the knife. But Kafka still clutched it firmly.

'You had better give it up,' he said.

Kafka shook his head angrily and set his teeth, but the Wanderer unclasped the fingers by quiet force and took the weapon away. He handed it to Keyork, who breathed a sigh of relief as he looked at it, smiling at last, and holding his head on one side.

'To think,' he soliloquised, 'that an inch of such pretty stuff as Damascus steel, in the right place, can draw the sharp red line between time and eternity!'

He put the knife tenderly away in the bosom of his fur coat. His whole manner changed and he came forward with his usual, almost jaunty step.

'And now that you are quite harmless, my dear friend,' he said, addressing Israel Kafka, 'I hope to make you see the folly of your ways. I suppose you know that you are quite mad and that the proper place for you is a lunatic asylum.'

The Wanderer laid his hand heavily upon Keyork's shoulder.

'Remember what I told you,' he said sternly. 'He will be reasonable now. Make your fellow understand that he is to let him go.'

'Better shut the door first,' said Keyork, suiting the action to the word and then coming back.

'Make haste!' said the Wanderer with impatience. 'The man is ill, whether he is mad or not.'

Released at last from the Individual's iron grip, Israel Kafka staggered a little. The Wanderer took him kindly by the arm, supporting his steps and leading him to a seat. Kafka glanced suspiciously at him and at the other two, but seemed unable to make any further effort and sank back with a low groan. His face grew pale and his eyelids drooped.

'Get some wine – something to restore him,' the Wanderer said.

Keyork looked at the Moravian critically for a moment.

'Yes,' he assented, 'he is more exhausted than I thought. He is not very dangerous now.' Then he went in search of what was needed. The Individual retired to a distance and stood looking on with folded arms.

'Do you hear me?' asked the Wanderer, speaking gently. 'Do you understand what I say?'

Israel Kafka nodded, but said nothing.

'You are very ill. This foolish idea that has possessed you this evening comes from your illness. Will you go away quietly with me, and make no resistance, so that I may take care of you?'

This time there was not even a movement of the head.

'This is merely a passing thing,' the Wanderer continued in a tone of quiet encouragement. 'You have been feverish and excited, and I dare say you have been too much alone of late. If you will come with me, I will take care of you, and see that all is well.'

'I told you that I would kill her – and I will,' said Israel Kafka, faintly but distinctly.

'You will not kill her,' answered his companion. 'I will prevent you from attempting it, and as soon as you are well you will see the absurdity of the idea.'

Israel Kafka made an impatient gesture, feeble but sufficiently expressive. Then all at once his limbs relaxed, and his head fell forward upon his breast. The Wanderer started to his feet and moved him into a more comfortable position. There were one or two quickly drawn breaths and the breathing ceased altogether. At that moment Keyork returned carrying a bottle of wine and a glass.

'It is too late,' said the Wanderer gravely. 'Israel Kafka is dead.'

'Dead!' exclaimed Keyork, setting down what he had in his hands, and hastening to examine the unfortunate man's face and eyes. 'The Individual squeezed him a little too hard, I suppose,' he added, applying his ear to the region of the heart, and moving his head about a little as he did so.

'I hate men who make statements about things they do not understand,' he said viciously, looking up as he spoke, but without any expression of satisfaction. 'He is no more dead than you are – the greater pity! It would have been so convenient. It is nothing but a slight syncope – probably the result of poorness of blood and an over-excited state of the nervous system. Help me to lay him on his back. You ought to have known that was the only thing to do. Put a cushion under his head. There – he will come to himself presently, but he will not be so dangerous as he was.'

The Wanderer drew a long breath of relief as he helped Keyork to make the necessary arrangements.

'How long will it last?' he inquired.

'How can I tell?' returned Keyork sharply. 'Have you never heard of a syncope? Do you know nothing about anything?'

He had produced a bottle containing some very strong salt and was applying it to the unconscious man's nostrils. The Wanderer paid no attention to his irritable temper and stood looking on. A long time passed and yet the Moravian gave no further signs of consciousness.

'It is clear that he cannot stay here if he is to be seriously ill,' the Wanderer said.

'And it is equally clear that he cannot be taken away,' retorted Keyork.

'You seem to be in a very combative frame of mind,' the other answered, sitting down and looking at his watch. 'If you cannot revive him, he ought to be brought to more comfortable quarters for the night.'

'In his present condition – of course,' said Keyork with a sneer.

'Do you think he would be in danger on the way?'

'I never think – I know,' snarled the sage.

The Wanderer showed a slight surprise at the roughness of the answer, but said nothing, contenting himself with watching the proceedings keenly. He was by no means past suspecting that Keyork might apply some medicine the very reverse of reviving, if left to himself. For the present there seemed to be no danger. The pungent smell of salts of ammonia pervaded the place; but the Wanderer knew that Keyork had a bottle of ether in the pocket of his coat, and he rightly judged that a very little of that would put an end to the life that was hanging in the balance. Nearly half an hour passed before either spoke again. Then Keyork looked up. This time his voice was smooth and persuasive. His irritability had all disappeared.

'You must be tired,' he said. 'Why do you not go home? Or else go to my house and wait for us. The Individual and I can take care of him very well.'

'Thanks,' replied the Wanderer with a slight smile. 'I am not in the least tired, and I prefer to stay where I am. I am not hindering you, I believe.'

Now Keyork Arabian had no interest in allowing Israel Kafka to die, though the Wanderer half believed that he had, though he could not imagine what that interest might be. The little man was in reality on the track of an experiment, and he knew very well that so long as he was so narrowly watched it would be quite impossible to try it. In spite of his sneers at his companion's ignorance, he was aware that the latter knew enough to make every effort conducive to reviving the patient if left to himself, and he submitted with a bad grace to doing what he would rather have left undone.

He would have wished to let the flame of life sink yet lower before making it brighten again, for he had with him a preparation which he had been carrying in his pocket for months in the hope of accidentally happening upon just such a case as the present, and he longed for an opportunity of trying it. But to give it a fair trial he wished to apply it at the precise point when, according to all previous experience, the moment of death was past – the moment when the physician usually puts his watch in his pocket and looks about for his hat. Possibly if Kafka, being left without any assistance, had shown no further signs of sinking, Keyork would have helped him to sink a little lower. To produce this much-desired result, he had nothing with him but the ether, of which the Wanderer of course knew the smell and understood the effects. He saw the chances of making the experiment upon an excellent subject slipping away before his eyes and he grew more angry in proportion as they seemed farther removed.

'He is a little better,' he said discontentedly, after another long interval of silence.

The Wanderer bent down and saw that the eyelids were quivering and that the face was less deathly livid than before. Then the eyes opened and stared dreamily at the glass roof.

'And I will,' said the faint, weak voice, as though completing a sentence.

'I think not,' observed Keyork, as though answering. 'The people who do what they mean to do are not always talking about will.' But Kafka had closed his eyes again.

This time, however, his breathing was apparent and he was evidently returning to a conscious state. The Wanderer arranged the pillow more comfortably under his head and covered him with his own furs. Keyork, relinquishing all hopes of trying the experiment at present, poured a little wine down his throat.

'Do you think we can take him home tonight?' inquired the Wanderer.

He was prepared for an ill-tempered answer, but not for what Keyork actually said. The little man got upon his feet and coolly buttoned his coat.

'I think not,' he replied. 'There is nothing to be done but to keep him quiet. Good-night. I am tired of all this nonsense, and I do not mean to lose my night's rest for all the Israels in Jewry – or all the Jews in Israel. You can stay with him if you please.'

Thereupon he turned on his heel, making a sign to the Individual, who had not moved from his place since Kafka had lost consciousness, and who immediately followed his master.

'I will come and see to him in the morning,' said Keyork carelessly, as he disappeared from sight among the plants.

The Wanderer's long-suffering temper was roused and his eyes gleamed angrily as he looked after the departing sage.

'Hound!' he exclaimed in a very audible voice.

He hardly knew why he was so angry with the man who called himself his friend. Keyork had behaved no worse than an ordinary doctor, for he had stayed until the danger was over and had promised to come again in the morning. It was his cool way of disclaiming all further responsibility and of avoiding all further trouble which elicited the Wanderer's resentment, as well as the unpleasant position in which the latter found himself.

He had certainly not anticipated being left in charge of a sick man – and that sick man Israel Kafka – in Unorna's house for the whole night, and he did not enjoy the prospect. The mere detail of having to give some explanation to the servants, who would doubtless come before long to extinguish the lights, was far from pleasant. Moreover, though Keyork had declared the patient out of danger, there seemed no absolute certainty that a relapse would not take place before morning, and Kafka might actually die in the certainty – delusive enough – that Unorna could not return until the following day.

He did not dare to take upon himself the responsibility of calling someone to help him and of removing the Moravian in his present condition. The man was still very weak and either altogether unconscious, or sleeping the sleep of exhaustion. The weather, too, was bitterly cold, and the exposure to the night air might bring on immediate and fatal consequences. He examined Kafka closely and came to the conclusion that he was really asleep. To wake him would be absolutely cruel as well as dangerous. He looked kindly at the weary face and then began to walk up and down between the plants, coming back at the end of every turn to look again and assure himself that no change had taken place.

After some time he began to wonder at the total silence in the house, or, rather, the silence which was carefully provided for in the conservatory impressed itself upon him for the first time. It was strange, he thought, that no one came to put out the lamps. He thought of looking out into the vestibule beyond, to see whether the lights were still burning there. To his great surprise he found the door securely fastened. Keyork Arabian had undoubtedly locked him in, and to all intents and purposes he was a prisoner. He suspected some treachery, but in this he was mistaken. Keyork's sole intention had been to insure himself from being disturbed in the course of the night by a second visit from the Wanderer, accompanied perhaps by Kafka. It immediately occurred to the Wanderer that he could ring the bell. But disliking the idea of entering into an explanation, he reserved that for an emergency. Had he attempted it he would have been still further surprised to find that it would have produced no result. In going through the vestibule Keyork had used Kafka's sharp knife to cut one of the slender silk-covered copper wires which passed out of the conservatory on that side, communicating with the servants' quarters. He was perfectly acquainted with all such details of the household arrangement.

Keyork's precautions were in reality useless and they merely illustrate the ruthlessly selfish character of the man. The Wanderer would in all probability neither have attempted to leave the house with Kafka that night, nor to communicate with the servants, even if he had been left free to do either, and if no one had disturbed him in his watch. He was disturbed, however, and very unexpectedly, between half-past one and a quarter to two in the morning.

More than once he had remained seated for a long time, but his eyes were growing heavy and he roused himself and walked again until he was thoroughly awake. It was certainly true that of all the persons concerned in the events of the day, except Keyork, he had undergone the least bodily fatigue and mental excitement. But even to the strongest, the hours of the night spent in watching by a sick person seem endless when there is no really strong personal anxiety felt. He was undoubtedly interested in Kafka's fate, and was resolved to protect him as well as to hinder him from committing any act of folly. But he had only met him for the first time that very afternoon, and under circumstances which had not in the first instance suggested even the possibility of a friendship between the two. His position towards Israel Kafka was altogether unexpected, and what he felt was no more than pity for his sufferings and indignation against those who had caused them.

When the door was suddenly opened, he stood still in his walk and faced it. He hardly recognised Unorna in the pale, dishevelled woman with circled eyes who came towards him under the bright light. She, too, stood still when she saw him, starting suddenly. She seemed to be very cold, for she shivered visibly and her teeth were chattering. Without the least protection against the bitter night air she had fled bareheaded and cloakless through the open streets from the church to her home.

'You here!' she exclaimed, in an unsteady voice.

'Yes, I am still here,' answered the Wanderer. 'But I hardly expected you to come back tonight,' he added.

At the sound of his voice a strange smile came into her wan face and lingered there. She had not thought to hear him speak again, kindly or unkindly, for she had come with the fixed determination to meet her death at Israel Kafka's hands and to let that be the end. Amid all the wild thoughts that had whirled through her brain as she ran home in the dark, that one had not once changed.

'And Israel Kafka?' she asked, almost timidly.

'He is there – asleep.'

Unorna came forward and the Wanderer showed her where the man lay upon a thick carpet, wrapped in furs, his pale head supported by a cushion.

'He is very ill,' she said, almost under her breath. 'Tell me what has happened.'

It was like a dream to her. The tremendous excitement of what had happened in the convent had cut her off from the realisation of what had gone before. Strange as it seemed even to herself, she scarcely comprehended the intimate connection between the two series of events, nor the bearing of the one upon the other. Israel Kafka sank into such insignificance that she had began to pity his condition, and it was hard to remember that the Wanderer was the man whom Beatrice had loved, and of whom she had spoken so long and so passionately. She found, too, an unreasoned joy in being once more by his side, no matter under what conditions. In that happiness, one-sided and unshared, she forgot everything else. Beatrice had been a dream, a vision, an unreal shadow. Kafka was nothing to her, and yet everything, as she suddenly saw, since he constituted a bond between her and the man she loved, which would at least outlast the night. In a flash she saw that the Wanderer would not leave her alone with the Moravian, and that the latter could not be moved for the present without danger to his life. They must watch together by his side through the long hours. Who could tell what the night would bring forth?

As the new development of the situation presented itself, the colour rose again to her cheeks. The warmth of the conservatory, too, dispelled the chill that had penetrated her, and the familiar odours of the flowers contributed to restore the lost equilibrium of mind and body.

'Tell me what has happened,' she said again.

In the fewest possible words the Wanderer told her all that had occurred up to the moment of her coming, not omitting the detail of the locked door.

'And for what reason do you suppose that Keyork shut you in?' she asked.

'I do not know,' the Wanderer answered. 'I do not trust him, though I have known him so long.'

'It was mere selfishness,' said Unorna scornfully. 'I know him better than you do. He was afraid you would disturb him again in the night.'

The Wanderer said nothing, wondering how any man could be so elaborately thoughtful of his own comfort.

'There is no help for it,' Unorna said, 'we must watch together.'

'I see no other way,' the Wanderer answered indifferently.

He placed a chair for her to sit in, within sight of the sick man, and took one himself, wondering at the strange situation, and yet not caring to ask Unorna what had brought her back, so breathless and so pale, at such an hour. He believed, not unnaturally, that her motive had been either anxiety for himself, or the irresistible longing to see him again, coupled with a distrust of his promise to return when she should send for him. It seemed best to accept her appearance without question, lest an inquiry should lead to a fresh outburst, more unbearable now than before, since there seemed to be no way of leaving the house without exposing her to danger. A nervous man like Israel Kafka might spring up at any moment and do something dangerous.

After they had taken their places the silence lasted some moments.

'You did not believe all I told you this evening?' said Unorna softly, with an interrogation in her voice.

'No,' the Wanderer answered quietly, 'I did not.'

'I am glad of that – I was mad when I spoke.'

Chapter 23

The Wanderer was not inclined to deny the statement which accorded well enough with his total disbelief of the story Unorna had told him. But he did not answer her immediately, for he found himself in a very difficult position. He would neither do anything in the least discourteous beyond admitting frankly that he had not believed her, when she taxed him with incredulity; nor would say anything which might serve her as a stepping-stone for returning to the original situation. He was, perhaps, inclined to blame her somewhat less than at first, and her changed manner in speaking of Kafka somewhat encouraged his leniency. A man will forgive, or at least condone, much harshness to others when he is thoroughly aware that it has been exhibited out of love for himself; and a man of the Wanderer's character cannot help feeling a sort of chivalrous respect and delicate forbearance for a woman who loves him sincerely, though against his will, while he will avoid with an almost exaggerated prudence the least word which could be interpreted as an expression of reciprocal tenderness. He runs the risk, at the same time, of being thrust into the ridiculous position of the man who, though young, assumes the manner and speech of age and delivers himself of grave, paternal advice to one who looks upon him, not as an elder, but as her chosen mate.

After Unorna had spoken, the Wanderer, therefore, held his peace. He inclined his head a little, as though to admit that her plea of madness might not be wholly imaginary; but he said nothing. He sat looking at Israel Kafka's sleeping face and outstretched form, inwardly wondering whether the hours would seem very long before Keyork Arabian returned in the morning and put an end to the situation. Unorna waited in vain for some response, and at last spoke again.

'Yes,' she said, 'I was mad. You cannot understand it. I dare say you cannot even understand how I can speak of it now, and yet I cannot help speaking.'

Her manner was more natural and quiet than it had been since the moment of Kafka's appearance in the cemetery. The Wanderer noticed the tone. There was an element of real sadness in it, with a leaven of bitter disappointment and a savour of heartfelt contrition. She was in earnest now, as she had been before, but in a different way. He could hardly refuse her a word in answer.

'Unorna,' he said gravely, 'remember that you are leaving me no choice. I cannot leave you alone with that poor fellow, and so, whatever you wish to say, I must hear. But it would be much better to say nothing about what has happened this evening – better for you and for me. Neither men nor women always mean exactly what they say. We are not angels. Is it not best to let the matter drop?'

Unorna listened quietly, her eyes upon his face.

'You are not so hard with me as you were,' she said thoughtfully, after a moment's hesitation, and there was a touch of gratitude in her voice. As she felt the dim possibility of a return to her former relations of friendship with him, Beatrice and the scene in the church seemed to be very far away. Again the Wanderer found it difficult to answer.

'It is not for me to be hard, as you call it,' he said quietly. There was a scarcely perceptible smile on his face, brought there not by any feeling of satisfaction, but by his sense of his own almost laughable perplexity. He saw that he was very near being driven to the ridiculous necessity of giving her some advice of the paternal kind. 'It is not for me, either, to talk to you of what you have done to Israel Kafka today,' he confessed. 'Do not oblige me to say anything about it. It will be much safer. You know it all better than I do, and you understand your own reasons, as I never can. If you are sorry for him now, so much the better – you will not hurt him any more if you can help it. If you will say that much about the future I shall be very glad, I confess.'

'Do you think that there is anything which I will not do – if you ask it?' Unorna asked very earnestly.

'I do not know,' the Wanderer answered, trying to seem to ignore the meaning conveyed by her tone. 'Some things are harder to do than others – '

'Ask me the hardest!' she exclaimed. 'Ask me to tell you the whole truth – '

'No,' he said firmly, in the hope of checking an outburst of passionate speech. 'What you have thought and done is no concern of mine. If you have done anything that you are sorry for, without my knowledge, I do not wish to know of it. I have seen you do many good and kind acts during the last month, and I would rather leave those memories untouched as far as possible. You may have had an object in doing them which in itself was bad. I do not care. The deeds were good. Take credit for them and let me give you credit for them. That will do neither of us any harm.'

'I could tell you – if you would let me – '

'Do not tell me,' he interrupted. 'I repeat that I do not wish to know. The one thing that I have seen is bad enough. Let that be all. Do you not see that? Besides, I am myself the cause of it in a measure – unwilling enough, Heaven knows!'

'The only cause,' said Unorna bitterly.

'Then I am in some way responsible. I am not quite without blame – we men never are in such cases. If I reproach you, I must reproach myself as well – '

'Reproach yourself! – ah no! What can you say against yourself?' she could not keep the love out of her voice, if she would; her bitterness had been for herself.

'I will not go into that,' he answered. 'I am to blame in one way or another. Let us say no more about it. Will you let the matter rest?'

'And let bygones be bygones, and be friends to each other, as we were this morning?' she asked, with a ray of hope.

The Wanderer was silent for a few seconds. His difficulties were increasing. A while ago he had told her, as an excuse for herself, that men and women did not always mean exactly what they said, and even now he did not set himself up in his own mind as an exception to the rule. Very honourable and truthful men do not act upon any set of principles in regard to truth and honour. Their instinctively brave actions and naturally noble truthfulness make those principles which are held up to the unworthy for imitation, by those whose business is the teaching of what is good. The Wanderer's only hesitation lay between answering the question or not answering it.

'Shall we be friends again?' Unorna asked a second time, in a low tone. 'Shall we go back to the beginning?'

'I do not see how that is possible,' he answered slowly.

Unorna was not like him, and did not understand such a nature as his as she understood Keyork Arabian. She had believed that he would at least hold out some hope.

'You might have spared me that!' she said, turning her face away. There were tears in her voice.

A few hours earlier his answer would have brought fire to her eyes and anger to her voice. But a real change had come over her, not lasting, perhaps, but strong in its immediate effects.

'Not even a little friendship left?' she said, breaking the silence that followed.

'I cannot change myself,' he answered, almost wishing that he could. 'I ought, perhaps,' he added, as though speaking to himself. 'I have done enough harm as it is.'

'Harm? To whom?' She looked round suddenly and he saw the moisture in her eyes.

'To him,' he replied, glancing at Kafka, 'and to you. You loved him once. I have ruined his life.'

'Loved him? No – I never loved him.' She shook her head, wondering whether she spoke the truth.

'You must have made him think so.'

'I? No – he is mad.' But she shrank before his honest look, and suddenly broke down. 'No – I will not lie to you – you are too true – yes, I loved him, or I thought I did, until you came, and I saw that there was no one – '

But she checked herself, as she felt the blood rising to her cheeks. She could blush still, and still be ashamed. Even she was not all bad, now that she was calm and that the change had come over her.

'You see,' the Wanderer said gently, 'I am to blame for it all.'

'For it all? No – not for the thousandth part of it all. What blame have you in being what you are? Blame God in Heaven – for making such a man. Blame me for what you know; blame me for all that you will not let me tell you. Blame Kafka for his mad belief in me and Keyork Arabian for the rest – but do not blame yourself – oh, no! Not that!'

'Do not talk like that, Unorna,' he said. 'Be just first.'

'What is justice?' she asked. Then she turned her head away again. 'If you knew what justice means for me – you would not ask me to be just. You would be more merciful.'

'You exaggerate – ' He spoke kindly, but she interrupted him.

'No. You do not know, that is all. And you can never guess. There is only one man living who could imagine such things as I have done – and tried to do. He is Keyork Arabian. But he would have been wiser than I, perhaps.'

She relapsed into silence. Before her rose the dim altar in the church, the shadowy figure of Beatrice standing up in the dark, the horrible sacrilege that was to have been done. Her face grew dark with fear for her own soul. The Wanderer went so far as to try and distract her from her gloomy thoughts, out of pure kindness of heart.

'I am no theologian,' he said, 'but I fancy that in the long reckoning the intention goes for more than the act.'

'The intention!' she cried, looking back with a start. 'If that be true – ' with a shudder she buried her face in her two hands, pressing them to her eyes as though to blind them to some awful sight. Then, with a short struggle, she turned to him again.

'There is no forgiveness for me in Heaven,' she said. 'Shall there be none on earth! Not even a little, from you to me?'

'There is no question of forgiveness between you and me. You have not injured me, but Israel Kafka. Judge for yourself which of us two, he or I, has anything to forgive. I am today what I was yesterday and may be tomorrow. He lies there, dying of his love for you, if ever a man died for love. And as though that were not enough, you have tortured him – well, I will not speak of it. But that is all. I know nothing of the deeds, or intentions, of which you accuse yourself. You are tired, overwrought, worn out with all this – what shall I say? It is natural enough, I suppose – '

'You say there is no question of forgiveness,' she said, interrupting him, but speaking more calmly. 'What is it then? What is the real question? If you have nothing to forgive why can we not be friends as we were before?'

'There is something besides that needed. It is not enough that of two people neither should have injured the other. You have broken something, destroyed something – I cannot mend it. I wish I could.'

'You wish you could?' she repeated earnestly.

'I wish that the thing had not been done. I wish that I had not seen what I saw today. We should be where we were this morning – and he perhaps would not be here.'

'It must have come some day,' Unorna said. 'He must have seen that I loved – that I loved you. Is there any use in not speaking plainly now? Then at some other time, in some other place, he would have done what he did, and I should have been angry and cruel – for it is my nature to be cruel when I am angry, and to be angry easily, at that. Men talk so easily of self-control, and self-command and dignity, and self-respect! They have not loved – that is all. I am not angry now, nor cruel. I am sorry for what I did, and I would undo it, if deeds were knots and wishes deeds. I am sorry, beyond all words to tell you. How poor it sounds now that I have said it! You do not even believe me.'

'You are wrong. I know that you are in earnest.'

'How do you know?' she asked bitterly. 'Have I never lied to you? If you believed me, you would forgive me. If you forgave me, your friendship would come back. I cannot even swear to you that I am telling the truth. Heaven would not be my witness now if I told a thousand truths, each truer than the last.'

'I have nothing to forgive,' the Wanderer said, almost wearily. 'I have told you so, you have not injured me, but him.'

'But if it meant a whole world to me – no, for I am nothing to you – but if it cost you nothing, but the little breath that can carry the three words – would you say it? Is it much to say? Is it like saying, I love you, or, I honour you, respect you? It is so little, and would mean so much.'

'To me it can mean nothing, unless you ask me to forgive you deeds of which I know nothing. And then it means still less to me.'

'Will you say it, only say the three words once?'

'I forgive you,' said the Wanderer quietly. It cost him nothing, and, to him, meant less.

Unorna bent her head and was silent. It was something to have heard him say it though he could not guess the least of the sins which she made it include. She herself hardly knew why she had so insisted. Perhaps it was only the longing to hear words kind in themselves, if not in tone, nor in his meaning of them. Possibly, too, she felt a dim presentiment of her coming end, and would take with her that infinitesimal grain of pardon to the state in which she hoped for no other forgiveness.

'It was good of you to say it,' she said at last.

A long silence followed during which the thoughts of each went their own way. Suddenly Israel Kafka stirred in his sleep. The Wanderer went quickly forward and knelt down beside him and arranged the silken pillow as best he could. Unorna was on the other side almost as soon. With a tenderness of expression and touch which nothing can describe she moved the sleeping head into a comfortable position and smoothed the cushion, and drew up the furs disturbed by the nervous hands. The Wanderer let her have her way. When she had finished their eyes met. He could not tell whether she was asking his approval and a word of encouragement, but he withheld neither.

'You are very gentle with him. He would thank you if he could.'

'Did you not tell me to be kind to him?' she said. 'I am keeping my word. But he would not thank me. He would kill me if he were awake.'

The Wanderer shook his head.

'He was ill and mad with pain,' he answered. 'He did not know what he was doing. When he wakes, it will be different.'

Unorna rose, and the Wanderer followed her.

'You cannot believe that I care,' she said, as she resumed her seat. 'He is not you. My soul would not be the nearer to peace for a word of his.'

For a long time she sat quite still, her hands lying idly in her lap, her head bent wearily as though she bore a heavy burden.

'Can you not rest?' the Wanderer asked at length. 'I can watch alone.'

'No. I cannot rest. I shall never rest again.'

The words came slowly, as though spoken to herself.

'Do you bid me go?' she asked after a time, looking up and seeing his eyes fixed on her.

'Bid you go? In your own house?' The tone was one of ordinary courtesy. Unorna smiled sadly.

'I would rather you struck me than that you spoke to me like that!' she exclaimed. 'You have no need of such civil forbearance with me. If you bid me go, I will go. If you bid me stay, I will not move. Only speak frankly. Say which you would prefer.'

'Then stay,' said the Wanderer simply.

She bowed her head slightly and was silent again. A distant clock chimed the hour. The morning was slowly drawing near.

'And you,' said Unorna, looking up at the sound. 'Will you not rest? Why should you not sleep?'

'I am not tired.'

'You do not trust me, I think,' she answered sadly. 'And yet you might – you might.' Her voice died away dreamily.

'Trust you to watch that poor man? Indeed I do. You were not acting just now, when you touched him so tenderly. You are in earnest. You will be kind to him, and I thank you for it.'

'And you yourself? Do you fear nothing from me, if you should sleep before my eyes? Do you not fear that in your unconsciousness I might touch you and make you more unconscious still and make you dream dreams and see visions?'

The Wanderer looked at her and smiled incredulously, partly out of scorn for the imaginary danger, and partly because something told him that she had changed and would not attempt any of her witchcraft upon him.

'No,' he answered. 'I am not afraid of that.'

'You are right,' she said gravely. 'My sins are enough already. The evil is sufficient. Do as you will. If you can sleep, then sleep in peace. If you will watch, watch with me.'

Then neither spoke again. Unorna bent her head as she had done before. The Wanderer leaned back resting comfortably against the cushion of the high carved chair, his eyes directed towards the place where Israel Kafka lay. The air was warm, the scent of the flowers sweet but not heavy. The silence was intense, for even the little fountain was still. He had watched almost all night and his eyelids drooped. He forgot Unorna and thought only of the sick man, trying to fix his attention on the pale head as it lay under the bright light.

When Unorna looked up at last she saw that he was asleep. At first she was surprised, in spite of what she had said to him half an hour earlier, for she herself could not have closed her eyes, and felt that she could never close them again. Then she sighed. It was but one proof more of his supreme indifference. He had not even cared to speak to her, and if she had not constantly spoken to him throughout the hours they had passed together he would perhaps have been sleeping long before now.

And yet she feared to wake him and was almost glad that he was unconscious. In the solitude she could gaze on him to her heart's desire, she could let her eyes look their fill, and no one could say her nay. He must be very tired, she thought, and she vaguely wondered why she felt no bodily weariness, when her soul was so heavy.

She sat still and watched him. It might be the last time, she thought, for who could tell what would happen tomorrow? She shuddered as she thought of it all. What would Beatrice do? What would Sister Paul say? How much would she tell of what she had seen? How much had she really seen which she could tell clearly? There were terrible possibilities in the future if all were known. Such deeds, and even the attempt at such deeds as she had tried to do, could be judged by the laws of the land, she might be brought to trial, if she lived, as a common prisoner, and held up to the execration of the world in all her shame and guilt. But death would be worse than that. As she thought of that other Judgment, she grew dizzy with horror as she had been when the idea had first entered her brain.

Then she was conscious that she was again looking at the Wanderer as he lay back asleep in his tall chair. The pale and noble face expressed the stainless soul and the manly character. She saw in it the peace she had lost, and yet knew that through him she had lost her peace for ever.

It was perhaps the last time. Never again, perhaps, after the morning had broken, should she look on what she loved best on earth. She would be gone, ruined, dead perhaps. And he? He would be still himself. He would remember her half carelessly, half in wonder, as a woman who had once been almost his friend. That would be all that would be left in him of her, beyond a memory of the repulsion he had felt for her deeds.

She fancied she could have met the worst in the future less hopelessly if he could have remembered her a little more kindly when all was over. Even now, it might be in her power to cast a veil upon the pictures in his mind. But the mere thought was horrible to her, though a few hours before she had hardly trembled at the doing of a frightful sacrilege. In that short time the humiliation of failure, the realisation of what she had almost done, above all the ever-rising tide of a real and passionate love, had swept away many familiar land-marks in her thoughts, and had turned much to lead which had once seemed brighter than gold. She hated the very idea of using again those arts which had so directly wrought her utter destruction. But she longed to know that in the world whither he would doubtless go tomorrow he would bear with him one kind memory of her, one natural friendly thought not grafted upon his mind by her power, but growing of its own self in his inmost heart. Only a friendly memory – nothing more than that.

She rose noiselessly and came to his side and looked down into his face. Very long she stood there, motionless as a statue, beautiful as a mourning angel.

It was so little that she asked. It was so little compared with all she had hoped, or in comparison with all she had demanded, so little in respect of what she had given. For she had given her soul. And in return she asked only for one small kindly thought when all should be over.

She bent down as she stood and touched his cool forehead with her lips.

'Sleep on, my beloved,' she said in a voice that murmured softly and sadly.

She started a little at what she had done, and drew back, half afraid, like an innocent girl. But as though he had obeyed her words, he seemed to sleep more deeply still. He must be very tired, she thought, to sleep like that, but she was thankful that the soft kiss, the first and last, had not waked him.

'Sleep on,' she said again in a whisper scarcely audible to herself. 'Forget Unorna, if you cannot think of her mercifully and kindly. Sleep on, you have the right to rest, and I can never rest again. You have forgiven – forget, too, then, unless you can remember better things of me than I have deserved in your memory. Let her take her kingdom back. It was never mine – remember what you will, forget at least the wrong I did, and forgive the wrong you never knew – for you will know it surely some day. Ah, love – I love you so – dream but one dream, and let me think I take her place. She never loved you more than I, she never can. She would not have done what I have done. Dream only that I am Beatrice for this once. Then when you wake you will not think so cruelly of me. Oh, that I might be she – and you your loving self – that I might be she for one day in thought and word, in deed and voice, in face and soul! Dear love – you would never know it, yet I should know that you had had one loving thought for me. You would forget. It would not matter then to you, for you would have only dreamed, and I should have the certainty – for ever, to take with me always!'

As though the words carried a meaning with them to his sleeping senses, a look of supreme and almost heavenly happiness stole over his sleeping face. But Unorna could not see it. She had turned suddenly away, burying her face in her hands upon the back of her own chair.

'Are there no miracles left in Heaven?' she moaned, half whispering lest she should wake him. 'Is there no miracle of deeds undone again and of forgiveness given – for me? God! God! That we should be for ever what we make ourselves!'

There were no tears in her eyes now, as there had been twice that night. In her despair, that fountain of relief, shallow always and not apt to overflow, was dried up and scorched with pain. And, for the time at least, worse things were gone from her, though she suffered more. As though some portion of her passionate wish had been fulfilled, she felt that she could never do again what she had done; she felt that she was truthful now as he was, and that she knew evil from good even as Beatrice knew it. The horror of her sins took new growth in her changed vision.

'Was I lost from the first beginning?' she asked passionately. 'Was I born to be all I am, and fore-destined to do all I have done? Was she born an angel and I a devil from hell? What is it all? What is this life, and what is that other beyond it?'

Behind her, in his chair, the Wanderer still slept. Still his face wore the radiant look of joy that had so suddenly come into it as she turned away. He scarcely breathed, so calmly he slept. But Unorna did not raise her head nor look at him, and on the carpet near her feet Israel Kafka lay as still and as deeply unconscious as the Wanderer himself. By a strange destiny she sat there, between the two men in whom her whole life had been wrecked, and she alone was waking.

When she at last raised her eyes the dawn was breaking. Through the transparent roof of glass a cold grey light began to descend upon the warm, still brightness of the lamps. The shadows changed, the colours grew more cold, the dark nooks among the heavy foliage less black. Israel Kafka's face was ghostly and livid – the Wanderer's had the alabaster transparency that comes upon some strong men in sleep. Still, neither stirred. Unorna turned from the one and looked upon the other. For the first time she saw how he had changed, and wondered.

'How peacefully he sleeps!' she thought. 'He is dreaming of her.'

The dawn came stealing on, not soft and blushing as in southern lands, but cold, resistless and grim as ancient fate; not the maiden herald of the sun with rose-tipped fingers and grey, liquid eyes, but hard, cruel, sullen, and less darkness following upon a greater and going before a dull, sunless and heavy day.

The door opened somewhat noisily and a brisk step fell upon the marble pavement. Unorna rose noiselessly to her feet and hastening along the open space came face to face with Keyork Arabian. He stopped and looked up at her from beneath his heavy brows, with surprise and suspicion. She raised one finger to her lips.

'You here already?' he asked, obeying her gesture and speaking in a low voice.

'Hush! Hush!' she whispered, not satisfied. 'They are asleep. You will wake them.'

Keyork came forward. He could move quietly enough when he chose. He glanced at the Wanderer.

'He looks comfortable enough,' he whispered, half contemptuously.

Then he bent down over Israel Kafka and carefully examined his face. To him the ghastly pallor meant nothing. It was but the natural result of excessive exhaustion.

'Put him into a lethargy,' said he under his breath, but with authority in his manner.

Unorna shook her head. Keyork's small eyes brightened angrily.

'Do it,' he said. 'What is this caprice? Are you mad? I want to take his temperature without waking him.'

Unorna folded her arms.

'Do you want him to suffer more?' asked Keyork with a diabolical smile. 'If so I will wake him by all means; I am always at your service, you know.'

'Will he suffer, if he wakes naturally?'

'Horribly – in the head.'

Unorna knelt down and let her hand rest a few seconds on Kafka's brow. The features, drawn with pain, immediately relaxed.

'You have hypnotised the one,' grumbled Keyork as he bent down again. 'I cannot imagine why you should object to doing the same for the other.'

'The other?' Unorna repeated in surprise.

'Our friend there, in the armchair.'

'It is not true. He fell asleep of himself.'

Keyork smiled again, incredulously this time. He had already applied his pocket-thermometer and looked at his watch. Unorna had risen to her feet, disdaining to defend herself against the imputation expressed in his face. Some minutes passed in silence.

'He has no fever,' said Keyork looking at the little instrument. 'I will call the Individual and we will take him away.'

'Where?'

'To his lodging, of course. Where else?' He turned and went towards the door.

In a moment, Unorna was kneeling again by Kafka's side, her hand upon his forehead, her lips close to his ear.

'This is the last time that I will use my power on you or upon anyone,' she said quickly, for the time was short. 'Obey me, as you must. Do you understand me? Will you obey?'

'Yes,' came the faint answer as from very far off.

'You will wake two hours from now. You will not forget all that has happened, but you will never love me again. I forbid you ever to love me again! Do you understand?'

'I understand.'

'You will only forget that I have told you this, though you will obey. You will see me again, and if you can forgive me of your own free will, forgive me then. That must be of your own free will. Wake in two hours of yourself, without pain or sickness.'

Again she touched his forehead and then sprang to her feet. Keyork was coming back with his dumb servant. At a sign, the Individual lifted Kafka from the floor, taking from him the Wanderer's furs and wrapping him in others which Keyork had brought. The strong man walked away with his burden as though he were carrying a child. Keyork Arabian lingered a moment.

'What made you come back so early?' he asked.

'I will not tell you,' she answered, drawing back.

'No? Well, I am not curious. You have an excellent opportunity now.'

'An opportunity?' Unorna repeated with a cold interrogative.

'Excellent,' said the little man, standing on tiptoe to reach her ear, for she would not bend her head. 'You have only to whisper into his ear that you are Beatrice and he will believe you for the rest of his life.'

'Go!' said Unorna.

Though the word was not spoken above her breath it was fierce and commanding. Keyork Arabian smiled in an evil way, shrugged his shoulders and left her.

Chapter 24

Unorna was left alone with the Wanderer. His attitude did not change, his eyes did not open, as she stood before him. Still he wore the look which had at first attracted Keyork Arabian's attention and which had amazed Unorna herself. It was the expression that had come into his face in the old cemetery when in his sleep she had spoken to him of love.

'He is dreaming of her,' Unorna said to herself again, as she turned sadly away.

But since Keyork had been with her a doubt had assailed her which painfully disturbed her thoughts, so that her brow contracted with anxiety and from time to time she drew a quick hard breath. Keyork had taken it for granted that the Wanderer's sleep was not natural.

She tried to recall what had happened shortly before dawn but it was no wonder that her memory served her ill and refused to bring back distinctly the words she had spoken. Her whole being was unsettled and shaken, so that she found it hard to recognise herself. The stormy hours through which she had lived since yesterday had left their trace; the lack of rest, instead of producing physical exhaustion, had brought about an excessive mental weariness, and it was not easy for her now to find all the connecting links between her actions. Then, above all else, there was the great revulsion that had swept over her after her last and greatest plan of evil had failed, causing in her such a change as could hardly have seemed natural or even possible to a calm person watching her inmost thoughts.

And yet such sudden changes take place daily in the world of crime and passion. In one uncalled-for confession, of which it is hard to trace the smallest reasonable cause, the intricate wickednesses of a lifetime are revealed and repeated; in the mysterious impulse of a moment the murderer turns back and delivers himself to justice; under an influence for which there is often no accounting, the woman who has sinned securely through long years lays bare her guilt and throws herself upon the mercy of the man whom she has so skilfully and consistently deceived. We know the fact. The reason we cannot know. Perhaps, to natures not wholly bad, sin is a poison of which the moral organisation can only bear a certain fixed amount, great or small, before rejecting it altogether and with loathing. We do not know. We speak of the workings of conscience, not understanding what we mean. It is like that subtle something which we call electricity; we can play with it, command it, lead it, neutralise it and die of it, make light and heat with it, or language and sound, kill with it and cure with it, while absolutely ignorant of its nature. We are no nearer to a definition of it than the Greek who rubbed a bit of amber and lifted with it a tiny straw, and from amber, *elektron*, called the something electricity. Are we even as near as that to a definition of the human conscience?

The change that had come over Unorna, whether it was to be lasting or not, was profound. The circumstances under which it took place are plain enough. The reasons must be left to themselves – it remains only to tell the consequences which thereon followed.

The first of these was a hatred of that extraordinary power with which nature had endowed her, which brought with it a determination never again to make use of it for any evil purpose, and, if possible, never even for good.

But as though her unhappy fate were for ever fighting against her good impulses, that power of hers had exerted itself unconsciously, since her resolution had been formed. Keyork Arabian's words, and his evident though unspoken disbelief in her denial, showed that he at least was convinced of the fact that the Wanderer was not sleeping a natural sleep. Unorna tried to recall what she had done and said, but all was vague and indistinct. Of one thing she was sure. She had not laid her hand upon his forehead, and she had not intentionally done any of those things which she had always believed necessary for producing the results of hypnotism. She had not willed him to do anything, she thought, and she felt sure that she had pronounced no words of the nature of a command. Step by step she tried to reconstruct for her comfort a detailed recollection of what had passed, but every effort in that direction was fruitless. Like many men far wiser than herself, she believed in the mechanics of hypnotic science, in the touches, in the passes, in the fixed look, in the will to fascinate. More than once Keyork Arabian had scoffed at what he called her superstitions, and had maintained that all the varying phenomena of hypnotism, all the witchcraft of the darker ages, all the visions un- doubtedly shown to wondering eyes by mediaeval sorcerers, were traceable to moral influence, and to no other cause. Unorna could not accept his reasoning. For her there was a deeper and yet a more material mystery in it, as in her own life, a mystery which she cherished as an inheritance, which impressed her with a sense of her own strange destiny and of the gulf which separated her from other women. She could not detach herself from the idea that the supernatural played a part in all her doings, and she clung to the use of gestures and passes and words in the exercise of her art, in which she fancied a hidden and secret meaning to exist. Certain things had especially impressed her. The not uncommon answer of hypnotics to the question concerning their identity, 'I am the image in your eyes,' is undoubtedly elicited by the fact that their extraordinarily acute and, perhaps, magnifying vision, perceives the image of themselves in the eyes of the operator with abnormal distinctness, and, not impossibly, of a size quite incompatible with the dimensions of the pupil. To Unorna the answer meant something more. It suggested the actual presence of the person she was influencing, in her own brain, and whenever she was undertaking anything especially difficult, she endeavoured to obtain the reply relating to the image as soon as possible.

In the present case, she was sure that she had done none of the things which she considered necessary to produce a definite result. She was totally unconscious of having impressed upon the sleeper any suggestion of her will. Whatever she had said, she had addressed the words to herself without any intention that they should be heard and understood.

These reflections comforted her as she paced the marble floor, and yet Keyork's remark rang in her ears and disturbed her. She knew how vast his experience was and how much he could tell by a single glance at a human face. He had been familiar with every phase of hypnotism long before she had known him, and might reasonably be supposed to know by inspection whether the sleep were natural or not. That a person hypnotised may appear to sleep as naturally as one not under the influence is certain, but the condition of rest is also very often different, to a practised eye, from that of ordinary slumber. There is a fixity in the expression of the face, and in the attitude of the body, which cannot continue under ordinary circumstances. He had perhaps noticed both signs in the Wanderer.

She went back to his side and looked at him intently. She had scarcely dared to do so before, and she felt that she might have been mistaken. The light, too, had changed, for it was broad day, though the lamps were still burning. Yet, even now, she could not tell. Her judgment of what she saw was disturbed by many intertwining thoughts.

At least, he was happy. Whatever she had done, if she had done anything, it had not hurt him. There was no possibility of misinterpreting the sleeping man's expression.

She wished that he would wake, though she knew how the smile would fade, how the features would grow cold and indifferent, and how the grey eyes she loved would open with a look of annoyance at seeing her before him. It was like a vision of happiness in a house of sorrow to see him lying there, so happy in his sleep, so loving, so peaceful. She could make it all to last, too, if she would, and she realised that with a sudden pang. The woman of whom he dreamed, whom he had loved so faithfully and sought so long, was very near him. A word from Unorna and Beatrice could come and find him as he lay asleep, and herself open the dear eyes.

Was that sacrifice to be asked of her before she was taken away to the expiation of her sins? Fate could not be so very cruel – and yet the mere idea was an added suffering. The longer she looked at him the more the possibility grew and tortured her.

After all, it was almost certain that they would meet now, and at the meeting she felt sure that all his memory would return. Why should she do anything, why should she raise her hand, to bring them to each other? It was too much to ask. Was it not enough that both were free, and both in the same city together, and that she had vowed neither to hurt nor hinder them? If it was their destiny to be joined together it would so happen surely in the natural course; if not, was it her part to join them? The punishment of her sins, whatever it should be, she could bear; but this thing she could not do.

She passed her hand across her eyes as though to drive it away, and her thoughts came back to the point from which they had started. The suspense became unbearable when she realised that she did not know in what condition the Wanderer would wake, nor whether, if left to nature, he would wake at all. She could not endure it any longer. She touched his sleeve, lightly at first, and then more heavily. She moved his arm. It was passive in her hand and lay where she placed it. Yet she would not believe that she had made him sleep. She drew back and looked at him. Then her anxiety overcame her.

'Wake!' she cried, aloud. 'For God's sake, wake! I cannot bear it!'

His eyes opened at the sound of her voice, naturally and quietly. Then they grew wide and deep and fixed themselves in a great wonder of many seconds. Then Unorna saw no more.

Strong arms lifted her suddenly from her feet and pressed her fiercely and carried her, and she hid her face. A voice she knew sounded, as she had never heard it sound, nor hoped to hear it.

'Beatrice!' it cried, and nothing more.

In the presence of that strength, in the ringing of that cry, Unorna was helpless. She had no power of thought left in her, as she felt herself borne along, body and soul, in the rush of a passion more masterful than her own.

Then she was on her feet again, but his arms were round her still, and hers, whether she would or not, were clasped about his neck. Dreams, truth, faith kept or broken, hell and Heaven itself were swept away, all wrecked together in the tide of love. And through it all his voice was in her ear.

'Love, love, at last! From all the years, you have come back – at last – at last!'

Broken and almost void of sense the words came then, through the storm of his kisses and the tempest of her tears. She could no more resist him nor draw herself away than the frail ship, wind-driven through crashing waves, can turn and face the blast; no more than the long dry grass can turn and quench the roaring flame; no more than the drooping willow bough can dam the torrent and force it backwards up the steep mountain side.

In those short, false moments, Unorna knew what happiness could mean. Torn from herself, lifted high above the misery and the darkness of her real life, it was all true to her. There was no other Beatrice but herself, no other woman whom he had ever loved. An enchantment greater than her own was upon her and held her in bonds she could neither bend nor break.

She was sitting in her own chair now and he was kneeling before her, holding her hands and looking up to her. For him the world held nothing else. For him her hair was black as night; for him the unlike eyes were dark and fathomless; for him the heavy marble hand was light, responsive, delicate; for him her face was the face of Beatrice, as he had last seen it long ago. The years had passed, indeed, and he had sought her through many lands, but she had come back to him the same, in the glory of her youth, in the strength of her love, in the divinity of her dark beauty, his always, through it all, his now – for ever.

For a long time he did not speak. The words rose to his lips and failed of utterance, as the first mist of early morning is drawn heavenwards to vanish in the rising sun. The long-drawn breath could have made no sound of sweeter meaning than the unspoken speech that rose in the deep grey eyes. Nature's grand organ, touched by hands divine, can yield no chord more moving than a lover's sigh.

Words came at last, as after the welcome shower in summer's heat the song of birds rings through the woods, and out across the fields, upon the clear, earth-scented air – words fresh from their long rest within his heart, unused in years of loneliness but unforgotten and familiar still – untarnished jewels from the inmost depths; rich treasures from the storehouse of a deathless faith; diamonds of truth, rubies of passion, pearls of devotion studding the golden links of the chain of love.

'At last – at last – at last! Life of my life, the day is come that is not day without you, and now it will always be day for us two – day without end and sun for ever! And yet, I have seen you always in my night, just as I see you now. As I hold your dear hands, I have held them – day by day and year by year – and I have smoothed that black hair of yours that I love, and kissed those dark eyes of yours many and many a thousand times. It has been so long, love, so very long! But I knew it would come some day. I knew I should find you, for you have been always with me, dear – always and everywhere. The world is all full of you, for I have wandered through it all and taken you with me and made every place yours with the thought of you, and the love of you, and the worship of you. For me, there is not an ocean nor a sea nor a river, nor rock nor island nor broad continent of earth, that has not known Beatrice and loved her name. Heart of my heart, soul of my soul – the nights and the days without you, the lands and the oceans where you were not, the endlessness of this little world that hid you somewhere, the littleness of the whole universe without you – how can you ever know what it has been to me? And so it is gone at last – gone as a dream of sickness in the morning of health; gone as the blackness of storm-clouds in the sweep of the clear west wind; gone as the shadow of evil before the face of an angel of light! And I know it all. I see it all in your eyes. You knew I was true, and you knew I sought you, and would find you at last – and you have waited – and there has been no other, not the thought of another, not the passing image of another between us. For I know there has not been that and I should have known it anywhere in all these years, the chill of it would have found me, the sharpness of it would have been in my heart – no matter where, no matter how far – yet say it, say it once – say that you have loved me, too – '

'God knows how I have loved you – how I love you now!' Unorna said in a low, unsteady voice.

The light that had been in his face grew brighter still as she spoke, while she looked at him, wondering, her head thrown back against the high chair, her eyelids wet and drooping, her lips still parted, her hand in his. Small wonder if he had loved her for herself, she was so beautiful. Small wonder it would have been if she had taken Beatrice's place in his heart during those weeks of close and daily converse. But that first great love had left no fertile ground in which to plant another seed, no warmth of kindness under which the tender shoot might grow to strength, no room beneath its heaven for other branches than its own. Alone it had stood in majesty as a lordly tree, straight, tall, and ever green, on a silent mountain top. Alone it had borne the burden of grief's heavy snows; unbent, for all its loneliness, it had stood against the raging tempest; and green still, in all its giant strength of stem and branch, in all its kingly robe of unwithered foliage. Unscathed, unshaken, it yet stood. Neither storm nor lightning, wind nor rain, sun nor snow had prevailed against it to dry it up and cast it down that another might grow in its place.

Yet this love was not for her to whom he spoke, and she knew it as she answered him, though she answered truly, from the fullness of her heart. She had cast an enchantment over him unwittingly, and she was taken in the toils of her own magic even as she had sworn that she would never again put forth her powers. She shuddered as she realised it all. In a few short moments she had felt his kisses, and heard his words, and been clasped to his heart, as she had many a time madly hoped. But in those moments, too, she had known the truth of her woman's instinct when it had told her that love must be for herself and for her own sake, or not be love at all.

The falseness, the fathomless untruth of it, would have been bad enough alone. But the truth that was so strong made it horrible. Had she but inspired in him a burning love for herself, however much against his will, it would have been very different. She would have heard her name from his lips, she would have known that all, however false, however artificial, was for herself, while it might last. To know that it was real, and not for her, was intolerable. To see this love of his break out at last – this other love which she had dreaded, against which she had fought, which she had met with a jealousy as strong as itself, and struggled with and buried under an imposed forgetfulness – to feel its great waves surging around her and beating up against her heart, was more than she could bear. Her face grew whiter and her hands were cold. She dreaded each moment lest he should call her Beatrice again, and say that her fair hair was black and that he loved those deep dark eyes of hers.

There had been one moment of happiness, in that first kiss, in the first pressure of those strong arms. Then night descended. The hands that held her had not been yet unclasped, the kiss was not cold upon her cheek, the first great cry of his love had hardly died away in a softened echo, and her punishment was upon her. His words were lashes, his touch poison, his eyes avenging fires. As in nature's great alchemy the diamond and the blackened coal are one, as nature with the same elements pours life and death from the same vial with the same hand, so now the love which would have been life to Unorna was made worse than death because it was not for her.

Yet the disguise was terribly perfect. The unconscious spell had done its work thoroughly. He took her for Beatrice, and her voice for Beatrice's there in the broad light, in the familiar place where he had so often talked with her for hours and known her for Unorna. But a few paces away was the very spot where she had fallen at his feet last night and wept and abused herself before him. There was the carpet on which Israel Kafka had lain throughout the long hours while they had watched together. Upon that table at her side a book lay which they had read together but two days ago. In her own chair she sat, Unorna still, unchanged, unaltered save for him. She doubted her own senses as she heard him speak, and ever and again the name of Beatrice rang in her ears. He looked at her hands, and knew them; at her black dress, and knew it for her own, and yet he poured out the eloquence of his love – kneeling, then standing, then sitting at her side, drawing her head to his shoulder and smoothing her fair hair – so black to him – with a gentle hand. She was passive through it all, as yet. There seemed to be no other way. He paused sometimes, then spoke again. Perhaps, in the dream that possessed him, he heard her speak. Possibly, he was unconscious of her silence, borne along by the torrent of his own long pent-up speech. She could not tell, she did not care to know. Of one thing alone she thought, of how to escape from it all and be alone.

She feared to move, still more to rise, not knowing what he would do. As he was now, she could not tell what effect her words would have if she spoke. It might be but a passing state after all. What would the awakening be? Would his forgetfulness of Beatrice and his coldness to herself return with the subsidence of his passion? Far better that than to see him and hear him as he was now.

And yet there were moments now and then when he pronounced no name, when he recalled no memory of the past, when there was only the tenderness of love itself in his words, and then, as she listened, she could almost think it was for her. It was bitter joy, unreal and fantastic, but it was a relief. Had she loved him less, such a conflict between sense and senses would have been impossible even in imagination. But she loved him greatly and the deep desire to be loved in turn was in her still, shaming her better thoughts, but sometimes ruling her in spite of herself and of the pain she suffered with each word self-applied. All the vast contradictions, all the measureless inconsistency, all the enormous selfishness of which human hearts are capable, had met in hers as in a battle-ground, fighting each other, rending what they found of herself amongst them, sometimes uniting to throw their whole weight together against the deep-rooted passion, sometimes taking side with it to drive out every other rival.

It was shameful, base, despicable, and she knew it. A moment ago she had longed to tear herself away, to silence him, to stop her ears, anything not to hear those words that cut like whips and stung like scorpions. And now again she was listening for the next, eagerly, breathlessly, drunk with their sound and revelling almost in the unreality of the happiness they brought. More and more she despised herself as the intervals between one pang of suffering and the next grew longer, and the illusion deeper and more like reality.

After all, it was he, and no other. It was the man she loved who was pouring out his own love into her ears, and smoothing her hair and pressing the hand he held. Had he not said it once, and more than once? What matter where, what matter how, provided that he loved? She had received the fulfilment of her wish. He loved her now. Under another name, in a vision, with another face and another voice, yet, still, she was herself.

As in a storm the thunder-claps come crashing through the air, deafening and appalling at first, then rolling swiftly into a far distance, fainter and fainter, till all is still and only the plash of the fast-falling rain is heard, so, as she listened, the tempest of her pain was passing away. Easier and easier it became to hear herself called Beatrice, easier and easier it grew to take the other's place, to accept the kiss, the touch, the word, the pressure of the hand that were all another's due, and given to herself only for the mask she wore in his dream.

And the tide of the great temptation rose, and fell a little, and rose higher again each time, till it washed the fragile feet of the last good thought that lingered, taking refuge on the highest point above the waves. On and on it came, receding and coming back, higher and higher, surer and surer. Had she drawn back in time it would have been so easy. Had she turned and fled when the first moment of senseless joy was over, when she could still feel all the shame, and blush for all the abasement, it would have been over now, and she would have been safe. But she had learned to look upon the advancing water, and the sound of it had no more terror for her. It was very high now. Presently it would climb higher and close above her head.

There were long intervals of silence now. The first rush of his speech had spent itself, for he had told her much and she had heard it all, even through the mists of her changing moods. And now that he was silent she longed to hear him speak again. She could never weary of that voice. It had been music to her in the days when it had been full of cold indifference – now each vibration roused high harmonies in her heart, each note was a full chord, and all the chords made but one great progression. She longed to hear it all again, wondering greatly how it could never have been not good to hear.

Then with the greater temptation came the less, enclosed within it, suddenly revealed to her. There was but one thing she hated in it all. That was the name. Would he not give her another – her own perhaps? She trembled as she thought of speaking. Would she still have Beatrice's voice? Might not her own break down the spell and destroy all at once? Yet she had spoken once before. She had told him that she loved him and he had not been undeceived.

'Beloved – ' she said at last, lingering on the single word and then hesitating.

He looked into her face as he drew her to him, with happy eyes. She might speak, then, for he would hear tones not hers.

'Beloved, I am tired of my name. Will you not call me by another?' She spoke very softly.

'By another name?' he exclaimed, surprised, but smiling at what seemed a strange caprice.

'Yes. It is a sad name to me. It reminds me of many things – of a time that is better forgotten since it is gone. Will you do it for me? It will make it seem as though that time had never been.'

'And yet I love your own name,' he said, thoughtfully. 'It is so much – or has been so much in all these years, when I had nothing but your name to love.'

THE WITCH OF PRAGUE

'Will you not do it? It is all I ask.'

'Indeed I will, if you would rather have it so. Do you think there is anything that I would not do if you asked it of me?'

They were almost the words she had spoken to him that night when they were watching together by Israel Kafka's side. She recognised them and a strange thrill of triumph ran through her. What matter how? What matter where? The old reckless questions came to her mind again. If he loved her, and if he would but call her Unorna, what could it matter, indeed? Was she not herself? She smiled unconsciously.

'I see it pleases you,' he said tenderly. 'Let it be as you wish. What name will you choose for your dear self?'

She hesitated. She could not tell how far he might remember what was past. And yet, if he had remembered he would have seen where he was in the long time that had passed since his awakening.

'Did you ever – in your long travels – hear the name Unorna?' she asked with a smile and a little hesitation.

'Unorna? No. I cannot remember. It is a Bohemian word – it means "she of February". It has a pretty sound – half familiar to me. I wonder where I have heard it.'

'Call me Unorna, then. It will remind us that you found me in February.'

Chapter 25

After carefully locking and bolting the door of the sacristy Sister Paul turned to Beatrice. She had set down her lamp upon the broad, polished shelf which ran all round the place, forming the top of a continuous series of cupboards, as in most sacristies, used for the vestments of the church. At the back of these high presses rose half way to the spring of the vault.

The nun seemed a little nervous and her voice quavered oddly as she spoke. If she had tried to take up her lamp her hand would have shaken. In the moment of danger she had been brave and determined, but now that all was over her enfeebled strength felt the reaction from the strain. She turned to Beatrice and met her flashing black eyes. The young girl's delicate nostrils quivered and her lips curled fiercely.

'You are angry, my dear child,' said Sister Paul. 'So am I, and it seems to me that our anger is just enough. "Be angry and sin not." I think we can apply that to ourselves.'

'Who is that woman?' Beatrice asked. She was certainly angry, as the nun had said, but she felt by no means sure that she could resist the temptation of sinning if it presented itself as the possibility of tearing Unorna to pieces.

'She was once with us,' the nun answered. 'I knew her when she was a mere girl – and I loved her then, in spite of her strange ways. But she has changed. They call her a Witch – and indeed I think it is the only name for her.'

'I do not believe in witches,' said Beatrice, a little scornfully. 'But whatever she is, she is bad. I do not know what it was that she wanted me to do in the church, upon the altar there – it was something horrible. Thank God you came in time! What could it have been, I wonder?'

Sister Paul shook her head sorrowfully, but said nothing. She knew no more than Beatrice of Unorna's intention, but she believed in the existence of a Black Art, full of sacrilegious practices, and credited Unorna vaguely with the worst designs which she could think of, though in her goodness she was not able to imagine anything much worse than the saying of a *Pater Noster* backwards in a consecrated place. But she preferred to say nothing, lest she should judge Unorna unjustly. After all, she did not know. What she had seen had seemed bad enough and strange enough, but apart from the fact that Beatrice had been found upon the altar, where she certainly had no business to be, and that Unorna had acted like a guilty woman, there was little to lay hold of in the way of fact.

'My child,' she said at last, 'until we know more of the truth, and have better advice than we can give each other, let us not speak of it to anyone of the sisters. In the morning I will tell all I have seen in confession, and then I shall get advice. Perhaps you should do the same. I know nothing of what happened before you left your room. Perhaps you have something to reproach yourself with. It is not for me to ask. Think it over.'

'I will tell you the whole truth,' Beatrice answered, resting her elbow upon the polished shelf and supporting her head in her hand, while she looked earnestly into Sister Paul's faded eyes.

'Think well, my daughter. I have no right to any confession from you. If there is anything – '

'Sister Paul – you are a woman, and I must have a woman's help. I have learned something tonight which will change my whole life. No – do not be afraid – I have done nothing wrong. At least, I hope not. While my father lived, I submitted. I hoped, but I gave no sign.

I did not even write, as I once might have done. I have often wished that I had – was that wrong?'

'But you have told me nothing, dear child. How can I answer you?' The nun was perplexed.

'True. I will tell you. Sister Paul – I am five-and-twenty years old, I am a grown woman and this is no mere girl's love story. Seven years ago – I was only eighteen then – I was with my father as I have been ever since. My mother had not been dead long then – perhaps that is the reason why I seemed to be everything to my father. But they had not been happy together, and I had loved her best. We were travelling – no matter where – and then I met the man I have loved. He was not of our country – that is, of my father's. He was of the same people as my mother. Well – I loved him. How dearly you must guess, and try to understand. I could not tell you that. No one could. It began gradually, for he was often with us in those days. My father liked him for his wit, his learning, though he was young; for his strength and manliness – for a hundred reasons which were nothing to me. I would have loved him had he been a cripple, poor, ignorant, despised, instead of being what he was – the grandest, noblest man God ever made. For I did not love him for his face, nor for his courtly ways, nor for such gifts as other men might have, but for himself and for his heart – do you understand?'

'For his goodness,' said Sister Paul, nodding in approval. 'I understand.'

'No,' Beatrice answered, half impatiently. 'Not for his goodness either. Many men are good, and so was he – he must have been, of course. No matter. I loved him. That is enough. He loved me, too. And one day we were alone, in the broad spring sun, upon a terrace. There were lemon trees there – I can see the place. Then we told each other that we loved – but neither of us could find the words – they must be somewhere, those strong beautiful words that could tell how we loved. We told each other – '

'Without your father's consent?' asked the nun almost severely.

Beatrice's eyes flashed. 'Is a woman's heart a dog that must follow at heel?' she asked fiercely. 'We loved. That was enough. My father had the power, but not the heart, to come between. We told him, then, for we were not cowards. We told him boldly that it must be. He was a thoughtful man, who spoke little. He said that we must part at once, before we loved each other better – and that we should soon forget. We looked at each other, the man I loved and I. We knew that we should love better yet, parted or together, though we could not tell how that could be. But we knew also that such love as there was between us was enough. My father gave no reasons, but I knew that he hated the name of my mother's nation. Of course we met again. I remember that I could cry in those days. My father had not learned to part us then. Perhaps he was not quite sure himself, at all events the parting did not come so soon. We told him that we would wait, for ever if it must be. He may have been touched, though little touched him at the best. Then, one day, suddenly and without warning, he took me away to another city. And what of him? I asked. He told me that there was an evil fever in the city and that it had seized him – the man I loved. "He is free to follow us if he pleases," said my father. But he never came. Then followed a journey, and another, and another, until I knew that my father was travelling to avoid him. When I saw that I grew silent, and never spoke his name again. Farther and farther, longer and longer, to the ends of the earth. We saw many people, many asked for my hand. Sometimes I heard of him, from men who had seen him lately. I waited patiently, for I knew that he was on our track, and sometimes I felt that he was near.'

Beatrice paused.

'It is a strange story,' said Sister Paul, who had rarely heard a tale of love.

'The strange thing is this,' Beatrice answered. 'That woman – what is her name? Unorna? She loves him, and she knows where he is.'

'Unorna?' repeated the nun in bewilderment.

'Yes. She met me after Compline tonight. I could not but speak to her, and then I was deceived. I cannot tell whether she knew what I am to him, but she deceived me utterly. She told me a strange story of her own life. I was lonely. In all those years I have never spoken of what has filled me. I cannot tell how it was. I began to speak, and then I forgot that she was there, and told all.'

'She made you tell her, by her secret arts,' said Sister Paul in a low voice.

'No – I was lonely and I believed that she was good, and I felt that I must speak. Then – I cannot think how I could have been so mad – but I thought that we should never meet again, and I showed her a likeness of him. She turned on me. I shall not forget her face. I heard her say that she knew him and loved him too. When I awoke I was lying on the altar. That is all I know.'

'Her evil arts, her evil arts,' repeated the nun, shaking her head. 'Come, my dear child, let us see if all is in order there, upon the altar.

If these things are to be known they must be told in the right quarter. The sacristan must not see that anyone has been in the church.'

Sister Paul took up the lamp, but Beatrice laid a hand upon her arm.

'You must help me to find him,' she said firmly. 'He is not far away.'

Her companion looked at her in astonishment.

'Help you to find him?' she stammered. 'But I cannot – I do not know – I am afraid it is not right – an affair of love – '

'An affair of life, Sister Paul, and of death too, perhaps. This woman lives in Prague. She is rich and must be well known – '

'Well known, indeed. Too well known – the Witch they call her.'

'Then there are those who know her. Tell me the name of one person only – it is impossible that you should not remember some-one who is acquainted with her, who has talked with you of her – perhaps one of the ladies who have been here in retreat.'

The nun was silent for a moment, gathering her recollections.

'There is one, at least, who knows her,' she said at length. 'A great lady here – it is said that she, too, meddles with forbidden practices and that Unorna has often been with her – that together they have called up the spirits of the dead with strange rappings and writings. She knows her, I am sure, for I have talked with her and she says it is all natural, and that there is a learned man with them sometimes, who explains how all such things may happen in the course of nature – a man – let me see, let me see – it is George, I think, but not as we call it, not Jirgi, nor Jegor – no – it sounds harder – Ke-Keyrgi – no, Keyork – Keyork Aribi – '

'Keyork Arabian!' exclaimed Beatrice. 'Is he here?'

'You know him?' Sister Paul looked almost suspiciously at the young girl.

'Indeed I do. He was with us in Egypt once. He showed us wonderful things among the tombs. A strange little man, who knew everything, but very amusing.'

'I do not know. But that is his name. He lives in Prague.'

'How can I find him? I must see him at once – he will help me.'

The nun shook her head with disapproval.

'I should be sorry that you should talk with him,' she said. 'I fear he is no better than Unorna, and perhaps worse.'

'You need not fear,' Beatrice answered, with a scornful smile. 'I am not in the least afraid. Only tell me how I am to find him. He lives here, you say – is there no directory in the convent?'

'I believe the portress keeps such a book,' said Sister Paul still shaking her head uneasily. 'But you must wait until the morning, my dear child, if you will do this thing. Of the two, I should say that you would do better to write to the lady. Come, we must be going. It is very late.'

She had taken the lamp again and was moving slowly towards the door. Beatrice had no choice but to submit. It was evident that nothing more could be done at present. The two women went back into the church, and going round the high altar began to examine everything carefully. The only trace of disorder they could discover was the fallen candlestick, so massive and strong that it was not even bent or injured. They climbed the short wooden steps, and uniting their strength, set it up again, carefully and in its place, restoring the thick candle to the socket. Though broken in the middle by the fall, the heavy wax supported itself easily enough. Then they got down again and Sister Paul took away the steps. For a few moments both women knelt down before the altar.

They left the church by the nuns' staircase, bolting the door behind them, and ascended to the corridors and reached Beatrice's room. Unorna's door was open, as the nun had left it, and the yellow light streamed upon the pavement. She went in and extinguished the lamp, and then came back to Beatrice.

'Are you not afraid to be alone after what has happened?' she asked.

'Afraid? Of what? No, indeed.' Then she thanked her companion again and kissed Sister Paul's waxen cheek.

'Say a prayer, my daughter – and may all be well with you, now and ever!' said the good sister as she went away through the darkness. She needed no light in the familiar way to her cell.

Beatrice searched among her numerous belongings and at last brought out a writing-case. Then she sat down to her table by the light of the lamp that had illuminated so many strange sights that night.

She wrote the name of the convent clearly upon the paper, and then wrote a plain message in the fewest possible words. Something of her strong, devoted nature showed itself in her handwriting.

Beatrice Varanger begs that Keyork Arabian will meet her in the parlour of the convent as soon after receiving this as possible. The matter is very important.

She had reasons of her own for believing that Keyork had not forgotten her in the five years or more since they had been in Egypt together. Apart from the fact that his memory had always been surprisingly good, he had at that time professed the most unbounded admiration for her, and she remembered with a smile his quaint devotion, his fantastic courtesy, and his gnome-like attempts at grace.

She folded the note, to wait for the address which she could not ascertain until the morning. She could do nothing more. It was nearly two o'clock and there was evidently nothing to be done but to sleep.

As she laid her head upon the pillow a few minutes later she was amazed at her own calm. Strong natures, in great tests, often surprise themselves far more than they surprise others. Others see the results, always simpler in proportion as they are greater. But the actors themselves alone know how hard the great and simple can seem.

Beatrice's calmness was not only of the outward kind at the present moment. She felt that she was alone in the world, and that she had taken her life into her own hands. Fate had lent her the clue of her happiness at last and she would hold it firmly to the end. It would be time enough then to open the flood-gates. It would have been unlike her to dwell long upon the thought of Unorna or to give way to any passionate outbreak of hatred. Why should Unorna not love him? The whole world loved him, and small wonder. She feared no rival.

But he was near her now. Her heart leaped as she realised how very near he might well be, then sank again to its calm beating. He had been near her a score of times in the past years, and yet they had not met. But she had not been free, then, as she was now. There was more hope than before, but she could not delude herself with any belief in a certainty.

So thinking, and so saying to herself, she fell asleep, and slept soundly without dreaming, as most people do who are young and strong, and who are clear-headed and active when they are awake.

It was late when she opened her eyes, and the broad cold light filled the room. She lost no time in thinking over the events of the night, for everything was fresh in her memory. Half dressed, she wrapped about her a cloak that came down to her feet, and throwing a black veil over her hair she went down to the portress's lodge. In five minutes she had found Keyork's address and had despatched one of the convent gardeners with the note. Then she leisurely returned to her room and set about completing her toilet. She naturally supposed that an hour or two must elapse before she received an answer, certainly before Keyork appeared in person, a fact which showed that she had forgotten something of the man's characteristics.

Twenty minutes had scarcely passed, and she had not finished dressing, when Sister Paul entered the room, evidently in a state of considerable anxiety. As has been seen, it chanced to be her turn to superintend the guest's quarters at that time, and the portress had of course informed her immediately of Keyork's coming, in order that she might tell Beatrice.

'He is there!' she said, as she came in.

Beatrice was standing before the little mirror that hung upon the wall, trying, under no small difficulties, to arrange her hair. He turned her head quickly.

'Who is there? Keyork Arabian?'

Sister Paul nodded, glad that she was not obliged to pronounce the name that had for her such an unChristian sound.

'Where is he? I did not think he could come so soon. Oh, Sister Paul, do help me with my hair! I cannot make it stay.'

'He is in the parlour, downstairs,' answered the nun, coming to her assistance. 'Indeed, child, I do not see how I can help you.' She touched the black coils ineffectually. 'There! Is that better?' she asked in a timid way. 'I do not know how to do it – '

'No, no!' Beatrice exclaimed. 'Hold that end – so – now turn it that way – no, the other way – it is in the glass – so – now keep it there while I put in a pin – no, no – in the same place, but the other way – oh, Sister Paul! did you never do your hair when you were a girl?'

'That was so long ago,' answered the nun meekly. 'Let me try again.'

The result was passably satisfactory at last, and assuredly not wanting in the element of novelty.

'Are you not afraid to go alone?' asked Sister Paul with evident preoccupation, as Beatrice put a few more touches to her toilet.

But the young girl only laughed and made the more haste. Sister Paul walked with her to the head of the stairs, wishing that the rules would allow her to accompany Beatrice into the parlour. Then as the latter went down the nun stood at the top looking after her and audibly repeating prayers for her preservation.

The convent parlour was a large, bare room, lighted by a high and grated window. Plain, straight, modern chairs were ranged against the wall at regular intervals. There was no table; but a square piece of green carpet lay upon the middle of the stone pavement. A richly ornamented glazed earthenware stove, in which a fire had just been lighted, occupied one corner, a remnant of former aesthetic taste and strangely out of place since the old carved furniture was gone. A crucifix of inferior workmanship and realistically painted hung opposite the door. The place was reserved for the use of ladies in retreat and was situated outside the constantly closed door which shut off the cloistered part of the convent from the small portion accessible to outsiders.

Keyork Arabian was standing in the middle of the parlour waiting for Beatrice. When she entered at last he made two steps forward, bowing profoundly, and then smiled in a deferential manner.

'My dear lady,' he said, 'I am here. I have lost no time. It so happened that I received your note just as I was leaving my carriage after a morning drive. I had no idea that you were in Bohemia.'

'Thanks. It was good of you to come so soon.'

She sat down upon one of the stiff chairs and motioned to him to follow her example.

'And your dear father – how is he?' inquired Keyork with suave politeness, as he took his seat.

'My father died a week ago,' said Beatrice gravely.

Keyork's face assumed all the expression of which it was capable. 'I am deeply grieved,' he said, moderating his huge voice to a soft and purring sub-bass. 'He was an old and valued friend.'

There was a moment's silence. Keyork, who knew many things, was well aware that a silent feud, of which he also knew the cause, had existed between father and daughter when he had last been with them, and he rightly judged from his knowledge of their obstinate characters that it had lasted to the end. He thought therefore that his expression of sympathy had been sufficient and could pass muster.

'I asked you to come,' said Beatrice at last, 'because I wanted your help in a matter of importance to myself. I understand that you know a person who calls herself Unorna, and who lives here.'

Keyork's bright blue eyes scrutinised her face. He wondered how much she knew.

'Very well indeed,' he answered, as though not at all surprised.

'You know something of her life, then. I suppose you see her very often, do you not?'

'Daily, I can almost say.'

'Have you any objection to answering one question about her?'

'Twenty if you ask them, and if I know the answers,' said Keyork, wondering what form the question would take, and preparing to meet a surprise with indifference.

'But will you answer me truly?'

'My dear lady, I pledge you my sacred word of honour,' Keyork answered with immense gravity, meeting her eyes and laying his hand upon his heart.

'Does she love that man – or not?' Beatrice asked, suddenly show-ing him the little miniature of the Wanderer, which she had taken from its case and had hitherto concealed in her hand.

She watched every line of his face, for she knew something of him, and in reality put very little more faith in his word of honour than he did himself, which was not saying much. But she had counted upon surprising him, and she succeeded, to a certain extent. His answer did not come as glibly as he could have wished, though his plan was soon formed.

'Who is it? Ah, dear me! my old friend. We call him the Wanderer. Well, Unorna certainly knew him when he was here.'

'Then he is gone?'

'Indeed, I am not quite sure,' said Keyork, regaining all his self-possession. 'Of course I can find out for you, if you wish to know. But as regards Unorna, I can tell you nothing. They were a good deal together at one time. I fancy he was consulting her. You have heard that she is a clairvoyant, I dare say.'

He made the last remark quite carelessly, as though he attached no importance to the fact.

'Then you do not know whether she loves him?'

Keyork indulged himself with a little discreet laughter, deep and musical.

'Love is a very vague word,' he said presently.

'Is it?' Beatrice asked, with some coldness.

'To me, at least,' Keyork hastened to say, as though somewhat confused. 'But, of course, I can know very little about it in myself, and nothing about it in others.'

Not knowing how matters might turn out, he was willing to leave Beatrice with a suspicion of the truth, while denying all knowledge of it.

'You know him yourself, of course,' Beatrice suggested.

'I have known him for years – oh, yes, for him I can answer. He was not in the least in love.'

'I did not ask that question,' said Beatrice rather haughtily. 'I knew he was not.'

'Of course, of course. I beg your pardon!'

Keyork was learning more from her than she from him. It was true that she took no trouble to conceal her interest in the Wanderer and his doings.

'Are you sure that he has left the city?' Beatrice asked.

'No, I am not positive. I could not say with certainty.'

'When did you see him last?'

'Within the week, I am quite sure,' Keyork answered with alacrity.

'Do you know where he was staying?'

'I have not the least idea,' the little man replied, without the slightest hesitation. 'We met at first by chance in the Teyn Kirche, one afternoon – it was a Sunday, I remember, about a month ago.'

'A month ago – on a Sunday,' Beatrice repeated thoughtfully.

'Yes – I think it was New Year's Day, too.'

'Strange,' she said. 'I was in the church that very morning, with my maid. I had been ill for several days – I remember how cold it was. Strange – the same day.'

'Yes,' said Keyork, noting the words, but appearing to take no notice of them. 'I was looking at Tycho Brahe's monument. You know how it annoys me to forget anything – there was a word in the inscription which I could not recall. I turned round and saw him sitting just at the end of the pew nearest to the monument.'

'The old red slab with a figure on it, by the last pillar?' Beatrice asked eagerly.

'Exactly. I dare say you know the church very well. You remember that the pew runs very near to the monument so that there is hardly room to pass.'

'I know – yes.'

She was thinking that it could hardly have been a mere accident which had led the Wanderer to take the very seat she had occupied on the morning of that day. He must have seen her during the Mass, but she could not imagine how he could have missed her. They had been very near then. And now, a whole month had passed, and Keyork Arabian professed not to know whether the Wanderer was still in the city or not.

'Then you wish to be informed of our friend's movements, as I understand it?' said Keyork going back to the main point.

'Yes – what happened on that day?' Beatrice asked, for she wished to hear more.

'Oh, on that day? Yes. Well, nothing happened worth mentioning. We talked a little and went out of the church and walked a little way together. I forget when we met next, but I have seen him at least a dozen times since then, I am sure.'

Beatrice began to understand that Keyork had no intention of giving her any further information. She reflected that she had learned much in this interview. The Wanderer had been, and perhaps still was, in Prague. Unorna loved him and they had been frequently together. He had been in the Teyn Kirche on the day she had last been there herself, and in all probability he had seen her, since he had chosen the very seat in which she had sat. Further, she gathered that Keyork had some interest in not speaking more frankly. She gave up the idea of examining him any further. He was a man not easily surprised, and it was only by means of a surprise that he could be induced to betray even by a passing expression what he meant to conceal. Her means of attack were exhausted for the present. She determined at least to repeat her request clearly before dismissing him, in the hope that it might suit his plans to fulfil it, but without the least trust in his sincerity.

'Will you be so kind as to make some inquiry, and let me know the result today?' she asked.

'I will do everything to give you an early answer,' said Keyork. 'And I shall be the more anxious to obtain one without delay in order that I may have the very great pleasure of visiting you again. There is much that I would like to ask you, if you would allow me. For old friends, as I trust I may say that we are, you must admit that we have exchanged few – very few – confidences this morning. May I come again today? It would be an immense privilege to talk of old times with you, of our friends in Egypt and of our many journeys. For you have no doubt travelled much since then. Your dear father,' he lowered his voice reverentially, 'was a great traveller, as well as a very learned man. Ah, well, my dear lady – we must all make up our minds to undertake that great journey one of these days. But I pain you. I was very much attached to your dear father. Command all my service. I will come again in the course of the day.'

With many sympathetic smiles and half-comic inclinations of his short, broad body, the little man bowed himself out.

Chapter 26

Unorna drew one deep breath when she first heard her name fall with a loving accent from the Wanderer's lips. Surely the bitterness of despair was past since she was loved and not called Beatrice. The sigh that came then was of relief already felt, the forerunner, as she fancied, too, of a happiness no longer dimmed by shadows of fear and mists of rising remorse. Gazing into his eyes, she seemed to be watching in their reflection a magic change. She had been Beatrice to him, Unorna to herself, but now the transformation was at hand – now it was to come. For him she loved, and who loved her, she was

Unorna even to the name, in her own thoughts she had taken the dark woman's face. She had risked all upon the chances of one throw and she had won. So long as he had called her by another's name the bitterness had been as gall mingled in the wine of love. But now that too was gone. She felt that it was complete at last. Her golden head sank peacefully upon his shoulder in the morning light.

'You have been long in coming, love,' she said, only half consciously, 'but you have come as I dreamed – it is perfect now. There is nothing wanting any more.'

'It is all full, all real, all perfect,' he answered, softly.

'And there is to be no more parting, now – '

'Neither here, nor afterwards, beloved.'

'Then this is afterwards. Heaven has nothing more to give. What is Heaven? The meeting of those who love – as we have met. I have forgotten what it was to live before you came – '

'For me, there is nothing to remember between that day and this.'

'That day when you fell ill,' Unorna said, 'the loneliness, the fear for you – '

Unorna scarcely knew that it had not been she who had parted from him so long ago. Yet she was playing a part, and in the semi-consciousness of her deep self-illusion it all seemed as real as a vision in a dream so often dreamed that it has become part of the dreamer's life. Those who fall by slow degrees under the power of the all-destroying opium remember yesterday as being very far, very long past, and recall faint memories of last year as though a century had lived and perished since then, seeing confusedly in their own lives the lives of others, and other existences in their own, until identity is almost gone in the endless transmigration of their souls from the shadow in one dream-tale to the wraith of themselves that dreams the next. So, in that hour, Unorna drifted through the changing scenes that a word had power to call up, scarce able, and wholly unwilling, to distinguish between her real and her imaginary self. What matter how? What matter where? The very questions which at first she had asked herself came now but faintly as out of an immeasurable distance, and always more faintly still. They died away in her ears, as when, after long waiting, and false starts, and turnings back and anxious words exchanged, the great race is at last begun, the swift long limbs are gathered and stretched and strained and gathered again, the thunder of flying hoofs is in the air, and the rider, with low hands and head inclined and eyes bent forward, hears the last anxious word of parting counsel tremble and die in the rush of the wind behind.

She had really loved him throughout all those years; she had really sought him and mourned for him and longed for a sight of his face; they had really parted and had really found each other but a short hour since; there was no Beatrice but Unorna and no Unorna but Beatrice, for they were one and indivisible and interchangeable as the glance of a man's two eyes that look on one fair sight; each sees alone, the same – but seeing together, the sight grows doubly fair.

'And all the sadness, where is it now?' she asked. 'And all the emptiness of that long time? It never was, my love – it was yesterday we met. We parted yesterday, to meet today. Say it was yesterday – the little word can undo seven years.'

'It seems like yesterday,' he answered.

'Indeed, I can almost think so, now, for it was all night between. But not quite dark, as night is sometimes. It was a night full of stars – each star was a thought of you, that burned softly and showed me where heaven was. And darkest night, they say, means coming morning – so when the stars went out I knew the sun must rise.'

The words fell from her lips naturally. To her it seemed true that she had indeed waited long and hoped and thought of him. And it was not all false. Ever since her childhood she had been told to wait, for her love would come and would come only once. And so it was true, and the dream grew sweeter and the illusion of the enchantment more enchanting still. For it was an enchantment and a spell that bound them together there, among the flowers, the drooping palms, the graceful tropic plants and the shadowy leaves. And still the day rose higher, but still the lamps burned on, fed by the silent, mysterious current that never tires, blending a real light with an unreal one, an emblem of Unorna's self, mixing and blending, too, with a self not hers.

'And the sun is risen, indeed,' she added presently.

'Am I the sun, dear?' he asked, foretasting the delight of listening to her simple answer.

'You are the sun, beloved, and when you shine, my eyes can see nothing else in heaven.'

'And what are you yourself – Beatrice – no, Unorna – is that the name you chose? It is so hard to remember anything when I look at you.'

'Beatrice – Unorna – anything,' came the answer, softly murmuring. 'Anything, dear, any name, any face, any voice, if only I am I, and you are you, and we two love! Both, neither, anything – do the blessed souls in Paradise know their own names?'

'You are right – what does it matter? Why should you need a name at all, since I have you with me always? It was well once – it served me when I prayed for you – and it served to tell me that my heart was gold while you were there, as the goldsmith's mark upon his jewel stamps the pure metal, that all men may know it.'

'You need no sign like that to show me what you are,' said she, with a long glance.

'Nor I to tell me you are in my heart,' he answered. 'It was a foolish speech. Would you have me wise now?'

'If wisdom is love – yes. If not – ' She laughed softly.

'Then folly?'

'Then folly, madness, anything – so that this last, as last it must, or I shall die!'

'And why should it not last? Is there any reason, in earth or Heaven, why we two should part? If there is – I will make that reason itself folly, and madness, and unreason. Dear, do not speak of this not lasting. Die, you say? Worse, far worse; as much as eternal death is worse than bodily dying. Last? Does anyone know what for ever means, if we do not? Die, we must, in these dying bodies of ours, but part – no. Love has burned the cruel sense out of that word, and bleached its blackness white. We wounded the devil, parting, with one kiss, we killed him with the next – this buries him – ah, love, how sweet – '

There was neither resistance nor the thought of resisting. Their lips met and were withdrawn only that their eyes might drink again the draught the lips had tasted, long draughts of sweetness and liquid light and love unfathomable. And in the interval of speech half false, the truth of what was all true welled up from the clear depths and overflowed the falseness, till it grew falser and more fleeting still – as a thing lying deep in a bright water casts up a distorted image on refracted rays.

Glance and kiss, when two love, are as body and soul, supremely human and transcendently divine. The look alone, when the lips cannot meet, is but the disembodied spirit, beautiful even in its sorrow, sad, despairing, saying 'ever', and yet sighing 'never', tasting and knowing all the bitterness of both. The kiss without the glance? The body without the soul? The mortal thing without the undying thought? Draw down the thick veil and hide the sight, lest devils sicken at it, and lest man should loathe himself for what man can be.

Truth or untruth, their love was real, hers as much as his. She remembered only what her heart had been without it. What her goal might be, now that it had come, she guessed even then, but she would not ask. Was there never a martyr in old times, more human than the rest, who turned back, for love perhaps, if not for fear, and said that for love's sake life still was sweet, and brought a milk-white dove to Aphrodite's altar, or dropped a rose before Demeter's feet? There must have been, for man is man, and woman, woman. And if in the next month, or even the next year, or after many years, that youth or maid took heart to bear a Christian's death, was there then no forgiveness, no sign of holy cross upon the sandstone in the deep labyrinth of graves, no crown, no sainthood, and no reverent memory of his name or hers among those of men and women worthier, perhaps, but not more suffering?

No one can kill Self. No one can be altogether another, save in the passing passion of a moment's acting. I – in that syllable lies the whole history of each human life; in that history lives the individuality; in the clear and true conception of that individuality dwells such joint foreknowledge of the future as we can have, such vague solution as to us is possible of that vast equation in which all quantities are unknown save that alone, that I which we know as we can know nothing else.

'Bury it!' she said. 'Bury that parting – the thing, the word, and the thought – bury it with all others of its kind, with change, and old age, and stealing indifference, and growing coldness, and all that cankers love – bury them all, together, in one wide deep grave – then build on it the house of what we are – '

'Change? Indifference? I do not know those words,' the Wanderer said. 'Have they been in your dreams, love? They have never been in mine.'

He spoke tenderly, but with the faintest echo of sadness in his voice. The mere suggestion that such thoughts could have been near her was enough to pain him. She was silent, and again her head lay upon his shoulder. She found there still the rest and the peace. Knowing her own life, the immensity of his faith and trust in that other woman were made clear by the simple, heartfelt words. If she had been indeed Beatrice, would he have loved her so? If it had all been true, the parting, the seven years' separation, the utter loneliness, the hopelessness, the despair, could she have been as true as he? In the stillness that followed she asked herself the question which was so near a greater and a deadlier one. But the answer came quickly. That, at least, she could have done. She could have been true to him, even to death. It must be so easy to be faithful when life was but one faith. In that chord at least no note rang false.

'Change in love – indifference to you!' she cried, all at once, hiding her lovely face in his breast and twining her arms about his neck. 'No, no! I never meant that such things could be – they are but empty words, words one hears spoken lightly by lips that never spoke the truth, by men and women who never had such truth to speak as you and I.'

'And as for old age,' he said, dwelling upon her speech, 'what is that to us? Let it come, since come it must. It is good to be young and fair and strong, but would not you or I give up all that for love's sake, each of us of our own free will, rather than lose the other's love?'

'Indeed, indeed I would!' Unorna answered.

'Then what of age? What is it after all? A few grey hairs, a wrinkle here and there, a slower step, perhaps a dimmer glance. That is all it is – the quiet, sunny channel between the sea of earthly joy and the ocean of heavenly happiness. The breeze of love still fills the sails, wafting us softly onward through the narrows, never failing, though it be softer and softer, till we glide out, scarce knowing it, upon the broader water and are borne swiftly away from the lost land by the first breath of heaven.'

His words brought peace and the mirage of a far-off rest, that soothed again the little half-born doubt.

'Yes,' she said. 'It is better to think so. Then we need think of no other change.'

'There is no other possible,' he answered, gently pressing the shoulder upon which his hand was resting. 'We have not waited and believed, and trusted and loved, for seven years, to wake at last – face to face as we are today – and to find that we have trusted vainly and loved two shadows, I yours, and you mine, to find at the great moment of all that we are not ourselves, the selves we knew, but others of like passions but of less endurance. Have we, beloved? And if we could love and trust and believe without each other, each alone, is it not all the more sure that we shall be unchanging together? It must be so. The whole is greater than its parts, two loves together are greater and stronger than each could be of itself. The strength of two strands close twined together is more than twice the strength of each.'

She said nothing. By merest chance he had said words that had waked the doubt again, so that it grew a little and took a firmer hold in her unwilling heart. To love a shadow, he had said, to wake and find self not self at all. That was what might come, would come, must come, sooner or later, said the doubt. What matter where, or when, or how? The question came again, vaguely, faintly as a mere memory, but confidently as though knowing its own answer. Had she not rested in his arms, and felt his kisses and heard his voice? What matter how, indeed? It matters greatly, said the growing doubt, rearing its head and finding speech at last. It matters greatly, it said, for love lies not alone in voice, and kiss, and gentle touch, but in things more enduring, which to endure must be sound and whole and not cankered to the core by a living lie. Then came the old reckless reasoning again: Am I not I? Is he not he? Do I not love him with my whole strength? Does he not love this very self of mine, here as it is, my head upon his shoulder, my hand within his hand? And if he once loved another, have I not her place, to have and hold, that I may be loved in her stead? Go, said the doubt, growing black and strong; go, for you are nothing to him but a figure in his dream, disguised in the lines of one he really loved and loves; go quickly, before it is too late, before that real Beatrice comes and wakes him and drives you out of the kingdom you usurp.

But she knew it was only a doubt, and had it been the truth, and had Beatrice's foot been on the threshold, she would not have been driven away by fear. But the fight had begun.

'Speak to me, dear,' she said. 'I must hear your voice – it makes me know that it is all real.'

'How the minutes fly!' he exclaimed, smoothing her hair with his hand. 'It seems to me that I was but just speaking when you spoke.'

'It seems so long – ' She checked herself, wondering whether an hour had passed or but a second.

Though love be swifter than the fleeting hours, doubt can outrun a lifetime in one beating of the heart.

'Then how divinely long it all may seem,' he answered. 'But can we not begin to think, and to make plans for tomorrow, and the next day, and for the years before us? That will make more time for us, for with the present we shall have the future, too. No – that is foolish again. And yet it is so hard to say which I would have. Shall the moment linger because it is so sweet? Or shall it be gone quickly, because the next is to be sweeter still? Love, where is your father?'

Unorna started. The question was suggested, perhaps, by his inclination to speak of what was to be done, but it fell suddenly upon her ears, as a peal of thunder when the sky has no clouds. Must she lie now, or break the spell? One word, at least, she could yet speak with truth.

'Dead.'

'Dead!' the Wanderer repeated, thoughtfully and with a faint surprise. 'Is it long ago, beloved?' he asked presently, in a subdued tone as though fearing to wake some painful memory.

'Yes,' she answered. The great doubt was taking her heart in its strong hands now and tearing it, and twisting it.

'And whose house is this in which I have found you, darling? Was it his?'

'It is mine,' Unorna said.

How long would he ask questions to which she could find true answers? What question would come next? There were so many he might ask and few to which she could reply so truthfully even in that narrow sense of truth which found its only meaning in a whim of chance. But for a moment he asked nothing more.

'Not mine,' she said. 'It is yours. You cannot take me and yet call anything mine.'

'Ours, then, beloved. What does it matter? So he died long ago – poor man! And yet, it seems but a little while since someone told me – but that was a mistake, of course. He did not know. How many years may it be, dear one? I see you still wear mourning for him.'

'No – that was but a fancy – today. He died – he died more than two years ago.'

She bent her head. It was but a poor attempt at truth, a miserable lying truth to deceive herself with, but it seemed better than to tell the whole truth outright, and say that her father – Beatrice's father – had been dead but just a week. The blood burned in her face. Brave natures, good and bad alike, hate falsehood, not for its wickedness, perhaps, but for its cowardice. She could do things as bad, far worse. She could lay her hand upon the forehead of a sleeping man and inspire in him a deep, unchangeable belief in something utterly untrue; but now, as it was, she was ashamed and hid her face.

'It is strange,' he said, 'how little men know of each other's lives or deaths. They told me he was alive last year. But it has hurt you to speak of it. Forgive me, dear, it was thoughtless of me.'

He tried to lift her head, but she held it obstinately down.

'Have I pained you, Beatrice?' he asked, forgetting to call her by the other name that was so new to him.

'No – oh, no!' she exclaimed without looking up.

'What is it then?'

'Nothing – it is nothing – no, I will not look at you – I am ashamed.' That at least was true.

'Ashamed, dear heart! Of what?'

He had seen her face in spite of herself. Lie, or lose all, said a voice within.

'Ashamed of being glad that – that I am free,' she stammered, struggling on the very verge of the precipice.

'You may be glad of that, and yet be very sorry he is dead,' the Wanderer said, stroking her hair.

It was true, and seemed quite simple. She wondered that she had not thought of that. Yet she felt that the man she loved, in all his nobility and honesty, was playing the tempter to her, though he could not know it. Deeper and deeper she sank, yet ever more conscious that she was sinking. Before him she felt no longer as loving woman to loving man – she was beginning to feel as a guilty prisoner before his judge.

He thought to turn the subject to a lighter strain. By chance he glanced at his own hand.

'Do you know this ring?' he asked, holding it before her, with a smile.

'Indeed, I know it,' she answered, trembling again.

'You gave it to me, love, do you remember? And I gave you a likeness of myself, because you asked for it, though I would rather have given you something better. Have you it still?'

She was silent. Something was rising in her throat. Then she choked it down.

'I had it in my hand last night,' she said in a breaking voice. True, once more.

'What is it, darling? Are you crying? This is no day for tears.'

'I little thought that I should have yourself today,' she tried to say.

Then the tears came, tears of shame, big, hot, slow. They fell upon his hand. She was weeping for joy, he thought. What else could any man think in such a case? He drew her to him, and pressed her cheek with his hand as her head nestled on his shoulder.

'When you put this ring on my finger, dear – so long ago – '

She sobbed aloud.

'No, darling – no, dear heart,' he said, comforting her, 'you must not cry – that long ago is over now and gone for ever. Do you remember that day, sweetheart, in the broad spring sun upon the terrace among the lemon trees. No, dear – your tears hurt me always, even when they are shed in happiness – no, dear, no. Rest there, let me dry your dear eyes – so and so. Again? For ever, if you will. While you have tears, I have kisses to dry them – it was so then, on that very day. I can remember. I can see it all – and you. You have not changed, love, in all those years, more than a blossom changes in one hour of a summer's day! You took this ring and put it on my finger. Do you remember what I said? I know the very words. I promised you – it needed no promise either – that it should never leave its place until you took it back – and you – how well I remember your face – you said that you would take it from my hand some day, when all was well, when you should be free to give me another in its stead, and to take one in return. I have kept my word, beloved. Keep yours – I have brought you back the ring. Take it, sweetheart. It is heavy with the burden of lonely years. Take it and give me that other which I claim.'

She did not speak, for she was fighting down the choking sobs, struggling to keep back the burning drops that scalded her cheeks, striving to gather strength for the weight of a greater shame. Lie, or lose all, the voice said.

Very slowly she raised her head. She knew that his hand was close to hers, held there that she might fulfil Beatrice's promise. Was she not free? Could she not give him what he asked? No matter how – she tried to say it to herself and could not. She felt his breath upon her hair. He was waiting. If she did not act soon or speak he would wonder what held her back – wonder – suspicion next and then? She put out her hand to touch his fingers, half blinded, groping as though she could not see. He made it easy for her. He fancied she was trembling, as she was weeping, with the joy of it all.

She felt the ring, though she dared not look at it. She drew it a little and felt that it would come off easily. She felt the fingers she loved so well, straight, strong and nervous, and she touched them lovingly. The ring was not tight, it would pass easily over the joint that alone kept it in its place.

'Take it, beloved,' he said. 'It has waited long enough.'

He was beginning to wonder at her hesitation as she knew he would. After wonder would come suspicion – and then? Very slowly – it was just upon the joint of his finger now. Should she do it? What would happen? He would have broken his vow – unwittingly. How quickly and gladly Beatrice would have taken it. What would she say, if they lived and met – why should they not meet? Would the spell endure that shock – who would Beatrice be then? The woman who had given him this ring? Or another, whom he would no longer know? But she must be quick. He was waiting and Beatrice would not have made him wait.

Her hand was like stone, numb, motionless, immovable, as though some unseen being had taken it in an iron grasp and held it there, in mid-air, just touching his. Yes – no – yes – she could not move – a hand was clasped upon her wrist, a hand smaller than his, but strong as fate, fixed in its grip as an iron vice.

Unorna felt a cold breath, that was not his, upon her forehead, and she felt as though her heavy hair were rising of itself upon her head. She knew that horror, for she had been overtaken by it once before. She was not afraid, but she knew what it was. There was a shadow, too, and a dark woman, tall, queenly, with deep flashing eyes was standing beside her. She knew, before she looked; she looked, and it was there. Her own face was whiter than that other woman's.

'Have you come already?' she asked of the shadow, in a low despairing tone.

'Beatrice – what has happened?' cried the Wanderer. To him, she seemed to be speaking to the empty air and her white face startled him.

'Yes,' she said, staring still, in the same hopeless voice. 'It is Beatrice. She has come for you.'

'Beatrice – beloved – do not speak like that! For God's sake – what do you see? There is nothing there.'

'Beatrice is there. I am Unorna.'

'Unorna, Beatrice – have we not said it should be all the same! Sweetheart – look at me! Rest here – shut those dear eyes of yours. It is gone now, whatever it was – you are tired, dear – you must rest.'

Her eyes closed and her head sank. It was gone, as he said, and she knew what it had been – a mere vision called up by her own over-tortured brain. Keyork Arabian had a name for it.

Frightened by your own nerves, laughed the voice, when, if you had not been a coward, you might have faced it down and lied again, and all would have been well. But you shall have another chance, and lying is very easy, even when the nerves are over-wrought. You will do better the next time.

The voice was like Keyork Arabian's. Unstrung, almost forgetting all, she wondered vaguely at the sound, for it was a real sound and a real voice to her. Was her soul his, indeed, and was he drawing it on slowly, surely, to the end? Had he been behind her last night? Had he left an hour's liberty only to come back again and take at last what was his?

There is time yet, you have not lost him, for he thinks you mad. The voice spoke once more.

And at the same moment the strong dear arms were again around her, again her head was on that restful shoulder of his, again her pale face was turned up to his, and kisses were raining on her tired eyes, while broken words of love and tenderness made music through the tempest.

Again the vast temptation rose. How could he ever know? Who was to undeceive him, if he was not yet undeceived? Who should ever make him understand the truth so long as the spell lasted? Why not then take what was given her, and when the end came, if it came, then tell all boldly? Even then, he would not understand. Had he understood last night, when she had confessed all that she had done before? He had not believed one word of it, except that she loved him. Could she make him believe it now, when he was clasping her so fiercely to his breast, half mad with love for her himself?

So easy, too. She had but to forget that passing vision, to put her arms about his neck, to give kiss for kiss, and loving word for loving word. Not even that. She had but to lie there, passive, silent if she could not speak, and it would be still the same. No power on earth could undo what she had done, unless she willed it. Neither man nor woman could make his clasping hands let go of her and give her up.

Be still and wait, whispered the voice, you have lost nothing yet.

But Unorna would not. She had spoken and acted her last lie. It was over.

Chapter 27

Unorna struggled for a moment. The Wanderer did not understand, but loosed his arms, so that she was free. She rose to her feet and stood before him.

'You have dreamed all this,' she said. 'I am not Beatrice.'

'Dreamed? Not Beatrice?' she heard him cry in his bewilderment.

Something more he said, but she could not catch the words. She was already gone, through the labyrinth of the many plants, to the door through which twelve hours earlier she had fled from Israel Kafka. She ran the faster as she left him behind. She passed the entrance and the passage and the vestibule beyond, not thinking whither she was going, or not caring. She found herself in that large, well-lighted room in which the ancient sleeper lay alone. Perhaps her instinct led her there as to a retreat safer even than her own chamber. She knew that if she would there was something there which she could use.

She sank into a chair and covered her face, trembling from head to foot. For many minutes after that she could neither see nor hear –

she would hardly have felt a wound or a blow. And yet she knew that she meant to end her life, since all that made it life was ended.

After a time, her hands fell in a despairing gesture upon her knees and she stared about the room. Her eyes rested on the sleeper, then upon his couch, lying as a prophet in state, the massive head raised upon a silken pillow, the vast limbs just outlined beneath the snow-white robe, the hoary beard flowing down over the great breast that slowly rose and fell.

To her there was a dreadful irony in that useless life, prolonged in sleep beyond the limits of human age. Yet she had thought it worth the labour and care and endless watchfulness it had cost for years. And now her own, strong, young and fresh, seemed not only useless but fit only to be cut off and cast away, as an existence that offended God and man and most of all herself.

But if she died then, there, in that secret chamber where she and her companion had sought the secret of life for years, if she died now – how would all end? Was it an expiation – or a flight? Would one short moment of half-conscious suffering pay half her debt?

She stared at the old man's face with wide, despairing eyes. Many a time, unknown to Keyork, and once to his knowledge, she had roused the sleeper to speak, and on the whole he had spoken truly, wisely, and well. She lacked neither the less courage to die, nor the greater to live. She longed but to hear one honest word, not of hope, but of encouragement – but one word in contrast to those hideous whispered promptings that had come to her in Keyork Arabian's voice. How could she trust herself alone? Her evil deeds were many – so many, that, although she had turned at last against them, she could not tell where to strike.

'If you would only tell me!' she cried leaning over the unconscious head. 'If you would only help me. You are so old that you must be wise, and if so very wise, then you are good! Wake but this once, and tell me what is right!'

The deep eyes opened and looked up to hers. The great limbs stirred, the bony hands unclasped. There was something awe-inspiring in the ancient strength renewed and filled with a new life.

'Who calls me?' asked the clear, deep voice.

'I, Unorna – '

'What do you ask of me?'

He had risen from his couch and stood before her, towering far above her head. Even the Wanderer would have seemed but of common stature beside this man of other years, of a forgotten generation, who now stood erect and filled with a mysterious youth.

'Tell me what I should do – '

'Tell me what you have done.'

Then in one great confession, with bowed head and folded hands, she poured out the story of her life.

'And I am lost!' she cried at last. 'One holds my soul, and one my heart! May not my body die? Oh, say that it is right – that I may die!'

'Die? Die – when you may yet undo?'

'Undo?'

'Undo and do. Undo the wrong and do the right.'

'I cannot. The wrong is past undoing – and I am past doing right.'

'Do not blaspheme – go! Do it.'

'What?'

'Call her – that other woman – Beatrice. Bring her to him, and him to her.'

'And see them meet!'

She covered her face with her hands, and one short moan escaped her lips.

'May I not die?' she cried despairingly. 'May I not die – for him – for her, for both? Would that not be enough? Would they not meet? Would they not then be free?'

'Do you love him still?'

'With all my broken heart – '

'Then do not leave his happiness to chance alone, but go at once. There is one little act of Heaven's work still in your power. Make it all yours.'

His great hands rested on her shoulders and his eyes looked down to hers.

'Is it so bitter to do right?' he asked.

'It is very bitter,' she answered.

Very slowly she turned, and as she moved he went beside her, gently urging her and seeming to support her. Slowly, through vestibule and passage, they went on and entered together the great hall of the flowers. The Wanderer was there alone.

He uttered a short cry and sprang to meet her, but stepped back in awe of the great white-robed figure that towered by her side.

'Beatrice!' he cried, as they passed.

'I am not Beatrice,' she answered, her downcast eyes not raised to look at him, moving still forward under the gentle guidance of the giant's hand.

'Not Beatrice – no – you are not she – you are Unorna! Have I dreamed all this?'

She had passed him now, and still she would not turn her head. But her voice came back to him as she walked on.

'You have dreamed what will very soon be true,' she said. 'Wait here, and Beatrice will soon be with you.'

'I know that I am mad,' the Wanderer cried, making one step to follow her, then stopping short. Unorna was already at the door. The ancient sleeper laid one hand upon her head.

'You will do it now,' he said.

'I will do it – to the end,' she answered. 'Thank God that I have made you live to tell me how.'

So she went out, alone, to undo what she had done so evilly well.

The old man turned and went towards the Wanderer, who stood still in the middle of the hall, confused, not knowing whether he had dreamed or was really mad.

'What man are you?' he asked, as the white-robed figure approached.

'A man, as you are, for I was once young – not as you are, for I am very old, and yet like you, for I am young again.'

'You speak in riddles. What are you doing here, and where have you sent Unorna?'

'When I was old, in that long time between, she took me in, and I have slept beneath her roof these many years. She came to me today. She told me all her story and all yours, waking me from my sleep, and asking me what she should do. And she is gone to do that thing of which I told her. Wait and you will see. She loves you well.'

'And you would help her to get my love, as she had tried to get it before?' the Wanderer asked with rising anger. 'What am I to you, or you to me, that you would meddle in my life?'

'You to me? Nothing. A man.'

'Therefore an enemy – and you would help Unorna – let me go! This home is cursed. I will not stay in it.' The hoary giant took his arm, and the Wanderer started at the weight and strength of the touch.

'You shall bless this house before you leave it. In this place, here where you stand, you shall find the happiness you have sought through all the years.'

'In Unorna?' the question was asked scornfully.

'By Unorna.'

'I do not believe you. You are mad, as I am. Would you play the prophet?'

The door opened in the distance, and from behind the screen of plants Keyork Arabian came forward into the hall, his small eyes bright, his ivory face set and expressionless, his long beard waving in the swing of his walk. The Wanderer saw him first and called to him.

'Keyork – come here!' he said. 'Who is this man?'

For a moment Keyork seemed speechless with amazement. But it was anger that choked his words. Then he came on quickly.

'Who waked him?' he cried in fury. 'What is this? Why is he here?'

'Unorna waked me,' answered the ancient sleeper very calmly.

'Unorna? Again? The curse of The Three Black Angels on her! Mad again? Sleep, go back! It is not ready yet, and you will die, and I shall lose it all – all – all! Oh, she shall pay for this with her soul in hell!'

He threw himself upon the giant, in an insane frenzy, clasping his arms round the huge limbs and trying to force him backwards.

'Go! go!' he cried frantically. 'It may not be too late! You may yet sleep and live! Oh, my Experiment, my great Experiment! All lost – '

'What is this madness?' asked the Wanderer. 'You cannot carry him, and he will not go. Let him alone.'

'Madness?' yelled Keyork, turning on him. 'You are the madman, you the fool, who cannot understand! Help me to move him – you are strong and young – together we can take him back – he may yet sleep and live – he must and shall! I say it! Lay your hands on him – you will not help me? Then I will curse you till you do – '

'Poor Keyork!' exclaimed the Wanderer, half pitying him. 'Your big thoughts have cracked your little brain at last.'

'Poor Keyork? You call me poor Keyork? You boy! You puppet! You ball, that we have bandied to and fro, half sleeping, half awake! It drives me mad to see you standing there, scoffing instead of helping me!'

'You are past my help, I fear.'

'Will you not move? Are you dead already, standing on your feet and staring at me?'

Again Keyork threw himself upon the huge old man, and stamped and struggled and tried to move him backwards. He might as well have spent his strength against a rock. Breathless but furious still, he desisted at last, too much beside himself to see that he whose sudden death he feared was stronger than he, because the great experiment had succeeded far beyond all hope.

'Unorna has done this!' he cried, beating his forehead in impotent rage. 'Unorna has ruined me, and all – and everything – so she has paid me for my help! Trust a woman when she loves? Trust angels to curse God, or Hell to save a sinner! But she shall pay, too – I have her still. Why do you stare at me? Wait, fool! You shall be happy now. What are you to me that I should even hate you? You shall have what you want. I will bring you the woman you love, the Beatrice you have seen in dreams – and then Unorna's heart will break and she will die, and her soul – her soul – '

Keyork broke into a peal of laughter, deep, rolling, diabolical in its despairing, frantic mirth. He was still laughing as he reached the door.

'Her soul, her soul!' they heard him cry, between one burst and another as he went out, and from the echoing vestibule, and from the staircase beyond, the great laughter rolled back to them when they were left alone.

'What is it all? I cannot understand,' the Wanderer said, looking up to the grand calm face.

'It is not always given to evil to do good, even for evil's sake,' said the old man. 'The thing that he would is done already. The wound that he would make is already bleeding; the heart he is gone to break is broken; the soul that he would torture is beyond all his torments.'

'Is Unorna dead?' the Wanderer asked, turning, he knew now why, with a sort of reverence to his companion.

'She is not dead.'

Unorna waited in the parlour of the convent. Then Beatrice came in, and stood before her. Neither feared the other, and each looked into the other's eyes.

'I have come to undo what I have done,' Unorna said, not waiting for the cold inquiry which she knew would come if she were silent.

'That will be hard, indeed,' Beatrice answered.

'Yes. It is very hard. Make it still harder if you can, I could still do it.'

'And do you think I will believe you, or trust you?' asked the dark woman.

'I know that you will when you know how I have loved him.'

'Have you come here to tell me of your love?'

'Yes. And when I have told you, you will forgive me.'

'I am no saint,' said Beatrice, coldly. 'I do not find forgiveness in such abundance as you need.'

'You will find it for me. You are not bad, as I am, but you can understand what I have done, nevertheless, for you know what you yourself would do for the sake of him we love. No – do not be angry with me yet – I love him and I tell you so – that you may understand.'

'At that price, I would rather not have the understanding. I do not care to hear you say it. It is not good to hear.'

'Yet, if I did not love him as I do, I should not be here, of my own free will, to take you to him. I came for that.'

'I do not believe you,' Beatrice answered in tones like ice.

'And yet you will, and very soon. Whether you forgive or not – that is another matter. I cannot ask it. God knows how much easier it would have been to die than to come here. But if I were dead you might never have found him, nor he you, though you are so very near together. Do you think it is easier for me to come to you, whom he loves, than it is for you to hear me say I love him, when I come to give him to you? If you had found it all, not as it is, but otherwise – if you had found that in these years he had known me and loved me, as he once loved you, if he turned from you coldly and bid you forget him, because he would be happy with me, and because he had utterly forgotten you – would it be easy for you to give him up?'

'He loved me then – he loves me still,' Beatrice said. 'It is another case.'

'A much more bitter case. Even then you would have the memory of his love, which I can never have – in true reality, though I have much to remember, in his dreams of you.'

Beatrice started a little, and her brow grew dark and angry.

'Then you have tried to get what was not yours by your bad powers!' she cried. 'And you have made him sleep – and dream – what?'

'Of you.'

'And he talked of love?'

'Of love for you.'

'To you?'

'To me.'

'And dreamed that you were I? That too?'

'That I was you.'

'Is there more to tell?' Beatrice asked, growing white. 'He kissed you in that dream of his – do not tell me he did that – no, tell me – tell me all!'

'He kissed the thing he saw, believing the lips yours.'

'More – more – is it not done yet? Can you sting again? What else?'

'Nothing – save that last night I tried to kill you, body and soul.'

'And why did you not kill me?'

'Because you woke. Then the nun saved you. If she had not come, you would have slept again, and slept for ever. And I would have let his dreams last, and made it last – for him, I should have been the only Beatrice.'

'You have done all this, and you ask me to forgive you?'

'I ask nothing. If you will not go to him, I will bring him to you – '

Beatrice turned away and walked across the room.

'Loved her,' she said aloud, 'and talked to her of love, and kissed – ' She stopped suddenly. Then she came back again with swift steps and grasped Unorna's arm fiercely.

'Tell me more still – this dream has lasted long – you are man and wife!'

'We might have been. He would still have thought me you, for months and years. He would have had me take from his finger that ring you put there. I tried – I tell you the whole truth – but I could not. I saw you there beside me and you held my hand. I broke away and left him.'

'Left him of your free will?'

'I could not lie again. It was too much. He would have broken a promise if I had stayed. I love him – so I left him.'

'Is all this true?'

'Every word.'

'Swear it to me.'

'How can I? By what shall I swear to you? Heaven itself would laugh at any oath of mine. With my life I will answer for every word. With my soul – no – it is not mine to answer with. Will you have my life? My last breath shall tell you that I tell the truth. The dying do not lie.'

'You tell me that you love that man. You tell me that you made him think in dreams that he loved you. You tell me that you might be man and wife. And you ask me to believe that you turned back from such happiness as would make an angel sin? If you had done this – but it is not possible – no woman could! His words in your ear, and yet turn back? His lips on yours, and leave him? Who could do that?'

'One who loves him.'

'What made you do it?'

'Love.'

'No – fear – nothing else – '

'Fear? And what have I to fear? My body is beyond the fear of death, as my soul is beyond the hope of life. If it were to be done again I should be weak. I know I should. If you could know half of what the doing cost! But let that alone. I did it, and he is waiting for you. Will you come?'

'If I only knew it to be true – '

'How hard you make it. Yet, it was hard enough.'

Beatrice touched her arm, more gently than before, and gazed into her eyes.

'If I could believe it all I would not make it hard. I would forgive you – and you would deserve better than that, better than anything that is mine to give.'

'I deserve nothing and ask nothing. If you will come, you will see, and, seeing, you will believe. And if you then forgive – well then, you will have done far more than I could do.'

'I would forgive you freely – '

'Are you afraid to go with me?'

'No. I am afraid of something worse. You have put something here – a hope – '

'A hope? Then you believe. There is no hope without a little belief in it. Will you come?'

'To him?'

'To him.'

'It can but be untrue,' said Beatrice, still hesitating. 'I can but go. What of him!' she asked suddenly. 'If he were living – would you take me to him? Could you?'

She turned very pale, and her eyes stared madly at Unorna.

'If he were dead,' Unorna answered, 'I should not be here.'

Something in her tone and look moved Beatrice's heart at last.

'I will go with you,' she said. 'And if I find him – and if all is well with him – then God in Heaven repay you, for you have been braver than the bravest I ever knew.'

'Can love save a soul as well as lose it?' Unorna asked.

Then they went away together.

They were scarcely out of sight of the convent gate when another carriage drove up. Almost before it had stopped, the door opened and Keyork Arabian's short, heavy form emerged and descended hastily to the pavement. He rang the bell furiously, and the old portress set the gate ajar and looked out cautiously, fearing that the noisy peal meant trouble or disturbance.

'The lady Beatrice Varanger – I must see her instantly!' cried the little man in terrible excitement.

'She is gone out,' the portress replied.

'Gone out? Where? Alone?'

'With a lady who was here last night – a lady with unlike eyes – '

'Where? Where? Where are they gone?' asked Keyork hardly able to find breath.

'The lady bade the coachman drive her home – but where she lives –'

'Home? To Unorna's home? It is not true! I see it in your eyes. Witch! Hag! Let me in! Let me in, I say! May vampires get your body and the Three Black Angels cast lots upon your soul!'

In the storm of curses that followed, the convent door was violently shut in his face. Within, the portress stood shaking with fear, crossing herself again and again, and verily believing that the devil himself had tried to force an entrance into the sacred place.

In fearful anger Keyork drew back. He hesitated one moment and then regained his carriage.

'To Unorna's house!' he shouted, as he shut the door with a crash.

'This is my house, and he is here,' Unorna said, as Beatrice passed before her, under the deep arch of the entrance.

Then she led the way up the broad staircase, and through the small outer hall to the door of the great conservatory.

'You will find him there,' she said. 'Go on alone.'

But Beatrice took her hand to draw her in.

'Must I see it all?' Unorna asked, hopelessly.

Then from among the plants and trees a great white-robed figure came out and stood between them. Joining their hands he gently pushed them forward to the middle of the hall where the Wanderer stood alone.

'It is done!' Unorna cried, as her heart broke.

She saw the scene she had acted so short a time before. She heard the passionate cry, the rain of kisses, the tempest of tears. The expiation was complete. Not a sight, not a sound was spared her. The strong arms of the ancient sleeper held her upright on her feet. She could not fall, she could not close her eyes, she could not stop her ears, no merciful stupor overcame her.

'Is it so bitter to do right?' the old man asked, bending low and speaking softly.

'It is the bitterness of death,' she said.

'It is well done,' he answered.

Then came a noise of hurried steps and a loud, deep voice, calling, 'Unorna! Unorna!'

Keyork Arabian was there. He glanced at Beatrice and the Wanderer, locked in each other's arms, then turned to Unorna and looked into her face.

'It has killed her,' he said. 'Who did it?'

His low-spoken words echoed like angry thunder.

'Give her to me,' he said again. 'She is mine – body and soul.'

But the great strong arms were around her and would not let her go.

'Save me!' she cried in failing tones. 'Save me from him!'

'You have saved yourself,' said the solemn voice of the old man.

'Saved?' Keyork laughed. 'From me?' He laid his hand upon her arm. Then his face changed again, and his laughter died dismally away, and he hung back.

'Can you forgive her?' asked the other voice.

The Wanderer stood close to them now, drawing Beatrice to his side. The question was for them.

'Can you forgive me?' asked Unorna faintly, turning her eyes towards them.

'As we hope to find forgiveness and trust in a life to come,' they answered.

There was a low sound in the air, unearthly, muffled, desperate as of a strong being groaning in awful agony. When they looked, they saw that Keyork Arabian was gone.

The dawn of a coming day rose in Unorna's face as she sank back.

'It is over,' she sighed, as her eyes closed.

Her question was answered; her love had saved her.